On the preceding page, we picture a delicious boy who is always on the prowl, Emilio Sands, from Boiling Point Productions' "Pleasure Trail," now available from STARbooks Press. Emilio and friends also appear on the cover. You may contact the producers at www.boilingpointxxx.com.

The main cover model appears courtesy of Ben Block, the renowned photographer, whose images often grace the pages of magazines such as *Vulcan*. Block operates Flashers studio in London and makes his prints available to collectors worldwide. For more information, write: 56 Byron Mews, Fleet Road, London NW3 2NQ. Ben operates a flashy new website, www.britishguyslive.com in addition to his website for photography, www.flasher.co.uk. Ben's E-mail: ben@mistral.co.uk

"I just got 'Intimate Strangers' and by the end of the week
I had read it all. Great stories! Love it!"
- *L.C., Oregon*

"'Superstars' is a fast read...if you'd like a nice round of fireworks
before the Fourth, read this aloud at your next church picnic..."
- *Welcomat, Philadelphia*

"Yes, it's another of those bumper collections of steamy tales from
STARbooks. The rate at which John Patrick turns out these
compilations you'd be forgiven for thinking it's not exactly quality
prose. Wrong. These stories are well-crafted, but not over-written,
and have a profound effect in the pants department."
- *Vulcan magazine, London*

"For those who share Mr. Patrick's appreciation for cute young
men, 'Legends' is a delightfully readable book...I am a fan of John
Patrick's...His writing is clear and straight-forward and should be
better known in the gay community."
- *Ian Young, Torso Magazine*

"...Touching and gallant in its concern for the sexually
addicted, 'Angel' becomes a wonderfully seductive
investigation of the mysterious disparity between lust
and passion, obsession and desire."
- *Lambda Book Report*

"John Patrick has one of the best jobs a gay male writer could
have. In his fiction, he tells tales of rampant sexuality. His non-
fiction involves first person explorations of adult male video
stars. Talk about choice assignments!"
- *Southern Exposure*

"The title for 'Boys of Spring' is taken from a poem by Dylan
Thomas, so you can count on high-caliber imagery throughout."
- *Walter Vatter, Editor, A Different Light Review*

*Book of the Month Selections in Europe and the U.K.
And Featured By A Different Light, Oscar Wilde Bookshop,
Lambda Rising and GR, Australia
And Available at Fine Booksellers Everywhere*

You are now entering the torrid zone....

Heatwave

A New Collection
of Erotic Tales
Edited By
JOHN PATRICK

STARbooks Press
Sarasota, Florida

Books by John Patrick

Non-Fiction A Charmed Life:
Vince Cobretti
Lowe Down: Tim Lowe
The Best of the Superstars 1990
The Best of the Superstars 1991
The Best of the Superstars 1992
The Best of the Superstars 1993
The Best of the Superstars 1994
The Best of the Superstars 1995
The Best of the Superstars 1996
The Best of the Superstars 1997
The Best of the Superstars 1998
The Best of the Superstars 1999
The Best of the Superstars 2000
What Went Wrong?
When Boys Are Bad
& Sex Goes Wrong
Legends: The World's Sexiest
Men, Vols. 1 & 2
Legends (Third Edition)
Tarnished Angels (Ed.)

Fiction
Billy & David: A Deadly Minuet
The Bigger They Are...
The Younger They Are...
The Harder They Are...
Angel: The Complete Trilogy
Angel II: Stacy's Story
Angel: The Complete Quintet
A Natural Beauty (Editor)
The Kid (with Joe Leslie)
HUGE (Editor)
Strip: He Danced Alone

Fiction (Continued)
The Boys of Spring
Big Boys/Little Lies (Editor)
Boy Toy
Seduced (Editor)
Insatiable/Unforgettable (Editor)
Heartthrobs
Runaways/Kid Stuff (Editor)
Dangerous Boys/Rent Boys
(Editor)
Barely Legal (Editor)
Country Boys/City Boys (Editor)
My Three Boys (Editor)
Mad About the Boys (Editor)
Lover Boys (Editor)
In the BOY ZONE (Editor)
Boys of the Night (Editor)
Secret Passions (Editor)
Beautiful Boys (Editor)
Juniors (Editor)
Come Again (Editor)
Smooth 'N' Sassy (Editor)
Intimate Strangers (Editor)
Naughty By Nature (Editor)
Dreamboys (Editor)
Raw Recruits (Editor)
Play Hard, Score Big (Editor)
Sweet Temptations (Editor)
Pleasures of the Flesh (Editor)
Juniors 2 (Editor)
Fresh 'N' Frisky (Editor)
Boys on the Prowl (Editor)
Heatwave (Editor)

First Edition Published in the U.S. in May, 2000
Library of Congress Card Catalogue No. 99-094936
ISBN No. 1-891855-08-5

Contents

Editor's Note

Most of the stories appearing in this book take place prior to the years of The Plague; the editor and each of the authors represented herein advocate the practice of safe sex at all times.

And, because these stories trespass the boundaries of fiction and non-fiction, to respect the privacy of those involved, we've changed all of the names and other identifying details.

"...The one with the blue eyes is whispering the things he would like to do on this sticky afternoon, and I am becoming aroused by what I can hear of the furtive conversation. I am just wondering what he would look like with the other's cock up his ass, how his mouth would open as he took the man's prick between his lips...."
— *Michael Thomas Ford, describing what can happen when the temperature soars*

HOT is the only word to describe porn star/stripper/escort Tony Cummings, long a favorite of the editor's. John Patrick's first meeting with Cummings is recounted in the Introduction.

INTRODUCTION:
WE'RE HAVIN' A HEATWAVE

John Patrick

"We're havin' a heatwave, a tropical heatwave," Irving Berlin wrote in that sexy song Marilyn Monroe made famous, and it seems that heat brings out the beast in us—at least we seem to get hornier than hell as the temperatures rise. My most memorable "affair" (paid for by the hour, you understand) began some years back on a *hot* day in July. For starters, the "feels like" temperature was over 100 degrees, and I was making one of my periodic forays to Tampa to visit Mike Shelden, publisher of the local gay magazine *Encounter*. When in Tampa, as I so often do, I stopped at Tomes and Treasures to see how our books were selling. I also always take time to scan the magazine rack because, although we get almost every periodical of interest to gay men, some of the slick photo journals we occasionally miss. Sure enough, a current *Jock* and *Blueboy* simply begged to be purchased. The *Jock* was especially noteworthy because of the cover model, who was treated to a dozen pages inside, including the centerfold. There, sandwiched (appropriately enough) between Max Grand and Adam Hart, was a fresh-faced looker named Tony Cummings. I chuckled over the name, imagining how they came up with it, and happily plunked down $6.95, plus tax.

After dinner with Mike, it was off to the local hotspot, the now-defunct Angels, to see who was stripping. This was also always a must for me, especially after I saw they were putting their bartenders in their ads—with lewd descriptions. We were greeted effusively by the owner and the bartender named Markie (famous for his Cowboy Cocksucker).

We asked where the stripper of the night was and, lo and behold, he was standing right in front of us, talking to a couple of guys seated at the bar. We didn't realize he was a stripper, of course, because he was still dressed in T-shirt and jeans. As we were introduced, I had a sense of *deja vu*, that I had somehow met this tall, handsome young man somewhere before.

A few moments later, I noticed the stripper had gone to the dressing room, gotten a magazine, and was showing it to the two men seated at the bar. It was the same magazine I had purchased earlier in the day and the stripper was none other than the centerfold himself in more or less the flesh! And here I thought the odds of my meeting Tony Cummings that night (or ever) were about as great as winning the lottery!

Tony began to dance on the little stage with the rainbow drape hanging behind it and I dragged Mike to a ringside table. By this time Tony had changed to a pair of bib overalls. Slowly he let the straps drop and then turned around to bare his butt. He wore nothing under his farm boy pants. I had to admit the pictures in the magazine didn't do justice to this incredible beauty in person. This was so *hot* I could barely contain myself.

When Tony finally came up to the table, he slid his body over my thigh and perched there for what had to be the most enjoyable few minutes in a public place I'd ever spent. He had the softest skin (even Mike was compelled to touch it, and agreed with me) and a physique that seemed just naturally perfect, without hours spent in a gym working on it.

While he rubbed his groin back and forth on my knee, he told us all about his new career in the adult entertainment industry. He had made six videos at that point for the top-rung companies such as Catalina, Forum Studios and Falcon Studios. Besides that, he was dancing here and there occasionally and doing some private gigs. Best of all, he lived right in Tampa.

One of Mike's staff people had already approached Tony about appearing in the centerfold of the *Encounter*. "Centerfold, hell," I said, "this is cover material!" Mike smiled in full agreement.

Tony said he couldn't leave with me that night; he was going to Orlando to party with some friends. That should have been a tip-off to his true nature, but I was too star-struck to see it at that time—and the heat, inside the club and outside, wasn't helping any.

We exchanged business cards that night. Tony's card was a lot more interesting than mine, of course, offering: "Adult Film Star, Exotic Male Dancer, Night Club Appearances, Full Party Services." Of course it was the Adult Film Star that would make me rush home to see him in action on my VCR, but it was the "Full Party Services" that had me calling his number, beginning a four-year affair that has cost me dearly. The moral is: never fall in love with a porn star! But that, as they say, is another story (or two, or three...).

The character Evan in Paul Lisicky's delightful novel Lawnboy, was luckier than I was in landing the object of his desire: "The hush overwhelmed. Above, dry palm fronds clattered in the heat," he says. "We were in his room. He sat on the bed while I swayed above him. He unzipped my pants and felt for my dick: hard, red, glistening muscle. He gripped it, cranked it around. 'Beautiful,' he rasped, gazing up into my face. He started sucking me off. It wasn't like I had expected. I mean, I'd fooled around before, but it wasn't serious sex, not in a bed or anything, and this, I supposed, was serious sex. I wasn't particularly excited. Maybe I was bored, even disgusted. I concentrated on the motions, trying to pinpoint the smells in the room. I thought: bleach, weeds, sweat, funk, hair.

"...We continued. We rolled around on the bed, when a thought, a full sentence, occurred to me: He is getting younger, while I am getting older. I didn't know what it meant. I thrust out my leg, kicked over the lamp, then rolled him over on his back, even though he was the stronger. I hiked his legs onto my shoulders, and to my astonishment, started fucking him.

"'That's it,' he muttered. 'Fuck your old man, boy. That's it. Keep fucking your daddy.'

"'Shut up,' I whispered. 'Just please shut the hell up.'

"...A thin cord of electricity quavered up my spine. I realized: this is what I'd always wanted. All at once I departed from myself, turning above the bed like a huge ticking wheel, watching us pushing against each other. My breath was sticking in my throat. I leaned over and kissed the harsh sandpaper of his face. I returned to myself, felt him clenching and relaxing around me, then pulled out, coming across his heaving stomach.

"I stood before the bathroom mirror. I stuck a coated finger in my mouth, pushing it around my gums, feeding myself. My body felt new: the blood enriching my face, the muscles sharper as if dug by fine tools. I had something. I had a power all along and hadn't even known it.

"But when I walked into his bedroom, I was only just high school boy again. I eased under the covers, punching him softly on his broad, freckled back, waiting for encouragement. ...It went on and on like this. Was there something wrong with all these people, or was it me? How could I not see myself as lucky when I looked at them, then looked at myself? How could I not stand in front of the mirror, stare into my cool, uncomplicated face, and not call myself one lucky son of a bitch?"

Later, the boy meets a boy named Jesus: "He was short, muscular, with blue-black skin, thickly lashed eyes, and a wet, enormous mouth curving upward. I'd met him in Lummus Park late one night, sitting on a bench beside the beach. The ocean scented the air with seaweed, tanker fuel. A reggae band thudded loudly in the distance. Soon enough we'd gotten to talking, then we were walking arm-in-arm up the street, laughing at things that weren't even funny, ambling toward his second-floor apartment off Meridian. We were lying together in his bed, holding each other. 'Man, you're sweet,' I said, pulling away from him.

"He smiled back at me. 'You too.'

"We continued to make love. It occurred to me I'd leave early in the morning after a quick cup of coffee to be back at the nursery. I knew I'd never see him again. But it was possible, I believed, to enjoy a stranger's company, to be a little in love with somebody, even if it was only for the moment...."

In his book *Flipping*, Ricardo Ramos talks about his hottest summer: "Not the summer of love, but a summer of incessant hot sex. Five white men to myself, four or five nights a week, way out in the mountains. I'm a city girl, but there's nothing to compare to servicing a work crew without any competition. The uncle who got me the job thought that doing physical labor building roads is supposed to be 'man's work,' right?—being outdoors with other real men would butch me up. Instead I had a monopoly of 'real men' eager to use me as a woman.

"...Olaf's night was Thursday, and he wanted me greased and lying on my stomach with my legs together when he came in. He wouldn't take off his clothes. He'd rub my smooth thighs, murmuring, 'Just like a woman, just like a woman, just like a woman ...' until he got hard. Then he'd push into me with his legs around mine. The first few weeks he had to tell me, 'Don't move. Don't move.' I thought it was pretty boring just to lie there, taking it up the ass, but it was over quickly. The Norwegian would get off me, then go shower. He didn't want a whole night in the rotation, just a quick fuck to hold him over until Saturday night when he could get 'the real thing.' I wonder if he told the whores not to move. Probably he was done before they thought of moving.

"When Olaf went to the shower, Paul would sneak in and use me more interestingly. He was the second youngest, and his designated night was Monday. The others wouldn't be horny yet after the exhaustion of their wild weekend. Paul was always horny, but he didn't always want the same thing every time, like the others did. He wanted to know that he was fucking a man, so he'd put my legs up. Or, when he wanted to fuck me from behind he'd put his jockstrap on me. I guess if you're fucking a smooth ass with a jockstrap on, it's some high school fantasy or memory or something. I hated gym classes and got out of several years of them. Yet, there I was, a high school graduate, wearing a jockstrap that hadn't been washed since Paul graduated from high school—or maybe junior high. Oooo, baby, baby! And with a long, pink cock rotor-rooting my ass....

"Both Jim and Matthew would let me jack off while they fucked me—not together at the same time, of course. Jim liked it doggie style; Matthew, with my ankles wrapped around his neck. Jim jacked me off a couple of times while he fucked me. I guess he was the only one who touched my cock deliberately and directly...."

British author Mark Simpson recalls when he and his old friend David Hoyle were taking the Brighton Express from London Victoria on the year's first truly warm day, through the bright sunshine and thickening heat, with trees and bushes sprouting bright, hopeful blossoms and fresh, tender new leaves eager to absorb another summer's energy flashed passed the window. "When the train stopped at Crawley and a very cute laddie looking like trouble ... entered our nearly empty carriage. Naturally, our inverted eyes followed his tender, perky booty as he walked—nay, sauntered—past our table. Now, mind you, this boy wasn't merely good looking. This boy hurt to look at. This boy was the sort that makes you sympathize with serial killers. Radiant, worry-free skin. Casually white teeth that probably only get a cursory brushing once a day. Cropped—but not too recently—strong, dark hair on his head; little downy blond ones on his thickening forearms. And an absurdly, impossibly cute little broken nose, so uncalculating in its perfect crooked beauty. This you understand was the kind of boy that you see walking across the other side of the street, driving a van past you at high speed, riding the up escalator as you ride down. This was the sort of boy who makes you think: well, I'm sorry, really I am, but looking like that you just don't have any right to live because you won't live with me. Killing people so they don't ever leave suddenly seemed to make sense.

"...This vision of frustration sat, with his almost as pretty blonde girlfriend of about the same age. 'Girls don't really appreciate men like that,' I complained bitterly and only slightly ironically.

"'No, you're right,' replied David. 'They don't get him to sit on their face and stick their tongues up his arse and swivel them around for hours and hours, do they?'"

"I must've looked very queer," recalls one of the gay men interviewed for the book *Telling Tales Out of School* from Alyson. "That was how I felt in my near-virgin adolescence on that hot-summer Los Angeles street. It was a new experience being cruised by this man in his slow-moving car; I didn't know I could have wanted him. I feared the unknown and certainly couldn't allow myself to take the ride. ...I guess it's no wonder I never wanted to know what I was thinking. For years afterward I plunged like a child naked and dazed out of focus, parts of myself disoriented, chose freely to wander sabotaged, and searching men seemed an adventure. Some were wonderful new experiences, exciting or tender, while others were a mistake from the onset, but still I kept on seeking men stripped to the flesh to hold. Half naked in shadows of adult movie theaters, my mind overactive and exhausted from days of methedrine and cocaine, I never found what I wanted, I never wanted to stop to wonder what I wanted. I didn't want to think, just follow the drug drifting, the ocean tides, midnight rides; and side road fucks under the stars were sweet, to have found somebody to be there with for a moment, unraveling sexual intensity and the passion of strangers touching just once, just one more time, and I never formulated any other plans, couldn't motivate any desires, so when the time came I got sober and my sex life just stopped; that was 1989."

Columnist Michael Thomas Ford describes what can happen when the temperatures soar, in more ways than one: "...I am sitting in the hotel bar sipping a drink and surreptitiously listening to a handsome young man with black hair and blue eyes as he tries to convince another man who is not his lover to come back to his room and make love. I know the man being pursued, who has honeyed skin and hair the color of mahogany, does not belong to this one because I saw the dark-haired man check in with another earlier in the morning, saw them kissing on the landing when his lover left to conduct some business.

"Now, the one with the blue eyes is whispering the things he would like to do on this sticky afternoon, and I am becoming aroused by what I can hear of the furtive conversation. I am just wondering what he would look like with the other's cock up his ass, how his mouth would open as he took the man's prick between his lips....

"A few minutes after the appointed time, I enter the dining room. It is crowded with people escaping from the oppressive heat, taking some comfort from the slowly circling overhead fans and glasses of gin. I see to one side the dark-haired man I'd watched in the bar earlier sitting with his lover. Several tables away is the mahogany-haired man, with a pretty woman I take to be his wife. The idea of these two men spending their afternoon in one another's arms (while the lover sat in a stuffy room doing business and the wife looked through the local stores for some small item to bring home to the waiting children) makes me laugh...."

ELECTRICITY

John Patrick

*"I started noticing: jaw, eyes, hair, smell, hands, feet, mouth.
There was a kind of buzz about him, a field of hissing electricity
that jerked with my ions and electrons. I felt myself getting hard.
I thought: now you've really gotten yourself into trouble."*
—Paul Lisicky, in the novel, "Lawnboy"

J.T. drew me to him, kissed my cheeks, nose, ears, until our mouths met. Gently, then with increased passion, we held each other and rocked. The hum of passion turned to groans, turned to a roaring deep inside me.

He unbuttoned his shirt, opened his jeans, then turned to face me. With his pale skin and vivid blue eyes he looked translucent in the glow from the street lamps, and suddenly fragile, vulnerable.

I shook my head no, but he knew I wasn't sure what I wanted.

As he pressed his body into mine, his tongue brushed my lower lip, and at the same time I felt him opening my shirt buttons.

"We shouldn't do this," I told him, but then immediately I realized how silly my words of protest sounded.

"Well, don't do anything, then. Stay like that." He unbuttoned my shirt, pulled it nearly off. His cool hands stroked my pecs, then he bent his head and sucked my nipples, sending little shivers up and down my spine.

In moments, he had my cock out and was sucking it. I held his head, face-fucked his mouth. In moments, I came, and he swallowed it all. Wiping the cum from his lips, he begged me to come home with him. I begged off, pulling my clothes back on, anxious because I had gone this far in a parked Lexus behind the restaurant where I worked.

I worked as a busboy at the Colony, where J.T. took his clients to dinner, and one day he handed me a card with his number. I knew what he wanted; he knew what I wanted. I called him, he called me back, from his office, saying that he was going through a break-up with his boyfriend. I told him I was too.

He said he would see me that night when I got off work. We sat in the car and talked until everyone had left. Then he made his move.

Feeling guilty after having let him blow me, I was anxious to leave. He didn't fight me; he told me we would meet again when we were both free.

Weeks passed, then I lost my job at the restaurant; I had simply been late too many times. It was my fault, I was trying to keep Jerry happy and failing miserably at it. J.T. missed me at the Colony and called me; he invited me to dinner. He wanted me to go with him to a motel. I couldn't, I told him, putting him off. I still had feelings for Jerry, I told him, but the truth was I was afraid of falling for someone else while I was still living with Jerry.

Finally I left Jerry and moved back in with Mom. Then she decided to take her annual mid-summer vacation at Aunt Edna's. She asked me, "Will you be okay all by yourself, honey?" I could barely contain myself. The day after she left, I called J.T. and invited him over. He was delighted to hear from me. Dinner first, in the dining room, then sex in my bedroom. That was my master plan.

But things never go according to plan. In this case, what happened was better than I ever could ever have imagined. I had expected J.T. at six and I had fussed all day in the kitchen before I realized that I hadn't finished mowing the lawn. I had stopped with half the front yard clipped. I had left the mower in the sun and fled into the house to escape the suffocating heat of midday.

I was just finishing the mowing when J.T. pulled in the drive. He was still dressed in his business suit and tie, and he looked so distinguished. I felt silly standing there admiring him clad only in my little red bikini. He seemed to be delighted with what he saw, however, and tried to hug me right there in the front yard.

I ran to the house, with J.T. in hot pursuit. We laughed as I pushed him away and begged to be permitted to take a shower and greet him "properly." He insisted I was "proper" just as I was: a sticky, sweaty, skinny kid with a bulging crotch, anticipating what I knew would come later.

I fixed him a drink and left him in the living room. I walked into the bathroom, leaving the door open and looked at myself in one of the mirrors as I stripped off my bikini. *Well, it's what you wanted*, I thought. I'd been drooling over J.T. for months and now what I hungered for was about to happen. I wondered whether J.T. realized how submissive I could be with the right man, how pliable, how anxious to please. Yes, he probably did realize it; J.T. impressed me as one of those men who realized everything.

Inside the shower stall, I turned the water on and adjusted the temperature. The spray felt wonderful on my body after the heat outside. I began lathering my body with soap, paying extra attention to my asshole, when J.T. slid the door open and stepped inside.

It was the first time I had seen him in all his naked glory. I sighed when I saw the huge slab of meat that dangled between his thighs. I cursed myself for waiting so long. I took the thick penis in my hand and stroked it.

He smiled at me. "Is it big enough?"

I nodded. "Yes, it's fine."

He looked at my body, a long and careful judgment that made me tremble inside because I was afraid he might not approve, might find me too skinny for his taste.

Then the looking was finished. He reached out to take hold of my cock, which was now fully erect.

"I like this," he said. "It's lovely." He bent over and sucked me. I closed my eyes and groaned.

He seemed amused by my response. "You're very hot for me, aren't you, kid?"

"Yes."

"God, I want it. I knew I wasn't wrong about you."

And then he put his hands on my shoulders and pushed me down gently but firmly enough so there was no mistaking what he wanted.

I slid to my knees in the shower stall and buried my face in his crotch.

The shower spray was behind him. I had a clear field. I wanted to look at it first, but J.T. slipped one hand behind my head and pulled me forward to get my mouth directly on it.

If I couldn't look at it, at least I could taste it. I sucked the head between my lips. I slid my hands up his thighs to his buttocks, and for the first time my fingers gripped that lovely ass. He hunched at me, rocking his body slowly to get more friction on his prick and send the shaft deep into my throat. He was completely stiff now. As soon as I started sucking it, he had the quick orgasm he'd said he wanted, the climax accentuated by a vigorous humping of his crotch against my upturned face.

After that, he stopped moving. He helped me to rise. "Now we're even," he said.

He kissed my mouth, then he made me turn my back. I wondered what was about to happen, and then when I felt his hand fondling me, and his cock pressed to my ass, I understood what he wanted and I leaned forward. His hand was soon reaching around to jerk my cock while he rubbed against me.

"Is it good?" he said.

I groaned. "Yes, it's marvelous."

Then I felt his finger pushing inside my ass, a long, slender digit inside my rectum. I was now possessed in both places. With one hand he continued taking me with his finger, then two fingers. Before long, I had a smashing climax that left me gasping.

He kissed the back of my neck as he slowly drew his fingers out of my body. "You're lovely, kid. You're quite lovely."

Soon after that we left the shower. We quickly dried ourselves and walked into downstairs to eat dinner—in the nude.

As we ate my baked potatoes and meatloaf, he said, "You come hard. I like that."

I felt myself blushing. "Yes."

"But it's wonderful," he said with a smile. "It's wonderful to come hard."

After dinner, he followed me back upstairs and he got on the bed. I moved on top of him, brushing his lips with a light kiss. I crouched above him. A whimper escaped his mouth when my lips found his nipple, then back to his cock.

My hands leisurely explored the curves of J.T.'s hairy body, the tight skin over ribs. I stroked the hardness of his belly, licked his cock. His moans turned to a thin gasp as my fingers teased him while I returned to sucking it again. The rhythm quickened. He pulled my hair gently, as I pressed my mouth to his cock. I sucked forcibly like a newborn who knows what he wants and how to get it. And he was so hungry for my pleasure.

Moments later, no longer content with sucking, I lifted myself over him. His limbs seemed weightless as, head thrust back, back arched, he brought the head of his cock to my asslips.

There was no turning back; we had come too far for that.

Whispering my desire to have him, I moved down to feel the pressure of his body. He lay motionless and tried to steady his breathing. Still shaking slightly, we held each other, fitting our curves together. His cock was all the way in. It hurt, but I got over it quickly as I moved up and down on it.

His hands gently followed the outline of my torso. We explored the subtle differences of our bodies by touch, sight, smell. He seemed to like my cock; God knows, I loved his: big but not too big, thick, hard.

After several minutes, he lifted me up and lay beside me, gently spreading my legs. I sensed he did not want to force his desire on me. Slowly his fingers stroked, then opened my asslips. He wrapped his arms around me and I writhed as he thrust his erection into me again. I didn't want the fuck to end.

I felt awkward again. I wanted him so much, had been wanting him for so long, the reality was frightening. But he went on fucking me with complete abandon, happy at the new intimacy between us. I felt a surge of happiness as he began shaking through another intense climax.

When it was finished, I rolled away from him with my legs wide open, my cock burning with need. He reached out, took hold of my hand and led it to my erection. "Jerk off for me," he said.

I had no will of my own. If that was what he wanted, I was happy to please him. I began masturbating, rubbing my sex with my fingers to get myself off. He lay there and watched me, and when I was close, he started kissing my balls, as if he were pushing the cum out of me. I came, not as hard as before, but it seemed to satisfy him. He took me in his arms and kissed me. "You look lovely when you come," he said.

I moaned and pressed my face against his chest as he urged me to sleep.

The next morning, I woke up an hour before J.T. did. I fixed coffee, toast. I waited. I heard the shower running, the toilet flush. Then J.T. appeared, dressed.

"I gotta go." He sounded half sullen, half apologetic.

"Why? Where do you have to go?" I said slowly, trying not to anticipate disappointment.

"The office. I'm late already."

"On Saturday?"

"Yeah. I work seven days a week during the summer. I'm in the air conditioning business."

"Have some coffee."

He shook his head. "I'll call you soon."

"Call me?! You're just going to run out the door and say you'll call me? You're crazy."

"Crazy in love," he said, hugging me to him. "You looked so happy after I fucked you, I'm scared."

I took in his words and his voice, forced myself to relax the knot in my throat.

"Oh, shit," I sighed. "I thought I was the one who was scacred."

He kissed me, as if somehow reassuring me.

I pulled away. "Here, have some coffee before you go. Come on, sit down."

We sat in the same position as the evening before, and we both looked out the window at the freshly mowed grass, the pine trees lining the road, the beginnings of one of those long, hot August days. My initial panic left me, replaced by a new resolve. I would get J.T. to ask me to live with him.

"I was too rough with you," he said. "I hurt you."

"No, it was fine...."

"No," he said. "I hurt you."

I was both sad and braced for further admissions.

He forced a tight smile. The incredible electricity of last night was now again a charge between us. He took my hand, squeezed it.

"I know what you're thinking," I said, my mind racing and numb. "You're thinking. You're thinking it won't work. But there's nothing to 'work.' It just happened. We had been wanting it to happen and it did."

"Yes, it happened. I know that. What can I say?"

"I'm sorry, I'm a hopeless romantic, remember? And, you,

you're so strong you don't need anyone else."

"I don't feel very strong right now."

He got up, stood at the window.

A power was rising in me. I knew he would let me move in with him. If not now, then soon. Very soon. "Last night was wonderful," I said. "You didn't hurt me, really."

Whether he had heard what I was saying or not I couldn't tell. I moved quickly to the other window, braced my back against the wall. He stared out the window, hypnotized by the sun. Finally I shrugged, went over to clear away the cups of now-cold coffee. I stood in the middle of the dining room, feeling tired.

He turned and regarded me. "Now you look sad. C'mon, lovely boy, this will work out."

"Okay," I said, brightly.

"But right now I think I'd like to be alone for a while."

"Okay," I said quickly, with a mixture of rejection and relief.

"I'll call you later."

"All right."

A hesitation, a quick shoulder hug, then J.T. left the house, closing the door softly behind him.

I busied myself tidying an already clean kitchen; paused only once, to hear his Lexus turn down the gravel driveway. I wandered through the house, healing myself with its familiar sights and smells. Slowly, against all expectation, I found myself smiling. I had let a man fuck me in my mother's house. How could I have done such a thing? But then that's probably what she expected, asking me if I'd be all right. Yeah, she was practically encouraging me.

"Oh, J.T. ... J.T. ... J.T. ... J.T. ...." His name floated on the morning air; I pushed it with a kiss to the vanishing Lexus, now climbing the rise to the road. *I love you, too,* I thought. More and more. Not any more for last night; not any less for this morning. I looked in the dining room mirror, chuckling wryly, loving the hurting in my ass and the strength of J.T.'s fucking that even now sent tremors between my legs. Yawning, I stretched my arms heavenward. Giving thanks, I looked forward to the night.

THE PLEASURE OF THE MOMENT

John Patrick

Jeffrey went down to the shore hoping to come upon them again. When he first saw them, they had their backs toward him, and he thought the two of them were luminous with youth.

When he saw them again, they were standing naked, knee-deep in a tidal pool, the dark-haired one behind and to the right of the blond one, his right hand on his shoulder, his left hand rubbing in slow circles at the small of his back. While Jeffrey watched them, partially hidden by a pair of side-by-side boulders, the dark-haired one slid his hand down over the blond's buttocks and then under him and through his legs. The blond laughed and turned around and they embraced and kissed.

Jeffrey moved back behind the boulders and waited. He looked about, a bit nervous about getting caught leering at these youths. Getting caught would be humiliating and he was genuinely afraid of it—and that mixture of real fear and sexual excitement, that was one of the things that made him do it. It felt powerful, intense.

Jeffrey waited a few minutes, and when he looked again, they were kneeling in the water, splashing each other playfully. He wished he had his camera to capture the moment. Then Jeffrey walked out from between the boulders and acted nonchalant, as if he had just accidentally come upon them, as if their naked bodies were nothing more to him than an amusement.

The dark-haired one seemed taken aback at first, but the blond met Jeffrey's eyes and smiled playfully.

Now Jeffrey was sorry he hadn't just turned and returned to his house. Now he would have to pretend that it was no big deal, finding them here, naked. He wouldn't be able to leer and stare; he would have to pretend that he didn't want to feel the weight of the dark one's big balls in his hands, that he didn't want to run his tongue over the blond's adorable cut cock, that he didn't want to reach down under him the way the dark one had. The truth was that he wanted to do all those things and more.

On the set at his studio, he was surrounded by stunningly beautiful men—all out of his reach, by his own choice, because he had a rule not to play around with his models. The tension was incredible. He wanted those men intensely and he didn't want them intensely—both at the same time. When an attractive man came near him, he looked at him as a potential model, not as a potential lover. If he did sign a model, photograph him, he would get off just seeing him in various stages of undress, nude even. That was enough, most of the time. In a sense, Jeffrey's voyeurism was a kind of compromise. He chose looking over acting. Most of the time. Roger was different, of course, because he already knew Roger was gay. At least open to suggestion. That was why Roger had come to the studio. Jeffrey was going to leer at Roger, but he wasn't going to make a pass at him. But of course he wanted Roger. He wanted to see Roger nude, to see the fabled cock he had so often heard about. To touch it. He wanted that cock. He didn't want Roger, really. It was maddening and confusing. It had always been maddening and confusing.

From watching from the boys on the beach, Jeffrey felt the familiar tingle of sexual excitement—and it surprised him. The blond stayed, extended his hand, while the dark-haired boy trotted away into the water, and yelped as he dove dramatically into the waves. The blond turned to watch his friend, then turned around and looked directly up at Jeffrey.

He expected the boy to follow his friend, but instead he found him reaching down to stroke his cock, still looking up at him, looking directly at him, as if he were engaged in a staring match and resolved not to be the first one to look away.

Jeffrey got about three feet away and just stood there for a long moment, looking down at the cock, hardening.

Then the boy turned around and walked slowly into the water. Jeffrey watched them all the time they were in the water. He sat on their towels, enjoying them, and he wound up feeling as though he were floating loose of the earth. He wound up feeling as though he were drifting. He leaned back and eventually fell to the sand completely and began to doze. When he opened his eyes, he saw that alongside him the blond lay stretched out on top of his towel. The beauty lay on his stomach, naked. He was asleep. His body was covered with a sheen of perspiration: a pool of sweat had gathered in the small of his back, and his hair looked as though he had just stepped out of the shower. Jeffrey was also soaked. He ran his hand over his hairy chest and stomach, and sweat ran down his sides in rivulets. He sat up and let himself awaken slowly to the sounds and sensations around him. It was quiet. And it was hot. Very hot. There was no breeze, and the heat was palpable: he could feel it on his skin like standing close to a fire. The only sound was the constant murmur of the ocean. It didn't take Jeffrey more than a few moments to decide he wanted to go for a swim. He stood and his bright red briefs clung to him tightly as a tattoo. He started walking towards the water.

Jeffrey found the dark-haired lad crouched in the surf. He was sitting on his haunches, now wearing a blue bathing suit, looking out over the ocean as water rushed back and forth over his feet and ankles.

At Jeffrey's approach, the boy turned around and smiled. "You believe this heat?" he asked.

Jeffrey knelt alongside him, immersing his calves and thighs in the water. He threw his torso forward as he submerged his face and hair in the surf, rubbing the cooling water into his scalp and forehead and eyes. He came up shaking his head, getting the dark-haired boy wet. "Oh God," he said. "That was good. I think I roasted there on the towel."

The dark-haired one laughed and wiped the water away from his face. "Is Willy awake?"

Jeffrey shook his head. "Still cooking," he said.

"He likes you, you know."

"He does?"

The boy turned around so that he was facing Jeffrey. He sat in water up to his waist. "Do you mind if I ask you something?"

"Go ahead."

"I'd better not," he said, and he looked away and then back, as if with that motion he had turned the page in a book and was now reading from a new script. "You live near here?"

Jeffrey smiled in response. It was an honest smile. He nodded. "So?"

"So, what?"

"The question," Jeffrey said. "The question you wanted to

ask."

The lad looked down and his expression changed suddenly. He put his hand on Jeffrey's knee. "Willy and I are not going to last," he said. "I mean, I doubt we'll be together for another month after this vacation."

Jeffrey looked off, past the boy, his face taking on an appropriate expression, a world-weary look of sadness for the unfortunate ways of this world. Inside him, however, the rate of his heartbeat picked up slightly. His mind was blank, but his blood was moving. "I'm sorry," he said. "You make a beautiful couple."

"It's not that things are bad," he said. "I doubt Willy has any idea. It's just that . . . he's such a little boy. He's sweet, but it's like being with a kid." He looked up at Jeffrey, as if wanting confirmation. He touched Jeffrey's hand. "He told me he wanted to fuck you. He wants to fuck all the time."

Jeffrey rubbed his eyes with his fingertips, hiding his face momentarily. Of course Willy was a boy. All-boy, in fact. It was the way he was, the way most boys were: promiscuous. Jeffrey remembered the process by which things fell apart for him when he had lovers: the faults real and invented that led to arguments followed by unhappiness.

Jeffrey removed his hands from his eyes in time to see the emotion gathering in the dark-haired boy's face, building second by second as he failed to respond.

"Of course," he said, finally. "He's a cute boy. He's comfortable in his skin."

The dark-haired one turned to Jeffrey and stared at him intently, waiting to read his smallest gesture.

Jeffrey had been here many times before, at this moment. It was the moment when he had only to touch the object of his affection and he would lean toward him and they would embrace.

He could kiss the lad now. He could touch him. He knew the boy wanted to be kissed and touched by him. This was the moment when it might begin, whatever it would turn out to be: an affair, love, a sexual adventure. He stood up and extended a hand down to the boy. "My name's Jeffrey. Let's walk a little," he said.

"I'm Kevin." He took his hand and lifted himself from the water. Kevin walked alongside Jeffrey in his dripping cut-offs and soaked sneakers.

They were walking toward a place where three boulders formed a semicircle on the beach and three more out in the water completed the circle.

Jeffrey's heart was beating fast as they reached the circle of boulders and Kevin stopped and looked around. The boulders formed a small private beach, a place protected from the casual view of others. "I'm going in here," he said, and he dropped his shorts, tossed them in a heap on the sand, and waded into a deep tidal pool that was still connected by a flowing stream of water to the ocean.

Jeffrey watched him for a moment, growing excited by the beauty of the lad's buns. He followed him into the tidal pool.

When Kevin turned around to face him again, standing waist-deep in water, Jeffrey stepped close to him, took his hands in his, and said, "You're the one, you know." When he spoke, he heard his voice change, the timbre turning just slightly more resonant, the tone dropping a note. It was his best acting voice and it had emerged out of nowhere, on its own. It surprised him, as did the tears welling in his eyes.

Kevin brushed the tears away with wet fingers. "You want me?"

"Yes."

"Willy doesn't understand me," Kevin said, and he bowed his head and covered his eyes with his hands.

Jeffrey laughed at the gesture, which seemed fake to him. He half expected to hear a director yell "Cut!" But Kevin pushed on. "I feel empty," he said. "We're lovers ... but I feel ..."

Jeffrey could hardly believe what he was hearing. "I know," he said, and he embraced Kevin, wrapping his arm's around him and holding him tight against him. He repeated: "I know. I know exactly."

Kevin pulled away and held Jeffrey at arm's length. "I saw you watching.... And it was like I could feel you, I could feel your eyes on me."

"I do that...."

"It's your eyes.... They're hungry. It's just, like, a hunger about you...."

"Professional hazard, I assure you. I'm a photographer."

"Oh," Kevin said. "But there's more. Like, earlier, I felt this connection between us. It was like something real between us.

I felt filled up by it. I can't explain, really...." He leaned forward, as if he were tired of stumbling for words, and he embraced and kissed Jeffrey, his lips pressing hard against the older man's lips, his tongue pushing into his mouth. Jeffrey returned the kiss, letting his hands move over his back, clutching and releasing his shoulders—but when his head moved lower, to Kevin's semi-hard cock. Kevin resisted. "Not here," he said. He stepped back from him. They had moved, while kissing, into shallower water, and Jeffrey was on his knees, looking up at the boy. Kevin ran his fingers through Jeffrey's wet hair.

Jeffrey took Kevin's hand and pulled him toward him. "Yes," he said. "Here. Now."

Kevin shook his head. "No. Willy might come by...."

"So?" Jeffrey said. He looked at the sky, at the wavering, late afternoon light. "No one can see us here," he said, and he ran his hand along the length of his thigh.

"Listen," he said. "There's nothing to life but moments like this. Intense moments like this."

He sucked a bit on the cock, and it grew erect. "We'd regret it forever," he said, "if we let this moment pass." He sucked on it a bit more. Then he stood, embraced Kevin and kissed him and turned his body around, moving them both toward shallower water, where he lay on his back and pulled off his briefs, releasing his own erection, and moved his body under Kevin's. He had, then, only to thrust his thighs up slightly and his cock slid right in. Above him, blocking out the bright yellow circle of the sun, Kevin's head was lifted to the sky as if in ecstasy or pain, lost in the pleasure of the moment. Jeffrey felt again as though he were floating—this time into a place of pure sensation, rising free of the gritty earth. Then he moved his hips, pushing into the heat of Kevin's body. Soon Kevin was moving rhythmically, pushing Jeffrey down into the sand and water. He held the lad's wrists, and behind him, from someplace beyond and above the boulders, he heard a sound like a rock might make being kicked in the sand. He wanted to turn around and look, but he was afraid of what he might see. He feared that Willy had indeed awakened and was above them on the beach looking down at them in the water. He closed his eyes and told himself these feelings would pass in a moment if he remained calm. Amazingly, Kevin appeared to have no idea there was a problem. Kevin was jerking himself, spiraling up and away. Jeffrey held on tight to Kevin, letting the boy bounce up and down on his cock while he orgasmed. Finished, Kevin started to lift up, but Jeffrey wouldn't let him.

"Just a damn minute," Jeffrey said, slamming his cock deep into the boy.

"Oh, god, that hurts...." Kevin groaned. "Oh! Oh!"

"Yeah," Jeffrey hissed as he shot his load into the boy's ass.

Breathing hard, Jeffrey held Kevin tight for a few moments before releasing him. As Kevin lifted away, Jeffrey's softening cock popped from the opening. As Kevin slowly made his way back to where his shorts had been left on the sand, Jeffrey heard something above him again and looked up to see Willy's smiling face. Jeffrey, stroking his cock to full hardness once more, smiled back....

AT THE CAR WASH

David Patrick Beavers

The room was stifling. Even with the windows open, even with the balcony door open and the turbo fan blowing, nothing seemed to dispel the almost fluid humidity that pressed all around him. Barry loved his apartment nine months out of the year, but during July, August and September, he often thought about giving up the space and character of his seventy-plus year old home to opt for the luxury of a more modern building with wonderfully frigid centralized air conditioning. Sweat and discomfort were no reason, though, to chuck the huge, two-bedroom abode with its hardwood floors and nine-foot ceilings and intricate tile work throughout kitchen and bathroom.

He had to remind himself as he turned on his computer and logged onto the internet that not every summer was as miserable as this one. This summer was one of the worst in a decade. Simply sitting still his body worked overtime to cool itself, sending veritable rivers of sweat running down his torso and back.

He'd given up wearing any sort of shirt indoors. Rather, he covered his desk chair with two beach towels, then stripped to his Jockey shorts before he sat down to work. The heavy cotton towels were perhaps a bit warm, but they were soft and absorbent. Some of his friends thought his set-up a bit primitive—even repulsive—but Barry had to work. His job enabled him to tele-commute almost daily, plugging into his company's wide area network to gather and send e-mail, most of his own offerings to others being engineering quote details for new telephone systems. Boring work, really, but financially rewarding. The company paid for his computer, his modem, his phone line and his internet service provider. Plus he could work hours that were the most convenient for himself.

But today was a Thursday. An extremely hot and humid Thursday by anyone's standards. His mind was not inclined to focus on boring engineering stats. So, rather than dialing into his work's network, he brought up a search engine and began to hunt the internet for all sorts of things from auctions to travel arrangements. He didn't really want to buy anything nor was he planning on taking a trip anywhere. He just needed to allow his focus to drift for a while.

It was during this time that he happened upon a listing of sites for travel and he spotted a link to gay travel sites. His mind immediately flooded with images of cruise ships sailing through Caribbean waters to exotic locales. Places where men stripped down to oiled-up skin to bake in the sun. A fleeting thought it was, but a strong enough image to make his thick, heavy cock stir beneath his damp briefs. Reflexively, he slipped his left hand beneath the waistband and shifted his member and his balls as his right hand manipulated the mouse and clicked on one of the links. The computer screen blinked and brought up the web page of an independent sojourner named Ty.

Barry leaned forward a bit and shifted the sticky towel beneath him. Framed by an azure sky and cool, green water was Ty, center-screen, his feet buried in golden sand, his lean, nearly naked form and smiling, handsome face beckoning anyone to venture into his website.

Barry leaned back into his chair and just stared at the image of this sun-bronzed young man with shaggy, coppery hair smiling at him. Barry felt his cock swell immediately, filling the pouch of his briefs with an almost painful strain. An unusual sensation this was, for Barry never found himself reacting to pictures. Not since adolescence, anyhow. Barry liked men like himself. Men in their thirties and forties with strong, substantial bodies. Men with a little gray around the temples, and with a few lines etched on their faces. Men with broad shoulders and backs and a moderate amount of thickness about the waist. Men who looked like men, not like boys ready for a night out in the dance clubs in the city.

Nonetheless, the image on his computer screen made his body react. He shifted in his seat and slipped his briefs down over his meaty thighs and granite calves, then kicked them aside, freeing his thick cock. His scrotum contracted sharply as the shaft of his penis swelled in response, his foreskin drawing back over the head, already slick with pre-cum. Wrapping his fingers around the shaft, he gripped his member tight and slowly began pumping his prick as he stared at the boy on the screen. The boy with the broad smile and bare lean, trim torso, smooth and bronzed. The boy in black diving trunks inviting him to visit.

Barry let go of his stiff cock and drew his chair closer to his desk. He clicked on the image of Ty to enter into the young man's web page. A directory appeared, each separate listing delineated by some sort of nautical or oceanic sign. Curious to see more of Ty, Barry clicked on a spyglass icon listed as the connection to Ty's personal cam site. A view into Ty's home. Into his private world.

While clicking the mouse was quick, the connection to Ty's screen froze. Barry sighed, relinquished his hold on his cock, then re-booted his computer. Evidently the Internet Gods were telling him to buckle down and get on with his real work. And that's what he did. Boring as it was for him, he soon managed to push those fleeting thoughts of mystery man Ty out of his mind and focus on the one endeavor that paid his bills.

Hours passed in a haze. When all his tasks were completed, Barry pushed back from his desk and stood up. The cotton towel stuck to his back. He peeled it away from his skin, just then realizing how damp it was. His entire body felt sticky and clammy from perspiration and humidity. A shower was needed. A long, cool shower. Leaving everything where it was, he headed into to the bathroom and stepped into the tub. A jet of cool water blasted from the showerhead and assailed his scalp, his skin. Soap felt good. Invigorating. Heat made him think of pools and streams and crashing waves along the beach. In his mind, the only time heat was welcome was when his body was or could easily be submerged in water. Water that reflected the sun and tanned his skin.

As he rinsed shampoo and lather away, he looked down at his body. In a way, it resembled his cock. Beefy. Solid. Probably too much fat around the midriff, but what the hell. He wasn't twenty anymore. He was twice that and then some.

As he stepped out of the tub, he cranked open the louvered window to let some air circulate in the bathroom. He slowly patted himself dry, studying his body as he did so. The man in the mirror was recognizable. A bulldog neck atop broad shoulders. Thick delts and tri's, bi's and an extremely thick chest that still felt like a slab of concrete. No, he had no problems with his body in that upper torso region. The gym work was taken slower nowadays and was a bit more painful at times, but he'd done himself proud there. His cock was still the mass of meat it'd always been. His legs, though a little slimmer now, were still as good as they ever were. It was the squish encircled his middle. The fat that covered marble hard abdominals. The squoosh that sat atop his hip bone. Call them love handles, call them grips, call them whatever, he still entertained the notion of having the gelatinous mass vacuumed out like so many other men he knew had done. Spend a few grand, restrict the diet even more and once again, he'd have the stomach he once had.

At least he still had it together above the neck. Thick, sable brown hair buzzed to a crew cut had very little gray in it. He ran a hand over his scalp, feeling the tickle of soft, bristle-like hair. A few lines around the eyes. A few faintly etched above his brow. His square, clean-shaven jaw still seemed sharp, taut, without sagging jowls. He had a few more years before those crept into place. If it weren't for his height, he'd look like a fire plug. At six-foot-three, he looked more like a defensive end than a systems engineer.

He sighed to himself as he left the towel behind and padded naked into his bedroom. A soft, welcomed breeze blew in through the open window. Warm as it was, it was air moving. He should dig out his other fans, he thought. Dig them out of his private garage and set them up throughout the apartment, in front of every open door and window. Get the air circulating. But that would entail digging through all the crap he'd stored away. Junk that filled the garage space while his car sat out at curbside under the shade of some huge, old Japanese maple trees that lined the street. Trees that made happy homes for fat, nesting, shit-dropping wrens.

He pulled on a jockstrap, then some old, baggy shorts. No zippers, no buttons, just deep pocketed, elastic waist shorts that were a decade old and frayed at the hem. Some years ago, he would've gone out without a shirt, but he wasn't as bold anymore. He slipped on an even older Hawaiian shirt that seemed to mold to his shoulders and chest. Shoes, though, were unappealing in the heat. A newer pair of thongs he wore around the house were fine, though they did make his size twelve feet look even bigger. All that mattered was getting out of the house for a while. Even if it was just to run to the do-it-yourself car wash to wash bird shit off the car.

He went back into his makeshift den and killed the computer

without a second thought, then stuffed keys, wallet and change into his pockets and headed out the door into the hallway. It seemed just a bit breezier out in front of his door, the gentle wind from outside slipping through an open window at the end of the hall. His neighbor must have opened it, for the landlord of the building, who lived down on the first floor, never opened any external windows. She said bees and flies and wasps tended to float on in and the last thing she wanted to do was to be annoyed with complaints about buzzing insects flitting about in tenants' apartments. Barry didn't much care for flying insects, either, but he couldn't understand why the landlord didn't just put screens on the window during the summer months. Sure, they would be kind of ugly, but it was only for a short period of time. That was another negative about the old building. The landlord. A rather grumpy woman of indeterminate age who was prone to hit on all the single men in the building.

The thought of her made Barry's cock wilt and retreat into hiding. He slipped down the stairs, exiting to the rear of the building, then walked down the driveway to his guano-covered car. For all the abuse his restored Valiant took, the white paint seemed to be impervious to the bird poop.

It was a short drive to the car wash. A series of connected bays one drove into, parked, then plugged innumerable quarters into the slot to pay for five minutes of scrub time. He quickly rinsed the car first with the jet spray, then switched to the soaping scrub brush and began the task of eradicating the splatters. As he scrubbed, he caught sight of an old, three-quarter ton GMC pick-up cruising right in front of him, then turning into the adjacent stall. The driver, though a bit obscured through the passenger window, seemed to be a good-looking guy. That wasn't unusual in this part of town, the Hollywood/West Hollywood border. A place lost between the Land of Twinks in WeHo and The Land of Raunch in Silverlake.

Barry continued scrubbing his car as he listened to the driver climb out of his pick-up cab and slam the door. He expected to hear the sound of quarters plunking through the slot, but no sound came. Barry realized his own timer was quickly winding down, so he scooted over, plopped in a few more coins for a little more time, then hurried to finish using the brush. He parked the brush back on its hook, then grabbed the jet spray hose and began to rinse away the suds.

"Excuse me..." the voice said dully. "You got change for a dollar?"

Barry turned to see the pick-up's driver standing just a yard from him. A Ty clone if ever there was one. The young man was about five-nine, with shaggy dirty blond hair and large brown eyes. He wore nothing but skateboarder shorts that were either too big or untied at the waist, for they had slipped down from his slim, tanned waist to rest on glaringly white hips. The contrast between tanned flesh and lily-white skin was more than titillating. The kid was holding out a thrashed, worn-out dollar bill. Barry fumbled in his pockets and pulled out a small fistful of quarters. He offered them to the boy.

"Take what you need," he said.

"Thanks, man," the young guy replied as he stepped up to Barry and fished four quarters from the pile in his palm. He tried to lay the bill in Barry's hand, but Barry pulled back.

"Keep it," Barry said. "Loan it to someone who might really need it."

The young man grinned. "Can I loan it back to myself?"

"Sure," Barry said.

"Nawww," the kid said as he leaned into Barry and shoved the bill into Barry's pocket. "Thanks for the offer, but I like to keep things square."

"It's your dollar," Barry replied as he stepped over to the coin slot of the timer and fed a few more quarters into it. "But I'll take charge of it if you want me to."

The young man started to walk back, then stopped. "Thanks again."

Barry pointed the jet stream nozzle at his car and let the rinse water blast. He nodded to the young man, then half-heartedly gestured to the lad's skateboard shorts. "You might lose those if you don't..."

The kid looked down at his waist, then hoisted up his shorts and tied the drawstring. "They're a little big, I guess."

Barry surreptitiously eyed the kid as he tucked the ends of the tied drawstrings deep into this crotch. The kid glanced at Barry just then. Barry turned a bit red faced, but the young man smiled. "That's a cool car...." he said.

"Wasn't so cool back when I was your age. This would've

been an embarrassment to drive. We went in for Chevys, Capris and GTOs, mostly."

"Capris?"

"Little car. Around 1974. Or maybe 1973. Kind of sporty. Then they changed the body style, around 1975 or 1976. Anyway, the later models didn't look as hot. They're next to impossible to find these days. Like old Ford Mavericks or Mercury Comets."

"Mom had a Maverick," the young man said. "Two door, white hard-top with eight cylinders."

"I think most were six cylinder," Barry offered.

"It was a cool car. Wish she'd kept it. I remember she traded it in for some nondescript sedan."

Barry continued rinsing his car, fighting with the pivoting hose strung from above, yet enjoying the feel of the splash-back of the water as he maneuvered around the front end of the Valiant to the passenger side. "You've a three-quarter ton," he said.

"My dad's old pick-up. It's a 1973. He got it the year my brother was born."

"He took care of it, I see."

The kid relaxed his stance and leaned against the damp, tiled wall. "Babied it, is more like it," he said as he absently slipped his hand below the waistband of his board shorts. "But I like the older models."

Barry felt his cock swelling in his jockstrap. The kid's comment was either just off-the-cuff or a come-on, he thought. Off-the-cuff would be logical, but the kid had slipped his hand down his shorts, his motion forcing the shorts to slide a little down, exposing just a slight band of white skin.

"There's old," Barry jibed, "and then there's museum pieces."

The buzzer sounded, signaling an end to the water supply. Barry let the time lapse. The Valiant was clean. He moved to the young man, who was next to the jet spray nozzle's sleeve. The boy shifted a bit so Barry could slip the nozzle back into place. Tiny droplets of water and sweat beaded on the lad's chest, ringed his neck. Barry felt cold sweat drip down from beneath his own armpits. A sure sign that he was a little nervous.

"You use a hard wax on it?" the boy asked.

"Huh? Oh! Not today," Barry said. "I'll just pull up and dry it off..."

"I could do it for you."

"Hard wax? How much?"

The young man shrugged his shoulders. "You help me wash my truck."

"Wash your truck?" Barry repeated.

The young man smiled slightly. "There's mud in the bed. You get in with the scrubbing brush and I'll blast the water?"

Barry's crotch strained as his cock inflated, painfully trapped beneath the sheath of the jockstrap. Even through his loose shorts, his hardness could be detected by anyone who chose to focus his eyes there, and he noticed the young man staring directly at his bulge. He nodded to the young man and extended a hand.

"I'm Barry."

"Phillip," the young man answered as he stepped close and shook Barry's hand.

Barry felt a bristling charge course through his body as they locked palms. Phillip's grip was firm, his fingers long and thin. Barry's prick strained hard, pushing itself out from beneath the side of the jockstrap pouch. He could feel his foreskin pulling back as the swollen shaft and swelling head stretched out long, thick and hard down his thigh. Barry tried to shift his stance so that the baggy leg openings of his shorts would somehow camouflage it. He pulled his hand from Phillip's and played with his shirttails.

"Let me move my car," he said hoarsely.

Phillip took a quick scan of the area. No one watching. No one around them. He quickly slid his hand up Barry's hairy thigh, pushing up the leg of Barry's shorts. Barry reflexively took a step back, but not before Phillip had exposed the tip of his aching dick. Phillip snickered a bit as Barry tugged at his shorts, trying to conceal himself.

"Nice fuckin' piece you got," Phillip said in a low, throaty growl.

Barry fumbled in his pocket for his car keys. "Um... I'm gonna pull my car ahead and dry it off."

He moved quickly, sliding into the car and starting the engine. He was about to put it in gear when the passenger door opened and Phillip slipped into the seat. He shut the door, smiled at Barry, then scanned the car's interior.

"Clean," Phillip said. "Real clean."

Barry said nothing but drove the few yards to the vacuuming-drying off stall in front of him. As he cut the engine, he noticed only two other cars remaining nearby. Two others there, then there was Phillip's pick-up.

"You're a little forward, aren't you?" Barry said.

"It's hot today," Phillip said with a grin. "And I think you're hot."

"If you're hustling, I don't pay."

"I'm just horny. Just like you." Phillip slid his hand over and squeezed Barry's thick rod through the cloth of his shorts. "You don't like younger guys?" he asked.

"Like?" Barry parroted. "We're in public here, Phillip. That's never been quite my style."

Barry could feel the sweat beading up on him. With the car's windows rolled up as they were, it was about twenty degrees hotter in the car. He wanted to roll down the window at least. The best thing, he thought, would be to just get out of the car and get on with drying it. He could already see the water on the hood and the windshield evaporating, leaving those little white water marks where the drops dried up. He reached for the handle to open the door, then Phillip suddenly pushed up the leg of his shorts and gripped his still-rigid prick.

Sweat poured freely from his neck, from under his arms, down his back as he panicked. But Barry didn't move. He watched Phillip's fingers gently wrap around his shaft. The boy squeezed his cock hard. Barry thought he was going to shoot his load then and there.

"It is a nice piece," Phillip whispered. He could feel the mass of meat, hot and sweaty and hard in his hand. He eased Barry's prepuce up over the glans, enjoying the sight of so much skin. "The skin's soft," he said. "Nice 'n' soft."

"There are people here, Phillip," Barry started his protest.

Phillip scanned the area. Two guys, each at his own car, on the other side of the car wash's lot. Two gay guys, obviously. And they were both eyeing each other as they lingered over their drying and polishing tasks. "Yeah," Phillip said as his other hand slipped up beneath Barry's shirt. He could feel the softness of the hair on Barry's stomach and chest. The buttons on Barry's old Hawaiian shirt seemed to ease through their button holes and open up the plackets, exposing even more of Barry's flesh. He leaned in and wrapped his lips around Barry's nipple, caressing the pinch of pinkish-tan flesh with his tongue.

Barry's body went rigid. His meaty hand left the door handle and pressed itself against Phillip's head, his thick fingers gripping a fistful of dark blond hair. He pressed the boy's face into his chest, relishing the feel of a hungry mouth on his nipple, his pec. Without thinking, he let his other hand light upon the lad's back, running down his spine to the base of his back. Within seconds, his hand was down the back of Phillip's skateboarder shorts, feeling the taut cheeks of that creamy white ass.

Phillip felt rivulets of Barry's sweat dripping down onto his face, wetting his bangs, running salty wetness all around for him to lick and lap up. The taste of a man. The clean, sweaty smell of a man. He pulled himself away from Barry's chest and brought his mouth up to Barry's. His tongue pressed inbetween Barry's lips, seeking its mate within. He ground his chin into Barry's, feeling the sandpaper roughness of stubble grate against his own smooth skin.

Barry fumbled for the lever of the seat, hit it and pushed the car seat back a bit, then pulled Phillip over as best he could into his lap. The boy liked to kiss. Barry liked to kiss. They locked their lips and tongues together for a good long time, savoring the taste of each other. When they finally parted, Barry stared into the deep brown eyes of the young stranger with him.

"I don't live far from here," Barry said.

Phillip pulled back a bit, then slid into the passenger seat. His hair was drenched with Barry's sweat, his torso just as wet and slick. Phillip smiled, looked around through the windows, then raised his hips a bit and slid down his board shorts. His slim, cut cock jutted up in the air, a very pale tan staff of velvety skin stretching up seven or so inches. He slipped his left leg free of the jumbled trunks at his feet, hit the door's lock with his right elbow, then shifted in his seat so that his back pressed against the door. He brought his left leg up onto the seat, spreading his legs apart, so that Barry could see his cock, his smooth tight ball sac, and more importantly, the tight puckered hole of his ass.

Phillip stuck his long finger into his mouth, sucking on it, wetting it, then reached down and pressed the tip of it against his hole. He shifted down a little further in the seat then slid his finger up into his ass. "I like to get fucked," he said. "Like it a lot."

Barry lost all common sense and reason and he bent down over the boy's crotch. His mouth was running as wet as the rest of him as he swallowed the lad's hard prick, letting the silky shaft and swollen head slam down his throat. The thatch of brown pubic hair pressed into his nostrils and he could smell the beach, the boy's sweat.

Barry sucked hard, his tongue massaging the shaft as throat constricted around the glans, and his head bobbed rapidly up and down. He wanted the boy's spunk right then and there. Nothing else mattered. Nothing. He wanted that hot load of the kid's cum in his mouth.

Phillip drilled his own hole with his finger while Barry sucked ferociously on his dick. His sphincter twitched and clamped down hard, wanting to feel something bigger and thicker. Phillip pulled his finger out then slowed Barry down. "You gotta fuck me, man. Fuck my hole."

Barry wouldn't relinquish Phillip's cock, though. He could smell the newly stirred desire on Phillip's finger. He wanted to fuck that hole, all right. He wanted to bury his face between the boy's tight cheeks and eat that tight butt out. But he first wanted to feel the boy cum. He clenched his lips around the lad's prick and continued pumping. He felt the young man's cock stiffen even more in his throat, felt the subtle tremor rising through the young man's groin. Phillip started to pant, a panting that seemed almost as if he was choking. Barry bore down even harder until his mouth, tongue and throat were a milking machine that would not stop. Phillip let out a growling groan, grabbed Barry's head and held him fast. Barry slammed down one last time, then felt the warm, thick fluid spurt across the back of this tongue. Barry swallowed and swallowed again, sucking down every last hot drop he could suck from the boy's prick. Finally, he sensed Phillip's body collapse. Barry pulled back off the young man. He swallowed hard, took a deep breath, then just stared at the pretty lad beside him.

Phillip eased himself back into an upright position and pulled on his board shorts. He looked around through the windows, then grinned. Barry glanced out the window and saw that the two guys were just a few feet away. They'd been watching.

"I don't usually do things like this," he said.

Phillip laughed softly. "Me neither, but sometimes... Hey, a little exhibitionism is good for a little voyeurism. Especially on a hot day like today."

"Hot. Yeah. You're fucking hot."

"So," Phillip said as he reached over and grabbed Barry's still-hard cock. "You haven't come yet."

"Takes me awhile," Barry said. "But you've given me something to think about while I work it myself."

"I was serious, man. I'm still fuckin' horny. I wanna feel that thick, hard prick of yours up my ass."

"You gotta wash your pick-up, still."

"I can do that later."

"So, what exactly are you saying?" Barry asked.

"It's fuckin' hot, man," Phillip said. "And when it's hot like this, all I wanna do is get it." Phillip pressed a finger against Barry's lips. "You wanna eat me out?"

Barry sniffed the faint, pungent odor still lingering on Phillip's long finger. "Yeah, I want to eat out that ass of yours, then lube you up and fuck that tight, cherry hole."

"Then why're we still sitting here?" Phillip asked. He reached in his pocket, pulled out his keys, then unlocked the door. "I'll follow you."

"My place isn't air conditioned," Barry warned.

"That's okay, man. Sweat's my speed," Phillip said with a smile. "Lead on."

JEDEDIAH, MY TADZIO

Peter Eros

The boy was standing in the shallow end of the pool, gazing off in the other direction. Swimming practice was over and most of the kids were already on their way to the locker room. The lifeguard lolled languidly on his stand.

I slid silently in at the deep end and swam underwater toward the neat red triangle of his bikini, intending I don't know what. To frighten him or to tease him, perhaps? Some unformed prank lay at the back of my mind. But just before I got to him he turned, and I rose up before him, my arms reaching up and outstretched.

The late-afternoon sun glanced off his shining golden curls like a radiant halo. As the dark blue, limpid eyes caught my startled gaze, a hint of a smile played on his perfect rosebud lips. I couldn't help myself. My arms enfolded him in a tight embrace, lifting him against me, and I kissed him full on the lips. With a little gasp his mouth opened and our tongues touched as our spandexed cocks preened against each other.

"I want you," he whispered as he gnawed on my earlobe.

At that moment I didn't know or care if anyone saw us. It was only after we emerged from the water that I realized the lifeguard had seen and appreciated our encounter, though he probably thought I was robbing the cradle. A smirk covered his blush, but the bulge in his shorts was almost as obvious as the swollen dicks practically poking out the top of our Speedos.

I suppose you could call Jedediah my Tadzio, though I'm nowhere near as old as Aschenbach. I'm twenty-eight and Jed is just eighteen, but with his gamin looks, slender frame and diminutive height, he could easily pass for thirteen or fourteen. Only the undeniable fuzz on his upper lip hinted at a reluctant innocence.

I didn't know it then but Jed had packed much more experience into his brief life than I had. His lesbian-inclined mother took him to Spain along with her lover when he was only six years old. He never knew his sperm-donor father, but the disparity of his looks compared to those of his dark-haired, a bit pudgy mother indicated that the boy received, from his anonymous dad, a considerable genetic gift.

The women ran a popular bar in the seaside resort Sitges, near the port of Barcelona. The bar served as a front for a drug distribution and prostitution ring. Apparently, failure to sufficiently pay off the corrupt local police got Jed's mother and girlfriend deported. They returned to San Diego when Jed was seventeen. By then, he spoke both Catalan and Castilian Spanish, German, French and Italian more fluently than his native tongue. He apparently hadn't cared for the English residents and tourists, and met few Americans.

I'm swimming and gymnastic coach at the school as well as being a twelfth-grade Spanish and English teacher. When Jed first turned up in my class I thought there had been some mistake. He seemed far too young, but was in fact a few months older than most of my charges. He'd had to repeat a year in Spain.

I'd never been a chicken-hawk and I'd certainly never been foolish enough to get involved sexually with any of my pupils. Even as a youth I preferred older, muscular men, mostly acquaintances from the gym, some leading to brief affairs. But all those relationships, for one reason or another, failed. I was pretty much habituated to a life of casual sex and one-night stands, so I was surprised and embarrassed by the effect Jed had on me. The most substantial thing about him was the impressive bulge in his crotch. Spanish trousers and jeans are styled to fit snugly, advertising a man's assets, and Jed obviously had plenty to display.

The first day in my class, his hand shook as he introduced himself was electric. His grip was firm and he didn't let go for several seconds as he regarded me with his large, candid, lustful eyes, and moistened his luscious lips.

"My name is Jedediah, but you may call me Jed, *professor*."

It was difficult to decide which was sexier: his dazzling smile or his charming accent. It was a warm day and having reached his desk he removed his sweatshirt, revealing a skimpy tanktop, which blatantly exposed his shapely pecs and pits. My nostrils longed to sniff, my tongue to lick. I found it difficult to concentrate on my teaching.

Thereafter, Jed had the unsettling habit of locking his eyes onto mine whenever I caught his gaze. At times he politely but firmly corrected my Spanish pronunciation or syntax and brought the class up to speed on latter-day colloquialisms. He was always accurate but never cocky or disrespectful about it. A hint of real amusement, but never mockery, gleamed from his impish eyes as he gravely addressed me as *"professor,"* provoking giggles from the other kids. When he handed in assignments at my desk, he usually managed to caress my hand, or even press my shoulder or brush my back with a trailing hand, causing an instant erection to tent my straining boxers. I enjoyed it too much, looked forward to it even, to ever reprimand him. I only wished to test how much of his charisma derived from sexual enthusiasm and versatility.

The SATs were concluded and school was winding down to graduation. I felt like it was now or never. I guess Jed did too. The showers were deserted, the rest of the kids just a distant shout. We shed our costumes and hugged beneath a warm jet, his lissome, extremely cuddlesome frame seeming very fragile in my muscular arms. He turned his face up to me and I swallowed his mouth, probing his throat as his tongue furled and sucked against mine. He took a handful of coconut-scented liquid soap and massaged my straining prick, expertly manipulating, squeezing and stroking, while sucking on my upstanding nipples, as my hands cupped and kneaded his pneumatic and well-rounded buns, and fingered his prominently ridged fuckhole. I was perilously close to cumming.

"No, not yet," he murmured, "I don't want to waste it. Take me to your place, please? I want you inside me. I want you to fuck me hard."

I was shaking with passion as his hands released me and caressed my palpitating chest and abs. We hastily dried ourselves, slipped on our shorts and headed for the parking lot. Jed grabbed his bike and folded it so I could stow it in the trunk. He nestled in the passenger seat. It was only a ten-minute drive but one I'll never forget. Jed slipped off his sandals, lay back against the window and kneaded my crotch with his bare feet. His toes were as agile as fingers, grabbing the tab of my zipper and sliding it open. As my cock sprang into view the nimble digits stroked and titillated me to explosive proportions. With an enthusiastic lick of the lips, the golden head descended to my crotch and with one suck he'd deep-throated me, the muscles of his esophagus massaging the seeping head as I groaned and writhed in my seat, trying to steer straight.

I yelped as I my zipper caught my pubic hairs while I leaping out of the car. He giggled wickedly and, to my surprise, led the way through the predominantly gay-owned complex to my apartment. I gave him an inquiring look as I unlocked the door.

"I've followed you home a couple of times, hoping."

He stepped out of his shorts before the door was fully opened and flung them ahead of him into the apartment. His swollen, uncut bone bobbed in front of him as I pushed him in ahead of me, hoping none of the resident predators had seen his bare-ass display.

As my shorts joined Jed's on the floor, he grabbed me gently by the prick and dragged me, without hesitation, into my bedroom, as though he were completely familiar with the layout of the place and at home in it. He inspected, approvingly, the scarlet-walled boudoir, with its framed Tom of Finland prints, strategically placed mirrors and discreet, indirect lighting. He pushed me down onto the imitation gray fur bedcover and fell into my embrace, kissing first my eyelids, then my nose, with side trips to each ear where his probing tongue almost sent me over the edge.

He held down my arms as his tongue briefly jousted with mine before a nipping, licking tour of my neck and my pecs. He sucked on each nub of nipple in turn, squeezing and massaging the other at the same time. Then he tongue-bathed my midriff, licking and nibbling on my ribbed abs, burrowing into my navel, finally sliding through my pubic bush to suck first one then both of my swollen gonads into his warm mouth, jiggling and probing with his hard tongue. He licked between my legs and briefly probed my anus. Then he switched to my bouncing prick, his tongue curling and sucking, before going down on my straining knob. He sucked me, without any effort or difficulty, right into his throat. The incredible suction and massaging action of his throat muscles was beyond anything I had ever experienced. My whole body teetered on the edge of orgasmic ecstasy. I cried out, *"Oh si! Sintiendo miembro asi, en labios!"*

As if sensing that I was about to blow, Jed withdrew and slid up to eat my face. Then he reached out to the nightstand, expertly tore open a condom and encased my swaying token of love, inserted a lube tube into his asshole and squeezed, then straddled me and slid down effortlessly to consume me with his ass lips. As my probe reached its limit within his depths, his butt settled against my groin, and his fingers grasped my rigid cock. He slid up and, momentarily, I felt his anal lips bite down gently on the glans, then slowly engulf my entire shaft again as he lowered himself back onto me. His lust-glazed eyes gleamed and his mouth fell open with a gasp. "Oh fuck ..."

His body arched as he rotated his ass and began a slow ride, pumping up and down, his twinkling baby blues fixed on my face, which must have reflected my overwhelming lust, joy and gratitude. He babbled on in Spanish as he plucked at my swollen nipples as he increased the pace of his slick hole's slide and gripped my swollen dick in a steady rhythm with his practiced colonic muscles. His hugely priapic prick bounced on my belly, and the prepuce skinned back to reveal the perfectly shaped head. The piss slit was wide open and dribbling pungent pre-cum. His spunk-plump scrotum bounced on my pubes.

Sperm surged in my balls as I happily surrendered to penis power, pumping my hips in time with his downstroke.

Jed shot his wad a few seconds before I did, splattering my straining body from chin to belly button with pungent streamers. He gasped, shuddered and then, just as my cum-throbbing length spasmed inside the embedded rubber sheath, he fell forward onto me and smothered my mouth with his own. He sucked desperately on my tongue and probed my Adam's apple. He tongue-bathed and nibbled my ears and my throat, his ass-muscles still clutching me tightly, not permitting me to soften.

As my cock inevitably deflated, despite his best efforts, and slid with an audible pop from his hot ring, Jed sighed and slid down to lay by my side, idly scooping his cum from my torso and swallowing it with evident relish. As I removed and tied the amply filled sheath, wrapped it in a tissue and dropped it on the floor, he homed in on my tits, sucking and nibbling with renewed energy. It was too much. I grabbed his curls and pulled him across me so that I could look at him directly. With my lust satisfied, for the time being, it was time to satisfy my curiosity.

"Wow, Jed, you're fantastic. I'm damn sure I wasn't as good

at this as you are when I was your age. When did you start? Where did you learn?"

He gave me a grave smile as he slid off me and lay on one elbow beside me, his free hand caressing my pecs. He told his story matter-of-factly, with occasional glances at me to see how I was taking it.

"Mom was always involved with the sex business. I grew up in the brothel. Sex was just a natural part of life in our house. We had *chico* as well as *chica* prostitutes. I guess I was only eight or nine when I first started sucking cocks. The other guys taught me. They were good. They were real careful not to hurt me. They fingered me and diddled my *culo* with dildos until I could take a regular cock. I was fucking and being fucked, and enjoying it, before I was twelve. I didn't come, but I enjoyed dry orgasms. Before I was thirteen I was shooting my wad regularly, for pay. But Mom was good to me. I didn't have to do it with just anyone, like the other kids. I was able to choose who I did it with. But I did do it with some really nice older guys. They were mostly gentle and taught me a lot. I did videos too. Are you shocked?"

"I guess, a little. You make my sex life seem like amateur night. Maybe you'll teach me a thing or two."

"I intend to, if you'll let me. I think maybe I love you. I would like to live with you to find out, if you'll have me. I don't just fuck, I can cook too, and I'm neat and tidy. I won't make a mess of your place. It's time I settled down with someone, but you're the only guy I know who I like enough to try it with."

"What about your Mom?"

"Oh, she's not likely to care much, and in any case I'm eighteen, I can do what I like."

"What about your future plans? Are you going to try for college or are you planning on taking a job?"

Jed surprised me when he gazed candidly into my eyes and said, "I suppose that I can keep on turning tricks, unless you object. It's what I do best, you know, and I can still save my best cum loads for you."

"Well...."

"Oh, and I've been approached to do videos and I reckon I can probably earn some good money doing them as well. Come to think of it, why don't you audition for them? You're really handsome and you have a terrific body."

"Well...."

"You could be a big hit. If you're really good at it you get to travel to all sorts of exotic location shoots too. It's worth a shot."

"Oh I'm flattered that you think so, but remember I've got a career—a teaching career! Much as I enjoy watching them ... God, I have got a closet full ... I can't imagine being in one! Have you any idea what would happen to my teaching job if someone got to see me in a video?"

"The only ones likely to see you in a video are other gay teachers, or parents, and they're not likely to object. It would be difficult to do without bringing suspicion on themselves. Most likely they'll just be envious. You never know who's swimming naked until the tide goes out. I read somewhere 'If you study malaria, you should live in the swamp.' You know you'd enjoy it. We could be a double act."

I couldn't believe he was serious to start with, but the more I thought about it the more my prick did a fandango. I'd have been lying if I said that it didn't seem an attractive proposition. Here he was offering to share my life while encouraging me to continue to play the field, especially if it was for money. He hushed my initial objections by smothering my mouth with his own, as he pushed my legs back and rested them on his shoulders. He slid down and primed my pouting manhole with spit-slick, probing tongue, then lubed fingers, before lodging his sheathed prick with one swift shove in my deepest recess.

"Oh fuuuck! Ooooh! Your cock feels so good inside me," I moaned.

"Well, you'd better get used to it. I need it a lot."

He pulled his cock back to where the bulb of the glans tugged at my anal ring, massaging my prostate with the swollen head until he thrust his shaft back in my ass even deeper than before, working his prick in and out, frictioning the nerve-laced chute and tender tissues, filling me again and again, his belly mashing against my own seething orbs, my straining dick bouncing between our taut and heaving abs. My asshole convulsed as Jed spurted a volley of cum, and ecstasy jolted my scrotum, pumping the cum up and out through my bouncing cock.

In the ensuing weeks, before our audition for one of the

major gay porn studios, Jed taught me all he knew, and that was a hell of a lot. On the appointed day I was nervous but undeniably excited, an excitement that was more than obvious in my 501s, uncluttered by underwear. The auditioning director fondled his own straining prick as Jed and I performed our well-rehearsed routine, while accepting and incorporating his suggested variations, and the cameraman zoomed in to catch every detail of our unbridled lust.

As I began to fuck Jed's athletic colon, the director stripped and joined the action, reaming my asshole before threading his rubbered prick through my greedy pucker. Then he rode me slowly and deliciously, my torrid wetness gripping him with spasms that made his hips jerk with pleasure, as beneath me Jed let out little cries of ecstasy and his cock jerked and swelled, cum arching in milky spurts between our arching bodies, each one matched by a loving contraction of my colon around the welcome intruder in my own butt. It was my first three-way, the first of many, at home and at work, feeding an orgiastic joy and a need I'd not previously known I had.

Jed and I, labeled with professional names that reflect our sexual skills and protect our real identities, don't always get to work together. We've both fucked and been fucked professionally for several studios now, mainly during the school vacations for me, but, believe me, the pupil has become the teacher.

Thanks to Jed, I've explored sexual feats that I'd never have imagined, and enjoyed every one. Our expertise and enthusiasm have netted us both nominations for the next Gay Erotic Video Awards. Despite our narrow field of celebrity I've been neither reclusive nor gregarious about my regular occupation, but have been fortunate in finding intimates among the producers and models who are instinctively protective of my privacy. I'm convinced that our vulnerable, recorded, public intimacy breeds deep affection and friendship between the participants. Most of us aren't just performing for the benefit of the camera, or working to get paid—we're high on sex.

But you'll have to excuse me now. You see, Jed is begging for another lesson. Care to join us?

THE VOYEUR

Frank Brooks

*"The boy-whore usually entertained two or three other men
before the old man arrived, and sometimes
one or two later in the evening."*

1.

I first spotted him three weeks ago, on one of those sultry
August afternoons that makes a man's flesh sweat and his
blood boil. When I first saw him, I mistook him for a girl, a
blond bombshell of a flat-chested teenage girl: my type of girl,
if you know what I mean. I can best describe him as the
spitting image of teen idol Leif Garrett in that old film *The
Medicine Hat Stallion*, so you get the idea. I was embarrassed to
get so turned on by what turned out to be a long-haired
boy—everybody knows how straight I am—but it was an
honest mistake, and of course the act of voyeurism in itself can
induce a certain breathless excitement that borders on the
erotic, regardless of what you're looking at. I used to
experience it even when I was a cop working a stake-out with
binoculars.

Yes, there he was, mincing nude around that tenth-floor
apartment two blocks away as I trained my high-powered
telescope on the apartment's large, uncurtained windows,
allowing me unobstructed views of his living room, kitchen,
and bedroom. With his shoulder-length blond hair and an
absolutely smooth, nubile body, and prancing around and
showing it all off like some willowy little princess—well, you
can see why I mistook him for a girl and got so excited—then
so let down when I spotted the rigid, pink-tipped rod sticking
straight out from what I expected to be his pussy-mound.
Then as he walked, his naked rod wagging side to side like the
stiff tail of a dog, I found myself disgusted by the obscenity of
it and I had to remind myself, to keep from getting downright
furious, that he didn't know—that he *couldn't* know—that I
was watching him, and that he was not intentionally flaunting
his sissiness at me and throwing me that inviting look.

You see, my telescope is so powerful that I can read a newspaper over the shoulder of a bum seated on a park bench three blocks away. So, when the boy happened to look toward me, it was as if his longing green eyes were staring straight into my own eyes from inches away—as if we were lovers staring into each other's eyes as we fucked. No, "longing" is the wrong word. His look was *lustful*—lustful in a female way, lustful like the eyes of a nympho. *Take me*, they begged. *Rape me hard! Violate my nubile young body!* But, of course, he had no idea I was there, watching him from my own, eleventh-floor apartment.

As I hinted, it's no secret that I'm not gay. Everybody knows I'm as straight and manly as they come. I'm the head night security guard at one of the major skyscrapers downtown. I bench press over 400 pounds at the gym. I was discharged from the Marines with citations and medals and served eighteen years as a police officer in this jungle of a city before settling into this cushy security-guard position. And I've banged more pussy than I'll ever remember—more than ten average men do in a lifetime—so you can see why the pouty, kiss-me gaze of that blond little pretty-boy made me grind my teeth, and why my mistaking him for a girl and my getting so hard and worked up embarrassed me so. On the street I'd have decked him in two seconds flat if he'd looked at me that way. As a cop, I'd have run him in just for looking the way he did—for impersonating a hot teenage girl, for christsake. There oughta be a law.

But I'm getting side-tracked. Yes, it was three weeks ago that I first sighted him, and over those three weeks I've found myself not watching much else than the three windows of his apartment. It isn't that I've lost complete interest in staking out other apartments and keeping an eye on my regulars. I still keep a cursory eye on them. Humans are creatures of habit, so I know exactly when to point my telescope at what window in what apartment building to catch a couple fucking, or a schoolgirl doing her homework and diddling her pussy, or—I could tell lots of tales, hundreds of them. No, it isn't that I've lost interest in my other windows and what's going on behind them, it's that I've been finding the blond sissy's windows more *interesting* than the others lately—disgusting, of course, but interesting—and I've had my telescope mostly trained on them. I've had to remind myself that I can't let him become an obsession, and I won't, but lately....

I must state up front that contrary to whatever myths there are out there about voyeurs, we are, in general, intelligent, scientific individuals. I consider myself a sociologist, psychologist, and anthropologist all wrapped up in one. I'm a scientist of human behavior, an objective watcher of the private quirks of the common people around me. So, when I come across a situation more interesting than usual, you can't blame me for paying more attention to it, even if it disgusted me as much as it fed my curiosity.

It wasn't so much that my Leif Garrett lookalike walked around nude most of the time—I've observed many chronic nudists over the years, most of them women—or that he was often in a state of apparent sexual excitation much of the time—what boy that age isn't? What I found interesting was that expensive apartment he lived in—by himself, it looked like—and at so young an age—and those visitors he entertained daily—and *how* he entertained them.

I can't deny that I've found it stimulating to watch him in action. Apparently, this is because my mind has fixated on my first impression of him as a nubile, flat-chested teenage girl and I've continued unconsciously to see him in that way. When I watch him fucking himself on his bed, his long, smooth legs waving in the air like those of a whore as he plunges a long, thick, life-like dildo into his asshole, I become almost blind to the plump balls squirming in their satin-smooth pink sac above his perineum, or his rigid cock, untouched, pulsing against his girl-smooth lower belly. When I watch him fuck his asshole as if it were a pussy, I must consciously forget that he's a boy, and this must be why I get so worked up. What else could it be?

In any case, there he was, this little blond sissy all alone in this big ritzy apartment, where he stayed put most of the time, rarely going out—no school, no work—so you can see why my curiosity got the better of me, why I kept my scope trained on his windows. I mean, what was he all about? I had to know. Well, it didn't take me long to find out.

He was sprawled on a big white couch in the living room on the day after I'd first spotted him, watching TV as he played with his balls and fingered his ass, when up he jumped suddenly and ran to the front door, which had just opened and through which was stepping a fat, graying, Wall Street type, who looked as if he'd just come from counting his money at the bank. The man had a key to the apartment and was inside before the kid could get to the door to open it for him.

It's the kid's grandpa, I thought. He had to be 60, maybe 65. But he didn't act like your typical grandpa greeting your typical grandson. I watched in disbelief as the gray-haired old fart wrapped his arms around the naked teenager and kissed him like Romeo kissing Juliet, actually feeding the boy tongue, which the boy sucked, for christsake! Watching them up close through my telescope, I nearly vomited. It's bad enough to watch two men kiss, but to watch a man that age kiss a boy that young—it was downright, well, *incestuous*, if you know what I mean, and it rubbed me the wrong way. Queers in general infuriate me, but this was the ultimate. But that was nothing compared to what happened next.

Just like that, the kid was on his knees, fishing the old bastard's snake out of his three-hundred-dollar dress pants with hands as deft as those of a pickpocket. I have to admit I was surprised, even shocked, by the size of the old fucker's penis and by its hardness. Sticking straight out and throbbing away as the boy licked it, it had to be eight inches long at least, and thick as a beer can. You think of older men as being shriveled up and impotent, but this old goat had a crowbar that a well-built 25-year-old would give an arm for. Maybe that's why sissy-boy went for him: because he had a huge one. They say that queers will go for *anything* with a big dick on it, even if it's a horse, for chrissakes!

So there I was, watching the young queer peel back the old goat's foreskin and lick the moist, shiny, maroonish knob as if he couldn't get enough of it. Then he went down on the thick shaft, which stretched his lips thin like rubberbands and nearly unhinged his jaws. As the boy bobbed his head, greasing the man's veiny prick with spit, the man took off his fancy clothes until he was naked, revealing a stout, hairy physique that wasn't completely saggy. Muscle was still evident under the layers of fat, as if Grandpa had been an athlete at one time, before going to seed on Wall Street or whatever.

The kid sucked like a well-trained whore, and soon it looked like Grandpa, from the way his eyes were rolling, was going to lose his load down junior's throat, but before he lost it totally, he pushed the kid away and his big old crowbar popped out, dripping with spit and shooting a few drops of watery juice onto the boy's downy, flushed cheeks. The kid caught the cum with his fingertips and licked it off them, looking up into the the the old fart's face like a seductive whore.

Grandpa was so red-faced and was panting and puffing so hard that I expected him to have a heart attack, but as soon as he'd caught his breath, he picked up the giggling boy-slut and whisked him into the bedroom like a groom carrying his bride over the threshold. There he dropped him onto the king-sized bed.

The boy, laughing, kicked his slender legs up in the air and spread his asscheeks as grandpa, watching him, lubed up his hard old cock with grease. Then the old fart got up on the bed and knelt there, holding the kid by the ankles, his grease-shiny cock so hard it was pointed at the ceiling and throbbing with lust. It was a sight—this old goat kneeling there, his missile-like cock poised for launching into the hungry, half-open asshole of this nubile kid. He didn't waste time. Just like that, the old fucker skewered the boy with a single, perfectly aimed thrust. I mean, he sank that big old hog all the way in with such a quick, smooth motion that it made the boy's mouth gape. The boy, pinned down, squirmed as Grandpa, pressing his hairy shoulders to the backs of the kid's knees, began to screw fast and hard, and so deep that I expected his naked dickhead to pop out of the boy's open, gasping mouth.

But instead of the shiny old cockhead, the kid's pink tongue slipped out of his mouth and, as man and boy fucked like wild animals, their mouths locked together, each partner feeding the other his tongue. They fucked in a frenzy, staring into each other's eyes, the man driving, grinding, the boy wiggling and rotating his butt. The kid wanted it, wanted it even deeper than he was getting it. Each time they broke their kiss I could read the boy's lips: "Fuck me!" he kept saying. "Fuck me!"

I stared through my scope, my big hog sticking straight out and throbbing like crazy, my right hand just itching to stroke it. But I didn't let myself. It was too perverted—this scene I was watching. It was just fucking sick!

It didn't take long before the old fucker's head snapped back as if he'd been shot. He started to shudder and jerk. There was no doubt about it he was pumping his cum deep into the kid's guts. From the way the kid squirmed under him, toes working obscenely, I guessed that he must be shooting off too, probably grinding his young dick against the man's hairy paunch, since he hadn't laid a hand on his own cock.

At last the man's movement's slowed and the kid unhooked his knees from over the hairy shoulders. Grandpa collapsed onto the kid and fell into a coma. I soon lost interest in watching them sleep. When I checked them out later, I found junior sprawled in front of the TV in the living room and Grandpa nowhere in sight. Apparently, he'd left.

He was back the next afternoon at the same time for a repeat performance, and the afternoon after that, and I soon knew that I could count on him stopping by every weekday afternoon after work for his piece of ass. The boy usually blew him, and he usually fucked the kid, the two of them repeating their perverted coupling of that first afternoon in different positions and with kinky variations. The only time the old geezer didn't fuck the kid was when he lost his load down junior's throat before he could get him into the bedroom for a fuck. Then he'd take the young cocksucker across his knees and spank him, presumably for getting him off prematurely. The old goat was only good for one load per session. The boy seemed to enjoy the spanking; more than once he shot off down Grandpa's hairy leg as the man's fat hand cracked across his pink ass.

It didn't take too many smarts to figure out what was going on. I'm an ex-cop, you'll remember. I've seen it all. It was evident that the old fart was keeping the kid—supporting him—keeping him like any *normal* rich old fart would keep a mistress. In life, the man was certainly a married, upper-class pillar of the community, a bank president or a politician—maybe even a judge—and surely a church-goer. No doubt about it. I've seen enough of these hypocritical old community pillars in my time. Every one of them has some filthy, perverted little secret that leaves him a sitting duck for extortion, and I could have blackmailed this old hypocrite if I'd wanted to, but I'm not that kind. I didn't give a shit about the old fart, it was the kid I was interested in, the boy-whore. Who was he? What made him tick? I'll say it again, so you won't get the wrong idea: my interest is scientific. I'm a student of human behavior.

Anyway, so there was the old geezer, secretly fucking a load into his kept pretty-boy every afternoon. Nice little secret, and I'm sure grandpa was smug about it. But the old man didn't know that pretty-boy had a secret of his own—he didn't know what pretty-boy was up to the rest of the day while he was sitting in the courtroom or the bank or the stock exchange. Grandpa didn't know that he was never pretty-boy's first visitor of the day. The boy-whore usually entertained two or three other men before the old man arrived, and sometimes one or two later in the evening. He had nearly a dozen regulars, and they all had three things in common: One, they were all rich, which was evident from the clothes they wore and the cars they drove. Two, they were all older men, in their fifties or sixties. Three, they were all poker buddies of grandpa and often attended his Wednesday-evening card parties, which were held in the boy's apartment. Unlike Grandpa, they didn't have an apartment key and had to ring up pretty-boy from the foyer of the building and get buzzed in before taking the elevator up to pay their horny respects. I kept tabs on all their comings and goings and couplings.

The scene dumbfounded me. What did this satin-skinned teenager see in these wrinkled, paunchy old daddies? I could guess what they saw in him, but what did he see in them? It had to be more than money. As soon as they rang him from the foyer, he would start squirming and masturbating as if he couldn't wait for them to arrive. As soon as they stepped in the door, he was all over them, squirming in their hairy arms and kissing them, feeding them his pink young tongue. Frankly, it made me want to puke! But it intrigued me. I mean, what was happening here?

As I watched them day after day, I began to take a wicked, almost profane thrill at the sight of their sick behavior. Unconsciously, I must have been seeing the boy as a girl, because my cock would turn splitting hard and pulse with such a maddening fuck-itch that finally I had to give in and jerk it. There was something about that almost-sacrilegious coupling that excited me like I've rarely been excited, excited me as much as it disgusted me.

So there I was, watching these old toads stopping by one

after another, and eventually I went down and staked out the boy's building so I could enter the foyer with one of them and watch the procedure for ringing up pretty-boy—in Suite 628, it turned out. I followed Oscar, Burt, Mike, and Jim separately into the foyer and listened to pretty-boy greet them and buzz them in. They used no special code word to gain access, just their names, and a few minutes later they were up in pretty-boy's suite, a tongue down his throat, a cock up his ass.

One of these old perverts is a foot fetishist and gets off on sucking the kid's toes while he's fucking him. Sometimes he get's so excited sucking those wiggling pink digits that his dripping cock almost shoots off before he gets it inside the boy. The toe sucking drives the kid bonkers, makes him grab his cock and beat off in a frenzy, his eyes almost popping out from the double stimulation of cock and mouth, and soon he's shooting rivers of cum across his heaving stomach. The old foot-fetishist, after a spastic unloading up the kid's ass, leans forward and laps up the boy's cum like a cat lapping up cream. He doesn't miss a drop. Gross, I admit, but I can't help but watch. Gross, but intriguing.

Then there's the sadistic old goat who fucks the boy doggie-style, with each humping motion yanking his cock completely out, then ramming it back in before the gaping pink hole can close. As he rams in, he simultaneously yanks on the kid's longish blond hair as if jerking the reins of a horse. The boy gasps and winces, but his cock never loses its straight-out rigidity. I must confess that this sadistic treatment of the young whore especially excites me. He's getting exactly what he deserves. I confess that I've lost my load while watching this scene—no doubt unconsciously imagining the boy as a vixenish schoolgirl getting exactly what she deserves.

Another of the boy's lovers can't get enough of sucking his cock. He couldn't care less about fucking that tight young ass. He sucks like a greedy calf at the kid's stiff, squirming cock for an hour or more at a stretch, teasing two, even three loads out of the gasping teenager and guzzling down every drop of it. Disgusting!

But even more disgusting is that the boy himself seems to relish sucking off these men as often as he can, his Adam's apple dancing as he guzzles their cum! With the one named Burt, he does nothing more than sixty-nine, he and the old fart bobbing their heads between each other's thighs for an hour at a time and sucking out as many loads as they can get. While watching them through my high-powered telescope, I can almost hear them as they grunt and slurp and gulp. I'm sure you've noticed that telescopes and binoculars have the quality of bringing sounds as well as sights closer, allowing you almost to hear through walls.

As I watched these scenes repeat themselves day after day, I couldn't help but think of that old film, *Harold and Maude*, in which the clergyman expresses his disgust at the idea of young flesh coupling with old. My sentiments exactly. You might wonder why I continued to watch queer scenes that sickened my straight sensibilities. I've mentioned my objective, scientific curiosity as the main reason. Also, I'll confess a certain sadistic satisfaction I find in watching these aging studs assault their young quarry and, in my opinion, give the boy exactly what he deserved.

And then there were the Wednesday-evening card parties. The boy's sugar daddy and secret lovers would all meet in the boy's suite and play cards around a table in the living room while junior ran around naked, bringing them drinks and snacks. The men, who were clothed, copped feels of the boy's butt and hard prick, and he took turns sitting on their laps. The only man who kissed him was the sugar daddy, but occasionally one of the others would secretly slip a finger up the boy's ass and make him squirm. I could see it close-up through my telescope—a fat finger sliding in and out of the kid's tight, pink asshole. If the sugar daddy only knew, I thought!

My hunch is that these parties were not just for playing poker and socializing, but for the sugar daddy to show off his prize, his kept pretty-boy. It's my hunch also—and I'm good at hunches—that the only one who knew that pretty-boy was making it not just with the sugar daddy, but with every man in the group, was the sugar-boy himself. The sugar daddy thought that he had the kid all to himself, and each of the other men thought that he, and he only, was fucking the kid behind the sugar daddy's back. What a bunch of dumb shits!

Now, get this: Always before the party ended, the sugar daddy would pull his boy onto his lap for a fuck right there in front of the other men. Taking his cock out of his fly, he would jack it to hardness, then impale the kid with it. He'd make him ride it as he continued to play cards and the other men watched.

I could tell that, before long, they were all going out of their minds, and I could also tell that pretty-boy, not just his sugar daddy, was enjoying the tease. I'd have loved to see that frustrated gang lose it and rape the little bastard right there in front of his keeper. You've gotta understand, one thing I can't stand is cock-teases, and that kid was a cock-tease. Like one of those vixenish, cock-teasing, jailbait schoolgirls who are forever batting their eyelashes at me, tempting and teasing me until I want to kill, that boy-whore deserved to be taught a lesson.

2.

Leif was running a brush through his hair when the buzzer rang. A long session of sixty-nining with Burt always left his long hair a mess. His heart pounding with anticipation, he ran to the intercom, wondering who was ringing. Jim wasn't scheduled to come by until two, which was nearly three hours from now, but, if Jim was early, well, Leif could handle it. In fact, his cock was already throbbing with the expectation that it would be Jim—who always delivered a good, hard, deep fuck. He stroked his smooth, stiff cock as he pressed the intercom button.

"It's Burt," the voice said. "I forgot my watch."

"No problem, come on up." Leif pressed the buzzer to allow him back into the building.

Burt's voice sounded a little hoarse, Leif thought with a smile. He must have given Burt's tonsils a good workout with his stiff prick—the cocksucker! Burt knocked, and Leif swung open the door.

"Wha—"

In a second, Leif was on the floor, a sweaty hand clamped over his mouth, a man on top of him and pinning him down, a big man with a Batman cowl over his head. The man kicked the door shut and was growling in his ear: "Give me any trouble and I break your neck. Understand? Understand?"

Leif blinked his eyes. He couldn't shake his head. He was

shaking so hard that he'd have been too weak to resist even if he'd wanted to, even if he'd dared to.

The man stuffed a wadded rag into his mouth. "Bite on that. Try and shout and you're dead meat."

The man got up to chain the door. His dark eyes glared through the holes of the cowl as Leif lay cowering at his feet. He dropped his black-booted foot on Leif's chest, nudging Leif's nipples with the toe of it, then his chin.

"OK, pretty-boy, spit out that rag and kiss my boot. Scream and I shove it down your throat."

Leif had to use his hand to get the rag out of his mouth. He found himself panting like a dog, his chest rising and falling with quick, shallow breaths. He was still shaking, but was aware of wild sensations pulsing through his prick in spite of his fear. He kissed the black-leather toe of the man's boot.

"Now lick it!"

Leif eased out his pink tongue and flicked it at the shiny black leather. The man glared down at him, rubbing his crotch through his jeans. As Leif continued to lick, he watched the man undo his jeans and pull out a hard, sweaty, uncut cock at least eight inches long. In spite of himself, Leif couldn't help but gawk at the big cock and be excited by it, and he found himself licking the man's boot with long swipes of his tongue and almost relishing it.

"Whore!" the man growled. "Cock-tease! Worthless hunk of shit!" He drew his boot scalpel-like down Leif's smooth stomach and shoved the black toe of it up under Leif's plump, pink, hairless balls.

"Please," Leif dared to whisper. "Don't hurt me. I'll do anything you want."

"You're goddamned right you'll do anything I want!" The man stroked his cock as he twisted the toe of his boot between Leif's asscheeks. "Fucking cock-tease! Unlace those boots!"

Cautiously, Leif rose to a crouch. Sitting on his pink heels and leaning forward, he unlaced the man's boots and pulled them off one at a time. He didn't wait to be told to pull off the socks. As the man watched him, he took off his shirt, then dropped his jeans and kicked them aside. Except for the cowl, he was now as naked as Leif and stood there towering over him, well over six feet tall, with muscles upon muscles, and pre-cum like hot raindrops dripping from his pulsing cock.

With a firm shove of his foot, he knocked Leif onto his back, then was on top of him again, grinding his sweaty balls in Leif's face, his rough hands wrapped in Leif's hair.

"Lick my balls! Suck my balls! Cock-teasing bitch!"

Leif didn't hesitate. In spite of his fear, he couldn't help but moan as he licked, sucked, and slobbered over the man's enormous hairy nuts, his eyes on the underside of the man's huge cock as it throbbed against his forehead.

"Christ!" the man panted as Leif tongued his balls, and, with one hand wrapped in Leif's hair, he used the other to stuff his sweaty cock into Leif's mouth. "Suck on *that*, whore-boy!"

It was like a fist being stuffed down his throat. Leif choked.

"Suck it!" the man ordered. "Eat it!"

As the man withdrew his cock slightly, Leif gasped for air. When the man plunged back in, Leif was ready for him, tightening his mouth to prevent the whole thick cock from sliding down his throat. Using his lips and tongue, he sucked and licked the man's churning, sliding fuck-tool. It was a big, hairy, juicy one, and Leif salivated as he pleasured the succulent hunk of man-meat.

"Aw fuck yeah!" the man growled, his fiery dark eyes rolling with delirium. His head nodded almost drunkenly, as if he was going to topple off Leif's chest.

Leif darted the tip of his tongue under the man's foreskin, whirling it round and round the moist, sizzling glans, tasting and smearing the pre-cum that continued to ooze from it. As he sucked rhythmically, he drove the tip of his tongue into the man's gaping cum-hole, which seemed to send an electric jolt through the man's body.

"Oh Christ!" The man was gasping, trembling like a volcano about to erupt. He clapped Leif's head between his big hands and began to ejaculate, pumping torrents of spunk into Leif's rhythmically sucking mouth. "Drink it! Oh Christ, take it all!"

Leif gulped and guzzled, sucked and slurped, drinking down every drop of the thick, sweet, sizzling load of his rapist. He extracted every last drop and continued sucking until the man gasped as if he couldn't take it anymore and toppled off him, then lay panting beside him, his eyes glazed over and half shut. He looked exhausted and helpless, and Leif thought about escaping into the hallway and screaming for help while he had time. He had a chance now to escape—he could sense it—but, as his mind raced with the possibilities, he found himself more interested in pulling on his cock.

He wasn't just horny; he was unbearably horny. Fear had fueled his lust—fear and the realization that he'd been raped. He'd never been raped before, except in his imagination, and he'd found the experience more wildly exciting than terrifying—as exciting as he'd ever imagined it would be, or more so. His rapist had such a big, sweet cock—and there it lay now against his muscular, hairy belly, shiny with saliva and still nearly hard. If only the man had raped him up the ass! As much as he loved a cock down the throat, he loved one up the ass even more.

Without another thought, Leif straddled the man at the loins, then lifted the man's cock upright and guided the fat, sizzling head of it between his asscheeks. He was still well-lubricated from having been fucked earlier today by Lou, and the big knob slipped into his asshole easily. Rotating his ass, he impaled himself all the way to the man's hairy balls. The man groaned, his eyes opening as if in surprise, then disbelief, his body writhing as Leif began to ride his eight inches of rigid prong. Leif smiled at the man, leered at him, fucking up and own, tugging at his own rigid cock as he bounced. He tightened his asshole, skinning the man's cock alive.

"What the—" the man babbled, gasping and squirming.

I'm fucking Batman! Leif thought, almost laughing at the image of himself as trusty Boy Wonder Robin riding Batman's cock. It was a fantasy of his, which was now, in a way at least, being fulfilled. *I'm Robin, and Batman is fucking my butt!* He contracted his asshole rhythmically as he rotated his butt, screwing himself up and down on the thick, veiny, rock-hard prong of the man who had broken into his apartment to rape him and who now lay helpless and squirming under him.

The man groaned, writhing as if tortured, his eyes glassy and rolling behind the eye-holes of his black cowl. Leif, as he bounced, thrust a bare foot forward to tweak the man's nipples with his toes. The man looked as if he were going to lose his mind and Leif smirked and leered, bouncing faster, tightening his asshole mercilessly. He felt the man's thick, slippery cock jabbing the pit of his entrails like a hot, striking cobra. His hand became a blur around his own cock. The orgasmic fire whirled to a climax in his tight loins and he grunted as his spunk shot across the man's chest and cowled face, splashing in milky streams. Trembling, the man arched up and exploded.

"Oh, shoot it!" Leif moaned, feeling the spurts of man-spunk deep inside him.. "Fuck me! Give it to me!"

The telephone began to ring. Leif, reflexively, slipped off the man's softening cock and ran to answer it. He was picking up the receiver when he heard the door chain rattle behind him and looked back. His cowled visitor, clothing hugged to his muscular chest, was slipping out.

"Don't go!" he called after him, but the man was already gone.

HOT REUNION

Rudy Roberts

I remember going up north as a child—spending all those summers at the cottage with my grandparents, an elusive tomcat and a fat, lazy black lab. There were rarely any other kids my age on the lake—not like today when the lake is swarming with children, like blackflies. I spent most of my free time talking to myself, making up imaginary friends, fishing, canoeing, swimming—anything to get out of the house. And away from my grandfather's incessantly repeated stories of "life during the Great War" and "the Great Depression." But out of adversity often comes a shimmering ray of hope. Because my fifteenth summer was different.

It was that summer that I met Bryan.

One hot July day, I took the rowboat out for a spin around the harbor.

"Be careful of the rocks off the point," my grandfather gruffly reminded me, as he always did. He never said anything without speaking gruffly. And, as though cursed, I soon found myself scraping against slime-slicked rocks that were just below the surface of the water. I must have looked like an absolute incompetent: oars flailing about, jabbing at the water to push off from the scouring boulders, careful not to puncture the ancient and often-patched hull.

Finally freed, I took a deep breath, sat down and turned cautiously back towards the cottage. And there on the shore—as I knew he would be—stood my grandfather, hands sternly on his hips, the brim of his hat casting a sinister shadow low over his face. Even though I couldn't *see* his face, I knew that the countenance was stern, bursting with disapproval and augmenting rage. Instead of returning to shore for the obligatory scolding as I should have, I quickly brought the boat around and scurried off into the mouth of the channel, out of sight—at least temporarily—of those judgmental eyes, behind the sturdy concealment of the pine-covered point.

And there he was. He was about my age, maybe a year older, sitting on a rock on the opposite shore, looking dejected, absently tossing stones and chunks of wood into the water. As children are wont to do, I instantly forgot about my grandfather and eyed this stranger with curiosity. At first, my presence went unnoticed. He just sat on the shore next to a fallen tree. His face wore a look of absolute boredom. He was barefoot. And peculiar.

"Hey!" I shouted, rowing as though I were a seasoned veteran of the sport. "Wanna ride?"

The boy looked up then, his face pale and thin. His lips, although pouting, were bright. Then something sparked in those blue eyes and that pout went away. I brought the boat closer to shore and he waded out for it.

"Is it yours?" he asked with a strong British accent, seemingly glad of the diversion. He was skinny, with knobby knees and pasty limbs. But he had been out in the sun—the red and peeling patches on his nose and cheeks attested to that.

"Naw," I said, trying to sound as nonchalant as possible, "it's Grandpa's. But he lets me use it whenever I want. You wanna go for a ride?"

"Are you sure it's alright if I join you?" he asked, climbing deftly aboard. He had excellent sea legs and didn't falter once as we pulled away from the shore. His bare feet, toes splayed, left wet footprints on the bottom of the boat.

"Where are you from?" I asked as he settled down on the seat opposite me.

"England," he replied, looking around as though he'd just realized where he was. "It's lovely up here, isn't it?"

Lovely wasn't one of the more commonly used words in my family—nor among fourteen-year-old boys, for that matter -- so I giggled. I felt instantly ashamed, though, when he blushed more fiercely than his sunburn.

"Sorry," I said. "I've never heard anyone talk like you before, that's all."

"You mean my accent? Haven't you heard anyone from England before?" he asked, regaining his composure.

"Sure," I lied, nodding.

"That doesn't bother you, does it?" he asked, his face becoming suddenly hard as stone, his brow dark and brooding as he prepared to defend his heritage.

"No," I quickly replied, shaking my head and leaning back

into my rowing.

"Because if it *does*, I wouldn't think twice about popping you right on the nose and tossing you over the side!" He sat up very straight then, his palms flat against his thighs, the thin fingers digging into his legs, his jaws clenched, ready for a fight.

"I don't wanna fight," I said, smiling, trying to set him at ease. An unruly curl of blond hair fell into my eyes. "So, you wanna go for a ride or what?"

His transformation was almost fluid—from a defensive, savage creature to a soft, docile boy once again. And, as before, he turned pale and meek, apologetic for his actions.

"I've never seen you here before," I said. "Have you been up long?"

"We just arrived a couple of days ago," he replied, his voice tinged with anguish. "We're going to stay all summer." He said this last sentence with heavy regret, as though he were a prisoner and a summer vacation were his sentence.

"Me, too," I said, countering his regret with exuberance. "We can hang around together, if you like. I don't have any friends up here and...."

"Really?" he asked, looking up and peering at me through veils of dark, silken lashes. "You'd play with me?"

"Sure," I said. "Why not? Are you an escaped convict or something?"

His laugh was fresh and reassuring. We chatted all around the bay. I could see my grandfather standing on the shore, waving at me to come home. But I ignored his signal, knowing already that I'd tell him later that I mistook it for a greeting. I took the opportunity, in the meantime, to become better acquainted with Bryan.

Bryan's father was a journalist, and had recently been transferred from London to Toronto. While the family home was being selected, his company had given him a cottage on our lake for the summer. I asked Bryan why they chose a lake so far away from anything. He, of course, had no idea. He wasn't meant to question his elders, he said, quite obviously disapproving of their choice. Even though he seemed to like the physical surroundings, it was clear that he wished he were anywhere else but in the hinterland of northern Ontario.

"And you come up here *every* summer?" he asked,

incredulous.

"Ya." He was now beside me, having offered to take one of the oars himself. We were like two prisoners on a Spanish galley. "But I like it up here," I said. "It's not like I'm being shipped off anywhere because my folks can't stand me or anything. I really like it up here. Well, sometimes it gets a bit weird with my grandparents and all, but mostly it's great."

"Well, *I* don't like it much," he replied, his face once more assuming that sullen pout, looking out across the lake like Moses over the wilderness. "I'm used to traffic and trolleys and crowds of people—as dense as the fog itself sometimes. Not this ... silence and ... and ... clean air." Sitting suddenly still, he took in a deep breath of this silence and appeared to be all the better for it. I smiled and pulled on the oar.

"I should probably be getting back," I said remorsefully, casting a glance over my shoulder at my grandfather who was, by now, prancing up and down the dock like a stalking cat. "My grandpa's waiting for me."

Bryan looked over at our dock and saw my grandfather. "He looks like a treat," he observed aloud, immediately regretting that he'd let the words slip.

I giggled and set him at ease. "Ya," I replied, heading back to shore, "he sure is."

The roof of a cottage poked through the tops of the trees about fifty yards above the north shore. "Is your father up here with you?" I asked, holding onto the dock as he clamored out.

"No," he said, his voice doing little to betray his disappointment, "just my mother. Father's back in the city working all week. He might be up on the weekend, but I doubt it. His work's pretty important to him. And pretty time-consuming."

"Then you'll have to come over and play," I said. "Because sometimes it gets a bit boring up here with just my grandparents. I've played too much euchre already. And if I hear another story of how the world was when *he* was a boy, I'll go crazy!" I made a face and persuaded another giggle from him.

He smiled at me then with such a sweet, cherubic look on his face. The sparkle in his eye captured me and I found myself inexplicably speechless. He was beautiful. But as a child, I didn't yet understand the appreciation of beauty in another of my own gender. I do recall, however, wondering what it would be like to touch his smooth, white, almost translucent skin— especially those plum-bright lips. Upon realizing my thoughts, I immediately shoved off and waved back at him.

"I'll call on you later," Bryan shouted.

"Great!" I replied, waving with both arms. And off I rowed, with all speed and might and confidence into the jaws of my surly grandfather. But I had a new distraction and that made my grandfather all the more tolerable for the time being.

● ● ●

Bryan and I saw a great deal of each other over the next few weeks. Grandpa took it upon himself to teach Bryan all the tricks of becoming an expert fisherman. Bryan, however, didn't take to fishing in a way acceptable to Grandpa. He didn't like the worms and absolutely would not touch the fish he caught. And, of course, he caught more fish that summer than anyone else. Needless to say, Grandpa didn't like Bryan very much. Mind you, Grandpa didn't like anyone. His disliking Bryan didn't surprise me in the least. In fact, the first thing he did was make fun of Bryan's accent, calling him a "Limey." I quickly took on the role of protector and Bryan and I became the best of friends.

His mother was extremely reclusive. Grandma had asked me one day to invite them both over for dinner but only Bryan came.

"Mother has a headache," Bryan reported dutifully, almost reciting a prepared speech, saddened but resolute, "and regrets that she cannot join us for dinner this evening." I loved the way he spoke, the way he formed his words. It was so different from what I was accustomed to. Yet, one couldn't overlook the sadness. I had a feeling that his mother's headaches were an excuse for something else.

Towards the end of August, my grandparents gave me permission to have Bryan over for the night. It took some serious coaxing on Bryan's part to secure approval from his mother. But he came. It was a beautiful, clear night and Grandpa had a fire going on the beach for marshmallows. Dinner had been good; my grandmother was a phenomenal cook. And we were giggling and carrying on on the shores of the lake while they sat inside reading and drinking their obligatory tea before bedtime. The radio was blasting Tony Bennett. We giggled at the sheer volume, not once thinking that we would also be of an age someday when our hearing would falter.

"Robert!" Grandpa called sharply and suddenly from the front steps, as though he couldn't stand to hear two people having so much fun. "Robert, you two boys get upstairs this instant! It's well past your bedtime!"

Bryan knew by this point that you simply did not disobey my grandfather. His staunch, British, boys' school upbringing had driven it into him to respect and obey elders at whatever cost. He almost marched whenever my grandfather spoke. Grandma even said one day that she found Bryan to be a "regular little gentleman."

"Where do I sleep?" Bryan asked as we climbed the stairs. Our cottage was without electric power back then and we had to carry lanterns from room to room. Bryan found this practice thoroughly barbaric but was intrigued nonetheless by its quaintness.

"You'll sleep right in with Robert," Grandma said. "I don't have any clean linens for the other bed, I'm afraid."

"Oh, that's okay, Bryan," I said, punching him in the shoulder. "My bed's huge." And it was. Grandpa had secured several cast-iron king-size beds from an auctioneer several years ago. God only knows how he got them up those steep stairs; they weighed a ton.

"Now, I don't want to hear a peep coming from this room after you've settled down," Grandma said, her voice scolding in word only. Her tone was always gentle and soothing. "Or your grandfather will have a word or two for you, I can imagine." Her warning was stern but polite.

We undressed in the dark. Bryan stubbed his toe on an armchair and almost yelled but I clamped my hand over his mouth.

"Grandpa will think we're horsing around!" I whispered.

"But my goddamned *toe* hurts! Fuck!" Bryan exclaimed, muffling the pain.

I suppose I'd lived a rather sheltered life up till then because I'd never heard anyone my age curse like that before. I especially didn't expect to hear such language coming from prim and proper Bryan. He instantly took on a new aura.

"Bryan!" I said, almost bursting into laughter at his expense. "I can't believe you said that!"

"Well, *you* try it and see what *you* think!" he said, stamping with his heel onto my big toe. I yelped aloud and instantly covered my mouth. Beneath my hand I yelled, "Fuck!" It felt good.

"You boys cut out all those shenanigans," Grandpa bellowed from the bottom of the steps, "or I'll come up there and skin you alive!"

I shrugged a giggle at Bryan and bit my lip to stop an outburst of laughter. "Sorry, Grandpa," I called, quickly resuming my sober posture. "I just stubbed my toe."

"Well, if you got into bed when you're *supposed* to, you wouldn't be stubbing *nothing!*" And I listened to hear him hobble off, hurling his own barrage of language at us. And, giggling, we crawled under the covers, burying our faces in the pillows to prevent our laughter from being heard downstairs.

After we calmed down, I slid off into sleep. It wasn't until much later that I felt Bryan beside me. At first, I didn't know what was happening. A storm had broken in the middle of the night and flashes of lightning lit up the room like a strobe. I looked across at the clock on the night stand and squinted to make out the time. Three-thirty. That's when I became aware of Bryan beside me. He was clutching onto me, his face buried against my back from behind. And he was crying, from the sounds of it.

"What's the matter?" I quietly asked, turning over to face him.

"I hate thunder storms!" he replied, his voice reedy and thin, wary of being caught. "They scare the shit out of me!"

"Shh!" I cautioned. Not only would we get a beating for causing trouble in the middle of the night but also for using such language. "Don't worry about the storm," I said, soothing as best I could. "It'll pass and you'll be all right. You'll see."

"I can't help it, Robbie! They scare me!" he said, digging his face into my shoulder and clutching me close.

I brought my hand up to his face then, determined to shove him away. But then I came into contact with that smooth, cool, alabaster skin of his and paused. He tensed slightly, then relaxed in my grasp. Before I knew what was happening, I was caressing his face, feeling that soft, dry skin against my fingers.

"Everything's okay, Bryan," I said, cooing gently into his ear. "You're with me. You're okay now. Nothing'll hurt you." And all the while I was stroking his face and smoothing his hair. And it felt good.

After several minutes, I realized that Bryan was no longer clutching at me with such urgency. In fact, his hands were feeling my shoulders with unusual tenderness. He then began to rub his face against my cheek. I found myself rocking him in my arms, embracing him tightly now. And he, too, wrapped uncertain arms around me. And rocked.

After a flash of lightning, I pulled away slightly and looked into his eyes. We were both confused by what was happening. At least Bryan didn't seem as frightened any more. And I smiled.

"Feeling better?" I whispered, cupping his face.

He nodded and gulped. His lips were quivering. I could hold back no longer and reached my index finger around to touch those full, red lips. I no longer cared that this was my friend—a *male* friend—and that I was enjoying the sensations of touching him. There were several unfamiliar twinges that I didn't understand that night. But I didn't stop.

And neither did Bryan. His lips parted and his soft, dark tongue poked out. At first, I felt that something very wrong was happening. But the feeling was fleeting and I continued exploring. He licked at my index finger now, curling his tongue around the tip of it and drawing the finger inside. I suppressed a nervous giggle and pulled back, unsure.

Not a word was spoken. Then I leaned back over and pressed my lips against his and we kissed with unknown passion. Neither of us could explain it; we just had to do it. We kissed with wild abandon. I was stroking his face and neck. He was rubbing my shoulders. And then his tongue returned, wet and peculiar, pressing against my lips, exploring beyond the pale. I instinctively opened my mouth and allowed the tip of his trembling, hot tongue inside. And I brought mine out to greet him. It was extremely clumsy as I recall, but strangely exhilarating. Then, with a sudden flash of lightning and a crash of thunder, I had an eerie vision of my grandfather with a look of absolute murder on his face. And I stopped abruptly.

"What's wrong?" Bryan asked, unsure of my hesitation.

I licked my lips and wiped them with the back of my hand. "Nothing," I said, not sure of my words or emotions at that moment. It was then that I realized that the vision of my grandfather was just in my head. I could hear him snoring at the top of his lungs down the hall.

"Did I do something wrong?" he asked, smiling so sweetly, the corners of his mouth curling.

I nodded and inhaled deeply. "No, I'm just scared," I said on the exhale.

"Just be quiet and nobody will hear," Bryan coached, interrupting. "And besides, *they* can't hear anything anyway." Smiling, he brought his lips closer again, puckered.

"Are you sure we should be doing this?" I asked, turning onto my back. I suddenly became aware of an erection in my pajamas.

"No, I'm not sure," he replied, moving closer, resting a hand upon my shoulder, "but I like it all the same." In the silvery darkness, his eyes twinkled like stars.

"I mean," I said, trying to explain myself, "I like you and all that ..."

"But you don't like me *this* much," he said, more a pre-concluded statement than a question.

"No," I clarified, "I'm just afraid of being caught. If Grandpa knew we were doing this, he'd *kill* us! He really would!"

"Then, we don't *let* him know," Bryan said, fiddling with my buttons.

This was thrilling. Here I was about to have an experience like I'd never felt before and not only was I totally unaware of my next move but I was totally afraid to make it. Instead, I showed no resistance and let Bryan have his way. Within moments, my pajama-top was undone. He pulled back the sheet to reveal my teenage chest in the glow of the night. My chest rose and fell rapidly. He rubbed the flesh tenderly, sending chills through me.

"Do you like that?" he asked, his lips pressed against my ear.

"Yes," I replied, my voice wavering, my body shivering

despite the summer heat.

"Good, because I like doing it." And he continued. His fingers ventured lower after a while to my pajama bottoms, playing with the drawstring. I put up no resistance whatsoever. I wanted to feel this as much as he did. I kept my lips tightly clamped shut to prevent any moans escaping. I was aware of the aching in my lungs as my nostrils fired air into them like a blast furnace. My teeth clenched.

He pried his hand down the front of my pajama bottoms then, and touched my erection. And he fondled me with tender sensuality.

"Stop for a minute!" I hissed, pulling his hand out of my pajamas. And I leapt out of bed, cautious of making any noise, and dropped my pajama bottoms to the floor, stepping out of them, my erection bouncing joyously against my stomach. "Easier access," I whispered, climbing back into the bed. Bryan, too, rose to his feet, standing tall on the bed, and undressed. In moments, we were completely naked and once again in each other's arms.

"This is much better," Bryan said, brushing a smooth yet bony knee against my testicles. And he reached back down to fondle my aching erection.

I took this opportunity to do a little discovering of my own and reached tentatively between our bodies for his throbbing pecker. Neither of us had much hair—we were, after all, only fourteen. And neither of us had a particularly large cock either. But that didn't stop us from rubbing and pulling and caressing and kneading.

"God, you feel good," Bryan said, licking my neck as he felt my smooth ass with one hand, my arched penis with the other. "Nice and smooth and hard."

I giggled at that observation, feeling his fingers pulling on my raging erection. I, too, had abandoned any former reticence and was enjoying every moment of our union. A quick look at the clock, though, told me that we had been at this for too long. The storm had since ceased raging outside.

"We'd better get our clothes back on," I suggested. "Grandpa will be up soon."

"Absolutely," Bryan said, showing no hesitation. "I'm not about to try explaining *this* to your grandfather. I mean, Robbie, he's like Hitler's cousin sometimes."

After we had dressed and returned to bed, Bryan said, kissing me sweetly on the lips, "Robbie, I always want to be your friend. Will you be mine?"

"Of course," I said, reaching down and rubbing his enraged pecker through the thin fabric of his pajamas. Deftly, I brought his stiff penis out for further molestation.

"Always?" he asked, strangely in need of an answer.

"Always," I assured him, kissing and groping. And we fell fitfully back to sleep.

It was difficult but there we were, later that same morning, with the sun just breaking through the clouds, propped up inside Grandpa's boat, barely awake, our fishing poles limply hanging over the sides. But we were happy. And, for whatever reasons, we were in love. We didn't really understand it, but, looking back, we were in love nevertheless.

We only had two other nights like that—one at his place and another at mine. We exchanged our love for each other as well as our addresses. The only time we would ever see each other would be during the summer months at the cottage—after all, we lived in different cities. But we were determined to keep in touch. In as many ways as possible.

Bryan left at the end of August. His father had come to take them home. I stood on the end of the dock and looked out across the bay at their boat as it sped away across the water. And there, in the back seat, was Bryan, sitting tall, waving with full arms. And I stood, waving back, crying. Because somehow I didn't expect to see him ever again.

As it turned out, Bryan's father was transferred eight months later back to England. The last letter I received was full of sorrow and anguish. He spoke of running away from home, of having my parents adopt him—anything so that we could remain together. But, of course, nothing happened. He moved back to England and I was sure I'd never see him again. The letters became fewer and fewer as time went by.

But the memory of Bryan remained strong in my mind. One's first love always does.

• • •

The years passed. I charged out of school into university

with an academic scholarship buoying me up. My study of philosophy and literature secured me a teaching post at a private boys' school in Toronto. In a strange twist of fate, it was the same school Bryan had attended for the six months he lived here.

Even now I think of Bryan often. After all, he was my first true love. I've been with a variety of people since then—most notably my lover, Peter, for three years at university. But Peter became increasingly unfaithful and, despite my undying love for him, I couldn't overlook his indiscretions any longer. And we went our separate ways.

It had been a difficult spring. We both had to find new apartments. I had to endure the nights, while we were still living under the same roof, when he wouldn't come home. I'd wake up at night hugging the pillow, alone in bed. I couldn't date for a while. It's only been recently that I've had the desire to go out. I've seen Peter, of course, in the clubs and that's been difficult. But we're progressing. Instead of feeling incredible loss, I now feel incredible rage. And that, oddly enough, is helping me to overcome him.

It was my father who suggested to me that I go to the cottage that summer. I was working on curriculum and the thought of such tranquillity appealed to me greatly. Fortunately, when my grandparents had died, Father had used part of the inheritance to install electric power at the cottage. So, I was able to bring along my notebook computer.

I packed light—just some casual clothes, my computer, writing paper, books and food. The cottage hadn't changed all that much over the years. If there was one thing good I could say about my grandfather, it was that he was a damned fine carpenter. Aside from the occasional repair— and a fresh coat of paint and new shingles from time to time—it was the same old place I'd grown up in.

At night, I'd sit on the front porch (now screened in against the mosquitoes and blackflies) and sip wine while listening to classical music and jazz. The loons called out across the water from an unknown spot on the lake. And I smiled, content at long last.

After a few days of settling in, I had to go into town for a few more groceries and some wine.

I saw that the town had changed. Where the old grocery

store once stood was now perched a shiny, new hardware store. A larger, brighter supermarket was down the road about a mile. And, like any city supermarket, there were people ramming their carts inadvertently into yours from all angles.

I was scanning the shelves for olive oil when the first crash came. I threw on a smile and nodded my head at an elderly woman in a Tilley hat with a bright grin, bluish hair and floppy dentures. The next crash came from behind. An elderly man this time almost took my heel off. It's a good thing I wasn't wearing sandals. As I soon discovered, these two crash-test dummies were together.

I thought they must have been running a bus tour when I received a third and violent crash. I had stuck the nose of my cart out into the aisle too far, I suppose, and nearly had it clipped off by a speeder. I still hadn't found the olive oil and was beginning to get quite annoyed at the inconvenience of this convenience store. When I came into full view of the aisle, however, there he stood—a tall, strapping youth with piercing blue eyes, sharp cheekbones, a shock of unruly, dark hair and a pair of full, red, pouting lips.

"I'm so sorry," he said, his English accent warm and distinct. "I didn't mean to...." And his eyes caught mine and all speech froze.

"That's quite all right," I said, smiling suddenly, unsure of myself as I pondered his appearance. "No harm done." And I languidly walked away.

We caught each other's eyes several times after the initial crash, strolling casually through the aisles, picking things off the shelves, suddenly in no rush whatsoever. It would be uncanny if this strikingly handsome man actually was actually Bryan. I couldn't allow myself to get too hopeful though. After all, I thought, the coincidence was far too great.

By the time I was at the check-out, however, I was sure it was him. Nobody had lips that sensuous. *Or* that pouty. I watched as he haphazardly perused a tabloid at the cash register, his cart only half-full: fruit, vegetables, whole grain bread, digestive biscuits, Earl Grey tea. God, but it *had* to be him.

The way he looked at *me* also made me wonder. He could melt a person with that stare of his—*whoever* he was—through those long, silken lashes. He had to be a model, I thought, he was so incredibly handsome. He was at least three inches taller than me. And his body had blossomed into that of a muscular statue. I caught myself wondering how well he'd grown all over. And I smiled to myself.

I guess he felt that the smile was for him because he winked subtly at me and the corners of his mouth curled upwards.

"Bryan?!" I asked, two line-ups away.

"Robert?!" he returned. His voice was rich and resonant. I'd forgotten that accent, and suddenly remembered why I loved it so much.

"*Little* Bryan?!" I repeated, holding my hand out in front of me, palm down, about half-way between my waist and shoulders.

"Were we *ever* that small?!" he returned, smiling fully now.

"My God!" I exclaimed "How in the world have you been?" I abandoned my cart momentarily and crossed to give his large, extended hand a firm shake.

"Sir," a local patron called, "you're next in line!" Her voice sounded pinched.

"Oh, I'm sorry," I said, yanking my cart out of the line. "I'll just go over here." And I pulled up behind Bryan.

"What brings you back to *these* parts after all these years?" I asked.

"Oh, I dunno," he said, shrugging massive shoulders. "I just got back into the country about a month ago. Thought I might head north and get in some rest and relaxation for a while before heading down to Toronto."

"Ya? What will you be doing in Toronto?" I asked.

"I've got a job there...."

"What do you do?"

"I'm a professor—English Literature." And he smirked.

I laughed aloud then, taking care not to draw too much attention. "This is so weird," I observed. "*I'm* a teacher at a boys' school in Toronto—literature and history. Can you believe it?!"

There was a brief pause as we surveyed each other more closely, wary of the small-town eyes that were inspecting us keenly.

"You look good, Robert," he suddenly said, voice lowered, smiling handsomely. I almost fell to my knees then, looking into those eyes, at that smiling face.

"Well, you ... you look ... good ... too," I managed, nodding. I must have looked like the giggly kid he remembered.

"Staying at the family place down the lake?" Bryan asked, emptying his cart onto the conveyor belt.

"Ya," I said, drawing up the slack in the line-up. "My grandparents passed away a few years back and Father inherited the place. Oh," I interjected exuberantly, as though I'd just won the lottery, "we have electric lights now!"

"Aw," Bryan said, pulling a pout, "that was part of the charm of the old place—having to grope about in the dark."

"That's true," I said, smiling mischievously at his remark. "But we still have the lanterns in case of an emergency. Heaven forbid."

The cashier was quick and efficient, catching every word of our conversation and furrowing her brow accordingly. I had to act quickly before Bryan left. And I invited him over for dinner that night.

"That would be lovely," he said, in the same tone he'd used the very first day we met. I smiled, remembering. "What time?" he asked.

"Six? We can have drinks and then a nice, long dinner. Catch up on all the lost years. I've got some red wine but you can bring anything else you might like."

"Good. I'll bring the scotch, then. You like scotch, Robert? They still call you Robert or Rob?"

"Most people call me Rob nowadays," I said. "Except, of course, my students. *And* my parents."

"Six o'clock it is, then," Bryan said. "It's great seeing you again, Rob. I'm sure we'll have lots to catch up on tonight."

"I'm sure we will," I replied, beginning to unload my groceries. I thought that he might wait for me but he grabbed his bundles and headed towards the door.

"See you tonight, then!" he called. And he was gone.

I was a nervous wreck for the rest of the day. Fortunately, or unfortunately, however you might look at it, there were only a few hours before dinner. And I had enough to keep me busy with the preparation of the meal to keep my mind focused. I also managed a quick swim before Bryan's arrival. I was just toweling my hair when I saw a boat scooting across the bay towards my place. And I gulped, as nervous and frightened then as I had been so many years before when we had been playing with each other under the covers in a proclamation of clandestine boy-love. Quickly, I combed my hair, threw on a shirt, and splashed on some cologne, ready to greet him.

I trotted on down to the dock in time for his official arrival. He swung the boat around and turned off the motor, using the momentum he'd built to bring him safely and neatly into a vacant slip. We fastened the boat securely and he proceeded to unload his loot.

"Scotch!" he announced, somewhat triumphantly, holding up a large bottle of Glenfiddich like a trophy.

"That's not just scotch," I commented, equally melodramatic, taking the bottle from him and carrying it with tremendous care, like a treasure. "This is ambrosia for the *gods!*"

Bryan threw back his head and laughed at me. Damn, he looked so incredibly hot. He also had a knapsack that had to get inside as soon as possible before "something" spoiled. So, we scurried indoors.

"The place is just as I remember it," he said, looking around. "Except your miserable old grandfather isn't around barking at us any more."

"Sometimes I wonder," I said, looking eerily at the ceilings as if able to see the spirit of the old demon hovering above us. "Beer?" I asked, heading into the kitchen.

"That'd be great, thanks. Oh," he said, leaping for the knapsack, "you'd better put this away before it spoils." And he removed a bowl covered in cellophane. "I took the liberty of bringing appetizers."

"Wonderful!" I said. And he reached into his knapsack, taking out a ceramic crock of pate and a jar of black currant preserves.

"Will you look at this," I said, exchanging the hors d'oeuvres for an icy bottle of beer. "You still know the way to a man's heart."

We clinked in a silent toast, eyeing each other suspiciously.

He sat across from me, in an armchair, and said, "You know, I can't believe that we're really back here again—in this cottage—after all these years."

"I never thought I'd see you again," I said, afraid that I was sounding silly. "I mean, after your family moved back to England and all, we just … drifted."

"Ya, that was awful. I was miserable for the longest while, I missed everyone so. But I eventually got back into the swing of things and grew up a bit."

"I'll say," I remarked, nodding at his physique.

He lowered his eyes and smiled, mildly embarrassed. "And you?" he asked. "What became of you, other than becoming a teacher in a boys' school? Sounds like it should be right up your alley."

I told him the highlights of my life. Remarkably, our schooling had turned out relatively similar. He and I had both excelled in literature, history and dramatic arts. We were both granted scholarships into our chosen universities. And we both became teachers—although in different capacities.

After our second beer, I broke out the appetizers. I fished around in the fridge for a jar of fancy mustard and some sweet pickles. Bryan smiled and lunged at the platter, obviously famished.

"So, tell me," he said, sitting back, wedging his beer bottle between his thighs, "why are you so nervous?" He munched on a cracker.

"Well, it's just so strange to see you here. I mean, it's been, what … fifteen, sixteen years?!"

"Fifteen years, eleven months, and … twenty-one days since we first met." Obviously, he'd done some calculations.

I was again stunned. He'd remembered that? *I* didn't even remember *that*. I just shrugged and nodded in agreement. "More or less," I replied. "But who's counting?" And I smiled.

"Are you here all by yourself?" Bryan asked.

"Ya. I'm doing some school work. Just taking it easy. And where did you say you were staying?"

"I don't believe I did," he said coyly. "Actually, I'm staying in a little country inn in town. It's really quite lovely." Then, almost with a tinge of disbelief to his voice, he added, "I'd initially wanted to rent the old place across the bay but I hear it's turned Catholic, or something."

I laughed, trying to explain. "Ya, well, I guess it was about ten years ago when it was bought by an elderly couple who use it as a retreat for nuns. Huh."

"Too bad," he sniggered, sucking back more beer, "it was a

nice place." And he returned his bottle between his lanky thighs, looking provocatively into my eyes the whole while.

We sat in silence for a few painful moments before I rose to go back into the kitchen to check on the dinner.

"Do you need any help?" he called, following me, beer in hand, jaws chewing.

"Oh, no," I said, checking the pots on the stove, "everything's in order. Can I get you another beer?" I asked, whirling about. He had approached closely behind me and I almost knocked the bottle out of his hand as I turned. I stopped dead in my tracks and stared into those blue eyes of his. And I could see a faint reflection of myself. Frightened and somewhat confused.

"Do you remember what we said to each other the last time we wrote?" he asked, his voice low and subdued.

I nodded. My mouth was dry.

"How you said you'd have to ... how'd you put it? ... love me alone? Do you remember?"

I nodded, my heart thundering in my chest.

"I trust that you weren't becoming a nun yourself, waiting for me to return?"

I chuckled. "No."

"Are you seeing anyone right now?"

"No, I just ended a relationship in fact. It was ... well ... messy wouldn't do it justice."

"I've never been particularly fortunate, either, in keeping a lover for much longer than about six months."

"I see," I limply replied, reaching around behind me to put my beer on the counter next to the stove. "So, you're single, just unreliable."

He smiled, reaching past me to deposit his bottle as well, pressing dangerously close, never losing eye contact. "Robert, you should know better than that."

"Well, it would seem that *neither* of us seems to be able to hold onto others for long. We make a fine pair."

"I've always thought so," he replied, smirking, laying one hand upon each of my shoulders.

I stood there with my mouth open, just staring into his beautiful face. Finally, after a lengthy pause, I managed to speak. "You turned out great, though."

"And *you*, my friend," he said, almost whispering, leaning

close, "became even *more* handsome than I remember. If that's at all possible. Your hair is even more golden now," he said, fingering my pony tail. "And longer. And you've filled out rather ... nicely," he said, checking me out openly now. "In all the right places, I'm sure."

"Ya, puberty hit full-force about a year or so after you left," I informed him, shrugging weakly, bringing my hands up to his arms, gently feeling his flexing and curved biceps through his thin shirt.

"I've missed you, Robbie," he whispered into my ear, inhaling me.

"I thought I'd never see you again," I replied, almost choking on my words, nearly in tears. "I didn't think I could ever go on ... without you."

"Then let's not screw it up now," was his only reply. And he had those lips back with mine, warmly mashing our mouths together, right where they belonged. They felt so hot, so familiar. I dug right in; we frantically struggled for each other's tongue. Finally, we broke, breathless and moist.

"Sure gets hot in the kitchen," he said, licking his lips. His long fingers caressed my neck, almost tickling.

"Oh, Bryan," I sighed. "It's so good to be with you again. It's almost as if we've never been apart, what with the way we ... fit together like this."

"Yes, it's familiar," he replied, "and it's refreshing, too. We've obviously both grown up quite a bit since we were last together. I'm also sure that our experience has enhanced our ... innate talents."

I grinned wickedly and said, "I don't wear pajamas any more, though."

"No? Well, I do—bottoms, at least." He smirked at the inadvertent pun.

His chest pressed against mine. It was expansive, flat and honed it seemed from many years of swimming. I immediately became erect, fearing that my over-excitement would catch his attention too quickly. I didn't want this encounter to be a writhing, slithering sexual tempest. I wanted it to be seductive and sensual, slow and tantalizing, loving and tender, the passion we were too young to understand but had since relived a thousand times inside our memories.

"Where will you be living in Toronto?" I asked, hoping to

avert blatant sexuality by inane chatter.

"I've got a place through the campus housing authority. Something that fits a professorial type."

"You'll have to wear glasses. Do you wear glasses? Little, round-rimmed ones would look incredibly ... professional." I smirked, raising an eyebrow seductively, unwittingly.

"As a matter of fact, I *do* wear glasses. I have for several years now. Weak eyes, I suppose. From all those years of my nose to the grind."

"Heaven forbid, it couldn't have been from reading porno magazines at night—under the covers, by flashlight."

Bryan laughed gently, resting his forehead against mine. His height dizzied me. I was trembling as though I were about to have my first sexual experience all over again.

"You still have that ... weird sense of humor, don't you?" And he kissed my forehead, brushing aside a stray curl of hair. His fingers were now fiddling with the elastic in my hair. Deftly, quickly, Bryan had my hair cascading in broad, damp curls around my shoulders. He framed my face and inhaled sharply. "My God," he whispered, "you're beautiful!"

I rose onto my toes to kiss him once more, unable to hold back any longer. A steaming pot broke our concentration and I turned back to the stove.

"Looks like we're not the *only* things boiling over tonight," Bryan said, pressing close from behind. I thought I could feel the pressure of his bulging crotch, but wasn't sure.

"Are you ready for dinner?" I asked. "I'm famished."

"Yes, I can see that," he hummed, nibbling at my earlobe.

I leaned back into his body then, feeling the broad strength of it, the heat. I couldn't wait for dinner any longer. Perhaps there was something in my mind that told me to make pasta that evening. Pasta is so much better when it's reheated.

"Or would you sooner have a nice *swim* first?" I asked, bounding out of his arms and out the front door, not waiting for a reply. I knew that he would be fast on my heels, so I scurried down the path, shedding clothes as I ran, straight into the lake.

I made a crashing dive off the dock into the water, kicking forcefully with my legs as I sliced through the murky depths. I was vaguely aware of another splash moments later and turned to see the approach of a large, dark body underwater.

I sped to the surface, breaking for air.

Bryan's head popped out immediately afterwards, snatching a lung full of air before he whooped. His voice carried with great resonance across the bay and back. I swam over to him and threw my arms around his neck above water, my legs around his waist below. His open mouth greeted me with a wet and wild tongue. We slowly sank beneath the surface, all the while dragging our limbs across each other's slick and hard body. His back was incredible—broad and muscular, with jutting shoulder blades. I didn't think twice before smoothing my flat palms down his back to that globular butt of his, rejoicing in its hairlessness. A moan started from deep within my throat.

Our mouths were full of tongue and water. My lungs ached for air and we struggled to the surface once again. Gasping, we held each other at arm's length. His eyes were glazed with passion. I began to laugh.

"What?" he demanded, his voice warbling.

"We're fucking *crazy*, that's what!" I replied, sputtering out words and water.

He panted, just staring over at me, a hint of something lascivious behind that full, bright smile. His tongue flickered at the corners of his mouth and he moved closer.

"Here," he said, reaching down, "let's have a look down below." And he wrapped his wide hand around the base of my tumescent penis. I didn't even flinch. After all, I'd been waiting for this for almost sixteen years.

"You don't change one bit, do you?" I said, pumping into his fist without provocation. "You've still got more nerve than a toothache."

"And *you* still need hardly any coaxing before you've got your legs in the air!" He reached with the other hand and cupped my balls. "Oh, shit! You've grown up *very* handsomely, Robbie. Very handsomely indeed!"

I was just as shocked to learn that his one-time skinny dick had grown into a hot, fat pecker of more than ample size.

"We'll probably *drown* out here if we keep at it like this, we're so goddamned horny," I said.

"Ya, but at least we'll have smiles on our faces when they find us," Bryan replied, diving below the surface of the water.

I didn't know where he had gone at first. He'd relinquished

my body—every inch of it—but I knew he was up to something. His fingers took me little by surprise, groping and prying my ass cheeks apart, slipping a long, firm digit into my puckered asshole. I let out a groan as he slid inside. His head reappeared immediately behind me, his tongue draped across my back.

"Goddamnit," he screamed for the world to hear, "but I love you!"

I smiled hugely and started to laugh, vaguely wondering what the nuns must have been thinking of all this. But that finger was insistent and aroused me tremendously. "Love me later," I urged. "Fuck me now!"

"Oh, you just know *all* the right things to say!" Bryan said, jabbing his finger in past another knuckle. I grunted at the sensation. Reaching behind me, I felt for his cock.

"Give me something else!" I coaxed, fondling his dangling balls. "Give me something *better!*"

"I'm afraid we should probably consider moving closer to shore, Rob," he said, breathlessly. "This might be a little trickier than I imagined."

Without a word, I pulled away, feeling his finger yank from my butt. I waited for him in the coolness below the dock, in a foot of water, against the soft sand. My hair swam around my head like Medusa's snakes. And my pecker poked above the surface of the water like the periscope of a submarine. Bryan swam up on his belly, crawling below the surface. I spread my legs and he drifted into the slip. His lips gently grazed my shaft. I instantly groaned and raised my hips. My inflamed cock rose above the water with incredible strength. And I reminded myself that when we had played around all those years ago, we hadn't actually performed any acts of sex—just a lot of groping and kissing. This was an entirely new sensation for us both.

"Jesus Christ!" Bryan gasped, wrapping his fingers around the thick shaft. "It's fucking *amazing*, look!"

I chuckled at the nuances of his native tongue. And I knew that I wanted to *feel* his native tongue wrapped around my frustrated and throbbing pecker even more. But all in good time, I told myself repeatedly. All in good time.

He looked up across my stomach and chest, into my eyes, panting. He absolutely dripped sex. His eyes were the color of the sky. His lips were sharp and pouting. A drop of water caressed his cheek, dipping into the hollow beneath the jutted cheekbone. There was a tiny cleft in his chin where a droplet of water rested patiently. His hair was slick against his skull. His shoulders bobbed just above the surface of the water, darkly tanned and freckled. His collar bone jutted from shoulder to shoulder. I could feel my excitement mounting at a furious pace.

He released me then and stood up, tall and hovering, splendidly muscled. His pectorals were heavy and flat, the nipples dark and tantalizing, pointing down at me from the curved muscle, almost accusatory. His washboard stomach was speckled with tiny hairs, hairs that increased in volume as they swirled down into his heavy crotch. His balls were low-hanging and large, like eggs with double yolks. I smiled at the analogy and savoured the sight of that dark, brooding cock— semi-erect and beautiful, remarkably sculpted. The head was plump and shapely with just the right amount of foreskin. I smiled then with a touch of triumph. Because, as handsome as it was, I realized that what he made up for in height and build, I made up for in dick.

He held a stance that caused his prick to jut outwards from his groin. I watched it openly as it grew in size, filling out its covering of skin, stretching into shape, the head shiny, darkening. He didn't even have to touch it. It grew at will to full erection. I was bewitched by that cock, by the sight of his arousal. Once more, my mouth was dry.

Without a word, I reached down and pulled my legs up over my head, exposing my pert, smooth ass. My puckered hole winked up at him. I found it difficult to keep my eyes off his handsome endowment. But I wanted to see his face as I surrendered to him.

Slowly, torturously, he lowered onto his knees. With one hand, he reached into my crack, rubbing my hole and exciting groans of approval from me. And all the while, a tender smile played at the corners of his mouth. He then lowered his eyelids, like veils, as he took his pecker into his hand. Lovingly, gently, he handled himself, almost as if inspecting a delicate instrument or a piece of bone china. A drool of saliva then fell past his lips onto the dark, fleshy head; his aim was impeccable. Another. And yet another. All the while, he was smearing his spit over the length of his glistening prick, preparing it for me. I wondered at his need for lubrication like that, given that we were both in a foot of water. But there was something to be said for foreplay that thrilled me. Then, with equal tenderness and accuracy, he spat onto my butt, working the hot saliva into my asshole. I twitched with anticipation, eager to feel his meat deep inside me. In sharp contrast, I could feel the grit of the sand against my back as I lay before him, my hair wildly askew.

Then he lined up his fat dickhead with my yawning hole. And slowly, with just the right amount of pressure, he pushed inside. I grunted and pushed out, allowing him to slide more of himself inside me. I sighed heavily and closed my eyes, lolling my head from side to side, the shallow water sloshing across my face. I took care not to swallow any and choke. I wanted nothing to interrupt us.

Bryan was soon totally encased within my hot, eager butt. With a sigh of accomplishment, he set about fucking me with slow, long, deliberate strokes. Each one, however, would be slightly harder, incrementally deeper. I had learned with Peter the pleasures of anal intercourse, including techniques of breathing. But Bryan's pecker increased in speed before my breathing could adapt. Exhalations were replaced by grunts and moans. His balls slapped against my butt gently, teasingly, and his thighs made sloshing sounds as his rhythm was established.

"I love you, Bryan!" I whispered hoarsely, my eyes straining to maintain eye contact. "I've always loved you!"

Tears welled in Bryan's eyes and his face softened. But he didn't lose momentum. With a quivering smile, he continued to plunge that dick of his into my tender yet experienced asshole, his chest pounding. And I brought my butt up to meet him with every stab. The water was sloshing all about us.

"Fuck me, baby!" I hissed. "Come on! Let me *feel* it!"

Not one to pass up a challenge, Bryan's face transformed into a smirk of mischief. He raised an eyebrow and increased the force of his thrusts. I was moaning louder now, holding my legs aloft, feeling that pecker pound into my butt. Sweat rolled off Bryan's chest, dripping like a leaky faucet from each nipple. How I longed to latch my lips onto each one and tenderly ravage him.

"Goddamnit, Bryan!" I rasped. "Fuck me!"

His thrusts began to splash water up over my stomach. I found the sight thrilling, yet comical, and chuckled. He, too, began to laugh, never once allowing the strength of his fucking to diminish. His strong fingers stroked my thighs as he held me in place, skewering me. His pelvis pivoted sensuously; his hips rocked back and forth; his chest rose and fell; his tongue danced about his lips as though they were drizzling honey.

This quickly became too much for me. I closed my eyes, feeling the force of my orgasm churning inside my balls. My moans were deeper, more elongated, louder. Tiny vibrations could be felt throughout our bodies. And I lost it.

"Oh, fuck! This is it!" And my cock belched out a volley of cum that sprayed across my chest, onto my face and into the shallow water. My tongue lashed about, trying frantically to contact a stray glob. I didn't think it would ever stop shooting off. And I thought Bryan would never let up. He continued to pound my ass with his fiery pecker despite my orgasm, *because of it*, perhaps. But even *that* tactic wouldn't last much longer.

"Oh, Christ!" he hissed.

I looked up at him then, seeing stars from the force of my eruption. And, panting, I noticed that his head was thrown back, his neck and shoulders straining. Every muscle in his body was alive then as his orgasm mounted. I reached up and twisted those nipples. And I gathered the last remaining ounce of strength and shoved back hard on his cock, tightening my sphincter around the thickness of his shaft. After a couple of deep, tight strokes, I knew that I had him exactly where I wanted him.

"Jesus *Christ*, Robbie!" And he came, a searing blast of cum inside me, burning me, singeing my bowels. His body was a monument to muscle as he stretched every part. It was as though his cum had been savagely torn from his body.

"Fuck!" he yelled repeatedly, his prick now amply lubricated by his voluminous load.

The well was running dry. I knew that it would only be another moment and his orgasm would end. I was a spectator now, privy to his remarkable body and the effects of orgasm upon him. I milked the last of his cum out with my practiced asshole, stroking the sides with my obedient and obliging sphincter. The erotic tenderness was too much for Bryan to endure; he had to pull out. His stomach muscles twitched, spasming. And I smiled.

We slid slowly back into a watery embrace, kissing with renewed and unbridled passion. I couldn't get enough of this man. And this was only the beginning. We hadn't even made it to dinner yet.

Inside once more, I turned the stove back on and simmered the sauce. Sore yet satisfied, I sat down at the table with a glass of red wine, careful of the angle at which I sat. It really *had* been a long time since I'd been really fucked. Bryan lingered outside for a few minutes, gathering his clothes and his senses. I sighed contentedly, watching him out the window. He stood, tall and resplendent, eyeing the lake, following the flight of a family of loons, inhaling the clean, cedar-scented air. His face, strong and striking, was happy. I could see something of the little boy in him. And I knew that my love for him hadn't weakened. Nor his for me. Despite the passage of time.

He eventually came inside. Silently, he sat in the armchair and relaxed. He looked tired. No wonder, after the performance he put in.

Presently the meal was prepared and dinner was served. Afterwards, we clamored into his boat and sped off down the lake to retrieve his belongings and check out of that lovely little town inn. Then we were ready to go back to my place.

The scotch felt good after our busy evening. The sun had set by the time we'd reached the hotel. What was left of the day, however, was clear and bright. Thousands of stars glittered like jewels in the dark sky. The occasional splash in the lake got us talking about fishing trips with my grandfather. We laughed so much that night, remembering. And, in the dark, we sat side by side, arms entwined, and we were deeply and passionately in love, recaptured.

"Okay," I said, sitting up, "this is getting a bit too romantic even for *me*. What do you say we tear each other's clothes off and make love all night long?"

"Are you sure you can take it?" Bryan smugly remarked, his hand rubbing the inside of my thigh.

"Hey, the question is: are *you*." And I crossed my arms to pull my shirt up and off.

Bryan grabbed the scotch bottle and carefully pressed me to

the ground. With expert fingers, he pried my eager mouth open and drizzled scotch across my tongue. I swirled the liquid around inside my mouth and swallowed. His mouth descended then and replaced the scotch. Presently we were both bare-chested and in a powerful embrace, our pants undone. But even the most experienced diver had to come up for air at some point. Our lungs ached as we broke from another passion-filled, devouring kiss.

"That first night," he began, lying on his side, playing with my erect cock, "you were as stiff as a board, like this. Remember?"

"Do I remember?!" I said with some amazement that he would even have to ask. "Of *course* I remember. You pretending to be frightened by a storm. When what you *really* had in mind was a little touchy-feely."

He laughed deep within his throat. And he licked at my stubbled jaw. "I was uptight. Give a boy a break."

"And do you remember how frightened I was that my grandfather would come in and find us together like that?"

We both laughed heartily as the reminiscences flooded back. "Oh, God, yes!" he replied. "You were something else."

"I was young," I said, smirking.

"And what's your excuse now?" he said, wrapping his legs around my waist, pulling his throbbing dick up against mine. They rubbed together and exchanged heat; I thought I saw a spark.

"God, but I've wanted you for so long," he whispered in my ear, his voice seething with passion.

I simply laid my arms at my sides and leaned back onto the grass. "Well," I said, "I'm all yours now."

His mouth met mine again, dragging a slippery tongue out across my chin and down my neck to nibble at my collar bone. His lips were more than just aesthetically pleasing. His tongue danced across my chest, pausing to spin around each nipple. Bryan moved lower onto my stomach then, reaching up with a stray hand to cup his fingers over my mouth. My cock was striking him in the chin now. His hands floated across my body. While he delved into my sensitive navel, his deft fingers popped the remaining buttons on my jeans, prying almost desperately for my turgid prick. I placed both hands on his head then, pressing down farther. I wanted so much, after all these years of fantasizing, finally to feel that hot mouth of his working up and down the length of my cock.

A laugh came from deep within his humming throat as he pulled my pants down, all the while averting the throbbing penis bobbing before his nose. Presently, I was fully naked, my jeans abandoned in the darkness. And Bryan was back between my outspread thighs.

"I can't believe how fucking amazing your cock is!" he said, perhaps to himself more so than to me. "And your thighs are like *granite*! What do you do to yourself?"

"The rewards of years of physical fitness," I replied, anxious to overcome the conversation at this point and get to the action.

"Mmm," he said, stroking my thighs, feeling the blond, downy hairs. Then, as if reading my over-zealous mind, his tongue came down in broad, flat strokes to replace his caressing fingers. He lapped at my thighs like a dog. I was drooling.

"Oh, man!" I hissed, grinding my teeth together. "Do me!"

Bryan chuckled again. His nose grazed my bloated balls as his tongue snaked its way further between my legs, forging a trail. I sucked in a ragged breath, suddenly aware of his desires. And I raised my butt, eager to make his access easier. His breath and his hot tongue lashed against the tender flesh of my scrotum. I, too, was breathing heavily as he proceeded towards his goal.

Then his large, broad hands reached underneath, prying my ass cheeks apart, as his tongue lunged into my pungent hole. I let out a yelp of excited passion as he wriggled around inside me, dribbling saliva out of my puckered butthole. His tongue was long and pleasing, reaching into me like no other oral instrument had ever before done. And I was insane, thrashing my head from side to side, my mouth filling with my own hair and grass.

Then he stopped, relinquishing me. I looked down and saw him stripping out of the rest of his clothes. My chest rose and fell heavily. I licked at my lips, out of breath but excited still.

"God, but you do something to me!" I hissed, struggling for the words.

I could just make out a seductive, almost wicked grin on his face and, silently, naked, he resumed his position. This time, however, his focus was slightly altered. With hot, dry fingers, he pulled my raging cock straight out from my body, a string of silvery pre-cum attaching it to my belly. He looked up at me only briefly before parting those luscious lips. I groaned and dropped my head back to the ground, even before he had begun.

He ran his tongue around the very tip of my cock. He felt alive, on fire. Slowly, intentionally, he dragged that pointed tongue of his down to the base of my cock, juggling my balls. The air was cool along that trail of spit. I was going crazy, digging my fingers into the grass at my sides. I couldn't wait much longer before exploding.

As if sensing this, Bryan brought his mouth back to the head of my prick and stuffed it inside. I'd discovered, from experience, that not just anybody can fall to sucking my cock without the slightest gag. But Bryan, as though prepared for this his entire lifetime, embedded my cock inside his throat. His nose was pressed against my pubic hair; his chin rubbed my aching balls. I knew I wouldn't be long.

Bryan worked me over with expert lips and tongue, licking and sucking with passionate ferocity, working the length into and out of his throat, slurping on the bulbous head. Presently, he began to crawl about, not letting up on my cock, dragging his own pungent dick over my chest to rest momentarily against my dry lips. I didn't have to be told twice; I instantly had that dick of his inside my mouth, slurping wildly, as though it were my last meal.

The night air was cool, washing over our bodies like moonlight. The grass was soft beneath us, like a blanket. There was one large stone, however, that poked into my back. But I wasn't about to stop what I was doing for one second, no matter how uncomfortable it got.

We sucked with wild abandon, equally hungry for pecker. I hadn't, after all, been with another man for several weeks and was literally starved for this kind of contact. But knowing that I was sucking on Bryan—for the first time in my life, after years of loving him alone—filled me with renewed vigour and passion. And, within moments, our passion erupted. Bryan only gagged slightly as I blasted his throat with my abundant load of cream. And then he regained his footing and swallowed valiantly. He, too, unleashed a pent-up load of cum that sprayed from the nozzle of his rigid dick. He tasted good, sweet and nutty.

I didn't want that moment to end so resisted releasing him. But his sensitive cockhead evoked spasms that threatened to hurl his knee into my face. So, not wishing to provide an explanation to the emergency hospital staff, I yielded. And we relaxed, at each other's side, panting with exhaustion, trying to re-fill our aching lungs.

I don't know what time it was; nor did I really care at that point. I simply stared at the clear, night sky and saw the millions of stars that dotted the blackness. And, regaining my strength, I sat up and reached out for Bryan. His fingers crept into mine and we sat silently for several moments, declaring our love before the universe.

"Let's get inside to bed," I whispered, kissing the top of his head as I rose to my unsteady feet.

"What about our clothes?" he asked, rising. "I can't see a damned thing out here."

"Ah, just leave them here," I said, heading up the path towards the cottage. "We'll get them in the morning."

Inside, I instinctively went to the cupboard and brought down an ancient lantern, not sure whether or not there was fuel enough in it to light it. It sloshed slightly and I set it down onto the counter. Carefully, I snapped a wooden match stick into life and lit the viscous, yellowed wick. And, turning around, I looked through the gloom and saw Bryan in full smiles across the room.

"Just like old times," I said, gesturing with my head towards the stairs.

We passed an ancient mirror on the landing, its silver peeling in patches. And I paused, holding the lantern aloft, casting eerie shadows across the wall behind us. The reflection was like looking at a tattered sepia photograph: warped and blurred, following the strange and distorted curves of the twisted reflection. But our eyes were intent and sparkling. Our faces were young, fresh and hopeful—our bodies strong and proud.

"C'mon," Bryan whispered, resting a hand on my shoulder. And then we went to bed.

THAT SIZZLING SUMMER

Thomas C. Humphrey

The temperature must have topped a hundred degrees in the stifling, tin-roofed roadside vegetable stand. To keep the produce, and myself, from wilting too much, I had just sprinkled the vegetables and poured half a bucket of water over my head to trickle down my bare chest and into the sweat-soaked waistband of my nearly threadbare denim cutoffs. I was shaking droplets out of my hair when I noticed the car.

I had done a good business that morning, but the scorching afternoon had crept on at a snail's pace without a single customer. I was so bored that I was ready for anything to break the tedium. I watched as the late-model Caddy slowed almost to a complete stop and the driver, a thirty-something, stout, pink-faced man, gawked at me until his eyes bulged. Finally, he slowly drove off and disappeared over the slight rise toward Beckley. A few moments later, though, he came back toward me and, this time, actually stopped in the road and rolled down the passenger window so he could gawk some more. His intense stare made me nervous. Without knowing why, I was relieved when he drove off again.

He didn't even go out of sight, though, before he pulled onto the shoulder, made a wide turn, and stopped beside the stand.

"You got some good ripe tomatoes?" he asked, getting out of his car. I saw that he had a big bald spot on the top of his head.

"Yessir, the freshest around," I said, giving him my best pitch. I moved to the tomato bin and hefted one in my palm. "Picked 'em myself this morning, right off the vine."

That was true enough. That summer, Pa would drive us out to his garden plot on one edge of Grandma Finnegan's farm early every morning, before the young sun had burned the mist off the distant Appalachian peaks and the cooling dew still lingered in the valley. Pa would sit, feet dangling out the open door of the battered pickup, chain-smoke his Camels, and occasionally spit out a cuss word or two when he thought we moved too slow at picking whatever vegetables were ready and loading them into the back of the truck.

When we had finished, he would drive to the roadside stand he had put together on the main highway above Grandma's. As he cussed and criticized, we would set up the stand. He would leave a couple of us—usually me and one of my little brothers—to operate the stand. He'd take the other kids home and then make his rounds in town, selling out of the bed of the old pickup. Around noon, the truck would be empty and he'd be thirsty. He would spend the rest of the day drinking at the bar.

We all dreaded to hear Pa come in the door when he'd been drinking. Sometimes he was in a jolly mood and would laugh and tell stories and sing Irish songs in his off-key tenor. Most times, though, he was mean as a mongoose and spoiling for a fight. All us kids tried to disappear from sight at those times. We hid out in various nooks and crannies of our rambling old house or sneaked out into the back yard to play and talk in whispers, frantically trying not to attract his attention. Invariably, though, he would stumble across one or two of us and find fault enough in our dress, or behavior, or attitude to beat hell out of us while we screamed and begged for mercy.

To escape Pa and my older brothers, who were nearly as bad, I had volunteered to run the stand every day all summer. I had begged and pleaded so much with Grandma that she let me stay with her almost every night and Pa would pick me up at her house next morning. But he insisted that one of my little brothers stay and work the stand with me.

The day the stranger kept driving by and staring, though, I was by myself. My brother Mark had gotten sick to his stomach and Grandpa had taken him home when he brought us a sandwich for lunch and found Mark all pale and trembly. As the man's stare made me more and more uncomfortable, I began to wish Mark were there with me.

The man walked over in front of me and picked up a few tomatoes one by one and turned them in his hand before putting them back down without really looking at them. He was too busy watching me out of the corner of his eye. Although I was a nearly completely innocent mountain kid, I finally caught on that he wasn't really interested in tomatoes, though I was still uncertain exactly what he was interested in.

"These are nice ones, but I don't actually need tomatoes," he said, picking up a cucumber. He held it by one end and slowly ran the fingers of his other hand up and down its length, staring at me with a peculiar grin on his face.

"I can give you a good deal on cucumbers," I said, ever the salesman.

"You live around here?" he asked.

"No sir, I live back in town," I said, gesturing south.

"And you're out here all by yourself," he said, eyeing me in a funny, intense way. His voice sounded like he was almost having to force the words out.

"Yessir, all by myself," I said. "But my grandma's farm is just over the hill there. She checks on me every once in a while." I didn't want him to think I was completely alone.

"My name's Jim. What's yours?" he asked, smiling broadly.

"Casey. Casey Boyle," I answered.

"Another Irishman, huh? I could have guessed, with those blue eyes and red hair." By then his eyes were slowly running up and down my body, and the expression on his face made me feel like I was standing there naked. Which I was, practically. Pa liked us to look as dirty and hungry as possible, so we could play on the sympathies of customers, particularly tourists who were there to gape at the poverty of the region. As usual, I was working barefoot, with a pair of ragged cutoffs, no shirt, and a beat-up straw hat.

"Has anyone ever told you you're a damned good-looking kid?" he said.

He had quit scanning my body, and his eyes were focused on the prominent outline of my dick running down the leg of my tight jeans. His tongue darted out and flicked at his lips, which were moist and red. Innocent as I was, I began to catch on to what he was really interested in. I had never done anything except jack off with a couple of friends down by the creek, but I'd done plenty of thinking about other things. I felt a slight stirring in my groin.

"I don't really want vegetables," he said, "but I might pay pretty good for something I do want." As he reached across the top of the counter to put the cucumber down, he let the back of his hand brush against my dick. "From appearances, you've got all that I could handle."

When I didn't move away, he reached for my dick and

squeezed it. "You ever do anything with this?" he asked.

"Once in a while," I said, looking down at my bare feet, my face flushed and my heart thumping in my chest. I wasn't sure whether it was from fear or excitement.

He gave me another squeeze. My dick grew rapidly in his hand. "Anybody else ever do anything with it?" he asked.

I just shook my head, and he reached to unsnap my cutoffs. "I've got to see that thing," he said. "It feels huge!" When he tugged my jeans down around my balls, my hard cock sprang out like a jack-in-the-box and climbed up my belly.

"Good God Almighty! It's a monster!" he cried out.

Some kids at school had talked about how big it was, but I didn't really have anything to compare it to. For an adult like Jim to admire it was more important. Without knowing why size should matter, I swelled with pride at his admiration.

After just holding it in his palm for a few seconds, he wrapped his hand around it and began sliding my foreskin back and forth. Under the strange touch of his hand, it thickened and lengthened to full size right away. I liked what he was doing, but it scared me at the same time.

"Uh-uh, don't," I said, stepping back. "Somebody might come by."

"Let's go sit in my car," he said in a throaty whisper.

"I can't leave the stand," I said. "What if a customer stops?"

"Could you use ten bucks?" he asked, and then answered himself. "Of course you could. How about if I come around behind the counter?" He was already on his way around, and, with the promise of more money than I'd ever had at one time in my life, I didn't try to stop him.

He turned me sideways and knelt in the dirt before me. He tugged my cutoffs on down to my ankles. When he exposed my full cock and balls, he sucked in his breath and then let it out in a big, "Whoosh!" "I've never seen such a big dick on such a little kid," he said just before he took it in his mouth.

I had presence of mind to ask, "You're going to give me ten dollars, right?" before the beautiful feeling of the first mouth that had ever been on my dick overrode all thought.

He wasn't in a hurry, and he dawdled and teased, nibbling at my foreskin and pulling it up over his tongue, and then pushing it all the way back to lick all over my cockhead, all the time diddling and juggling my balls in his palm and rubbing my bare abdomen and pinching at my nipples. Everything he was doing felt so strange and so good that I just stood with my eyes closed and my head thrown back, occasionally licking my lips and rubbing my chest. As the pleasure grew, I started gyrating my pelvis, hunching my dick in and out of his mouth.

Without warning, he shoved his mouth all the way down, and I felt my cockhead graze along his soft palate, felt it slide between his tonsils and on down deeper and deeper, felt his throat muscles massaging the shaft. I reached down to make sure and found that his lips were smashed tight against my pubic hair and my whole dick was buried in his mouth. It excited me so much that I almost shot my load, but he quickly backed off and started teasing my foreskin with his tongue until I cooled down a little.

Time after time, he swallowed all of me down and then pulled back to lick and tease the head of my dick, squeezing and tugging at my balls all the time. He had me so excited that I was gasping for breath and trembling all over. My knees went so weak I had to brace myself against the counter. I knew I was going to shoot any moment.

"Stop! I'm about to come!" I warned, trying to pull his mouth off my dick.

"Uh-uh," he muttered around my cock. He grabbed both my ass cheeks and pulled me toward him, feeding my dick deeper and deeper into his mouth.

I held back as long as I could, but a terrific sparkling sensation started in my toes, sped up my legs and into my tight balls, and exploded like a Roman candle in my dick. I grabbed both handfuls of his hair and jabbed into his mouth a couple of times and blasted my cum into him with a force I had never managed jacking off. It was like all of my energy spurted out of my dick in an almost steady stream until it made a last twitch or two and we both stopped moving and he just held me in his mouth.

When he finally eased my sensitive dick out, I took a deep breath and let it out in a long, "Whew!"

"Was that pretty good?" he asked, standing up. I saw that his own dick had blossomed in his pants.

"You better believe it!" I said. "Nothing's ever been so good before!"

He moved close beside me and gently massaged my chest

and stomach. "It was good for me, too," he said. "But right now let's give this big fellow some more action; he doesn't seem tired at all." He dropped to his knees and took my dick in his mouth. I grabbed him by the back of the head and thrust forward, giving him free access.

When he had me as hard as a steel spike and trembling all over like an aspen in the wind, all at once he popped my dick out of his mouth and stood up. He unfastened his belt and slipped pants and underwear below his knees, exposing a short, stubby dick. Afraid that he was going to try to make me suck it, I backed away, tugging at my cutoffs, planning to dodge around the shelves until I could grab something to protect myself with.

"Whoa! I'm not going to hurt you!" he said, grabbing my dick. When he moved close in against me, he spat a big glob on my shaft and spread it around with his fingers. He stepped back against a shelf and pulled me with him by my dick.

"I want you to butt-fuck me," he said. "I want to feel that big thing up in me." He turned his back to me, leaned over the shelf, and tugged me closer, until the head of my dick was poking between his cheeks.

"Uh-uh, I don't want to," I said, turned off by the strange idea of putting my dick there. But as he pulled me closer and my dickhead made contact with the soft, warm flesh of his buttocks, my reluctance faded.

"Come on, you'll like it," he promised, pushing his ass back against my throbbing cock.

I started probing around, trying to find the opening, and he reached back and parted his cheeks, opening up for me. I jabbed forward and felt the whole crown of my dick slide into the velvety warmth of him. I caught my breath to keep from crying out loud with pleasure and steadily pushed forward until I had entered him all the way.

"That's it! Now fuck me hard!" he moaned. "God, your big dick feels good!"

Going strictly on instinct, I began moving my virgin dick in and out of the tight wetness surrounding it. As it got to feeling better and better, I reached for his hips with both hands for leverage and began pounding him for all I was worth, sometimes pulling out completely before driving back in full length with one hard stroke. Jim collapsed on the vegetable shelf, moaning and cooing and begging me to fuck him harder. Finally, he reached under and started stroking his dick.

With him almost screaming in pleasure, I felt the cum boiling in my nuts, felt them draw up against my belly so tight it was almost painful, felt the tube on the underside of my shaft expand as thick as my finger, and then felt my jism exploding out with such force my whole dick jerked and spasmed with every spurt. When I was through, I collapsed across Jim's back, having to fight for breath. I had never been so drained and yet so fulfilled before in my life.

"Maybe I'll stop another day soon and we'll do it again," he said, as we pulled up our clothes and zipped up.

"You can't do that," I said. "One of my brothers is usually here with me." Then all at once I knew I had wanted something like this for a long time, knew I wanted it again and again in the future. "But I could meet you here most any night if you let me know ahead of time."

"You could, huh?" he said. "How about Friday night, say about eight o'clock? Maybe we'd have time for me to show you a couple of other things I think you'd like."

"Sounds okay to me," I said. I was willing to try anything if it felt as good as what we'd just done.

"Friday night at eight it is, then," he said. He reached to squeeze my dick, which was still rock hard. I knew then that some of my nights that summer were going to sizzle as much as the days.

When Pa finally came to get me just before dark, I sank contentedly back against the truck seat, a ten dollar bill tucked securely in my pocket and a warm glow still in my groin. I felt so good that I even risked whistling one of Pa's bawdy pub songs, and before long he was singing along with me in his off-key tenor voice. All in all, it had been a good day.

ON A BED OF GRASS

John Patrick

Around noon on a burning, bruising summer day, Mrs. Tinsley heard the roar of a motor in the yard. She looked out. A convertible drove up outside, the exhaust from the tailpipe raising a little dust.

"Your friend is out there," she said.

Jody turned around slowly. He was just getting over a cold and had a headache from all the dust.

Outside, Adrian, dressed only in worn denim shorts, slid out of the car and came rushing toward the door of the farmhouse with a smile. His dust still floated over the road.

Mrs. Tinsley gazed at Adrian as he approached the house. "There's some around you know who'd as soon cut him and make sure he don't breed no more half-wits, maybe calm him down some."

"He ain't no half-wit," Jody said. "I told you, he was in a bad car wreck. There's no harm in him, but he was hurt bad."

"Well, I understand all that. And I'm sorry about it. But it seems like there's a part a him that ain't hurt, don't it, he's so eager to show it off."

"Whatdaya mean, Ma?" Jody giggled, playing dumb.

"You know damn well what I mean. He can't hide that thing of his."

Jody stopped giggling when he saw Adrian, standing outside on the porch, peering into the kitchen. Yes, it certainly was obvious to anyone with two eyes that young Adrian was hung like a horse. Today, the shorts he was wearing were so short that the head of his cock hung out under the torn hem. "He was hurt but he's a boy like anybody else."

"I don't know any boy that's...."

"That's what?"

"That's, well, got what he's got. Man, either. He's a freak of nature, that boy is."

Adrian tapped on the door. Jody hesitated. The only pleasure the boy had in life was his time with Adrian. Adrian and his big dick. Jody *lived* for Adrian and his dick.

Mrs. Tinsley served them iced tea and they sat in rocking chairs on the porch. Adrian looked wretched, hair matted, hands and arms dirty, but he was, as always, oblivious to it.

"Adrian," Jody whispered, "I need to talk to you. Now you pay attention. You can't go on doin' like you been doin'."

"How's that?"

"Look," Jody said, pointing to the cockhead thath lay against Adrian's deeply tanned thigh.

"You can't show yourself like that. You're scarin' people."

Adrian blushed, tried to pull the denim over the cockhead. "I guess I've just outgrown these shorts all of a sudden."

Jody chuckled, remembering the swimsuit Adrian wore the week before when they went to the pond; and the jeans that would be baggy on anybody else that Adrian wore to the movies the week before that. Mrs. Tinsley had said that Adrian showing off like that was downright obscene, but now, seeing the huge cockhead poking out, the old woman was speechless.

They stood up and while Jody delivered the empty tea glasses to the kitchen, Adrian pushed his shorts down as far as he could to cover himself.

Moments later, they were in the old convertible, heading to the pond.

They were bathed by the sun that forced its way through the trees, dazzled by the fierce glare off the tall grass, and their bodies were covered with perspiration by the time they reached the pond. They were, as always, alone in this idyllic place.

After only ten minutes or so of swimming in the refreshingly cool water, Adrian's eyes became cloudy with desire. His flesh throbbed languidly. He did not know why, but he could stay here no longer. He got out of the water. He had to get out. He had to get rid of the feeling. And he had to do it right away. Jody followed Adrian to the place, their place, behind the trees.

Jody's diligently combed hair was now wet and glistening. The tanned cheeks of his long, oval face were covered with thick, long hairs, like weeds. Now their voices buzzed with an intimacy few teenagers could ever approach.

Jody was trembling now in anticipation of being hurt,

fiercely desired to be hurt once again by the enormous cock.

"Oh my god!" Jody cried out over and over and shivered. But his cock never lost its hardness. Adrian skinned it back, and licked the wet crown as it pulsated on his tongue. Adrian slurped slowly down the tapered shaft. He swallowed hard. He could take all Jody had and not gag. Jody couldn't take but a few inches of him. Adrian was proud of this; he loved sucking on Jody's cock. Jody's cock was like everybody else's, not a freakish thing like Adrian's.

Jody gagged, took a breath, and tried it again, groping mounds of taut, tan assflesh. He took more of it than he ever had, but still it was too much. He pried his lips away to lap the dark sac of Adrian's low-swinging balls. He was so hungry for him, there was no limit to what he would do for Adrian. Adrian moved his head back to his bobbing dick. Jody's tongue suctioned its large, juicy head as two fingers tapped and drummed the long, dark, rubbery shaft. The spittle-soaked nuts kept slapping at Jody's chin, and they established a rhythm. Jody was bobbing his head and sucking with such vigor, with such an expert pause at the bottom of his stroke, and another, longer, kissing pause at the top, Adrian was ready to come.

Unattended, Jody's cock poked the hot air. As Jody continued sucking Adrian off, Adrian reached behind him and stroked Jody's cock. Jody took a deep breath, flexed his throat muscles and burrowed down the long, choking shaft until he gagged. Jody's gagging only made the monstrous prick throb. But the bloat of Jody's cheeks seemed to set something off in Adrian. He pulled away, the long, wet meat tumbling from Jody's lips.

Jody knew it did no good to tell Adrian to take it easy now. There was no other way Jody could do it. He got on his hands and knees and lifted his ass to Adrian. He laid it on Jody's back like a swan's neck, then smearing the moist tip of it between Jody's buttocks, he grinned at Jody again as he placed it against the asshole. He put one hand on his shoulder to pull him forward to embed the whole purple bulb of the head. Then, having thus carefully set it, like a screw, he put both hands on his shoulders and gripping them, pulled, driving it all the way home. There was no other way Adrian could do it: it had to be accomplished like this and in one swift, furious plunge; to do otherwise would mean a loss of some of the hardness, and it would hurt even more.

The dickhead went in, then inch after inch of the shaft. Jody let out a garbled moan as the shaft flexed, burrowing in to the hilt. Adrian nestled up against Jody and gently kissed his young lover's shoulders. He dipped his hands down to curl his fingers around Jody's cock, which stiffened with his urgent touch, and quickened the pace of his stroking being done in time with his thrusting in Jody's ass.

Jody began to moan; his knees were shaking, his shoulders trembling as he came, cum spurting out of him onto the bed of grass. Adrian seemed to pause now, holding his cock at the root to give it extra rigidity, as if it needed it. Then he sent it back in to the hilt. "Oh," Jody sighed, his sun-burnished body coated in a sheen of sweat.

Moments later, Adrian's cum flowed into Jody. When he was finished and his cock slid from the opening, Adrian affectionately rubbed the boy's ass and closed his eyes. At this time they lay silently together, catching their breath, and taking pleasure in the thought that it might always be like this.

When the boys returned to the farmhouse, Mrs. Tinsley was jabbing at a boiling pot full of halved potatoes.

"Dinner!" Mr. Tinsley shouted at the boys, taking a last long swallow of his whiskey. "Dinner! Eat it or go hungry."

They ate without talking, finishing all of the pot roast.

Over coffee and freshly baked chocolate cookies, Mr. Tinsley, scratching his salt-and-pepper beard, finally confronted Adrian. "Boy, they are gonna hurt you one day. I've been told they got the word out they'll cut you if you don't quit pesterin' the girls. You understand what I mean?"

Adrian blushed, stared at his cookies.

Mr. Tinsley went on, "You understand what I'm sayin' to you when I say *cut*?" He snapped a cookie in half to make his point.

Adrian nodded, oblivious, but Jody found it disconcerting. Jody shot Adrian a sly look and began to laugh. Adrian joined in then, and the Tinsleys had no choice but to laugh too, even though they had no idea what was so funny.

In the dark that night, Mr. Tinsley confessed, "I don't know if that boy got a thing I said. I don't think he did. He laughed his head off. Christ, I wish there was some way you could tell what goes on in that poor boy's mind."

There was a silence and Mrs. Tinsley whispered, barely audible, "Well, you could take him down to Laramie. You know, visit one of those houses." In the dark, she blushed just to speak of it.

"Why, no," her husband said, truly shocked that his wife would even think it. "I couldn't do no such thing."

HOT AND WET AND READY

William Cozad

Some men follow their cocks through life, not looking for love but looking for sex. I'm the first to admit I'm one of them. That passion brought me out to Golden Gate Park and the windmills near the Great Highway and the Pacific Ocean.

Several years ago, a friend had given me a crude map spotting the locations of all the outdoor toilets. I went to the park, and prowlers told me they were afraid. There had been a lot of busts. The park was patrolled by cops on horses and those with the small Italian trail bikes that can go anywhere. After a while, fear got the best of me and I stopped going there.

But then I heard that the cops had laid off so I went back again, checking out the area of the windmills. A dowager had paid to restore them so that they'd irrigate the park. I thought of her rolling over in her grave....

It was very warm, the middle of what in San Francisco would be considered a heatwave, and I could see there was a lot of activity. It made me think of animals dragging fresh meat off into the bushes. I'd been a hard-core cruiser of bathhouses and arcades for some time and recognized some men only by their dicks, not their faces.

A tall man in a black T-shirt and jeans started talking to me. He had a denim jacket slung over his shoulder.

"What are you doing here in this heat?" he asked.

I wasn't sure what he meant. All I could do was show him. I groped him and led him off into the bushes.

Kneeling down, I freed his cock and began sucking him. He held my head steady while I took his cock all the way down to the pubic hairs and tugged on his hairy ballsac. He pumped his meat down my throat, clearly enjoying himself.

It seemed that his cock got harder and harder until he grunted, then it exploded, sending cum into my mouth. I swallowed some of it before I could pull myself off the cock.

He grunted again, buttoned up and took off, making a show of slinging his jacket over his shoulder, leaving me there on my knees alone. Just then a young blond appeared, as if out of nowhere, rubbing the bulge in his jeans. But a stocky older man carrying a black leather jacket came up and he led the blond away from me and deeper into the bushes.

I got up and trailed discreetly behind to watch them. They stopped in a clearing and started to kiss. They really were into it, and I wondered if they knew each other.

The blond dropped to his knees and the leather daddy whipped out his cock. It was a stubby cock with one of the biggest heads I'd ever seen. He took hold of the blond's head while the blond sucked him.

Watching them get it on made me even hornier. The blond pulled down his jeans and hugged a tree. The leather daddy stuck his erect cock into the blond, and once he was all the way in, grabbed the buttcheeks in both hands and began the fuck.

I pulled out my prick and beat it as I watched the leather daddy's cock slide in and out of the blond's butthole. The blond humped back. I could hear him beg, "Fuck me. Fuck my ass. Yeah, that's it. Do It. Shoot your fucking load."

The leather daddy fucked like a piston for a long time. I approached them, but stayed a couple of feet away. The daddy smiled at me several times, pleased that I was enjoying their show, then he suddenly pulled his cock out and his cum rained all over the blond's smooth assheeks. He wiped his cock off on them, then zipped up and motioned to me, as if to say, "I got mine, now you get yours."

Curious, I stepped over to the blond, who remained there, waiting, hugging the tree. I touched his ass and felt the leather daddy's cum. I lubed my own cock with it and at first I thought I'd jack off all over his ass.

But then he begged me, "Stick it in, please."

His asshole was hot and wet and I held onto his soft prick while I eased my cock inside him.

"Fuck my ass. I need more cock."

It didn't take many strokes before I started to come. He sensed this and clamped his butt muscles around my meaty cock.

"Oh, yeah, come inside me."

I crammed my cock in to the hilt and shot my load deep inside him.

I continued playing with his cock but it didn't harden.

Finally I pulled out, zipped up and stepped away. He didn't move, just stayed hanging on the tree with his ass exposed, waiting for another hard cock.

Back by the windmills, among the other cruisers, was a short man with a big basket. Licking my lips, I brazenly approached him, groped him. In return, he groped me, satisfied that I packed enough meat for him. When he walked away, I followed him.

Surrounded by bushes, he got down on his knees to service me. I hadn't cleaned my cock after fucking the blond, but the short man got excited by the smell and the taste of my cock. He held the head of my prick while he slurped up and down on the shaft.

"Eat it," I demanded. "Eat that big dick that was just up somebody's ass!"

The tone of my voice set him off; now he really went to work sucking my cock, slicking it with saliva, as if he were getting ready to have it up his own ass. While he worked on my cock with his mouth, he fisted his own cock in sync.

I got off watching him while he furiously jacked his cock until it blasted gobs of cum all over the ground, but rather than letting me fuck him, he just stood, zipped up, and ran off. That was that. I stayed in the bushes, enjoying the sun on my face after the fog burned off. I stroked my now-sopping cock and I became aware of the traffic sounds on the nearby highway. I closed my eyes and enjoyed beating my meat with humanity zooming by just yards away. Then I heard footfalls and my eyes snapped open. There, right in front of me, grinning, his eyes intent on my hard-on, was a swarthy, muscular stud wearing a black tank top and white pants. He looked up and lewdly licked his lips. I took my hands off my cock in invitation. The cock bounced in the breeze and the stud started to jack it. As he did, he took out his own fat, uncut cock. Holding our two dicks together, he jacked them at the same time. I liked the heat and friction from his cock.

Bending down, he took my cock in his mouth. I tried the same gambit, "Yeah, suck that cock that was just up the blond boy's hot ass."

At that, the stud bolted.

"Can't win 'em all," I mumbled as I watched him disappear into the bushes toward the highway.

I slipped my cock back into my jeans and went in the opposite direction, taking the winding path until I saw a kid with long dark hair. He was just sitting on a rock, drinking from a bottle of wine.

He smiled. "Want a nip?"

"Sure."

I took the bottle and tasted the wine. It was warm, sweet—not to my taste. I grimaced.

He chuckled. "I hate it too, but it's so hot and I was thirsty and...."

Then, incredibly, he just passed out—or pretended to. The bottle of cheap wine fell from his hand with a thud. I felt up under his cut-offs and his cock hardened to my touch. I unzipped his cut-offs and pulled them down over his hips. His cock was long and uncut. I jacked it slowly while I rolled my tongue around inside the foreskin. He didn't say a word or make a move. But playing with him gave me a hard-on. I freed my cock and jerked it while I sucked him.

When he didn't respond to my machinations, I began to think that maybe he really had passed out from a combination of the heat and the cheap wine. It became obvious that he wasn't in any hurry to shoot. My cock began throbbing when I squeezed his hairy balls and nipped at his foreskin.

When the time came, I aimed my cock at his brown pubic bush and spouted cum drops all over it. Then I abandoned him, leaving his half-hard erection blowing in the wind.

I wandered around some more. Nobody interested me. I figured I had gotten about all the action I was going to get here, so I decided to walk over to the beach and watch the waves roll in.

But no sooner had I made that decision than I saw my ideal man. I shook myself, thinking perhaps the wine had really been a drug and I was dreaming. But he was real. A butch young stud with his shirt off. A face as handsome as Matt Dillon's, my current silver screen favorite, with jet black hair and crystal blue eyes.

As if in a trance, I approached him.

He smiled and wiped his sweaty chest with his T-shirt, as if he was inviting me to touch him there. I sucked his nipples one at a time. He was real. He moaned softly.

Pulling him down to the ground, I got on top of him.

Straddling that rippled chest, I began a slow worshipping of his body. I bathed his chest with spit, lapping up his sweat, feasting on his smooth, salty flesh.

His crotch bulged and I ripped open the metal buttons of his jeans. He wore sexy black bikini briefs, which contrasted with his milky white skin.

I slobbered all over his underwear, wetting them with spit until the outline of his dick was clear. I tugged his jeans down to his knees. His cock was drooling when I pulled his briefs down around his thighs. I had the urge to see him completely naked. He didn't object when I took off his sneakers, his calf-length white socks, his black denim jeans and the black bikini briefs.

With his head pillowed on his clothes, he closed his eyes and, his hands at his sides, allowed me to enjoy his beauty. He was truly one of the most handsome young men I'd ever seen. I now regretted that I had had a steamy afternoon of sex. On the other hand, I could now take my sweet time, and he seemed in no hurry to leave.

When I have a hot stud, I have to taste all of him, lick him everywhere, and so I feasted on his thighs, his hairy ballsac, ignoring his six-inch, cut cock for now. As I finished on the balls, he spread his legs, and I nuzzled my face in his asscrack. I savored the bittersweet taste of his butt. He must have thought I was getting him ready for a fuck.

"You wanna? Go ahead. Stick it in."

I shed my clothes, something I rarely did outdoors. In the unsual heat, I wanted to feel him against my sweating body, skin-to-skin. He had his eyes closed, and he kept his legs spread wide as I got back between his thighs.

Lubing my cock with spit, I rubbed it against his asscrack, then I pushed the head inside. He was hot and wet and ready. As the first inch of the shaft slid in, he scissored his strong legs around me.

"Oh yeah, fuck me."

More inches went in and he begged some more. In response, I picked up my speed.

"Harder! Oh yeahhh."

I sat back on my heels, I gripped his legs and pushed them apart, watching my cock slide in and out of his beautiful butt.

His cock throbbed and drooled pre-cum. He wrapped his

fingers around it and stroked it. Just seeing him beat his meat while I fucked his ass took me to the brink.

Ramming my cock all the way up, I came. Spurt after spurt of my jizz squirted into him.

His head tossed from side to side like he was throwing a fit. I'd never seen anything quite like it. While he furiously jerked his prick, he humped back at my cock, which was wilting fast.

"Oh, God! Oh, shit! Fuck, I'm coming!"

Rivulets of creamy jizz landed all over his smooth chest and belly.

My cock finally slithered out of his butthole.

Suddenly I was aware of the other guys standing around us. I don't know how long they'd been watching us. I raised myself up and grabbed my clothes.

The young Adonis just lay there with a smile on his face. I counted a total of six guys moving in towards us with their cocks out, some looking at him, some looking at me; all were beating their meat. Among them I saw the long-haired boy with the uncut cock who had passed out on me; he seemed to have revived, and the blond with the torn T-shirt. Others I didn't recognize. As I dressed, they moved closer. The blond came up to me, but I pushed him away. Soon I moved out of everybody's way, but I stood back to watch them. In the light of dusk, it became a surreal spectacle. They seemed to be performing some sort of ancient ritual. They were touching each other as they jerked their cocks. The blond made the first move, dropping to his knees between the Adonis' wide-spread legs. As the blond sank his cock in where I had just come, the young Adonis writhed on the ground, jerking his meat to semi-hardness.

The swarthy man who had left me so abruptly earlier suddenly appeared at my side. He looked at me, stroking his cock, but I ignored him, intent on watching as the blond got up and the long-haired guy with the uncut cock replaced him. Watching that long cock slam into the Adonis made my own cock jump. Meanwhile, the swarthy man stepped up to the others and, after the long-haired kid had finished, he knelt down to shove his cock into the Adonis. The Adonis must have loved the feel of that fat, uncut meat because now the Adonis went wild again, as he had done with me. One after the other, the guys who remained, turned on by this lewd display, stepped over to splatter their seed on the Adonis' smooth stomach.

By the time the swarthy man was climaxing inside the Adonis, everyone had gone, and the Adonis put his arms around the man and pulled him toward him, forcing the man's cock back into him.

As they embraced and kissed, I could watch no more; I turned and hurriedly made my way out the park. The show was over—for another day.

HOT WHEELS

J. Freeman

That sizzling summer morning in 1969, anything seemed possible. Cruising the highways in my 18-wheeler, I'd had more sex that summer than I'd ever dreamed of. But none of the many men I'd been with compared to the young hunk who asked me for a ride to San Francisco that morning.

I'd barely finished a greasy breakfast at a truck stop when he approached me. I nearly choked on my last bite of pancakes when he asked if I was heading north, and wondered if he could join me on the four-hour trip.

He looked like a typical college kid did in those days, with a cherubic face framed in soft, dirty blond curls. Both his cut-offs and button-down shirt with the sleeves torn off were a size too tight, revealing an even tighter body. Broad, tan shoulders melted into chiseled biceps and pecs. Best of all, he sported a third leg that practically burst through his frazzled fly.

I readily agreed to take him with me. He accepted my offer to buy him breakfast and proceeded to gobble every morsel like he hadn't seen any food in days, which he later admitted was the case. As I watched him slurp his coffee, I was already imagining what that wet tongue could do to my pulsating gloryhole.

As we talked, he asked me if I knew my way around San Francisco. I hinted that I'd gotten around there quite a bit, and he displayed his white teeth in a knowing smile. Then he quickly changed the subject, leaving me unsure if he was as naive as he looked or just teasing me.

Soon we got into my rig and began our journey. There's something about driving down a long lonely stretch of highway that always brings out the secrets of a stranger, and Benjamin Packard, as he introduced himself, also had a story to tell. He said he was from Montgomery, Alabama, where he'd always sensed that he was different. By the time he turned nineteen, the month before he met me, he knew he had an intense attraction to men, but wasn't able to act on it at home because of his strict upbringing. So he'd hitched his way

expectation. I undid my pants and Ben eyed the hard tirejack that sprouted between my hairy thighs.

"I want you to lick me everywhere, Ben," I explained, half-turning and reaching around to finger my anus. "That's called rimming and it may be addictive, I warn you."

With a serious expression, he hunkered down between my legs, and I positioned my naked ass above his pretty head.

At first, he just sniffed my ass like some curious lapdog, but then I guess my scent made him hungry. When I felt Ben's warm tongue connect with my ass crack, I instinctively pushed my butt closer to his face.

Ben's tongue immediately slipped into my hole. Being a novice, he was really careful about not hurting me. But when I pushed into him even harder, he became bolder, and his tongue rubbed against each of my ass-folds with increasing ferocity.

"Mmm, yeah, Ben, you're really good. Don't worry about doing it harder. I love it, man. Go ahead, fuck me with that wet tongue of yours, real hard. Yeah, real hard!"

He pulled back a little, and I could feel him hesitating a bit against the sensitive skin of my perineum. Then he dove down again and really got into it. His tongue swirled in and out of each of my crevices and then spiraled back again. My woody was harder than ever, and I put Ben's hand on me so he could also jerk me off. He got the idea real fast and got down to work, jerking me off with long, smooth pulls.

All the while, he kept rimming me harder and harder. I was so hot that I thought my knees would buckle under me, and my head reeled, dizzy with lust. His other hand gripped my balls and clenched them, his fingers pulling at the curly hairs there. Tingles seared through my sensitive skin, and I found myself rocking back and forth to the rhythm of his enthusiastic hand job.

Spurred on by the hand-to-cock contact, his tongue flicked around wildly inside of me, always reaching higher and deeper. Finally, he hit my prostate. It was as if he actually lit my fuse over and over until my whole body caught on fire. The heat spread to my balls and then started to explode into my erection. The skin of my cock contracted as my woody instantly filled with my cum. And at the same time, his incessant tongue-flicking continued to put my ass in overdrive.

When I reached my pinnacle, I shot my first round of slime balls. They ricocheted out so fast and hard that they sprayed all the way up to my face. Then a second round hit me so fast that my chin and neck dripped with my own jizz. Beneath me, Ben was still going at it, squeezing my balls dry with the combined action of his hand, lips, and tongue.

Even after I expelled the last drop of cream, Ben went on licking my ass. He kept me going long after the orgasm had blasted its way through me. With every pulse of my sphincter, his tongue widened and spread and then thinned out again, stimulating me right through to the end—so to speak!

After a while, he had to come up for a breath. He sat up and saw the pungent cum dripping off me. Without any prompting, he licked the jizz right off my hot skin, slurping up each sticky drop and savoring it on his flexible tongue. His hand returned to my soft cock, playing with it as he lapped me clean. In no time, my boner surged back to life, harder than before.

"I want to be your first fuck, Ben. I'll go real slow and make sure you have something to remember," I said, brushing my fingers against his own cock, once again stiff, as it jumped into my hand with renewed appreciation.

"Yes, I want you to be my first one," he answered and turned his body around so he lay with his stomach on the ground.

Then I wiped the sweat off his ass and mixed it with the pre-cum oozing off the crown of his cock, creating my own brand of ass-lube. I slopped the sticky glob onto his tight pink asshole, making sure to moisturize every hill and valley and prepping his nervous butt for the big game with my fingers.

He reacted by raising his ass to my teasing and allowing me to give him a sneak preview of a genuine ass-invasion. Ben grunted loudly, enjoying every second of it. I took my time relaxing him, making sure he would enjoy feeling my stiff cock barrel into him.

When his hole began to widen slightly from my fingerfucks, I took the opportunity to insert my cock inside him. At first, he clammed up on me, but instead of retreating I pushed in a little farther. He gasped, "Oh, yes, that's good, so good," and brought his ass up to meet my thrust.

Before long, I was halfway in, and then with a long, slow

push, my entire cock submerged in his virgin ass. He was tight and hot, and felt better than a mouth around my rigid slab of meat. Then I really started to fuck him, and Ben groaned with lust every time I pushed myself deeper inside him.

Before long we were really going at it, and I felt my load descend once again. Then as if I hadn't come moments before, I started to jizz like crazy, filling him with my hot cum. His ass soon overflowed and some of it spilled over. His hands ducked down and wrapped around his own prong, pulling it like crazy.

Then I heard him groan as he came again, his jizz splattering and mixing with the mud. We both kept it up until we were dry from all the screwing.

Ben glowed from his first experience, and we enjoyed several more stops along the way until I dropped him off in the heart of the city. I had a feeling I left him with something to remember even though we never kept in touch.

All the same, I'll always remember the hottest day of the summer of 1969.

RUPERT BARE

Tony Anthony

You may think you know the guy you love, but have you seen him in his home town? The sort of thing I'm writing about here used to be known as the English vice.

It was the first time I had been to Greg's place in the country and I was impressed. Old walls clad in ivy, white frame windows looking out on playing fields, boys playing cricket in whites reflecting the hot summer sun.

"Glad you could come, old chap," he said when I arrived. "I have to go out. I'll be back in no time. Make yourself at home."

I looked around in the room. Framed photographs on a wall showed Greg, youthful in school sports teams; later ones had him stockily built and hairy in adult teams. There was even one showing him and me in our rugby team.

I was settling into a chair to watch the cricket when there was a quiet knock at the door.

It came from a good-looking boy, barely nineteen I judged, but remarkably fresh-faced. He was physically small and his pink cheeks and dark eyelashes gave him an innocent choirboy's looks.

"My name's Rupert," he said, almost whispering. "Greg told me to look after you until he gets back."

He seemed quite at home in the place and I realized that this was a friend Greg had not mentioned to me. I knew Greg was gay, of course; we had discovered each other soon after he joined my rugger club. This boy was obviously good-looking and I wondered whether Greg was letting his preference be known out here in the country as well as in town.

"I'm going to take a shower," Rupert said quietly. "I hate feeling sweaty."

From where I was sitting I could see into the bathroom and Rupert did not bother to close the door. I wondered why, but guessed that anyone knowing Greg was probably mad about sport and accustomed to showering without excessive modesty.

I tried to watch the cricket through the net curtains at the open window but kept looking back to see the shower stall and an indistinct pink figure behind the tinted glass panel. The possibility of trying for a closer acquaintance crossed my mind, but I decided that it might be unwise to risk spoiling Greg's possibly blameless reputation locally.

I went back to watching the cricket, but couldn't get the fresh-faced boy off my mind. When English boys are good looking in that way they really are something special. I could imagine a perfect body in the shower, skin gleaming wetly, black hair slicked down.

With an effort I wrenched my mind away. Greg might not appreciate my seducing an innocent young friend.

One of the boys playing cricket hit a six, and a faint cheer came through the window. It was a classic summer scene.

"Could you help me wash my back, please?" Rupert called out.

Going into the bathroom I wondered what exactly was on his mind.

"I'm sorry to be a nuisance," he said, and added, "Sir."

"No problem," I said. He had his back to me and the picture was perfect. Pure white skin, faintly pink in places, and a flawless little butt.

He looked over his shoulder at me.

"I'm sorry to impose on you, sir," he said. "But I can't bear being sweaty for long. Could you do my back please?" He handed me a cake of soap and backed away from the falling water.

I took the soap and began working on his back. How would Greg feel about this? Was I intruding on a private relationship? Was I imagining things about the boy only because I wanted him? Maybe he was simply obsessional about personal cleanliness.

"I was a junior at Greg's school," he said.

I knew it was an old English private school, the kind they call a public school. That might explain his calling me 'sir.' Maybe it was the custom there.

I soaped his shoulders and watched the white bubbles form a rivulet running down his back and into the clean cleft between the cheeks of his butt. My soaping hand went down to his waist. Should I take a chance and let it slide down and over the swelling globes? Maybe if I did it quickly I could laugh it off somehow if he reacted with hostility.

He half turned and was sideways on to me and I caught a glimpse of a long, white dick hanging from a dark bush of hair. I looked at his eyes and the curved eyelashes.

"It's very kind of you, sir," he said, glancing at me shyly.

To hell with it, I thought, and slid my soapy hand over his butt. It felt fantastically good, and I wondered what he would do.

He looked down, eyes half closed, his whole attitude passive.

I moved my hand slowly, caressing the sweetly swelling curves. He stayed motionless and I let my fingertips find his soft spot. He half turned and bent forward, bowing, offering his butt.

"Stand up," I said.

He straightened smartly. "Yes, sir. I'm sorry."

"Go back under the shower," I said. "I want this soap off you."

I felt that I wanted to take care of him somehow. He was a lot smaller than I, and something made him seem almost childish and needing to be cared for. When he was out of the shower I put a towel around his shoulders and began rubbing him dry. He let me do it, moving his body to aid the process.

When I got to drying his groin the long dick was stiffening, arching out fine and white. While I dried his chest he held his arms up and placed his hands behind his handsome head, exposing armpits with the beginnings of dark hair.

His nipples were little pink rosebuds; and I kissed them briefly, letting my tongue feel the tiny nubs.

His dick grew hard and cylindrical, like a length of broom handle. I kissed the shaft, letting my lips slide along its length while my hand cupped the balls hanging in the water-slackened white skin. With my fingertips I drew back his foreskin, loving the way the pointed pink head emerged, looking fresh and virginal.

He was so perfect I wanted suddenly to hold him. Putting my arms around him I pulled him close and kissed his slender neck. He did not respond in any way except to allow me to do it.

I was still embracing him when the front door opened and Greg breezed in. I barely had time to brace myself for possible trouble.

"Hello," he said. "I see you've met."

I felt embarrassed. Greg and I had only ever had one-on-ones and I wondered how he would really feel about me grappling with his young friend. I relaxed my bear hug and stood back.

"Don't stop on my account," he said. "Be with you in a second."

He disappeared into a bedroom and emerged naked, hairy body short and solidly built, stubby dick pointing horizontally, big grin on his face.

"Still fully dressed?" he said to me. "What's the matter? Are you queer or something?"

I had to laugh, and stripped off my clothes, glad to be free of them in the afternoon heat.

"Boy," he said, "make us a pot of tea."

"Yes, sir," Rupert said, and went into the kitchen.

Greg winked at me. "One of my adoring admirers."

"Do you pay him,?" I asked. I had never known him so abrupt and arrogant.

"Not at all," Greg said airily. "Treat him like a dog. He loves it. Well educated."

Rupert brought a tray of tea things in and squatted on the floor, his long dick only half hard now, foreskin modestly hiding the pink head.

Greg poured the tea and chatted with me, ignoring the boy as though he did not exist. When tea was finished and Rupert had taken the tea tray back into the kitchen Greg summoned him with a click of his fingers. "Fetch my condoms—and the lube."

The boy brought a small carton to Greg and stood at the side of his chair. Greg fingered the boy's long dick.

"Have you been good while I've been away?" Greg demanded.

"Yes, sir."

"Hmmm. I wonder. Get on your knees, suck me."

The boy knelt between Greg's hairy legs and sank his head over the hairy groin.

My eyes were on the boy's buns and the wide-open gap between them. I wanted to kneel behind the boy and get my fingers into him. My dick was stiffening rapidly.

"Get on with it," Greg commanded the boy. "What are you waiting for?"

"I'm sorry, sir," came the muffled reply.

Greg was looking down at his own groin. "Damn you. Make it stand."

Rupert's head bobbed energetically.

"Put a condom on it," Greg said. "Dark red."

Rupert did it and I admired Greg's dick again. It starts off stubby but it's a lot bigger when it's standing.

"Now go to my friend," Greg ordered. "Get him hard."

Rupert's beautiful lips closed on my dick and did not need to do much before the probe was as stiff as a cricket bat.

"If he isn't doing it right," Greg said, "give him a smack across the head."

It was the last thing I wanted to do to Rupert, and I caressed his dark hair.

"You'll spoil him," Greg said. He went to the window and looked out. The net curtain billowed in a slight breeze.

"Won't you be seen there?" I asked. He was stark naked and his rigid dick was sheathed in a bright red condom. Any cricket fan happening to look back might be a little startled.

"No, no," Greg said. "Curtains do the job. Fetch me a towel, boy."

Greg draped the towel over the back of an arm chair. "Bend over."

Rupert bent over the chair and gripped the arms to support his weight. When his butt was stretched tight, Greg drew a hand back and brought it down in a stinging smack. The boy's head snapped back and his mouth opened silently.

"That's for nothing," Greg said. "Now just do what you're told." He lubed three fingers and began opening the boy's hole.

"D'you mind if I do it?" he asked me. "I can't wait to get into the little swine."

I shrugged, wondering what the books of etiquette would say, I being the guest and he the host. This was a side of Greg I had not seen before. I was glad he hadn't tried it with me, but my dick seemed to find it all very stimulating—it was rigid in expectation.

Greg took his fingers out of the boy's butt and shuffled forward. Holding his dick at the base, Greg positioned it and pushed. It didn't go in.

"Damn you," Greg said to the boy. "What are you playing at?"

"I'm sorry, sir," Rupert said.

Greg inserted fingers again, glistening with lube. I could see Rupert's eyes closing and mouth clenching.

Greg shuffled forward and tried again. The red-clad dick stayed in view.

"Stand up," Greg ordered. Grasping the boy around the waist, Greg pulled him back against his penis, probing the gap in the white butt.

"Is it on the spot?" Greg asked.

"Yes, sir."

"Bend forward slowly," Greg said. "See if that gets it in." He pulled with his arms while the boy slowly bent forward. Greg's hips suddenly slipped forward a fraction and the gap between his groin and the butt closed.

Rupert's eyes blinked and his mouth opened silently.

Greg too closed his eyes and he bit his lower lip. The pair of them stayed like that for a while, tied in a junction of sexual passion.

My dick was standing like a rod of iron and I stroked it slowly.

Greg began working his hips in long thrusts, his muscles bulging and relaxing smoothly, body broad and rugged. He made Rupert, bending before him, look younger than he really was. The picture they made together was timeless: two men fucking, beautifully united.

Greg's thrusting speeded up, driving his dick with more determination. I got out of my chair and crossed to them.

Looking at Greg's groin I could see the red phallus entering and leaving, sinking into the boy's body and emerging, disappearing and reappearing. The shaft looked very thick. Watching inspired a sort of awe in me ... it always does. My dick stiffened and I circled my fingers around the base and pushed against my groin, letting the shaft project forward hard and straight. The plum-dark skin enclosing the head seemed tight enough to burst.

Unexpectedly Greg pulled his dick out and walked away from the boy. "Are you fucking me around?"

"No, sir," Rupert said.

"If you want trouble I'll give it to you."

"Please sir, I don't want trouble."

I guessed that Greg had invented a problem, justifying what he did next.

He went back to the bending boy, put his dick in the cleft and pushed. For a while there was resistance. The boy spread his legs wider and arched his back, lifting his butt.

Suddenly the dick went in and the boy gasped. Greg immediately pulled out and placed the head against the anus again. He pushed until it went in, then pulled out again. He repeated the move several times.

Rupert gasped and jerked his head back at each re-entry. Eventually he said, "Please, sir."

"Well, don't fuck me around," Greg said.

"No, sir. Never."

Greg resumed his steady fucking. It was like watching a well-oiled machine, silent except for a slight grunt from the boy as each thrust went home.

I put my hand on Greg's hairy butt and let the fingers feel into his cleft. Greg gasped and stopped fucking. His stomach muscles tightened and his whole body trembled in a spasm.

I thought my fingers had triggered his orgasm, but when I took my hand away he continued his rhythmic probing.

From the cricket game outside the window came a faint cheer. It seemed almost to celebrate Greg's performance. I nearly laughed.

It was a crazy situation. The three of us engaged in an act of carnal intercourse, a red sheathed penis plumbing the depths of a young man's rectum, while outside a cricket game proceeded in the calm of a sunny afternoon.

Greg's rhythm was speeding up, the meaty muscles of his back beginning to flex seriously. He is no slender weakling and his stocky, hairy body working hard was an impressive sight. His mouth opened and he began breathing heavily.

The boy dropped his head and I could see his hands were gripping tightly on the arms of the chair. He looked pink and vulnerable against the hairy man behind him.

I felt under the boy's groin and found his long penis jammed against the towel that hung over the back of the chair. He inched back until his dick was standing clear, long and thin. With my finger tips I eased his foreskin back and closed it again, and opened it over and over again while I rubbed my other hand along my own length.

I felt an early surge of nearing orgasm electrify my penis. Shortening my strokes I wondered how close Greg and Rupert were to their coming.

Greg's eyes were closed and he was thrusting hard with his pelvis. Looking down at the gap in Rupert's white buttocks I watched Greg's red rod plunging and reappearing. Another near-orgasm seared into the head of my dick. I stopped jacking myself and watched the drama unfolding before me.

Greg raised his face, eyes closed and mouth twisted in a grimace. He was gulping air noisily, going *uh, uh, uh,* in time with his thrusts.

I put a hand on his shoulders and slid it down his back until my fingers were clasping his butt. Then I lifted my hand to his shoulders and ran it down again. I went on stroking him, faster and faster.

"Fuck-ing-hell," Greg gasped. "Yes, yes, yes."

"Go for it," I said. "Let it all come out now."

Rupert raised his head and was making little whimpering sounds.

When my hand was next in Greg's cleft I let it go on down and under, between his legs, and grasped his hairy balls.

"Oh fuck, fuck, fuck," he said.

I felt another surge in my own dick and realized I had started masturbating it again. My stomach muscles were tensing spasmodically, making my hips give little jerks.

Greg suddenly stopped fucking and gave a few slow and massive thrusts. His mouth opened as he gasped, "Yesss. Yesss. Ye—ss." His buttocks clenched hugely as he drove his dick in.

Quickly I felt under Rupert's groin. His semen ran over my hand, slicking it wetly as I rubbed his long shaft, making him come completely. The feel of his liquid orgasm gave me an urgent need to come.

An electric surge went through me and I moved my hips close to Greg and watched as a long spurt of semen looped out of me onto his hairy back. My eyes closed as the anguish of orgasm scorched into the head of my penis. My legs were shaking uncontrollably as I rose onto my toes, thrusting my dick forward as it spurted and spurted and spurted again.

Bowing my back I tilted my pelvis quickly, thrusting my dick forward frantically, blindly seeking the end of my orgasm. The ecstasy was agonizing.

And in a while it was all slowing down, my desperate need easing.

Gradually we regained control of our minds. The reality of day returned. Our breathing slowed to normal.

When my head cleared, I saw Greg looking down at his red dick as though he hadn't seen it before. He looked at me and smiled while Rupert used the towel to wipe up the white remains of our passions.

The boy disappeared into the bathroom with the towel and the limp condom. When he came back he was fully dressed.

"May I go now, please, sir?" he asked Greg.

"Yeah, get out," Greg said.

"Thank you, sir. Thank you very much," Rupert said.

At the door he paused and looked back at Greg expectantly.

"Well done," Greg said.

The boy's face lit up in a seraphic smile and he let himself out.

"A bit hard on him, weren't you?" I asked. "That was a fantastic fuck. For all of us."

"Don't worry about him," Greg said. "He loves being used roughly. Just like that."

I looked him in the eye.

"Honestly," he said. "He really likes it. You should have asked him."

"Maybe I will," I said. "Next time?"

"Certainly. There must be a next time. Enjoyed your company. Cup of tea now, or a bit of action first?"

Afterwards, we went to a pub and celebrated. It had been a very hot day.

SMOOTH
(A Tale of a Peerless Boy)

Kevin Bantan

It wasn't a big deal. It was just a stone. A smooth, brown stone. I turned it over in my palm. Funny, the things that fascinated me. But it was so smooth. I'd found it in the alley on my way home. It was lying there in the middle of the pebble-strewn blacktop, as if it were an orphan puppy wagging its tail in the hope that I would pet it. Then fall in love with it. Then adopt it. But it was just a stone. Albeit smooth. I learned that word from my stepfather. He was educated. And he had money. Which was why my mother and I didn't live in the projects anymore. Which was why I was sitting on the sturdy wooden steps of this humongous house in the fanciest section of town I'd ever seen. Holding a smooth stone.

It felt good to the touch. Like Charlie Moss said Doris the Can's ass felt under her panties. As if I believed that his hand ever got there. But with Doris the Can you never knew. She was supposed to be sweet for me, the rumor was. As if I needed a girl to be liking me, especially because it got the guys riding me about it. Doris was pretty, I admit. But that was the extent of my interest in her. Or any girl, for that matter. I didn't care how smooth her ass was. Now, Alexander Bascom's was a different matter. I stroked the stone, imagining that it was Alex's skin. God, he was beautiful. It's the only way I could describe him. It was the way my mom and stepdad described me. My mom's very light-skinned, but she has brown eyes, so that doesn't explain why I look the way I do.

Because I'm an oddity. People stare at me for that reason. I'd swear that my real father was white, but that doesn't untangle the mystery of my chocolate skin, especially given how light my mother is. It might explain my blue eyes, though. But how did I get creamy brown skin and blue eyes? Mom says that people stare at me because my looks are so arresting. In the projects that's what the cops were always doing to people. But we didn't live there anymore. We lived in a good part of town. But little Mark Dwyer still had cornflower blue eyes looking out at the world, surrounded by chocolate skin. As I said, a real oddity. Not like Alex, with his stunning emerald green eyes and that soft tan coloration that white boys can manage for the summer, happily. And I loved Alexander Bascom. I stroked the stone. And his smooth, tan skin.

I first did it with Rasheed Holloway on the decrepit basketball court at the projects. It was one night after the basketball players had left, because the darkness prevented them from seeing the ball, or themselves, anymore. There in the darkness, doing it with Rasheed, the smell of boy sweat still lingering in the air. Doing it with Rasheed, and not even knowing what I was doing. But I wasn't in love with him. I liked him. We were friends. And doing something natural with each other. But just friends doing it. I was eleven. Now I was fourteen and in love for the first time in my life. Really in love. A feeling I knew I'd never have for Doris the Can or any girl, no matter how pretty she was. Alex was beyond pretty. Alex was beautiful. I started, dropping the stone.

"Sorry, Mark. I didn't mean to scare you."

"It's okay, man. I was just lost in thought." *That one being you*, I didn't add. Being short for my age, I knew when to keep my mouth shut to avoid becoming creamed corn at the fists of another guy my age, who was always taller than me.

"Hey, I wondered if, well, maybe, like you might want to hang together or something?"

Or something sounded like a winner, but I said, "You mean it?" God, his blond crew-cut hair looked so good next to his tan. My new neighbor messed so much with my hormones, I was afraid that I'd run out of them. I was pretty ignorant about hormones, except for knowing that I had them. And that they went wild around males. Well, specifically around Alex Bascom, who was Fair Hills Middle School's poster boy. And it was strange, because he was kind of shy, you know? Like his looks embarrassed him. I wondered if Doris the Can was sweet for him, too. Who wouldn't be? I even overheard Michael Fagin, our star basketball player, joking once that he would stick his six inches in Alex in a heartbeat, he was so pretty. I wondered if Alex really was mortified by his prettiness. Another word my stepdad used. It was catching. Words, I mean. I picked up the stone.

"Yeah. But only if you want to."

"Yeah, I really do."

"What do you have there?"

"Just a stone I found in the alley. It's really smooth, though." I walked to the fence and showed it to him.

"It is." He stroked it with his index finger. I licked my lips, thinking about how good that finger would feel stroking me anywhere on my body. Just touching me. Making me a lump of goose pimples, it would feel so good. Making me hard, just because that little patch of soft skin belonged to Alexander Bascom, the boy god I loved. Thank goodness he didn't know it. The last thing I needed was to be known for the faggot I was.

"So, um, what do you want to do?" I swallowed hard, watching his finger repeatedly touch the stone like that. *Inside me, Alex. As far as it'll go. And then in my mouth, making me clean you for having been in me like that.*

He shrugged. "I don't know. Just to hang, you know?" He looked into my eyes, and those gorgeous emerald irises were pulling my soul from my body. He managed a shy smile with lips fuller even than mine. I would often go to sleep at night pretending I was sucking on his overripe lower lip. If only he knew.

"Okay, sounds good." *God, Mark what unbelievable control, considering that you're imitating a Tootsie Roll down there. What an absolutely cool fourteen-year-old you are.*

"Want to come over? We can play music in my room."

"Cool." But it wasn't. I could smell him. That soft teenage boy smell he gave off from being slightly sweaty. His room would be worse. His sheets would give off that scent the whole time we were in there.

But I appreciated the fact that he seemed to want to be friends. Even if he was almost a head taller than I was. And blond. And gorgeous. And making a part of my body into a Tootsie Roll. I closed my eyes, imagining him licking that Tootsie Roll.

"You okay, Mark?"

"Huh? Sorry." Busted. Man, this was dangerous. But I leaped the fence, anyway. *I love you, Alex Bascom, but you'll never know it, because little Mark Dwyer can act like the cool guy he really isn't, dangerous hormones notwithstanding.*

The scent hit me like a spilled perfume bottle. It made me

stir again, damn it. I wanted to dive onto his bed and die smelling him, dead from being intoxicated by the rich boy aroma of beautiful Alex Bascom. But dying happy. Being held by him, my dying breaths inhaling his crotch, overdosing me with its fragrance, speeding my demise.

"It's hot today," he said, pulling his T-shirt over his head. *Please, don't do that, Alex,* my brain warned. Besides, what was he talking about? The central air was on. "Can I see the stone again?" he asked sitting on his bed. The bed that hoarded his wonderful boyish scent.

"It's just a stone," I said, holding it out to him from a safe distance. Was there such a thing? Here? Where the object of every affection I didn't have for my folks slept? God, the smooth, tanned chest with those hard breasts and the little brown nipples. Better than Doris the Can's jugs, in a squillion years. Heaven. "Sit?" Not on your life, man.

I sat. Not too close, but too close, because I could feel his heat, smell his sweat, which should be bottled so that I could bathe in it, cover my body with it, smell like him. *You're going nuts, Mark,* I warned myself.

"How do stones get this smooth?" he asked, doing his damn stroking again. Tootsie Roll City for Dwyer again, as a result.

"Um, from being eroded by water, I guess. I read that once." I'd also done it with Rasheed once, so did that make me an expert on that, too? Fool.

"It must have taken a lot of water." We laughed, mine more high-pitched and gay than I ever meant it to be. Fool. All of a sudden his hand closed on the stone. My eyes went past his hand to his crotch. No, his dick couldn't be tenting his khaki shorts. It had to be something else. I looked up, quickly, afraid he'd seen me staring at his private boy place. His eyes were closed. His lashes looked longer and more curved without the distraction of those glinting green marbles of his. Now he opened them and asked, "You ever do it, Mark?"

"Once," I blurted without thinking. Now we were beyond dangerous, into beaten-to-death territory. Hell, if I were going to be killed by the fists of my beloved, what did I have to lose? I would be out of my misery, never having to look at his blond fur, his emerald cat's-eyes, his perfect tan again.

"Really? What was she like?"

"No clue." That's it, Mark. Now go for the jugular. "His

name was Rasheed."

"No shit? What was he like?" The question threw me. I was expecting the first fist in my face, bracing for it. What was wrong with this picture?

"Like?"

"Yeah. What did you do?"

"I don't know. We just kind of kissed a little. And played with each other. You know. Exploring. That's what we called it. Exploring."

"Did you like exploring?"

I was going to have big shoulder muscles shortly, I was shrugging so much. "Better than he did."

"Do, uh, I mean, do you still like want to do it?"

"Only with you."

At that moment my life ended. I could feel the heat rise on my cheeks, the redness spread. Fool. Total Fool! Kill me, Alex. I deserve it. Bust my pitiful faggot ass, calling me that all the while you do it. The fool faggot.

Against all logic, I opened my eyes and looked at him with blush-stained cheeks. The green of his eyes was more brilliant than I ever remembered it being, although I'd hardly seen it more than a dozen times close up, we hadn't known each other that long.

"I feel the same way about you." Now I knew I was dead, because this is what I imagined heaven was like. It was a boy, a beautiful one with blond hair and green eyes and perfect white teeth hiding behind lips that should be illegal. Attached to a body that God made Himself to show what the perfect boy would look like, if he existed. And he did. His name was Alexander Bascom, and he was telling Mark Dwyer that he wanted to do it with him. Why couldn't Mark Dwyer's brain stop short-circuiting? Why couldn't he stop his head from inclining to those Eden lips? To brush his own against the pug nose to end them all? Why didn't he have any sense left, except for the searing pleasure on his lips? Why did only a being named AlexMark exist now?

Our arms were in motion, our hands desperate for contact. My hand feverish on his left pectoral. Beyond Eden. His nipple hard against my palm. My cock hard against his.

"I love you, Mark." Beyond heaven. Was that possible? His hot breath scorching my ear with pleasure as he breathed the words.

"I love you, Alex."

Now a tangle of teenage arms and legs on the bed, in a freefall of boy lust, stoked by substances coursing through our bodies that we hardly knew the names of, let alone the reason they made us do this. But we did it, in spite of that.

Although shorter, I found myself pinning Alex to the bed and looking at him with the same heavy-lidded eyes that were staring back at me.

"I love your blue eyes, too." I lowered my face, depriving him of the sight of the cornflower irises, my lips tasting his, gently sucking his sweet breath into my mouth. Aware of his erection pressing through the khaki cloth, through my denim shorts, through my skin, into my being. I held his head as I kissed him, delighting in the feel of the blond stubble that made him a golden god. To the impossibly smooth skin, sunkissed to a color to seduce the world. Alex. The world was Alex. That's all it was. One boy. It was more than enough. It was overwhelming.

I have no clue how we became naked on that bed, but we were. And exploring each other with an unexplainable tenderness as opposite as our initial frenzy had been. Unbelievably, we were making love. Two horny teenage boys were actually consummating their love by doing the real thing. His hand on my thigh. Mine on his surprisingly hard ass cheek. His sliding the hand up my Tootsie Roll, gently, as if it were a fragile thing. Kissing his neck. Kissing his face, feeling the tide of emotions return. Playing for keeps. Frantic again. Telling each other, over and over, that we loved each other. Because we did. This was the beloved, our hearts pounded out to us in emphatic, hurried beats. *This is the one you love. The smooth body of your dreams. Do it. Do it with him, because he's all that matters. Only he exists for you. No one else ever will.*

I rubbed my circumcised brown cock against his lighter dark pink cock. "Oh, god, Mark."

"God, I love you, Alex."

"Oh God, Mark, do me with your dick. Do me! Make me come, beautiful."

I rubbed his sex like a demon, unable to think of anything but how perfect it was, how hard it was, how much it loved me.

Our convulsions were heroic as our come lurched from us and spread between us, mingled in boy happiness. When our spasms stopped, we looked at each other through the same lowered lids of love, and kissed.

I remained lying on Alex as we told each other how great a lover each of us was, replaying what we had just done, almost announcing it as if we were doing a play-by-play. Then kissing again and feeling the need rise as sure as the sun. The need to be coupled with the object of our love and hormones. Still wet. And hard again. Luxuriating that hardness in the slick essences we'd given up to each other. Sliding frictionless now. As smooth as a baby's bottom. As smooth as Alex and Mark's, newborn lovers. Holding the god of the universe as my rigid maleness moved against his. Way beyond whatever heaven could be imagined. Beyond words. Only smells and nerves now. Of the only person who existed. And smooth. Smoother than any water-slicked stone. Smoother than anything. Alex. Kissing him as if my fever might abate from covering his neck with my lips. Making the fever worse. Rubbing fast, needful. No resistance on his sweet come, only sleekness. Like his smooth, boyish body. Come to me, love. Come to me, you peerless boy.

"Sooooo smooth. God," Alex breathed and arched his back, making our coital contact complete. Alex Bascom and Mark Dwyer. In orgasm.

And smooth
. Totally, utterly ... smooth.

IN CERTAIN SITUATIONS TOES BEGIN TO SWEAT

Carl Miller Daniels

tall and slender,
blond and good-looking,
the big-dicked blue-eyed boy
sometimes beats off 3 or 4 times a day,
maybe more.
this seems like a lot to him, and he wonders
if other boys beat off that much.
but he's too shy to ask anybody.
he washes the washrag he spurts his
cum into at the sink in the bathroom that
adjoins his room,
and often the washrag has
no time to dry out between uses,
and is still damp
when he spurts fresh cum into it.
3 or 4 times a day sure seems like a lot to him.
now,
he sits in his desk at school
in algebra ii class
and he thinks about
being at home in his room lying on his back
on his bed on top of his smooth soft light blue bedspread
beating off
and while he's thinking about
that,
his dick gets hard, and as he
sits there in algebra ii class aware
that his dick is hard and waiting for it to get
soft,
he is looking at the back
of the neck
of bruce macheson the star swimmer on the high
school swim team,
looking at the broad shoulders of bruce macheson,
looking at the backs of the ears of bruce macheson

he sits there looking at bruce macheson,
listens to formulae and the scrape of chalk,
wishing he were home in his own bedroom
on top of his light blue bedspread,
a little bothered by the thought
that bruce macheson might be
there in his bedroom, too,
a bit troubled to find his thoughts tentatively
prodding the possibility of bruce macheson, naked,
sitting on top of the soft blue bedspread,
bruce macheson naked and smooth beyond any sensible
expectation for smoothness,
bruce macheson's smooth muscular butt pressed tight
against the soft blue bedspread,
the smooth, little-nippled bruce macheson chest waiting
to be gently and
brazenly
licked.
he is disturbed by thoughts
of this nature in regard
to bruce macheson.
he stares at the pink
backs of bruce macheson's
sexy compact ears.
he wonders just how many times a day
bruce macheson
beats off.
at that instant, bruce macheson turns around,
looks at him
squarely in the eyes,
and softly says
"three." then,
bruce macheson
winks
knowledgeably, with
genuine
affection,
and that's when all those
toes really
begin to sweat.

LOCKERROOM HEAT

R.J. Masters

I must admit that I love sucking cock. I love the feel of it coming to life on my tongue, sliding into my throat. I especially love the hot, sticky cum exploding from the tip of a jerking, twitching monster. Even when a latex sheath keeps me from tasting the sweet cum, there is a special excitement when that first burst of cum erupts against the back of my throat.

I knew I was gay in high school and began savoring the delicacy of prime, teenaged cockmeat when I was a senior. I had devised many ways of seducing my fellow jocks, and as a result had sucked off the majority of my varsity teammates.

There was one exceptional cock I never thought I would get to suck though. It belonged to my best friend, Luke. Luke was handsome and sexy, with sandy blond hair and a body to die for. His arms, chest and abdomen were a mass of muscle. Below his narrow waist, trapped within his jock was a huge bulge of cockmeat and lemon-sized balls that made me drool.

Every day in the locker room, he unknowingly teased me until I could barely contain my lust. My horny cock stiffened, coming to attention as he stripped off his sweaty uniform, stepped under the warm water and lathered the soap over his smooth, hairless chest. I watched out of the corners of my eyes, trying to appear indifferent, while he stroked the thick, uncut eight-incher. I longed to drop to my knees and worship the beautiful specimen, to run my tongue along his hot, throbbing length and flick my tongue against the soft, fleshy fold of foreskin.

Instead I would try to conceal my arousal, wash and dress quickly, and go home to whack off, alone and frustrated.

But everything changed the night of our state championship basketball game. Luke had been playing well, and was our high scorer. But it was still a close game. No one was surprised when Central's defense became more and more aggressive as the game wore on, and Luke was their obvious target.

Late in the last quarter they finally succeeded in eliminating Luke from the game. He was taken down on the hardwood floor with a loud thud, and two Central players fell on top of him. He held onto his back as he was helped to the locker room. Our team was barely able to maintain our lead, but we won the game by six points, while Luke nursed his injury.

We all ran back to the locker room, whooping and hollering, to find Luke standing under a hot shower, letting the pulsating spray massage his sore back. His face was pale and it was obvious that he was in pain. Everyone shook his hand and told him how great he had played, but then disappeared for a victory celebration. Even the coach didn't hang around. But I couldn't leave Luke to suffer alone. It was only because of him that we had something to celebrate. So I stayed behind, taking my time in the shower. I dried off and pulled on a pair of jockey shorts, then turned to Luke.

"I could rub some liniment onto your back if you want me to," I offered, not even thinking this could be my chance to get my hands on my sexy friend.

"Okay," he mumbled, lying down, stark naked, on the padded table in the center of our locker room.

I climbed up on the table and straddled his back. I put some liniment onto his shoulders and began to rub them, feeling the large muscles beneath my fingertips. I worked my way slowly down his spine, massaging the knots from his injured body. The liniment made his skin hot to the touch, and I was enjoying the sensation of rubbing his smooth, hard flesh.

"Oh yeah, that's good," he moaned, as my hands continued to ease his pain. "My back's starting to feel a lot better."

He relaxed even more, the tension and knots leaving his tired body, as he surrendered to my touch. When I realized he was enjoying this contact, even after his pain had subsided, I began to fantasize about having him. I imagined how it would feel to have his eight-incher in my mouth, jabbing into my throat. My balls churned with my long pent-up load, and my cock stiffened, pushing against the front of my shorts. I was so horny, I could hardly stand it. This was like a dream come true. I wanted to whip out my sword and plunge it into his prone form, to finally conquer my fantasy lover.

I wiped my hands on a towel, as my imagination took over and reality became distorted. I got more daring, letting my hands move lower, until I was massaging the tops of his fleshy mounds. When he didn't object, I let my hands move even lower, letting my fingertips creep into his hairless asscrack.

My cock was oozing its pre-cum juices into the cotton fabric, and a warm, wet spot was forming where the swollen head rested. I used my free hand to grope my horny meat, through my shorts, wishing it were his hand fondling me. I stroked my length, squeezing and yanking on it. I was so hot, so filled with desire for Luke's hard body, that I became more bold than I had ever been.

I grabbed a handful of assflesh in each hand, openly massaging them. I let my fingertips rest in the warm, moist crack just above the entrance to his body, waiting for his response. When he didn't protest, didn't pull away, I lightly caressed his tight, pink asshole. I fingered the unyielding opening, then pushed one digit inside, stretching the inflexible muscle-ring. I was surprised when he humped upward to meet my touch, letting my finger sink even deeper into the heat of his body. I couldn't believe I was actually finger-fucking my sexy friend, but he seemed to really be getting off on it.

When I pushed a second digit inside him, he moaned loudly, obviously enjoying the sensation. Finally I couldn't stand it any longer. My brain had long ago surrendered control to my horny cock. I slipped an arm around his waist and encouraged him to turn over. My eyes widened at the sight of his throbbing boner protruding from his golden bush. Apparently the massage had done more for him than ease his back pain.

I lay my hands on his chest, rubbing the bulging muscles. I stole a glance at his beautiful face. His eyes were squeezed shut, as he concentrated on my roving fingers. The large pink nipples were already standing at attention, but got even harder when I pinched and twisted them roughly. He gasped as sensations of pleasure-pain filled him.

"Oh man, that feels so good," he groaned.

My hands crept down over his washboard belly. I let my fingers curl around the awakened monster and stroke his length, gently squeezing tiny drops of pre-cum juices from the fold of foreskin that covered his sensitive glans. I tugged the hood from his deep red helmet, desperately wanting to shower it with kisses, to make love to his magnificent tool.

He moaned and thrust upward to meet my touch, signaling his willingness to let me jerk him off. But I could not settle for merely fisting his beautiful cock. I wanted it in my mouth, to feel the heat of his arousal on my lips, to have his length sliding over my tongue and pounding into my throat.

I quickly jumped off the table and retrieved a crisp foil wrapper from my jeans. I tore into it, eagerly applying the sheath to his thick eight-incher.

As soon as it was dressed in its latex armor, I lowered my lips and kissed the quivering flesh. He didn't open his eyes, but moaned in appreciation.

I parted my lips and let only the very tip of his impressive cock into my mouth. I swirled my tongue around the rim of his supersensitive cockhead, causing him to shudder beneath me. I sucked gently on my captive, drawing him slowly into my throat, until I had swallowed the first three inches of his nearly wrist-thick rod.

The excitement was building up within him, and his oversized balls had pulled up close to his body in preparation for the impending explosion. But I didn't want him to cum too quickly. I wanted to prolong this moment, make it last as long as possible. My own cock was aching for attention, for his caress, but I was focused only on his horny meat.

I let his throbbing monster slide from my mouth. I teased it with heavy, hot breaths, then lapped it, causing him to hump upward. I ran my tongue along the pulsating vein until my nose was nuzzling his hairless nutsac.

"Oh suck it, please," he pleaded, as I kissed and lapped the crinkled skin.

I sucked on his tender balls, drawing first one, then the other into my warm, moist mouth and drenching them in my saliva. His cock twitched and jerked in front of my face, his need now more urgent than before.

When I finally clamped my lips around his swollen pole, he entangled his fingers in my dark hair. He pushed his incredible cock into my throat until my nose was buried in his curly blond bush, nearly gagging me before he allowed me to retreat. I gasped for air, as the thick invader plunged into my gullet once again.

I couldn't pull away, as he repeatedly rammed into me. The sensation of his smooth, hard flesh sliding over my tongue and violating my throat caused my balls to churn. I knew I couldn't hold off much longer, but I didn't want to cum in my shorts. I wanted my wand buried in his sexy body when I shot off.

His cock began to wiggle and squirm as the first blast of hot, creamy cum exploded against the latex covering. The sheath swelled with his huge load, then his fingers released their hold on my hair. He relaxed back onto the table, while my cock throbbed in my shorts.

He had scarcely finished coming, when his arms circled my waist and he pulled me down on top of him. I ground my horny cock against his, my painful erection still held captive in my briefs. He mashed his lips to mine, his tongue forcing its way inside my mouth and thrashing around my own.

Before I could even think about what was happening, we were wrestling playfully on the table. He was powerful, with his bulging biceps and muscular thighs, and it took little effort for him to reverse our positions so that I was lying face down beneath him. I was soon pinned on the table with him straddling me, his thick monster pressed against my ass. I didn't try to resist, only waited to see what he intended, while my heart pounded in my chest.

He moved quietly, adeptly cloaking his still-solid prick. My shorts were yanked from my body, exposing my bubble-butt and leaving me vulnerable to whatever torture he wished to inflict upon me. His fingers unexpectedly slithered between my fleshy asscheeks, dragging them apart. My virgin hole twitched in anticipation as it was forced open for his inspection. I moaned as his fingertips pressed against my tight ass-ring, stretching the resisting muscle until it allowed them to invade my body. He teased my prostate, nearly causing my boiling load to explode, then retreated.

I had never been fucked before and I was more than a little nervous, but I knew I wanted Luke to pluck my cherry. I wanted that hot cock plundering my unexplored cavern.

Then the menacing cockhead was at the entrance. I gasped when the thick monster shoved its way into my body, forcing my tight chute to accommodate its girth. The intense pleasure-pain ripped through me, as he filled my aching emptiness.

But still my horny cock was being neglected. I humped desperately against the table, urgently needing to get my rocks off, but inadvertently allowing his lengthy weapon to plunge even deeper into my belly. A jolt of excitement filled me when his balls slapped my fleshy mounds, his hot stick buried to the hilt in my tender love tunnel.

He used slow, deliberate strokes, letting his cock slide out and then re-invade my body. I was hotter than I had ever been, desperate to shoot off as my fantasy hunk jabbed my violated manpussy. I rammed my cock into the table beneath us, while he tormented my horny hole.

"Fuck me," I moaned. "Take me hard and fast," I pleaded, the desperation apparent in my voice.

But he continued his methodical torture, repeatedly bringing me to the brink of orgasm. I was becoming angry and frustrated that he was intentionally denying me release, but there was nothing I could do. Then his hand slithered around my waist and his fist clutched my cock. I knew he had never held another man's cock in his hand, and the thought that he was groping my wand thrilled me. He yanked me off, tugging roughly at my smooth, hard meat, in the limited space beneath us, while his menacing weapon plowed into me.

Each time he thrust forward, slamming into my gut, I humped even harder into his hand. Seconds later, his snake began to jerk and twitch within me. Just as his load was launched into the protective sheath, I exploded against my belly.

I was disappointed that my spunk had not been deposited within his sexy body, but I took comfort in the fact that he was still holding my throbbing boner in hand as he collapsed on top of me. He lay there for a while, nuzzling my neck, his cock still buried inside me.

I looked back at him and he brushed his lips softly across mine. He smiled his disarming smile and raised his body off mine, letting his cock slide from my newly-explored manpussy. I felt suddenly empty and disappointed, but at least I had fully experienced the wonderful world of hot mansex.

When he got up, I rolled over and looked at him. He was gazing in my direction as though he couldn't believe what had happened. My heart went out to him, as I recalled my first man-to-man encounter and the confusion it caused.

"Are you okay?" I asked, concerned about my friend.

"Yeah, I'm fine. I hope you don't think I'm a prick for jerking you off like that, though. I just didn't think I was ready to suck you off."

"It's okay. I wouldn't want you to do anything you're not

comfortable with," I answered honestly.

He picked up a towel and headed toward the shower. "Are you coming?" he asked, looking back at me.

"Yeah, in a minute."

"You don't want to wait too long," he encouraged, grinning mischievously. "You never know what you might miss."

AT THE OLE SWIMMIN' HOLE

David MacMillan

I was standing on the soft, sandy shoulder of an unpaved road from nowhere to nowhere, one that meandered forever through the tobacco and cotton farms of south Georgia. I was also hoping somebody would stop and give me a lift—though that was about as likely as a Catholic like John Kennedy getting himself elected President of the United States of America. I had just finished a tour of duty in Beirut where Ike had sent me, and was making my way home to Ma and the farm.

It was late June, and south Georgia was hot. Hotter than I ever remembered it being that time of year. I trudged through more sand spurs and told myself for the hundredth time I should have written Ma and told her to meet me at the bus station in Soul. Walking fifteen miles through the heat of a Georgia summer was what I got for wanting to surprise my best girl. I brushed gnats out of my face and remembered the creek where I had a swimmin' hole when I was a kid. It was at the edge of our property and couldn't be more than five more miles. I smiled through the swarm of gnats.

A '55 Chevrolet came down the flat dirt road and began to slow down as its driver spotted me. It pulled along beside me and stopped; its driver was smiling as he reached over and opened the door for me. "Sort of warm to be walking," he offered good-naturedly.

I gave the man a quick once over. Young and tall—almost as tall as my own six feet—with sandy hair and a boyish face. He certainly wasn't anybody I knew. He was even wearing a tie and slacks, and couldn't be more than four or five years older than my own twenty years.

There was something—that indefinable something—that reminded me immediately of some of the Yankee drivers I'd met when I was stationed up near Boston at the beginning of my service. I grinned. If he was queer like them, my dick was ready for him. It'd been more than a week since it got any exercise, and it was sure hurting when I let myself think about it. Yeah! My grin broadened until it went from ear to ear. I was definitely interested if he was!

"Yeah," I answered as I got in the car. "But, then, there's a swimming hole just at the edge of our property not too far from here." I glanced over at him as he started the car. "I sort of thought I might cool off down there before I got home."

I saw he looked at me out of the corner of his eye. And he was taking in the front of my jeans. Just as I'd suspected! I grinned again, as warmly as I could. "You've got to be hot too, decked out in a tie and all," I offered innocently. "Maybe you ought to take a minute or two out and get cooled down yourself?" There was a thin film of perspiration beginning to form on his forehead and upper lip. "By the way, Mister, my name's Buddy."

"Maybe I ... uh ... could do that at that." The sandy-haired man grinned uncertainly. The car was moving down the flat road again, picking up speed. "Where's this swimming hole of yours anyway?"

"Not far ... maybe five to ten minutes from here. Where y'all from?" He had a Southern accent all right, but it wasn't rural south Georgia like everybody from around here. I already had the man pegged for a traveling salesman going from farm to farm ... maybe, an insurance salesman even. I didn't care what he did just so long as he did a good job on my dick. Two years in the service, with most of my time spent outside of Boston, had taught this Georgia cracker how to have a good time cheap. Besides, this one wasn't bad looking at all. Fact was, he was sort of cute.

He pulled the car off the road where I told him just past the wooden, single-lane bridge. "That's the creek down there," I told him pointing.

"Where're we going to swim, Buddy?"

I looked back at the water and then him. "What do y'all mean?"

"That's pretty open space down there and I don't see either one of us having a swimsuit."

"You ashamed of what you got?" I chuckled and he reddened.

"No. But then, I don't see any cause for getting arrested for indecent exposure either."

I laughed, liking the man's sense of humor. Maybe something could develop here. "See that clump of trees and brush down there?" I asked pointing to a wooded spot about five hundred yards down the embankment and away from the road. He nodded dubiously. "Well, we'll be as private there as y'all can want."

We climbed out of the car and made our way down through the underbrush that fronted the creek. I found a fallen tree and sat down, looking back up at the sandy-haired man. "See? You're hidden and there ain't a soul around." I pulled off my shoes and socks, rubbing my feet to get the circulation going. Then, I unbuttoned my shirt and pulled it out of my jeans.

He stood there staring down at me and I looked back at him as I pulled off my shirt. "D ... do you know what I'd like, Buddy?" he stammered. He was looking everywhere but at me. He was scared of what he wanted and equally scared not to try to get it.

"I've got me a good idea," I laughed and unzipped my pants. "I sure hope you're good, mister, cause I'm close to hurting." I stood up slowly and glanced down at the front of my pants. "You want to take them off ... or me to do it?"

The sandy-haired man sighed and mopped perspiration from his forehead. "Thank God!" he groaned. "This could've been a very uncomfortable moment."

I grinned back at him. "But it isn't. I've been around awhile and know pretty basically what's up. So, which is it going to be, mister?"

"I'm pretty new at this kind of thing," he said, his voice dreamy now. "Fact is, you're the first guy I've ever picked up in my life."

"But not the first one you've had, I hope." I eyed him suspiciously.

"Oh, no .. I had a lover back at school—at Emory. And I've ... uh ... been around the block a couple of times, I guess you could say." He smiled then. "Let me undress you ... I haven't ever done that, and I think I might like it."

I grinned. "Be my guest, Mister!" He stepped in front of me and touched my chest hesitantly, his thumb and index finger encircling my closest nipple. His lips found the other one. It felt wonderful; I hadn't had good man-sex in more than a month. My dick struggled to hardness in the confines of the denim of my jeans.

His hands slipped inside the waistband of the pants, finding my asscheeks and squeezing them as his tongue explored downward and my jeans slid down below my hips. He pushed my pants down to my knees, massaging my legs as his fingers came back up my thighs. "Feels real good!" I moaned as both of his hands and his tongue found my dick at the same time.

His hand encircled it, pulling back the foreskin so my big shiny, purple knob was bared, his other hand found my cheeks and squeezed. His tongue washed my cockhead before he let it slide into his hot, hungry mouth. I was almost ready to explode right there, the wad churning in my balls with all his stimulation; it'd been so long. "Jesus!" I groaned and humped further into his mouth, my hands grasping his head and pulling him farther onto me. His hand left my ass and came around my hip to take my balls in their grip, pulling gently on them.

"Hurry!" I demanded, my voice husky. "I'm so damned close!" I grabbed his hair in my hands, pulling him onto me.

His head was bobbing up and down on my shaft, his hand around it guiding it into his mouth. I could feel the explosion coming, rushing up out of my balls, unstoppable in its need. "I'm gonna come!" I cried, fucking his face hard. His hands went to my hips, pulling me hard against him as I erupted.

Weakly, I began to push him away, the sensations in my dick were so intense; but he kept pulling me back, draining me and swallowing it all. Finally, he did release me and I fell back against the fallen tree.

"I'm sorry," I mumbled a moment later.

"For what, Buddy?"

"For coming so fast." I grinned sheepishly at him. "Tell you what ... why don't we take a swim and cool off. After that, if you want, I can show you a real good time."

The sandy-haired man grinned back at me. "Only if that means you'll be cornholin' me," he answered. "I haven't had a good fuck since I left Atlanta two months ago."

I laughed. "I got no problem with that one except-"

"What's that?"

"I don't fuck nobody unless I know their name."

"I don't give my name in situations like this unless it looks like more than just a quick romp in the hay."

I scratched my head. I knew what he was saying, I thought. He wanted a commitment to see him again. The question was did I want anybody around the county to know I even thought of doing queer sex? I knew the answer to that one - if anybody even guessed, it would be the kiss of death for me. I just wouldn't be able to live here.

Yet, I'd been gone for two years. It'd take me a while to get to know girls again enough to get it on with any of them. I was pretty sure this man was only a traveling salesman; I'd see him once a month or so. He sure wouldn't be going around telling anybody about us. Besides, for some reason I couldn't understand, something about this sandy-haired man attracted me. There was a gentleness and acceptance about him that appealed to me far beyond just his good looks.

"Well?" I smiled up at him.

"Are you saying...?" I nodded, still smiling at him. "I didn't think anybody in south Georgia would be willing to."

"Don't go explaining things to death," I told him as I pulled my jeans over my ankles and stood up butt naked. "Either we see each other whenever ... or we don't."

"My name's Drew ... Drew Forrester ... Buddy." I went to him, grinning and took him in my arms, hugging him to me.

"Drew, my name's Buddy Varnadore and it's sure good to meet you." I pulled away and looked at him critically. "Of course, you've got to get naked to go skinny dipping." I started walking toward the water, a smile on my lips and a swing to my ass. What I suddenly could see developing was a sure sight better than the life of a subsistence farmer that had been waiting for me if Drew Forrester hadn't stopped and picked me up.

I swam across the creek and had started back when the blur of Drew running into the water startled me. I laughed, feeling good with the cool water having washed away the sweat and grime of my ten-mile walk and the basest of my sexual urges satisfied. As I approached him now, I was downright frisky—even giddy—with the feeling of freedom Drew had somehow given me.

"For a guy who's just asked me to cornhole him, you sure are shy about being naked!" I told him.

"I...." He blushed. "Buddy, I guess I ought to apologize."

"What for?" Grinning, I reached toward him, my hand knifing the water as it grabbed for his dick. My eyes grew large as it found its target. I gasped in surprise. "My God, you're a big one, aren't you, Drew?"

He turned redder still as he hardened. "You don't have to do anything, Buddy ... I'm willing to let it go on like it is."

"What's that supposed to mean?" I asked, that big long tube coming closer and closer to occupying the center of my attention. I gave it a tentative tug.

"I mean I'll do all the sucking and take all the fucking. I'm not asking you to do anything back."

I looked hard at his dick then as it rode just below the surface of the water. It was big, bigger than mine even, but there was something strange about it, too. Different, as I really looked at another man's dick for the first time in my life. Hell! The son of a bitch was fucking pretty! That was an incongruity I couldn't fathom.

My hand continued holding onto his dick, stroking it slowly now under the water. I found myself thinking thoughts I'd never thought before. I was wondering if I could even get it into my mouth and what it'd be like to do that.

I forced myself to turn away from the invitation it seemed to be presenting me but found my eyes following his creamy white torso up toward his nipples, which also seemed to beckon to me. Escaping their enticement, my eyes found his and were suddenly falling into those deep blue orbs. Unconsciously, my hand continued to pull on that tube of meat just beneath the water.

His face seemed to be swimming toward mine and I was wanting it to. I wanted it closer and willed it to be so. In another moment, our lips brushed each other's and I almost gasped. His tongue invaded my mouth and my free hand went behind him and pulled him against me. We kissed and my knees were as weak as all those love stories say they become as he held me against him.

"You've got to be careful, Buddy," he mumbled, breaking for air. "I could easily fall in love with you."

"I think it's too late," I gasped, barely able to believe my own words. "I think I already do love you." Instinct led me to lower my head as I touched each of his nipples with my lips. Instinct turned my mind onto its autopilot channel and left it there. I knew what I was doing ... yet, I didn't. I was doing what I wanted to do; but I had no sense of doing it.

"Buddy?" Drew queried, but I wasn't listening. My eyes were on the head of that tube sticking now out of the brown creek water and inviting me to taste it. He backed away a couple of steps, bringing more of his dick out of the water and my mouth found it, suddenly hungry for the first time in its life.

I gagged as his skinned knob found its way beyond my lips and he told me: "Take it easy, Buddy - it's not going anywhere. Just lick and nibble at it in the beginning-" I started back down the thick pole of rigid flesh and started treating it the way he'd treated mine - like those men in Boston had done me. Soon, he was fucking my face and I was taking it. And enjoying it.

He was coming, giving me the first taste of a man I'd ever known. I was strangely proud of myself for being able to do it. And I knew with everything in me that I was falling for this tall, gentle sandy haired man with the beautiful blue eyes and slim body.

Later, as we were dressing, he looked over at me wistfully. "I wanted you to fuck me."

"Don't we have all the time in the world together, Drew?" I asked, glancing back at him and adoring the way the sun behind him made his hair seem like a golden halo. "You aren't through with me already, are you?"

"Never!" He smiled. "It would be nice to do it on a bed, to make love to each other leisurely. Why don't you come over Sunday afternoon? I'll feed you dinner and you can stay the night?" He quickly jotted down an address in town; I put the scrap of paper in my pocket and looked back into his face. "I'll be there ... you know I will!"

All day Saturday, Ma kept after me to go to church with her on Sunday. I just wasn't interested—not in all that hell and brimstone junk I'd been brought up with. Besides, I was still trying to recover from my shock at what I'd done down at the creek. I was one twenty-year-old man who was absolutely stunned to find out he was queer!

I had to have time to work it out—me being queer and being in love with a man at the same time. It wasn't like guilt or feeling the wrath of God; but it was unsettling. And Ma's nagging wasn't helping my frame of mind any. Finally, I agreed to go just to shut her up.

Drew had given me his address in town and, as we drove to church, I figured I'd see exactly where he lived so I could find it when I came back to see him that evening. We got closer and closer to the church, but I hadn't seen the side road he'd told me about. Then, we were at the church and I saw the street - right by the church! We were actually turning onto it to find a parking place. We found one and my stomach gave a lurch at the thought of being that close to the house of God when I came back to be with Drew.

Ma dragged me inside and we sat down in front where she could be seen by all her friends. Her baby boy was home and at church with her. I was her prize exhibit. Me— the queer.

I didn't look up. I sat there contritely holding my hands and wishing I was back at the creek, skinny-dippin' with Drew. Then, the congregation around me was standing to sing the entrance anthem and I had to let that dream go. I glanced up at the pulpit and almost fainted.

There was Drew standing up there, smiling ever so sweetly out at his flock of sheep. I grabbed the pew in front of me to support myself because my legs had suddenly become rubber.

Drew Forrester was the Methodist minister in town! My Drew! The man who'd sucked my dick! Whose dick I'd sucked! Him. The preacher up there. That man of God.

And he was just another queer like me. My mind went on, closing out the sermon and everything else around me. I went through my loss of faith in God and this man I'd been so sure I loved as well as the questions of whether I did love him in that hour of religious pageantry.

By the time we were filing past him, I'd come to the decision a man could be homosexual and have a calling to any job. And I knew I really did love the Reverend Drew Forrester—no matter what he was to other people. I smiled at him as Ma and I came abreast of him; and he colored quite a bit when he saw me.

Ma introduced us, and I said: "Hello, Reverend," just like Ma's good little boy.

There was a twinkle in my eye though and he saw it. "I don't know why, but I feel I know just about everything about you," I told him as he released my hand. He turned even redder then.

I was chuckling when we got to the car and Ma wondered if I was all right. "You're actin' goofy, boy."

I told her I was okay; it was just the new minister.

It was almost supper time when I drove back into town, heading directly to the rectory and parking in the driveway. Drew greeted me at the door. "I was beginning to think you weren't coming, Buddy," he said opening the screen door for me. He shut the door behind me, locking it.

"Why shouldn't I, preacher?" I asked innocently.

"Because ... Buddy, please don't."

"Don't what?" I asked and couldn't help but grin. "Don't make fun of my calling ... or what I feel for you. I love you now like I did Friday. I want you now like I did then ... only, I am what I am." He looked down at his hands. "I hope you still feel the same way you did then."

"Look, I'm pretty confused right now," I confessed, getting as serious as he was. "I think I was okay until we pulled God into the picture."

"Oh God loves us all, Buddy. He asks that we love each other and I haven't found where He puts any sort of limits on that. But, let's leave Him out of this. How about you? Do you feel the same way as you did Friday?"

"I still feel the same way," I answered slowly. "And that's pretty messed up ... my brain is, anyway."

"That makes me feel a whole lot better, Buddy." He sighed and smiled then. "The whole human race stays pretty messed up; so I suspect you're in pretty good shape if you know you're in love and keep yourself on an even keel. I'm not the best cook in the world, but I think you'll maybe agree I can't ruin franks and beans."

I laughed then, beginning to feel good about me and us again. "You're too much!"

I stared at him hard, making the moment grow between us. "Come here and greet me proper," I told him finally. "Then, let's find a bed and take up where we left off back at the creek."

"All of that before supper?" he asked, stepping into my arms.

"Greet me right and we'll hold everything else off, til after we eat."

I had to kiss him to wipe that silly grin off his handsome face.

TWICE THE HEAT

R.J. Masters

*"...My fingers crept around the fiery flesh and began to
knead it—the feel of the smooth hardness sliding back
and forth in my fist was working us both into a heated frenzy...."*

It was so damn hot. The sun was pounding down and the
sweat was pouring off me. I lay sprawled on the grass under
the huge maple tree, the gentle summer breeze blowing my
sandy hair into my face, while I watched two of the most
incredible men I had ever seen playing a heated game of
one-on-one. Their hard, athletic bodies, covered only by
skimpy gym shorts, were drenched in perspiration. They
jumped and played, their thick black chest hairs matted against
their damp skin.

I had never seen identical twins up close and it was an
amazing sight to watch them locked in such a fierce
competition. One of the brothers went in for a lay-up as the
other tried desperately to intercept him, causing their hard
bodies to collide in midair. Both struggled to regain their
balance, but one was not successful and fell backward onto the
ground, landing with a loud thud.

He collapsed back on the grass and rested, catching his
breath while his brother stood over him. "Ready to admit
defeat?" he taunted. But the other was not ready to give up.
When his brother extended his hand, he hauled him roughly
to the ground. The two of them rolled around, each vying for
the competitive advantage—the opportunity to pin the other
and force his submission.

Their biceps bulged, and the muscles of their tree-trunk
thighs protruded as they struggled to defeat one another. I
couldn't take my eyes off them, these two examples of manly
perfection, wrestling closer and closer to where I sat. I was
certain they were performing for my benefit, trying to elicit
some reaction from my reclining form. My breathing grew
heavy as their animal-like display of aggression fueled my
desire, drawing me into their primitive ritual. I wanted them,
needed their untamed energy and excitement, and knew I

could not leave the park that afternoon without having them.

The heat of the afternoon sun was no match for the warmth that was overtaking me, as a familiar throbbing swept through my groin and my cock began to swell. My hot cockmeat began to stiffen and rise in the confines of my tight jeans. It struggled to free itself of the restricting fabric, becoming harder and hornier with each passing second. The sound of them panting and grunting, as one gained the advantage over the other was nearly more than I could bear without exploding a hot wad into my jeans.

I reached down and squeezed my aching boner, then unzipped my fly and hauled my prick out into the daylight. My fingers circled around the smooth shaft and began to stroke slowly, teasing and massaging until it lengthened in my fist. The angry red cockhead glistened with my pre-cum juice. I smeared the sticky goo down my thick stalk, so that my hand slid easily over the hard, hot meat.

"I win!" he howled, proclaiming victory. "Say Uncle!" he demanded.

He straddled his brother's chest, his knuckles turning white where he held the other's wrists to the grass, then looked in my direction. Our eyes met for an instant, those sparkling blue eyes capturing my attention and hypnotizing me. Then his gaze was drawn to my fully-erect, drooling seven-inch member, as my hand slid from the wet, sticky head to the curly bush at its thick base.

My heart raced, wondering how they would react to seeing me openly jacking off over them, but I managed to smile at him. I relaxed as he smiled back, and continued to work the pre-cum juices down my shaft so that my fingers glided over the slick skin.

"That was quite a show, guys," I called.

"Yours too. But there are other things we're much better at," bragged the victor. "Care for a demonstration? A little two-on-one action?"

"Get off me," his brother demanded.

"I can't. You didn't say 'Uncle'."

I smiled at their boyish taunts.

"All right, all right. Uncle. You satisfied?" he asked, sounding more than a little annoyed.

"Yeah, I guess I am," he said, rising and walking toward me.

"I'm Steve Richards, and that's my brother, Scott."

"I'm Todd."

"So, would you be interested in a little two-on-one?" Scott inquired seriously, breaking into the conversation.

For a moment I was speechless. This was like a fantasy come true. My eyes were instinctively drawn to the large bulge in the front of Steve's gym shorts. My cock twitched as he stared down at the swollen knob poking from my clenched fist. The boiling load in my bloated ballsac begged for release. I continued to massage my meat, but could not take my eyes off his impressive, pulsating prick.

I wondered if his brother was equally aroused by their tussle, so I stole a glance at Scott, who was still lying on his back on the grass. Appearing to read my thoughts, he smiled at me, then grasped his hard cock in his strong hand "This what you're looking for?" he teased.

The heat of embarrassment flooded into my cheeks and I didn't know how to respond.

"Maybe you'd like to check it out up close," Steve added.

"Maybe I would," I replied, sitting up and leaning my back against the tree. "Why don't you both come on over and keep me company on the blanket," I stammered, slightly distracted by their overpowering presence.

"Sounds great," Scott answered, quickly getting to his feet.

Steve stripped off his shorts and underwear. I could feel my heart thumping in my chest and gobs of pre-cum oozed from my horny meat when his cock bounced free. It slapped against his belly, the glistening tip coming to rest in the forest of thick, black hairs on his abdomen. He was a magnificent sight standing there, his tanned body reminiscent of a bronzed Adonis: broad shoulders, narrow hips and powerful thighs.

Not to be outdone by his brother, Scott stood up beside Steve. He quickly stripped off his clothing, so that the two of them were standing side by side, their sameness mesmerizing me. Their proud nine-inchers stood at full attention. My mouth watered and I couldn't wait to get at those juicy pieces of steak. There was no question that they were equally well-hung, with huge baskets that dangled between those mammoth thighs. I licked my lips in anticipation, anxious to find out how well they used their incredible equipment.

I pawed in my backpack until I recovered an unopened box

of condoms, then placed it on the ground in front of me. "Think these will hold us over for the afternoon?" I asked, teasing my handsome duo.

They each smiled and took a foil-wrapped shield into their hand. I watched as they tore into the packages and outfitted their lengthy shafts, then likewise cloaked my own wet, sticky boner while they took their places on the blanket.

While Scott watched, Steve's fingers began to caress my smooth chest. Tiny fires were ignited on my bare flesh and my nipples tingled with anticipation, when his fingers moved closer to the already-erect nubs. I gasped for air when he pinched the tender pink buds between his thumbs and forefingers and rolled them gently. I could not contain the excitement I felt when his touch became rougher, twisting and tugging the reddened pebbles until I thought they would be torn from my body.

I looked into those incredible eyes and recognized the intense desire that was filling him, the same need that had drawn me to them. He flashed me a boyish grin, then his strong hands dropped lower, grazing the latex-covered cockhead. Erotic shock waves shot through me, sending shivers down my spine as I felt my jeans and white briefs being pulled from my body, leaving me naked and vulnerable. The cool breeze teased my bare skin and my head was spinning as the passion built up inside me. I yearned to feel those two stiff tools jamming into my cock-starved body, filling the emptiness and satisfying my desperate longing.

Scott began to kiss my neck and shoulder, his hot breath arousing me further, while his hands explored my naked body. He cupped my crinkled nutsac in his palm gently rolling my delicate balls between his thumb and fingers as his rigid cock brushed against my thigh. My fingers crept around the fiery flesh and began to knead it—the feel of the smooth hardness sliding back and forth in my fist, working us both into a heated frenzy. I moaned and thrust upward as Steve's fingertips caressed my engorged shaft, dancing along the bulging vein, then lightly circling the supersensitive cockhead.

My body was jolted as though an electric current had shot through me, sending it into spasms when Steve's lips touched the quivering head, then let it slide into his mouth. His tongue swirled over and around the nerve-filled glans, making me wriggle in ecstasy. He sucked gently, cautiously taking my length into his throat, teasing my horny cock, pushing his tongue against the cloaked pee-slit, until I cried out. I was certain I would shoot off any second, and tried desperately to prolong the thrill.

I was frustrated when his lips left my aching cock, but was rewarded when he began to lap and kiss the loose skin of my balls. When my nuts were drenched in his saliva, he carefully drew one ball, then the other into his hot, wet mouth. He sucked them gently, rolling his tongue over and around the tender orbs until I could contain my desire no longer.

"Oh, suck it, please," I pleaded.

He returned his attention to my throbbing cock, at the same time letting his index finger push against my virgin hole. I moaned as his finger slipped into the heat of my body, awakening feelings I had never experienced before. The intruder rubbed my inner walls, massaging the previously untouched nerve-endings until I was squirming with delight.

Scott's lips found mine and his tongue invaded my moist, warm mouth, exploring every inch of my being. I wrapped my arms around his neck and held him close, mashing our bodies together while enjoying the sensation of their two hot, hungry mouths bringing me closer and closer to release. My pleasure was building minute by minute, their slow, methodical touches teasing my tormented flesh. I moaned and thrashed, desperate for the moment when my balls would be relieved of their oversized load.

I knew I couldn't hold off much longer when Scott crawled up next to my head and eased his pulsating monster into my mouth. I took him all, letting him slide deep into my throat as Steve's lips released my cock from the warm wetness of his mouth and began to flick his tongue against my tight virgin manhole. He lapped and nibbled at the reluctant ass-muscle before his tongue burrowed into my body. I sucked harder, nearly swallowing Scott's squirming snake, as Steve continued to tantalize the sensitive nerve-endings of my unexplored cavern.

Scott rammed his swollen cock head against my tonsils, coming closer and closer to an explosive climax. I was so focused on his twitching monster that I was almost unaware of what Steve was doing. He spread my legs wide and moved between them, his latex-covered cock demanding entrance to my stretched manhole. The unyielding ass-muscle resisted his advance momentarily, then gave way as the massive intruder forced his way into the heat of my body. He was motionless for only a moment, then the two of them began to move in unison. Scott's cock slammed into my gullet, his crinkled ballsac slapping against my chin, while Steve's huge slab of meat rammed deeper and deeper into my gut. The monstrous cock repeatedly banged into my tiny prostate until I could hold off no longer. I moaned and my body convulsed, as I was overtaken by the most powerful orgasm I had ever experienced. My cock twitched and jerked as it spilled my hot creamy load into the protective covering. My lips locked around Scott's cock and my ass-muscles contracted involuntarily around Steve's massive invader. Within seconds of each other, both Steve and Scott erupted, their condoms swelling inside my body.

Though they were spent, they continued to move their softening tools within me, feeding my voracious appetite, until I was again thrashing and moaning. Again and again they teased me to the point of inexplicable pleasure. Finally I could stand the teasing no more. My cock jerked and twitched obscenely as a second smaller explosion overtook me. I moaned and purred as though my passion had never before been freed, as more of my white, sticky cream spewed into the latex sheath.

When I was completely exhausted, we lay there on the grass for a while enjoying the sensation of the light afternoon breeze on our naked bodies. We were fortunate that the park was so deserted on that Thursday afternoon, but agreed that the next time we met, it would be in a more secluded location where we could take our time and truly enjoy each other's body. I watched my handsome studs pull on their underwear and shorts, while I pulled my jean over my firm, round asscheeks. They headed off toward home in one direction, while I walked off in the other.

I clenched their address and telephone number in my fist, confident it would not be long before we got together for another afternoon of hot, horny man-to-man-to-man action.

THE PLAYGROUND

Blaise Bulot

It was the hottest summer I could remember. It was too hot yesterday to go jogging, but I did anyway. Force of habit. It was so hot I skipped the shirt and the jockstrap. I just wore my running shorts. I was hot. I was sweating, but I thought I was jogging along just fine. Until I looked down at myself. My shorts were soaked with sweat, clinging to my body, and the wet fabric was almost transparent. Everything showed—and I mean, I might just as well have been streaking naked in public. And my cock. I could see it, flopping back and forth with every stride. And so could everybody else. So I started for home, taking the route with the least people along the way.

But the revealing shorts were not my only problem. Bad hair day! All of a sudden, with no warning, I had to take a crap. Real bad. Did you ever have to take a crap in the city? It's not that easy. I looked for bushes—none. No fences, no walls I could get behind. No abandoned buildings—they've been all torn down. No dead-ends or alleys even. So I jogged on. Well, not really jog. That was the last thing I wanted to do. I tried to keep my asshole as tight as I could. But for how long? With every jog, with every jarring step, I thought my bowels would let loose. Home, the bathroom, seemed such a long, long way away.

The playground looked endless. It looked miles to get by. There was a bunch of black boys shooting hoops. Like me, shirtless with just their shorts on.

And hey! Praise the lord! There was a toilet. I'd forgotten about it. You don't notice them 'til you need them! A public toilet. Well, sort of.

I made it to the door. Almost. A little something ran down my leg. I entered the toilet. What a mess! Filth, filth, filth. Graffiti all over the walls; litter, and worse, all over the floor. The windows were broken out, the doors, including the doors to the stalls, were gone, the glory holes were cut so big you could crawl through them, one of the urinals was running over, and the floor was covered with water. I made it to the first stall. The last user hadn't flushed. I raised my foot to push the flush lever. Wow, I almost lost it. At least it flushed.

I didn't want to drop my shorts on the wet floor so I carefully stepped out of them. Put my arse on that filthy toilet seat! I'd get twenty kinds of diseases. So I just kind of squatted over the seat, not touching it. And shit, shit, shit, shit. Boy, did it feel good. I'd made it. I was emptied. The world was a great place again. Maybe I could rinse my shorts out at one of the sinks, but first.... Oh, oh, wait a minute, there was no toilet paper- of course. And those kids, their voices were getting closer, they're coming here! The thunk, thunk, thunk of the dribbled ball. Closer, closer. I remembered seeing a newspaper amongst the litter on the other side of the room. I rushed over to pick it up and wipe myself. It wasn't the *Times Picayune*; it was the *Wall Street Journal*! But I couldn't be choosey. Newspaper in hand, I started back to the stall. Too late. The gang came tumbling through the door, making a bee-line for the urinals. One pulled his cock out through the leg hole of his shorts to pee. The others dropped their shorts down around their knees.

I tried to cover myself with the newspaper. At first they didn't seem to notice me. But then the tallest, who seemed to be their leader, flashed a broad grin at me and came in my direction hand extended. So I extended my hand to shake his offered hand. Oops! I forgot about the newspaper. It fell to the floor.

"Hey man, " he exclaimed, grinning even broader, "Y'all butt nekked as y'all can be!"

"I was trying to take a crap," I tried to explain.

"Well, lookie here," he yelled at the others, "We all got ourselfs a nekked white boy."

"There's no toilet paper," I said limply.

They dropped their shorts and gathered around me, seven or eight nude, sweaty, black guys. The tall one, still grasping my hand, with his other grabbed my cock. What could I do? How much control do you have over your cock? In his hand mine grew and got stiff as a log.

"Well," remarked the thin one, tightening his grip on my hand and my cock, "Y'all sure ain't got a little pink worm like most white boys."

Letting go of my hand, but not my cock, he pushed my face down against his chest.

"Suck them titties," he whispered. I did. The nipple tasted salty and swelled between my lips. He pushed my head down farther.

"Lap that belly."

I did. It was tight and smooth—and salty. Farther down he guided my head. My face was buried in his pubic hair. Quite a bush. It was thick and kinky. Like a Brillo pad. I half expected soap suds to ooze out of it. He gave my head a final push.

"Suck that black dick! Suck that *real* cock, white boy."

Well, I tried. It was a gagger, I must say. Huge! I didn't think I could stuff it all into my mouth. But I didn't give up and, eventually, I did.

The other boys were giggling, making smart-ass comments, and enjoying the show immensely.

Then, as the tall one bent me down, another one grabbed my buns and spread my pearly gates.

"Lawdy," he exclaimed "Y'all sure do have a dirty white boy ass." The others roared with laughter.

"Y'all wants me ta clean y'all up real good?"

I couldn't answer—my mouth was full.

Without waiting for a reply he picked up the newspaper where I had dropped it and started rubbing it, very vigorously, in my opened crack. Rub, rub, rub. Soon I must have had the cleanest arsehole in the Big Easy.

"Does he have to do that good a job?" I asked myself. But the tall one was now hanging on to my shoulders with both hands so I couldn't budge.

The boy behind me started spitting on his fingers and wetting my crack with them. Rub, rub, rub. Then his fingers, pushing in. I could feel my arsehole swelling and pushing up against his fingers, eager-like. He spread my cheeks wider and spat right into my bunghole. His aim was very good. Then he thrust a finger right up my butt. I jerked and both of them laughed. And the others joined in.

He pushed his finger in deeper and deeper, then a second finger, then he wiggled them around. He pulled his fingers out and I felt something wet and warm in my crotch. At first I thought he was trying to fuck me. But it wasn't his prick; it was his tongue. He lapped my crack and then my rosebud. Slurp, slurp. Then he pushed his tongue up my hole.

"Finger-lickin' good," someone shouted.

"My turn," someone else. More laughter.

The tall one withdrew his prick from my mouth and stretched his nude body out before me on the dirty floor. He wanted me to straddle him on my hands and knees. Which I did. His cock again in my mouth; mine, and my balls as well, in his. The other youth repositioned himself behind me and stuck something else into me. Not a finger, not a tongue. Something long, hot, and hard—like a cock.

"Oh my goodness," I said to myself, "I'm getting fucked by a big black dude."

So there I was, stark naked, all my holes full and busy, except my ears and nostrils. A cock up my butt, a cock down my throat, my cock in a mouth. God, it was heavenly.

When I think about it now I get so hot and horny I have to pull on my meat and work my finger up my butthole.

The thrusting into my behind got harder and faster. The guy began to grunt and groan. And so did the tall one. The strokes quickened. I wasn't going to swallow it, but I forgot. I was helpless. I couldn't stop or even slow down. Then, all if a sudden, the three of us carne all at once. Cum up my ass, cum down my throat, and me squirting too!

I was hot. I was spent. I was tired. But I was so happy, I just flopped over and lay on my back on the filthy floor. The other dudes and the two who had been working me over gathered around me in a circle, jerking off. Their naked sweaty black bodies twisting and jerking spasmodically. Then plop! The first big hot blob of cum, like a monstrous snot, splashed right in my face. Plop! The second landed on my chest. My body was covered with cum; my face, my chest, my belly, my pubic hair and cock and balls. Running down my sides off me.

Strange what you think about sometimes. Looking up at those naked black bodies, those stiff juicy cocks, those straining faces, their tongues between their teeth, hearing their grunts, groans, and ejaculations, all I could think was, "Where the hell are my shorts?"

HEATWAVE

Daniel Miller

It was the summer of 1978, and my fellow Chicagoans and I were suffering through one of the worst heat waves ever to hit our fine city. Though my office kept the air conditioning cranked to the maximum, that feeble trickle of cool air wasn't enough to lower my soaring blood pressure. It was distracting enough to look out at the white-hot mist hanging motionless over the distant skyline and think about the sweaty, sleepless night that was sure to follow. But what really had my nerves in a jangle was the virtual mirage that shimmered in the glass of my big picture window. There, balanced on a wooden scaffolding, a hot young stood wielding a squeegee, wearing nothing but a low-slung pair of white denim cut-offs and a glossy film of clean, clear sweat.

He'd been out there ever since lunchtime, making his way from window to window. Now it was nearly five o'clock, and my cock had become a hot poker burning against my leg. When he absently reached for his bare chest and flicked a droplet of sweat off the tight cinnamon bud of his nipple, I suppressed a horny moan. I shifted back and forth in my chair, but couldn't seem to relieve the aching pressure that had built up in my nuts. My cock began to throb in earnest when he spread those long, sinewy legs and leaned forward on the toes of his tan workboots to balance himself. When he reached up with his rag, the top button of his snug cut-offs accidentally popped open. My whole body went tense with lust as my gaze followed the shimmering trail of soft gold hair that bisected that lean, narrow torso.

The more I tried to control myself, the more lost I started to feel. Though I shuffled and reshuffled the papers on my desk, all I could focus on was a mental picture of that light, honey-colored fuzz dusting his lean flesh, and the slow pulse of muscle beneath it. How easy it would be to crack open the window, snake my hand down into those paper-thin shorts, and stroke his wiry bush until his shaft rose hard and hot as a live poker against my steady fingers....

I was shaken from my bliss by the harsh sound of fingers

rapping on glass. My head snapped up to find the window washer crouching down on the scaffold, his earnest blue eyes scanning my office. I could just make out his shouted words through the glass.

"Hey, man," he was saying, tapping harder this time. "Hey, can you hear me?"

Swallowing, I felt my crotch to make sure there was no wet spot on the front of my suit pants. Then, moving slowly, I walked over to the window, unlatched the bottom pane, and twisted my head around to look up at him. Unlike in my vision, I didn't reach through to stroke the gorgeous crotch that loomed only inches in front of me. But I admit I was sorely tempted.

"Sorry to bother you, but one of these pulleys seems to be stuck. I can't get up to the next level, and I don't dare to go back down and get my ass stuck somewhere between the ground and the tenth floor. Mind if I crawl in there and use your phone?"

"Oh...no, that would be fine," I said, backing away as he thrust one booted foot, and then his entire leg, through the window. When he'd squeezed the rest of his wiry body through the impossibly small opening, he stood there looking at me with a grin playing over his plush lips. I couldn't help imagining how good they'd look wrapped around my meaty shank, pulling the cum up through me like an extra-thick milkshake from a straw.

He was looking around my desk, and I belatedly remembered that he hadn't come in here to feed my fantasies, but to use my outside line. Hastily I stepped between him and the handset.

"Before you make that call, maybe you should sit down a minute and have some ice water. You look pretty heat-beat."

"Sure am," he agreed slowly, sinking his perfect ass onto the corner of my desk. My hands trembled as I fetched him a paper cup of water from the cooler in the corner. He quaffed it in one quick toss, tilting his head so far back that I could see his Adam's apple bulge against the velvety skin of his throat. Again he raised his hand to tweak his own nipple, apparently a habit with him. Before I could turn away, my cock lurched up at a forty-five degree angle in my pants.

My face burned hotter than the pavement outside when I

saw him looking down at my brazenly swollen crotch. I was even more mortified when, at last, I saw a tiny damp spot forming beside my fly as my pre-cum slithered out of my inflamed cocktip.

The guy lowered the paper cup to his sculpted thigh and eyed me in surprise. "Hey, man, did I do that to you?" he asked.

His voice was so earnest that it startled me for a moment. "Well, uh....Guess I got a little carried away looking out the window." I stammered. "It's been a long, hot morning."

"Yeah, it sure has been," he agreed, his brows drawing together in a frown. At first, I worried that he might be offended, even angry, at my confession. Instead, he merely looked thoughtful, like he'd stumbled upon a situation he wasn't quite sure how to react to. When he looked up again, his ice-blue eyes were sharp with agitation–and a physical arousal he couldn't conceal. He shifted his ass on the desk, like his balls had started itching, and ran a nervous hand over the telltale mound that had started to rise there.

It was now or never, I knew. Two more minutes and he'd bolt. "Listen, uh...."

"Curtis," he supplied, the word escaping his lungs in a breathy rush.

"...Curtis...ever had a blow-job from another guy?"

"Nope," he said, the muscles in his face going tighter still. "Not from a girl, either. Have...have you?"

He sounded so innocent that I couldn't help laughing. "Sure, lots of times. There's nothing like it, let me tell you."

Again he fell silent, like he was weighing my suggestion very carefully. Though it amused me that he was making such a big deal over something as simple as a quick blow-job, I kept my expression serious and respectful. After I'd glided over to lock my office door, I returned to stand in front of him.

Probably because of my gentle, reassuring attitude, Curtis didn't so much as tug away when I knelt down between his splayed legs and pulled down the shiny tab of his zipper. The flaps of the white cut-offs parted to reveal tight black Jockey shorts stretched taut around a half-hard cock and plush, grapefruit-sized balls.

He moaned a little when I pushed the leghole of his underwear to one side and hooked the elastic band around the steaming base of his cock. His nuts popped free, too, the wrinkly sac turning a deep maroon while I watched, fascinated. The tip of his long, skinny cock emerged berry-red from a thick, rubbery foreskin. My mouth literally watered for a taste of hot cherry.

"I'll take this nice and slow," I whispered, meaning every word I said. Curtis shifted his buns on the desk as I leaned forward and nestled my mouth against his hot slab of stiff meat. He groaned a little as I extended my tongue as far as I could and lapped around the jutting flange of his cockhead. I spent a long time gently pushing his fleshy sheath down from his pointed dome, inhaling the tangy aroma of sweat, pre-cum, and untouched manhood.

The idea that I was the first guy on earth to taste this delicious concoction turned me on all the more. It took a real effort not to lunge down and start sucking the living cum right out of his balls. But I remembered my promise to go slow. It took a real effort on my part, but I managed to keep my lip-action steady and measured. Using my tonguetip, I traced each bumpy vein that crisscrossed his shaft, then raised my head and nibbled softly on his chunky dome.

Curtis was getting into it, I could tell. Though he whimpered and twitched a little, and nervous sweat poured from his crotch and armpits, he was soon humping his hips softly into my face. Slowly but surely, his tool stiffened and unfurled against my churning mouth.

"Oh, it's great, man," Curtis rasped, twisting his fingers through my dark hair. He jerked my head forward in a sudden spasm of lust, spearing my throat with his now-rigid shaft. "Oh, yeah, that feels good! Really good!"

"Told you," I managed to murmur, seconds before his cockhead crashed past my tonsils. Instinctively, my jaws clamped around his shank and hauled it down as far it would go. Warm spurts of spicy pre-cum slithered down my throat, setting my esophagus on fire. Curtis was totally lost in pleasure, fucking my face as hard as he could, grunting every time his full balls crashed into my chin.

Reaching down, I wrenched open my pants and let my own bulging hard-on curl into my open hand. While I sucked Curtis, I squeezed and rolled my shaft in my fingers, paying special attention to the bulging, dome-shaped head that emerged above the loose sheath of foreskin. My mind was blank, my consciousness totally consumed by the fiery electrical storm zigzagging up and down the rigid length of my shaft. My balls, nestled deep in the sweaty nest of my overgrown pubic bush, soon began to expand as a heavy load of cum gathered deep in their cores. Shifting on my knees, I managed to stimulate them by crushing them against the insides of my sweating thighs.

In no time flat, I'd brought Curtis to the point of no return. His cock gave a sudden lurch in my mouth, and his scarlet nuts drew up tight in their wrinkly sac. He choked out a single, drawn-out cry as he blasted my mouth with his virgin seed. Three powerful spurts later, the sweet, milky torrent had filled my guts and bubbled up through my lips. My own cock snaked out another couple of inches into my fist as his burning spunk spouted from the corners of my mouth and coursed down my chin.

I couldn't help crying out as I came hard and fast right along with him. My own husky cries mingled with the throb of my pulse in my ears as my body jerked involuntarily again and again, depositing a white sea of sticky cum onto the plush pewter carpet beside my desk.

Literally drained, I sagged back on my heels in a state of utter exhaustion. Also wiped out, Curtis lay back on my desk with his shorts halfway down his thighs, his sculpted chest rising and falling as he took deep, shuddering, satisfied breaths.

"So how'd you like it?" I managed to ask, reaching down to close up the front of my pants and wondering how I could get the cum off the rug without anyone seeing—or smelling—what had been going on. "Was it as good as you expected?"

Slowly, Curtis sat up on my desk and looked down at me. His cheeks were flushed, and his blue eyes smoldered with lust. Gone was all the awkward self-consciousness he'd displayed at first. To my surprise, he didn't answer me in words. Instead, moving with the grace of a panther, he slid to his feet and crept toward me.

I let out a sharp gasp as Curtis bent down and yanked my trousers back down to my calves. As I lay there bare-assed on the carpet of my office, he shoved one hand down and shucked off his open shorts. He hovered over me completely naked except for his tan work boots and white striped socks, his huge prong rearing up again from his cum-spattered patch of honey hair. The exposed shank curved in the middle, and the thick, spongy head split the tender flaps of his foreskin.

"It was terrific," he said, pivoting around so his plump balls dangled right above my cum-flecked face, and his own mouth drooled down into my tangled bush. "But now I'd say I owe you one."

I didn't protest as he bent down and closed that exquisite mouth around my own throbbing shank. Instead, I lifted my head to haul him deep into the back of my throat.

"Listen," I gasped, after we'd each slurped another load from the other's trembling balls, "it's almost quitting time. Why don't you come home with me for a couple of cold beers?"

Curtis sat up and blushed a little, licking the cream off his face like he'd just remembered what he'd been up to. Then that dazzling, somewhat shy smile crept across his face again.

"Sure, why not? Just let me make that call about my ... ah ... equipment failure, and I'm sure they'll let me knock off for the day."

As he sprang off me and went to the phone, I looked out my sparkling clean window at the sweltering horizon outside. All day, I'd been dreading the long, steamy night that lay ahead, when I had to leave my temperature-controlled office and head back to my stuffy top-floor apartment.

Now, for some reason, the idea of lying around for a few hours with my naked body bathed in sweat didn't seem so intimidating.

CROWNING ACHIEVEMENT

Thomas Wagner

Before I came to college, in many ways I was very sheltered. I'd jacked off over a few guys in the locker room during my senior year of high school, but they never turned me on that much. Then, the summer after I graduated, I discovered our gardener, Rafael, who looked like a real man. I can still remember that first hot afternoon in my parents' potting shed. My spit-coated mouth was hungrily worshiping his fat, coffee-colored cock while the sweat dripped from his dark brown nipples and musky, overgrown pubes. In the middle of the blow job, I reached down and opened my khaki shorts to let my raging boner spring free.

All of a sudden, Rafael stopped fucking my face, though he left his thick prong wedged between my tonsils. When I glanced up at his face to see what was wrong, I saw that his dark eyes were wide, and they seemed to burn with fresh lust. Since I couldn't exactly open my mouth wide enough to ask what was wrong, he pointed down at my crotch and said something in Spanish. It was a slang I didn't understand, but the jist was clear enough. Rafael was both surprised and incredibly turned on by the fact that my cock was intact. In fact, after I got done sucking him, he could hardly wait to return the favor. That guy blew me so enthusiastically that I've never forgotten how wonderful his lips felt on my shaft, and how hard I exploded in his apparently bottomless throat. The whole time he was drinking my cum, he just kept mumbling praises for my size and stamina, though his mouth was so distorted against my shaft that I could understand the tone of his comments rather than the actual words.

Naive as I was at the time, that experience was a major revelation to me. Up until then, I'd been nervous about revealing my dick to another man precisely because it was uncut—and, I feared, an ugly turn-off. Knowing that I could make a horny man crazy for me just by revealing it gave me exactly the burst of confidence I needed to go out there and pursue the sex life I wanted so badly.

Unfortunately, soon after that incident in the shed, my mom

got wind of what was going on, and Rafael was discreetly fired. For a long time, I moped around, horny as hell and masturbating constantly. I had no idea how to find Rafael, or any other swarthy, hairy man who was ready to latch onto my foreskin-wrapped plunger! It seemed I was destined for a life of celibacy until I went off to college a couple of months later.

Then, a few weeks into my first semester, I spotted the custodian in Barrows Hall, the big gloomy building where my Bio 101 class met every Wednesday night. "Juan," as I heard people call him, was in his late thirties, about the same age as Rafael had been. Juan reminded me of my former gardener in other ways, too: he spoke the same broken English, the same coarse five o'clock shadow darkened his firm jaw, and he stood a head taller than me with hair-covered, sinewy forearms. His right bicep bore the tattoo of a wolf, which looked like it was walking as he lifted heavy garbage bins and moved furniture around after the night session was over. Whenever I saw him, I'd think about that sticky afternoon in the potting shed, and my dick would swell up so hard I could barely walk.

I started hanging around long after class had ended, and I'd look at his ass whenever he bent over to swab the floor or pick up a stray cola can dropped by a sloppy student. The dark, hair-filled crack of his ass always edged over his black leather belt when he dipped down, and his faded jeans and sleeveless red flannel shirt would go taut over the planes of his body. I said hi to him whenever his eyes met mine, but that was the extent of my contact with him. He might have looked like Rafael, but I doubted he shared our gardener's sexual tastes. I figured I'd have to content myself with looking for the time being.

Before long, I knew his routine inside and out. Best of all, I'd learned that he spent half an hour every night scrubbing the toilets and urinals in the ground-floor men's room. And after he was finished cleaning and polishing the place, he'd take a long break—and a long whiz—himself. I liked to listen to the heavy stream shooting out of him. Eventually, I found a way to slip into the bathroom and stand just inside the door so that I could actually see the thick yellow stream whirling from his juicy prick.

That night I had another wonderful revelation: Juan was uncut, just like I was. His meat was even bigger than I had expected, with a purplish tinge and slight veins throbbing though the loose, translucent foreskin folded around his fat prick. His bloated balls had a decidedly maroon tinge under a mass of thick, black hair which covered his groin and crept outward onto a well-rounded, olive-colored ass.

In fact, his piss stream went haywire because Juan hadn't bothered to push his foreskin all the way back, and it hung so loose and low that it half-blocked his piss-slit. Golden froth was spraying everywhere, even onto the rounded toes of his tan work boots. It made me imagine how much cum a fleshy tube like that could hold.

At that point, I couldn't stop myself. Just as the last bit of piss dripped onto his worn-out briefs, I took my own uncut beauty out of the hatch. Then I leaned against the wall and jacked my flesh-covered dick until I'd blown my own wad all over the freshly scrubbed tile wall. At first, I started to grab a paper towel and wipe it away. Then I had an idea. If Juan saw it there when he came back from the urinal, he'd figure out what had happened. Then I'd have a chance to find out just how that tough Latino stud would feel about another guy staring at his prong like that. Even if he wasn't interested, I'd have the satisfaction of knowing I'd made contact with him, however one-sided it might have been.

I hung around outside the bathroom until I heard him walking toward the door. Suddenly, the footsteps ceased. I knew he was looking at the cum stain on the wall. I heard him release a low, admiring whistle. I hid again as the door swung open, and as he walked by I saw the front of his jeans pushed out by an obvious boner.

I managed to stuff my boner back into my pants and went back to my dorm room hornier than ever. Luckily, my roommate wasn't there. Flopping onto my bed, I opened my pants again and yanked my still-throbbing tool back out. I shook the fat mushroom from my fleshy pocket, and imagined that Juan was looking at me the way I'd spied on him.

I wiped some of my pre-cum from my exposed cockhead, imagining that it was Juan's, and wiped it onto my shaft. The ooze crept into my sensitive skin. I lubed my hands with it and got a tight fist around my cock. It throbbed in my grip and grew steadily, stiffening and becoming hotter to the touch.

My foreskin was stretched to the limit. The soft flesh tightened around my base. The veins bulged and expanded. When my cock had risen practically parallel to my belly, the bruised-looking crown poked out all the way. Working fast, I squeezed its rock-hard dimensions and raced down the length of it from base to tip and back again, using my foreskin like a small towel to scrub the core of my boner. My fist gripped it as hard as it could. Up and down, I greased my palms and prick with the sticky cum, and used my other hand to give my swollen, hairy balls a sharp twist. The vision of Juan spouting all over my body seared in my mind's eye as I jacked off.

Then, suddenly, my prick exploded all over my sweaty chest and belly. I rubbed it into my skin, dipping my fingers into the glop. Then I licked it off them, savoring the tangy flavor of the bitter cum.

Now I fell asleep, exhausted—and truly satiated for the first time since that day in the shed. That night, I dreamed of Juan's orgasmic studmeat, as I did on many other nights that followed.

Finally, one humid night, I decided I had to fuck Juan for real.

After class, I went downstairs to wait until he got off work. I knew where he usually parked his beat-up van and waited next to it. I didn't have to wait very long.

I turned when I heard footsteps and grinding gravel in the parking lot. There was Juan carrying a heavy toolbox. His flannel shirt was now tied around his waist, revealing a white undershirt smeared with dark grease stains. But as he came closer I could see the thick black hair covering him and the faint outline of his hardening nipples, aroused by a slight breeze.

I'm not sure whether Juan knew how much I wanted his attentions, but in any case I was ready to tell him how I felt. I spoke to him in Spanish. *"Hola."*

He stopped and looked at me curiously. *"Hola."*

"It's a nice night," I said, casually shifting the massive weight in my pants.

"Kind of hot," he commented, wiping his slick brow with a worn, blue bandanna he yanked from his back pocket.

"Yeah, it's hot, all right. Where are you goin'?" I asked as I thought of him pissing like he had the other night.

"Home," he answered, not meeting my gaze.

"Not yet," I said, and moved over to the door of his van.

Shrugging, he slid open the door and I climbed into the back. He'd set up a portable tool shop in there. Scraps of metal and oily rags dotted the floor, but there were also a few beer bottles strewn around a gym mat that smelled of man. Juan sat down on it, stripped off his undershirt, and sat there looking at me expectantly. I could see by his expression that he'd found the wad of cum on the wall, and that he knew who'd done it. There was no need for either of us to say anything.

I walked over to him and hunkered down next to him. I ran my hands down his muscular torso, the mound in my groin pressing against his while I undid the zipper of his soiled jeans and pushed them down his muscular hips. That uncut cock I'd drooled over popped up against the thin cotton of his white underwear. The damp spot on the cloth told me it was drooling for me, too.

"You make me hot, Juan. I like your body." I flicked a drop of sweat from his ear with a rough swipe of my tongue, then stood up again.

I stripped slowly as Juan watched with intense anticipation. Then he helped me along, unzipping my jeans. My boner popped out right in front of his face because I purposely hadn't worn any underwear that night.

Grunting, Juan slid down until my cock jutted right in his face. A spurt of hot pre-cum immediately clouded the tip of my crown and oozed out over my foreskin. Juan half-closed his eyes and opened his mouth with a moan. He started to lick my fuzzy balls, pulling at the fine hairs with sharp white teeth. At the same time, he rubbed my foreskin back and forth, swelling my hot core inside its fleshy sleeve. My body was tense with need as I started pushing my boner into his scruffy face.

His five o'clock shadow rubbed against my crotch as the pre-cum from my mushroom oozed onto his lips. Juan made sure to pull my foreskin back all the way to get every drop. He began to flick his tongue in and out of the crease, but I was pumping out more as fast as he slurped.

"Show me how much you want me, Juan. Suck me," I demanded, reaching down and pushing his face into me.

Juan promptly licked the last bit of pre-cum off my tip and swallowed it, then licked his parched lips. With the tip of my boner still on his tongue, I rammed all my weight into him, shoving my heavy prick way past his tonsils into his hot throat.

I heard Juan gag for a second, but then he seemed to adjust. I fucked his rough face harder. My foreskin was stretched to the limit, filling his warm throat until I felt it bulge out against my low-hanging nutsac.

Just at that moment, my balls clenched up and I fired a perfect slimeball into his throat. His nostrils flared as I unloaded shot after shot, filling his mouth, riding him until he was gasping for air. I rode his face even after I'd emptied my scrotum. It was like my boner had taken on a will of its own, and it tried to punch a hole through his neck.

When I finally pulled out of his mouth, Juan went right back to my cock and started licking every stray drop of cum off the folds of my foreskin. He didn't sit back until he'd cleaned off all of my pubes and nutsac. I guess his training had conditioned him never to leave a mess behind!

Moaning, I crawled up on the mat and stretched out next to him. For a moment, Juan sat next to me, smiling and licking his own lips and chin. Then, gradually, his face changed.

"Now me," he said, pointing to the gigantic slab of studmeat pulsating between his dark thighs. I looked down, drinking in the sight of that enormous red shaft and blazing foreskin. Before I could say anything, Juan rolled me over and heaved himself on top of me.

He wrenched apart my ass-cheeks and split my tight crack with an enormous, well-aimed push. The tender folds and muscles in my ass-canal wrestled with his flared cockhead, clutching his shaft like a fist as he plunged into me with all his considerable strength. There was pain, and there was pleasure. Mostly there was pleasure. I groaned, bouncing my stomach up and down on that spunk-covered mat. All the while, Juan polished my prostate with his flaring cockhead, the foreskin shoved way down and his hot bulb spearing my guts. Even though it was pressed flat between my stomach and the mat, I felt my cock let loose a second hot torrent of jizz. Seconds later, Juan filled my juicy ass with a load of boiling seed. I twisted my head around just in time to see his body tighten and spasm abruptly. He whipped his head from side to side in sheer elation as the scum continued to pour from his hose. In no time he'd filled my ass and was gushing out all over the interior of the van. Soon the mat, my butt-cheeks, and even the wall beside me were all dripping with his froth. There was even more cum than I'd imagined on that night when I'd watched him piss gallons.

Finally, his cock flew out of my hole with a sticky pop, the loosening skin still oozing hot oils. After giving my own balls a last, drawn-out squeeze, I let go of them and groped my way back to rub his now-flaccid cock. He did the same for me, playing with the flaps that had covered my cockhead again, then pushing them back and poking the sensitive tip with his index finger.

Laughing wickedly, I turned my head and gripped his meat in my fingers. While he moaned, I slurped his whole fleshy helmet inside my mouth and chewed his rubbery meat until he was begging me in Spanish to finish him off.

My mouth slid down past his distended cockhead and along his hot shaft. After a while, I figured out just how to apply my teeth to stimulate his base and balls and just when to tighten and release my lips to prevent him from actually coming. Reaching over with my right hand, I raked my fingers through the slick, musky hair surrounding his balls while he thrust his hips rhythmically to my mouth's diving lunges. He was moving his body back and forth, trying to force his cock farther down my greedy mouth with each stroke.

Soon my back teeth grated against the loose skin around his shank, my nose nudging his base and expelling my hot breath into his sweaty, saliva-drenched bush. He was swollen now nearly beyond tolerance, splitting the bulge of my tonsils with every thrust. My tongue was almost painfully aware of every pulsing vein I slid over. I could tell how much more this aroused him, because his downstrokes suddenly became almost savage. I moaned and shivered against him even as the sweat poured down my neck and into the crack of my bare ass.

Suddenly, I felt his balls distend against my chin, throbbing urgently. Juan began driving faster into my mouth, wedged his blunt fingers against the back of my head, and let out a low, animal cry as he spewed another blazing load into my obliging body.

I began swallowing as his hot salsa filled me, his coarse foreskin scraping the roof and sides of my mouth wonderfully raw. It slowly dawned on me that this experience had surpassed even the one in the shed.

And I knew that Rafael and Juan wouldn't be the only men who would want me. There was a whole college full of hot men who were probably willing to give me the most complete education I could ever have imagined.

PROVINCETOWN HEAT

Matt McCarthy

There are two reasons I'll never forget the heat last summer at Provincetown. Reason number one was that the thermometer went over 100 degrees that afternoon. As for reason number two, the only thing hotter than the sand at the beach that day was the man I met. He changed the meaning of sex for me forever.

My day at the guesthouse started off like any other: coffee and toast, and then the beach. I was about to leave when I noticed the new arrival who would occupy the room next to mine. He glanced up at me while he was unlocking his door, an expensive suitcase at his feet. Before I could get my tongue to stammer out a greeting, he gave me a polite nod and disappeared inside his room.

Though I was disappointed, I tossed my towel over my shoulder and went my own way. The sun was still low on the horizon when I reached the sands of Herring Cove, and I had the exhilarating feeling of having the beach all to myself.

I gave a cursory look to make sure no one was around. Then I stripped off my swimsuit, rolled it up and stashed it under my head, and wrapped my fist around my throbbing boner. I started yanking myself hard, the salty breeze creating a burning sensation as it fluttered over the tender skin of my exposed shank.

Before long, I felt a warm inner wave of my own bubbling up inside my groin. My balls gave a sudden lurch, and my naked ass-cheeks clenched up against the folds of my towel. I closed my fingers tighter and jerked myself hard and fast. The downstroke, while the tense ring formed by my fingers and thumb massaged my swollen cockhead every time I yanked upward. In no time at all it seemed, I was unleashing a white-hot geyser of volcanic proportions, my steamed cream flowing down over my hand to drench my flushed thighs and abdomen.

Drained, I fell back onto my towel, breathing hard. The heat that day was going to be intense: already, the white-hot sun was slamming down on my naked body, covering my skin with a sheen of sweat. I'm generally not crazy about swimming in the Atlantic—the cold water always feels like a vise on my nuts. Still, in my presently overheated state, the chilly waves looked unexpectedly inviting, the pointed blackish waves stabbing the humid air.

I staggered down to the shoreline, steeled myself for the blast of cold that I knew would hit me in a moment, and plunged into the water, rinsing the pungent film of sweat and jizz off me. When I got back to my towel, I was astonished to see a tall, dark-haired guy standing there, looking at me. His thin lips were curved upward in a horny smile.

"That was quite a show you put on," he said, laughing. Instinctively, I glanced at his crotch and saw that he was wearing a skimpy red thong suit. My own exposed cock stirred between my legs as I looked at him, stretching down almost to the middle of my thighs. It was hard to say which part of my anatomy was redder just then!

"I ... uh ... uh ... I didn't know anyone was watching," I stammered. "Where *exactly* did you come from?"

Still grinning, he tilted his head toward a sloping dune about fifty feet away. "I was thinking I'd have this stretch of sand to myself," he told me. "Now I'm glad it didn't work out that way. I'm Tom, by the way."

"Matt," I murmured, but my eyes were riveted to his hand as he reached down and cupped the growing bulge between his legs. He spread his fingers a little, outlining his rigid, domed cockhead and plump balls. They pressed against his scarlet thong like they were struggling to burst free at any moment. Softhearted guy that I am, I couldn't help but reach out to give them a little help!

His whole body seemed to tense and tilt forward when I extended my fingers to peel aside the left side of his thong. One thick ball dropped free into the salty air, followed by the eager head of his cock. Taking a deep breath, I pushed the suit back farther, finally exposing both nuts and the full, impressive length of his stiff meat. His fingers shot out and coiled through my hair, twisting my curls until the roots stung in my scalp.

Slowly, he guided my face toward his crotch, stopping only when my nose touched the heavy, club-like head of his cock.

He hunched his hips suddenly, slapping his low-swinging balls against the curve of my chin. A thin trickle of pre-cum spurted from his flared piss-slit, trickling down my upper lip and spattering my outstretched tongue.

I took the liberty of pulling his suit down to his ankles as I dove straight for his fierce boner. Hanging onto the backs of his thighs in order to balance myself, I started thrashing my head from side to side like a hungry shark going for its meaty prey. Tom leaned back with pleasure, raking his fingers over my scalp with increased ardor as his boiling juices boiled up from his nuts and filled his shaft. It grew so full and heavy that it pressed down on my tongue like a solid steel pipe as I closed my lips and slurped him hard, his bittersweet juices flooding my throat.

"Oh, yeah," he groaned, sawing his hips back and forth desperately, his thigh muscles going rigid against my groping hands. I paused to tug on his balls a little, noticing that they'd become as throbbing and white-hot as a pair of coals from a fire pit. Tom started to spurt a moment later, bucking and grunting like a rutting wild beast.

He made small, spasmodic pushes with his hips, and his groin rose to meet my manhandling like a horse wheeling around to suit its master's prickings.

I grasped him as tightly as I could and pushed my mouth down his impressive hilt's full length, tightening my throat—muscles with all the power I could muster. I chewed and rubbed and slurped him raw, his skin almost flying off from my intense exertions. His tight ass bobbed up and down while his fat balls smacked up against my face. My knees dug hard into the sand, and I could vaguely feel the gravel dig into my skin. The hint of pain only spurred me on, however. His grip on my head became stronger as he came closer to coming.

When the first sizzling droplets of cum bathed my tongue, I dug my head into his groin and started swallowing up his juices. Warm and bubbly, they flowed over my tongue and dripped from the corners of my mouth. At the same time, I reached around and jabbed a finger up his silky ass, feeling his ass-muscles alternately contract and relax to allow me deeper access. I twisted myself in, adding a second and then a third finger to the mix as he groaned and pushed back at me.

"Yes, Matt. I'm there," he croaked. "Suck it up, man. Faster, Matt, faster. Now! Now! Now!"

I slurped and sucked and bobbed my head, never stopping until I'd milked his ball-sauce down to the very dregs. At that point, he suddenly went soft and pulled away. His still-bulging cockhead slapped my pursed lips like a billy club. He stood there a while, panting and moaning with pleasure, leaning back on the fingers I still had wedged up his ass. Two trickles of steamy cum were steadily oozing down the sides of his deflated rod.

"Mmmmm, that was great," he murmured, finally slipping his hands from my scalp. I could see a few of my dark, curly hairs clinging to the sweat on his fingers where he'd pulled them up by the roots. He held out that same hand to me, helping me back to my feet. My own boner had now swelled to achingly huge proportions, the round head practically glowing with lust.

"My turn now," I whispered hoarsely.

He looked at my face for a long time, making me suffer until he finally reached between my legs and stroked my stiff pole and bulging balls with his fingers. "Come with me," he said, and started for the water without releasing my burning meat. I hardly had time to consider the double meaning of his words before I was thigh-deep in the chilly water, Tom's fist still securely fastened around my throbbing shank. Icy tendrils spiraled up my legs and splashed my groin, but luckily my hard-on was intense enough that even the assault of cold water couldn't wilt it.

"But I don't like the water...." I started to yelp, then left the rest unsaid as Tom hunkered right down in the waves and slid my boner into his throat.

I filled his gaping mouth instantly, sliding all the way back to his tonsils in a single rough lunge. He clamped his skillful jaws around me as I started to pound his face. A tidal wave of jizz billowed up through my body, my whole torso quivering. My need was so intense that I completely forgot that I'd brought myself off less than twenty minutes ago. Instead, I held onto Tom's shoulders and pumped like crazy, cramming my pole down his gullet until I felt a giant second load descending. I could hardly believe I had any left, let alone what felt like a whole waterslide's worth of the stuff!

Wincing with concentration, Tom clamped his hand around my shank and kept jacking me off with his mouth and throat. In what seemed like mere seconds, my cock went off like Old Faithful. I blew my load into his mouth while he sucked me down hard, but it turned out that I had even more to give than he could handle. My hot geyser blew with such force that a giant gob of it spurted from his mouth, splashing my chest and neck and thoroughly dousing his chin and cheeks.

In the brief instant before the next waved lashed out and rinsed it away, I had a wonderful glimpse of his slack face, hot with desire and streaked with my cream. In that delicious moment, I forgot all about the cold water and my instinctive distrust for the sea. It almost seemed like we were both immersed in a swell of warm cum, our naked bodies merging with a surging sea of lust.

"There's nothing like doing it in the ocean," Tom grinned, then stretched his head up like a turtle and gave my protruding right nipple a playful nip. "It's the whole reason I come to Provincetown every summer."

Next, he spit a stream of salty water on my chest, doing a perfect imitation of a horny sperm whale. I got back at him by plunging headlong into the water and grabbing for his submerged nuts. When I got them in my hand, I ducked my head under and crushed them briefly against my lips. Then I held my breath as long as I could, wrapping both hands around his new erection.

Tom's hips jerked underwater, and his cock wagged against the current and my grasp. The flow of the water helped my hand get him off by exerting pressure against his flailing cocktip. I could feel Tom's drifting balls swelling once again to full capacity.

Briefly, I ducked my head above the waves for a quick gulp of air. "Okay, Tom," I rasped, "time to shoot for points." When I submerged again, I shoved his pulsing tool right into my mouth and floated up so that my stuffed face floated just above the surface. He was brewing a full load in those furry nuts, I could tell, and I didn't want to miss a drop. While the forceful billows tantalized his blushing crotch, I started a powerful suction-force with my jaws that must have rivaled any ocean predator's toothy grip.

Just as his cock began to sputter, an enormous wave slammed into us. Some of his cum sprayed the inside of my mouth, but another good spurt of it got knocked to the side. It hosed the air and then arced back down, mixing with the ocean froth that rose and fell around us. I dutifully licked off his balls and dick one last time, then pressed my body against him as we floated on our backs.

Eventually, the sun began to set on the first day of the most orgasmic vacation on record. Tom and I went back to his room and went at it again. We didn't even stop to eat until much later the next day. He didn't bring it up, and I was too busy satisfying my hunger for the richest meat I'd ever tasted—in Provincetown or anywhere else.

ROCKY MOUNTAIN FEVER

Jason Carpenter

When my parents decided to move from the temperate climes of south Texas to the nut-frosting cold of Denver, I hated the frigid country and it seemed to hate me. My first week in our new home found me with a cold of historical proportions. I felt like I had been dipped in shit and shrink-wrapped.

Mom fluttered around me, taking my temperature, fluffing my pillow, even offering to make chicken soup. Having experienced her chicken soup, however, I declined, not wanting to add to my misery.

Besides being sick, I felt a gnawing loneliness. All my friends in Texas were probably having a great time while I lay shivering. Butts were being fucked and dicks were being sucked back home. Two weeks had passed since I last had my mouth wrapped around a nice hard dick. The thought caused my young meat to jerk to attention beneath the heavy blanket covering me. Hmm. *Maybe I'll feel better if I release some pressure,* I thought. I stroked the length of my dick and closed my eyes, willing images of past lovers to frolic through my imagination.

Rigid nipples, taut, rounded buns dusted with fine blond hairs, and gently up-curved, purple-headed dicks danced in my memory. I slipped my hand inside my pajamas and encircled my dick with my fingers, beating my meat enthusiastically, in need of a quick orgasm. Then my mother's voice broke through my pleasant daydreams. "Jackie?"

My eyes snapped open, but my dream continued. Standing beside my mother was a Nordic god. Pushed over the edge by the sight of the handsome boy, I felt hot cum gush between my fingers. I caught my breath as my juice soaked my pajamas in a spurting flood. Mom frowned. "Jackie, you're all flushed again."

"I ... I'm okay, Mom," I stammered, unable to take my eyes off the stranger. The tent pole beneath the covers slowly subsided. Hopefully, they had not noticed.

"This is Bradley. He lives next door. His mother had him bring us a fresh apple pie as a welcome to the neighborhood. Isn't that nice?"

"Very nice," I said, checking out Bradley's copper-colored hair. He wore it brushed back and pulled into a long ponytail. His eyes were as clear and blue as a mountain stream. He appeared to be about my age.

He stepped to my bedside. "Good to meet you, Jackie."

Shit! I couldn't shake his hand. Mine was dripping with jizz!

He grinned down at me. "I'd shake hands...." My breath caught in my chest. "...But I have a bad blister from skiing," he finished.

Whew!

"Well, I'll let you boys get to know each other," Mom said. "while I go over to Bradley's house and introduce myself. I hope we become good friends."

The bulge in Bradley's tight jeans looked scrumptious.

When we heard the door close downstairs, he laughed. "You can get up and wash the cream off now."

He knew! "Uh ... what?"

"I saw the look on your face when you saw me. I made you shoot your wad. Besides, man, I can smell cum a block away. Shame you wasted it."

Be still my heart! "There's more where that came from," I said, climbing out of bed and walking bowlegged to the bathroom with liquefied cum oozing down my inner thighs. I washed up hurriedly and went back to the bedroom bottomless.

Bradley sat on the edge of my bed. "Come here," he said.

I stepped between his spread knees. He nestled his mouth and nose in my pubic hairs and inhaled deeply. Lifting my semi-hard dick, he leaned forward, and ran his tongue around my crown. He nipped at my foreskin with delicate bites, then sucked my responding meat into his soft mouth. I clasped my fingers behind his neck and ground my pelvis against his lips.

As my tube filled with blood, lengthening and swelling, Bradley gripped my buns in his hands and urged me to fuck his face. His tongue played snake-like over my pulsing crown and up the sensitive underside of my shaft. I spread my feet and thrust between his lips and down his silken throat, watching my meat slide in and out of his pursed lips.

But it was too soon. I could tell I was not yet able to cum again, despite the erotic circumstances and Bradley's talented mouth. I withdrew my spike and dropped to my knees. The sudden motion made me dizzy. Only then did I remember I was ill. But some things are worth a little discomfort. I unfastened Bradley's wide belt buckle, unzipped his jeans, and tugged them off. His man-fucker stood up as rigid as re-bar from a cushion of blond curls.

I lowered my mouth over his bulging totem pole, tasting his salty flesh for the first time, wetting him with my saliva. Ambrosia! I licked his shaft and sucked at the fringe of his foreskin. He wriggled excitedly under my ministration, running his fingers through my dark hair. When he moaned with pleasure, I stopped eating him.

Dizzy, I tried standing up again, fell back, tried again. Finally I was able to straddle his thighs, then squatted until the velvet tip of his cock prodded my asshole. He put his arms around my waist, balancing me, so I could wrap my legs around him. I squirmed until his dickhead popped through my clenching ass-ring then let my weight lower me until I was fully impaled on his thick tool.

We kissed hungrily, wet tongues flashing and dancing as we rocked together. His dick up my ass felt wonderful as it bore into the depths of my guts. I bounced gently, driving him even deeper. "Shit, you're tight. And so fucking hot!" Then he added, "You've got a fever, man.".

"What I've got his a fever for your cock. Buttfuck me, hard."

He gripped my ass and thrust upward as I bobbed on his pole, harder now, and faster. The feel of his flesh slipping and screwing up me got my heart beating like a tom-tom. My prostate quivered deliciously each time his dickhead prodded it. Pre-cum bubbled out of me.

Bradley clasped my dick and fisted me with long, slow strokes as I covered his face and neck with kisses. His thrusting became more frantic and I knew he was close. I tightened my sphincter muscles, squeezing his dick hard. "Ohh! Unngh!" he moaned, throwing his head back and pumping up me. "I'm shooting my wad up your sweet ass ... way up you. Do you want it?"

"Give me all you've got. Fill me up. Use my ass, Bradley," I breathed. He fucked into me with single-minded resolve.

Seconds later, I felt his cum splash inside my anus. Now I rode him until he was dry, pumping up and down in short strokes to maximize the intensity of his orgasm.

We rolled, still connected, until I lay beneath him. Though I thought he was spent, his hard-on did not dwindle. I locked my ankles behind his broad back and complacently let him slow-fuck my asshole. His flat belly rubbed the hairs of my balls and my thumping prick, making me crazy with desire for him.

He unbuttoned my pajama top and dipped his head, licking and biting my pea-hard nipples. In and out, he fucked. The room smelled of my insides. He seemed able to go on forever. But nothing lasts forever. "I'm cumming again," he said, rotating his hips. He screwed into me deeply, rapidly. His balls pounded my asscheeks in rhythm with his pounding thrusts. When he shot his load, he stabbed so far up my rectum I nearly cried out. His ten solid inches was the most I had ever taken. At last, he dragged his cock out of ass and rolled off me.

"Great way to get to know your neighbor," I told him.

"Yeah. A real Rocky Mountain 'Hi'," he joked.

I sniffed, coughed, and felt my head swim. *Maybe I'm too sick to fuck,* I thought, then decided that wasn't possible. I still had a pulse.

I wound my fingers around Bradley's sexy ponytail and urged him downward. "Suck me off," I said.

Bradley licked a tingling path from my nipples to my navel. He darted his tongue into my navel, reaming it out, then licked down to my pubic hair. Teasingly, he detoured around my cock and continued down my inner thigh. I hunched upward in frustration. "Patience," he said. The tip of his tongue traced maddening circles over my balls. He lifted them and made a trail along my perineum, poking at my puckered, freshly fucked asshole. When he sucked my whole nut-sac into his mouth and rolled my balls with his tongue, I arched upward, stabbing my eight inches toward the ceiling.

Enough foreplay already! I tugged his ponytail. Bradley smiled up at me, spit out my balls, then toyed with my crown. His worked his tongue around the head and parted my dick slit, taking my pre-cum onto his tongue. "Tastes like honey. I hope you've got a big load for me." He opened his mouth wide and lowered it over my throbbing cock.

He compressed his lips and bobbed up and down the length of my meat. His teeth raked the tender underside of my shaft, sending electric tingles into my balls. Mmm, he sure knew his way around a dick. My crown glided along the roof of his mouth and part way down his throat. He worshipped my dick with loving licks and kisses. But I wanted more.

I rolled, taking him with me, and straddled his head. I fucked his sweet lips like I would an asshole, plunging deep. He cradled my balls in his hand and rolled them, squeezing firmly. Yeah. With his other hand he lightly slapped my ass,, then ran his knuckles along my spine, urging me on. I felt my cum building in my balls. My ass clenched. Then I was coming. Burning cum raced through my pumping shaft and spurted out my dick slit, into Bradley's gulping throat. He timed his sucking perfectly, siphoning my fuckcream in long drafts, drawing it from deep inside me. Before I was completely empty, he took my dick in his hand and pulled it from between his lips. Looking down the length of my body, I watched as he milked the last of my cream from my cock, letting it dribble into his open mouth. He swallowed every drop of my cum, then tongue-bathed me clean.

I moved off him and he crawled up beside me. We lay side-by-side, dick-to-dick, kissing. I tasted my own cum on his lips. We each stroked the other's cock, basking in the afterglow of our heated sex. My eyes fluttered, and the dizziness swept over me again. Bradley's face suddenly went out of focus. I heard him calling, "Jackie? Jackie! Jack....", but I drifted away.

"Jackie!" My mother's voice broke through my fever-induced sleep. "You passed out, honey ... are you all right?"

I looked blearily around the room, confused. My head throbbed with pain. My eyeballs felt too big for their sockets. No Bradley. Had the whole damn thing been a dream? I felt like cursing. Then Bradley walked out of the bathroom with a damp washcloth. He folded it and tenderly placed it on my forehead. "You scared me, neighbor. We were talking and, all of a sudden, you blinked out on me. Your mother came running when I called home."

I saw that Bradley was dressed, as was I beneath the cover. My sexual escapade had been just a delusion caused by my high temperature.

"I'll go down and get you some aspirin, dear," Mom said.

"I'd better be going, too," Bradley added.

I looked at him longingly.

He watched until my mother started down the stairs then came back to my bedside. He bent down, kissed my lips, and gave my dick a squeeze through the blanket. "Tomorrow'll be even better," he said, smiling.

Relief flooded through me. My delirium was real! "I'm going to love Denver," I told him.

CRAZY WITH THE HEAT

Lance Rush

If you live here long enough, you grow accustomed to the dry heat in Texas. But when the temperature reaches a blazing 107 degrees in the shade, you're too lazy to do anything except lie down and sweat.

Well, that's just what I'd caught Gregory doing. And it wasn't even quitting time. Granted, I was exhausted from the day's work and the heat, but then I came upon Gregory's lazy ass, laid up in that old hammock, his jeans undone. But instead of resting, the stud was jackin' off! I couldn't believe it! And imagine my surprise when, as I drew closer, I saw Gregory had at least nine-inches of prime meat to play with! The hammock swung back and forth and, suddenly, as a bright beam of sun hit him just so, cum came gushing from the big head of that monster prick!

Understand that I had lusted for him ever since he'd strode onto Mr. Roundtree's office at the ranch, like some muscle-bound colt, looking for work. He was a lanky stud in a Stetson, with lots of attitude. Once he was hired, I was able to observe that his cock hung in his faded jeans like a freak third leg, begging to be noticed, touched, pulled free, and sucked.

Now the stud of my dreams gazed vaguely up at me, and asked, "What the hell you lookin' at, kid?"

"Your freakin' dick!" I said boldly. "You're lucky it's me, and not old man Roundtree; he'd fire your loafing ass. It ain't quitting time, yet."

"Shit! I pull my fuckin' weight around here, kid," he grunted, slowly pulling up his jeans. His rod swung to and fro, cum still dripping from it.

I stared at him, finding it amusing that he was having trouble wrangling the meat back inside those filthy, very tight jeans of his.

It was still hot as hell on Friday. It was payday, and I imagined Gregory took paycheck and his big cock into town to squander all his earnings and drain that cock dry in some cathouse. Still, I had no proof of what he did; he was the mystery man on the ranch. Oh sure, he "pulled his weight" all right, but he was even more of a loner than I was. A sour man in his late 30's, everybody thought he was just too conceited to mix.

My paycheck wasn't cold in my hand before I headed into town to prowl one of my favorite haunts: the local adult bookstore and theater. The place wasn't gay, but I've found that a hard cock has no conscience. There would always be some straight guy wrestling with his out-of-control boner. If he was horny enough, he'd stick it into any hole it fit.

After my eyes became accustomed to the dark of the theater, I spotted a blond boy flogging a suck-worthy prospect. So I sat close by, and caught a real eyeful. He made that dick dance, shot me a look, stood, and went to the john.

I followed him. The blond was in there with a shorter, swarthy guy in chaps. They stood at adjacent urinals, both cocks sticking out, hard as crowbars! I figured, the way they were smiling at each other, that they knew each other. As I pissed in a nearby urinal, both of 'em turned and wagged those pricks in my direction. I admit I was simply too goddamn horny to resist. Flushing, I turned to the blond one. He was waving a good-sized cock, and its head was just starting to juice. I reached out and stroked his beet-red tube as it drummed heavily in my fist.

"Suck it!" he said, pushing the rod in a slow fuck motion inside my grasp. I couldn't refuse him.

The moment my head dove for that shiny dick-cap, his thighs clamped tight around my neck. He wasn't about to let me go until he'd come. A sweet moan escaped his lips as I crawled along his corona, then enclosed that pulsating knob. A jumble of veins pushed all across its shaft, every one thumping! I surged down, started slurping. It leaked a bitter ooze, but shit, I didn't care. Then, the short one moseyed up, prick poking from his chaps. Every dick's got it's own personality, but these two could've been twins. Both were long, red, meaty staffs, with juice-dripping mushroom heads. Well, the short dude slaps his drooling tube all over my sucking face. "Suck mine ... here! Stick both our big dicks in that fuckin' mouth." He tried to force-feed his slimy meat through my cock-stuffed lips. "Go on! Take it!" I was surrounded by bucking thighs, nuts thrusting, and choking on two hard insistent dicks! Things were getting rough. Suddenly the night had taken a decidedly vicious turn. The short guy punched my chest, so hard it stung! Then, the blond hauled me to my feet, and slammed my face to the wall.

"You ever been double-dicked, huh, faggot?" he asked gruffly.

"You know he has, fucking dick lover!" the other moron chipped in, hauling down my jeans.

Was it the heat? Or were these guys just stone crazy? I felt that bare cock on my ass, and he pushed me to the filthy floor. I'm pretty swift with my fists, but there were two of them—both hard, strong and bullying. Still, no way was I going to let those bastards double-dick me! Flipping over, as the blond straddled me, I hauled off and hit him with a left cross. He staggered back, more stunned than hurt. The other one raised his fist, but, as he was about to strike me, someone grabbed his wrist. Soon as he swung around, he was punched in the face! The buffed blond, who I'd hit, bounded up and jumped on the man's back.

As I looked up, I saw that the man who'd come to my rescue was none other than my ranch-hand pal Gregory!

Well, they both flew backward, and Gregory slammed the blond so hard to the wall, the fucking place reverberated.

We punched, we kicked, and we brawled. When both men ran, bruised and battered, Gregory dusted himself off and laughed. Dazed, all I could do was stare at him. I was lying on the filthy floor, bruised but otherwise intact.

"Man, that felt good! Got some fight in you, boy!" he grinned. "Now. Let's get outta here!"

We jumped in my pickup. I drove around aimlessly, listening to Gregory chiding me for trolling strange toilets, looking for dick.

"That shit, back there, it almost serves you right! Shouldn't be slutting around places like that!" His rugged features caught a blade of moonlight, and he looked more menacing than ever.

I kept listening to his tirade, thinking I would interrupt him, to ask what the hell he was doing in that place, instead of spending his time at the whore house up the street, but every time I opened my mouth, he'd start in again.

At one point, I glanced over to see the tattoo on his left bicep moving slowly up and down. Once when I saw him fondling that long stiff protrusion in his jeans, I swerved into the other lane.

"Easy! You still shook up, dizzy or something? Hey, maybe you ought to pull over. Yeah, that's it, pull over."

"What?"

"You heard me. Pull the fuck over, damn it!"

"Here?"

"Yeah, here. Middle of nowhere, kid."

It was the middle of nowhere, for sure. Although it was one of the entrances to the Bar-B-X ranch, the gate was padlocked so we could only go down the road a short distance.

"That fight got me hard. Why don't you suck me off?"

I skidded, hit the brakes, and parked just outside the locked gate. Gregory was actually going to let me sample that dick! Soon as I pulled down his zipper, the sight of that cock sent a shiver through me. Even in near darkness, it was a the biggest cock I'd ever laid eyes on, and it wasn't even hard!

"I know you been wanting some of this. Now's your chance."

"Hmmm," I moaned as I planted a kiss on that big heart-shaped knob. Taking the bulb in my lips, I lapped all around that long, fat, salty rod! The roused shaft lunged across my tongue and past my jaw like a rattler! Had to be the thickest cock I'd sucked to date, but I sucked it hard, fearless now. My cheeks bloated against its burgeoning size as it pulsed, lengthened, thickened by the second. Beneath it, his ripe furry balls hung loose, bouncing against my spit-coated chin. I teased its oily foreskin as its seeping pre-cum salted my dragging tongue. I surged down, gulping bloated meat, spitting slick saliva on all its roping veins. His deep groan confirmed for me that he was ready, and I took his load in record time.

"We'd better get outta here," Gregory said, zipping up.

Back at the ranch, it seemed it was hotter than in town. We stood on the back porch of the bunkhouse, smoking cigarettes. The rest of the guys were in town, so Gregory and I had the place to ourselves.

"God, it must be 100 degrees out here, tonight. Steam's risin' off the tin roof."

I wondered if this how it was going to be: making small talk about the weather, ignoring what had gone on between us? Didn't he want to take things further?

Well, hot as it was, and hot as he'd made me, I wasn't going to push it.

We sat on the stoop and finished our cigarettes.

Then, he started chuckling again. "So, how long you been sucking dick?" he asked straight out.

"Not too long. I do a lot of beating-off, thinking about it, though. I think about sucking cock all the time."

"What about fucking?"

"Yeah...? What about it?" I asked, my prick hardening at the question.

"Well, some guys ... well, they'll just fuck anything, you know what I mean?"

"Yeah," I said.

"I suppose you've had guys like that, right? Guys that'll fuck anything?"

"No, not really. I've heard about it, but, well, I don't think I could do it."

"You've never had a cock up there?"

"No."

He tossed his smoke away and led me to his favorite spot, the hammock. He took off his jeans and laid back and I began to do him again. The hammock rocked back and forth as his mighty shaft kept unfurling in heavy throbs into my throat.

My head bobbed up and down as I tried to harness as much of Gregory's cock as possible. I loved his cock. I wanted to give him the best head he ever had in his life and make him come again.

Then, to my surprise, he yanked the slab from my sucking lips. The night suddenly grew hotter as he turned on his belly. Gregory ran his big ham hands along his tanned globes, gyrating, tempting me with every nasty swerve. He reached down in his boot, and suddenly tossed me a rubber. Then, in a wordless move, he winced his asshole in and out, calling my dick forth. Was he for real? As virile and manly as he was, did he really want me to fuck him? Well, one look at those rounded mounds heaving in moonlight and I knew he did.

"You said you knew about guys who'd fuck anything...."

"Yeah, but...."

"Well, I'm waitin'."

The night grew hotter still. But a different kind of sweat broke out all over me as I stripped for action. I spit on my cock, then opened him to wet the chute. I entered him in a slow, delicious plunge. It was so tight, I thought I might shoot before I could even begin to fuck him. I pulled back, grabbing his waist, drawing him in close, and I lunged. I couldn't move. I let my prick remain static for a moment, soaking in the warm vise of his fuckhole. I was amazed how his hole seemed to mold like warm rubber along my cock. With a smooth glide of my hips, I fucked him slowly. But Gregory was insistent. He wanted more. "'Fuck me! C'mon. damn it! Fuck me!" he called out. He ground himself into my boiling dick.

I moved my hips in sharp, stabbing motions. The heat was getting to me, but fucking his ass soon became my bliss. He didn't want it soft and swerving. No, he needed it hard and fast.

I reached down and grabbed his cock. It was erect, and I flogged it rapidly, whipping it to my rhythm as it filled my fist with strands of sticky sap. Gregory's pre-cum aided in my glide. His dick pitched in my sliding hand. His ass clutched tighter. I knew I didn't have much more fuck left in me. His hole was milking my load forth with every blazing stroke. Being a man of experience, Gregory must have sensed my climax was nearing.

"Ah! Mmm. Hold it. That's enough. Here, let me do you," he moaned.

I grudgingly gave up his butt. We switched places in the hammock. Maybe it was the heat, but I never felt so exhausted, and yet invigorated. Gregory bent down and ran his cheek along my warm, pulsating shaft. His stubble caused a thousand tiny shocks to my cock's skin. Then, he let his tongue flick its head.

"Mmmmm.... You're so fuckin' hot, kid," he sighed.

He looked so sexy with my dick crown wedged between his lips. His lips wrapped around my throbbing plum. He lapped my shaft. Ah, yes! That tongue spun and spun, sending warm gobs of saliva sliding down my porous dick skin. Ah! I began to throb as I surged deeper down his gullet. As my sweaty balls churned beneath his chin, I saw his pants fall, and he pushed them past his glorious ass that I'd just fucked.

There he stood with his dick jutting so high, so startlingly hard, it cast a shadow across the porch. When he wagged it at me, it looked both seductive and menacing at once. There we were, alone and naked, not a peep from the bunkhouse, only the rickety noise of the hammock.

"This night's about to get a whole lot hotter, kid" he huffed as his lips dove back to my pulsing prick. Ah, yes. I couldn't believe it, but there was Gregory, with my prick in his mouth, sucking me off! His teeth raked my pulsating shaft as his tongue sailed to my prick's root. A country breeze stirred up my butthole as he brought my knees to my chest. He glided down and lapped my nuts. That long, wet tongue rattled the skin of my burning sac, then whipped inside my asshole. It truly startled me! Was this what he meant about the night getting a 'whole lot hotter'? If things had gotten any hotter, I would have lost consciousness.

I lay back in the swinging hammock, gazing at the stars and at Gregory. I grunted as the wide crown burrowed up my wincing crack. He was so thick, so fucking engorged, I thought my little brown ring might explode from the heat and the girth of him! He pressed down; more inches passed through, making my rectum shudder and burn. Initially his dick brought on far more pain than pleasure. I'd never felt anything like it.

I thought that hammock would break when he pulled back and punched through my asshole a little more forcefully. First, gliding, smoothly, then with a sound jolt, I felt he'd split me in half! The heated night just grew hotter. A river of sweat coursed down my chest. Then, with the bucking force of a rough rider. It felt like this horny ass-fucker was trying to pound me senseless! Then, he drew back and tore even deeper, and I swear, I almost wept! My body thrust forth, and that hammock swung to and fro in wild pitches! That charging dick was battering through my fuckhole so hard, it would gape for days after he was done! Electric chills shot through my bouncing body. I buried my face in my arm as he pumped in short, rapid strokes, his strong legs smacking my blistering cheeks.

The scorching heat didn't seem to affect him in the least. The rhythm of the fuck was hard, jolting, desperate with his aching need to orgasm. I could feel myself opening wider and wider to his thrusting cock. Each time he rammed and withdrew, I anxiously awaited that next jab.

"I'm coming!" I warned him, and my cum sprayed in thick, frenetic spurts between us, pumping up my belly, my chest, and onto his. Gregory pulled out and stood, finally, on wobbling knees, beating off, sending that hammock swinging precariously. Swift as rockets, cum discharged in vaulting spurts from his prick.

"Some piece of fucking ass you got there, buddy!" he wheezed, as he fell hard in an exhausted fit on top of me. Our cum and his weight cemented us in the heat of that night.

"Did you ever.... I, mean ... Well, I heard you were fucking Mrs. Roundtree. Is that true?".

He laughed. "Hell, no! At least, not yet...." he teased, humping me playfully. "Now that I've had this, I may never need to try anything with her."

And then it happened. The old hammock just gave way and broke, sending us crashing to the porch floor.

"Damn it! You all, right?" he panted.

"No, I'm not all right. My fucking ass is sore as a hell."

He stared at me.

"But it's got nothing to do with the fall," I cackled.

From that night on, for the rest of the summer, until I went off to college that fall, I was his and only his. By then, of course, there were many stains on my Stetson, so crazy with the heat were we.

TOWER PARK BOYS

Ronald James

Cruising Tower Park one hot summer day, one of the young pretty ones waved me down. I'd picked him up a few times before, a cute kid, slender as a blade of grass, shaggy, dirty blond hair, full lips—but his name? I couldn't recall.

He opened the passenger door and slipped in, shorts riding up a bit: long legs, when he got his height those legs would be up to his neck.

"Guess what?" he asked, big smile on his face.

"What?"

"I can come now!"

"No shit!" Matthew, Matt, his name was Matt. "When did you start?"

"Last month. Wanna see?"

Down went his shorts before I could answer—no underwear —and he began stroking it.

Nice cut cock a little bigger than my middle finger, not a hint of fur, nuts already drawn up in a lightly textured sac, a dream boy.

"Hang on, Matt. Stop!"

He stopped and looked at me.

"Slide over, babe. Let me have some of that."

He slid next to me close as he could and began rubbing my crotch.

"Easy, babe. Sit back up."

I handled his cock, ran my hand down to play with his balls.

"Babe, you are too much."

"This is a great car, a gangster car."

It was a 1976 Sedan de Ville, black inside and out, windows tinted darker, far darker, than allowed by law.

"What did you do with the Seville?"

"Traded it for this. Bucket seats in the Seville made getting close to you too hard. The bench seat makes it easy. And speaking of hard, babe, get my dick out for me."

I pulled away from the curb, heading for some fairly deserted streets I knew of.

Matt unsnapped my trousers and unzipped them.

I rose up a bit and worked them down to my thighs.

"Play with it, Matthew. You know I like it while I drive. That's why I had the windows tinted as dark as they are. Nighttime, dark windows, dash lights out—nobody can see in."

"Nice, babe ... play with my rod ... play with my nuts. Lay across the seat, babe, and put your mouth where it will do some good ... yeah, that way I can play with your beautiful ass while you do me."

So this beautiful near-naked youth stretched across the seat giving me head while I played with his creamy pink ass, really too small to fuck, but too beautiful not to.

"Like me playing with your ass?"

"Yeah ... last time you sucked it."

"I remember."

"You gonna do it again?"

"C'mon, babe, you gonna go back to sucking my cock or do I have to spank your pretty butt?"

Obediently, he went back to my dick, sucking, licking, kissing the head, the shaft down to my nuts, then my nuts. I didn't have to tell him what to do, I just *liked* telling him what to do. I think he liked it too.

"Suck me off, babe. Suck me....!"

"Ummm...." His mouth was full of dick.

"Eat Daddy's balls now. That's good, babe, that's so good... eatin' Daddy's balls, eatin' Daddy's cum-filled nuts. Head, babe, eat the head while I jack it. That's it babe, give Daddy head while Daddy jacks off in babe's mouth. Suck the head, suck my babe makin' dick head while I jack-off in your mouth. Gonna cream in your sweet mouth. Here it comes babe... I'm gonna shoot ... swallow it, babe, swallow it ... here ... here ... oh, oh babe, fuck, oh, fuck ... swallow it babe, swallow it."

I pumped my nuts dry into that sweet, young mouth.

He came off my dick, "Did you like it, babe?" I asked.

"Yeah... want me to jack-off now?"

You want to jack-off or you want me to blow you?"

"A blow job!"

"Okay, we'll go back to the park. We can go into the trees and I'll blow you there, okay?"

"Cool."

We returned to the park, parking on a side street.

"I'll walk into the trees, then you follow."

I crossed the street, entered the park, stopped at the first line of trees. Matthew was just starting across the street in his sneakers and shorts; I'd never seen him in a shirt. As he passed beneath a street lamp, his mass of hair shone momentarily like spun gold.

He joined me and together we moved farther in, farther away from the light.

We stopped when I felt we couldn't be seen. I backed him into a tree, feeling him up then pulled him to me, into my arms, running my hands from his shoulders to his ass, then back against the tree.

On my knees now, I got his shorts down and swallowed his babe cock, squeezing his ass, licking his balls, now sweet dick, nuts, dick, nuts....

"Feel good, babe?"

"I'm ready to shoot."

"Not yet ... not yet ... make it last. Turn around."

He turned bending slightly; I licked his crack, then tongue fucked him. He moaned as I pushed my tongue into his hole.

Twigs cracked. I jumped up facing the sound.

"It's cool man. Don't worry. I been watchin' y'all." A young black approached. Even in the darkness I could see his dick was out.

"I been comin' here ever' night, but I ain't never seen what you be doin'. What you doin' that boy?"

"You've got a big dick," I said.

"Y'all wanna suck it? You sucked his good. You wanna suck mine?"

I hesitated. "How old are you?"

"Ol 'nough."

He was with us now, a circle of sorts.

"Y'all got a big un too?"

I unzipped and pulled it out.

"Yeah...." He reached for it. "Y'all got a big un too."

"Suck me."

"I don't do that."

I reached for him, wrapping my hand around his cock, and began stroking it. I've always been a sucker for jacking uncut cock. The skin moves so easily, like a well-oiled piston, and this was no exception.

"Make you a deal, kid," I said. "Suck my dick and I'll have this pretty little white boy deep throat that big black hose of yours—what do you say?"

"He gona suck it for sure?"

"For sure."

He dropped to his knees.

I guided his head forward. "That's it, take it, suck it....."

After a few moments, my dick slipped from his mouth. "'Nough?"

"Not yet, man. A little more. Suck my cock a little more ... and play with my balls."

His head bobbed between my legs, and his fingers set my balls on fire.

Matt watched at my side, hands at his sides, shorts bunched at his knees, cock still up and ready.

Finally I said, "Enough, man. Enough. Get up, drop your pants, lean against that tree."

He did as he was told,.

"Okay, suck him, Matt. I wanna see you take it all."

"I'm not suckin' no...."

I stopped him in mid sentence. "Come on babe," pleading with him. "Suck it just a little and I'll suck your ass some more. Come on, babe ... we'll have some fun."

He hesitated, then knelt before the black youth.

"Go on, Matt ... just a little."

"You suck my ass?"

"I'll suck your ass, then suck you off."

He took the enormous head of the black's dick in his mouth.

"Oh man!" the black boy shouted as Matthew went to work on that prick. Pretty soon, the black was shouting, Matthew's blow job was so good, as I knew it would be once he got started..

"Quiet, dude!" I warned him. "Quiet! Keep it down."

"Okay man, okay, sorry ... man, I ken get off now."

"No, no. Up, Matt. Get up." I took his place, swallowing the black's thick rod, pulling it back into my throat. Once, twice I took it deep. He placed hands on my head, and he was practically squealing when he came.

"Jesus, man, y'all swallow it?"he asked when he was done.

"Yeah, why?"

"My cousin spit it out."

"You too? You spit it out?"

"Yeah, me too! What you think!"

"Well, what I think is this. I sucked your dick, you sucked my dick, Matt sucked your dick, now you suck off Matt's pretty dick."

"I ain't swallowin'...."

"Then you suck him 'til he's ready to pop, you in front, me behind."

"What you mean?"

"You suck his cock, I eat his ass."

He shook his head. "Man you a for-real faggot!"

I dropped to my knees behind Matthew and the black boy slowly got to his knees in front of the boy.

"Suck him now," I demanded. "Suck that nice white dick."

The boy sucked Matt's cockhead into his mouth while I ate Matthew's sweet ass.

Almost immediately, Matt was hollering, "I'm gonna come." Matt pulled his dick from the black boy's mouth just as I shoved my tongue as far up his ass as I could get it, pulling him back onto it, while he exploded, shooting his jism into the night air. The black boy got his head out of the way just in time.

Then I turned Matthew around, licking up the last bit of cream from his cock.

"Man," said the black boy, standing up, "you crazy for dick ... you be here ever' night?"

"Most every night, why?"

"I be here tomorrow."

I smiled. "I'll meet you, then. But while that hose of yours is still hard, how about jacking it off for me now ... I love to see young dudes get a nut."

He stroked it. "Okay, you watch."

I watched for a couple of moments, then moved closer. I played with his good-sized nuts while he beat off.

"Here it come, man," he screamed at last. "Here it come!"

A long rope of cum shot from his dick. When he finished, I stroked his softening cock, finally licking it until he made me stop.

"I gotta go man." He pulled up his trousers, "You be here tomorrow I'll bring my cousin. You can suck his dick too. He's even bigger 'n me."

"See you tomorrow then."

He disappeared into the trees.

"You meetin' him tomorrow?" Matt asked, pulling himself together.

"Two of them? Are you kidding? Anyway, you feel all the curly that boy had?"

"Yeah, he had a lot."

"You know I like my dick smooth ... like yours. Come on, I'll drive you home."

On the way he asked, "You ever fuck anybody? I mean a guy ... up the ass?"

"You want to get fucked, babe?"

"I'm too little. It'd hurt bad."

"Who told you that?"

"My brothers."

"Brothers? More than one brother?"

"Yeah, they're twins."

"The three of you do dick together?"

"Sometimes ... they're older."

"You gonna let me meet 'em?"

"If you want."

"Maybe later. Know what I want right now?"

"What?"

"I want to meet you tomorrow night. I'll get a room someplace, and you fuck me up the ass. Want to fuck me up the ass, babe?"

"Yeah, cool. Hey, did you pay the black kid?"

"No, babe." I handed him a twenty. "I only pay *you*."

BEYOND BEAUTIFUL
(Or, DANGEROUS WHEN WET)

Lance Rush

Each summer, they'd sit like brawny sun-kissed gods in their high towers, gazing out at the ocean. I'd admired them from the time I realized I liked dick. They were saviors, patrolling the hot, white sands. They were men among men. And in the golden summer of 1979, I became one of them: a lifeguard.

And of all the hot young guards on duty, no one could set my juices boiling quite like Gaetano. The instant I laid eyes on him, cum hummed in my balls, and I proceeded to pop a throbbing 18-year-old boner, the urgent, cock-strong kind of hard-on that defied all the laws of gravity.

Being of black and Italian heritage, Gaetano his skin was a luminous shade of honey. Everyone called him "Guy," he was, to put it simply, beyond beautiful. He stood five-eleven and weighed a sturdy, muscle-packed 185 pounds. An, fascinating to me, he showed a wickedly long protrusion in his red Speedo.

When wet, and lit by a noon day's sun, Guy's buffed body virtually glowed with the hot, oozing, boundless possibilities of steamy sex. But I didn't know which way he leaned. Both women and men had eyes for him. Some even faked drowning in hopes Guy would swim out, wrap a burly arm around them and lead them back to shore. Though dusted in black fur, his torso was a perfect V-shape, similar to my own. I was naturally thin, and needed leg work. But Guy possessed long, hot, hairless legs. His quads and calves were rivals in size. His hamstrings jutted in magnificent bulges. Watching them tense and flex as he used the weight machines would send me dashing for a cold shower.

Late one night, after working out in the weight room, Guy walks in, freshly pumped and hulking with sweat. He looked enormous. There I was standing under ice cold water, my joint showing serious shrinkage. He grinned, pointed at my cock, and said, "God, that water must be cold, man!"

"Yeah? Well, it wasn't so puny a few minutes ago!" I yelled, hoping he'd catch my drift.

"Oh yeah? Well, was it big as this motherfucker, here?" he asked, dipping inside his shorts.

Just then, he yanked the waistband, peeled down his jock, and out it flopped. To simply call it a cock would be a gross understatement. Even in its vaguely turgid state, his tool was one hell of an impressive shank of meat. So big and hot in its natural state, its mold was big and brawny.

"So, junior, was it the size of this one?" he teased.

"Ah .. uh, not hardly," I mumbled, absolutely stupefied. He proceeded to get naked, and stepped under a separate nozzle. Man! Seeing him in the raw made me even hotter for him. The vision has burned in my brain throughout my cock-beating life! Ah: His long downward curve. His large, low, hairless nuts. How his dick tumbled down in a shroud of mahogany skin and gathered into a blunt nipple at the tip. Right then, even under cold water, my stubborn bone betrayed me. In seconds the fucker arched and kept lifting, tilting up until it was hard and vertical. I turned and quickly soaped my ass, hoping he hadn't noticed the bold specter of my erection.

But he had. Hell, who could miss it? From the corner of my eye, he was the hottest thing since sunburn. His taut brown chest glistened like proud armor above washboard abs. Guy was blessed with the kind of muscular thighs, I would've killed for! His naked bubble ass resembled two basketballs fused into one perfect globe. A steady stream drained from his pisshole, down his nuts. It simply wasn't fair. Some guys had all the luck.

As I lathered my butt with my back to him, he drew closer. Soon his beefy body was right next to mine, and I swear I could felt the heat of his eyes on my ass.

"So, after a long shift, you ever, uh, jerk off in here, man?" he asked a slow meandering way.

"Oh, all the time, man. Especially when no one's around. In fact, I'm so horny now..."

Guy shut off his nozzle. I heard the whack of wet prick slapping to his thigh as he said, "Well, turn around, man. Let me see it."

I turned slowly, erect cock punching from my soapy fist, and give him a peek of my stuff.

"Damn, dude! I sure couldn't tell it a few minutes ago, but you've got good size dick on you!" he said, surveying my seven-inch rod. "Man, you're full of surprises!"

I looked down at his dick. It was a long, wet monument. To me, it looked like raw, naked sex incarnate. When he skinned the foreskin back, I gasped. Damn all the beach restrictions, the bullshit rules forbidding sex on the job. I wanted nothing more to suck him off. Now!

And, surprisingly, he seemed to feel the same way too. "C'mon, let's stroke these and see whose shoots the most," he suggested, pulling his cock up his belly. Then he let it slap down his thigh with a wet, sudsy whack.

"Oh ... okay. Sounds ... like ... a ... plan," I panted in agreement, staring at what had to be the hottest dick on the beach. He slowly raked back his foreskin from the awesome cockhead, and played with his cum-packed balls.

Then, smiling slyly my way, he jacked his soggy copper cock with slow, lazy strokes.

Excited, I began in earnest, ruggedly flogging my reddening boner. He watched intently. There was a silent charge between us. We found a kinky rhythm to our strokes. He posed and teased better than all those shiny boys on film and I began jerking off with a vengeance. He was the only fodder I needed. His soap-laden cock was now sliding recklessly in his fist, making hot, whipping noises. Guy spread his brawny legs wide and ran both hands along that stout brown log, beating it, working it white with glossy bubbles. I pretended that big tanned dick was inside me, fucking me raw. I imagined taking it deep up my ass. The pain of it, the heat, the thrust. I closed my eyes and let the fantasy take hold...

But then, Gaetano sort of snaked his hand in back of me, and boldly clutched my wet cheeks. "You gay guys have the best little asses. Real nice. Think you can take a finger or two?"

My eyes shot wide open. Before I could stammer my answer, he was jabbing a long, blunt digit up my chute. I flinched, felt instantly weak. My knees buckled from the anticipated jolt. I dipped down, a breath away from his ripe dark nipples. I grabbed one, twisted. Every muscle flexed as his body vaulted from the pleasure. "Ah! Yes!"

I began sucking his luscious brown man-tits, and he shivered, loving it. His prick banged hard against my belly.

His finger moved deeper inside me, jabbing, stabbing it, making my heated asshole even hotter. He slid his finger out. He slowly guided my lips past his nipples, down his hard pounding belly. I darted my tongue impulsively, licking every well-defined sinew. He gently nudged me further down where his looming dick awaited.

Breathless, I snatched its spongy crown up in a greedy gobble.

"OOOOOhhhhhh!" he cried.

He was so full, warm, with every nerve-ending pulsing, throbbing, twitching on my tongue. I wanted to consume him whole, but that was clearly an impossibility. My throat, my jaws were swollen with meat. Though I'd sucked dick before, I was forced to slurp and gurgle in strange, foreign and noises.

When he lunged, his cock choked me. Pulling back, I massaged his firm bubble ass, gliding the spheres slowly into my motion. He settled into my grip and began a crazed litany: "Oh damn! Suck it, man! Oh yes! Suck my big dick, man! Oh! Aw! Shit, yessss! Ooh! You're good at this!"

I grabbed his swinging balls, forcing one polished orb into my mouth, then quickly lacquering other. His hips spun in erotic waves.

Slowly he eased his cock through my lips again. Now I'm even more aroused by the weight, by the incredible heat of it. Wild animal noises consumed the shower room as I thirstily took on the brunt of that dark, pistoning rod.

I yanked my meat as my spittle ran down his hefty balls. Those hot thighs began trembling. I knew he was bound shoot soon. But I wanted more.

"You close?" I asked, looking up into his eyes.

"Oh! Oh yeah! Real close, man!"

"Don't shoot! Not yet. I ... I want you to fuck me," I whispered.

He was simply too hot to trot to refuse me. I realized it would be a challenge, but one I was willing to take. I stood, and he drew me close. Both our raging young dicks met, in a slow, slick glide. He clutched my cheeks, pulling them apart as he stared into my eyes. He looked so fine, all dripping and wet. I wanted to kiss him, then. But some guys get weird by the mere thought of kissing another man. I did lick his pounding jugular, and I began swerving my body in a slow, churning motion, matching his.

"You really want me to fuck you, man? You think you could take it?" he asked in that warm purr of his, sending two long fingers deep up my wincing chute. I shuddered. "Yes! Oh, shit yeah! I want it!"

He pulled away and spun me around, tapped that cock on my wet ass. It felt so hot, so heavy as he drummed my cheeks. He picked up a bar of soap and lathered his hands and cock.

Then he rubbed the soap inside my twitching hole making me slippery wet. He led his cockhead in real slow. My legs spread wider, and wider. I let out a grunt as the wide head and long, thick shaft plowed through with a sharp and wicked pain. My ass wiggled in mad protest, but he steadied me.

"Shit, you got a big ol' dick!" I howled.

Halfway inside, he paused as I trembled around him. "You want me to stop, huh? Tell me now!" he demanded, panting and throbbing inside me.

"No! Oh no. Please, just give a second," I huffed, taking deeper breaths. He did. He paused. Finally, I was ready: "Go on. Give it to me!"

He eased it inside my gaping passage. My gripping ass walls flinched along every rigid inch of him. Then he pulled back and began to thrust it in and out of my butt.

I ached right down to my knees.

Then he slowed his pace. In, out, in, out he moved, gently, yet efficiently, with a slow yet driving purpose..

"Damn! This is good, man!" he groaned.

"Oh shit, Guy! It's bigger in my ass than it was in my mouth!" I groaned.

All we could do was groan as he worked my hot cock with his soapy fist. I moved my ass, flowing with his every humping gyration. Reaching back, I grabbed one beefy thigh, pulling him in, not wanting to miss an inch. He saw it as a sign of aggression. Immediately his rhythm grew more intense. His hips quickened. His dick lunged full speed. His big galloping balls pounded my aching cheeks so hard.

"Are you close?" he asked.

"Yes! yes! Oh! Damn! I'm gonna, shoot, man!" I cried, cock jumping in his rushing fist.

He tightly squeezed the base, stalling me just at my climactic edge. He pulled that bull's cock from the depths of me, and panted, "Not yet! Let me try suckin' your dick."

He wanted to blow me!? Wide-eyed, I turned, and he dropped before my outstretched prick, My well-fucked ass felt empty without him pulsing there. Soon my mushroom cockhead was in his mouth, then the full length of me entered him.

At this point, even if the whole squad of lifeguards had walked in, I wouldn't have cared; taking such a risk only heightened the excitement.

As his sucking increased in intensity, below me, his cock bobbed and weaved, untouched. Then ... well, it happened. I pushed him away the moment of orgasm. Jism bounded from my slit in high roping arcs, leaping like headlong divers to his chest. He pulled himself off and, soon, he aimed his cock at me and likewise bathed me in his cum.

Well, as you might imagine, Guy and I bonded that summer. We became two sweat-slicked buddies, patrolling the warm, treacherous shores by day; drowning in our cum by night.

WHITE-HOT

David MacMillan

I gripped the steering wheel and collapsed against the seat. I couldn't believe everything that was happening to me all at once. It was Friday, and school was finally out. I had just turned eighteen. My parents were letting me spend June with my English cousins. I had only three weeks before I graduated from high school. I'd finally made it—I wasn't a kid any more. I watched the convertible top rise and the white-hot sky spread above me.

"Hey, Alec! Wait up!"

I turned to face the sprawling, single-story brick schoolhouse I had just left and saw Tommy Taylor trotting across the pavement toward me.

Tommy and I had become good buddies at school. He was really cool: open, unaffected, friendly. He was also several months older than me, but wasn't stuck up about it.

He had the nuttiest Bible-pounders in the county for parents, and most of the guys at school felt sorry for him ... and we went out of our way to cover for him so they didn't know he was being normal when out of their sight. Tommy Taylor was also the best-looking boy in our school and I was too aware of it, even if he wasn't. I even imagined him naked when I jacked off.

"I sure hoped I'd catch you, Alec," he said as he reached the car and gripped the passenger door to look in at me. "I missed my bus. Think you could give me a ride home?"

I nodded and watched him slide onto the seat next to mine. "Just give me directions," I told him and started the car. I wished I could see him nude on the car seat as I had seen him in gym. Just once. Far from prying eyes. With a hard-on.

"I'd do anything to be in your shoes next month," he said as we passed the city limits. "I'd be away from this bullshit ... and I sure wouldn't come back," he growled and looked out at a field of corn as we approached it.

"Not anything," I chuckled.

"I would too. Anything ... but kill somebody ... or hurt them for no reason."

"You wouldn't suck somebody off ... or let them fuck you?"
I pressed.

Silence grew between us as we passed the corn field, a copse of pine trees, and a cotton field. I finally forced myself to glance over at him and found him watching me.

"Maybe ... if everything felt right about it."

"Tommy Taylor!" I stared at him in shock.

"Get your eyes back on the road, Alec. I want you to be alive when you get back from England."

"Tommy, you can't mean...?"

He laughed. "Which one of us do you think has the bigger dick?"

"Jesus Christ!" I groaned above the wind racing past us. I already knew who had the biggest one. I did. We had had gym together the past four years and I had practically drooled every one of those days when we were in the showers. He had a nice fat piece of meat. But, soft, it was a solid two inches shorter than mine. It didn't take a rocket scientist to project lengths out to erections.

"I'll bet you a blow job I'm bigger than you are."

I stared at him and only pulled my eyes back to the road when he reached over and put his hand on the steering wheel. I was cold and clammy all over. "What do mean bigger ... length or width?" I asked quietly.

"You call it, Alec. I'll let it be your call all the way."

I could feel the heat of my blush spreading across my scalp. "Where?"

"Let's go swimming," he suggested and smiled at me. "I know a real quiet place not too far from where I live."

I stared at column after column of pine trees and heard the breeze soughing through their boughs above us. I hadn't seen a house for miles. "You come here often, Tommy?" I asked as we pulled to a stop. I was beginning to wonder if he had really meant it when he said he'd go bobbing between my legs.

"Enough, I guess."

"Where's this swimming hole you mentioned?"

"Just the other side of the trees." He opened the door and hopped out, and I was keenly aware of him standing there and staring back at me. I turned and was looking directly into his eyes. "We still got our bet?" he asked and my heart was back in my throat.

"You really want to suck me off, Tommy?"

"You want me to? Really?"

I stared at him, my jaw sort of falling and my eyes getting wider. "Yeah ... I guess I could get into that."

He grinned. "Okay, then, I'll suck you off. You want anything else while you're at it?"

My jaw fell some more and my eyes started bulging out of my head. I was sure I wasn't hearing him right. "You being funny ... or something?" I demanded.

"Nah ... you want a piece of my ass to go along with that blow job?"

I stared at him in shock. "What're you sayin'?"

"Do you want it?"

"I guess so. Why?"

"I got me a need, Alec. A real itch."

I stared at him. "You've done it before?"

"My cousin's banged my butt every day the last several months ... only, well, he joined the army last week and I've been hurting ever since."

"You're saying you're queer?"

"I'm saying I like a big dick to help me out now and then." He smiled again. "I hope you aren't gonna spread this around town."

"Shit!"

He laughed. "C'mon then. We're standing here getting hotter by the minute and I'm betting you've got what it takes to cool me down!"

I was numb as I climbed out of the car and obediently followed him in among the pine trees. I could see his butt as he walked in front of me and something inside me kept telling me it was damn cute as it stretched and rode his jeans. I was hard as hell knowing I was about to get it on with this lad. I wondered what it'd be like to fuck him.

He pulled off his shirt and sat down on a stump near the edge of a slowly moving stream and pushed his shoes off his feet. He looked over at me and smiled hesitantly. "You don't mind helping a buddy out, do you, Alec?" he asked.

I shook my head as I forced myself to look out at the stream flowing past us and felt the solitude of this place.

"Is this where you and your cousin came?" I asked.

"Yeah. It was pretty good, too. I hope it can be that way for us while I've got you here."

I pulled my T-shirt over my head and turned to look at him. He was naked already and I let my eyes travel over his smooth, compact body and wasn't surprised to find myself wanting to touch it and feel it against me. His pole stuck straight out of a mass of curly hair and was smaller than mine by a good inch but just as thick. I knew suddenly he had been banking on that. He had been planning all along to go for what he was hoping I'd do for him. I grinned then, all doubts forgotten.

I smiled and shoved my jeans over my hips. My briefs followed them quickly to the ground and I was stepping out of them naked as the day I was born and harder than I could remember being. I saw his eyes were glued to my favorite part of myself and I grinned even more broadly. "You like what you see?" I asked.

He nodded his head slowly. "You got a nice one all right ... you do yourself up proud." His eyes came up to mine. "Can I hold it?"

I shrugged and he came closer and took it in his hand. He jacked it a couple of times, staring down at it and the way the skin moved up over its helmet and peeled back easily as his hand started for my balls.

"I thought you wanted to do more than just touch it," I mumbled in anticipation of having a man swing on my meat.

"You want me to suck you off now?" he asked, his eyes searching mine for some answer I didn't know the question to.

"Yeah." I smiled at the sensations his fingers on my rigid pole were giving me. "I think I'd like that."

He dropped to his knees in front of me. One moment he was standing before me and the next he was kneeling. He pushed the skin back and stared at the angry red head of my dick. "It's been so fucking long," he groaned and I watched as my dick disappeared between his lips. His tongue greeted each new inch as he pulled me into him and I shivered with excitement.

He buried his nose into the mat of dark hair that grew at the base of my meat and his hands went to my naked asscheeks. Both of his hands quickly gripped my butt so he could direct my pole's movement against his tonsils and down his throat.

My mind switched off and I gave myself up to the sensations spreading over me from my dick and what he was doing to it.

My balls tightened in their sac instantly and his fingers dug into my crack. "Jesus!" I grunted and humped his face harder. His fingers caressed and kneaded my backside and I couldn't believe how good my pole was beginning to feel and how that was making me feel all over.

Tommy could make a vacuum behind his lips the physics teacher at school would have loved to patent if she had known about it.

His hands began to travel familiarly over my abdomen, and then, my chest, and I knew I'd be hard-pressed to find anybody in this world who could make me feel as good as he was making me feel right then.

Too soon, my balls rode the underside of my mast and rumbled with the load I was ready to shoot. I had both my hands on his head, guiding his movement on my dick, and couldn't imagine ever letting him go.

I shut my eyes and pushed away from him as my first blast barreled down my dick. It hit him between the eyes. I jerked and convulsed like somebody was feeding electricity directly to my balls. He bent his head and came up underneath my spurting rod and started to lick my balls. Tommy's fingers wrapped around my shaft and squeezed me dry. I pulled away from him and pushed him away at the same time. I stared down at him full of awe and surprise.

He licked his lips and grinned back at me. "You liked it?"

"That...!" I stared at the boy still kneeling before me and knew then that I thought he was bloody cute. His face was impish, his body was tight and nice, and his butt was two cute bubbles. I grinned when I realized I'd be between them and feeling them up close before the day was out.

I stepped back and laughed. "Don't let what you just did get around town ... or you're going to have every guy in the county asking for a chance to come out here with you."

"I didn't want anybody but you, Alec." His eyes were on mine and his voice was quiet. As I met his eyes, I felt like I was falling into a bottomless chasm of warmth and friendliness.

"What makes me so special?"

"You." He grinned. "Remember, we've been putting out the school paper for the better part of a year now. You've just got the warmest, sweetest personality I ever saw in a boy."

I took a step toward him and didn't understand why. I had my blowjob from him. Almost any other boy in town would be climbing into his clothes and running to his car. And, later, most of them would let everybody around know about the queer who had sucked him off.

Only, I liked Tommy. I realized I thought his body was better than nice. I wanted it against mine. I wanted to touch him and was pretty sure I could get into sucking him. I wanted to fuck him. Only, I didn't just want to stick my rod into his butt. Tommy had picked me ahead of every one of them. I wanted to make love to him.

"You are my best and most special buddy," I told him. "What you just did, what we both just did, was a lot more than just you sucking me off. We *made love* just then ... and, if you want it, we'll *make love* again."

He seemed to loved the way I added emphasis to the words. "You mean it?" He pulled himself between us and his cock dueled mine between our bodies.

"Yeah, I mean it," I answered and wondered at where I was getting all these insane thoughts.

"Then hold me, Alec."

I didn't hesitate; my arms went around his back and pulled him hard against me. He lay his head on my shoulder and relaxed while his meat stayed hard against my stomach.

He pulled away and looked up into my face. "When you screw me, would you let me face you ... at least, the first time?"

The look on my face must have shown him how puzzled I was. "I mean, you can fuck me like a hound dog mounting a bitch in heat or you can face me between my legs. I want to face you ... I want to see your face when you're plugging that dong of yours into my butt the first time."

"We'll do it the way you want to, Tommy," I told him. I was hard just from touching him. "How about us both cooling off and having some fun?" I let go of his arms and started toward the stream at a trot.

We swam and played for quite a while and my thoughts repeatedly returned to what we had done on the shingle of sand earlier. I actually *liked* holding him against me. I liked the feel of his rod hard against my stomach. I liked the way he placed his head so trustingly on my shoulder.

His hand on my shoulder brought me back from my thoughts into the reality that he offered me. And I was looking into all that warmth that were his eyes. "What're you thinking, Alec?" he asked quietly. He grinned. "Don't lie. It may have been months ago, but I can still remember some of the things going through my head after my cousin talked me into it that first time."

I shrugged. "I was thinking how tight you're going to be."

He chuckled. "Alec, I'm not asking you to do nothing but sit back and get your rocks off. What I'm asking isn't queer. There isn't a boy in town who wouldn't let me suck him off or who wouldn't dick my ass if he thought I'd let him ... and none of them is queer I know of. So, what we do isn't gonna make you anything but what you already are."

I grinned. "Sounds reasonable to me."

"It is." He smiled and his fingers found my hip on their way to my cock. "And, right now, I'd sure like some of that loving we were talking about a bit earlier." I was hard against his hand.

"You really want me to fuck you?"

"I sure as shit do. Shit, man, I got an itch up my ass I need your dick to scratch. C'mon." He started toward the bank.

I grinned. "I've got a feeling I'm going to like this," I mumbled as I followed after him.

He yanked his wallet from his jeans and took out a foiled packet. He glanced back at me and smiled. He stepped to a patch of pine needles where he dropped to his knees. "Come here," he commanded.

When I reached him, he licked my helmet well before his lips slid down the shaft. He leant back on his haunches and tore open the packet. He smiled up at me as he unrolled the condom along my dick.

Tommy lay back. "Do I need to give you directions or can you figure it out from here?" he asked as I squatted at his feet and looked down at him from between his splayed knees.

"I doubt it'll be too hard." I grinned back at him. He raised his legs and I reached out to take them at the ankles. My hands slipped down his calves as he laid his feet on my shoulders.

His ankles crossed behind my neck as my hands traveled down the back of his thighs. He grinned as I leaned into him to raise his ass off the pine straw and bring it closer to my throbbing dick.

His fingers found it and guided it to his asslips. "Last chance to back out, virgin boy," he grunted as my cockhead found his pucker.

I leaned farther into him and felt those lips spread in welcome as my meat started to sneak between them. "That feels good," he moaned beneath me and his hands grabbed my backside to pull me into him. "Oh, yeah ... so fucking good!"

I looked down my chest and saw his ballsack and, behind that, less than half an inch of my dick connecting him and me. Almost eight inches of me was deep into his guts.

"You're starting to scratch my itch good," he mumbled and wiggled his butt around on me.

"Sweet Jesus!" he grunted, and I watched in amazement as he blew a load without touching himself.

"You gonna do something with that dick you got shoved up my butt?" he asked a moment later and looked up between his legs at me in anticipation.

"You seemed to be having fun all by yourself ... I didn't want to interrupt you."

He chuckled. "Well, now, I'm ready for us to have some fun together! Start humpin' me, Alec."

I began to pull away, but his hands stopped me after only a few inches and pulled me back into him. We established a pattern with that first tentative movement. He directed my movement in his ass with his hands firmly on my buttocks. My thoughts turned off and I bumped and ground and humped him as he wanted me to, as he was directing me to with his hands on my ass.

He grunted and tried to grind against me with each new downstroke. "Give me all of it," he ordered. "All of it! Fast and hard!"

He leaked continuously. All I could think of was how tight his ass was on my dick as it moved in and out of him. My balls crashed again and again against his bubbled backside as I shoved as deep as I could into that hot creamy tightness that pulled at my rod as his throat had done when he was sucking on it.

"I can't believe it but I'm gonna blast another load!" he cried.

I looked down in time to see a rope of hot cum hurl over his chest toward his face. It struck him on the cheek and, with a whoop, Tommy scooped it up and plopped it into his mouth.

"Oh, shit, yeah!" he groaned and grabbed his balls with the hand he had freed from guiding my ass. His finger inched down below his sack to touch the top of my dickshaft as it moved in and out of his hole.

My balls tightened and rode high on the underside of my mast as I crept over the edge into my own orgasm. I looked down into glassy eyes staring unseeingly into mine as I pressed hard into him and ground my thatch against his asslips and shot my own load into him.

"Oh God!" I moaned and ground my hips until I didn't have any more in me. I fell against him then and gasped until my breathing finally returned to normal. His lips nuzzled my cheeks as my softening dick slipped out of him. His fingers slipped down to my backside and made concentric circles over them.

"You like it?" he whispered against my ear.

"Oh, yeah ... hmmm ... that was better than fine."

"Well, then, I guess you're gonna be giving me a ride every day from school then?"

I smiled ... and nodded.

TALLY HO, TEENS

Peter Gilbert

"...You're a cheeky boy. Drop your pants ... and those. That's right. Come and lie over my knee."

I remember the day it started as clearly as if it was yesterday. In fact it was ... let me see ... I'm thirty-six now and I was sixteen then. My God, twenty years ago! Unbelievable.

It was an oppressively hot day, but we were out anyhow, on the trail of a particularly crafty one. In retrospect I can honestly say that I have never known a boy like that one. We were tired, dusty and thirsty. The batteries in the hunting buggy were almost flat. We'd been after him for hours. We'd spot him in the distance; dash towards him—only to see him some considerable way away—often in the direction we'd just come from. International Hunting Rules were stricter then than they are now. You had to be near enough to the quarry to be able to dispatch him instantaneously with one shot. Shots in the distance indicated that others in the party were having more luck than we were.

Not for the first time, I cursed the Hunt Master for assigning me to Ralph and Alan. It was obvious that they didn't want me with them either. They were renowned for never bagging anything. The two guys I'd been with on previous weekends were quite different. They were both superb shots and I learned so much from them. It was from them I learned that our sport is not just of value to the community. It's art in the highest form and well practiced skill rolled into a series of sublime experiences. It was from them that I learned to appreciate the beauty of a naked boy. I'd stand up on the balcony of the hunting club with them looking down at the milling crowd in the pen and they'd tell me how to spot a boy who'd give the best sport. The best boys, they said, had long legs for running and a slim but not thin build. A tight, jutting butt was a good indication of stamina and there should be some sort of expression in the eyes. The ones who stared listlessly and who stood still were probably resigned to their fate and anxious to get it over with as soon as possible. The best boys had a wily, sly expression and spent a long time whispering to the others—which gave us time to appraise their physiques.

Now, I guess it may be that you, like my buddy Keith Miller, think it's a cruel sport. The obvious answer to that is to ask you what's better—to keep criminals in penitentiaries for years and years like they used to in the old days, or let them provide enjoyment? Believe me, there is nothing so enjoyable as hunting; especially teen hunting. They enjoy it too and there's always a chance—okay, not much of a chance—that a boy will get to the boundary fence and once his hand's are on that, he's free. Not one of the boys they selected ever got near the fence. They were uncanny. They'd watch the direction the boy sprinted in when the gate went up; we'd wait for the statutory three hours and then go after him. Trevor, the oldest of the two, could bring a running boy down at 150 yards. It was describing a day I'd spent with them that led to the rift in my friendship with Keith.

Keith Miller was a welfare assistant at school. He'd chosen to do that instead of compulsory military service. If you lost a button, had some sort of problem you wanted to talk about, you drifted down to Keith's little office. He was, I guess, about twenty-two. One day (and the memory is as clear as if it were yesterday), I took my copy of *Tally Ho Teens!* to show him. I think I must have been about thirteen. I'd only just joined the club and was still practicing on rabbits. *Tally Ho Teens* was my favorite magazine. It combined all the elements I've told you about. Some of the reports of hunting parties were really exciting. The photos were good too. They were generally carefully posed shots of boys, showing you the best places to aim for but they were, nonetheless, beautifully artistic.

Keith said something about hunting being a sublimation of lust and how our rifles were penis substitutes. I took no notice.

"What about this one?" I said opening the center spread. The caption was on the other side so I lifted it slightly and read it for him.

'John Mayhill (pictured overleaf on the previous day) gave the members of the Green Vale Hunt a worthwhile run on June 21st. Despite the heat, the 17-year-old firearms offender and thief covered eleven miles before being stopped with a perfect shot through the heart by Hunt Master Peter Cribbold."

"He's beautiful, isn't he?" I said. John had been photographed from the front and back. His hands were secured behind his back and his ankles were linked by a short length of chain. I'd studied that picture pretty carefully at home so I knew every detail by heart; his convict-cropped hair and his thick lipped mouth. He had that defiant stare that still turns me on.

"Did you ever see a cock like that?" I said. John had a really thick bush and a cock as thick as a broomstick, which hung down to a point only a few inches above his knee.

"I prefer them younger," said Keith.

"Do you?" I asked, eagerly. I thought I'd made a convert. My two mentors had little time for boy hunting. According to them, boys didn't give much sport. They lacked the stamina to run far and lacked that wily quality that every teen seems to have. More often than not, they didn't go out if there was a boys-only hunt on. We'd go down and look at them, of course. Some boys at that young age are *really* pretty and make attractive trophies. Paul Marsh in our club specializes in boys and he's got some really beautiful heads in his trophy room.

All this I explained to Keith. "I could introduce you to Paul," I said. "He's a really nice guy. I'm sure he'd take you out with him. There's a boy hunt at the end of this month."

"Why go out and hunt one?" said Keith. He stood up, walked over to the door and turned the key. Then he came back and sat on couch next to me. He took the magazine out of my hands and looked at the picture for some moments before he spoke. "What would you like to do with him?" he asked. I stammered something about not having much of a chance to bag a boy like that.

"But if you did...."

"Well, I'd cut his head off, of course. I've got a superb hunting knife. I haven't used it yet."

"I guess you've got something else equally superb which you haven't used yet," said Keith.

"Like what?" I asked and jumped as his hand landed on my groin.

"This," he said.

I knew I ought to tell him to keep his hands to himself. I knew that sort of thing was illegal. Whether it was as a result of the pressure or looking at the picture I didn't know, but my cock started to rise in my jeans. Worse still; Keith felt it.

"I thought so," he said in a low voice. "Now then, let's just forget hunting for a moment. Suppose someone were to let you do anything you like to John Mayhill when he was alive. Let's assume that he's manacled like he is in the photo. Then what?"

I was lost from that moment. It was almost as if he knew the secret thoughts I'd enjoyed in my bedroom with that picture spread open in front of me.

"Well, I'd ... I'd...."

"What?"

"Play with his cock." I said it in one breath.

"Good for you. Good for him too. I guess he'd like that and just imagine it going stiff in your hand. That's a great sensation."

I did nothing to stop him. He undid my buckle, slid my fly down and groped for a few seconds before bringing it out into the open. "Beautiful!" he exclaimed and began, very gently, to slide the foreskin up and down. His touch was infinitely better and more effective than my own solitary pumping efforts. I began to feel light-headed and, somehow, all my fears, all my inhibitions, seemed to vanish. In my imagination I was licking John Mayhill's fuzz-covered thighs, moving up slowly to his huge balls.

"And then I'd take hold of his cock," I gasped.

"Why not?" said Keith. He took hold of my right wrist and placed my hand on his fly. I could feel his shaft throbbing under the material. It took some time to bring it out into the light. I'd never seen an erect, adult cock before that very moment. I remember wondering when mine would take on that strange banana-bend. Now that I've seen a good few, I can honestly say that Keith's was the most peculiar penis. I didn't know that then. I peeled his foreskin back, a process that he seemed to find painful at first.

"You can suck it ... if you want," he said.

I didn't want.

"Oh go on, boy. It feels great," he said.

For a few minutes I managed to convince myself that it was John Mayhill's giant member which was causing my jaw to ache but then I choked and gave up the attempt. Keith lowered his head onto my lap. That was different. Very different. I just left this world. For a second or two he was John Mayhill. Then he reverted to being Keith. After that my mind was full of images of boys in pens, all with erections and waiting their turn to do whatever I commanded. Several of them were my seniors at school; boys I had never seen naked but whose genitalia I had feverishly conjured up in the dead of night when it was too dark to find someone suitable in *Tally Ho Teens!*.

I don't even remember the final moment. I was dimly aware of Keith sitting upright again and wiping his mouth with a handkerchief. My heart was pounding and I was panting as if I'd just run a race.

"I guess I'd better get back. We've got Mr. Wolfe and he gets mad if you're late," I said. Keith said he guessed so too. I never felt so guilty or so worried in my life as I was when I left his office. Not one word of Mr. Wolfe's lesson went in. I felt as if I'd gone through a door and found myself on the brink of a precipice. The door had closed behind me and there was no way back. Instead of dreaming about boys that night, the same theme returned, only that time I actually started falling.

But I went back for more. I knew it was wrong. Men who did what they called "sexual things" with boys ended up as trophies but, according to the reports in *Man Hunt* and the other magazines for adult-hunters who had "lured the boy" to their homes or offices. This boy, it seemed, went willingly. I hoped that might make a difference. It wasn't long before we both ended up naked and lying on Keith's sofa clutching each other, feeling each other and sometimes even kissing. And I have to say, in all honesty, that I loved every minute and everything we did. I loved licking up Keith's thighs until I got to his balls and then sucking them into my mouth one after the other. After that I took his cock into my mouth. That wasn't so easy but I knew that, if I kept on long enough, he would do the same to me.

Months turned into years, and my hunting skills greatly improved. What Keith used to refer to as my "little rosebud" turned into something as thick as a young tree with a mulch of hair at its base. My "dear little balls" got bigger and delivered their load more quickly and more copiously. More importantly, my guilt dissipated. I became able to enter a classroom and say "Sorry I'm late, Mr. Wolfe. I was with Mr. Miller and didn't notice the time," without blushing.

Naturally I never told anyone about Keith. I'd gotten really fond of him but never even mentioned his name at school and certainly not in the hunting club. I'd learned that Keith was one of what the hunt members called the "Welfare Weirdos"—the people who patrolled the perimeter fence at night hoping to find a convict who had survived and made it to the fence. International Hunting Law said that once a runner had a hand on the fence he was free. Free for Keith and his buddies to try to rehabilitate.

One day I was lying on the sofa in Keith's room as usual, wiping his spunk off my belly. There was no hurry to get dressed that day. He'd sent a note to the teacher saying that I was unwell. "How about spending next weekend over at my apartment," he said. "Would your parents agree?"

"There's no need to tell them where I am these days," I said.

"That's great. We can have a real good time."

"We have a good enough time in here," I said.

"Yeah ... but what I have in mind is best done slowly."

There was no doubt in my mind as to what was in his. For almost a year he'd worked on my asshole with his fingers and, on that particular day, with his tongue as well. That had been a mind-blowing experience. Half of me welcomed the prospect. The other half wondered if that extraordinary bent cock would be painful. I guessed that he wanted to screw me at home so nobody would hear me yell. Fortunately I had a watertight excuse. I said I'd love to but there was a hunt planned that weekend.

"Couldn't you miss it for once? I've already laid in extra food," he said.

I said that was a bit premature. He ought to have asked me first. Then he became totally unreasonable. I couldn't believe what I was hearing. I was uncaring and selfish. I was unreliable. There had been days when I promised to pay him a visit but never turned up. I tried to explain that it was difficult sometimes. I'd get involved in something and couldn't say, "Sorry guys, I have to see Mr. Miller."

"Excuses, excuses. You only think of yourself, don't you? You're quite happy to leave a buddy just to go off and get your kicks by killing some poor sod!"

"But, Keith, listen. You'll be busy yourself that weekend with your border patrol," I said, trying to keep the discussion rational.

"I've already arranged for someone else to take my place. I thought you'd like for us to be together. I thought you were my friend."

There was no point in continuing. I got dressed and left him. That time Mr. Wolfe did notice that something was wrong but when he'd elicited the fact that I'd been with Mr. Miller and made a few sarcastic remarks to the rest of the class about people who couldn't manage their own lives, he shut up and the day continued normally.

I was upset though. I still was when I arrived at the Hunting Club and my misery was made even worse when the Hunt Master told me I'd be with Alan and Ralph. You're not allowed to go out on your own till you're eighteen. It's too risky. Someone made a joke about sending out a truck to collect the trophies they were sure to bag and someone else advised me to stand well clear if one of them as much as raised a gun. Feeling utterly fed up, I went down to the pen to find them.

Since getting to know Keith, I tried to spend as little time as possible at the pen. My secret thoughts had a tendency to come to the surface and have a visible effect, if you know what I mean. There were about a hundred of them that day. Some nice ones too. The sight of all those legs and swaying cocks made me wonder if I might have been better off with Keith after all. I introduced myself to Alan and Ralph. Alan shook my hand. Ralph didn't. Totally different from my previous mentors who made me feel really welcome. These two ignored me and resumed looking through the thick, double fence.

"Nice ass on that one in the corner," said Alan.

"Spoiled by the scar on his face," said Ralph. He had a point. The boy concerned—from his dense bush and the line of hair leading up to his navel, I guessed him to be about seventeen—was beautifully built. He had the butt and legs of a good runner but it was highly unlikely that his head, mounted on a shield, would send any connoisseur of boy beauty in raptures. It was also, as I knew too well, very unlikely that either Alan or Ralph would get near enough to dispatch him, so the conversation was purely theoretical. The one they should have gone for was a rather pretty young one. There was something wrong with his right leg. He walked with a decided limp. They could have got him easily and he had a really pretty face. I couldn't say anything of course. I just let them indulge in their dreams.

"What about the blond, that one talking to the Afro-American?" said Ralph. "He's really nice."

He was too. Seventeen, maybe just eighteen and tall. His legs were superb—probably the most graceful legs I'd ever seen— and his butt was perfectly round. It gleamed in the morning sun. Probably conscious of the fact that he was being talked about, he turned to face us.

"Wow! That's decided me!" said Ralph. "What an incredible cock!"

Now, cock sizes are a good indication of age but not of a boy's potential. I guessed that Ralph was one of those people who kept pickled cocks as trophies instead of heads. There had been an article in *Tally Ho Teens* that told the reader how to do it, but I'd never met anyone who actually had. Being as inept as everyone said he was, he wouldn't have had to spend much on preserving fluid and jars.

"That's the one for me," he said with all the confidence in the world. "What about you?"

"I've already chosen," said Alan.

"Who?"

"I'll tell you later. Hello. Starters orders."

Two men came out of the club house. They looked at their watches simultaneously, then at the clock on the tower. The boys stopped talking. Some of them got down into start positions. One man nodded to the other and the gate went up. There was a terrific rush. I felt the wind on my face as they streamed out, separating soon after they were through the gate. Some pairs stayed together but very few. Soon they were specks on the horizon and then there was nothing. Just a vast, empty landscape.

We went into the club house for the usual ceremonies and the compulsory wait. The Hunt Master read out the

International Hunting Rules. We all confirmed that we knew them. The club chaplain prayed that the boys would find forgiveness for their sins in heaven. He's an interesting man. He's a crack shot and only goes for really little boys. Once a kid's got a bit of hair round his cock, the Rev. Simpson loses interest. He uses his trophies in his Sunday School. I'd forgotten all about his lessons until the business with Keith started. It was probably one of his lessons that made me feel so guilty.

"This is Tim," he said, holding up the head so that we could all see it. "Tim did dirty things. Nasty things. Tim let men play with his private parts. He was just ten years old. Can you imagine that, boys and girls? He's better off dead. Now we'll put him back in his case and sing a hymn."

Alan and Ralph went to the bar. Most members were out on the verandah checking their guns. I did the same. My last mentors were there.

"Why, it's our old buddy. Sorry you're not with us this time," said Trevor. I explained that the Hunt Master had reallocated me.

"So I heard," said Trevor. "They asked for you apparently."

That staggered me. I said there must have been a mistake. It was obvious that they regarded me as a nuisance. Unfortunately, our Hunt Master was a retired general and hardly the sort of guy a 16-year-old can complain to. It would have to wait till the following Monday and I'd get my dad to call him. Knowing that this would be my last hunt with Alan and Ralph made me feel better.

The time ticked by. The buggies were all lined up for us. Most people checked the batteries. Ralph and Alan didn't appear so I checked ours. They didn't come out until about five minutes before the start by which time most people were sitting in the buggies and raring to go. I helped them load their gun cases and took the jump seat. The Hunt Master appeared with his starting gun. He too, looked at his watch and the clock. Then he fired and we were off.

Ralph's boy had apparently run due west, which gave us both disadvantages and advantages. A boy against the setting sun is a good target. On the other hand the very sun, that illuminates the boy blinds the hunter. There was no word of where Alan's boy had gone. I just sat back and felt miserable again. We were going to travel for miles and miles and come back empty-handed.

We'd gone about fifteen miles when I spotted a movement on a rock ledge. It was sheer luck. I just happened to be looking in that direction. I pulled out my binoculars and, with some difficulty, focused on the spot. A boy was crouching up there holding his head in his hands.

I got Alan to stop the buggy and passed the glasses to him. "Not ours," he said.

I was astounded. This wasn't just single-mindedness. It was sheer stupidity. We could have got him so easily. You're not permitted to fire at a boy if he's not moving but we could have started him with a shot to the rocks behind him and then he'd have been a good sideways on target—good for someone who knew how to shoot. Trevor would have got him with a shot through the buttocks to spin him round and then one through the heart. I'd have loved to have had a go at him but the rules said that boys under eighteen could accompany hunters but not kill. My function was to cut the head off and I knew all too well that my brand new hunting knife was going to remain in its sheath.

We set off again. I turned round in my seat to watch the boy. He'd raised his head and was staring, as well he might, at the dust cloud behind us. He was out of sight when we heard a gun go off twice in rapid succession. Someone with more skill had obviously spotted him.

The day wore on. We stopped to eat our packed lunch. The sun was getting stronger and stronger and I was feeling more and more miserable. We set off again. Ralph looked at his watch. "Somewhere near here. In those rocks I guess," he said.

"What makes you so sure?" I hoped that he would detect the sarcasm in my voice.

"Mixture of powerful running and walking. Six hours since he was let out. Average speed for a frightened lad of his build would be about seven miles per hour. He's going for the boundary. He's exhausted now. He's done forty-five miles. Figure on the clock just forty-five miles and he's too tired to make any significant progress. He's as good as mine."

"Ha!" I thought. I might even have said it. I don't know. We stopped by the big rock outcrop and searched it thoroughly but there was no trace of the quarry. We'd just got down to the buggy when I spotted him. The winter rains draining off the rock had carved a sort of gully in the earth below. He'd covered himself with earth but some of it had rolled off his butt. If it hadn't been for those few flecks of pure white I wouldn't have spotted him in a thousand years. The very attribute that Ralph had admired gave the boy away. I nudged Ralph, who grinned and put a finger to his lips. He went to the buggy and opened his gun case. I was about to throw a stone to start the lad but Alan restrained me and shook his head.

Shocked so much that I couldn't move, I watched Ralph approach the gully. He put the gun to his shoulder and fired. Not a sitting target. A lying down target! I was astounded. It only needed a report to the Hunt Master to have him drummed out of the club and banned from hunting for the rest of his life.

Then common sense returned. The report of the gun hadn't been the eardrum ringer I was used to and the splash of gore you'd expect from a shot at that close range hadn't appeared either.

All three of us went to the gully. In his final spasm the boy had shaken off most of the earth. He lay there quite still and apparently intact. For a moment I thought Ralph had missed and then I saw it. A tiny little red-feathered dart was stuck in his right buttock. A stun-gun dart.

"And now what?" I said, expecting Ralph to get out a real gun and finish him off. He didn't.

"I'm not taking his head off until he's dead," I said. "That's final and when we get back...."

"His head is staying firmly in place," said Alan. "Now then. Where? That's the question?"

"Up on top of the outcrop. Nobody will see us up there and we'll spot anyone coming," said Ralph, and Alan, for some reason I didn't understand, found this amusing. He and Ralph went down into the gully. Ralph pulled out the dart and took hold of the boy's arms. Alan took his legs and they lifted him out.

"What are you going to do with him?" I asked, still fearing that yet another flagrant breach of the rules was going to be committed and I had no wish to be any part of it.

"We're not going to harm him. I promise," said Alan. "You'd better lead the way. He's heavy."

So, against my better judgment, I did so. The outcrop wasn't very high. Twenty feet at most and the path leading to the top wasn't very steep. Nonetheless, the two of them were panting when they finally laid the boy down on his back.

"He's certainly a good one," said Alan, fingering the boy's cock. For a dreadful moment I feared he might ask to borrow my knife.

"So, now he's up here, would one of you mind explaining what you're going to do?" I asked.

"We're going to drive him to the boundary fence," said Alan.

"What? Set him free?" I said.

"That's right. Later. After dusk."

"What about the one you chose?" I asked. "When are we going after him? It's getting late."

"Oh I don't need to go after him. He's here."

"Oh, I see. You chose the same...."

"No."

"Then what..?"

"You're Keith Miller's friend, aren't you?"

"How did you know?"

"Keith told us. You're the boy in Mr. Wolfe's class who likes lying on Keith's sofa. 'The most beautiful boy in the school.' That's what Keith said. And willing too by all accounts."

"The bastard. What an utter bastard! Wait till I get back to school on Monday. I'll sew him up good and proper. I'll have his head on someone's wall before the month is up."

Alan put his hand on my shoulder. "Don't get the wrong idea," he said. "Keith never told us your name. He wouldn't. But when he said that there was one boy in the school interested in hunting and that he was a member of this club, we put two and two together. In fact, to be honest, we didn't think you would be here for this hunt. Keith said you wouldn't come."

"Because he'd cottoned on to our plan," said Ralph. "Keith isn't into sharing whereas we are."

"In a big way," said Alan, bending down to feel the boy's flaccid cock again. "As you will see," he added.

Anger gave way to curiosity. "How?" I asked. Watching him finger it had made my cock stir.

"This lad is strong and powerfully built, eh?" he said.

"Er ...yeah. I guess he is," I replied, staring down at the boy's heaving chest.

"Just right for a boy of your age to work on," said Alan. "Not many of them have cocks like this. This is a real beauty. You'd like to have a taste of it, wouldn't you?"

I nodded. I couldn't speak. Ralph left us at that moment and for some reason I felt even more apprehensive. With good reason. Alan stood up and put his hand on my butt. "And you're just right for me to work on," he said squeezing my buns. "This is just how I like them. Soft but tight. You're going to be good."

I think I might have said, "Fuck off," or at least offered some sort of resistance but Ralph appeared again. He'd been down to the buggy to collect his gun-case. It was a magnificent thing; one of those rectangular leather cases that holds several guns and all sorts of other paraphernalia as well. To be honest with you, I'd laughed in the gun club several times about that gun-case. The really good shots like the Hunt Master have pretty simple canvas gun cases. Reverend Simpson goes out with a single gun, a cartridge belt round his waist and a pocket full of old supermarket bags to carry the heads in. The stuff Ralph carried would have been sensible enough if he was up in their class. He pulled out four of those tools that mountaineers use to secure their ropes. Again, Reverend Simpson might have found them useful. One of his favorite techniques was to climb to the top of an outcrop and just wait. Very little boys, as he explained to me in the club house one evening, always pee against a vertical surface.

Their elders aren't so particular. "I just wait up there until he's got his little cock in his fingers. They have such lovely expressions on their faces when they're having that last pee," he said. "Then I give him a warning shot; wait till he's running and within range and then line up on the cleft in his little cherry-bum. Up slightly and 'Boompf'! Little Johnny is no more. And, do you know, they're often still peeing when I take their heads off; shitting too, some of them."

My doubts about Ralph's ability took a knock when I watched him hammer those pitons in the rock. He stretched the boy out in an X-shape with his arms and legs as far outspread as possible. Then, finding little cracks in the rocks near as possible to his hands and feet, he hammered the pitons in and attached the boy's ankles and wrists to them with thick elastic ropes. It was all done in less than ten minutes. I know that because I was all too aware of Alan's hands kneading my backside and silently praying that he would stop ... not because I didn't like it, but the sight of that magnificent body held taut in the ropes combined with his massaging hands had started to wake my sleeping cock.

I was vaguely aware of Ralph undressing. He was out of sight but I could see the mounting pile of clothes on a neighboring flat rock. "Beautifully flat belly. I love 'em like that," he said. Alan's hands left my backside and slid up under the front of my shirt. "Me too," he said. Ralph walked over to the boy. The hair on his chest was nothing to what was lower down. I'd never seen anyone like it. His groin and his thighs were a mass of dark hair, and his cock swung like a thick, outward-pointing pendulum as he walked. He knelt down and touched the boy's flaccid cock. That did it as far as I was concerned. Mine sprang up. Alan touched it through my jeans. "I think our young friend is ready," he said.

"Ready for what?" I asked. It was a silly question. I had a pretty good idea of what was in store for me.

"You can have the pleasure of waking him up," said Alan. "If you're as good as Keith says you are, it won't take long."

"Go ahead. He's all yours," said Ralph. If he hadn't said that I might have been able to maintain some self-control. Keith's words came back to me. "Suppose someone were to let you do anything you like with John Mayhill...." John Mayhill was decorating someone's wall then but the boy Ralph had bagged was even more beautiful. My legs felt like jelly as I walked over to him. "Anything you like...." I knelt between his legs and took his enormous scrotum in my hand. Then, bending down, I took the tip of his cock between my lips. It felt delightfully floppy. I'd never had one in that state before. It fitted perfectly into my mouth. No gagging on a throbbing giant member that time. The taste was better than Keith's too. I stretched my legs backwards so that I was lying down. My lips were buried in wonderfully bristly pubic hairs and the tip of his cock was at the back of my tongue. I sucked and felt the foreskin move slightly. One of my companions started to undo my boot laces. I didn't mind. Still holding his balls, I sucked and licked. He tasted strong—small wonder, I guess, after the number of miles he'd covered. It was a good taste though. It made my mouth tingle.

The soles of my feet felt cold. Fingers went round my middle and found my belt buckle. Before I was really aware of it, my jeans and shorts were off.

"What a beauty!" Alan exclaimed. He might as well have been speaking for me. The beauty I had in my mouth had started to wake up. I could feel it pulsing and swelling. Then all hell broke loose. I don't think I've heard so many swear words delivered at such a volume in all my life. He struggled and bucked. There was nothing for it but to let it slip out of my mouth but I was slightly too late. That hard belly that Ralph had admired hit my nose so hard that it started to bleed slightly. The screams and yells continued. If there had been any other hunters in the area they would certainly have heard and the three of us would have ended up on the mat in the Hunt Master's room. If a boy screams more than twice it means you weren't quick enough and you get a reprimand for unwanted cruelty. But nobody came. Just as well. I dread to think of what they would have thought.

Ralph was talking to him, caressing his heaving, struggling chest as he did so but the boy continued to struggle. It didn't do any good as Ralph pointed out to him. Those elastic ropes had been tested to two tons' breaking strain and they were attached to tungsten steel pegs, each firmly anchored in hard rock. His joints would go long before any of the kit holding him. Slowly, he ceased fighting and just lay there panting and staring defiantly upwards.

"What did you do?" asked Ralph after some minutes had elapsed. My nose seemed to have stopped bleeding.

"Took a truck for a joy ride," said the boy.

"Did you indeed? Then it seems only right and proper that someone should take you for a joy ride and, believe me, it really will be a joy. But think yourself lucky. A cock feels much nicer than a bullet and when we've finished with you, we'll take you to the boundary and let you go. And now our young friend here can carry on."

Their young friend was only to happy to oblige. His struggles had turned me on even more. I got called a "filthy cocksucking cunt," and several other awful things, but didn't mind in the least. All the fight seemed to have drained out of him. My job ... and I hoped desperately that I wouldn't make a mess of it ... was to drain him of something else and, from the feel of his balls, there was going to be a lot of it. His cock hardened in my mouth until I could manage only the top few inches. Not that it mattered. I had the best part. It felt like a very hard boiled egg at the back of my throat.

Exactly as Keith had done, Alan ran a finger up and down over my asshole. I wanted to tell him to ease up but my mouth was full. It was the worse thing he could possibly do at that moment. Keith had discovered that doing that made me come in seconds. Sure enough, I felt as if I might faint. I fell forward and choked as a cock bigger than Keith's ... and straighter ... battered against the back of my throat.

"Time," said Ralph.

I felt Alan's hands on my waist and he lifted me off as if I were a toddler who'd been crawling on the floor. I was in such a state that I couldn't walk. I remember staggering, with his help, to the boulder on which Ralph had put his clothes. Alan swept them off and laid me down over the stone. I remember that it felt warm against my groin, but colder against my chest. I looked over toward Ralph. One of the boy's legs had been secured to the same peg that held his wrist. I watched as Ralph unhitched the other ankle. I heard the boy groan as that leg rose and I heard the click when Ralph secured the elastic rope. It must have been uncomfortable to say the least. The boy's back was rounded and all his weight was on his shoulders.

The strange bottle marked "gun oil" in Ralph's case wasn't. At least, I'm fairly sure it wasn't. I watched with a sort of fearful fascination as he shoved the nozzle between ass-cheeks stretched so tight that it looked as if the skin might tear. The boy groaned. I looked away. Alan was naked. He grinned down at me. I was more interested in what he was holding. It was big. Bigger than Keith's, I thought, though it was difficult to make a comparison. Alan's was straight and circumcised as far as I could see. More significant; it was thick.

Which of us said "No. Don't do it. Please don't do it!" I can't rightly remember. Perhaps we spoke together. Alan's finger went back to work on my asshole. I was really scared. I think I might even have struggled a bit but not for long. It was just the same as it had been with Keith. "No, Keith. Not that!" But Keith, like Alan, took no notice. Keith said he couldn't wait to get me to his apartment. I was able to delay that. Alan, I knew all too well, wouldn't brook any delay at all.

"Christ, you're going to be a lovely fuck!" he said. I was conscious of the oil. I felt it running down the back of my legs. After that? It hurt. It hurt like hell but it was a strange sensation. It was as if I could transfer the agony to the boy who deserved to be punished. I didn't look at him. I couldn't. Alan was holding me too tight. I could hear him though; hear him cry out and gasp; hear the slapping noise. He had to suffer. He deserved to suffer. My pain was his pain. Like the time Reverend Simpson found Mickey Masters' cigarettes in my pocket at Sunday School.

"But they're Mickey's cigarettes. I was looking after them for him."

"Telling lies is another sin. How old are you?"

"Twelve, Reverend."

"And a very, very cheeky little boy."

"I've never cheeked you!"

"Nonetheless, you're a cheeky boy. Drop your pants ... and those. That's right. Come and lie over my knee."

And Mickey had to stand there, embarrassed as hell, and watch my butt being slapped.. Afterwards, when it was all over, the Reverend Simpson promised he wouldn't tell my parents and I shouldn't say anything either. He gave us both a lecture about Jesus being innocent and suffering for other people's sins and that made me feel better.

I wasn't in the least embarrassed some forty-five minutes later, after I'd got my witnesses together. Watching Mickey's black butt writhing on the Reverend's lap gave me quite a kick. Mickey deserved to feel pain. So did the boy impaled on Ralph's cock. What had the Reverend said? "Pain is good for boys.' He was right. The first seconds had been agonizing but now I actually wanted it to last as long as possible.

It didn't, of course. There was no way I could hold back. No way Alan could either. I just wish I could remember which of us came first and exactly how it felt when Alan's spunk flooded my colon but I can't. I remember him saying "Boy oh boy, you're beautiful!" but that was after he'd taken it out. I'm sure it was because I was able to see that Ralph's boy had been unhitched and was lying on his back, panting while Ralph licked the spots of semen from his belly. I always regret not having seen the moment when he came. I've seen several since then. I guess that makes up for it.

It was getting dark when we reached the boundary. We put Joe (that was his name) in the back of the buggy with a sack over his head so that, if any other hunters spotted us, they'd assume we were dumping a headless corpse. As it happened we saw nobody. We didn't have to wait very long and I wasn't too surprised to find that the guy who came along the road first was Keith. Joe muttered something as he climbed into the car. Whether it was curses or thanks, I don't know.

"How are you? That's the main thing," said Keith, addressing me.

"He's fine," said Alan.

"Great! How about that weekend?"

"Out of the question I'm afraid," I said. "I'm hunting with these two."

ONE HOT FUCK

John Patrick

I had not had a good night. Even with air conditioning, it was just too hot to sleep. I turned over in my bed to lie on my stomach and, burying my face in the pillow, moved against the hot sheets as if I were lying over Greg, the kid in drama class at college who occasionally let me poke him. But when the friction increased the fever in my body I stopped myself. It was no use. Heat or no heat, it really wasn't a surprise: I always had trouble sleeping at my parents' small house. I hated coming home. I couldn't believe I had grown up here. It had become a strange, disorienting, threatening experience. I tried to avoid staying overnight but on this occasion I had no choice. Fortunately I had only to endure my parents for one night, and then they would be off on an extended holiday, celebrating their freedom, I guess, the idea that I was finally out of the house and in college. I soon would have the place all to myself, me and the cats and the plants. I was looking forward to the solitary life for the summer after months of straight roommates and tedious classes.

It was two when I gave up and took a sleeping pill, so when I woke again, past nine, I was groggy. I could hear my parents, who had been up since eight, keeping their voices down for my sake but already starting in on the day's arguments. Dad was downstairs in the kitchen. When I got there, Dad was saying, "Well, here ... listen to it." He held the telephone out toward the refrigerator, which had ratcheted up again and was drumming loudly and at high speed. "Can you hear that?" Pause. "Can you?"

Whoever was on the other end of the line apparently could because an appointment was made for the next day. "My son's watching the house while we're gone. He'll take care of you."

I smiled. *Yeah, sure,* I thought. I should be so lucky, here in this backwater of a town.

But I was in for the surprise of my young life. The next day, when the repairman arrived, I was rendered nearly speechless by the tall, tanned, muscle-bound stud in tight jeans who smiled at me and asked, "You're having a problem?"

"Come in," I said. "Thank you for coming so quickly. The refrigerator's right in here."

Now the old refrigerator was humming quietly. Inaudibly, really; it was hard to hear that it was on at all.

"It was making quite a lot of racket yesterday," I explained, somewhat embarrassed.

The repairman wore a green shirt with JERRY embroidered on the pocket. He put down his toolbox in front of the refrigerator. "Well, let's just see what the problem is here," he said, not answering me.

"I guess maybe they had too much food in there, but I threw a lot away this morning."

Jerry stepped in front of me to get at the back of the refrigerator. I got a good whiff of his heady sweat. He wrestled the refrigerator gently out from the wall.

"I can't imagine being overloaded was really what was wrong," I went on, even though it was obvious Jerry wasn't paying any attention to me. "Maybe it's like the car, when you take it in, whatever was making noise suddenly stops."

The refrigerator was shuffled farther out from the wall, toward the crammed kitchen table. Jerry emerged from behind the refrigerator and knelt on the floor in front of it with a screwdriver. He paid no attention to me.

"Are you having any luck?" I finally asked the repairman, who was peering into a mysterious opening he had created at the front of the refrigerator.

"Well, we haven't solved the problem yet," Jerry said, turning to look at me. I saw his eyes travel from my face down to the crotch of the Speedo I was wearing (that was all I had on, my usual summer attire when I am home and we are forced to keep the A/C at 78 degrees), then back again. He smiled for the first time since I met him at the door, and went back to work..

I blinked as I sat down at the table and gazed at the stud's strong back, thick neck and unruly brown hair. How I would love to run my hands through it....

"Well, I'll be damned. Here's the problem," Jerry said suddenly, backing away on his knees from the refrigerator.

"What is it?" I asked, smiling at him.

Jerry held up a yellowed newspaper clipping. "CRESTVIEW SCORES HOLE-IN-ONE" was the headline.

"Oh, my goodness," I said, holding out my hand. I shook my head. "I guess Dad has been wondering where that was. That was his moment of glory five years ago. He had it up on the door, stuck on with a magnet. And that's what was making all that noise?"

"Yep," Jerry said. He was back inside the black hole again, replacing everything.

As Jerry stood up, I was sticking the clipping back on the refrigerator door and I made a sudden intimate acquaintance with the flowing script over Jerry's pocket.

"Sorry," I said, flustered, and backing away.

"It's okay," Jerry chuckled.

I backed up a bit farther, falling backwards onto the table.

Jerry said, "Careful, there." He caught me by the waist, held me briefly.

"Sorry," I sputtered.

"Well, I'm all through now," Jerry said, wiping his hands on his jeans. "Is there anything else you need?"

"No," I said weakly. I was helpless, impotent in the presence of such hyper-masculinity. Telling Jerry the truth, of course, would get me smacked upside the head. "No, everything here is fine now I guess," I said finally.

But it wasn't. My close encounter, and lack of sex for nearly a week, had produced a hard-on. Jerry couldn't miss it. In fact, he did a double-take, then he smiled again. "I really hate to charge you but I have to, you know."

"Yes, I know."

He looked down at the hard-on again, then looked toward the sink. "Could I trouble you for a glass of water? It's so damn hot outside...."

"Yes, it's a regular heatwave...." I said, rushing over to the sink and filling a glass with cold water.

The stud finished off the glass in two gulps, set it on the counter. "God, I hate to charge you fifty bucks for this call. You sure there's nothin' else I can do while I'm here?"

Again I saw that his eyes had become riveted on my hard-on, which just wouldn't go down.

"Well...." I said, moving closer, but tentatively. Part of me wanted it to continue, another part of me wanted it to stop. I didn't want to touch him; I wanted him to make the first move.

And he did. "Well, it sure looks like there's something here that needs takin' care of...." he said, stroking my bulge. "Needs takin' care of real bad."

Emboldened now, I reached down and stroked his crotch. "You should let me take care of *you*, stud, you've been so nice...."

I couldn't wait any longer. I dropped to my knees before him and unbuckled his pants, and, as I pulled them down, Jerry's briefs were straining to hold everything in.

I grabbed the sides of his briefs and pulled them down below his knees. His flaccid dick hung at least five inches straight down. It was uncut with circles of thin wrinkles around his cock. The wrinkles started about a third of the way from the base, about the same place where the skin that hung down to his ballsac began its descent. His two huge, hairy balls hung next to each other just below the end of his dick. The skin that held them in place ran up near the sides of his dick, forming a convenient pocket. The head of his cock bulged under the skin, and the foreskin rounded off the end of his dick, all of which seemed to rest softly against his balls. I had seen only a few uncut dicks and only in the shower, so I was fascinated with this magnificent specimen.

I cupped my hand around Jerry's dick with my thumb and index finger toward the base. The dick moved around freely in the skin, like a piece of thick sausage in a loose plastic bag with all its natural juices intact. I pulled the skin out and let it retract back in my hand. Then I pushed it all back to the base, trying to expose the head.

I stroked it, wondering if it was going to get fully hard. I worried that maybe Jerry thought my folks would return at any moment. Each time I pushed at the base, Jerry moaned. "I'm here all alone for three weeks, maybe a month," I said.

"Hmmmm," Jerry said in response.

The first couple of strokes I could pull my hand out past the end of Jerry's dick, but I still saw no sign of the head. Soon I began to see the piss-slit at the end, peeking through his tender foreskin. After doing this for a few moments, I realized I really did have quite a piece of man-meat in my hand. I stared at the now-throbbing, thickening cock. The head was starting to curve outward, and I could just see its definition.

Jerry begged, "C'mon, kid, make me hard."

Before continuing my hand strokes, I brought my mouth

around the end of Jerry's dick and sucked all the skin out, giving me a mouthful. Then I moved towards the base. When I reached the base, Jerry moaned loudly.

Jerry seemed to be taking the scene in stride. I grunted, and proceeded, but cautiously. It was such a huge prick, and it was so beautiful, that I knew I would come the moment I started sucking it.

"Oh, yeah, suck it," Jerry ordered.

I obeyed, sliding the head of the prick in my mouth.

"That's right, kid. Suck me."

He grasped my head and pulled me forward. The familiar excitement and longing began. My cock was throbbing, ready to spurt, and I pulled it from my Speedo. I jerked it while I moved my mouth back and forth, varying the pressure of my lips as I had learned to do sucking Greg's penis, which was puny in comparison to this. Greg had taught me what precious little I knew about sex, and now I was suddenly grateful to him. While I had begun to avoid Greg, finding him way too "dramatic" and demanding, now I would have to make up for it with an extra poke or two when classes resumed.

I took the giant cock out of my mouth and gave it a lick or two. Jerry loved this, so I kept it up for a bit, using my tongue and hands as best I could to keep him stimulated. I knew he was close, but I didn't want him to come just yet. I put my hand at the base to slow him down a bit and returned to deep sucking. I kept up my in-and-out in the slow, sensual pace that Greg had taught me, and I had no time to grow bored with this. First I came, gushing quite a load onto the linoleum floor. This was apparently what Jerry had been waiting for because he grabbed my head and pulled me back so that the cock slipped from my mouth and we both watched as the cum splattered all over my face and dripped onto the floor.

"Oh, kid...." Jerry groaned, releasing my head. "That was really great."

I grinned as I stood and went to the sink, wetting a towel and cleaning off my dick and face. I stepped over to Jerry and cleaned him off as well. He held me close and I thought for a moment he might kiss me. But he pulled away, seemingly embarrassed now, and put his cock away.

"The office will be sending you a bill," he said as he gathered his tools.

"Why don't you deliver it yourself?" I suggested, following him to the front door.

"Three weeks, eh? You're gonna be alone here for three weeks?"

"Yep."

"Well, then maybe I could," he said with a smile.

I watched him climb into his truck. After backing out of the driveway, he looked up and waved as he drove away. After I slammed the door closed behind me, I thought about what the next three weeks might bring—and I was hard again!

I had given up hope. Once or twice over the next few days, I thought about calling and saying the fridge was on the blink again, but then I feared they'd send somebody else. I had only three days to go before the folks returned and I was fixing dinner when there was a knock on the door. I looked out to see the "MISTER FIX-IT" truck in the driveway. I rushed to the door.

There he was, smiling. He held up a slip of paper. "The office says this here bill is overdue and they sent me here to collect."

"Well, come in."

The scene, right there in the foyer, began much the same way as the previous one, but during the course of the blowjob I managed to undress him completely, to feast my eyes on his muscular body, the medium body hair, and the generous thighs. I was careful not to force an orgasm, because I had something more in mind this time.

I glanced up into his eyes as I licked his hard cock and said, "I want you to fuck me...."

He smiled, ran his hand through my long dark hair and said, "Okay."

I led him upstairs to my bedroom. I prepared myself and rolled a condom over his still-erect cock. He said nothing until I got on the bed and spread my legs wide for him. "You sure?" he asked. "It might hurt you."

"I'm sure," I said.

I had only been fucked once before, by Greg, so I didn't know what to expect, but I knew anything that large would definitely take some getting used to.

"Well, let's see if you can handle this," he said, pushing the head against my asslips. As he entered me, slowly, tenderly, tears began running down my cheeks. I groaned when he got the head in, and he pulled out, but then plunged in again. Inch after hard inch went in. But this was only the beginning. Slamming himself hard against my ass, he fucked me—long and hard. I quivered and screamed as he pressed tightly against me, all the way in. I began to come, and he pulled back to watch it gush onto my belly.

He pulled out completely now, and jerked off onto my stomach, his cum joining mine. My own jerking slowed and my heart stopped racing. Dripping with sweat, he climbed off the bed and went into the bathroom and took a shower. I stayed in my bed, relishing the fact that I had two hefty loads of spunk on my stomach.

I followed him downstairs and watched him dress. When he was finished he took the bill in his hand and ripped it in half. "Paid in full," he said, chuckling.

"Full is right."

As he eased out the door, he said, "Call me if you have any more trouble."

"I will," I said, easing the door shut. I leaned against the door and looked down to see my cock again was hard.

GIVING A BOY A HAND

Frank Gardner

Intercepted Letter

Dear Dad:

Golly, I sure want to write and thank you for raising my allowance. The twenty dollars you sent in your last letter, sure makes life easier here at Camp Pisquash. We just had supper, and I'm writing this in the recreation room. I didn't think I'd like it here at first; darn, there's a guy practicing on a guitar just across the room. Oh well, he's just learning too.

Like I told you, I wanted to work this summer, but you're right Dad; there sure is a lot of interesting stuff to do here at Camp Pisquash, even if it is hotter than hell here this summer. Everybody's runnin' around with next to nothin' on (and sometimes even nothin' at all!)

Do you remember the Pisquash motto over the gate, Dad? It is, "WE GIVE BOYS A HAND."

And, you know, it's true, Dad, it really is!

Sure thing, I remember why you sent me the money. You know, like we talked about it, and how you didn't want me to play with myself and all. And how the twenty dollars is to encourage me not to be a loner, but to reach out to other people. Boy, that's sure good advice, Dad. I gave ten dollars of it to Stud (that's what I nicknamed him, that's not his real name, of course). He's a counselor here at Camp Pisquash, and he sure is a *good* counselor. Did I spell that okay, Dad?

Stud sure knows the ropes; he teaches swimming and hiking and stuff like that. He's good at reaching out too, better than I am, anyway. He's the best teacher I ever had. He's patient with me, and I can learn from him.

Stud has shown me a lot of stuff, like different ways to exercise and make my muscles grow, and different ways of looking after myself, like keeping it good and clean and how to skin it back and wash it good. He says lots of boys don't do that, and they should.

Stud says that when I shit, excuse me Dad, but I don't know any other way to say it, I should squat down like the Indians if I can, and this will keep my asshole muscles in better shape.

He says that when I get done, I ought to wash it if I can, and keep that clean too. He's sure a good teacher, and he tells you stuff no one else will tell you.

Stud has his own way of doing things, though. When I gave him ten of the dollars you sent me, I said something about how you didn't want me to be a loner and all, and just be tied up with myself.

He grinned and thought for a while; then he nodded and asked me if I wanted to go hiking and camping out at the other end of the lake.

I said sure, and we got a beat-up Ranger tent that was kicking around, and we went up there the next day.

Gee, I sure want to thank you, Dad, for the money—but not just the money, but the advice too. It's sure good advice, Dad.

We got the tent all set up Saturday night, and cooked us some swell hotdogs and beans, and had some coffee; Stud showed me how to make coffee. I know you don't want me to drink very much of it, where I'm still growing and all, so I just had one cup. It made me feel all warm, and Stud likes it too.

He gave me a smoke. I know you don't think I should smoke, Dad, but I just had a couple of puffs; and Stud said it was just like the Indians.

When he handed me the smoke, he said, "In peace." Just like we were smoking a peace pipe. Then we had a good talk about things, and we turned in.

We got up early Sunday morning. The sun was just getting up, too. It was all quiet and there was this mist on the lake, and the birds were singing like they were just stretching their muscles, kind of like they were saying "There's work to be done," and getting ready to go out looking for food and stuff.

Stud had an awful time waking me up, he had to tickle my belly, and that made me dream about food, and then I woke up and laughed like an idiot. He told me to take off my briefs, that I didn't need them for swimming because no one came around there. I didn't want to at first, you know how I am, Dad.

He finally said, "Do you think I will faint?" I laughed and just pulled them off.

We dove right in the water off a rock. Boy, that's sure a quick way to wake up. Wow! The water was cold as the dickens!

Stud sure is husky, and I'm going to try and get a tan like the one he's got. We horsed around, swimming and splashing around like a couple of idiot kids I guess, then we came up to the tent, and Stud got a blanket spread out and we sat there drying off. The sun was high enough to shine on us, and a little breeze was blowing so that helped.

I remember looking up at the leaves in a maple tree right over us, the breeze was turning them over and the sun was flashing off them, when Stud cuffed me easy on the back of my head.

"What are you thinking, Soldier?" he asked me.

"Oh, nothing much, just watching the sun on the leaves."

"Idiot child." He picked a blade of grass and chewed on it for a while. Then he looked at me and asked, "Just what did your pa say?"

"Oh, nothing much."

He laughed, "Boy, you're a great talker."

I picked me a blade of grass too, and started chewing, to cover up my embarrassment, I guess. I tried to be casual, "Oh, just that he doesn't want me to play with myself."

"Uh-huh. Anything else?"

"Well," I said, "just that he was sending me the twenty dollars to encourage me not to—and that he didn't want me all tied up with myself, and wanted me to learn to reach out."

Stud rubbed something on the inside of his thigh, and scowled. Boy, when he scowls, he looks ferocious. He was thinking I guess. Then he smiled and turned towards me and gave me one of his straight looks.

"Go ahead," he said. Sometimes he talks just like he's shooting an arrow. He said it like that. He could see I was puzzled, so he said it again, "Go ahead and reach out. That's not playing with yourself."

"Gee...." I got real red in the face, "You mean it would be okay...?" I just couldn't spit the rest of it out.

So next thing I know, Stud reaches over and scratches my head. "Maybe this will help you think," he said.

"You mean it would be okay ... with someone else?"

"Sure," Stud replied, "and someone else with you. That's how it works, see?"

"Yeah, I guess."

I guess he could see I was pretty confused so he didn't make fun of me. He just said, "Give me your hand."

I finally found the darned thing, I mean my hand. I guess I

was looking at it like I didn't know what it was for.

Stud reached his hand over and took mine and put it between his legs. Then he lay back on the blanket, and showed me how to reach out. Stud sure was patient with me, Dad.

I remember how a maple leaf came down on his chest, and how it shone in the sun.

You know, Dad, Stud can be as tough as hell, excuse me, Dad, I know you don't like rough language and all, but sometimes Stud can get—golly, the most peaceful gentle look on his face, like he's just in love with the whole world.

Then, after a while, he said, "Now, I'll give you mine."

He reached over with his hand. I remember how tanned it was on the back, and he's got calluses on his palm, Dad.

Golly, sometimes he moves his hand like it's full of hope, and like it's got all the tenderness and joy and sorrow in the world held in it.

I could hear the water on the rocks and the beach, and I could feel a light breeze on the inside of my thighs and Stud's hand, and golly....

After a while, I asked him, "Say, Stud, you said something about how you have a cow on your place, didn't you?"

"Yup."

"And I'll bet you milk it too, don't you?"

"Yup."

"I thought so," I said, then I lay back again and really relaxed. Now I knew why he had such a peaceful look on his face!

Finally Stud smiled and said, "Cream."

"Yeah," I replied, "and my belly-button, that makes a pretty good cup, doesn't it?"

"Sure as hell does, Soldier," he said, with a big grin spreading across his face.

Well, anyway, I want to thank you again, Dad.

And, oh yeah, Stud just came in the recreation room, and it's almost time for lights out, so I'll stop here. But you sure are right, Dad. People should learn to give boys a hand!

Love, Sonny Boy

RED-HOT, IRON-HARD

Barry Alexander

"Lance's cock was a huge, throbbing, juicy fat cylinder of turgid, gleaming, wet, scarlet, succulent man meat. Randy's velvety-smooth, milky white quivering bubble butt was speared fast and sharp by Lance's awesome, red-hot iron-hard love weapon. So round, so firm, so fully packed."

Jeff tossed the manuscript onto the growing pile of stories waiting for rejection slips. He didn't need to read any further to make a diagnosis: adjectivitis with severe loss of verb function, accompanied by acute sentence fragments. Prognosis: terminal.

Jeff sighed as he picked up the next one. He'd thought this was going to be a lot more fun than his former job as a medical technician. Someone was actually going to pay him to sit around reading dirty stories and meeting the hunky models who strutted through the pages of *Hot Stuff.*

But it didn't work out like that. Jeff spent most of his day running errands, answering the phone, and processing subscriptions. When he had the time, he sorted through the ever-growing mountain of slush on his desk. Models never stopped in. Writers did. Bulging biceps and massive torsos were confined to their stories. Writers looked like, well, writers.

Jeff skipped to the last page of the next story, "Jocked Off." *"The quarterback had just pulled out of me when the coach walked into the locker room. I smiled up at him, jock jizz oozing out of my tight end. 'You were wrong, Coach. You said I'd never make the team. Well, I just did. I made the whole fuckin' team.'"*

Yeah, right. After only three months at *Hot Stuff,* Jeff had read at least a dozen getting-fucked-by-the-team fantasies: the football team, the hockey team, the soccer team, and one really kinky story about a polo team and its ponies.

Jeff had two problems: He needed a decent story for the next issue, and he needed to get fucked. He hadn't had a good ass-pounding, cock-pumping, all-night fuck since his lover left.

He looked across the room to the editor's closed door and sighed. Marcus was tall and leanly fit. A shock of silky black hair tumbled over his broad forehead. Beard stubble shadowed his square-cut jaw and rimmed his full lips. When the office was hot, Marcus would remove his jacket and tie and open his collar. The sight of all that lush black hair curling under a crisp white shirt gave Jeff fantasies of endless summer. Marcus was friendly, but Jeff never forgot that he was the boss. He didn't want to risk losing another job. So far everything was on a strictly professional level.

Jeff picked up the next story.

"Rod's big ripe tomatoes pulled up to the base of his hot dog, and the plum-shaped head mushroomed over his crisp, oiled stalk. His plump, spicy sausage exploded, drooling thick cream all over the sweet honey buns of the little tart beneath him."

Nothing like a well-balanced meal, Jeff thought. Salad, main course, and dessert. Wonder if he'll give me his recipe? Jeff checked his watch and decided to break for lunch.

In the break room that *Hot Stuff* shared with the other departments of Magnum Publishing, Jeff sat down and shoved aside the junk cluttering the long table to make room for his sandwich and soda. There was no one to talk to, so he picked up a copy of *New Age Writer* that someone had left behind. He flipped through the magazine's pages that promised great writers' secrets and surefire success. He couldn't help laughing at the ads.

SAY GOOD-BYE TO WRITER'S BLOCK--
EX-BLOX KEEPS THOSE WORDS FLOWING!
STOP STRAINING TO FILL EMPTY PAGES--
NATURAL, THERAPEUTIC AGENTS
PROVIDE GENTLE OVERNIGHT RELIEF!

WHERE DO WRITERS GET IDEAS?
EVERYWHERE THEY WEAR WRITER'S KAP!
ELECTROMAGNETIC DISKS CHANNEL PSYCHIC FORCES
INTO STORY-PRODUCING IDEAS
(BATTERIES NOT INCLUDED)

NO MORE REJECTIONS!
WRITE THE STORY YOU'VE ALWAYS WANTED TO WRITE!
EDITORS READ THE STORY THEY'VE ALWAYS WANTED
TO READ!

SUPER SUBLIMINAL PAPER
GUARANTEES ACCEPTANCE!

Writers would believe anything. Jeff tossed the magazine aside and finished his lunch. He was probably one of the few people in the building without delusions of writing the Great American Novel. He took the job to help forget the lover who'd walked out on him and because he thought he'd get his rocks off reading the stuff. Well sometimes he did, but not often. After three months of stories about pizza boys, truck drivers, and cops with turgid, bloated, and engorged dicks, cocks and fuck poles shooting, blasting, and exploding rivers, pools, and oceans of cum—he didn't find many of the stories erotic.

Jeff groaned as a lavender cover letter fell out of the next big yellow envelope. Damn! Not another one from him. Every week for three months, Clarence Twait had submitted the worst stories Jeff had ever read.

"Hi ya, Ed! Ya gotta love this one! My lover swears it's the hottest thing he's ever read, especially when the big, butch leatherman goes spelunking for the peanut butter and marshmallows. Be sure you put it in next month's issue. I want to surprise him for his birthday. Hornily yours, Clarence!"

I must be a masochist, Jeff thought. Experience should have taught him that he'd find nothing usable here. He fingered the heavy stock of the manuscript in surprise. The guy should spend his money on writing lessons instead of on such obviously expensive paper.

The beginning wasn't half bad. By page two, Jeff's cock was starting to sit up and take notice. He double-checked the author's name; the expensive paper confirmed it: Clarence Twait. Jeff couldn't figure it out. It definitively wasn't the horrifying story Clarence had described in his letter. Somehow Clarence had learned to write. Perhaps the Good Editor's Fairy had at long last taken pity on him.

The main character sounded exactly like Marcus: lean, muscular build, silky black hair, and dusky blue eyes. By page three, Jeff ached so badly he couldn't wait to turn the page. How in the hell did Clarence know what he wanted Marcus to do to him? Everything was perfect, exactly as he'd imagined it to be. Surreptitiously, he stroked the hard bulge straining against his Calvins. He teased his fingers up and down the thick cock, imagining they were Marcus's fingers. His breath quickened and his face flushed as he read more, turning the pages with one hand. He eased his zipper down. The hard mound of his cock welled into the opening, the thick white bulge of cotton already moist and throbbing.

Jeff longed to open his pants fully and slide them down his slim hips so he would have full access. He didn't dare. Even at a porn magazine, you can't sit around beating your meat. If he had a private office like Marcus, he could lock the door and do what he damn well pleased. He could open his shirt and stroke his nipples into hard little points. He could run his hands over the light coating of hair on his inner thighs. He could take the lube out of his desk and slick it all over his long pink cock until it glistened under the fluorescent lights. He could pump it slowly up and down, listening to the moist sound of flesh on flesh, speeding up when the fat helmet flared and darkened with the powerful surge of blood up his engorged shaft. Then, when it got close, when he couldn't stand it another second, he could....

He couldn't; he didn't' have a private office. He could only squirm his fingers inside the opening and touch his hard flesh, cock and balls squashed together in the tight confinement of his briefs. Damn! It just wasn't the same.

Jeff worked for a few more minutes before he gave up. The short, furtive strokes just weren't going to do it, especially when half his attention was focused on the office door he feared would suddenly open. He pushed the painfully hard mound back inside his trousers.

He could finish the manuscript at home, but he had a better idea. Trying to ignore his demanding dick, he waited until his tumescence was under control. He hesitated outside Marcus's door. Maybe it wouldn't work. Maybe Marcus wouldn't even notice the similarity of characters—or care if he did. In three months he'd never made a move. Jeff took a deep breath and knocked.

"Come in," Marcus said in his clear baritone. He looked up and smiled when Jeff entered. "What's up?"

Jeff couldn't help blushing. "I've got the perfect story for that hole in our November issue, but I'd like you to take a look at it, Marcus." Jeff tried to let his enthusiasm show without being pushy. He struggled to keep from fidgeting.

Marcus leaned back in his swivel leather chair and looked at him curiously. Jeff knew the boss was probably picking up on his anxiety, but he couldn't help it. Just looking at that strong, lean body only inches away was arousing his cock. He clutched the papers in front of him for cover.

"You caught me at a good time. I just finished checking the model releases, and that new photographer canceled his appointment, so I'm free. Let's see it."

Back at his desk, Jeff tried to keep his mind off his squirming cock. He picked up a manuscript, then tossed it back on his desk. Marcus had to want this one, had to want him. He jumped when Marcus called him back into the office.

"Well, that was some story."

"Yeah, I thought so," Jeff said awkwardly. He didn't know what to do next. He couldn't read the expression on Marcus's face.

Marcus handed him the story across the desk. His white shirt tightened across his broad chest, showing a hint of nipple as he stretched. Jeff was so intent on the little peaks that he dropped the manuscript. Paper fluttered all over the desk and floor. Jeff made a wild grab, missed, and knocked a pencil stein over. It bounced off his foot and rolled under the desk.

"Oh, shit!" Jeff scrambled under the desk and rescued the ceramic stein. He scooped up the scattered pens and pencils. "I think it's OK. I don't see any cracks," he said breathlessly. He didn't know if the cup had a special meaning to Marcus, but he sure as hell didn't want to break something that might have been a gift from a lover. Spotting another pencil under the desk, he dived for it and surfaced right between Marcus's sprawled-open legs. For several seconds, he stared wordlessly at the bulging basket just inches from his face.

"Everything all right down there?"

Jeff blushed as he looked up at Marcus's dancing eyes. "Uh, yeah. Great." Jeff gulped. "I got it." He held up the maverick pencil.

The corner of Marcus's mouth twitched. "Sure you weren't looking for something a little thicker?" Jeff started to get up before Marcus's meaning registered. Then he felt a pair of big warm hands pressing down on his shoulders. "Don't. I think you've wanted to be down there for a long time."

Marcus reached for his zipper. Mesmerized, Jeff watched the teeth part slowly, one by one, until something big and hard and purple surged outward. He couldn't believe it! Marcus, the conservative dresser, always so formal and businesslike, sported a bright scarlet jockstrap!

He stared at the full package, swathed in scarlet silk and waiting to be unwrapped just like a birthday present. Sheer fabric revealed the clear outline of a thick shaft. A wet circle clung to the deep red cock head. Jeff's hands shook as he reached for the enticing mound. Heat burned through the silk as he petted the hard shaft. It arched beneath his touch like a cat being stroked.

Jeff pressed his face against the mound and inhaled. The warm musk of Marcus's crotch sent a fresh surge of blood into his own dick. He rubbed his face back and forth, feeling the moisture against his cheek. Marcus groaned and pushed Jeff's face harder against his groin. Jeff mouthed the fat cylinder twitching under his lips. Slipping his tongue under the edge of the pouch, he lapped the furry balls. He bunched the fabric until the fat orbs escaped, one on each side of the gathered silk.

"Oh, yeah, suck those balls...." Marcus said. Spreading his legs wider, he raised his hips and shoved his slacks down, exposing the flattened rings of black hair on his muscular thighs.

Jeff tongued the damp inner flesh of his thighs and savored the salty sweetness of his sweat. He teased Marcus for several minutes, and then he ripped the jock off. Marcus's big cock bounced free, all eight inches of fat, heavily veined stud-meat. Jeff caught it in his fist before it finished bouncing, and it throbbed and jerked against his grasp like some trapped, wild creature.

Suddenly Marcus pulled away, yanked open his desk drawer, and dug frantically through its contents, spilling junk all over the floor. "Oh shit! Where are they?"

Jeff laughed at the mess Marcus was making. He stood up and reached into his pocket. "Hey, Marcus, you looking for one of these?" he asked with a big grin as he held up a condom.

"Give me that thing," Marcus ordered.

"Uh-uh." Jeff danced back, holding the little packet out of reach. "I've waited for you for three months. It's your turn to wait."

Jeff tucked the packet down inside his briefs. While Marcus watched, he slowly unbuttoned his shirt, then ran his hands over his solid chest and flat stomach.

Jeff smiled at the feverish look in Marcus's eyes; this little performance was getting to him. Marcus thumbed his cock downward, aiming it straight at Jeff's crotch. He stroked it from the hairy base to a flaring head as red and silky as his jock.

Jeff shivered in anticipation, but he wanted to prolong the excitement. He undid his pants, spun around, and shoved them down past the small, hard mounds of his ass. He bent as if he were going to push them all the way off, then yanked them back up after flashing his tight pink pucker.

Marcus groaned. "Get over here, you damn cockteaser." Without waiting for a reply, Marcus crossed the room in two steps, grabbed Jeff in his arms, and thrust his tongue down his throat and his hand down his pants. Jeff responded eagerly to both probes. The kiss was hot and wet and passionate. Jeff couldn't breathe, but he didn't care. He worked frantically at Marcus's shirt buttons so he could bury his fingers in that lush black forest. He ground his hips against Marcus, trapping Marcus's hand inside his briefs.

When he finally came up for air, Marcus pulled his hands free and triumphantly held the condom packet aloft. His hand was wet from Jeff's pre-cum, and he wiped it in the black thicket on his bared chest.

Marcus grabbed him by the back of the neck and pulled his face close. Eagerly Jeff went to work, licking his own juice off the sweat-dampened hair. He slid his hands under Marcus's open shirt and explored the firm muscles of his back and shoulders. His lips brushed over the hard point of Marcus's nipple, and he sucked it in. He bit lightly, then rubbed his tongue over the rubber peak. His lips trailed the narrow line of hair leading to the heavy pubic bush, licking and kissing. He wanted to linger, but he moved downward, pulled irresistibly by the thought of what lay ahead. Jeff dropped to his knees and stared, hypnotized by the swaying cock just inches from his mouth. "I gotta have it," he groaned. "Put it on."

Marcus dropped the packet into his hand. "Do me."

Jeff ripped open the packet, caught the cock, and covered it. He crammed it into his mouth and swallowed it in one gulp, mashing his lips against Marcus's wiry pubes. Suctioning it back to the head, he held the shaft in his fist and swirled his tongue over the glans.

"Oh, man, that feels great." Marcus sighed. "Get it sloppy. I'm going to drive this rod right up that cute little butt of yours."

Given that kind of incentive, Jeff went into a power suck, impaling his throat with the fleshy sword, time after time. He polished it with hot foamy spit until it gleamed.

"Good enough." Marcus panted as he pulled away. He had to hold Jeff's head back when Jeff tried to dive for more. Marcus wiped a thread of drool from the corner of Jeff's mouth and grinned at the glazed look on his face. "You want it that bad?"

Jeff nodded.

"Then get that ass over this desk and prepare to get fucked." With one sweep of his arm, Marcus cleared his desk, knocking everything to the floor. He pushed Jeff face down and pulled his cock back until it swung between his spread legs. Marcus ran his finger over the fat tube to the ridge of Jeff's smooth, pink cock. Clear juice shot out of the slit. Marcus gathered the abundant lubricant and slicked it all over the throbbing target.

Jeff shuddered at the intimate touch and parted his legs even wider. His cock jerked, bumping against the desk edge and smearing a snail trail of pre-cum over the polished wood.

"Yeah, that's what I like to see," Marcus said, " a nice tight ass, all pink and spread and greased." He nudged his cock against the opening.

Jeff moaned, thrusting his hips backward, searching for the giant cock he had fantasized about for so long. "Hurry! Don't make me wait any longer."

Marcus pulled away and rubbed his cock over the smooth white globes of Jeff's ass. "I don't believe you really want this. Tell me how much you want it."

"I want it. I want it really bad."

"Nope, not convincing." Marcus slid one finger down the narrow chasm and tapped it against Jeff's frustrated hole.

"Damn it, Marcus, stop horsing around. Shove it in." Jeff rocked his hips backward, trying to capture the finger that was teasing tight little circles around his sensitive pucker.

"Better, but I'm not quite convinced." Marcus said. He

dropped his heavy shaft in the slick divide and drove it upward over the gaping hole.

Jeff whimpered at the delicious friction. "Don't do this to me," he pleaded. "It's been too long. I need it. I need you. Please, Marcus."

"Okay, I'm convinced."

Immediately Jeff felt the cockhead at his portal. He pushed backward, opening himself wide and welcoming the hard shaft that slowly entered him. Inch by inch, Marcus's cock filled him until he felt the tough pubic hair against his ass. "Oh, yeah!" Jeff sighed.

Marcus leaned forward and kissed him between the shoulder blades. He lay against h him for a moment, letting him get used to the size of the cock inside him. Jeff enjoyed the heat and weight of Marcus's body covering his. The rough pelt of his chest rasped his back, and the hard nubs of Marcus's nipples poked his skin.

"Fuck me, Marcus. Fuck me hard!"

Marcus pushed back, bracing himself with his hands on the desk. His cock slid free until the head stretched the opening again. He lunged, slamming the entire length of his cock deep inside. Jeff grunted.

"Like that?"

"Yeah, ram that big dick in me!"

Marcus rode him hard, rocking his body with the force of his thrusts. Jeff clutched the desk corners to prevent his sweaty body from sliding across the slick wood. His cock thumped against the table edge every time Marcus's big balls slapped against this ass.

Marcus shortened his strokes, fucking him with the last couple of inches. He caught Jeff's throbbing cock in his fist and worked it while his hips pistoned faster and faster.

Jeff whimpered. The big warm hand drove him closer to the edge. He wriggled his hips in delight, clamping down and trying to give as much pleasure as he was receiving. The desk creaked in rhythm with the wet slapping of flesh on flesh. Their ragged breathing formed a stereo medley of gasps and grunts as Marcus's cock massaged every inch of Jeff's guts.

Sweat dripped off Marcus's heaving chest and trickled down Jeff's spine into his asscrack. Jeff couldn't feel Marcus's balls slapping against his butt anymore, they must have tightened as he became more inflamed. Marcus was almost there. His fat cockhead flared, opening Jeff even wider. Marcus locked his hips in place, bucking wildly as he drove himself deep and faster into Jeff's quivering body.

It was too intense. Jeff went over the edge. He moaned and whimpered as he came again and again, pumping a thick white fountain all over the side of the desk. His guts convulsed, clamping down on Marcus's cock and milking it. "Give it to me, man! Give me everything!"

"Take it all! Take that hot load!" Marcus roared. He clutched Jeff's hips as if his life depended on it, gave a final ass-pounding fuck, and sprayed the biggest load of cream Jeff had felt in a long time. His cock thrashed around in Jeff's ass like a fire hose out of control.

Marcus collapsed on top of Jeff, his weight warm and heavy. Jeff could have stayed that way forever, with Marcus's breath hot and moist against his neck and his heart thudding against Jeff's back.

All too soon, Marcus eased off Jeff's satiated body and helped him back to his feet. To Jeff's delight, Marcus took him in his arms and kissed him. "That was wonderful! Boy, you didn't need to go to so much trouble. I've wanted to do that since the first day you walked into the office. You didn't need to write a story to seduce me." Marcus held Jeff in his arms and stroked his back slowly.

"I didn't, but sure as hell would have if I'd thought it would work." Jeff turned his head against Marcus's chest and sighed. "I couldn't believe it when I read it. It was exactly what I'd fantasized since I met you." He looked up and grinned. "I'm just glad Clarence didn't submit the story he described in his cover letter—peanut butter and marshmallows. Yech."

"It was exactly the way I imagined it too. Right down to the black Stetson and spurs."

Jeff looked puzzled. "I don't remember spurs."

"How could you miss them?"

"I didn't read it all the way through; I was in such a hurry to show it to you. But I'm sure I would have noticed spurs."

"Whatever. Just as long as it worked." Marus tilted Jeff's face up and kissed him again, then swatted him gently on the butt. "Speaking of work, you'd better write that guy an acceptance letter."

"We better make sure we have all the pages!"

The two men scrambled over the floor collecting the scattered sheets. "Hey, Marcus," Jeff said ruefully as he held up a handful. Come splattered the paper and dripped onto the carpet. "How are we going to tell him we need another copy?"

Marcus laughed. " Here, let me. I'll tell him the truth. I don't think he'll mind."

Marcus picked up the title page and scribbled across the top: "Dear Mr. Twait: We are pleased to accept your manuscript for publication in *Hot Stuff*. Please send...."

"Marcus?" Jeff asked in a strained voice, "can you finish that later?"

Marcus looked up. Jeff was sitting on the edge of his desk, a handful of pages in one hand and a handful of erect cock in the other. "I started reading it again, and...."

Marcus was right. Clarence Twait didn't mind a bit. The acceptance letter was exactly the one he'd always wanted to read: *"You are the hottest new writer to hit the scene since John Preston. I'm tripling our usual fee and including a $1000 bonus. Please send me everything you have. And you must come and see me. I know you have a giant dick. No one could write this well without having a fantastic body and a huge cock. I am dying to worship your awesome throbbing manhood. Please come soon. I just can't wait."*

Clarence put on his "Writer's Kap and" rolled a clean sheet of the heavy lavender paper into his typewriter. He'd have to remember to thank his lover for that box of "Super Subliminal Paper". It had really done the trick. He'd been waiting for an acceptance letter like that his whole life!

HORNY AS HELL

Sonny Torvig

It was one of those days when, for no particular reason it seems, you wake up horny as hell and even a quick jerk in the shower doesn't relieve the tension. Unfortunately for me, it couldn't be a day devoted to searching out a willing partner because there were too many deliveries to make. Being the boss and the delivery driver rules out a great deal when it comes to recreation! The business being very new, I was devoting every waking minute to its welfare. I kept telling myself the long-term benefits would be worth the sacrifice. With that hope and an enthusiasm fueled by youth, I crashed headlong into each day. So, I crammed my starving cock into straining jeans and hit the streets.

It was turning into a real hot one, and I began to feel schizophrenic, leaping from the roaring heat of the van, loping up people's gardens in crackling temperatures, then entering homes with from air-conditioning. The first deliveries went all right, everyone at home to receive their arrangements, and things running vaguely to schedule; but nothing diminished my feeling horny!

Midday shot by, and I was into a second clean shirt, momentarily refreshed by its dry fabric before I had to leap out into the inferno again. I sprinted up the narrow driveway, all the room left beside the firemist blue Eldorado, taking a minute to gaze into its sumptuous leather shadow, the holy grail of 'climate control' visible amongst the many extras. I glanced back at my Apache, a present from Dad when I'd set the business up. The cab was a furnace, but the cooler box on the back was a welcome breath of cold air when taking out a delivery.

Into the momentary shadow by the door, I rang the bell and waited. The large arrangement in my arms was mostly gardenias, their scent wonderfully relaxing, thankfully. I waited some more. There were no sounds from within, so I headed down the side of the house, searching out the back door. Sometimes that works. I knocked, and looked around. It wasn't a blatantly expensive home, but there was something about its architecture that breathed pure taste. I put a hand to the cool granite, a change from colonial white timbers. There was sound from inside, so I tried again.

Eventually, I saw the frosted shape of humanity approaching the glass door. I straightened up. The door opened. A woman smiled at me. I was a little taken aback because she was wrapped in just a small towel, water droplets running down her dark skin, her cleavage with uplift a magnet for the droplets. Her wet hair clung close to her head, and a small puddle of water formed at her toes. "You want cash for *that*?"

I regained my voice, and muttered that would be fine. She beckoned me in, told me to bring the arrangement through. Of course I've had the occasional lady make a pass, and this seemed to have all the ingredients already in the mixing pot. I grew jumpy. "In here, handsome." Oops.

I peered around the door into a minimalist seating area. White seemed to be in favor, I kicked my sandals off, and padded to the low glass table indicated. A wall of glass threw sunlight across the thick pile carpet, the gardenias looking perfect as I perked up the slightly astray arrangement. I got lost in my work, because it took me a moment to realize I was being watched. I flushed, and straightened up. "That's my youngest son, Keir." She was occupied with finding cash, and I had opportunity to study Keir. He was lying by the pool, naked, and the color of maple. With a good helping of oil his body had a sheen like polished wood, every muscle emphasized by strong light and shadow. He was studying me just as closely, slowly uncurling himself from the lounger and moving towards a towel. Damn!

"He just loves showing off his wares." I heard a hint of something in her voice, perhaps of an issue between mother and son. My distracted silence caused her to turn back. "You are quiet. Is it my semi-nakedness that embarrasses you, or my son's nakedness?"

She was teasing me. I think.

I stammered, "Uh, yeah. Both."

I could feel my ears on fire, acutely aware of the figure behind me reflected in every polished surface, padding towards the sliding windows. At last I remembered why I was there. "That will be eleven dollars sixty, please, ma'am."

She seemed merely amused, and while she counted the money out on the coffee table, gaping cleavage soft and damp,

I took the opportunity to rearrange my jeans. A hand in one pocket did a lot to diminish the obvious difficulties I was having.

She looked up, far too slowly, and smiled unchecked. "Ah me, the innocent abroad. I wish I could help you with your discomfort, honey, but I have appointments to keep. You take the money...." She uncoiled from her seat and patted my cheek on the way past. "We'll have gardenias again for next Friday, yellow this time, for sonny's birthday." She was already at the door. "You know your way out."

And she was gone. I let my shoulders relax again, and pulled my hand free of its confines. If I just rearranged my hard-on before I took off....

I froze. With my belt unbuckled and jeans open two buttons, I had a hand buried in my pants getting my rigid cock comfortable. And watching me from the door was the glowing Adonis. Did I thought for a moment about an explanation, but I decided it was simply too complicated. I grinned, and withdrew my damp fingers, buttoning my fly and quickly fastening my belt. "Gotta go."

"Oh, don't rush off on my account, and you best know that you've buttoned up wrong. You look even worse than with a hard on." He leaned on the door frame, a thumb hooked into the top of the small towel, the first strands of black hair just visible against the bleached white fabric. I looked down to see my error and began to fumble. "Let me know if you want a hand."

I glanced up in my embarrassment, to see him gently stroking down the front of his towel, a swelling luxuriance visible beneath its rough surface. Was this guy for real?

All in order, I pocketed the money, and headed for the wide doorway. He peeled himself from the frame and padded to the door, opening it for me. I smiled as I stepped past him, and took a chance. He felt warm and hard under my gentle squeeze, and with my eyes locked on his I angled past. "See you next week?" I paused in the hot shadow of the house, looking back at his unruffled pose.

"You can put a bet on it. You got a name?"

"Ronan." I raised an eyebrow.

"Keir, I gotta shower and cool off some. See you around."

As if I had already gone, he turned from the door and

padded away, the towel slipping from his hips before he disappeared. The last I saw of him was his beautiful glossy back and absolutely luscious ass vanishing round a doorway. I leaned my head against the wall and bumped lightly in frustration. If only his siren of a mother hadn't been around!

I spent the rest of the day in a daze, forgot two deliveries, and had to fend off one really abusive customer. Oh, and dented the rear fender on a stone gateway. I was never so glad to see an empty work sheet as early that evening. I then spent what felt like the rest of the time in the shower, tossing away the frustrations of the day. None of my attempts released my intense need however, and all there was left was to cruise down the strip. I took a look at the cash situation and slumped, I could afford a hand job, maybe a cheap blowjob.. But no more. The vision of Keir kept flickering in my mind, naked, oiled, hot. I wondered on the odds of his mother being out for the evening. Of him being in on his own. Even as the light began to fade he haunted me still.

This was sheer madness! The drive had been empty of the Eldorado and the majority of the ground floor unlit. It all looked very promising. And now here I was lurking in the shrubbery, eyes fixed on the upstairs balcony, behind that a floor-to-ceiling French-window. Behind that, a naked Keir was working out with free weights, a jutting cock the focus of my being. I didn't smell the stocks, nor sense the honeysuckle that loaded the night's air. But, in fact, I wasn't taking much notice of anything other than Keir. I crept closer, sizing up the big sycamore near the house. With a bit of nerve, I reckoned I could make his balcony, and then we'd just have to see what came next. Me, I hoped.

Trying to be quiet while struggling up an unlit tree is difficult, and I was breathless and lichen-stained by the time I faced the balcony rail. It would just take a leap of faith, and I'd be there. He came to the window and opened both doors wide, the evening loud with crickets and the distant background of the highway. He stood there for minutes, left hand slowly rubbing his engorged cock. I licked my lips, my own cock threatened to burst the metal buttons off my jeans. He turned, his sweet ass silhouetted against a low lamp. I almost had to wipe drool off my chin. This was it, now or never. I hesitated until he had vanished into the bathroom, and then committed myself.

The noise I made as I grabbed the railing for a better hold must have been enough to alert him, but no movement came. I froze, ears almost swelling on my head in an effort to hear more. It sounded as if he might be in the shower, in which case, I was safe to play Hendrix flat out without discovery. "All Along the Watch Tower." The music I could now hear in his white room was new to me, different, strange. I padded to the doors and slipped quietly in, why I didn't know. He was still in the shower. I saw the album sleeve on the large bed and tiptoed over. A cool guy singing, "These Foolish Things (Remind Me of You)." I made my way to the bathroom door, and chanced a peek through. My breath froze. The room was white-tiled floor to ceiling, the shower pounding away. Keir stood beneath it in all his glory, pounding at his meat, head arched right back under the water's flow. I watched in my desperate need as at last he reached his orgasm, his arching cum lost in the cascading water. From his movements and vocalized pleasure though, it just kept pumping. I ran my fingers down over my own cock, and felt the damp even through my jeans.

Turning back to the room I wondered for the first time how to work this. "Gardenia perfume lingering on my pillow...." perfect! I slipped into the darkened landing and then down the wide stairway to the ground floor. It didn't take a minute to find the main room, and less to pick the largest of the blooms from the table display. With a smile already on my lips I raced back upstairs, and placed the bloom on his satin pillow, the bedding thrown back in readiness. He was bound to notice that. Then what? Look round? Call 911? Pick up a hidden gun? I suddenly felt a twinge of fear settle in my stomach. I looked around frantically, then spotted my place. Outside on the balcony. I slipped into the deep shadow to the right of the doors, letting him come to me being the logic behind my move. It seemed sensible.

What felt like hours later, I heard the shower turned off, the album long since finished. The footsteps I didn't hear, but side two I did. A shadow spilled out onto the decking, growing longer as he moved to the doors. I braced myself. If the worst came to the worst I could just take off over the balcony on the left, and hope that the honeysuckle trellis would break my fall, and not me.

"That you, Ronan? Man you're cool, just makin' your own way around my house. Whaddya think I should do? Maybe call 911? Huh, get your ass busted? Or you goin' to humor me and come out to play awhile?" The shadow remained still, then grew to touch the railing. I stepped out quietly, my own shadow moving into his. He turned to me, dripping, hand on angled hip. Beautiful. "So tell me something, why you takin' the risk, man?" So where the hell did this guy come from, the Bronx? I shrugged.

"Couldn't get you off my mind, so I called by to say hello." He relaxed a little, and softened a bit. He turned away, stepping over the threshold and back into the light. I followed.

"You better get yourself a drink, you must have lost some sweat getting in here. The bar has the small choice Mum will allow me for entertaining."

I looked: beer, red wine and ready-mixed martini. I took a chilled beer. "Where's the heavy accent gone?"

He slowly turned from the stereo, putting his hand on hip once again.

"It's for the play I'm in at the moment, a musical set in New York." He was perfect with his hooker's pose. I nodded my admiration.

"I could've sworn you was from the wrong side of town, man. You playin' a heavy, or a hooker?" I sounded really fake to my own ear.

"Neither. I'm in the chorus, but I want to understudy the lead. So I'm working on my lines. I need to get noticed." He turned away and leaned over the turntable, his ass still shining with water droplets. I just wanted to lick him dry.

"You don't need to do anything to get noticed. I've had a hard-on since I arrived!" I put my beer on the low table and unbuckled my jeans, slowly, trying to look both determined and provocative. He just looked over his shoulder as my buckle clinked, smirking in defiance.

"So, you think that all it takes is a single meeting, then to turn up uninvited and flash your cock at me, to get laid? You like what you see so you think you'll just take it for your own amusement?"

He had turned back to me, and despite his defiance, I noticed his gorgeous cock taking an interest, swelling gently with the intention of looking me straight in the eye. He stepped closer. "Well, listen, honey. If you come into my home, then you have to keep in line with house rules. So you just keep on peeling your fruit, but just remember, you are at my disposal, tonight I call the shots." He stepped to within arm's length, and tugged at my belt. I was on an adrenaline rush, tearing my kit off as if there were a strict time limit. The warm evening air felt good on my bare skin as at last I stood naked in front of him.

The moment dragged for hours, the pair of us just looking. His skin was taut over the subtle definition of muscle, the occasional droplet of water still shining in the light. Large, dark nipples highlighted his Mediterranean coloring, with light curling hair beginning down his breastbone. The softness of his belly was slightly proud of the muscle beneath, a lovely little hooded eye of a bellybutton above darkening hair, leading tantalizingly down to his proud and upstanding cock. He was so excited that the shape of his cockhead was tight beneath uncut skin, the tip visible where it forced aside its warm sheath. The slit glistened with excitement. I saw how tightly his balls hugged the base of his shaft, and longed to suck them into my hungry mouth. I breathed loudly, suddenly aware that I had been holding my breath. "God you're beautiful. I've never wanted anyone as much as I want you this minute!"

"You better get onto the bed, boy." His warm fingers closed around my throbbing cock. "Get onto the bed, and surrender yourself to me. You are, after all, the intruder." He squeezed, and pulled me with him as he padded backwards to the bed. He had little idea of just how willing I was!

Delirious with lust, I threw myself onto the satin covers, my pride and joy jutting and bouncing over my belly. He stood over me, a half-smile bathing his full lips. "Hands above your head, boy. I have plans for you." He leaned over and placed my arms high, his grip on my wrist light but firm. I felt the cold metal against me, but not until the click and ratchet grip did I realize what he had done. I tried to tug free, but without success. He smiled. "Hi, there. Welcome to my world." I felt dizzy with sexual power, and to be honest I didn't feel under threat. I felt excited, but somewhere inside I knew that there was nothing he could do that I wouldn't enjoy, coming from him anything was acceptable.

He gripped one of my firm nipples and twisted hard, I squirmed. "My pet, my own prisoner to lust." He bent low over me and his hot pink tongue lapped the side of my face. I tried to turn into a kiss, but he twisted away. "Ah-ah-ah, bad boy. You do that again and you'll get no treats. You hear me?" I nodded eagerly. Anything! The hot tongue continued downward, sliding down my neck and over my collarbone. I shivered in anticipation as his came closer to my aching nipples. Suddenly, his teeth gripped one of my pert buds. I jumped in shock as pain erupted through my chest, which only made him more eager. He leapt to my other, leaving that too flushed and tingling in aftershock. My focus was now entirely on what he intended next, my skin alive with expectation. Teeth nipped their way down over my belly, a mouthful of hair tugged to the point of pain. Keir was obviously a wildcat when it came to sex. My cock pounded feverishly, aching to be engulfed in something wet and warm.

Oh God, here it came, his mouth descending over my full length. I gasped as he bit, moaned as he sucked. My hips were jerking off the bed, as faster and faster Keir worked on me, a tremendous pressure building up to scream out my orgasm. More and more fierce grew the electric charge running through my entire body, focusing somewhere in my groin. I felt my ass being raked by his sharp nails, then gripped in eager anticipation of my coming. Nearer and nearer I climbed, all the while his slurping sounds music in my ears. And then he did it. He had been tickling my hole gently, but as my cock began to jerk in preparation he slipped a finger inside me, then another, and another. I almost erupted off the bed! Hot cum pumped endlessly from me into him, his sucking and licking so intense my skin was on fire. I cried out in release, and writhed against my bondage.

Very slowly I began to come down from my stratospheric heights, my cock so alive that any touch was almost too much. But Keir knew what he was doing, his fingertips merely tickling down my soft and wet length. Again and again he ran his fingertips over my tingling skin, murmuring his pleasure in my frustration.

The sensations rushing through my body ripped me down the middle, all my desire blossoming in its tethered captivity. He ran hot lips and tongue over me, lapping up my lost cum, my ass tingling from his intimate invasion. My cock rested against the warmth of his cheek as he nipped and licked at its base, his grip so tight on my almost painful balls.

He eased back to my mouth, and I tasted myself for the first time, his tongue slipping between my lips. His hands stroked my ribs, my cock enthusiastically nuzzling his warmth. He rose above me and looked down, my vision filled with his own rearing length of mansex. I smelled the musky scent of him as he wriggled away from my reach, hands behind his back, a smile of anticipation bathing his features. I felt my cock in his slippery fingers, sensed what was to come. He half closed his eyes and eased back, and I felt him. A tight muscle pressing against my desperate cockhead, the weight of him forcing the issue. His bud relaxed its resistance, and I slithered up into his hot suction. He was prepared, slithering, my cock gripped in a soft vise as he sighed down onto my hips, filling himself with all I had to offer.

He stayed stationary for a short while, eyes tight shut, rocking back and forth in slow motion. He moaned low and slow, and then eased up my slippery shaft. I felt the cool air on me, all the while half my length buried in hot and tight ass. He had his hands on his thighs, his length jerking and bobbing before my eyes as he slowly rode me. I was his sex toy, and he took his own time to fuck himself with my hard and horny cock. His rhythm grew faster and faster, a hand occasionally straying to grip his own cock, tugging the skin back to reveal the wet and flushed head. My mouth watered. I licked my lips. I was bucking up at him in harmony, and at last I felt the beginnings of my release tightening in my groin, heating my balls to aching infernos.

He was in his own world now, fucking himself as if this were the last time, bucking up and down on me, my cock buried deep in its own moist heaven. The fact that I was unable to do anything but watch his orgasm was no great frustration, my own taking all precedence. He began to lose his rhythm, and I saw his head snap back in ecstasy. A great arch of hot cum burst onto my face, splashes of his creamy semen running down my cheeks, pooling over my lips. I licked his salty gift, to be rewarded with my own roaring cock erupting deep inside him. He gasped in pleasure as hot cum filled his insides, nails raking down my chest as he rode me like a bucking bronco.

Eventually our pumping decreased to a gentle heaving, our sweat-and-cum-sticky bodies smearing our cum over each other's skin. I looked into his eyes, and saw an edge of something threatening. He bent low and slipped off my softening length, the slap as my wet cock hit my belly a full stop, period. He licked at my aroused nipples, teeth edging nearer to the pain threshold. I winced and tried to move, but he continued to increase his bite, I breathed quickly as I was forced nearer to crying out, my inflamed flesh like two small fires on my chest.

He dug nails into my belly and raked downward, and I was dragged into the realms of being dominated. He looked up to see me wince, a hand lashing out to slap me across the cheek.

"You're the one who broke the law, so now you're subject to mine. I'll do with you as I please."

He squirmed down my chest, all the while his fingernails leaving what felt like ripped furrows. I froze as his teeth slipped down my cock, still soft and lying warm on my belly.

Shortly I began to swell between his teeth, only this time his teeth didn't allow for that. Soon he had my tender skin screaming with agonizing excitement. I squirmed, trying to get away, but he pursued me, moaning his own pleasure as my skin was dragged roughly back from my cockhead. He was almost eating me, for goodness sake! My balls were the next to feel his unfettered oral pleasures. Tugged and dragged moaning into his hot mouth, lapped and nuzzled to a tingling focus of attention. Above them my rearing cock quivered red and rampant, head glistening with saliva and pre-cum. He continued down, lifting my legs to hang above his shoulders. He lapped the back of my thighs, rubbing his chest against the damp skin. His cock nuzzled between my soft inner thighs, he used my body to rub its skin back and forth in a hypnotic rhythm. Without my first being aware, I found he was doubling me back, my hamstrings as tight as wire as I almost managed to touch my toes, his firm grip propelling my feet to the bed head.

I was too high to bother about the soft rope, its tightening around my ankles only making me the more horny, There I lay, like a chicken ready for the roasting tray. Ready for stuffing. He nuzzled his firm head against me, nudging in a slow and methodical rhythm. More and more firmly he pressed, my ass unwilling to admit him until ready. Cool goo slithered between his hot cock and my tight rosebud, and like a password for admittance he slipped slowly into me. His heat and solidity filled me to capacity, and more, stretching and straining my every practiced muscle. He was buried up to the hilt in me, pounding mercilessly, driving the breath out of my lungs, the bed banging against the wall in time to his fuck. His hips slapped against my wet asscheeks, the noise accentuated as gel smeared out over our skin. He pounded on, eyes shut, lips drawn back over perfect teeth.

He was using my legs as a support now, and as his levels of excitement stole his strength away he thrust more fiercely into me. He was panting, moaning deep and low in his chest. I was squirming, whimpering at the strength of his assault. The pleasure and pain seemed to merge into one intense semiconsciousness, the light around the periphery of my vision growing dark as my entire being concentrated on our joining. I felt my own level of excitement growing close to erupting, even as his moaning began to slip into a rising rhythm. Louder and louder he grew, and more and more fierce. His slicked hips slapped loudly against my bound thighs, cock rampaging in and out of me. I was a hole to be fucked, and his raking nails told me how close he grew.

When he did collapse into jerking and arching ecstasy, my already heated insides flooding with superheated cum, his breathing subsiding into primal panting and moaning, total domination. I was there for his pleasure. It was purely by chance that his domination included suddenly seizing my delirious balls, my own cum triggered in its explosive eruption. Hot juice pumped out over my chest, oozing down my rib cage, trickling up to form a warm puddle in that hollow where collarbone and trachea meet. There was a sound beyond our passions, one that made Keir grin, still buried hot inside me. I froze, not that there was much else I could do. He gently rocked inside my well-greased hole, stroking the backs of my legs now, hands reaching up to untie my feet from their bondage. He eased me out as he eased himself out, and lay slippery and hot on my chest, tongue lapping in the cum puddle like a cat with its milk.

I heard sounds again, footsteps now. Closer. I felt my nerve go, wanting more than anything to be unbound. He felt my agitation and smiled again. "Don't worry, Ronan, it's only Mom. She won't mind us. I relaxed a little, and gave way to a kiss. He was gently now, and in the afterglow I soaked up the affection like a sponge.

"You having a good time there, honey?"

I would have sat bolt upright, had I been able, but the best I could manage was to look across to the doorway. There she stood, housecoat unfastened, her soft curves glowing in the warm light. "Did you save any for me?"

"Sure did, Mom. He's nice and secure, and by the look of this he's ready and willing." His soft fingers stroked my already rampant cock. One of those times when, despite your feelings on the subject, the adrenaline that comes with fearfulness pumps up your manhood to proud proportions. I looked down at my cock, glistening with gel and cum, then fleetingly at the door. She was coming toward me, silk robe billowing out to reveal her ample physique. Keir slipped away from me, still grinning down at my writhing figure. He blew me a kiss, his beautiful body aglow with love juices and sweat, and teasingly stroked my cheek with his wet cockhead. "I'll see you later, Ronan, when Mom has finished with you."

Warm fingers were already slipping around my aroused flesh, and as a hot tongue lapped my bared cockhead I knew for the first time the powerlessness of genuine bondage.

COOLING OFF, GETTING OFF

David MacMillan

Sex was the furthest thing from my mind. I was climbing the highest hill in Athens, Georgia, on my way home from my last class of the day. I was sweating buckets in the heat of an Indian summer and I just wanted to cool off.

A VW Bug pulled up beside me, and the guy inside grinned and motioned me over. I stepped to the curb and bent my six-five frame over to peer at him through the wound-down window. I took in blond hair, blue eyes, with puppy dog grin amid a sea of freckles.

"Looks like you could use a ride."

"Yeah!"

"Well, hop in."

I slipped into the bucket seat beside the driver, my knees forced up nearly even with my face. Bugs were not the most comfortable cars for guys like me, but they were cars. The door shut behind me and I was crunched into the little car.

"Name's Julian," he offered and stuck his hand out, brushing my knee in the process.

I took the proffered hand, my leg hair standing straight up from the touch like I'd just been electrocuted. "I'm Max." I grinned at him. "And you're a life saver."

"Baxter Street's a killer," he agreed and laughed softly, "but you've got the body to hike it." He grinned sheepishly. "Can I invite you for a beer?"

"Sure," I answered and leant back in my seat, thinking a cold one would definitely hit the spot.

It took us two beers apiece to go through each other's life story. Julian, who looked much younger than his years, was a graduate assistant in philosophy, and from a hole in the wall near Brunswick on the Georgia coast. I was a newly minted sophomore in the College of Liberal Arts, and, most recently, from an Air Force town in the middle of the state.

There had been a continuous, underlying energy between us since I had entered the man's car. It was there sparking between us as Julian came back into the room and handed me another bottle of beer. I was confused by it, though. I mean, I couldn't remember once being interested in my buddies that way as I was growing up. Now I was. I wanted Julian naked. I was pretty sure he wouldn't mind and that he'd like me that way too.

I was nowhere close to being drunk. Now I was cooled off, I knew I was horny. I sort of hoped something would happen. I hoped all the strange energy was sexual. I smiled as I took in Julian's long, sun-bronzed legs, my eyes moving leisurely up to the basket encased in tight-fitting cut-offs.

I knew in the back of my mind that I ought to be shocked at what was going through my head; but my curiosity and the intrigue of the unknown held me firmly in their grip. And the sunny warmth of everything I had come to know about the man made it all comfortable.

"You must be feeling pretty grubby," he said as he sat down on the couch beside me.

The bubble of my acceptance and heightened sexuality threatened to burst. I figured he was pushing me to leave. "I'm pretty dry now," I replied. "But I guess you're right, I am pretty bad off." I stood up and sniffed under my arm and made a face.

"You can use my shower if you'd like." He grinned as I glanced down at my shirt and shorts. "I'll throw your clothes in the wash while you're getting cleaned up."

The bubble of comfort surrounding me settled again and I grinned back at him, telegraphing my relief to him. "Okay. Thanks."

"But finish your beer."

Our eyes met. There wasn't anything like hearts and flowers or song, but we both understood what we wanted to happen. That it was going to happen.

His lips slowly broke into a smile and his whole face was quickly taking it up, radiating its warmth out to me. "Why don't you slip out of your things and I'll get them in the wash while you're still on that beer?"

I luxuriated in the sexual energy that crackled in the room around us, and the strange, easy acceptance of stripping before another man that came with it.

I pulled the nearly dry T-shirt over my head and let it drop to the floor at my feet. Julian whistled softly and I glanced back at him. "You've got one hell of a nice body, Max," he offered, his voice filled with ego-pleasing awe. I smiled in appreciation, unzipping my shorts.

He reached out and wordlessly pulled my shorts down over my hips. I sighed as his fingers came back up my thighs and began to edge inside the elastic of my briefs. He came off the couch to get closer and went down on his haunches. His hands cupped my asscheeks. That was the greatest feeling I'd known; my knees nearly buckled as his body heat transmitted itself to me through his palms on my ass.

"They're nice," he mumbled, edging my briefs over my butt while keeping me cupped in his hands. "So nice."

"That sure feels good," I groaned, my cock springing fully to life behind the briefs bunching around it.

He tongued the tube of my meat through the still-sweaty cotton and I gasped.

"It's going to feel a whole lot better in just a minute or two," he promised and brought his hands around my hips, pulling my underwear down onto my thighs and forcing my cock out of its cloth sheaf. As the cloth fell down my legs, his lips found the thick knob of my finest feature and pulled it into his mouth.

My gasp quickly became a moan of pure pleasure as inch after inch of me pushed over Julian's tongue on their way down his throat. Instinctively, my hands went to the back of his head, pulling him farther onto me. I groaned loudly and began to fuck his face.

His fingers closed around my balls, tugging gently on them. His other hand joined his mouth on my cock, encircling it and moving up and down it in conjunction with his lips. Sensations I'd never imagined were erupting out of my virgin rod and sweeping over my body like tidal waves.

My muscles locked and I shuddered all over. My knees threatened to buckle, and Julian's hands on my ass steadied me. My balls contracted despite his tugging on them, and I moaned like a whore on Saturday night was supposed to.

I felt it all too soon.

The sense that pervades a man just before he erupts into orgasm spread out over me, and I forced myself to pull my prick from his throat. Julian's lips slipped down the side of my shaft and his tongue lapped at my balls. I watched as my spunk rained down on his shoulders.

He buried his nose in my nuts. His hands spread out to grip my cheeks, pulling me against him. I continued to erupt as his tongue worked the shaft of my suddenly very sensitive cock. That action was wiping me out, sending wracking spasms coursing through my body. He held me to him until I was dry.

"Holy shit!" I gasped when he finally released me.

"You taste good, Max," he told me, his voice matter-of-fact, like we were discussing which wine goes with spaghetti.

"Shit! How can you say that?" I gulped. "I've got to taste like sweat—and smell a lot worse."

"You're a virgin?" He gazed up at me.

"In every way except jerking off." I grinned then. "Or, I was...." I looked down at him and found myself becoming lost in his blue eyes.

He grinned. "Okay, virgin, how'd you like it?"

My eyes rolled toward the ceiling. "I'm just glad I didn't know what I was missing back in high school."

"You've got a lot more to learn, Max. You feel like a crash course this afternoon?"

I grinned at him. "If the rest of it is anything like the first lesson, you couldn't beat me away with a stick!" I plopped down on the couch and he joined me, our legs touching now because that was what I wanted.

Julian laughed and kissed my cheek. "Drink your beer before it gets as hot as you are. I'll get these things of yours in the washing machine." He scooped up my clothes and I noticed his balls trying to escape down one side of his cut-offs. His cock spread wide beneath the crotch of his pants. My eyes widened.

He saw my eyes were on him and glanced down at himself and chuckled. "That's an entirely different lesson and you're going to have to wait till I get back before I teach that class."

I watched his ass flex against his cut-offs and studied his long legs as he headed toward the kitchen with my things. I wanted to see the rest of him. To taste him. Lying back against the couch, I didn't care that I was naked. I didn't feel shame at having had my cock sucked. And I didn't fear what else would happen between us. I wanted to try it all, to sample this new world of sex. And I wanted to feel Julian's naked body against mine.

My eyes were shut and I was immersed in the peaceful

euphoria that I was to learn was the aftermath of good sex. I heard him return but didn't pull away from the feelings flowing through me. His fingertips on the inside of my thighs were like the kiss of a butterfly.

"You're really beautiful, Max," Julian said, his voice a gentle whisper deep in the security into which I had sunk. "All over. Beautiful body, beautiful face, and beautiful dick."

I smiled beatifically like some long-dead saint.

"And beautiful long legs and a butt most men would die for."

I spread my legs wider so the fingertips had easier access to my balls. They were joined by a tongue that explored both my cock and nuts before going on to find its way behind them. I spread my legs even wider and sank deeper into my serene euphoria as my cock grew harder.

Julian's lips and tongue explored along the seam that extended from my ballsac to my asshole. His fingertips explored my crack and soon centered on the puckered entrance into me. I moaned as he began to massage my asslips. The gentleness of his massage served to heighten my euphoria—as did what his tongue was doing with my balls.

The gentle massage of my asslips ended and I mewed like a kitten for more. A glob of something cool and greasy touched them and I jerked, threatening to come out of the serene rightness that cradled me. His hot, wet mouth descended my cock toward its base and the greasy chill at the entrance to my ass quickly disappeared, leaving me to float again in the sea of contentment that held me. His fingers returned to caress the puckered wrinkles at my hole, teasing them and slipping beneath them to push into me.

My legs were lifted one at a time onto Julian's shoulders and I didn't resist. Individual hairs from his head fell on my abs, caressing my navel. His mouth working my cock retreated farther and farther toward its head, pulling it toward my bellybutton. A moment later, even the lips were gone, leaving my meat wet and exposed and alone.

His tongue rimmed into my navel. My knees were pushed back against the sides of my ribs. His tongue trailed wetly over my chest until it found a nipple and began to suck on it. A thumb and forefinger sought and found my other nipple hidden under my knee and began to tweak it.

Fingers from his other hand returned to my ass and teased the puckered lips there. I moaned as his first finger breached my hole and slipped into me. I tightened on it and Julian toyed with my ass muscles with its knuckle. I ground my hips against it. I humped his chest with my hard dick. He slipped another finger into me. My balls tightened and threatened an earth-rending blast.

His cockhead touched my balls, shoving them to either side of their sac as it made its way beneath them. Julian slipped a third finger into me.

"Like it?" he asked.

I knew what was coming. What had to come. But that didn't frighten me. I was awash in the sensations spreading over me from my butt. I moaned softly and smiled.

His fingers pulled out of me and I felt empty and alone for the moment it took his wide knob to find its way to the pucker guarding my ass. There was a shift beneath and above me. His cockhead pressed against my asslips and the tongue on my nipple moved up to my ear. "I've already got a rubber on, Max," he whispered.

Pressure built at the entrance to my guts. The tranquility that had held me grew brittle. My eyes flew open as his lips suddenly pressed against mine. I saw my feet reaching for the ceiling above us. His weight was on the back of my thighs. My ass spread wide.

I still found it hard to believe. My hand went to my asscheeks. My fingers found the wide flange of his cockhead at my rear entrance and slid along its hard shaft down to his pubes. They followed it slowly back out until my asscheeks stopped them. The head of his cock was embedded in my pucker, at the ring of muscle. He humped forward and my asscheeks pushed my fingers back onto the shaft of his cock as his knob punched into my canal.

Pain shot through me. It erupted over my body. I opened my mouth to cry out but it filled with miles of tongue immediately when I opened it. His cock seemed to dig deeper into me until, finally, my cheeks were pressing my fingers hard against his bush.

"Oh shit, it hurts!" I groaned, finally twisting my face away from his.

"Keep your fingers on my dick," he whispered. His face was

above mine, his eyes looking down into mine. "How does it feel up inside you?"

"It fuckin' hurts!"

"I'll stay where I am for a minute; that'll give you a chance to get used to me being there." He grinned. "You're going to love this. Really you will."

"It's going to have to change pretty fucking drastically," I grunted between clenched teeth. But the pain was already ebbing, being replaced by a fullness I had never known before. I chuckled suddenly.

"What's so funny?" he demanded, sounding hurt.

"How I must look, with my legs up in the air and my ass wide open."

He smiled down at me. "It's not that open. In fact, it's pretty full of dick right now." He pulled a couple of inches out of me and I stared up at him, showing how startled I was at its movement inside me. "But you look beautiful like this. Really. And don't worry, virgin ass," he said, "I'm not about to quit. I'm going to fuck you good." He plunged back into me and I gasped as his cock massaged my prostate. He started nibbling at my earlobe as he settled into a slow, steady rhythm.

The tranquility that had cradled me was gone. But the pain too had evaporated. There was a whole army of new sensations marching out of my ass as he plundered it. I was wide-eyed as I tried to catch each one and experience it.

I pulled on my cock and it grew hard as he pummeled my ass. My hands went to his asscheeks, holding on for dear life as I rode his rod toward an eruption. My meat rode his chest. My balls tightened and I felt the second coming of that sense of overwhelming release pervading me.

"I'm going to shoot!" I cried in wonder, staring up at his smiling eyes watching my face telegraph my surprise. "Oh, Jesus!"

I pulled him deeper into me. My asscheeks ground against his pubic thatch, exulting in being impaled on his cock. "Jesus! Oh, sweet Jesus!" I moaned, gyrating faster. I felt his cock grow inside my chute. "Shoot! Damn it all, come with me! Come inside me!" I hissed between clinched teeth.

I was firing wad after wad of cum. I saw the first glob hit him in the center of his chest, and I writhed with crazed abandonment on his pole. My second shot hit just above his navel. "Shoot, damn you! Shoot!" I growled, humping his groin with all the instinct in me. My third blast hit me in the chin.

I felt it then: His cock grew larger and harder in my ass. I felt him coming up inside my gut. His blast sprayed into the reservoir of his condom. His spunk didn't exactly scald my insides, but I could feel it pumping into me. I would've felt it there—even if I hadn't been able to watch his body jerk and shudder with each blast of his cum inside me.

He collapsed on top of me, his cock still embedded inside me. We were both covered with sweat and my spunk.

He lifted himself slightly and found my lips. We lay there, him on top of me, in each other's arms, our tongues dueling for supremacy, his cock staying in me.

After Julian pushed off me and sat back on his haunches to watch me I tried to make my feet find the floor. I glanced at him and smiled tentatively as he pulled the rubber off his softening dick. "That was your second lesson, Max," he said, smiling back. "How'd you like it?"

I struggled to my feet, my ass aching but feeling good too. "What else can you do to me?" I asked, impulsively reaching out to touch his smooth chest and hoping to show him even a few of the emotions crashing around inside my head. "Whatever it is, I want a steady diet of these first two lessons...." I focused on his eyes watching me. "Promise me, Julian."

He chuckled and his fingers spread possessively across my closest asscheek. "Well, right now, I'm going to suggest we both take a shower and get cleaned up."

"Sounds good to me," I answered and followed him as he started toward the back of the apartment. "Julian...?"

He turned back to face me. I grinned happily. "Yes?"

"You can fuck me anytime you want."

His arm went around my waist then and the two of us together continued on toward our shower. His lips nuzzled my cheek and I turned to step into his arms. "You want to spend the night?"

My ass muscles clinched at the mere thought of him spreading me open again, sticking it in....

I grinned. "Just try kicking me out!"

A.K.A. DICK ADAMS

Mike Johnson

"Damn that phone!" I groaned. It was nearly two in the afternoon and I seemed to have been on the phone since early that morning, talking to publishers and other potential customers. Since going on the Internet, there had been quite a bit of interest from card companies and magazines in a number of countries I hadn't sold to directly in the past, but it had meant getting on the phone and making personal contact to find out exactly what they wanted. I had thought I was done for the day, but now the phone was ringing again. I expected this was one of those people in Australia calling me back.

"Is that you, Mr. Johnson?" The voice asked. There was a short pause. Then, "The photographer?"

"Yes, that's me."

"Well, hi. My name's Adam. Adam Richards. A mate of mine gave me your number."

"Who was that?"

"Steve Royale. You know him I think."

I smiled. I had known Steve for about five years and he'd been one of my most successful models in terms of getting published. I had sold pictures from every shoot I had done with him. And he was also good fun to work with, with a great body and an especially nice cock.

"Yes, of course I know Steve. What can I do for you?"

"Well, he said I'd make a good model and I have always wanted to give it a go."

"He told you the type of photographs I do?"

"Sort of. Nudie stuff, right?" he asked in his furry northern accent. Couldn't work out if he was from Manchester or Yorkshire.

"That's right." I smiled to myself. "Can you tell me a bit about yourself? Build, age. That type of thing."

"Well, I'm 20 now."

"Good."

"But I'm only five seven. Is that okay?"

He sounded a bit worried about that, so I said, "Don't worry about your height. You only have to be over six feet if you want to get into fashion photography. Height isn't so important for me." I thought to myself, "And I prefer working with shorter lads."

He carried on: "Brill. Anyway, me other measurements are 40-inch chest, 28-inch waist and I take size 10 shoes."

"Any other details?" I laughed as I asked the question.

"What? About me dick, you mean?"

Before I could answer he carried on, "Well, it's uncut, quite thick and about nine inches. And I've fairly big balls."

"Impressive. *Very* impressive."

"Not had any complaints." I could hear both pride and a smile in his voice.

"What about body hair and hair color?"

"Well, I've a little bit on me chest. A really hairy bum and legs and it's dark brown. My eyes are brown as well. And I've a tattoo. Is that okay?"

"Perfect. If you look as good as you sound I am sure you'd be ideal for me. Obviously before we could go ahead with a shoot I'd need to see you. Just to confirm you have the looks I want."

"Sure. No prob', mate. I've got to come down through your place next week. Got a delivery to do not far from you. I could call in. If that's okay?"

"Sure. When will that be?"

"Next Monday."

We then agreed on a time and I gave him directions on how to get to my office. We chatted a bit more about the type of work he wanted to do. Basically, he didn't mind posing in the nude but didn't want to do any erotic work

A little after three on Monday, the doorbell rang. I went down and opened the door to a really cute-looking skinhead. "I'm ... I'm Adam" and he stepped in. He was cute, no doubt about it, but he had a slightly rough look that made him even more appealing to me. Personally, I tend to prefer street urchins more than the clean-cut collegiate types I usually photograph for magazines.

I showed him my office. I work alone so there was no one else around to distract him as he leisurely inspected some of my photographs on the wall.

"Nice. Me girlfriend would like some of these."

Well, that answered one question I always had when first

meeting a model.

We chatted again about the sort of photos I thought he'd be good for, and went through the model release with him. To make sure he knew the photos would be offered for publication. It is always amazing to me how many lads do the work, get paid, and then are surprised when their photos appear in a magazine or on a postcard or something.

We also agreed on his professional name, the name to be used when the photos got published. Knowing he had an impressive cock, I suggested "Dick Adams." Not very imaginative, but he liked it. We also set a date for his first photo shoot. It was to be in two weeks' time. It tied in with another delivery he'd be doing. "Right, mate. I ought to be off soon. It'll take me about three hours to get back."

He stood and I got up to show him to the door. "Before I go do you want to see it?" He smiled. Before I could reply he kicked off his trainers and pulled off his sweatshirt. His chest was well defined and he had a wonderful six-pack. A dark line of hair disappeared into the top of his jeans. I smiled as the jeans were completely removed. Dick Adams indeed.

He stood there before me nude, hands in fists on his hips and a big beaming smile. "Well? What do you think?"

I just looked at his beautifully formed body and watched his cock filling and rising in an impressive curve upwards. He hadn't exaggerated about anything. His legs and bum were covered in thick dark hair and his dark, hard, uncut cock looked all of the excessive length he'd said it was.

"Not bad," was all I could think of saying.

"You want a closer look?"

I nodded and he stepped toward me. My hands explored his body. They worked down to his hairy bum and started to knead the fleshy, round, firm mounds. I could feel his hard cock pressing between us. I started to work my way down his body with my lips. Kissing his neck, sucking on his pert, oval nipples. He squirmed in pleasure as I did that. Finally I got to his balls. They were the size of large walnuts and churning around in his ballsac. My tongue went under his balls to that sensitive area between the legs.

"Ohhh … fuck, that's good," he moaned. And I slowly pushed him back onto my desk, lifting his legs over my shoulders

I sucked on his balls. First taking one into my mouth, then the other. He was really enjoying it. My right hand slowly pumped his hard cock and my left tweaked his nipples. "Suck meeee! Please! Please... suck ... meeee," he pleaded.

I was happy to oblige and worked my tongue up the underside of his hot, pulsing cock. Nine inches at least, I decided. Maybe more when he was really turned on. Pre-cum was oozing out and pooling on his belly. I pulled the foreskin right back to reveal his thick, juicy cockhead. He had a big slit.

I flicked my tongue over the slit. Lapping up the pre-cum. Then I licked the underside. Adam writhed around

"Yeahhh. That's...." He didn't finish the sentence as I took his shaft deep into my throat. "Ohhh. yeah...." he moaned

With his cock in my mouth I looked up to his face and saw Adam looking at me with a smile of pure pleasure on his face. I went up and down on him in a steady rhythm. He responded by pumping his hips.

I could feel he was building up to shoot.

"Will you swallow?" he gasped.

"Mmmmmmmmm," was all I could say. After all my mouth was full of his hot cock.

"I'm gonna shoot...!"

With that, my mouth was filled with his cum. I swallowed all he delivered. He pumped hard into my face. At last he eased off. I carried on sucking until I was sure I had got every last drop.

I looked at Adam and smiled. He grinned back.

In almost a whisper he said, "Hey, that was fucking great, man. Best head I've ever had." With that he got up off the desk and quickly got dressed

He then headed for the door. "See you next Monday. Bye mate. And thanks." And with that he was gone. After the door was closed I thought to myself, "We'll see." To be quite honest, I never expected to see or hear from him again.

But, much to my surprise, I was wrong.

At three on the day we had planned to do the shoot, the doorbell rang. I went to answer it and found Adam standing there with a great, beaming smile.

"Hi, mate. I'm ready for action." He stepped in. "Where'll we be working? You said it might be out in the countryside or something?"

"That's right. I know some old barns that I have been planning to use for some time. Plus it's such a nice day it would be better than working in the studio."

"Brill. I've always fancied getting me kit off outside—in the heat." He smiled again.

I gathered up my camera gear and we both walked out to my car.

"Is it far? This place we're going to?"

"No. It only takes about ten minutes to drive close to it. Then we have to walk a bit. But that wont take long. Don't worry. We won't be back too late. I know you have a long journey home."

"No worries there, mate. I told me girlfriend I wouldn't be back till tomorrow mornin'. I hope that's okay with you."

"Certainly. There is a spare bedroom if you want."

We both just smiled and I drove off. I took him to two old barns. They were in a bit of a state but made a really interesting location. They were far enough off the beaten track for us not to be disturbed by any groups of people out walking. Also a friend, who didn't mind me using them, owned them.

I had asked Adam to wear an old shirt, jeans and boots and he duly had obliged. It was a more appropriate style of clothing for the setting. Even if he wasn't going to be in them for long. It was a warm, sunny day with just a bit of clouds, which meant it was comfortable, but without the strong shadows that sometimes cause problems when shooting outside.

I started the shoot by getting Adam to stand in front of an old stone wall. He opened his shirt and played with his nipples. He was obviously enjoying being photographed immensely, and I only had to suggest a pose and he was right into it. At one point, he turned his back and dropped his jeans down to his ankles and placed his hands on his buttocks. He looked over his shoulder and gave a sexy smile. "You like?"

I just smiled and nodded.

He then pulled his hairy cheeks apart and leant slightly forward. I told him, "If you take you jeans off, you'll be able to spread your legs more." Adam needed no further instructions. He pulled off his boots and pants, spread his legs farther and placed his hands back on his firm, tight ass. Again he started to pull his cheeks apart and started to poke his hole with the index finger of his right hand. "How's that mate?" again looking over his shoulder.

"Great. I thought you said you didn't want to do erotic?"

"Oh, forget that shit. I'm kinda enjoyin' this." And with that turned to face me. Again he smiled. "Hey, mate, get a shot of this," he said pointing to his hard cock, which was dripping pre-cum.

"My God!" I cried, staring at his cock. "That is quite something, Adam. And do you always ooze that much?".

"Yeah, I'm afraid so. And me girlfriend hates it. Just hates it! She always says it's messy and she don't like getting it on her. She won't even play with it when it's dribbling. And she don't like the taste." And he grinned.

"She doesn't know what she's missing."

"Well, she did try it once, but gagged and nearly threw up!" he laughed. "Never tried it since. It's a pity 'cos I love getting sucked off."

"I know. How *well* I know," I said, and proceeded to photograph him from various angles to get the best shots of his body and his luscious, very hard cock.

"What about you, mate?" he asked. "What do you like? Have you only had it with lads?"

"Yes. I did have girlfriends when I was at school. But never anything physical. Couldn't get a reaction when any of them made a move. I always thought it was because I had been brought up to think that you should only have sex once you were married."

"Really!?" He seemed surprised, and chuckled.

"Yeah. Then I realized that when I was kissing a girl I was actually thinking about one of my mates. It was then I knew girls weren't for me."

"What's it like going with a lad? Does it hurt? You know...." He didn't have to explain what he meant.

"If you're not relaxed, it certainly does. The first time I was so tense it really hurt. But the guy was gentle and I got used to it. But I prefer giving rather than receiving."

"Hmmm." He smiled that sexy, very cute smile of his. I almost felt like going down on him then and there.

He quickly changed the subject and started chatting about his job. The town he lived in. That type of thing. The shoot lasted nearly two hours and I had Adam pose in every possible location in and around the barns I could imagine. All the time he kept stroking his cock to keep it hard. He was glistening with sweat by the time we finished. It was a very horny session. He obviously enjoyed posing.

"Cheers! That was a great shoot," I said at the end. "I am sure I have got some great material."

As I packed my camera away in its case, I realzied I had taken about six rolls of film.

"You think the mags you sell to will be interested in me then?" he asked while putting on his shirt.

I looked up at him adoringly.

He stood smiling, just wearing his open shirt and a pair of white terry-cotton socks.

"If they aren't, they have no taste. Simple as that."

He smiled back then. His cock, which had been getting softer, began to suddenly firm up again. I was still kneeling down as Adam walked toward me. It was obvious now what he wanted. I smiled.

He stood in front of me, his hands firmly planted on his hips, with his incredible, dripping cock pointing in a steep upward curve. My tongue licked up the salty pearl that had formed at the slit. He put his hands on my head and pulled me forward My mouth opened and I took the head of his thick cock into my mouth. I inhaled the pungent musky smell of him and tasted his salty juices. I sucked on him gently and he slowly rocked back and forth. Then he stepped back. "Stand up," he instructed.

Not sure what was going to happen next, I got up off my knees.

He then started kissing me. This took me completely by surprise, but soon our tongues wrestled with each other and our hands were all over each other. He grabbed my crutch and started rubbing my own stiff cock. He found the zip fastener and pulled it down. All through this we kissed. He then knelt down in front of me and pulled my hard cock out of my straining pants. He sat there looking at my uncut shaft and gently stroked it, pushing back the foreskin to reveal the pulsing head.

He looked up at me, his eyes gleaming. He licked his lips, then took my cockhead into his mouth. He went down a bit too fast and gagged a bit. He pulled back, then took it more slowly. I could feel his tongue working round my shaft as his lips went back and forth from the glans to the base. I was so turned on about this shoot that I soon felt my balls churning and pressure building in my cock. Seldom had I reacted quite so irresponsibly. Normally, I held back, not wanting to jeopardize what could well become a long-term relationship with a model. Yes, this was anything *but* normal, in every way.

"I'm gonna shhhoooooot...." I groaned.

I expected him to stop sucking and wank me but Adam never moved off. He just carried on sucking. Then I came. I could feel my warm spunk filling his mouth and he gulped it down.

After I shot my load, Adam licked his lips. Some of my cum was dribbling down his face.

I sat back on a bale of hay that was behind me and watched Adam close his eyes, squeeze his nipples and slowly jerked himself. He was clearly enjoying himself.

After a few minutes, he grunted and spurt after spurt of cum shot out over the barn floor.

We just smiled at each other as we got dressed and walked back to my car.

"I can't believe it. That was the first time I've ever sucked a bloke."

"Really?"

"Yeah. Was I okay?" he asked.

I was surprised because he had been so good. "Well, you were definitely okay. More than okay."

He smiled back. "You know, it tasted better than I thought it would..." He drifted off, and when he spoke again, he changed the subject, talking about his family.

Twenty minutes later, we were back at my place. I showed Adam where the bathroom was. He said thanks and a few minutes later I could hear the sound of water filling the bath. Adam popped out wearing a towel round his waste. "Er, Mike, any chance of a cup of tea? White, two sugars?"

"Sure," I answered.

"Cheers," and he disappeared back upstairs into the bathroom. I made the tea and took his up to him. I found him lying in the bathtub, eyes closed, gently caressing his body. And I couldn't believe it—his prick, his glorious big prick, was hard again!

His eyes snapped open and he saw where I was looking. He laughed, and I laughed too. I handed him his tea. "Here, this should calm you." Chuckling, I went back down stairs.

About an hour later, he came downstairs wearing a short white toweling dressing gown loosely tied at the waist. He looked stunning. His chest was exposed and, as the gown only came down to his knees, his hairy calves were clearly visible. "I found this hanging up behind the door of the bathroom. Is that okay?" he explained. Then he asked to see some of my published photographs.

I love showing people where my work has been used and showed him the filing cabinet where I kept copies of everything I'd had published. "Have a look through. I've just got a few things to finish, then I'll fix us something to eat. "

I left Adam looking through my files while I finished some paperwork. When dinner was ready I called him through to the lounge. It was only spaghetti with meat sauce, but he seemed to enjoy it. At least he didn't leave any on his plate.

Over dinner, he asked about the lads he'd seen in the photos. If I kept in contact with any of them and if any of them did duo work. Then he said, "If you ever want to pair me up with anyone, I wouldn't mind giving it a go."

"Were there any guys in particular you'd like to work with?"

"Nah, not really. So long as they are about my age and not too muscled or too queeny. Normal. You know...." He took a long swallow of the brew I had given him to go with the meal.

"Okay, I'll think about it."

We carried on talking till midnight , when I said, "Well, I have to be up at seven, so I'd better show you where you'll be sleeping."

I showed Adam upstairs and opened the door to one of the spare bedrooms.

"Nice,' he said, his eyes scanning the furnishings. "And where'll *you* be sleeping?" he asked

I pointed to my room across the landing. "Over there."

"Okay. Goodnight, then." He smiled again and went into the spare room and I went into the bathroom to get ready for bed.

After I'd showered, I put on my bathrobe and went into my bedroom. As I climbed in to my king-size bed when a quiet voice in the dark said, "I never thought you'd ever finish."

He was sitting in the chair in the corner. He walked over to the bed and put his arms round me.

"I'm sorry," I said. "I thought I was finished."

"Nah. Not yet."

Again we kissed. Then he shoved me forward so I could suck on his hard cock. He knelt over me and pushed the duvet off. Because the curtains were open I could see his naked body in the light of the half-moon. I wished I had my camera, so lovely was the view.

As I sucked on him, my fingers worked their way into his deep, hairy asscrack until they found the opening of his moist hole. My fingers gently probed.

With a mouth full of my cock, Adam mumbled, "Gentle there. Please be gentle...." and returned to sucking my cock and playing with my balls.

I leaned across to my bedside cabinet, opened the drawer and pulled out a tube of lube. I found his hole again and squeezed some of the lube at the entrance. I then started easing my index finger in. He was tight but didn't stop me; he just kept sucking on my hard cock. Adam then rolled over on to his back and lifted his legs presenting me his hot hairy ass. "You got a rubber in that drawer?" he asked in a hoarse whisper.

I leaned across and got a small foil packet out of the drawer. "Are you really sure you want to do this?" I asked as I gently stroked his hard cock.

"Oh, yeah," and he held his legs apart even further.

I opened the pack and rolled the rubber over my hard cock, and put some lube on it. Then I positioned myself so my cock head gently pressed against his asslips.

"Oh, Mike, please be careful. I've never done this before you know."

I was. After all, I didn't want to hurt him. As my cockhead pushed against his ring I could feel the resistance. He was really tight.

"Relax. Just relax," I said as I pressed in. I kept on stroking his hard cock and bent forward so I could suck on his nipples. That did it. He suddenly opened and I slipped in.

"Ahhh fuck," Adam groaned, wrapping his legs round my back to stop me from pulling out. I got into a steady rhythm thrusting in and out, going a bit deeper each time. I leaned forward again and sucked hard on his nipples. He grunted and it was obvious he was really getting off on having his nipples sucked whilst I fucked him. Then he yelled, "I'm gonna shoot!"

I lifted off him in time to see his spunk splatter across his belly, chest and face. Seeing that he could hold back no longer and pumped hard into his virgin ass. Within a few seconds I was shooting my own load into the condom that was deep in his ass.

Then I collapsed on top of him. We kissed briefly, his spunk acting as a lube between the two of us. "That was fantastic," I said after I'd caught my breath. I could see Adam's face in the moonlight smiling as he just said in a quiet voice, "I'm glad you liked it, mate."

After lying next to each other for a while we got up and showered together. We then returned to my bed and fell to sleep. Adam's head was resting on my shoulder and his arm draped over my chest. My arm was around him. We were soon fast asleep.

Early the next morning, we got up and had breakfast. Adam was smiling a lot, but he made no reference to what had happened the night before. I thought he might be regretting it so didn't bring it up.

Just as he was getting ready to go, he said, "Hey, you know, I really enjoyed the shoot...."

"I'm glad."

"But more than anything, I enjoyed what we did last night."

"I'm glad."

"Can I call in again sometime ... you know, to do more photos—or something?"

"Whatever, whenever...." I said as I kissed him goodbye.

Well, all that happened two years ago now. In that time, he has dropped in about once every three months or so when he is down this way making a delivery. He's done quite a few photo shoots in that time and he always stays overnight so I have plenty of time to work out just the right angles.

ECSTASY

John Patrick

The club was still pretty empty when I arrived on an insufferably hot night in July. I ordered a beer and was cruising a couple of bodybuilders in tank tops who were dancing more or less together when Marty came in. He was with a new boyfriend, all right, but it wasn't just any boyfriend—it was *Tony.* I couldn't believe it! My two most recent fucks strutting in the door with their arms around each other, jeans so tight, their asses so perfect. They came up to the bar around the corner from me, moved two stools together, and proceeded to sit almost in each other's lap, flirting and laughing and glancing in my direction every once in a while like they were talking about me and wanted me to know it. They even had matching longneck beers. Really, those bottles were the only long things they'd have in their hands that night.

You see, I knew they both liked big dicks, the bigger the better, and they were both "average." Well, if I wasn't upset enough by the fact that they were in there together for all the world to see, I was driven to near panic when it occurred to me that they might be comparing notes about what I was like in bed. My mind filled with memories of Tony sitting on my cock, and then Marty sucking my cock and licking my balls for nearly an hour and then sitting on my cock....

My revelry was detonated by the image the two of them locked in an embrace, maybe after taking turns, maybe using the huge black dildo I remember seeing Tony kept at his bedside.

They both smiled at me. I know they liked what we did, but I couldn't even bear to think they were complaining about me now. I felt my ears turn red. As if reading my mind, they started laughing and talking even louder, using cryptic hand motions now. I couldn't stand it. I had to go somewhere where I wouldn't have to watch them. Grabbing my Bud, I slid off the stool and started edging by the two offenders, heading toward the dance floor. When I was directly in back of them, Tony turned. He was stroking the bulge in Marty's jeans. "Why, John," he said. "Why didn't you tell me Marty's such a hot number?"

A hot number! Well, Marty is, but I sure didn't want to hear it from Tony. In fact, I never thought I'd hear such a thing from Tony, knowing what a hot bottom he is. Marty as a top? I couldn't believe it. But the smile that spread across Tony's face told me everything I needed to know. I was being drawn into their web. I was helpless against the two of them. Tony drew me toward him with his other hand. I looked down at the bottle of beer clutched in my hand. I felt like hitting Tony over the head with it, but his hand was busy at my crotch and I was about to forgive him everything.

Somehow, we became tangled together, all three of us, rocking to the beat of the dance music thudding from the juke box. I noticed the man next to Marty turned to his neighbor. The second man's face bobbed forward to get a look at the three of us. A *menage a trois*, with me in the middle. I knew Tony would have come to the club ready for action, so my hand found its way into his shorts, pushing down into his crack. A clean, greased-up hole ready for a quick, one-time-only fuck.

Generally it doesn't take much time for a boy as cute as Tony to hook up with some horny stud whenever he ventures into a club. Tony always takes a hit of Ecstasy when he gets to the club, washes it down with a beer, and then a couple of glances, a dance or two, a little conversation and before you know it, Tony is getting the shit fucked out of him in a dark corner of the club, in a car in the parking lot, or back at the stud's hotel room.

"Let's dance," he said to us, brushing away my adventurous hand from the crack of his splendid ass.

After about half an hour, the three of us were in a dark, all-too-familiar corner of the club. Tony was unzipping me, pulling my jeans down to my knees as he bent down in front of me. I was wearing white briefs and, without hesitation, Tony began gnawing at the growing bulge through the fabric. I moaned, bringing my hands to Tony's head to control his wild tearing at my prick.

"Suck it, baby. C'mon, suck it," I whispered.

But Tony continued to tease me, soaking the full length of my ten-inch cock through the fabric. Meanwhile, he was stroking Marty's bulge and Marty began to kiss me as he moved in tighter on Tony.

Instead of taking my cock immediately into his mouth, Tony took Marty's prick out and, since Marty never wore underwear, the hard-on flopped in Tony's face. Tony sucked it while he stroked my sopping hard-on through the cotton. Finally, he rescued my cock from its captivity, flicking his tongue at my ball sac, then taking one ball into his mouth, gently sucking, then taking the other.

"Oh, Tony...." I groaned.

He released my balls and ran his tongue up and down the middle of my thick shaft, flicking his tongue at the tip. He was bent on making this moment last.

When he finally took my cock into his mouth, I sighed loudly, grabbed his head hard, and shoved my cock all the way into his throat. He used every effort to keep from gagging. Soon I was fucking his face with the long, powerful strokes he loved, pulling my cock out so the tip was just barely touching Tony's lips, and then shoving it back in all the way so his nose was buried in my pubic hair.

Kneeling in front of me, Tony managed to push my jeans and underwear down to my ankles without missing a beat. Then Marty got behind Tony and began munching on the lubed ass lips and inserting his middle finger into Tony's hungry hole. Tony began moaning. He was so hungry for it, his cock was hard as he stood now. His dick was not quite horizontal and had a nice upward curve the entire length. His dick so hot, coated with pre-cum. "Fuck me, John," he begged, stroking my organ, pulling at the foreskin, bending over and sucking on it again.

I realized I was in fact getting harder, hard enough to fuck him certainly. Every time Tony pushed firmly at the base, the skin behind the head became taut and pulled its flared edges downward. As he stroked outward, the skin began to bunch up behind the head and then with a snapping motion, it suddenly lurched forward over the edge and down around the slope of my glans. When he finally let go, Marty moved in next to Tony.

They held their dicks together, and I saw first-hand their cocks were nearly identical. When Marty pushed down on his so it was horizontal like Tony's, Tony moaned. "You fuck me, too, Marty. Both of you fuck me," Tony begged.

I started to stroke both dicks, which took both of my hands

to wrap around them.

But the heat of the moment could no longer be contained. "I'll open him up for you, John," Marty whispered. Marty spit on his dick over and over and, with Tony bent at the waist, he slowly inserted his cock into Tony. Tony went back to sucking me. Watching Marty working at Tony's ass really got me going. Tony knew I wouldn't hold out much longer. It was time for me to replace Marty in Tony's ass. Marty generously pulled out and stood next to me as I lined up my cock and shoved it into Tony. Marty reached down and felt my cock as I fucked. "Oh man," he said as he looked up.

I looked up as well to see three strangers standing in front of us. It was odd, but part of me was excited by this. I had never before fucked anyone with an audience looking on. My heart, which was already beating incredibly hard, thumped even faster.

One of the men stepped up to Tony and held his dick out for Tony to kiss. Tony opened his mouth and let the man feed him his long, thin penis.

My dick started to quiver. The excitement was almost too much. I could only moan as Tony wriggled back, allowing me to push all of my cock into him.

"Wow!" Marty moaned at the sight of me completely buried inside Tony. "That's ... that's fucking incredible."

I began rotating the head of my cock the way I knew Tony liked it. I pulled back a bit, but he pushed up trying to keep all of me inside him. Marty reached down as I slid part of the way out, and held my shaft. We kissed then, and I thought I'd go mad if I didn't come. Finally I started the slow fucking I knew Tony loved: thrusts to the hilt, then pulling almost completely out, again and again. My cock now slid effortlessly in and out of him.

Before long I was leaning over Tony's sweaty back, whispering in his ear, "Oh, baby, oh, baby, I'm gonna give you my cum ... it's coming all for you, Tony!" I began trembling as I shot my load up inside him, groaning heavily in his ear. At the same moment, the man Tony had been sucking came all over Tony's face.

Slowly I pulled out and stepped back so Marty could also finish inside Tony. It was then that Marty exhibited talents I did not know he possessed. I reached down and held his hard cock as he had mine while he slammed in and out of Tony. Our kisses as he fucked Tony were almost as good as watching him fuck. Meanwhile, Tony took the other two guys into his mouth at once, sucking them with an eagerness that was mind-boggling.

Sweat was streaming off Marty as he got close. "Oh, Marty," I whispered in his ear as he was dumping his load into Tony, "I wouldn't have missed this for anything." He kissed me as he pulled out of Tony. Then Marty and I held each other as one of the men came 'round to also finish inside Tony while Tony sucked the other man to orgasm.

When the strangers left, we pulled Tony onto the floor and held him tight, kissing his torso while he jerked himself to orgasm. As he came, Tony's eyes were squeezed shut in ecstasy.

BEST LAID PLANS

James Hosier

"You just get hotter and hotter," said Greg, whispering in my ear. "You are one hot fuck, I must say."

"Well, you're pretty good at it yourself," I replied. His cock was twitching limply in my ass and the spunk-laden towel under me was cooling fast. He started licking my shoulder blades and my neck. I just lay there making appropriate noises. It wouldn't be long before somebody else would be in my place. Everything depended on Luke. He wanted to get screwed by me every Sunday and I was anxious to oblige. My regular Sunday appointments had to be off-loaded. Greg was the first.

"Oh well," he said at last, "I guess we'd better get up and get ready." I felt his hands on my asscheeks. He pulled out and stood up. I followed suit and we went into the bathroom. He slung the rubber into the bin. As usual, I took the tub and he took the shower.

"Silver Firs again?" he called over the sound of the streaming water.

"Would you mind very much if we went to the Burger Bar in town?" I asked. He turned off the shower.

"The what?" he asked.

"The Burger Bar."

"Yeah, but it's an awful place. Let's go somewhere better than that. What's wrong with the Silver Firs?"

The Silver Firs was his favorite eating place. He was known there. The price of one meal there could keep a person eating well at the Burger Bar for a week.

It was time to start my well-rehearsed campaign. "Well, the truth is that I've got a buddy in Sussex College. They're only allowed out on Sundays and I said I'd try to meet him there. We hardly ever get a chance to meet and my eighteenth birthday is coming up. Then I'll be away at college and I'll probably never see Luke again."

I let the message sink in. "You never told me you had a buddy in Sussex College."

"It's not a thing you shout about in a High School like ours,"

I said. "You're likely to be branded as a snob or a social climber."

"I see." He turned on the water again and finished showering. He was obviously thinking. I hoped his mind was working on the right lines. All too soon I would be away at college and he would have to spend his Sundays alone, jerking off over memories or dirty books.

I climbed out of the tub, toweled myself down and let the water run away.

"I'll tell you what," he said, as we dressed. "Why don't we go to the Burger Bar, collect this guy Luke, and take him to the Silver Firs? My treat of course."

I said it was very generous of him and that Luke would enjoy it. We got into the car and drove into town. "I'll sit in the car and wait for you. I don't think I could face the Burger Bar," said Greg. "Besides, the chances are that some of those spotty kids are patients of mine."

If it hadn't been for his invitation to the Silver Firs the plan would have gone haywire there and then. That's what happens when you try to plan things. I could see what he meant about not wanting to enter the Burger Bar though. It was packed. Thank God none of my buddies was in there. Most of the customers were what I would call mini-teens. The music was loud. Paper-hatted girls slapped burgers onto plastic plates as fast as they could but the queue didn't seem to get any shorter.

Luke and the other guy stood out like sore thumbs. They were sitting in a corner, both in their immaculate Sunday walking-out suits.

"Here he is," said Luke as I approached. "James, this is Martin. Martin, meet James Hosier."

Martin stood up and we shook hands. Boy oh boy! Luke had done well, I'd say that! Martin was about average height. He had very short hair, broad shoulders, long legs—just right!

"Sudden change of plan," I said. They both looked disappointed. "Greg wants to take us to the Silver Firs. His treat," I said.

"That place on the right outside town?" asked Martin. I liked his voice. If you spoke to him on the phone, you'd know you were talking to a boy, not a man, but you couldn't possibly mistake his voice for a girl's. Do you know what I mean?

"That's it."

Martin whistled. "Lead on," he said.

"Don't you want to finish your meal?" I asked.

"I think I could forgo it for a meal at the Silver Firs," he replied in that superior tone that Sussex College folk use when they're speaking to mere people. They followed me outside. "Come again, won't you?" the manager called. None of our crowd ever gets asked to come again. When tradesmen see a Sussex College kid, you can almost spot the dollar signs in their eyes.

"Greg, Luke's got a buddy with him. Is that all right?" I asked, bending down to talk to him through the car window.

"Sure."

I got into the front seat. Luke and Martin climbed in the back. Greg turned round and shook hands with them. On the way to the restaurant there was the usual stilted conversation you get when people meet for the first time and can't actually talk face to face. Did they like being at Sussex College? It was okay. Yes, it was a bit like a prison. They were only allowed out on Sundays.

We arrived at the restaurant and, as usual, were bowed in by the doorman. Luke and Martin didn't give him a second glance and probably thought they were getting the usual Sussex College treatment until the head waiter bustled forward. "Doctor Turner and Mr. Hosier!" he said, ignoring Luke and Martin. "Welcome!"

"We're four this time," said Greg.

"Of course. This way!"

"You're a doctor, are you?" said Martin. "Local G P?"

"Professor of Dermatology actually," said Greg.

That put Martin in his place. He actually blushed slightly. "My mother is a gynaecologist," he said.

"Oh really? Where?" But Greg didn't know his mother or the hospital where she worked. "Are you going to follow in her footsteps?" he asked.

"No way. It's a messy business."

"How right you are. I stick to skins." We laughed.

It was in the middle of the meal, over the steaks that things started to go wrong.

"What do you think this is, on the back of my hand?" asked Luke. He put down his fork and held his hand over the table.

Now, if there is one thing that upsets Greg, it's being asked to work in his free time. 'Opening the consulting room,' he calls it and you normally get slapped down fast. To my amazement, he took Luke's hand in his and held it up to his face.

"Don't do that. It looks like you're proposing to him," I said. Martin laughed. So did I—at first.

"Some sort of simple dermatitis. Nothing to worry about. I'll give you the name of a cream you can get. You got long fingers."

"Have I?"

"Amazingly long. How old are you?"

"Sixteen."

Greg continued to hold his hand. I was beginning to feel annoyed.

"You know what long fingers indicate, don't you?"

"Musical ability?"

"Haha! No, a big penis," said Greg. "See this finger here?" He touched Luke's middle finger."

"Yes."

"If we fold it back into the palm, like this, as far as it will go, like this, that dimension is the exact size of your penis when it's erect."

Luke looked down at the palm of his hand. "I don't think so," he said. Martin folded his own finger back. I watched carefully. "I think it might be," he said. I hoped it was. Not that Greg was really a cock man, but eight inches is eight inches—and certainly more than Luke had.

Greg released the hand and we continued the meal.

"Do you come here often?" Luke asked.

"Mostly. In the summer we go farther afield. The coast sometimes."

"You and your wife?" Martin asked.

"No, James and I. I'm not married."

"Oh." You could see what Martin was thinking. I didn't mind him coming to any conclusion he liked. In a few weeks' time it would be Martin, not me, sitting in the Silver Firs with an aching asshole, and I would be free to fuck Luke. On the other hand, I didn't want Luke to know the truth. I think I was afraid he might think less of me if he knew about my secret life.

"I service Greg's car for him," I lied. The truth was that I had once recommended that he should take it in for a service. BMW engines are way beyond my capabilities. "Not for much longer, unfortunately," I added. "We're going to Europe in the summer vacation and then I'll be away at college."

"I shall have to find someone else," said Greg. "Either of you know about cars?"

I was delighted. At last the plan was beginning to work. The fish was nibbling the bait.

"Not me," said Luke which was just as well.

"Nor me," said Martin. "I just about know the difference between a piston and a cylinder."

"One slides up and down inside the other," said Luke with a giggle. The wine was beginning to take effect.

"And has to be well lubricated," I said. He giggled again. I think we were both remembering how I'd had to use my mom's hand cream on his asshole.

"What are you interested in?" Greg asked. Martin was apparently into electronics. Luke, to my surprise, said he grew cactus plants.

"That's where you got that rash," said Greg. "I'll bet my bottom dollar," and so, for the next ten minutes, all attention was on Luke again. What sort of cacti did he grow? Had he scraped the back of his hand against the spines at any time? I was left to talk to Martin who obviously knew a lot about electronics and seemed determined to get me interested as well.

Greg stood up to go to the toilet. "I'll come with you," said Martin. "You can show me where it is." That was a good sign. I had to stand up to let him get out and Luke and I were left together.

"You know something," said Luke when they had gone.

"What?"

"I reckon your friend Greg is a homosexual."

"Could be, I suppose. I'd never thought about it."

"I think he is. Making all that fuss about my hand and that business about cock size."

"Possibly," I admitted. "We can soon find out."

"How?"

"Why don't we fix him up with Martin and see what happens."

"Oh! Is that why you asked me to bring along one of Dr. Gotham's favorites?"

So much for the superior intellects of Sussex College pupils! I thought he'd clicked straight away. All my careful cross-questioning had been a waste of time. As my father says, when his secretary doesn't click on something straight away, 'It's like working with Lassie!' Luke had given me the background on a number of boys. He'd been pretty circumspect at first. Of all the boys in the school, apart from himself, Martin was most often sent for by the Principal and, one day, Luke had actually caught him in the showers pushing a soapy finger up into his asshole.

"It might work," Luke said, doubtfully. "How would we do it?"

"That's easy. When do you two have to be back in school?"

"Not till ten."

"So we get Greg to drive us back to his place. He'd do that anyway. Then you remember something important, like your dad's due to call you. I'll take you on the back of the bike and that leaves Martin with Greg."

"But you wouldn't actually take me back to school? You'd take me back to your place." He grinned.

"Well, my folks won't get back till nearly midnight," I said. "I guess that gives us long enough."

"For you to give me long enough," he said, licking his lips.

Greg and Martin returned. "Greg, what's the plan after this?" I asked.

"That's up to you and these guys." He turned to Luke.

"We're happy to do anything," Luke said. "We don't have to be back in school till ten."

Greg laughed. "It's easy to tell you come from the secluded world of a private school," he said.

"How so?" Luke asked.

"You'd never get James here to say he was prepared to do *anything* with a relative stranger," he said.

For some reason that annoyed me. I suppose I should have been grateful but I was the guy he'd been fucking every Sunday for almost a year and to be portrayed as some prissy, puritan kid needled badly. I fell silent but he paid no attention to me and carried on chatting with Luke and Martin. In the past he'd always been hyper-sensitive to my moods.

"Well, let's get on the way," he said and paid the bill. We were bowed out of the restaurant and were soon speeding back into town.

"You were a bit quiet back there," he said.

"Was I?"

"I thought so. Thinking about being eighteen and going to college perhaps?"

"Maybe."

"I guessed so. Ah! Here we are."

"Is that your bike?" asked Martin as we drove into the garage.

"That's it."

"Looks great. Wish I had one."

Greg unlocked the door and all four of us traipsed in. Luke and I sat on the leather sofa which still bore the stain of my first visit. Martin sat opposite. Greg fixed some drinks and put some music on. Somebody had to start the ball rolling, I thought. It might as well be me....

"What Greg said about finger length and cock length is absolutely right," I said. "I checked it out."

Luke gazed at his hand as if he had never seen it before. "I'm sure it wouldn't work with me," he said. "I'd like to believe it was right."

"That reminds me," said Greg, standing up again. "I wonder if I've got any of that cream in the house. I may have." He left the room and we heard him going upstairs.

"I think it's right," said Martin.

"It would have to be proved before I believed it," said Luke.

Greg returned with a packet in his hand. "In luck," he said. "I found a sample tube. Are you quite certain that it's only your hand which is affected? Do you itch anywhere else?"

"Well... er...." Luke blushed.

"I think I might as well have a proper look at you," said he who had once blasted me for asking how long one of the swimming team members would be off swimming through some sort of rash on his back. The two of them went upstairs.

"That really is some bike you've got!" said Martin. "Would there be any chance of you giving me a ride on it one day?"

"I'd be glad to," I replied. "If I'd known you were interested I'd have brought a spare helmet along."

"What about next Sunday?" he asked.

"I think I'm going to be busy next Sunday," I said. So, for that matter, was he— as soon as this silly medical examination was over and I could put the plan into operation.

"I've always wanted a motor bike," he said. "There's no chance though. My parents are dead set against them. I've never even ridden on the back of one."

That set me off. I told him about all the bikes I'd had and how fast (or slow) they had been and about the places I'd been to on mine. He seemed really interested and I forgot all about the time until we heard some sort of a bump from upstairs.

"They're sure taking their time," I said.

"Probably checking the finger trick," said Martin.

I said I doubted it. After all, Luke and I had an appointment that evening. I looked at my watch. Very shortly, he would remember that his dad was due to call him and we'd both be on the way. Pity that he would be without a helmet for the first part of the journey but it was only a short distance to my place and I had a spare one there. There would be plenty of time for him to undress—slowly this time—and then I'd fuck that delectable little ass of his. My cock stirred at the thought.

"Greg's very thorough. He'll want to see if that rash has broken out anywhere else," I said as the minutes ticked by. I was beginning to get a bit concerned.

"If he finds a rash in his ass, it'll be nothing to do with horticulture," said Martin. "Luke hasn't been sitting on a cactus plant. It's a condition associated with private schools, especially Sussex College."

"Yeah, he sort of hinted about something like that," I said.

"Stands to reason," said Martin. "He was the only boy in the school over the Easter vacation and getting it at least once a day. Now the others are back, it's small wonder that he's itching for cock. Sounds to me like your buddy Greg's giving him some."

It was true that there were some strange sounds coming from upstairs but they weren't the sort of sounds I associate with someone getting screwed. Then I remembered how silent Luke had been when I fucked him.

For a moment or so, I was furious. I see now that a lot of my anger had been groundless. After all I had planned to replace myself. I think what upset me was that the plan had gone wrong. Luke was good-looking and a *very good* fuck, but Martin had a lot to commend him. On the non-physical side he was interested in bikes and Luke wasn't. He had long legs and, if the finger trick was universal, there was a potential eight-inch tool tucked away under those smartly creased pants!

"Do you suffer from it too?" I asked.

"Sometimes. Not today. This butt of mine got screwed three times last night. In fact the last time was at eight o'clock this morning."

"And when's the next time?"

"Who knows. Not for about three weeks at least. It's Sherakowski's turn with the principal next. Then there's the guy from Nigeria. The twins are due for their sixteenth birthday at the end of the week. They'll keep him busy."

"You'll have to find someone else," I said. "Another boy perhaps?"

"Out of the question. Very strictly not permitted."

"So it looks like you're going to go onto hand jobs," I said, "Unless...."

"Unless what?"

"I wouldn't mind...."

I'd been looking at him in a new light. In fact, he was better looking than Luke. He was more powerfully built somehow. Luke's narrow waist and cute, little-boy butt were attractive ,but Martin looked more muscular. There was a lot of power there, plus eight inches of cock! In swimming terms (and I didn't know then if they were swimmers), Luke would cut through the water elegantly with hardly a splash. Martin would plough through it—and win.

"Not here," he said. "They'll be finished soon."

"My place," I said. "Leave it to me. We'll go on the bike. It's not far. I can lend you a helmet there and take you back to school afterwards."

"Hey! That'd be great!" he said. I couldn't help noticing a considerable lump in his pants that certainly hadn't been there a few minutes earlier.

Somebody upstairs flushed the toilet. We heard Luke laughing and they came downstairs. I wonder if you know that superior 'I know something you don't know' look? I get it from school kids if a teacher has let slip that James Hosier isn't exactly the prodigy he makes himself out to be, and from my parents when I drop hints about acceptable birthday presents and the item in question is already wrapped and in their bedroom. Both Luke and Greg were perfect examples of it.

"Did you find any more itchy places?" I asked.

"No," said Luke.

"You spent long enough looking for them."

"You can't be too careful with skin infections," said Greg. I caught a glimpse of his wrist. Sure enough, there was a red line. He'd been wearing a rubber glove, just as he had when I first lay face down on the couch and he was looking for a rash. He would have gotten his finger into Luke's ass more easily than mine. That was for sure. Possibly more besides.

"Martin's just remembered that he ought to go," I said. "His father is due to call him tonight."

"Yeah, I know. From London, so I ought to be back for the call," Martin added. Luke's face was a study. I was waiting for him to say 'Hey! That's my line!'

"And I really ought to...." he stammered.

"Don't say that your father's going to call you too," said Greg.

"Well... er, he might. He often does?"

"But he's in West Africa, you said."

"That's right. He's in the embassy there."

"Good. You can call him from here and save him the expense," said Greg. "I'll get you back to school in time."

Martin and I said our goodbyes and thanked Greg for the meal. Greg saw us to the door. "Thanks a lot, James," he said when Martin was out of earshot and standing by the bike.

"Guess you won't want to see me on Sunday?" I said.

"Are you sure you don't mind?"

"Sure."

"Tell you what," he said. "Why don't you come round at say, six o'clock and we can go to Silver Firs. I still want to be your friend."

"That would be great," I said. "Do you mind if I bring Martin?"

"Why? Are you and he..."

"Not yet but we very soon will be," I said. "Have fun with Luke."

I drove home very slowly; not so much for safety reasons as for the feel of Martin's warmth against me. I had to show him how to sit, pushed up as close to me as he could get. At first he put his arms round my middle and clutched me so tight that I could hardly breathe. Slowly, he got a bit more confident and relaxed a bit, holding on, as he should, by clutching my butt between his legs. By the time we turned into Ashgate, I had a raging hard on under my leathers. I pulled up in the drive and he climbed off. I had no cause to feel embarrassed. His pants stuck out in the center too!

"That was great!" he said. "How fast were we going?"

"Not more than forty,"

"It felt faster than that."

"We'll make the next bit as slow as possible to make up for it," I said.

"The next bit?"

"When we get indoors."

"Oh, I see. Yeah, sure."

I led him indoors, double-checked to make sure the folks were not at home, and then we went upstairs.

"Nice room," he commented. He walked round, examining my posters, the computer and the rarely used exercise machine.

"What's your room like at college?" I asked, pulling off my leathers.

"A monk's cell. One bed, one desk, one chair; end of inventory." He stopped in front of my favourite poster. It's a huge cut-away drawing of a Harley Davidson, my dream bike which I shall have one day when I don't have to explain to my folks where the money came from.

"There's a hell of a lot in a bike, isn't there?" he said, staring up at it. I moved close behind him and put my hand round to his front.

"There's a hell of a lot in here too," I whispered stroking the lump. It grew even bigger. I could feel it throbbing through the material.

"This is the crankcase," he said, touching the poster.

"Right!" I pulled his hand down and placed it over my cock. "This is the con-rod," I said. His fingers wrapped round the shaft. "Leading up ...that's right... to the piston." I felt his fingers exploring the shape of my cockhead.

"Which slides up and down in the cylinder," I added.

"I'll bet it's a tight fit." He squeezed my cock.

"The tighter the better," I said. "The cylinder has to be well lubricated." I took my hand away from his front and slid it up and down in the furrow of his butt.

"You'll have to show me some time," he said.

"That's what I had in mind."

"Not today, though," he said. "This cylinder had more than enough piston last night and this morning."

I of all people should have known. I could have kicked myself. After a session with Greg my ass burns. Michael isn't so bad but I still wouldn't want to take another cock in it for some time. There have been times with Greg when I could hardly sit on the bike afterwards and I am eighteen and well used to it. Martin was only sixteen.

"So,. what are we going to do then?" I asked, putting both hands round him and trying to undo his belt.

"We'll think of something. Here. Let me."

We were both undressed in record time. Clothes seemed to go everywhere. He turned around to face me or, rather, it seemed, to *point* at me. Most cocks have a habit of pointing upwards and outwards when they're aroused; his stood out at exactly ninety degrees to his belly!

"The finger trick certainly works for you," I said. I put the palm of my hand under it. The first inch was buried in dense black hair. The rest was as hard as steel. It was uncut. Just the shiny, purple tip of his cock head showed.

"You've got a big one too," he said, admiringly. "What shall we do?"

"Well, that's up to you."

"I don't know really," he replied.

"Well, let's get up on the bed." I couldn't take my eyes off his ass. It was milky white; not so well-rounded as Luke's but certainly bigger and it looked softer. Dimples formed in the sides as he clambered up onto the bed. We lay side-by-side, looking at the ceiling.

"All yours," he said.

"I was about to say the same thing to you," I replied. His hand went to my cock and slowly retracted the foreskin. That felt good. I reached over and took his between my finger and thumb. I was in a quandary. The truth is that I didn't know what to do!

Having found out with Luke that ass-fucking is a thousand times better than *being* fucked, all I wanted to do was to get my cock in him.

"Why don't you suck it?" said Martin.

Damn, I was afraid he might say that. Having your cock sucked feels great, but my experience was limited to having it done; not doing it. There were some drawbacks after all in retiring from passive life.

What was I to say? 'I'm not really into that'? Back to square one and a spot of mutual masturbation? Not with Martin. He was too good for that. He and Luke were bound to talk about their experiences at school the next day....

'How did you get on with Greg, Luke?'

'It was great. He sucked me and fucked me till I could hardly stand. How about James?'

'Oh, we just tossed each other off.'

I wasn't having that! No, no.

When you've been on the receiving end as often as I have, you realize that cocksucking is an *art*. And Michael is superb—a real master. He artfully uses his tongue a lot and applies suction at just the right times. Being sucked by Michael is mind-blowing. Greg's pretty good, but perhaps a bit too quick. All he seems to want is a throat full of spunk and yesterday was too late if you know what I mean. Andy starts by sucking my toes, and works up my legs. This does nothing to me and, by the time he's got to the fountain, he's gotten so excited by my feet that he shoots all over the place and loses interest.

Worse still, and in a class by herself, is Janet. One of the guys in the swimming team; a real beauty of a boy called Jeffrey Selsey, once had some of us in fits and some of us wondering by announcing in the changing room that, in his view, girls couldn't suck cock.

"Which guys have you tried it with?" somebody (guess who?) asked. He was furious. Said he meant it in a general sense like 'Birds can't swim' or 'Fish can't fly' and he tried to find out who said it so that he could punch the filthy sod's face into a pulp. It was a narrow escape but I think he was right.

For a start, Janet calls it her 'little action man'. That's pretty sick-making for a start as I think you will agree. It is also not little. It might not be huge or enormous like they are in books but I draw the line at 'little'. She has to be in the mood, and then she says, "Let me see my little action man." Fumble, fumble. "There he is, trying to hide. C'mon then, little man.... Oh look, he's standing to attention. Isn't he sweet? Let's just pull his scarf down a bit shall we? Can't have his little head covered like that. There! Oh look! He's blushing. Let me give him a little kiss...." It's all so silly. Then, after several minutes of painful teeth scraping, she wants to see him fire his little gun.... "Naughty little man. Some of that went on Janet's tits. Now James will have to lick it off."

There was no way I was going to let Martin go back to Sussex College and say, "High School guys can't suck cock." If I was going to do it, it was going to be good. What did Michael do? Well, for a start he stroked the inside of my thighs. I sat up, put a hand on Martin's left knee and worked it slowly up to his balls.

"That's nice. Kinda relaxing," he said. I did the same thing to his other leg. He enjoyed that. He spread his legs apart and I got the first really good look at his balls. Would you understand, I wonder, if I describe them as a large peach with the surface of a walnut? It's the best description I can think of. The sac was an almost perfect globe, wrinkled on either side of the median line.

A bit more of the stroking and then phase two of the Michael treatment. I got him to bend his knees and bring his feet back up as near his butt as possible and then got in between his legs. It was a bit difficult at first but I got there in the end. With my hands supporting his thighs I started tonguing his balls. Just gently playing with them at first with the tip of my tongue, feeling the wrinkles and the few soft hairs that sprouted from the surface. He spread his legs even wider and lifted his body right off the bed. In that respect he was better than I had been. Michael had to tell me what to do. I got further in and sucked on the surface of the sac as if trying to pull his balls out through the skin. He began to moan slightly.

Farther still ... hold the balls up... even farther... tongue out to its farthest extent....

That really turned him on. He gasped at first and then started wriggling round, pushing himself down onto my mouth.

I didn't think I would enjoy it at first. Certainly there was a hint of gas down there that deterred me from trying to get in as far as Michael does with me. I think I might have stopped if it were not for the effect it was having on him. It dawned on me that he was completely and utterly mine. I could have done anything with him. A muscular sixteen-year-old, strong enough to floor me with a single punch was writhing around on my bed willing me to do what I wanted. I could have fucked him pretty easily but there was always next time. It was time to move on to his cock. I pulled my head out.

"Go on! Keep going!" he gasped. I let him sink back on the bed. His cockhead was streaming. I don't think mine ever gets as sticky as that. It certainly doesn't when Janet's playing with it.

Not wanting any of that stuff in my mouth, I wiped it as best as I could with my forearm. A mistake! I should have remembered something Michael used to say. I never looked at what he was doing but felt his finger tips playing gently on my cockhead. Then he'd say something about a boy's pre cum being the best aperitif in the world and lick round my slit until I was ecstatic.

Gingerly, I touched it with my lips and tongue. That's when I realized what a mistake I'd made. I can't say that it tasted particularly nice but there was something about it which made me want more. It was his secret essence, straight from his secret organ, which few people, apart from me, had seen; and even fewer had done what I was doing.

Being very careful to cover my teeth with my lips, I moved my mouth down on to it and took as much as I could.

"Oh! Yeah! Yeah!" he moaned.

Then what was I supposed to do? I wished I'd asked Michael a few questions. I managed to move my tongue around a bit. He liked that, so I carried on doing it. I pushed down farther. Another mistake. I choked and had to release it altogether. I was embarrassed and furious with myself. Martin was used to the practised ministrations of Dr. Gotham. I bet he hadn't choked over it.

Then I had an idea. I'd heard about the sixty-nine position; even seen a picture in a magazine but I'd never done it, not even with Janet who thought it was dirty. It was worth trying. He shifted sideways to make room for me. I felt my cock slap against some part of him but all I was conscious of was a close-up view of his. The veins on the surface stood out and it was still glistening with my spit. Very gently, I took it again and then.... were those lips against mine? Was he really going to? All doubts vanished as I felt it being sucked into his mouth.

His fingers played with my balls. I just went crazy. From that moment, I couldn't have cared less if it choked me to death. I sucked and licked as hard as I could. I put my hands round his ass cheeks and kneaded them. He did the same to me. After that I experienced an extraordinary sensation that I'd never had before. It was as if we had become one. We seemed to move together. Neither followed the other's lead. I sucked at exactly the same time as he sucked and kneaded the same part of his soft buttocks as he had found on mine.

His butt muscles stiffened and shuddered slightly. For an instant I was aware of a throbbing and a strange taste in my mouth. Then it happened. I felt it jetting out of him, filling my mouth and overflowing down my cheek. I tried to swallow but couldn't. It just seemed to keep coming and coming. It's funny. I knew it was going to happen and had steeled myself for the moment. I wanted to know what it really tasted like. Michael always said something like 'utterly delicious'. Greg (on the few occasions he'd made use of my cock rather than my ass) said 'It tastes like you,' and Andy was more enamored of the taste of my toes and usually pulled away at the crucial moment so I splattered over him and the furniture.

I still don't know. I was too far gone to pay much attention to the taste. There was a hint of swimming pool water maybe? I don't know. I was only conscious of the dull ache in my balls that meant that my own load was on the way. I couldn't warn him. My mouth was full. I think I must have tried to shove it further in because he made a sort of gagging, gurgling noise as I spurted into him.

As carefully as I could, worried about what my mother might say about farther strange stains on the bed cover, I pulled away and swallowed what I could. My cock suddenly felt cold as he did the same.

He sat up, swallowed hard and smiled. "You've done that a good few times before, haven't you?" he said.

"What makes you think that?"

He put his fingers round my limp, sodden cock. "You're brilliant at it, man. If you suck like that I can't wait to get this in my ass."

"Next Sunday," I said.

Perhaps there is something in the theory that compliments make you big-headed. My helmet seemed tighter than usual as we rode to Sussex College. My very first one, dating back to my 100 cc days, fitted him perfectly. I took the suburban streets slowly but out on the freeway I opened her up for him. Sixty, seventy, eighty. The needle flickered up towards the ninety mark—about all my bike is really capable of with two people up. His hands gripped my waist and his knees wrapped round my butt. A nice feeling. Even nicer, though a bit scary for a second, he started playing with my cock through the leather. I wound the throttle forwards and the bike slowed down. We were soon pottering along at a steady thirty and the scowling drivers we had overtaken passed us, grinning happily this time. They couldn't have been aware of what Martin was doing. I guess they thought I'd had a piston blow.

By the time I drew up outside the gates of Sussex College I had a hard on again. So, I was glad to see, did he as he clambered off and undid the helmet.

"That was great!" he said. "We'll do it again on Sunday, eh?"

"We'll do a hell of a lot on Sunday," I said. "I'll pick you up about ten, okay?"

"Sure. A bit earlier if you like."

"Nine-thirty then." At that point another boy rode up on a push bike. He was tall, and dark haired. He waved to Martin and at that moment I noticed his feet. They were enormous. He pedalled the bike in such an ungainly way that his heels were close to the rear wheel.

"Who's that?" I asked.

"Steve Barratt, otherwise known as Big Foot," Martin replied. "He has to have his shoes made specially."

Steve's buttocks rolled on the saddle as he pedalled away down the drive towards the school buildings.

"Nice ass," I observed. "Does he...."

"He wouldn't be allowed out on Sunday if he didn't. Those who object get kept in until they change their minds. Trouble with Steve is that he can't afford cab fares into town; hence the bike."

My brain went into overdrive. Andy would go crazy over a boy with feet that big. He'd pay for it too. He was more than generous with his money. Cab fares and an allowance for Steve and the rest for me. Martin would get a share too if he would act as a go-between....

"Does he swim?" I asked, thinking of Andy's vast basement

pool.

"Yeah. He doesn't need flippers with feet like that. Why the interest? You're not thinking of having it off with him, surely?"

"No way! I've got you but I know someone who'd like to meet him. Someone with a swimming pool and loads of cash."

"Who?"

"A friend. Acquaintance really. Look, tell Steve to stand by next Sunday. How can I get word to you?"

"Drop me a line. Something not suspicious. Some of our letters get looked at. I'd suggest something like 'My friend says he can fix Steve's bike.' Or something like that."

"Good idea. Till Sunday then." He turned away and started to walk up the drive.

"Martin!" I called. He turned round.

"Thanks for everything."

"It was nothing. See you," and he continued up the drive.

"Eight inches is hardly nothing," I muttered as I started the bike. On the way home I thought hard. Greg had Luke. Andy would have Steve. There was just Michael to worry about. I was beginning to look forward to my 'retirement'.

LEARNING THE HARD WAY

Peter Gilbert

"Just look at him go!" raved Michael, leaning over Richard's shoulder and staring at the monitor.

Richard didn't answer.

"He's got a nice ass on him too," Michael added and, again, received no reply. Richard was thinking.

It was a hot Wednesday night. The last of the domestic staff had gone home and the two of them met, as they always did, for what Michael referred to as 'appreciation of solo performances.' The star of that evening's show was Peter Bauer. Peter was still a teenager, thin, blond, long-legged and, Richard had to agree, absolutely beautiful. But he was a problem.

"I think we're going to have to weed him out," said Michael.

"Give him a bit more time. He may well come round. It's happened before," said Richard.

"We could try to force the issue, so to speak," Michael replied.

Richard leaned back in his leather chair. "Coming from you, I find that quite funny," he said. "I thought 'gentle persuasion' was your motto."

"It is but it's not working with that one—and yet, just look at him go!"

He leaned even farther forward, almost obstructing Richard's view of the screen.

"That's it, Peter," he murmured. "Give it all you've got. Oh yes! That's good. Let's see the cream spurt."

It was apparent from the moment Peter started to undress that they were in for a performance different from those they were accustomed to watching. Michael had classified them. There were the 'undercover wankers.' Boys who lay with open mouths and closed eyes in beds which looked as if two dogs were fighting under the quilts.

Infinitely more entertaining were the "cast inhibitions aside" brigade. Boys who threw the quilt on the floor, removed whatever they wore in bed and lay fondling their cocks lovingly before pumping semen onto their bellies.

Peter Bauer was in a class of his own. They had watched him undress, carefully remove the quilt from the bed and lie on his back. He parted his legs, grinned and put his right hand under his balls. He closed his eyes and lay still for some minutes. If it wasn't for the gradual rise of his cock, he might well have been asleep. It twitched upwards, lengthening and thickening as it did so. Finally, all eight inches of it was parallel to Peter's flat, white belly. He took his hand out of his crotch and fingered it. Then he drew up his knees so that his feet were flat on the mattress, raised his butt and started. His rasping breath came over the loudspeaker. The bed creaked as he waggled his butt from side to side.

Finally, unaware that the eyes of the Principal and Vice principal of the Loxley Academy were watching him, he gave a long, drawn-out moan. A jet of semen like a white flash shot upwards and splashed down on him, followed by another and then another. He sank back on the bed, wiped it up with his hand and sucked his fingers.

Like all the others, Peter had queried the purpose of the TV camera high up in the corner of his room and like all the others, he'd been reassured by Mr. Loxley's explanation. They were, Mr. Loxley assured him, very rarely used but in an institution housing nearly a hundred young men, some of whom had criminal tendencies it was regrettably necessary to have some means of monitoring them. He didn't tell the boy about the infra red floodlights that, on that Wednesday evening, had turned a darkened bedroom into a film studio or about the microphones hidden behind the wall coverings that were picking up the squeaks of the bed and Peter's rasping breathing.

All the teachers, the counsellors, the domestic staff and the parents of the inmates held the Loxley Private Corrective Academy in high regard. Parents were appreciative of Richard's 'mentor' scheme, by which certain carefully screened rich men befriended their sons and visited them at weekends. They were unaware of the services their sons provided. The academic and maintenance staff attributed the boys' Monday morning exhaustion to the extensive sports and exercise program the Academy provided. None of them knew the truth.

As for the boys: Richard found them quite amusing. They invariably arrived resentful and often fighting mad at the thought of being confined. A few days alone in a comfortable bedroom gave them time to think and, of course, they picked up snippets from the other boys at meal times. Then Michael went into action.

Michael had been a great find. When Richard first met him he was in despair having just lost his job at an exclusive boys' boarding school. News of his changing room activities had reached the school authorities. He was a good sportsman, a superb athlete, he was good looking and, more importantly, all the boys liked and trusted him. This was extraordinary because Michael never showed them the slightest affection. He treated his young charges as a gardener might regard a selection of attractive but hardy perennials or a farmer his herd of prize cattle.

"Pleasantly tight but agreeably responsive," he would say after a night with a new boy, or "Satisfactorily hung. Nice balls too."

All the boys would agree, were you to ask them, that Michael was the only 'bent' one on the staff. They had no doubt that the principal, Mr. Richard Loxley, was as straight as they come. If Mr. Loxley ever found out about Michael or their mentors, they said, he'd go ballistic—which was how Richard had planned things. If anything were to go wrong, he'd be in the clear and Michael would be the one who went down for several years; a fact of which Michael, being no fool, was well aware.

"We'll have to do something about him," said Michael, still watching the screen. Peter was dropping off to sleep.

"If we force him, he'll run away and tell someone and then you know what will happen, don't you?" Richard replied.

"It's almost worth the risk," his colleague replied. "A cock like that and a butt like a rubber ball. We'd make thousands out of him if only he'd play along. Stupid little idiot!"

"Give me time," said Richard, stifling a yawn. "I'll try to think of something."

"Make it soon," said Michael. "Good night."

"'Night, Michael."

Richard got up, switched off the monitor and left the office. Something, he thought, as he undressed for bed, would have to be done—but what? To send the boy home would be an admission of failure, and something that had never happened in the ten years the Academy had been in existence. Not to introduce a boy so good looking; not to mention randy, to a suitable mentor would be a failure of another sort.

Wearily, he climbed into bed. Ten years, he thought. It was a long time but it was working; thanks to Michael and thanks, too, to David Atkinson....

He was in his third year of college and, because of pressure on accommodation in the halls, he'd had to find lodgings, ending up with the Atkinson family about a mile out of town. Mr. Atkinson was a nice enough guy. Mrs Atkinson was kind and a good cook. The only drawback had been their sixteen-year-old son, David. He was a good-looking lad, but a loud-mouthed show-off. He was the sort of boy you'd see in the streets with his disreputable buddies throwing rotten apples at cars or calling out rude remarks to passers by. At home he was equally difficult. Mr. Atkinson seemed to ignore him—even when David said things to him that would have earned Richard the hiding of his life if he'd spoken to his father in that way. It was left to Mrs. Atkinson to restrain him and, faced with a tall sixteen-year-old, she didn't have a chance.

For his part, Richard got on reasonably well with the boy, helping him with his homework and listening to his accounts of the latest exploits of his friends.

Then, one weekend, Mr. and Mrs. Atkinson went away for a long holiday, leaving the two of them in the house. On Saturday night, David came home not just slightly tipsy but blind drunk. He'd been to a party and drunk a whole bottle of Bacardi—most of which he'd vomited up all over his front. Somehow or other, Richard managed to haul him upstairs to the bathroom. David lay on the floor, choking and muttering to himself. There was nothing for it but to undress him, which, with some difficulty, Richard managed to do. There were so many chains on his jacket and jeans that it was difficult to distinguish the real fastenings from the decorations. Richard took a sponge and wiped his face and neck. Richard had enjoyed several pleasant glimpses of his landlord's son-and-heir since he had been in the house. There had been the time when David stood at the top of the stairs in his boxers shouting for his jeans or a clean shirt to be brought up at once; little incidents which Richard would play over to himself in the solitary night hours.

Naked, David looked good—very good. Even in its drink-induced sleep, his cock looked beautiful. It was fairly long, and tapered to a puckered point. His balls were large and loose hanging and he was as hairy as Richard had imagined him to be. Sadly there was neither time nor opportunity to gloat. David was sick again. Patiently, Richard wiped it up. He managed to drag the almost unconscious boy to his room and heaved him up on the bed. He intended to sleep on the floor but it was cold and very uncomfortable and there was, after all, room in the bed for the two of them. David lay still and snoring as he clambered in. Richard was absolutely determined to do nothing. David had the world's biggest mouth. Richard would be followed everywhere he went by teenagers calling him a 'fucking queer' or a 'homo'—and seducing his landlord's son would bring his university career to a sudden end. No way!

And yet... the boy's warmth did things to Richard. His cock rose steadily as the minutes went by. He dozed off but woke up again. It was even stiffer. He tried desperately to go to sleep again but sleep wouldn't come. There was only one thing to do. He reached out for a tissue and with his back towards David, he began, very gently, to masturbate.

"Wharra yer doin?" He felt David's breath on his neck.

"Nothing. Go back to sleep."

"Do me if you want."

"You're too pissed. Go back to sleep."

"No. Go on. Do it to me."

Richard turned over to face him. "You've got a hard on," said David with a giggle. Richard reached down and took the boy's flaccid member between his fingers. "Go on. Do it to me," said David. Richard slid a hand up and down the boy's thigh.

"Feels good," David murmured. Richard moved the foreskin back enjoying the damp warmth of David's substantial cockhead, but there was no reaction at all. He might as well have been holding a piece of wet rope.

"Try and think of something nice," he murmured. "Your girl-friend maybe?"

"Haven't got one anymore," said David.

That, at least, was encouraging news but it didn't help. It flopped around in his fingers.

At least fifteen minutes passed. Nothing happened and Richard's wrist ached. "Shall I keep on?" he asked. There was no answer. He asked again. Still no reply. David had gone to sleep. Richard gave up the attempt and returned to his own pressing needs.

He woke up shortly before nine o'clock in the morning. The sun was streaming through the window and the solitary bell of St. John's church on the other side of the road was clanging.

"I never knew you were a homo," said David.

"What gave you that idea?"

"You tried to wank me off last night."

"You asked me to."

"Did I?"

"You did but you were too pissed to get a hard on."

"Oh yeah. I remember now. Where are my clothes?"

"In a disgusting heap in the bathroom. I'll put them in the washing machine." He went to get out of bed.

"Not yet," said David.

"Sooner the better. They smell disgusting."

David grasped his arm. "Not yet," he said again.

"Why?"

"I don't need them and I can do it now. If you want to, that is."

"It's what you want that counts," said Richard.

David smiled. "Mum and Dad won't be back till Monday night. There's fuck-all to do here on a Sunday. Why not?" he said. He pulled back the sheet to reveal the boy's cock was as stiff as only a teenage cock in the full glory of youth can be! The head peeked out from the enveloping foreskin as if it were taking its first look at the world.

Richard was fairly certain that it wasn't the first time that David had been masturbated by someone else. He made no embarrassed apology when he shot his load all over Richard's chest. Neither did he bat an eyelid a few hours later when Richard swallowed the next ejaculation.

But he'd never been fucked. Of that Richard was quite sure. It took hours of persuading and reassurance to get him into position. He squealed when the first well-lubricated finger penetrated. He screamed when Richard's cock finally slid past his tight muscle ring and began the slippery ascent into him. He writhed, kicked and screamed but Richard held on to his legs as hard as he could and just kept on pushing. When his cockhead reached the point of no return he was able to relax his grip slightly. David was impaled as firmly as a butterfly on a board—and knew it. Slowly, his mind accepted the fact. The agonised writhing turned into joyful wriggling and, if he didn't smile, the grimace left his face.

It was if Richard's cum had some magical property. The parents noticed the change in their son soon after they got back. By that time Richard's cock had jetted four loads into David. Twice during the day on Sunday and twice on Sunday night. He was quieter and more thoughtful; altogether a much nicer person.

By the following Friday, there were signs that the old David wasn't quite dead but on Saturday morning (Richard having slipped into his room in the middle of the night) he was considerably subdued. On Monday morning, apparently untired after no less than six injections, he went off to school and, for the first time in his life, actually buckled down to learning.

The amazing thing was that David never breathed a word. Not even after he'd got married. The inmates of the academy were the same. Their parents were gushingly thankful for all Mr. Loxley and his devoted staff had done. The boys went off to colleges or careers and often visited, "Just to see the old place again." It was almost impossible to imagine that those upright, handsome young men who often arrived with their fiancees or wives, had once (indeed, more than once) wriggled delightedly as they learned to comply with the wishes of their elders.

Next morning, he was back in his office, dealing with the usual reams of paperwork when the telephone rang. He was pretty certain that someone was setting him up. A man purporting to be Jake Blake's personal assistant said he was speaking from the recording studio in town. Jake had been given the number by a good friend and would like to call at the Academy at three o'clock to discuss private business. It was, Richard thought, almost certainly one of the boys playing a joke. He called the studio back. To his amazement, it had been a genuine call.

Never having entertained an internationally acclaimed pop

star, Richard was unsure of what to do. Should he tell the boys and arrange some sort of reception? Certainly they would like to know. Most of them were Jake Blake fans. On those grounds Richard decided to say nothing. It was pretty obvious to him that the purpose of Jake's visit was philanthropic and it was probably better that he didn't meet the boys. One hint that all was not as it appeared could be disastrous.

At three o'clock, he stood by his window and watched the enormous stretch limousine glide to a stop by the main gate. A man got out and the limo pulled away again. He watched the man enter the gate and begin to walk up the drive.

He returned to his desk. It was probably better, he thought, to appear to be working and to take a casual approach, as if visits by world-famous stars were a daily occurrence.

There was a knock on the door. "Come in!" he called and continued to check the grocery invoices.

"I want a word with you." It wasn't the voice of an adult singer. Startled, he looked up to find Peter Bauer standing in front of the desk.

"Not now, Peter," he said. "I'm very busy and I'm expecting a visitor."

"This can't wait," said Peter.

"I'm sure it can. Come back in an hour. I should be free then."

"You either listen to me now or I go to the police."

Richard looked at his watch.

"Make it quick then," he said.

"I want to make an official complaint about your vice principal. If any guy had the right title he has. He came to my room last night. He'd been spying on me through the keyhole."

"What were you doing?"

Peter flushed. "That's not the point," he said. "He made some pretty nasty suggestions. If you only knew what went on here behind your back. I know he's done it with some of the others but he's not doing it with me!"

"Do what?" said Richard, frowning.

Peter blushed again. "Oh nothing. Just tell him to keep away from me that's all."

There was another knock on the door. There was no time to say either "Come in," or "Just a moment." The door opened and in walked Jake Blake.

It was a surprise to see the man in an ordinary suit. Jake was famous, on stage, for his elaborate costumes.

"Gee. Sorry. Am I disturbing something?" he said in the familiar drawling voice.

"No, no. We've just finished," said Richard. He stood up and put out his hand. "A real pleasure, Mr. Blake. Do sit down. That'll be all, Peter. I'll deal with the matter right away."

But Peter didn't go away. He stood there with his mouth open, looking like a stranded fish.

"Excuse... Excuse me," he gasped. "Aren't you Jake Blake?"

"Sure am, son. Who might you be?"

"P...P...Peter Bauer."

"Glad to meet you, Peter." Ignoring Richard's still outstretched hand, Jake took Peter's and shook it warmly. "And you're one of the inmates here?" he asked.

"Yes."

"And how old are you? No, wait, let me guess. I'd say just about eighteen."

Peter grinned. "Not bad," he said. "As a matter of fact, I'll be eighteen in three months!"

"Good age to be. Just the age I like 'em at. Got yourself a regular *friend* here have you?"

"No. I haven't been here that long." Peter blushed yet again.

"Well, it looks like this is my lucky day. Roy Carpenter said all the boys had mentors."

"Colonel Roy Carpenter?" Richard enquired. His legs felt weak. Colonel Carpenter was a long-serving mentor. Until that moment, Richard would have awarded him full marks for discretion. He arrived every Saturday afternoon to visit Tommy Gearing. As always, Michael met him and took him to Tommy's room. Michael met all the mentors and took their money when they'd finished. The Colonel always stayed with Tommy for exactly three hours before taking him out to dinner and returning him just before lights out. More often than not, he decided it was better to stay the night rather than drive home to his dog-breeding (and apparently devoted) wife.

"Sure. Roy's an old buddy of mine from way back. He told me about the place and gave me the number. Well, I'm doing a tour here soon and we're recording the album at the moment. Thought I'd come by and pick me a boy....."

"You can go now, Peter," said Richard, urgently. He was

beginning to feel faint. It wasn't, on second thoughts, so much Colonel Carpenter's fault but his. He'd told the Colonel that all the boys were just as keen as Tommy.

"Ah, gee. Don't send him away. We're just getting acquainted, aren't we Peter?"

"Er... Yes. I've always been a fan of yours, Jake. Ever since I was about eleven. You know 'Tumble-weed on an Empty Road'?"

"Should do. That was a long time back."

"That was the first one I bought. Then there was 'My Old Home' and then 'Sundown on the Sea Shore'..."

"You've missed out 'When I Was Lost'," said Jake.

"Oh yeah! That was the one you made with the Circus Boys."

"Good name for them," Jake muttered.

"And then you made that film, 'Spring Vacation.' That was terrific!"

"Glad you liked it."

"I saw it about five times. Was that really all shot in Italy?"

"Every bit, except the scene in the hotel bedroom. That was done in the studio."

"With Maria Maroni?"

"That's right."

"Was it real? I mean did you actually...."

Jake laughed. "With about fifty technicians standing round the bed? No way. I'd be hard pressed to get an erection with just one. Anyway, who'd want to have sex with Maria Maroni? I can think of several people I'd rather spend a night with. One in particular...."

"I really think it would be better if Peter left us," said Richard but he might as well have been addressing empty air. The torrent of adulation continued.

"Then you did the European Tour and you came back to do the Winter Gardens concert."

Jake laughed. "You must have a spy among my roadies," he said.

"No, but I cut out everything from the magazines and papers about you. But I've only got three albums of your cuttings. Why don't you give interviews like the other stars?"

"Because I like a private life, that's why. There's not more than a dozen folks who even know where I live."

"Or whether you're married or what your hobbies are...."

"Well I'm not married and, as for my hobbies, I've got several. Guess you'll find out what the most important one is."

Richard interrupted him. "You must have some studying to do, Peter," he said. "Don't use this as an excuse."

"Finished it, Mr. Loxley," he said.

"All of it?"

"Every bit." He turned to Jake again. "It said in the paper that you and Val Martin are mad on gardening and you live next door to each other and have competitions to see who can grow the biggest vegetables," he said.

Jake laughed. "Val Martin lives about a mile and a half away from me. I hate gardening and so does he. He's got a beautiful garden but only thanks to about thirty-five full-time gardeners and truckloads of synthetic fertilizers. Never believe what you read, especially about me. It's all a load of cock. Speaking of which....."

"I really think it would be better if we continued this conversation in my apartment," said Richard. "Perhaps you'd like a drink..."

"Sure would, but what I have in mind ain't in your drinks cabinet," said Jake.

"Do you have time to autograph my albums?" said Peter, still gazing at the man as if he were a visitor from another planet."

"Sure. Where are they?"

"In my room. I'll go and get them."

"No. I'll come with you."

"Haven't you got business to discuss with Mr. Loxley?"

"No need now." He stood up and smiled down at Richard. "I'll call in before I leave," he said.

Like the proverbial drowning man, images from Richard's past flashed through his brain. Piles of hundred dollar bills on his desk on Monday mornings; grateful mentors shaking his hand; grateful parents doing likewise. Like a sandcastle on a beach, the Loxley Academy was about to be washed away.

He shuddered at the thought of standing, handcuffed and next to Jake in the dock while Peter Bauer gave evidence to a sympathetic judge.

"We don't allow visitors to...." he spluttered and then stopped. That story wouldn't work. Both Peter and Jake knew better.

They closed the door behind them and he sat for some minutes with his head in his hands wondering what to do. He couldn't throw the blame on to Michael for this one. Michael had done nothing save have a disastrously risky conversation with the boy. Maybe that was a way out. He could say, truthfully, that Peter had complained about his vice principal and that he was about to take the matter up when Jake had arrived.

"I had not the slightest idea that he was homosexual," he would say. *Neither*, he thought, grimly, *had Jake's fans*. In many ways Jake had more to lose than he had.

It wasn't a good story but it might work—especially if he could be seen to be taking action. Yes, that was it. He rummaged through the files in his drawer, found one, opened it and dialed a number.

"Mr. Bauer?" he said. "Loxley. How are you? Good. Mr. Bauer, I have to tell you some disturbing news. No, no. He's very well."

(Probably at that very moment punching an internationally famous star on the nose, he thought.)

"No," he continued. "The fact is that Peter has made a serious allegation against one of my staff. Needless to say I am investigating it thoroughly and if there is any truth in it, you may be sure that the man in question will be dismissed at once. In the meantime, though, I think it would be a good idea for Peter to go home at least for a few weeks. The incident has obviously distressed him and I wouldn't want him to be here. There's bound to be a certain amount of tension in the air..... Oh, that's kind of you. It's a long journey for you but it would be better if you could collect him. Incidentally, do you have the correct time? My watch has stopped and there isn't a clock in the office as you know ... Good God! Is it that late? Thanks a lot Mr. Bauer. I look forward to seeing you again tomorrow. Goodbye for now."

'So far, so good,' he thought. Peter would come bursting into the office at any moment. To be seen working normally would be the best thing. He studied the file. 'BAUER - Peter James. Aged seventeen.' He scanned through a long medical report, most of which he didn't understand. Then came the familiar pages of notes he'd made. Under-age drinking, petty theft, belligerent attitude, truancy from school, undesirable company.

It was a familiar history. Most of the files in that drawer could tell a similar story.

He came to the end and then read it through again. He looked at his watch. At least twenty minutes must have elapsed. A frightening thought came to him. What if Peter had struck Jake so hard that the man was seriously injured? He could even be dead. Peter would be wondering what to do—or maybe, he'd left the man there and run out of the building in a panic. It was the sort of thing a seventeen-year-old would do in a crisis.

One of his strict rules was never to use the monitor when a guest was being entertained. That was mostly to keep Michael away. He'd been tempted several times. Michael had pleaded with him to do it. "It's would be a total and immoral invasion of privacy," Richard had said. "Out of the question. Period."

But this wasn't such an occasion. He pressed the switch and then the button for Peter's room.

The monitor screen took several minutes to warm up. He could hear Jake's voice singing. A record obviously.

"Tumble weed rollin' just like me. Rollin' all day but never free...."

"Oh yeah, that's good! I like that." Peter's voice, breathless. It was funny, Richard thought, how music got to them... Suddenly, he sat upright and stared, open-mouthed at the screen. The naked soles of Peter's feet, looking unnaturally large-faced the camera. The boy's legs were propped up on Jake's bare shoulders. His hands were behind his head. His mouth was open. So was Jake's though Richard couldn't see it. It had to be to accommodate several inches of Peter's cock.

Peter wriggled slightly. Jake put his hands on the boy's hips to restrain him. Slurping, greedy, sucking sounds came from the loudspeaker.

"Oh! Yeah! Oh yeah!" Peter gasped. He appeared to be staring straight at the camera. Richard felt uneasy. Did the boy realize he was being watched? No, he couldn't possibly know.

"Oh yeah! Oh yeah!" he gasped. His movements became so violent that Jake had trouble holding on to him. He heaved upwards, sank down and then gave another powerful upward thrust and collapsed, panting, onto the bed. Jake stayed for a moment, bent forward and then, slowly, stood upright. He wiped his mouth with the back of his hand.

"By Christ, you're good!" he said. Peter smiled.

"Like it?" asked Jake.

"Did I ever! It's like a dream. I mean— me and you. To think I used to wank off to your picture and now here you are in the flesh."

That was true enough, Richard thought. Quite a lot of flesh as it happened. He caught a glimpse of it as Jake turned slightly.

"We'd better not do it here any more," said Jake. "My hotel's a bit more comfortable. Reckon this guy Loxley will let you out?"

"He would for you," said Peter. He reached for a tissue, wiped himself and then stood up to dress. Jake started to put his clothes on.

"Mr. Loxley doesn't know anything, so be careful about what you say," said Peter, pulling on his jeans.

"Shit! I thought he did. Roy Carpenter said...."

"No. He's straight. It's the other one who handles the sex side. He tried it on me last night."

"What did you do?"

"Told him to fuck off. I reported him to Mr. Loxley."

"Good for you kid. You're my boy now. Come here."

Richard stared, unbelieving, as their arms went round each other and their mouths came together.

Richard was, both Jake and Peter agreed that night in Jake's suite, wonderfully understanding about letting Peter spend a night away. It was better, he said, that the boy should be off the premises while he got to the bottom of Peter's story.

"All I could do to keep a straight face when he said that," said Jake.

"Me too," said Peter with a happy sigh. "If only he knew."

"About time I got to the bottom again," said Jake. "Ready?"

"Sure," said Peter.

"Turn over then. Jeez! That sure is a pretty little bottom."

• • •

"I have to say that I'm considerably relieved by what you've told me, Mr. Loxley," said Mr. Bauer on the following morning.

"Why so?"

"I'm afraid we weren't entirely honest with you when we first met. The boy has a history of er … that sort of behavior. To know that he has rejected this man's advances is a great comfort to us.

"It was a horrible shock when we found out what he'd been doing. My wife and I can hardly bear to talk about it. To come home from the office and find your son in bed with a telephone repairman…"

"They were in our bed too!" said Mrs Bauer. "Horrible!" She shuddered. "We've had to buy a new one. I just couldn't.…

Her husband interrupted her. "What's this Peter tells me about meeting Jake Blake, Mr. Loxley? A bit of teenage imagination, I guess."

"Not at all. Jake will be Peter's mentor when the boy returns. He's taken a great interest in Peter."

"Jake Blake!" said Mrs Bauer. "Peter's always wanted to meet him. He's the boy's idol. Oh I am glad! We have so much to thank you for, Mr. Loxley."

"Not at all. As I'm sure Peter has told you, Jake has offered to look after him during the time we're looking into this business. With respect, that's probably the best thing. It's never a good thing for a boy to go home after such a short time here. They fall so easily into their old ways."

Mr. Bauer looked thoughtful. "Sounds a good idea to me," he said. "We're both too busy to keep an eye on him all the time. Are you sure Mr. Blake doesn't mind?"

"Not at all. As I'm sure Peter has told you, I called on Jake at his hotel last night. He's very taken with the boy. We made an arrangement that, when he's away on tour, Peter moves into my private apartment."

"That's kind of you and a great weight off our minds," said Mr. Bauer.

"He's a changed boy already," Mrs Bauer interjected. "We both noticed it when we saw him this morning. He's more relaxed. More, er, docile if you know what I mean."

"He's learned his lesson," said her husband. "A lot of boys have to learn it the hard way."

"I'm sure there will be times when Peter will find it hard," said Richard.

"All the better for him," said Mr. Bauer. "If he doesn't come up to your high standards, make it as hard as you like for him."

Richard crossed his legs under the desk, leaned back in his chair and smiled.

"We will," he promised. "We will."

A HOT SATURDAY NIGHT
(AT THE POOL HALL)

Corbin Chezner

The traffic was so heavy through Cestehova that night, a good portion of the drivers lost their cool before they even got to the dance. But in the summer, that was to be expected. From June through August, on Friday and Saturday nights, a solid line of traffic clogged the two farm-to-market roads that bisected the tiny Czech community. The drivers had one destination in mind: the giant dance hall five miles outside town.

On the way, most remained oblivious to the Cestehova townsite, which was little more than a block-long business district that was nearly deserted and an amber caution light at the intersection of the two roads.

The onslaught of weekenders far exceeded the populaion of Cestehova itself, who lived in a scattering of shabby houses plopped helter-skelter on lots vegetated primarily by prickly pear cactus and mesquite scrub. The mesquite that reached tree status were bowed north by persistent winds off the coastal plain. And tonight, Tantrum, a popular country-western band from Kerrville, had attracted revelers from a four-county region of the South Texas brush country.

By 11 p.m., tension already hung heavy in the giant dance hall, better known as the Bottoms Up Club. Couples in western gear carrying Longnecks two-stepped to the pulsating music, cigarette smoke thick as pea soup trailing them.

Had it not been for the irresistible draw of the popular band, most of the celebrants from the region wouldn't have been caught dead under the same roof together, particularly here in the middle of nowhere. Despite being scattered over a 300-mile radius of South Central Texas, many of the dancers knew each other or knew of each other or at least knew someone who knew someone. School and rodeo rivalries, not to mention family feuds, had taken their toll, and couples eyed each other warily as they danced.

The cigarette smoke and the tension had left Billy Ray Thompson, one of the few people at the dance who actually lived in Cestehova, with a throbbing headache. The stubborn pain had persisted through eleven Longnecks. As the crowd jostled toward the dance floor for the "Cotton-Eye Joe," Billy Ray finally pushed away from the long, wooden table and stood up. Tossing his blonde hair away from his eyes, Billy Ray plucked his oversized black cowboy hat from the back of a chair and placed it on his head. Grabbing his Longneck off the table, he headed outside for some air.

A parking lot the size of ten football fields surrounded the club, situated on farmland due west of the Cestehova townsite. The club sold beer only, and Billy Ray hankered for a snort of whiskey from the bottle hidden beneath the seat of his pickup. On the way, he stopped short suddenly, slinging one hip of his tall, lanky frame lower than the other.

Peering through his smoldering green eyes across the giant parking lot, he sighed in frustration. How the fuck could he find his truck now? Twenty acres of vehicles stared back at him, pickups and SWs outnumbering cars two to one. No small challenge considering that some jerk had shot out the lights in the parking lot.

Billy Ray was meandering through the sea of steel when a door slammed nearby and a woman suddenly emerged from the shadows. Vickie Lynn Somers stomped past him in a fury, her red hair flying.

Billy Ray turned and tipped his hat. "Evenin', Vickie Lynn."

No answer. Vickie Lynn and Jimmy Lee Sims had had another falling out, Billy Ray reasoned. A safe assumption considering it was Saturday night. Just then, Billy Ray spotted Jimmy Lee's green Datsun pickup. Sidling up to the little truck, he bent down to look in the window. "You okay, Jimmy Lee?"

Jimmy Lee was buttoning up his Levis. He looked over at Billy Ray. Even in the faint light from the half moon, Billy Ray could see that the dark-haired dude was pissed. "Damn that Vickie Lynn!" Jimmy Lee fumed, darts streaming from his shining brown eyes. "Every time we come out here she pulls the same ole shit. If I even look at another woman. Hell, even if I stop to shoot the shit with another dude, she throws a damn tantrum."

"Mind if I join you?" Without waiting for an answer, Billy Ray climbed inside Jimmy Lee's pickup. Looking over at his handsome, dark-haired friend, Billy Ray offered, "Got some whiskey in my truck. Want a snort before you go back inside?"

"You bet." Jimmy Lee smiled, perfect teeth a gleaming contrast to his bronzed skin. The cleft in his chin deepened and crescent dimples appeared on both sides of full, sensual lips. "But no sense in goin' to all that trouble." Jimmy Lee reached under the seat and pulled out his own bottle. "Try some of this."

The blond took the bottle gratefully. He twisted off the cap and arched his head back against the seat and let some of the whiskey drain down his throat. Closing his shimmering green eyes, he swallowed and the whiskey settled warm in his stomach. Lifting his head away from the seat again, he replaced the cap and sighed with pleasure. "Aahh!" Wiping his mouth on the sleeve of his pearl-snap western shirt, he added, "Damn good stuff!" He handed the bottle back to Jimmy Lee.

"I'll say." Jimmy Lee took the bottle and drank some of the whiskey himself. "Cost me most of ten bucks!" Fondling his crotch, he added, "Damn that bitch! She gets me all worked up, then throws a hissy before I have a chance to shoot."

"I hear you." Billy Ray rubbed his own crotch. "You wanna see if we can round up Wanda Sue or somebody to blow us?"

"Hell, I don't think I can wait that long. I'm on the verge now. You wanna whack off?"

Billy Ray shrugged. "Suits me."

Jimmy Lee raised off the seat and ripped open his button-fly Levis. He pulled down his Levis and white boxer shorts, exposing his dick and balls. Desire shot through Billy Ray's loins as he peered at his dark-haired friend's dick and balls. Jimmy Lee's dick was thick and it had a good shape with purple veins protruding along the shaft, and a mushroom-shaped head that pointed downward.

"You got a damn good-lookin' cock on you, Jimmy Lee." Billy Ray took out his own cock then, which was already hard and throbbing from just watching Jimmy Lee. Billy Ray compared his dick and balls to Jimmy Lee's. Since he was a true blond, the skin on his own cock was lighter than his friend's. Billy Ray's cock was longer than Jimmy Lee's but a tad thinner. The head of Billy Ray's cock was bigger than Jimmy Lee's and Billy Ray's head pointed upward instead of down like Jimmy Lee's. Billy Ray's balls were bigger than Jimmy Lee's.

Jimmy Lee looked over at Billy Ray, his brown eyes

smoldering with desire now. "Damn good cock yourself...."

He was pumping his dick and was already breathless, and now Billy Ray joined in. They were both so horny it only took the dudes a couple of minutes to shoot.

Jimmy Lee came first. Suddenly, he jerked back against the seat and wailed, "Oh, man!" as his dick shot a heavy load of cum against the floorboard. An instant later, Billy Ray sighed, "Shit! " as his own load plopped heavy against the floorboard.

They were shaking goo off the end of their dicks when suddenly shots rang out from across the parking lot. Both men sank down reflexively in the seat and looked at each other.

"Sounds like some shit's about to come down, " Jimmy Lee said.

Billy Ray nodded. "Yeah. Better get the fuck outta here before the sheriff comes. You game for some pool?"

Jimmy Lee knew just what Billy Ray had in mind. Hell, wasn't a dude in South Central Texas who hadn't got his cock sucked in the Cestehova pool hall pisser one time or another. The pool tables were good, too. Jimmy Lee smiled and reached for the ignition. "Cool."

"Hold on. What about Vickie Lynn?"

"She can take care of herself."

"You sure? She'll be pissed big-time come tomorrow."

"So? She'll either get over it—or she won't. Ain't gonna bust my balls worryin' about it. "

"No use." Billy Ray took the bottle back and gulped down some more of the whiskey.

The Cestehova Pool Hall was on Main Street, two doors down from the Nighthawk, a four-booth tavern for serious beer drinkers. People like Lee Roy Bagley and Dakota downed brew at the Nighthawk. Natives drank Shiner, a dark beer brewed in a nearby town of the same name.

Legend had it that Dakota's cock was so big he'd actually worked years ago in a carnival sideshow. Billy Ray didn't know Dakota's age. Although Dakota's hair was silver he had a tall, lanky body like Billy Ray's and that made Billy Ray speculate that Dakota's hair had turned silver before its time.

Dakota's specialty was the pool table. Everyone wondered how the pool shark had managed to keep his good looks despite a long-running love affair with the bottle. Dakota had an aquiline nose and a broad, handsome forehead. He slicked his silver hair straight back which gave him an air of cool detachment. Leona Donley, a longtime local whore, whose specialty was sucking married men's cocks beneath school stadiums during football games, claimed Dakota looked better now than when he was 25.

When Billy Ray and Jimmy Lee stepped inside the pool hall, Dakota was hustling some young dude. Billy Ray could tell by looking the dude was not from Cestehova, or any of the other small towns in the area, for that matter. He had short brown hair cut in a semi-punk and dancing blue eyes that never seemed to focus. He wore frayed shorts and a blue T-shirt thin from too many washings and some kind of sandals made of rope.

"Well, look who the cat dragged in!" Jake Kingsly, the bald, genial owner of the pool hall, called out to Jimmy Lee and Billy Ray: "About time you two got your butts back in here. What's your pleasure?"

Jimmy Lee and Billy Ray each plucked a pool cue from the wall rack next to the empty table. "Take a couple a cold ones," Jimmy Lee said.

"The usual?" Jake opened the cooler and reached inside.

Jimmy Lee and Billy Ray nodded and Jake pulled out two Longnecks. Billy Ray had decided long ago that baldness suited Jake Kingsly damn good and it made him feel better about the fate that befell some men. Jake slammed the frosty Longnecks against the bar, and Billy Ray went up to pay for them while Jimmy Lee set up the pool table.

"What's happening?" Jake asked.

Billy Ray shrugged. "Nothin' much. Somebody was shootin' outside the dance hall a while ago."

"Anybody hurt?"

"Didn't appear so."

"Might keep your eyes on those two." Jake nodded toward Dakota and the young dude, and smiled wryly. "Expect we'll see some action directly." Jake leaned so close then that Billy Ray could smell whiskey on the pool hall proprietor's breath. "Dakota done set the kid up."

"Don't he always?" Billy Ray returned Jake's smile. "Who is he?"

"College dude. Says his name is David somethin' or other. He mumbled his last name, but I done forgot. "

Everyone in Brush Country knew Dakota's style. That's why Dakota preferred preying on dudes who didn't know any better.

Jimmy Lee and Billy Ray played a game, all the while keeping an eye on the next table. The sly pool hustler was going easy on the fellow named David, setting him up for the kill. David had a cocky grin and a swagger, a false sense of security, thinking he still had a chance to win. Dakota liked it that way. Without discussing it, Jimmy Lee and Billy Ray and Jake all knew the college dude was on the verge of losing his young asshole to Dakota's huge dick. If Dakota was feeling generous they'd all get to watch while Dakota plowed the kid. Usually, the pool hustler liked claiming his prize right there in the pool hall. Sometimes, though, if Dakota's ornery streak had set in, the silver fox would get selfish and take the dude off by himself to fuck.

Dakota was generous that night. After he'd clearly won two out of three, Dakota ordered the college dude to lower his pants and bend over the pool table. As was customary, Jake walked over to the plate glass window that faced Main Street and lowered the blinds. David's cocky attitude had dissolved and now he looked scared. Dakota pulled down his own pants and underwear and David trembled when he looked around and saw the size of Dakota's dick and balls. "I ... I don't know about this," he muttered, his voice trembling.

Dakota threw his head back and chortled. "A bet's a bet, dude." He leaned David over the pool table. "You'll be beggin' for it."

"No way."

"We'll see."

David clawed at the table as Dakota inched his huge cock inside the college dude's ass. Dakota had fucked enough butts over the years to know how to do it right. He knew that if he was patient the kid would take it all and then some. So he kept on inching his cock deeper, all the while fondling the college dude's dick and balls. Every once in a while, he'd bend down and throttle David's ear with his tongue. That would make David squirm and thrash his head against the table.

Finally, Dakota drove past the dude's sphincter. David clucked and hissed and moaned, "Oh, man!" as the base of Dakota's pole met the crack of David's ass. Dakota had staked the claim now, and he began his slow, rhythmic fucking: slow and steady at first, then faster. Out, then in. Out, in, out, in, faster, harder. David clawed wildly now, his hair dancing as he thrashed his head against the table.

Billy Ray and Jimmy Lee and Jake got so hot watching they all pulled out their meat and started jacking off as Dakota continued fucking the kid. After he knew the kid was his, Dakota stopped short suddenly. "Hey, dudes," he said, looking toward Jimmy Lee and Billy Ray and Jake. "Any of you wanna fuck this hot butt here?"

The kid looked back at Dakota. "Don't stop now. Fuck me all the way. "

Dakota laughed and pulled out. Then Jake took over. Since Dakota already had the kid loosened up, Jake had no trouble plowing into him right off. Jake went at it like a master, thrusting fast-paced into the college dude. Before long Jake arched his bald head toward the ceiling and hissed, "Mother fuck!" and he slammed his load into the dude's butt.

And then Dakota allowed Jimmy Lee and Billy Ray take turns fucking David. Jimmy Lee went in first, and, after a spell, he slammed his load into the dude. Then Billy Ray took over, fucking the dude good, shooting his cum inside him.

When Dakota climbed back in the saddle with his big cock good and hard, the kid was really loosened up. In fact, the kid's hole was so lubed with cum and spit and grease that Dakota kept sliding out. Finally, developed a faster, harder motion and, suddenly, he was squeezing the kid around the waist, arching his head toward the ceiling and pumping a huge load into the kid's butt, all the while groaning, "Aahhh!" over and over.

After Dakota pulled out and was cleaning his cock, Jake announced, "Time to close 'er up, boys. "

The college dude was flushed and trembling as he sauntered toward the door on the way out. Stopping short, he looked over at Jake and asked, quite timidly, "You open week nights?"

This got a hearty laugh out of Jake.

Jimmy Lee drove Billy Ray back to the blond's pickup at the dance hall. As Billy Ray climbed out, Jimmy Lee said, "How about let's do somethin' different next weekend."

Billy Ray brightened. "Fine with me. I'm damn tired of the

same ole shit. "

"Yeah," Jimmy Lee said. "Nothin' ever happens in this sumbitchin' town, does it?"

SWEET REVENGE

David MacMillan

It was typical middle-of-summer Georgia weather—insufferably hot and muggy—as I left the folks' car in the parking lot and started for the brick and concrete administration building to pay for my fall quarter at Mercer University. Sweat was pouring off me by the time I entered the building and started climbing the stairs to the Registrar's office on the third floor—and got into line.

An hour later, I was chilled from the air conditioning and handing over the check that paid his fees for the quarter. I grinned my pride at being officially registered to the students lined up outside the office as I left, waiting to do what I'd just done.

One boy stood out as I walked down the corridor, passing the line of students waiting to do what I'd just done. Blond and blue-eyed, tall and slim. My eyes didn't wait a second; their gaze zeroed in on his crotch. He glanced up, grinned, and raised his eyebrows in invitation.

And I wasn't even queer! No fucking way! But his dick welcomed my attention and started growing. I pulled my eyes away from his denim-covered basket, sped up my step, and got past him. Taking the steps two at a time, I hurried from the admin building and into the heat of late September.

Normally, I would have strolled through the Quad and given myself up to my return to the old ivy-covered brick buildings; they were what had held me to the small Baptist college in the center of the old town of Macon most of the past three years. Instead, I glumly crossed the parking lot, my hands shoved in my pockets.

I was not a happy camper. I didn't want to be queer. That was nowhere close to my plans for myself. I ignored the orange and yellow leaves of the newly planted maple trees—the school's attempt to beautify its new parking lot was the furthest thing from my mind.

I wasn't exactly sexually inexperienced as I entered my senior year at Mercer University in Macon, Georgia. Perhaps, it'd be more accurate to say I wasn't exactly straight that late in the game. But I sure as hell was still doing my best to convince myself I wasn't all the way queer.

Abandoned stores and dilapidated houses that had once been student apartments until the owners let them run too far down faced Napier Avenue as I drove to my own apartment. Now, they were boarded up with weed-choked yards—or are homes to poor black women and their children. My apartment was on the other side of Pio Nono Avenue, in a white working-class section of town, but the crime rate was a fourth of that around Mercer.

My old roommate had graduated at the end of the summer. He was a good egg and had taken care of the place. It was ready for me, all I had to do was change the lease and utilities to my name alone. I turned on the air and quickly unpacked the clothes and sound equipment that filled the back seat and trunk of the folks' car.

I needed a shower when I was finished and started for the bathroom, stripping off as I moved through the apartment. The phone caught me as I was pulling off my briefs.

"You're back," Gene Butler's voice greeted me before I had the receiver all the way to my ear.

"You're that tired of Megan that you're ready to crawl into my bed?" I kidded the red-headed boy who had been my closest friend since our first days at Mercer.

"Funny, asshole."

"How is she?"

"Megan? Ready to take on the whole male establishment with one arm tied behind her back."

I chuckled as I was meant to. "Did you two stay in town for the summer?"

"Naw ... Well, we made it back most weekends. Megan signed us up to beg money for Greenpeace. I've never knocked on so many doors in my life." There was a pause while he caught his breath. "Want to grab something to eat at that coffeehouse off Ingleside—and maybe take in a movie?"

"That old farmhouse you guys made into a hippie commune getting to you already?"

"Vic...."

"Sorry," I told him and wasn't. Gene knew how quickly I got bored out there in the middle of the county with nothing to do. "Sure, I'd love to get some good food before I have to start eating my own—and a movie would be great too."

"We'll be over to pick you up in an hour then."

I was hard as I stood and started for the shower. Gene had been able to do that to me since I first saw him. I had come to live with it but still frowned as I studied my dick. The damned thing seemed hellbent on keeping me from all the things I wanted in life. Thank God my brains were in my head and not down there.

What my dick wanted would never work with Gene Butler. It'd probably have him running in the opposite direction everytime he saw me, if he knew I got hot for his tight body. And Megan would probably claw my eyes out if she ever found out. She was ferociously protective, and Gene had been hers most of the past three years. I accepted that I could pull my pud to fantasies of him and was glad that was as far as it would go for me.

• • •

I met Mike Lynn once before he moved in on me—the day he answered Dad's ad in the Post paper. He was good-looking with curly black hair and was a bit shorter and only marginally stockier than me. He was also intelligent. There was a strangeness to him, however, that I didn't recognize but that stayed at the edge of my consciousness and served as a warning signal. He followed me to Macon..

Mike arrived two days before classes began. I helped him move his shit in under the careful eye of Colonel and Mrs. Lynn and accepted the parental invitation to join them for lunch. We picked at rabbit food and pretended to like Macon's attempt to be French. Back at the apartment, Mike and I watched the Lynns start back to Savannah. I wondered vaguely what I had on my hands.

I didn't have to wonder long. He whooped the moment the car was out of sight and turned to face me. "Do you let your hair down?" he asked almost shyly.

"Sometimes," I allowed and wondered even more what I was getting into.

He ran to his bags in his bedroom and was back with me in less than a minute. He had the biggest leer on his face I had seen. "This shit is Thai—it'll blow the top of your head off."

"Yeah?" I had smoked home-grown grass a couple of times and it hadn't done a damned thing for me. No buzz. No nothing. But I had heard the Asians had some weird shit—the Jamaicans and Colombians too.

"Yeah!" He quickly rolled a joint and offered it to me to light and take the first hit.

I was seeing colors before I released that first toke. I stared at him in wonder as I passed him the joint.

"Good?" he asked.

"God!" I groaned.

He grinned knowingly and I realized he had a nice body. I mean, a damned fearsome body. He had a real cute face full of freckles and big brown eyes, a pug nose, and full, pouty lips. I started imagining what it'd be like to have those black curls of his touching me as he licked me in places that hadn't been touched except by me.

"Take another hit, Vic," he told me and I took the joint from him. By the time I handed it back I was floating away on the hot September sunlight and was mindless.

"Hey, Vic!" I tried to focus on him through the colors swirling around my head. He grinned. "You're all right."

"Thanks," I mumbled, wanting to be alone to enjoy all these new experiences playing around in my head.

"I hope you're really all right, you know?" I looked puzzled and he laughed. "I guess we're good enough friends now that I can let you in on a secret or two."

"I hope we are," I told him indignantly, focusing on him again with difficulty and feeling a rush of interest all over again.

"Well, then ... shit! I get hornier than a buck rabbit in a warren of does when I get high ... you feel like helping a buddy out?"

I stared at him. "Me?" I yelped.

"You," he grinned.

"What're you getting at?" I asked as I started imagining him naked, my fears and inhibitions forgotten.

"I like ass, Vic ... blowjobs too. And I sort of got the impression back when we met that you wouldn't have too many hang-ups about either." He let his words hang in the air between us like a dare. Whoever spoke first lost.

I was having trouble keeping my thoughts in any sort of

order. He was nice. I would like to get him naked. And I knew my way around a bed with a guy in it. A nagging memory of there being some reason why I didn't want to do that again bothered me for a second or two, but it wouldn't materialize into anything I could make sense of. "Sure, I can help you out," I told him.

He laughed and opened the door to the apartment. "Let's go find your bed and get stripped for action then. God, am I ever more hurting!"

I was sitting on my bed and sort of wondering why I was naked when I looked up and saw Mike Lynn standing beside me. The man was boasting *el toro grande* as he started toward me. "You like what I've got?" he asked as I stared at the two-by-four jutting out of his pubes at me.

"Jesus!" My eyes were wide as I continued to stare at his pole and tried to guess at its dimensions.

"You're nice too, Vic. But, then, I was pretty sure you would be."

I mumbled incoherently as I tried to digest the signals my eyes were sending me. Mike Lynn's cock was long, and it was thicker than any I had seen in a long time. I was reminded of a beer can at its base. I wondered if I was going to get my jaw unhinged enough to take it. I even allowed myself to wonder what it'd feel like in my ass.

He sat down beside me and formed a fist around my dick. He pushed the cowl down along its shaft and smiled. "It's a nice one, all right. Lie on your back and let me give you a workout."

"Let's make this a two-way affair," I suggested with more coherence than I could imagine. I wanted to taste his meat and swallow it if I could. I already saw it as a challenge.

He grinned. "Shit! I don't mind some mutual foreplay before we get down to the real stuff." He climbed onto the bed over me so that his pole was in my face and mine in his. Before my eyes had adjusted enough that I could concentrate on his slab of meat, he had gripped both my asscheeks and was burying his nose in my balls, his throat open to my seven inches.

Soon enough, his balls slapped the bridge of my nose with his every downward thrust and my jaw was able to unhinge enough that I was taking him all the way to his pubes with each downstroke. He gobbled up my Southern-fried prick and spit it back out like it was a piston. All I could hear was our slurping on each other's dick.

His fingers maneuvered toward my asslips and, before too many seconds, he had an index finger pumping my hole in time with his dick-sucking. Before it fully registered what he was doing with his finger, he had shoved another one into me and both of them were massaging the hell out of my loveland.

I didn't have a chance. I was erupting like Mount Pelee and he was taking all the goo I was shooting. He pulled off my dick and got to his knees. I looked up in confusion at his hard, trimmed prime and wished I still had it down my throat. I wanted to taste him. I was softening as he crawled around me so that he was at my feet.

"I'm sorry," I offered. "I came too fast."

He grinned as he reached to the top of the night table. "I wanted to get you off, Vic. I like dick okay...." He laughed softly and tore open the condom packet he'd picked up. "It gets the guy damned pliant when I'm ready to take him." He rolled the latex down onto his shaft. "Are you going to need some lube?"

I stared up at him without comprehension. "What for?" I managed.

"My dick's pretty big and I like to give pleasure when I'm fucking a guy, not pain."

"You want to fuck me?" I asked, beginning to understand what was going on.

"You've got a cute set of buns ... I intend to be spreading them for you from now on out." He lifted my legs to his chest.

I stared down my body at him. I saw his tight body and much too-big dick as he spread my legs and leered back at me. "You're in for the fuck of your life now, Vic. You've never had anything that'll compare to what I'm going to give you."

I thought I should protest, though I wasn't sure why. "Mike, I...."

He stared at me suspiciously. "You aren't a virgin, are you?"

I shook my head slowly and saw the grin spread across his face again.

"Jesus, baby, you had me worried there for a minute. Okay, you know the score. So, look, just lie back, relax, and leave the driving to me, okay?"

He put his dick to the entrance of my lovechute. I felt it

spread my lips as he leaned into me. I pushed down automatically and opened my assring to let him through. He was kissing me when I felt his pubes scratch the insides of my globes and the bottom of my ballsac. I was flying on instinct as my hands went to his buttocks and I ground my butt against his thighs.

I was full; my asshole had never been stretched as wide as it was now. And I was leaking like crazy.

He pulled back enough that he could look down at me. "We're going to have us a good time this year," he cooed and started to plow my hole, slow and easy. His teeth nipped at my neck and shoulders. My hands held his backside and guided his thrusts into me.

Soon I came and floated away momentarily, lost in the afterglow.

My mind came back sometime later and he was still plundering my butt with the same slow and steady strokes he had started with. "You're fucking loving this, Vic!"

"Yeah," I mumbled and gripped my dick.

"Tell me what you like."

"I like to get fucked," I mumbled and felt my pole begin to jerk under my stroking fist.

"And who fucks you best?"

"You do, Mike. You fuck me best of all."

"What do you want?"

"I want you to fuck me, Mike," I grunted. "I want your dick in my ass." He crashed back into me and I stared at him in surprise at his roughness, at how good it felt. "Fuck me, Mike! Fuck me hard."

My cock was jerking between us and my balls were tight against its shaft. "Oh, shit," I moaned. "I'm going to shoot again."

"Hold it, baby!" he commanded and speeded up his tempo. "Let me come with you." His thrusts got faster and shorter, becoming rough little jabs into my ass. His breathing got hoarse.

"Jesus!" I shot another wad that glanced off his chest and still managed to hit me in the face. He banged into my hole and ground his pubes against my tender cheeks. I felt him grow even thicker inside me as he ground against me.

"Here!" he gasped and pulled me even closer against him.

He shuddered over me, then fell on top of me, his dick sliding halfway out of me. "Let's just lie here," he gasped."Just for a minute."

"Okay,' I responded, content.

I had already crossed the Rubicon of my sexual direction and hadn't even noticed it. Mike had quietly but firmly taken me into homosexuality and my body knew where it belonged by the end of our first night together. A lot of relationships would have to be reworked and plans redirected, but the basis of everything was no longer in doubt.

I woke the next morning to find Mike slipping into bed with me, erection throbbing and condom already in place.

"Slide your butt over here, Vic," he muttered against my ear as his fingers found my already hard dick. He chuckled. "We both need some relief, I see."

His arms encircling my chest, his dick moved into the already-established rut that led through my pucker. I didn't even cringe as it spread me wide. I was already leaking when his fingers encircled my pole and began to jack it in time with his movement in my bottom. I gripped his other hand and brought it to my lips.

I didn't believe I was in love with Mike Lynn. Only, that was the easiest way I could explain how comfortable I felt with him fucking me. It was more than just the lust I had had with Paco the year before. I had the same need but I was relaxed about it with Mike, accepting that he was my means of fulfillment. Kissing his open palm, I gave myself up to the first eruption of the morning beginning to develop in my ballsac.

"Feel good?" he asked as he nuzzled my ear and I creamed the sheets.

"Hhhmmm." I was happy in the flow of good sex and the feel of him inside me. In appreciation, I wiggled my butt as he pushed back into me.

His teeth gnawed gently at my shoulders, his fingers rubbed my tits carelessly. My erection stayed with me as he rode me through all the pleasures there were to being fucked well.

"I'm going to come," he groaned against my neck, his teeth still nipping at my shoulders. He grabbed me around the chest and started to hump me fast. I gasped and erupted again as he spewed goo into his rubber buried in my guts. I ground my cheeks around on him as I felt him softening inside me.

"Vic, baby," he groaned as he slipped out of me, "we need something to eat."

"I've got eggs and bacon in the fridge," I mumbled, floating on the gentle swells of satiation.

"Want to rustle us up some?"

I shrugged, not really wanting to get up. I was already beginning to understand it was my part of our arrangement to get him what he wanted, however. I sat up and found my briefs on the floor. Smiling, I pulled them onto my butt as he watched me.

I clanged a couple of pans around and heard him go into the toilet. I listened while he took his first piss of the day and wondered why he hadn't shut the door. He followed with a brief shower and came out dripping water about the time I finished frying our bacon and eggs. "Where are the towels, babe?" he asked and watched intently as my eyes traveled over his body.

He grinned as he started to grow hard. "I guess that's a dumb question, isn't it?" He approached me more slowly, letting his dick reach its full potential. "You like what you see?" he asked as he turned me to face the bar.

I nodded and smiled.

"Let's fuck then."

"Get a raincoat, Mike," I told him.

Moments later, he was back with the rubber already in place. He jerked my briefs down to my knees and rubbed his wide slab of meat against my asscheeks. "Grab the bar, Vic, and I'll take you doggie style this time around."

Fingers spread my cheeks to expose my crack. "Nice, baby," he mumbled and directed his dick to me. His hands came up to grab my waist. "Brace yourself, baby, I'm going to make it rough this time." He pumped his hips forward and my assring was caught unaware as his dick barreled past it in one blinding burst of speed.

"Jesus!" I yelped at the rush of pain spreading out of my hole and looked at him in surprise over my shoulder.

He grinned back at me. "A little rough livens up the fun, baby." He started to hump me as hard and fast as he could.

"Oh, God!" I groaned and tried to hold myself still against the fury with which he fucked me.

My dick rode against the ridges of my stomach. My balls bounced against my thighs. His bush scratched my cheeks and my lovegland overloaded. I shot a load that dribbled on the carpet at my feet. He held my waist and pounded my butt until I didn't have any feeling left in it.

Minutes later, he held himself against my bottom and grunted as he deposited more cream in yet another rubber buried where the sun never shines.

He stepped back and ran his hand over my backside. "You've got just about the cutest buns I've ever seen, Vic."

"Thanks," I mumbled and stood up weakly.

"Let's eat something."

"It's probably cold by now."

He grinned and bent in to kiss my cheek. "Baby, it'll never get cold with your ass and my dick in the same room." He picked up a plate and sauntered over to the table in the dining alcove. "Do we have coffee?" he asked as he sat down.

"Yeah, and it's made," I answered as I wondered if I even should get back into my briefs. They hadn't proved to be much protection with Mike Lynn around and they wouldn't be covering anything he hadn't already seen and claimed as his own.

"I take one spoon of sugar and just a dab of milk," he called as I started to pour two steaming mugs.

When I went to take a shower, he joined me and filled me up again. We went back to bed and he had me straddle him to give us a new position. I picked up the apartment and found his fingers spreading my bare cheeks before I had bent over twice. I cooked spaghetti for dinner and got taken once while I was dicing onions and the next time while my pasta boiled. I wondered at how big a supply of raincoats this boy had.

"We've got to talk seriously without your dick finding its way up into my butt, Mike," I told him as I sat bare and prim at the table to eat my dinner. My bottom felt funny with a chair under it instead of his dick inside it. And I was thankful that Gene would never see me like this.

"Talk away, Vic ... you've got my ears," he said around a forkful of pasta.

"One thing is grocery shopping...."

"I'm not particularly choosey about what I eat ... I'll just give you twenty a week and you buy whatever you want to fix."

I nodded. I already saw that this was going to be a strange relationship. I just didn't know if getting fucked a hundred times a day was going to be worth being his servant.

"Second is booze."

"I like scotch and rum. Will fifteen every two weeks be enough?"

I nodded. "Then there's condoms. We're going through even the economy packs like there's no tomorrow."

"We'll split that cost down the middle. I'll get down to the post in the next week or two and pick us up a month's supply."

"Fourth thing is I'm going to have to study starting day after tomorrow. I can't walk around all day long bare-assed knowing you're going to hop my ass at any moment."

He looked at me curiously. "What would you suggest?"

"We relegate our sex to late nights and early mornings."

"What if I need a piece of ass in the meantime?"

I stared at him in amazement. "You have that big a sexual appetite? Jesus! How did you ever make it through that junior college?"

He laughed. "I lived at home and my main squeeze had a room right off campus ... we'd have at it when I got to school in the morning and after classes until I had to go home."

"Well, we're going to have to tone it way down or I kiss Harvard Law goodbye. Mike, I study best at home in an easy chair or on a bed—not in a library." I glanced over my shoulder at the door. "Besides, you know what it's like around Mercer. I'd stand out if I had to walk back from the library every night."

He nodded. "Okay, so you're off-limits until eleven. If I get a hard-on any other time of the day, I go find a piece of strange ass to liven up my day."

I looked away, unwilling to meet his eyes. Suddenly, I was no longer comfortable with him. I lusted after him; I wanted sex with him. I was no longer comfortable and relaxed about us, however. I accepted that I was nothing more than his fuckbuddy, that was all I had been these past two days - and I didn't like the feeling.

Yet, I knew he'd do whatever he wanted to anyway. Even if I knew he was screwing some other guy, I'd still be out of my clothes and spreading my legs for his dick. So, why fight it?

I shrugged. "Fifth thing is I've got friends around from last year and before—guys I'd just as soon didn't know I was getting dicked all over this place. Macon, Georgia, isn't exactly Sodom, you know."

"Will they be coming over here?"

"Sometimes. Mike, some of these people I go back with for three years. I want to include you whenever we get together - but I want us to keep them out of our sex life."

"You mean you wouldn't go for a threeway every once in a while?"

"A three..?" My eyes rounded with shock and I felt myself blush.

He laughed. "There was a time when your ass hadn't known a dick. But we both know how much you like it now."

I wanted to hit his open, smiling face. My eyes dropped to his meat and I wanted to cry.

"Look, Vic, I'll make you the same promise I made myself, okay?"

"What's that?"

"I'll never rip a guy's clothes off. But, if he drops his pants himself, he's fucking fair game for anything. Is that fair enough?"

"I guess." I had the most depressing idea that I would soon be sharing my bed with somebody in addition to Mike, somebody I knew and whom I had always thought of as heterosexual.

"Let's go to bed, Vic. I want to watch you ride me to glory again." He put his plate on the bar and waited as I rose from the table, uncomfortable with my erection jutting out in front of me as I joined him. "You can clean the dinner dishes afterwards."

The next morning, I started class, and, that afternoon, I started back to the apartment. My steps got shorter the closer I came. Really, I didn't really want to go home, not yet— not to get naked and fucked the rest of the day. Too much of a good thing was proving to be still too much to my way of thinking. In my case, it was sex. All I had to do was look at Mike Lynn and I had a hard-on. And, it seemed he was very much the same way about me. My assmuscle was calling foul, and loudly. It needed a rest.

In addition to the need to rest my sphincter there was the other thing. I knew I needed to talk with myself about that. A long, hard talk. What exactly existed between Mike and me?

I hadn't seen him putting his dick anywhere near my mouth since that first time. He hadn't done anything with mine but jack it since that first time. It was definitely just his dick and my butt. Just as it had been with Paco; only, now I knew there was more to good sex than me getting plowed. My ass was crying foul. So was my heart ... or, at least, some of my heart strings were.

What I really wanted most was for Mike to miss me. Just a little. I wanted to hear that he did. Some of those hearts and flowers romance writers make big bucks writing about it. I didn't want to hear there was going to be even one extra fuckbuddy near the apartment I'd lived in for nearly two years. Somehow, his big dick and my heart had formed a connection that had me caught by the short hairs.

I told myself I needed the exercise and convinced myself to keep walking when I got to the turnoff to the apartment. It was only another mile down to the shops at Little Five Points on the south end of campus and I could get our two week supply of booze while I was out and avoiding Mike. Two quarts of rum and two of scotch proved to be heavier and bulkier than I expected, especially after I had added a couple of twelve packs of beer to what I was carrying.

I was glad to see the tree-lined drive to the small, quiet complex when I turned the corner. The heat had already got to me and a line of sweat trickled down my back between my shoulder blades and had me itching madly.

I set the bags on the porch and eased the door open. I was starting to pick up the first bag when I heard a low moan from the bedroom. I stepped through the door and listened, my heart in my throat.

"Oh, God! That feels...." A voice groaned and I was almost sure I recognized it. "Shit! Not so rough, asshole," the guy continued. "Sweet Jesus, I'm going to blow a load with your dick up my ass!"

"You're doing good, babe," Mike told whoever it was.

I wanted to run back to the bedroom screaming for both of them to get out. I wanted to run out of the house and find a quiet place to cry. I wanted just about anything but to hear

Mike giving some other guy that dick I was so used to already.

Instead, I carefully put my purchases on the bar and moved through the house to stand in the doorway of the bedroom. Mike Lynn was between a pair of legs and it was obvious as hell he was banging the guy's butt ... just as he did mine. It even looked to be his favorite position too. I took a step into the room and saw the face under him turn glassy eyes toward me.

I froze. Gene Butler! Redheaded, slim, cute, freckle-faced Gene. Gene with the girl he slept with at the communal house up the street where most of my American friends lived. Gene the theology student who had been a friend of mine the past two years. Gene Butler, whose naked images I jerked off to more than once before Paco first came along to fill my hole whenever I needed it.

"Oh, Jesus!" The eyes staring at me weren't glassy any more. "Mike, stop it! Let me get up now." Gene was trying to push himself away even as his ankles crossed each other behind Mike's neck. "Jesus, Vic's watching us!"

Mike glanced over his shoulder at me and kept right on plowing Gene's hole. "Hi, Vic," he grinned. "Want to join us?"

"What?" Gene yelped, pushing ineffectively against Mike's chest even as his body shuddered with each of my roommate's thrusts into his ass. "No! Oh, Jesus! Vic, I never ... Oh, God!" I watched as an arc of Gene's goo shot out of his dick and headed for his face.

"Eat it, babe," Mike told him, emphasizing his command with a rough lurch in the boy's butt.

Gene's face decided to turn as red as his hair. His wad began to ooze onto his neck, and Mike continued to massage his lovegland. "Eat it!" Mike commanded again.

Slowly, hesitantly, one of my best friends brought a finger up to his neck and lifted the rope. Shutting his eyes, Gene Butler stuck his finger and his wad of goo in his mouth.

Mike chuckled. "That's better, Gene. Now, we're going to shift positions. You're going to ride me so Vic can get to your dick." He grinned down at the redhead beneath him. "You're going to love this ... getting fucked and sucked at the same time will be a real treat."

Mike spread his knees wide and shifted his weight to them. His hands went under Gene's backside. He lifted my buddy straight up as he sat down on the bed. Gene's eyes were wide and his face burned with his shame. Mike's dick was as deep into Gene as he could get it. They were facing each other and I saw their connection still held. I also saw Gene had a cute bubble butt as he sat there on Mike's lap.

"Now, Gene," Mike told him, "I'm going to lie back so you can get your leg over me. Don't worry, babe, you're still going to keep my dick in your ass ... you're just going to turn around so Vic can give your dick the attention it deserves." Mike's hands on his hips guided him as well as kept him impaled, and Gene was soon turned to face me.

He wasn't large where it counted. He was maybe average. Six or so inches of pretty pink dick with a skinned helmet that glistened with arrogant pride despite his embarrassment.

"Okay, Gene, get your feet on the bed frame there so you've got some leverage and start riding this piledriver you've got in your ass. Vic, get down there and give our buddy some TLC."

I knelt and took Gene's dick in my mouth. I had already forgotten my resistance to Mike having anybody but me. This was Gene Butler, I had wanted him. Now, I was going to have him. My fingers cradled his balls and I felt him start to respond to what I was doing for him.

I deep-throated him. I gave him a vacuum a physics teacher would kill to have. I bobbed merrily up and down his shaft. I heard him gasp above me and tasted his pre-come as he pistoned himself up and down on Mike's dick, his embarrassment forgotten.

Sweat glistened on Gene's body. He arched his back and his eggs were growing tight in their sack again. "Can't you come?" he grunted to Mike from above me and shot his wad down my throat.

"I'm not ready yet, Gene," Mike chuckled from beneath us. "I like the feel of your ass squeezing my dick. Ride this thing harder, babe."

Gene pistoned himself and Mike lay back enjoying it. I kept sliding up and down on Gene's moving dick. "You like this, Gene?" Mike asked and my red-headed friend moaned. "Answer my question, boy! Do you like it?"

"Yeah." His answer came through gritted teeth and my tonsils had another wad of Gene's goo splattering them.

"I like it too ... but Vic's sort of getting left out of some of the fun. Vic, get out of your duds and let's all three have a good time."

I let go of Gene's dick and started peeling off my clothes.

"Now, Gene, this change's going to be easier than the first one. I want you to put your feet between my legs and stand up. Don't worry, I'm not going to leave you unplugged. I'm going to be right behind you and riding you doggie style while you bend over and give Vic some of the loving he's been giving you."

It took my friend a few minutes to catch Mike's new drift. He was, after all, getting his prostate rubbed good. Gene stared at me in immediate horror. I watched his eyes travel down my chest and stop at my briefs. I could imagine what he was thinking. He was always a bit too quick to accept an offer of free dope and it wasn't hard to figure Mike had made him the same offer he made me.

Naked, flying high, and lying back on the bed with Mike already between his legs, Gene never had a chance. His butt had been turned up and his chute invaded before he knew what was happening to him. My sucking his root hadn't touched what was left of his heterosexual heart. But him bending over and sucking my dick, even with one up his ass while he was doing it, scared the shit out of him.

"Pull his briefs down and look at a really nice dick, baby," Mike told him and patted an asscheek affectionately. "You're going to love this, Gene."

I realized that I didn't have it in me to be the one to go denying Mike his fun, especially when it was my fun too!

When Gene was pulling on his clothes and trying hard to ignore how wide his hole felt, he wouldn't look at me. Mike had dicked him so much he was as cowed as I was. But he wasn't happy at how his body had betrayed him over and over.

"Stop by around three tomorrow," Mike told him as he edged toward the bedroom door and his escape from the two naked and sated men in the room with him. I felt Mike's hand cup my nearest buttcheek. I glanced down and saw he was already tumescent.

"Huh?" Gene grunted and turned back to face Mike, his jaw gaping.

"Come over after three. We're going to have lots of fun while

Vic here is studying."

"I...."

"Gene!" The redhead cowered. "You're not going to do anything you haven't already proved to yourself that you like," Mike told him like he was explaining something to a recalcitrant child. "Besides, I'd hate for the Dean of Men's office to hear how you like to take it up the ass."

Gene's head jerked up and he was staring at Mike with both fear and hatred in his eyes. "You wouldn't!"

"Come by tomorrow at three."

Gene's Adam's apple bobbed a couple of times and I could have sworn I saw tears glistening in his eyes, but he nodded and found the door to his temporary escape.

"You interested in some fun?" Mike asked as he squeezed my butt.

"You don't come anywhere near me with that weapon," I told him. "Not until you've washed it off and have it covered with a clean rubber."

"I guess I could use a shower. You want to join me?"

"Not until later, Mike. I'm going to be hardnosed as hell about this."

He grinned. "I'll go along with this one, Vic. You've got a right to that hang-up."

I was hard as hell the whole time he was taking a shower. I wanted his dick. And it didn't matter that he was going to be balling Gene Butler every afternoon. I wanted him in me. I wanted the sex.

I was naked and lying on the bed when he came back into the bedroom. I grinned when I saw he was hard too. "Thinking of me?" I asked and spread my legs.

I knew what Mike was to me then. He was pure sexual energy. As he rolled a rubber down his shaft, I also accepted that he'd never be anything else.

Gene met me as I was coming out of class the next morning. His face was crimson but he pulled me onto the quadrangle and out of the flow of bodies. "How did he get you?" he demanded.

"That damned Thai shit of his," I answered. "Two tokes and we were sucking each other. Before I knew it I had his dick up my ass."

"Yeah! It was the same with me ... only, I didn't suck his dong. Jesus! You're the first guy I ever did that with! And getting fucked ... Oh, God!"

"You seemed to be enjoying it," I offered, pointing out the obvious.

"I've got Megan I live with, damn it! I've got all the sex a man could want."

"Do you come with her as much as you did with Mike yesterday afternoon?"

"Huh?" He stared at me. "You've accepted being queer because of him?"

"Does she get you off as much as Mike did?" I insisted.

"No, damn it! But that doesn't mean I'm ready to run up the white flag and swish around, Vic! I'm no fucking queer!"

"I never said you were, Gene," I told him quietly.

"I don't want to go over there today, Vic. Why don't you go ahead and drop your shorts and bend over for him?"

"I already do, Gene. At night. But I'm going to study and I can't do that with a dick plowing my damned ass."

"He's a fucking sex machine. Holy shit! He had to be fucking me for over an hour."

"Try at least twenty times the day before." I smiled ruefully. "After I got over my shock, I was sort of glad it was you and not me taking that afternoon ride."

"Jesus! What the hell are we going to do about him?"

"Shit if I know," I answered, allowing myself some feeling.

"Jesus! I'm going over to your place this afternoon and get dicked like some girl."

"If I remember correctly, you were getting off on it quite happily yesterday. How many times did you blow a load while you were riding him?"

"That doesn't mean jack shit, Vic! I don't have to be queer if I don't want to be."

"Then, don't. Just say no."

"And he drops it at the Dean's office that I'm queer. I sure couldn't pass a lie detector if they ever asked if I sucked a dick or took one up the ass. Jesus! Do you know what this would do to my parents?"

"About what it would do to mine."

"Vic!"

"Maybe you should stop in this afternoon?"

"And get my ass dicked good!"

"Or don't, and let the university kick you out for being queer."

"Jesus! We've got to find a way to get to him!"

"We?"

"Are you ready to admit you're a queer to the whole world, Vic?"

"I'm ready to admit to you and Mike that I like dick , up my ass and in my mouth." I grinned. "I even imagine I'd like to fuck ... if I ever got the chance."

"Do you want Mike leading you around by the nose?" Gene demanded, looking for another avenue by which to enroll me in whatever he could come up with.

"No." I did not like the situation— at least not beyond the sex he and I had. I'd had a chance to look at it with my head instead of feeling it with my butt. But I also knew that Gene was every bit as Irish as was his red hair. The boy went off half-cocked more times than he aimed at the target. I didn't want to get caught in the backfire. I'd think of something to get myself out of the situation I was in. Myself.

"Then, help me find a way out of this."

"Do you have any suggestions?"

"No." He studied me for a moment, like an insect or something. "But I'm not going to stop trying to find something to get out of this."

"Me either, Gene. But, for the time being, I guess that I'll see you this afternoon." I looked down at my hands to hide the fact that I knew I wanted this boy's butt. "I may even join you guys."

"Vic!" He was glaring at me when I looked back at him.

"If looks could kill, I'd be dead right now," I told him. "You want him bringing in somebody else?"

Gene's eyes filled with terror. "Oh, sweet Jesus!' He stared at me. "He wouldn't, would he?'

I shrugged. "I was sort of surprised to find you there when I walked in yesterday, Gene. What's to stop him from finding somebody else—or several of them even? You could become part of a real orgy."

"That'd be the time you'd be sending him packing."

"Not very likely. Do I want the good Air Force civilian manager and mummy dearest up here because I'm getting kicked out for being queer?"

He studied me for several moments in silence. "We're caught by the short hairs, aren't we?"

"Yeah. Look, I know you won't like this idea much but hear me out...." I scratched my head and tried to put the jumble of impressions I had into words. "Our boy's a psychology major and he's playing a mean head game on both of us. Why don't we watch him for his own little areas where he's weak ... sooner or later, we're going to find out where he hurts."

"In the meantime, he bangs our asses whenever he wants to?"

"Are you ready to go home in disgrace?"

Gene blushed when I answered the door and he didn't say anything as he went to the bedroom.

"Hi, babe," a naked Mike greeted him from his bed. "Come on in here. I've got a real hurt going and you're just the guy to help me out of it."

I wished they had the decency to shut the door so I didn't have to hear Gene gurgling like a drowning school girl. But, then, Mike didn't even shut the door to the john when he was taking a dump.

Soon enough, my red-haired buddy was yodelling like a Swiss maid until Mike was firmly imbedded in him and he was used to him being there again. I was finding it pretty hard to concentrate on the specifics of Plato's concept of a philosopher king while Gene moaned and groaned and the bedsprings squeaked continuously. My dick was hard and, soon, I was almost ready to take it out and start stroking it.

The springs stopped squeaking on the other side of the wall behind my chair. There were muted mumblings from the bedroom but Gene wasn't moaning any more. I dove into Plato with both feet.

"Vic?"

I glanced up from my book and saw a red-faced, naked Gene standing just inside the hallway.

"Mike and I thought you might like to take a break from studying."

"Yeah?"

"Maybe you could ... uh ... join us for a while?"

I shrugged and put my book down. I walked into the

bedroom and found Gene staring at me like I was some kind of monster. "Go ahead and ask him," Mike told him.

"Mike thought it might be fun if we got into a real threeway," Gene said, hanging his head. "And I'd like it if you'd fuck me."

I glanced from him to Mike and back. "You really want to get into that?' I asked.

"Come on, Vic!" Mike boomed. "Don't go looking a gift horse in the mouth." He had effectively shut Gene off. "Besides, you two can trade off whenever you want."

Gene wouldn't look at me but he nodded his head in agreement.

"Sure, why not?" I said and peeled off my clothes. Gene stared at me as I started back toward them. His eyes were blank and I couldn't read him as he sat down on my bed and lay back with his legs spread.

"Looks like you're going to get a piece of something you've wanted for a long time, Vic," Mike observed with what sounded like satisfaction.

"How's that?"

He grinned. "I just got the idea you'd wanted to get something on with Gene for a while and, now, you are."

I moved in between Gene's legs and smiled down at him as he raised them to my chest. I raised my brows into twin question marks as I pulled the cowl back along my shaft and slipped a rubber over the helmet and onto the shaft. He just looked blankly into my eyes. I raised his butt up to meet my dick as Mike came up alongside us stroking his own slab of meat. He grinned and cupped my nearest asscheek.

"I've never done this position, guys, so it's going to be a new experience for all of us," he told us. "Go on, Vic, and dick him ... I'll take you when you're settled in."

Gene was wide open, stretched that way by a half hour of Mike's dick. I slipped into him easily and bent over him. "Spread him open for me," Mike told the boy under me and Gene's hands grasped the cheeks of my backside and spread them.

Gene's eyes locked with mine as Mike's dick shredded my assring. "Vic, you just fall into him when I'm all the way into you ... just stay in synch with me and we're going to have one hell of a fuck."

I saw a tear roll down Gene's cheek and ducked down to nuzzle it away so Mike wouldn't see it. My red-headed buddy was humiliated enough and didn't need any more of Mike's nonsense than he was getting.

Gene grabbed my face and brought my mouth to his lips while Mike fucked me and I fucked him.

• • •

The quarter moved toward mid-terms and I had taken to studying in the library. I couldn't sit down in my living room and try to read a textbook with Mike pumping Gene's backside in the bedroom—not with Gene liking it as much as he did. Shit! The man acted like he wanted the whole neighborhood to know it when he was getting filled with dick.

My friendship with the redhead I had once drooled for was put on hold from the day I dicked him. It was almost as if we both were contending for the same man and Gene wouldn't mind if I just disappeared and left Mike to him.

That second day of Mike's dick in his butt seemed to have pushed Gene over the brink. He stopped fighting his daily meetings with my roommate in our bedroom. Within a week, he even started staying at the apartment later, making himself into Mike's main sextoy. The boy was singing soprano to Mike's baritone and seemed to be in a perfect orbit around his sun.

I let it ride and went on making sure I would have Harvard Law when I got out of Mercer. Besides, I went home every night to more than enough of Mike's dick to satisfy me before I got to class the next morning.

I hadn't realized just how completely Gene had surrendered to Mike until Halloween, when I went to a party at the communal house where the redhead lived with his girlfriend. I had a beer in hand and was talking about law school with a guy who lived at the house. They walked in then. Side by side. Gene smiling at Mike and Mike with his hand spread across Gene's blue jeaned butt. I stared, surprised to see how publicly Mike possessed Gene in front of everybody. It wouldn't take a university degree to read what Gene was getting from my roommate.

"Look at that! God, those fucking queers!" the law student

I was talking with sneered.

"Oh?" I asked, playing it dumb. "Who?"

"Those two," he answered. "Everyone at the house knows about them. I hear tell that Megan is getting ready to drop Gene."

"Oh...?"

"She's going to have to now. What in the hell has gotten into that boy, being so damned obvious?"

It was a shock to see Gene waiting for me as I came out of the Philosophy building. It was the middle of November and a cold, raw day. He stood at the foot of the steps, his hands dug deep in his pockets and his face even gloomier than I'd seen it when he accepted me between his legs that one time.

"I need to talk with you, Vic," he greeted me, real urgency in his voice.

"Hi, Gene, how are you?"

"Like shit! Let's go out in the graveyard...." He pointed in the direction of the small, walled-in resting place of former rectors and religious leaders from the time when Mercer was strictly a theology school for Baptists. "I really do need to talk with you."

I shrugged and followed him out into the blustery November morning. "It feels like it might rain," I opined.

"Fuck that shit! Vic, Megan knows and, worse, she's letting him dick her."

"What are you talking about?"

"Your roommate."

"The one you were so ready to scuttle our friendship over?" I asked mildly.

"C'mon, Vic. You're just about the only friend I've got left!"

"Start from the beginning," I told him as I leaned on a headstone almost as old as the republic.

"You know how Mike is when we go out?"

"Well, I know how obvious you both were at the Halloween party. Even the CIA would have you two figured out in a couple of minutes ... and they still leak worse than a sieve."

"Maybe, I don't know." He looked around at the bleak wintry scene, like he was seeing it for the first time. "Anyway, she started making noises about me two-timin' her ... about me being ... uh—queer."

"You have real problems with that word, Gene. Accept what it means! You like dick as much as I do."

"I know I do ... Shit! It was getting to where I could barely fuck Megan when we were in bed together. I had to imagine him in me to do it."

"I bet you still get hard quick enough for Mike." He blushed brightly and I let the subject drop.

"She apparently ran into him back in October sometime." He hung his head. "He invited her over to your place and offered her some of his Thai shit. They've been spending every goddamn morning over there with him plowing her just like he does us."

"Our boy does seems versatile, Gene."

He ignored me. "Yesterday they were both there when I showed up naked as jaybirds—and me standing in the door gawking at them."

"I guess that would have been a surprise." I smiled.

"He got me naked and hard enough to go in her. Then, he took me."

"Like he did me when I stuck it to you that time?"

"Yeah." He didn't even blush.

"Did you like it?"

"Well, it was one of the best fucks I've ever had—with either of them."

"Okay, now, you can have a happy three-way ... with you the permanent middle. What's wrong with that?"

"She wants to leave me—says she can't stand two-timing sons of bitches."

"Did you tell her to leave your mother out of it?"

"Vic!"

"How does Mike feel about it?"

"Shit if I know."

"Maybe you've got the answer to your problems." I permitted a smile to play across my lips. "And me mine ... he moves in with her."

"How does that answer my problem?"

"You get free of them both."

"But...." His eyes widened in sudden realization.

"You love him, don't you?"

He hung his head and his face turned white. He looked down at the ground. "I don't know if I've ever thought it through. But, damn it, I do love that dick of his."

"Okay. You give him a demand—either he moves in with you somewhere—or you quit. That way you may have a crack at him." I thought about it another moment. "I'll bet you anything he digs guys more than girls, Gene. You'd most likely get him."

"Then, I'd lose her."

"Do you love her too?"

"I...." He stared at me. "No, not really."

"She's just your last claim to not being queer?"

He grimaced before he nodded.

"You don't like the options, do you, Gene?"

"No, I don't."

"You've lost her, no matter what. There's not a woman around who's willing to let her main man spread his legs for another guy ... she's got to believe she's the best sex he can have."

"Then, everybody'll know I'm queer as a three dollar bill."

"Not if you don't go around broadcasting it ... like you have been."

"That'd mean giving him up too."

"I'm sure there's somebody around with as large a dick who'll probably love you a lot more than Mike Lynn ever will."

"I don't like it."

"Why?"

"Mike won't make a choice ... he makes other people make choices."

"What did he use on you when you were so hellbent on denying him?"

"He said he'd go to the Dean of Men and tell them I was queer."

A small suspicion had been bumping around in my mind since we'd entered the graveyard and I decided to explore its possibilities. "When you were fucking Megan, did you use rubbers?"

"Yeah. The pills makes her sick or something."

I grinned.

"How long did you say they've been getting it on?"

"Three or four weeks. I don't know."

"Would Megan talk to me and keep it serious?"

"Maybe. I don't know ... Shit! I haven't been able to really talk to her since I started seeing that bastard."

"Let's meet her over at that communal house you people all share after classes. I'd like to see if we can get something worked out here."

"Why?"

"Because I want a new roommate in January ... studying in the library hurts my fucking ass."

I had no reason to suspect that Mike might be fucking Megan bareback. Our bedroom was still the center of his operations with her, as it was with Gene and me. The boy had a condom supply sitting there right at his fingertips.

Only, I couldn't get it out of my head that there had to be some reason beyond sex that had him porking a girl. Something more even than that she was still technically Gene's girl. My roommate was on record as liking the boys. Between Gene and me, he probably got five or more fucks a day; so adding a girl to his harem didn't make any sense ... if that was all there was to it. He also possessed Gene; so, porking the boy's girl too was overkill. That was not something Mike Lynn went in for.

I knew Mike now. His game was to find a man's weakest link and possess him through it. His favorite game appeared to be going after the boy who wasn't out of the closet yet and pulling him out screaming. With me, I had surrendered in record time and accepted being his servant around the apartment. But I drew lines and he had pretty well accepted them. Maybe that was because we were roommates, and he needed a relatively peaceful home base to develop the games he played with other people. I wasn't sure of that one, but it felt right.

Gene had not surrendered quickly and quietly. He had resisted for a couple of days to my knowledge and probably longer. He had especially resisted accepting that he was gay. So, Mike made him into a sex slave publicly. It didn't matter where Gene Butler went nowadays, it was obvious he was fruity.

So, why had Mike gone after a girl? And Gene's girlfriend specifically? I was hoping that it had something to do with her head ... because Megan was a full-fledged feminist before she was anything. She'd tell anybody a woman had every right to get laid, just as much as a man did. Getting laid had nothing to do with getting pregnant for her, though. I'd even gotten the impression that Megan had a fear of that one; and I wasn't even a budding psychologist.

If Mike had set out to dominate her as he did Gene and me, I was hoping he'd let the macho lizard side of his brain take over his human one. That meant him possessing her even more completely than he could Gene or me. That could well mean he was doing it bareback, hoping to get her pregnant. Pregnancy would take a huge chunk of the wind out of the girl's sails.

Megan's hair was as red as Gene's and she was a bundle of energy as I walked into the big old house with her ex-beau. She was attractive in an aggressive sort of way that didn't appeal to me—even if this had been before Mike took me across my own personal Rubicon. I wondered what Gene had seen in her. If anything, she tried to have more balls than he. But I could see why she'd appeal to Mike. She was a lot to tear down and retrain; she'd be a real challenge to someone with his ego and his inclination to mind games.

She was chewing on a sandwich when we approached her. She looked up and saw us, her face become a snarl when her gaze landed on him. A moment later, she was staring at me like I was a tiger she had to tame. "I think we need to talk," I told her.

"I don't talk to fucking queers!" she spat and looked directly at Gene.

"Gene is part of the problem I need to talk to you about."

"Shit!" She reached to the table and grabbed a glass of milk. Never taking her eyes off me, she downed the glass. She took another bite from the sandwich and began to chew. I knew she was trying to intimidate me. Normally, I'd have gotten up and walked away. But there was Mike and the budding possibility of my being able to rid myself of him. Then, there was the beginning of a renewal of my interest in Gene. The boy was definitely nice, and it seemed like there might be room for something between—if, in fact, Mike was out of the picture.

She glanced over at Gene finally. "Go away, little fairy. I'm no faghag."

"Cut it out, you two. I want to be serious." I took both their elbows and headed in the general of the walled-in patio behind the house.

Once we were all sitting in the November chill, I turned to

face Megan. "I hear you've been getting together with my roommate."

"What of it?" she demanded, her eyes flashing. "I've got as much right to fuck as you have. Besides, I thought I'd see just how good he was if he could turn a simple little piece of shit like this turd...." she pointed at Gene, "into a queer."

"How long has it been going on, Megan? Your seeing Mike, I mean?"

"A month ... almost a month and a half."

I breathed a sigh of relief. Now, all I had to do was pray that Mike had set out to destroy her whole self-image. If he had, then all we needed was for nature to have taken its course.

"Megan, Gene was queer a long time ago," I told her, starting off carefully. "He just didn't know it and didn't want to know it." He cringed beside me but kept his mouth shut.

"He picked the wrong girl not to know it with," she growled, not ready to start forgiving ... especially not in front of someone she barely knew and had never controled.

"Actually, you were the right girl—or the rightest possible one he could've hoped for," I offered, trying for even a modicrum of curiosity.

She glared at me, her mind racing through synapses that I couldn't even imagine. "What're you trying to say, Vic?"

"Nobody wants to be queer, for God's sake!. There's a whole lot of hate out there for gays and lesbians. Some of the preachers are fomenting it even more. Gene sure didn't. He didn't even think he was—and was happy with you. Until Mike came along and started playing mind games with him. Did he give you a few tokes off a joint of Thai shit?"

"Yeah...." She stared at me as if I'd just grown a second head. "Why?"

"Because he did the same thing to Gene and to me." She stared at me in surprise and growing suspicion.

"You?"

"The day he showed up at the apartment I got a couple of tokes ... the next thing I knew I had that big-assed dick up my butt and was singing soprano." She giggled and I knew I had her. "I swear, the next day, I just left my briefs off because he was fucking me every time I turned around—it had to have been at least twenty times."

"Jesus! Twenty times?" Her eyes glassed over at the thought

of that much sex in separate, individual doses.

I nodded. "I was confronted with something I hadn't been ready to admit to myself. I was being forced to admit that I liked dick and I liked it in my ass. I mean, when you've been dicked as many times as I was that first day, you sort of know what the score is from there on out."

"Why'd he put the make on Gene?" She was right on cue.

"Because ... well, I told him I wasn't up to blowing my future on what he was doing to my butt. I study, Megan. Getting to Harvard Law takes A+'s from a school like Mercer. He found he couldn't control me ... he didn't have me locked up like he does most people he plays with. Maybe it was just that I wasn't resisting and he didn't have to keep forcing me to face up to what I was. Then, Gene came along looking for me."

"Did you ever get it on with him?" She pointed at her ex-lover.

"I've wanted to from the first day I saw him. Gene was too straight for me to seriously think of getting into anything with him. Besides, I was sure I was going to be one hundred percent heterosexual. I'd only done something with one guy before Mike...." I shrugged and smiled ruefully. "And I had myself convinced that there wasn't going to be anybody else putting a claim on my ass. But, then, I don't have the ego Mike Lynn has, or the psychological know-how either. Gene got to puff Mike's Thai stuff and thought he was going to get a blowjob when he took off his clothes. Instead, he got what I got."

I decided to spread it on thick. At least, a little thicker than I suspected was the truth. "Only, he tried to resist. He tried to hold onto what he had. And he didn't have the full force Mike can bring to bear on you when he's got you day and night in the bed next to his. Gene lasted a couple of weeks while I lasted a couple of minutes." I smiled and knew I was succeeding in buttering her up. "Because he had you to hold on to."

"He still fell."

"Sure he did! He likes dick just as much as I do. After Mike had him, he had to finally accept himself for what he was sooner or later or blow his mind. Imagine being a lesbian who suddenly falls in love with dick—you can't keep straddling the fence."

"Yeah." She glanced sideways at Gene and smiled weakly.

I figured it was about as close as the boy was going to come to an apology, given Megan's reputation.

"Mike had played with my head about all he could when he got me to accept myself ... but he tried. He'd leave the door open when he took a dump, he left me to clean up, and he expected me to cook for him like a good little hausfrau. I wouldn't rise to the bait; Gene did. He fought all the way."

"Poor baby," she mumbled.

"And, then, you came along."

"What did he see in me? I sure as hell don't look like a boy."

"Anger, frustration, confusion, anxiety, brights, pride - take your pick. He's a psychology major—and damned good at applying the practical stuff."

"Yeah," she mumbled, nodding and accepting this assessment of what she'd probably seen as a plaything until now. She had the reputation of being a tiger in bed and Gene was the only boy she'd ever settled down with.

I suspected she was realizing just how much of a fool she'd been played for. I decided to take the plunge. "Gene says you're allergic to the birth control pill?"

"So what?" Her glance at Gene this time wasn't a kindly one.

"So Mike may not have used rubbers...." The fear I saw in her eyes told me I'd been hoping right. I'd just gotten luckier than anyone deserved to be. So had Gene. "How long has it been since your last period?"

"A...." Her eyes widened in shock. "A couple of months," she answered in a small voice.

"And the only two making love to you these past two months were Gene and Mike?"

"The fucking bastard!" she growled, her anger taking an intuitive leap. "First, he screws us all up and, then, he leaves me with a fuckin' kid."

"His father's a full colonel, Megan. They have property in the Carolinas as well as Georgia and Virginia."

"So...?"

"The baby's paternal grandparents are financially well off."

Speculation began to dance in her eyes. Quickly it was moving with wild abandon. "I could never live with a guy who did that kind of shit to other people," she observed doubtfully. "And I'd always be wondering what cute guy he had between the sheets when I wasn't around."

I grinned. She was on the right track. "Marriages legalize babies more than anything else, Megan. You could divorce him right after it's born and make out like a bandit." I wrote out Mike's address on base in Warner Robins for her.

"I'd still be a good girl too." She grinned, accepting the idea. "What do we have to do?"

"He likes to use threats on other people. He threatened Gene. He said he would tell the Dean of Men about his being queer to keep him coming back for more."

She glanced at her ex-boyfriend and both of us understood the look of pity in her eyes. "Say no more, Vic. I've got the picture and I'm better at those kinds of games than he'll ever be —girls always are." She glanced at Gene again and smiled. "Take care of this boy, Vic—he's sort of sweet at times." I nodded while Gene turned crimson.

"What now?" Gene asked without looking at me as we took the walk out to Montpelier Street. He was looking over his shoulder at the large antebellum house with its many bedrooms and communal spirit. I noticed his eyes were misty.

"You find a new bed ... or a couch ... for the rest of the quarter." I grinned. "Just stay away from Mike ... and let her take care of the rest. She's got him by the balls and she knows it."

"What about you?"

I studied Gene Butler for a moment before I spoke. He was a handsome. My old desire for him had been right there all along, just below the surface of my thoughts. Then, he had been just a fantasy; now, he could be reality. He liked dick as much as I did, and we both knew it. I suspected the next two quarters at Mercer, my last two, could be pleasant ones with him as my roommate. "I think I can give up sex until he's moved. But I am going to need a new roommate come January."

He smiled slightly and faced me. "Are you asking me to move in?"

I returned his smile. "Yeah."

Gene looked back at the large house and was silent for a while. "I think I've outgrown this place." He smiled slowly. "I think living with you just might be fun."

"It might at that," I allowed.

I was not a happy boy as I stood before the door to the apartment I had rented the past three years. The thing with Mike could turn nasty at any moment now that Megan had him in her sights. I was not one for staying around when the shit started to fly. Still, though, the apartment was my home.

Mike was naked and pacing the living room floor when I let myself into the apartment later that afternoon. He stopped in the center of the room and frowned at me. "Where the fuck have you been?" he demanded.

I faced him. "It's none of your business, but you might remember that I have to go to the damned library to be able to study since you moved in."

"Have you seen Gene?" I noticed he was avoiding my dig at him.

"I thought he was avoiding me ever since he accepted he wanted your dick up his ass."

He looked at me suspiciously. Mike Lynn was nothing if he wasn't smart. I hadn't been this defiant in the two months he'd been living with me. "What're you fixing for dinner?" he finally asked.

"I thought I might go down the street ... they've got good hamburgers there."

"You aren't going to cook?"

"No."

"Want some company?"

"Not yours."

So, now it was out. Or most of it was. The part about him and me was. Now, I had to worry about how uncomfortable things were going to be for the rest of the quarter.

"Okay, Vic, hit me with it: are we breakin' up?"

I stared at him in surprise. "What did we ever have to break up?"

"I thought you loved me."

"You destroyed any chance of that when you brought Gene into the picture and made him into what he's become." I took a deep breath. "I would like you to find another place to live next quarter though ... I'm tired of studying in the library."

"You're just going to kick me out?"

"Either you leave or I leave, Mike. And I need to know

which one by the first so I can get another place if that's what I'm doing."

He sagged against the bar and looked down at his hands. A moment later he looked back up and smiled. "It's been fun."

"A real learning experience," I admitted.

"You loved it."

"I know I like dick now, if that's what you mean."

"Want some now?"

"Thanks, Mike ... but I'm giving up that particular brand of meat for the duration."

"You taking up with somebody I know?"

"There's plenty of dick around campus ... and I've been told that I've got a nice body."

"When do you want me out?"

"As soon as you can go ... tomorrow?"

He chuckled. "That's too fast. Give me the couple of weeks until Thanksgiving, okay?" I shrugged. "It really has been fun, Vic."

"I'm glad you liked it."

Mike was married during the Thanksgiving holiday and Gene moved in the day of the wedding. He looked around the place while I fixed us both drinks. "I can't believe he's really gone," he mumbled as he took his. "It doesn't look any different in here."

"It will."

"Vic, I...." He studied his drink for long moments. "I've got to get my grades back up ... so, we're going to have to keep our sex down to nighttime stuff."

"We don't have to do anything, Gene."

"Shit! I need to get laid. Do you have any idea how hard it's been to do without these past few weeks?"

"And you want me doing the honors?"

"I'm here, aren't I?" He grinned. "Besides, I remember you having some really nice equipment."

"I'd like to share, Gene."

"You mean you want me dicking you too?"

"Wouldn't Megan give you a recommendation?" He laughed. "Maybe she would at that."

IN HEAT

Thomas C. Humphrey

Without glancing back, I know Otis will be tagging just a little way behind me. We have played this game too many times for me not to know. He has been at it every chance he got since I was nine and he was thirteen. But, as I round the corn crib and head for the branch which separates the farmyard from the cornfield, I turn to look anyway. Sure enough, he saunters around the edge of the barn, as if he is just out for a casual stroll and not hungrily trailing me.

A combination of stifling July heat and the mind-numbing repetition of the country music Daddy and Uncle Ben and my two brothers produce has finally driven me off the front porch and toward the back yard. I hate summer Sunday afternoons. After a sumptuous dinner that Mama, who has stayed home from church, sets before us, usually I am stuck with washing dishes while Mama sits and fans and the rest of the family makes music on the front porch. I have lucked out on dishes this time, because Aunt Lottie volunteers to help Mama, giving them a little gossip time together, but out of politeness, I have had to endure at least some of the music before I could escape.

Otis got there just as my brothers were getting guitars out and Uncle Ben was tuning his fiddle. Otis lives the next farm over. He spends so much time at our house that traveling salesmen sometimes mistake him for another member of my family. Short and compact with mousy brown hair, liquid chocolate eyes, a short, slightly flared nose, and an open, uncomplicated face, he is seventeen, the same age as my brother Jess. He arrived wearing his baseball uniform, carrying his long socks and spiked shoes, his feet covered with dust from the country road. As soon as a few other players get here, they will load into Daddy's pickup and take off somewhere for the afternoon's game.

One of Daddy's overriding passions in life is baseball, and he coaches a teenage American Legion team that plays other amateur teams, adults as well as teenagers, in all the surrounding small towns. Both my older brothers play on his team; Otis is the starting catcher. I am a big disappointment because I refuse to play.

Another family passion is country music. My brothers are pretty good, and have even organized a band that performs on Friday or Saturday nights at nearby high school auditoriums and dance halls. Again, I am a big disappointment because I never even learned to chord a guitar despite my brothers' efforts. Otis has no musical talent, either, and he sat as bored as I was until I hopped off the porch and started for the back, the sun baking my bare shoulders, as Uncle Ben sawed and screeched away on his fiddle and everybody broke out stomping their feet and singing, "Bile Them Cabbage Down."

At the branch, I stand for a moment under the canopy of huge, ancient oaks, sweat streaming from my forehead, and look out at the ragged granite shelf over which in winter or after a heavy summer storm water cascades some four feet down to a shallow pool where minnows dart and shine silver below the sun-dappled surface. In the midst of a midsummer drought, that cascade has shrunk to a puny stream trickling down through a narrow trough that years of erosion has gouged in the rocky surface.

I vault down to the lower level and relish the sensual coolness of the ankle-deep water on my bare feet as I slosh over to the narrow sandbar against the overgrown embankment toward our house. I sit on a hip-high boulder, smoothed and rounded by the ages until it looks like some giant prehistoric egg. I turn in time to see Otis jump from the ledge and head toward me, beads of sweat glistening on the soft fuzz of his upper lip.

Without saying a word, he gropes at my crotch. I don't want this today; it's too hot, I almost say out loud. But, of course, I do want it, with some skewed emotion centered somewhere between anger and lust. Enacting a long-practiced ritual, I stand up and reach for him. I knead and squeeze the tight woolen fabric as his already-stiff dick struggles against the imprisonment of his jockstrap. His growing excitement stimulates me, though it does not fill me with stomach-trembling desire. Beneath his touch, my own dick languidly hardens and snakes down the leg of my baggy, hand-me-down khakis.

He fumbles with my belt and opens my fly. My now-fully erect cock jumps up as if it is spring-loaded. He tugs my pants down to clear my balls. He hefts my wrinkled, hairless ballsac and then lightly folds his hand around the shaft of my cock, just holding it for a few seconds. I can almost feel him losing interest in it, intent only on the urgency of his own need.

"Take mine out," he instructs, his voice husky and strained.

I open his uniform pants and wiggle them down, taking a moment to cup his taut jockstrap in my hand. I grab the waistband and slide it down. Freed from confinement, his cock stands tight against his belly, its thick veins dilated almost to bursting, the foreskin already in retreat, its inner folds red as a wound. As I wrap my hand around it, I am again aware how huge and overpowering it had seemed when I was nine, yet how small and ordinary it actually is compared to my own fully developed one and especially my friend Howard's, which I have recently discovered.

"Suck me," he says.

He pushes down on my head and I sink to my knees before him. He forces his rod away from his belly with his thumb and shoves his cockhead toward my lips. I inhale the rancid-sweet aroma of stale sweat trapped in the woolen uniform, which has not been washed since the last game, maybe not all summer. As he presses tighter against my face, the musky smell of piss and come on his jock mingles with the other aroma, a not completely disagreeable combination I am accustomed to. I open my mouth and take in most of his shaft, then back off slightly and put my tongue to work. He locks his fingers behind my head and moves back and forth in my mouth, clenching his ass with each forward thrust, gyrating and groaning with animal pleasure.

As I almost disinterestedly service him, my mind drifts, and I wonder how many times I have done this. I think back to his early seduction, to the first time, in the three-foot high space under our kitchen in broad daylight while Mama sat on the front porch visiting with a neighbor. He had rubbed and squeezed through my pants until my little peter was stiff, and then took it out and slid the foreskin back and forth with spit-dampened thumb and forefinger. He freed his dick and encouraged me to take it in my hand. It was the first man-sized erection I had seen, and I stared in awe and hefted it in my palm until he instructed me to squeeze it tight and slide my hand up and down on it. He kept manipulating mine until it tickled so much I shrank away and stopped his movement with my hand. A few minutes later, as he bucked his ass off the ground, moaning and trembling like I was hurting him, his dick erupted and spilled thick white fluid all over my hand and arm....

"Just a minute," Otis breaks my reverie. He pops his dick out of my mouth. He kicks off his uniform pants, hurriedly sheds his shirt, and stands naked except for his baseball cap, which he shoves back at a rakish angle, freeing his sweaty bangs to tumble down his forehead. He backs up a couple of steps and rests his ass cheeks on the arc of the boulder, legs spread wide, thighs clenched, heels digging into the sand. He leans back and supports his weight on outspread arms behind him, elbows locked.

"Now get back on it," he rasps out.

I raise up and duck-walk toward him, pants tangled around my shins. I stop to kick them off and kneel between his legs, completely naked. My lips close around his throbbing cock. As I suck him, I look up into his face. His eyes are closed, and he has a beatific smile, broken occasionally when he wrinkles his brow, purses his lips, and inhales sharply as my tongue sends an extra jolt of pleasure to already ultra-sensitive nerve endings.

It did not take much coercion to lead me from that narrow space beneath our kitchen to this long-habituated routine. Even before that first sex-driven time, Otis had given me more attention than anyone else. To my brothers I was just a pesky kid to be ignored whenever possible. Although I had friends at school and at church, I led a lonely existence on the farm, a bookish, introverted child who never quite seemed to fit in with my family.

Otis did not really fit in, either. He had been held back twice at school, and, except for sports and hunting, had little in common with kids his age. Since he was at our house all the time, it was only natural that we spend a lot of time together. Otis always was willing to help repair my bike or to tramp in the woods looking for birds' nests or hike the three miles to fish or skinny-dip in the creek. Nobody ever questioned our association, even after he matured physically and the sex began....

"Suck on my balls and let it rest some. I don't want to come too quick," he brings me back to the present.

I take my mouth off his rigid dick, which plops against his belly. I bury my face between his thighs, and tongue his nutsac. His groin is sticky and steaming with sweat, and the heat from his thighs flushes my cheeks. I am hot and uncomfortable, but I burrow deeper until my lips close around one of his balls and I slip it into my mouth. His loose scrotum is covered with long, wiry hairs that wriggle and scratch unpleasantly against my mouth and tongue.

Not like Howard's. His tight, wrinkled pouch is completely hairless. It reminds me of a paper bag that has been crumpled up and then smoothed out before two large plums are dropped in. When I am buried in his groin, I like to trace the grooves all over before I slip a plum in my mouth and try to swallow it whole without chewing. Just thinking about Howard and our time behind the preacher's house this morning during church service makes my dick buck and throb, and I reach down to stroke it.

Howard is not a farm kid. His father owns a general store in the village, and the family lives in a large brick house next door. Howard and I were never really friends until this past spring. For reasons that I still don't understand, I began noticing him more and more at school and creating fantasies at night about him instead of Otis. After weeks of teasing and hinting around, too scared to actually try anything, I finally got him alone one afternoon and, my heart in my throat, found enough courage to reach for his dick. Without protest, he let me unzip his pants and wrestle into the open a longer, thicker, more beautiful cock than I had ever created in all my fantasies. But the highest excitement of my life came when he freed my dick, dropped to his knees, and took it in his mouth....

"Stand up," Otis says, catching me off guard.

He pushes forward and almost topples me over into the sand. As I rise to my feet, he circles behind me. I hear him spit in his hand.

"Lie down on the rock. I'm going to fuck you," he says, crowding tight against my back.

I drape myself over the boulder, one forearm pillowing my head. Otis steps between my thighs and shoves them wider apart with his legs. He digs fingers of both hands into my cheeks and spreads them with his thumbs. His hot, moist dick probes around and then slides all the way into me with one quick jab. As accustomed as I am to it, I flinch away from the pain of his rough intrusion. Otis drags me back into position with a strong grip on my hips. He sets up a steady pounding rhythm, his balls slapping against me with every thrust. Gradually he eases down until his torso covers my back.

He works himself into a frenzy, grunting and moaning and driving into me harder and harder. We both are sweating like crazy, and his chest squishes against my back noisily with each thrust. He flings off his baseball cap, and sweat drips off his forehead and the tip of his nose onto my neck and shoulders. His breathing becomes strained and ragged.

I tune out his animal sounds and concentrate instead on Howard in the thick shrubs behind the preacher's house. Unlike Otis, who is completely lust-driven, Howard likes for us to take our time, hugging and kissing and teasing before we get into serious sex. With pants around our ankles, we lay entwined for a long time before he moved down to take me in his mouth. I soon switched around so we could sixty-nine. As usual, I studied Howard's beautiful dick for a long time before I started sucking him. I am fascinated by the perfect little pink circle created when his foreskin, too tight to slide over the broad crown of his cock, is forced as far back as it will go without unbearable discomfort.

Before I got too close to exploding in his mouth, I positioned Howard on his knees and fucked him slow and easy for maybe twenty minutes before I let go deep inside him. Then I stretched him on his back and brought him off, making it as good as I knew how, secretly glad that his foreskin problem keeps him from fucking me with that huge cock, which is almost as scary as it is beautiful.

As soon as he climaxed, Howard started in on how we were sinning and how we were going to hell for our behavior. I find it curious that the guilt sets in after he loses his load, never when he is hard as a rock and begging me to satisfy him. Maybe Howard's more religious than I am, but instead of worrying about going to hell, I was concerned about catching hell for grass stains on my dress pants....

Otis' trembling thighs and short, rapid jabs let me know he's on the verge of orgasm, and I wonder if he'll suck my dick, or at least get me off by hand afterward, as he has done less and less often lately. My thoughts of Howard have left me in urgent need of relief.

My brother Jess' shrill whistle followed by his bellowing baritone, "Otis! Time to go!" kills whatever desire was building in my groin.

"Damn!" Otis says, halting his thrusts and raising up off my back. He pulls part-way out of me. "Screw it! I'm going to finish this first," he says. He shoves back into me roughly.

Standing up now, he grabs both my hips and pounds away, but the climax he had carefully built toward has faded with the interruption. The harder he works at it, the more elusive it becomes. Grunting like a pig and spraying my back with sweat from his soaking hair, he finally reaches his peak, hunches and groans and drives as deep as possible. He collapses onto my back as his dick pulses and spurts in me.

"Otis! We're loading up. Come on! Now!" Jess calls out.

Otis backs away from me. "Yeah ... Coming!" he yells.

Without even wiping his slippery dick on a leaf or something, he steps into his jockstrap, hurries into his uniform pants, crams his cap on his head, and scrambles up the ledge, buttoning up his shirt as he goes. He lopes out of sight, tucking his shirt into his pants.

I sit on the boulder toying with my nearly flaccid dick, which stiffens immediately. As I idly stroke it, I know that I am just about through with Otis' selfish, impersonal sex. Howard has so much more to offer, physically and emotionally.

At the thought of Howard, I quit stroking my cock. Instead, I begin to hatch a plan. Howard has mentioned that his parents will attend the evening worship service and that he will be at home reading a new book. If I just happen to show up at his house shortly after his parents leave, I can coax him into making love again, except this time in the luxury of Howard's bed, something I have only dreamed of. Because my mother and Otis' oldest sister are always home, in my entire life, I have never had sex in a bed.

I will my erection away with thoughts of higher pleasures in store. As I get dressed and trudge back to the house with a long afternoon to kill and chores to complete before I can see Howard, I don't care if what I'm planning for the evening does send me to hell. It'll be worth it.

HOT SUMMER NIGHT RENDEZVOUS

Antler

The two boys embracing in the thunderstorm
Don't care if they get drenched,
Don't care if as they strip each other
  their clothes drop in lightning light
    into puddles,
  and are kicked laughingly into the mud.
It's the first time they've kissed each other,
The first time either of them ever kissed
  a boy
And neither has ever kissed
  a girl
And neither ever kissed before
  with his tongue.
They had no idea how passionate
  passion could be—
    they can hardly believe it,
That merely putting their lips together
  could be so...
    ah.
For a moment they stand apart
  silently gazing at each other
    in the flashes and thunder,
Centuries of Boyhood, Aeons of BoyLove
  proud in their playful smiles,
Knowing just what they're going to do,
  even though they never did it before,
Knowing that before long
  each of them is going to jack off
    the first boy he ever jacked off
  besides himself,
Knowing both of them can come
  and giving in, giving themselves
to boyfriendship's topsecret gesture,
Knowing they both know
  how to jack off real good
    and aren't going to stop frenching

while they whimper toward the brink.
Sure, it's beautiful to see a boy you love
  ejaculate in the lightning in the rain,
Crying with pleasure while the thunder thunders
  and the sky ejaculates millions of raindrops
As you squirm in rapture
  on the muddy grass
  under the tossing trees.

HEAT

K. I. Bard

When you're twelve
a week is a very
very long time.

Saying it now
sounds too foolish
for belief,
but I blamed Eve.
Almost twelve,
I was disturbed
by sex,
by the messy,
unruly,
vulgarity
I was supposed to disdain
but found so compelling.
Having found
no other way
I blamed Eve,
and with her
an entire gender
of evil temptresses.
It was girls
who'd damned us
out of paradise,
and I decided
I didn't even like
apples.
And yet,
we were taught
(if being lectured is
teaching)
to forgive the sinner,
and with that crutch
I managed
haughty tolerance

of anything in dress or
skirt.

It is most perplexing, then,
that I must confess
my own adoption
of temptation.
To tempt,
one needs someone
temptable,
and who better than
girls?
Already known to be weak,
they were easy game.
If there was anything
definite
in my plan
it escapes me now.
All that's left
is a memory of desire
to lure,
and by allure
to gain power.

Exact details
don't favor poetry
where the outline
studded with images
should convey
the feel
or perhaps texture,
of events within the heart.
So you will have to leap
in faith
to accept, as did I,
a fortunate circumstance

finding myself
the lone male in a trio,
or as I saw it,
a rose between two thorns,
one a year my junior,
the other a year ahead.
I was parked
in their world
for a week
while my parents
conducted business
out-of-town,
no room for a
tag-along boy.

Feeling rejected
was, perhaps, enough
to welcome revenge
using temptation.
But looking into
your own heart
you will know
there are murky deeps
that spur events
as children kick spurs
into an imaginary horse,
slashing at it,
riding hard
toward escape or
to inflict hurt upon an
imaginary steed.

Sharp currents flow
through children,
as through adults,
and like a well-schooled
hunter
I saw my chance
in a particular look
(you know it:
flush-faced and eager)

on their faces.

They found me interesting.
I was their boy to play with
for an entire week.
Seeing how their eyes
seldom left me
gave power to the hunt.

Every chase
is kin to others
and is built
of elemental bricks
known to every child.
In the hunt
everything matters,
place, time, temperature.
All are used,
employed to a particular
end.

In what can only be
described
as the prey's cooperation
with the predator,
it was soon decided
the dreadful-dull
board games they provided
would be played
in my "guest" room,
an attic location
far at the front
of the house.

Having them on "my"
ground,
even if it was but
borrowed,
set the developmental
stage.
Attic rooms are steamy

warm.
On summer afternoons
they swelter.
Precisely what I wanted.
Heat.
Claiming discomfort,
I removed my shirt,
from the corner of my eye
watching them watch me.
In simple stages I drew
yet more attention
to a body I had yet to
understand,
but which provided
so convenient a platform
for exploration.
In such a hunt
the sides are equal,
successful suggestion
requiring willing
agreement.
A hint from me
about what I was thinking
had to be balanced
with their response.
Scales of childhood
equilibrium.

With heat as my ally
I complained of having
no shorts
other than the swim trunks
I'd packed on a whim,
just in case
my week included
a nearby pool or beach
outing.
Hint, hint, hint
with word and body
I laid the possibility
before them.

Snapping at the bait
as huge goldfish gobble
chunks of bread cast on
water,
the girls, playing hostess,
invited me to change,
if I'd be more comfortable.
"Should I change here,
or in the bathroom?" I
wondered aloud,
the question very much
out of character
but essential to the hunt.
"We won't watch."
I was assured,
in meanings I couldn't
miss.

The fundamentals of
deception
are well learned early.
I had to be cunning enough
to appear innocent
to voice aloud
a question
really an invitation.
The girls,
by vowing indifference,
assured me
of their interest.
In mutual assent
who stalks whom?
In conducting
child-foolish games
is one fool bigger
than another?

For more such questions
than I can count
I've no answer
other than to recount

events transpired.
Having spied opportunity
I stepped on stage
casually disrobing
in deliberate calm,
the only thing missing
the well known chant;
Take It Off!
Unpracticed at striptease,
I took my time
carefully matching,
with nerve-shaking hands,
left sock with left shoe
and right with right.
Barefoot, I absorbed direct
the feel of a strange room
where I found myself
about to remove my
trousers
before an audience
who feigned indifference
while memorizing
my every move.
Caution inspired my final
move.
My back to view
I skinned down my
undershorts,
a culmination that made
my heart hammer-whack so
wildly
I wobbled on my feet
while behind me
the sound of bodies
moving,
straining, stretching to see.

Those sounds conveyed all
I needed to know.
Reassured, I took my time
pulling on my trunks.

By the time I turned
to rejoin the girls
I already knew
to provide a repeat.
Their darting eyes and
flushed faces
already told
of garden hose wars
in the back yard,
a strong spray of water,
surrogate fingers,
played along the body.
Feeling their eyes on me
foretold of afternoons
playing dress-up
in outlandish costumes,
the girls running me
through
a score of changes
before their urgency dulled
and we'd move to yet
another game
with an object
much the same as the last.

Between my cooperation
and their compliance
lay days of curious,
cautious exploration,
each risk
parent to a pause.
A day or two
are spent in care
before the time feels right
for me to turn in profile,
doing so as if I simply
forgot
I was bare.
Once having done so
there was nothing more to
hide.

I turned, then, to face
them,
looking intently at their
faces
wondering what they saw
wondering why I let them
see.
After that
our game went swiftly
because I was no longer me
but had become
another of their dolls
to be dressed and changed,
moved and positioned,
pampered and lectured,
spanked for my wrongs
comforted for my pains.
With listless arms and legs
I played doll boy
keeping my face
expressionless calm,
almost bored,
except for anticipation.

When you're twelve
a week can be
a very, very long time.

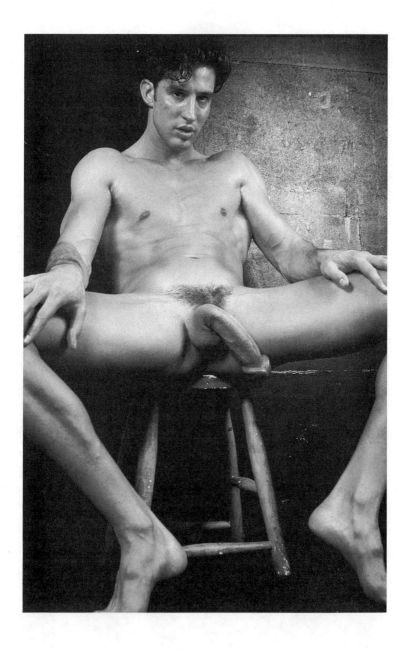

The too-weird adventures of the Lotus Boy...

The Boy
with the
Golden
Cock

An Erotic Novella by
Kevin Bantan

STARbooks Press
Sarasota, Florida

*"...He liked boys, preferably with long lashes
and a certain melting look around the eyes.
He particularly enjoyed them if they
had no experience of men before...."*
—John Pearson, 'Profession of Violence' (1972)

PROLOGUE

I saw Alex turn his head toward the restaurant entrance. My eyes followed his gaze. A very pretty boy had entered, sexily attired in a snug, sleeveless white T-shirt, skin-tight black jeans, and leather boots with heels only gay boys can walk in. He was slim, which seemed to add to his grace in the trendy, feminine boots. He joined another young man clad in a rugby shirt, baggy jeans and brown leather hiking boots. They kissed, as if they were boyfriends, and the boy sat. I noticed that he was wearing dangling earrings and light, tastefully done makeup. He could get away with that considering that the restaurant was gay.

"Typical Alex. He goes for the fem ones all the time," Nicky said.

"Well, what does that say about you, dear?"

"That it doesn't hurt to be the mirror image of a Narcissus."

"Good answer," Seaton said. "Besides, if they were all as pretty as he is, I'd take a fem boy in a minute."

"Oh, you would, huh?" I said.

"Well...."

"Uh, huh." He shrugged.

"Well, there's a lot to be said for pretty fem boys," Alex said.

"Just don't bore us with the details right now, Alex," Nicky said.

That made us laugh. In truth, Nicky was a little on the nelly side, himself, which was strange, because he and Alex were identical twins. Alex, on the other hand, was just your average straight-acting gay boy. They had been sent to military school to masculine Nicky up, but of course it didn't work. However, it did draw the brothers even closer to each other. Alex defended Nicky against any slight, real or perceived, at the academy. It was one thing that attracted Seaton to the twins. Another was that he guessed correctly that they were gay. They became best friends at school.

And as roving an eye as Alex had, that was all that roamed. He was completely dedicated to his brother. They were our best friends now, too. And lifesavers, along with Seaton. And although how I needed to be rescued is a tale too weird to be believed, it's true.

One

Seaton and I had a fairly typical childhood, if you didn't count the death of our beloved brother, Chris. We adored Christopher Cho, who was two years younger than Seaton and two years older than I was. We all got along great, but we each loved Chris more than we did each other. He was a special guy. He was a better athlete and better-looking than we were. (Although you'll get arguments on that latter point from others, but none whatever from us. Chris was a god. Period.) But he was just the neatest, nicest guy we knew. So his death devastated us—and it was so needless.

He was out drinking with some buddies at the local high school football field. It was locked, so they had to climb the ornamental wrought-iron fence that surrounded the stadium. The fence was topped by sharp points, like spear heads. Anyway, when they were climbing back over, he was high. He slipped and impaled himself on the points. He died there on the fence top before help came. His pals told us that the only thing he said was "Cee-tie," before he passed out. Or died. Cee was for Seaton, and Tie was for Ty, or Tyler. He was telling us he loved us with his last breath. That only deepened our grief.

You might be wondering how two boys with a surname like Cho came to have such uppity English names. Well, that was the point. Our mother was of English ancestry. Her maiden name was Seaton, and her mother's name Tyler. My father, although proud of his Chinese heritage, wanted his sons to have American-sounding names. His was An, which I think is a beautiful name, but he was having none of it. How Christopher got between us, when he should have been given my name, I can't tell you. Neither could our parents. But we both think it's the most beautiful boy's name, naturally. Sea thinks his name is dumb, but I don't agree. "It's so teddibly British, as if I looked it." Well, what we look like are Americans.

It bothers my father's family, of course, just as his marrying our mom did, mightily. But Sea and I have the gorgeous almond-shaped oriental eyes, softened by our mother's caucasian genes. Which I think is so cool. I also think that Sea is a fox, however prejudicial that testimony is. But I want to get back to Christopher.

As boys were wont to do, Chris began dating in grade school. He was the cutest boy in his class, after all. But he came to me soon after he started going out.

"Ty, I have a problem."

"You do? What is it?"

"Well, I'm dating Gina, you know, and, well, I don't think I'm a very good kisser."

"Really?" There wasn't anything that Chris couldn't do.

"Yeah. See, the thing is, it just doesn't feel right. Ty, I was wondering if I could practice kissing with you."

"With me? Chris, you know I don't kiss. Not even mom and dad. What do people see in it? Yucky."

"It's really cool. And you're going to want to do it pretty soon, too, whether you know it or not."

"Not."

"Ty, please."

"You know I would do anything for you, Chris, but kissing you? I don't know."

"I'll give you my Swiss Army knife."

"Okay, deal."

It was more of a deal than I could have imagined. I remember sitting on his bed and feeling his full, rosy, moist lips on mine. And not feeling yucky at all. But also feeling strange. Very strange. To the point where my penis was sticking straight up, which was a horrible development, let me tell you. I had no idea what was happening. On the other hand, his lips felt so good. Finally, I stopped him.

"Chris, you made my dick stiff."

"Huh, you made mine that way, too." He felt me down there. "Feel mine." I did. It was. And it felt good to feel that hardness. It was Chris's. "I think that's what kissing's supposed to do."

"Really? With my brother?"

"What does it matter? Nobody will ever know."

"That's true. Kiss me some more, Chris."

He did, and I began to ache down there, it felt so good. The next time we stopped, we were both panting.

"Chris, this is awesome."

"Yeah it is."

"Keep kissing me. And do whatever else you want with me."

"I'm not sure what else to do, Ty, but I sure want to."

He suggested that we undress. Once naked, I lay on his bed. He lay beside me and began to kiss me again. His free hand roved over my body, making me squirm from his touch. I wrapped my arms around my beautiful brother's neck and held us together. My little cock was actually bobbing, it was so excited. Then he got on top of me. Although he was bigger, his weight felt good. Well, all right, I hardly felt it. But I did feel his dick rubbing against mine down there, and I was like a crazy boy writhing under him. Before long, we were both freezing and experiencing orgasm. Neither of us came. That would have been too much for my brain to take.

"Well, good luck, Gina," I said, spent and mystified by what had just happened.

"Really. And good luck to us."

"Us?"

"Well, I'll still need to practice."

"You will? Great."

And it was. We began to learn all sorts of things together. Kissing more than lips. Nipples. Other places it felt good to touch or kiss. I suspected that Chris was spending more quality time with me than Gina, but I didn't say anything. I already kind of knew what the word faggot meant, so there was no way that I was going to hint that he was one of them. Nor me, for that matter.

At some point, unbeknownst to me, Chris decided to seduce Sea, and damned if our elder brother didn't fall for him. In fact, they got to the point of actually having real penetrating sex together. They would try out things Sea heard in the locker room at school that guys talked about doing with girls. Chris came to like being fucked, and Sea says that's why he's as good as he is today; hours and hours of practice on our brother's beautiful bottom. I doubt it, but he means it as a tribute to our brother, so that's fine.

Chris and I never went further than sucking each other off, and I was happy as a clam doing that with him. Which we did right up until he died.

Please don't misunderstand, though. My memory of my brother isn't clouded by the sex we had. I never fell in love with him the way I did with Sea. Chris really and truly was a great guy. Even if he was cheating on both Sea and me with each other. After all, we were family, and he was gorgeous.

And it was Chris's death that was the foundation for Sea's and my relationship. We began to sleep together after it happened. Although neither of us voiced it, I think it was because we were afraid of losing each other next. As sad as we were, those nights were great. Sea would hold me tightly to him and rest his head on mine. I fell asleep faster than I ever had in the reassuring arms of my brother.

We continued to share a bed after Chris was buried. Our parents didn't think anything of it, probably because they knew how much we were suffering and our need to circle our emotional wagons. Despite my consuming sorrow, I loved Sea's touch at night. He smelled good to me. I tried to remember if I ever smelled Chris, but I couldn't.

One night a few weeks after the funeral, we were snuggled together as always. I could feel Sea's erection pressing against me, as it usually did now before we fell asleep. I was used to his having them by then, so I didn't think anything of it. At least not in the context I had with Chris, because Sea and I didn't have sex. Still, my brother holding me often gave me a hard-on from the close physical contact.

"Ty?"

"What?"

"Do you love me?"

"Of course I do. You're my brother."

"I love you, too. A lot."

"Same here." After a few minutes, he said, "Ty?"

"What, Sea?"

"I used to make it with Chris."

"Make what?"

"It. Sex. I fucked him." My body froze and my eyes flew open.

"You...you did?"

"Yeah."

"Man. We fooled around, too."

"Really?"

"Yeah. We used to blow each other."

"Man. We were both having sex with him?"

"Evidently."

A wall of silence rose between us as we digested the stunning revelation that Chris had fooled with both of us.

"Ty?"

"What?"

"Um, would you maybe want to have sex with me?"

"Yes, Sea." I surprised myself by answering so quickly. I didn't yet realize just how much I loved my surviving brother.

In response Sea kissed me on the cheek. Then he reached around and took hold of my dick, which had shriveled at the news of Chris's unfaithfulness. He stroked it back to life, kissing me several more times. God, that felt so good.

"Lift your leg a little."

"Why?"

"You'll see."

Oh, did I. He slid his erection down my crack and nudged the tip of it against me. I inhaled involuntarily as his cock head pushed into me. It was more shocking than painful, although it did hurt. Sea assured me that it would go away. It didn't, but I was more focused on the fact that my brother's cock was easing into me. Then moving in me, fucking me. I was actually being fucked. Even Chris hadn't done that to me. But Sea was. Through the pain I realized that there was something about this act which was different from anything that I had done with Chris. Sea and I were joined as closely as two guys could be. He was using my body to get off. Something about that thought thrilled me. As did realizing that his come was inside me after he yelped into my neck. Once he stopped moving, I felt myself swell in his hand and spasm.

"Oh, god, Ty. That was great."

"It was. But it did hurt."

"It won't, the more we do it."

"Did Chris hurt?"

"A little, at first. But it's us now, baby brother."

"Us."

"As long as you want it."

"Always, Sea. If it won't hurt. Well, maybe if it just hurts a little."

"I love you, Ty." He turned me on my back and kissed me tenderly.

"I love you, Sea."

When we were lying like spoons again, I said, "Sea, are we faggots?"

"Naw. We're just brothers who dig each other." Maybe he was right. Maybe all brothers fucked together before they were finally attracted to girls. But, despite his assurance, something inside me wasn't so sure.

Two

Notwithstanding our blossoming relationship, Seaton was slowly going into a nose dive. I understood. No matter how close we were growing, we weren't able to get rid of the ghost of Chris. We had his photo on the dresser of the room which, for all practical purposes, we shared. I would go into the room after school, look at his picture and cry. I would think of him slumped and helpless on that fence, his blood running down the iron uprights. Occasionally, I would go there and kiss the bars to try to... I don't know what. Hope that he saw how torn up I still was that he was dead? But at least I was dealing with his death.

"You never cry about Chris."

"So what? That doesn't mean I don't miss him."

"But you never cry, Sea."

"Get off my case, Ty, for crying out loud."

"You shouldn't keep it bottled up."

"Shut up, faggot!"

After the verbal slap began to burn in my brain a second or two later, I ran. Seaton had never, ever said a word in anger to me that I could remember. So the hurled epithet hurt that much worse. My mind was a confusion of thoughts it couldn't handle. Everything came at once as I crouched behind a forsythia at the rear of the yard. I chose that space between the bush and the stockade fence, because I didn't want anyone to see me crying, something I seemed unable to control in the least now.

"Ty."

"Go away."

"Ty, I'm really sorry."

"Go away, Seaton. Leave me alone."

"Ty."

"Leave me the fuck alone!"

Although we did make up, things only continued to change for the worse. Our father didn't believe in shrinks, which was exactly what we needed. I mean, Chris had been our lover, in addition to being the guy we adored. But no shrinks for the Cho boys. We'd get over it. Yeah, just like my dad had. He had developed a heart condition after Chris died. He, too, refused to shed a tear over the star of the family, keeping everything bottled up inside. He got hypertension next. Mom, like me, wept from time to time. Sometimes I would go to her to be held, and we both would cry our eyes out over our loss.

But not Sea. And not Dad.

When things started to go really south for Sea, Dad decided to send him away to a military academy. The East was full of them, and Valley Forge was supposed to be one of the best. It was in Pennsylvania, so we would be separated, and by a couple hundred miles, for the first time in our lives.

I was in shock, as if I needed another one. So was Sea, but he refused to show how upset he was. I told him that he was a nut case, and he slapped me. That was the first time he had ever hit me. That time I didn't run. I just stood looking at him in disbelief as my cheek reddened and seared with pain. He returned my stare, not believing either what he had done. Then he slumped onto the bed and broke down, telling me how sorry he was through his tears. As angry and hurt as I was, I felt pity for him and held him.

And, true to form, I let him fuck me that night. He was taking me on my back now, and I was really getting into it. It felt good, and it was my brother's cock that was inside me. Whom I was coming to love in a relationship sense now, our lovemaking having become so serious. Which made his leaving so much harder for me.

Sea was sixteen when we left him in Wayne that day; I was twelve. I wrote to him several times a week, usually with tears in my eyes, I was so lovesick. He would write back every week or so to tell me that he missed me, and that the guys thought that his girlfriend was pining for him back in Rhode Island, because of all the mail he got. She was, although I didn't refer to myself that way.

Dad got worse and had a series of heart attacks, the last one fatal, before Sea ever came home for a visit. When he did then, he looked absolutely stunning in his gray uniform. And, despite Dad's death, every night Sea was home he fucked my brains out. About three times each. I worshiped his cock with my mouth, ecstatic to have it there again. And in my welcoming ass.

He was more muscular than he had been, and that turned me on all the more. Seeing him after those months apart made me realize how handsome he was, too. Different from Chris, but not that different. He told me how he got some grief from guys, because of his Asian looks. Nothing new there, I thought. He also told me about Alex and Nicky. How they were identical twins and how beautiful they were. And that they were becoming good friends.

"You don't have sex with them, do you?"

"No, little brother. I don't have any. Except with my hand while thinking about you."

"Good, because I really love you, Sea."

"I know. I feel the same way, Ty."

Sometimes, though, it didn't seem that way. He had changed in attitude, too, because of his military training. He was bossier and making love was more one-sided during that short stay. Truthfully, I was almost glad to see him go back; he was beginning to get on my nerves with his pushiness.

But only almost. Soon after he left I felt the void again. I hoped that I had enough of his come in me to last until he came home again, but I knew I would miss him mightily that very night. My horniness seemed even worse after he left. Were I straight, I probably would have gotten a girlfriend pregnant. I had begun to come a little now, which made me feel grown up, like my brother.

And if everything else weren't bad enough, Mom turned weird after Dad's death. I was suddenly the only male in the household. Half of them were dead, and one was missing all the time. Despite my suggestion that she bring Sea home, she didn't. Often she seemed to be in a trance.

For some reason, she turned to Eastern mysticism. Maybe to try to connect with her husband's spirit. I came to the conclusion that she was crazy, and I was right. I told Sea that. But it didn't save me. Her weirdness caused me to go on that strange journey. And it sure wasn't *The Rocky Horror Picture Show*. That would have been too easy.

Three

I had come to the conclusion that there were enough religious wackos in Boston and New York to fill Fenway Park. See, sometimes I would accompany my mother on her trips to see these guys. And it was always guys. Dressed in silk robes and socks, most of them. What my mom thought she was trying to do was to make sense of Chris's and my dad's deaths. In reality, she was losing it, becoming a first-class loon.

This was not what I needed. I desperately needed a shrink and stability, but the more she got into these oddball religions, the less inclined she was to believe in conventional things. Even Sea was seeing a psychiatrist at the academy, and he said that it was helping him a lot. But Tyler only got crystals waved at his face.

He also got his hand on his dick every night and thought about Seaton, who fucked me with his uniform on, cap and all. For his cock, I used the neck of a beer bottle I'd taken from the refrigerator. I didn't even drink the beer, the swig I took tasted so lousy. I poured it out and washed the bottle. In my bedroom I would take it out of the closet, where I had it hidden behind my hockey stick and baseball bat. I would get in bed and go down on it, pretending that it was my erect brother. Then when I had it slicked up with spit, I would lie down and insert it into myself until the wider part kissed my cheeks. Then I'd jerk off while urging my absent lover to cream my insides. Sometimes I went to sleep with it in me, the way Sea had on occasion. But the beer bottle wasn't Sea, and neither was my fantasy of him. I was getting pretty depressed. I seemed to be matching my mother, depth for depth, albeit with a different mental problem.

I always got excited when Sea would come home. He just got better and better looking. And he was practically an animal, he was so hungry for my body. I was afraid that we made so much noise that my mom would wonder what the hell we were doing in that bed. He thought the beer bottle was pretty funny, until he realized that it wasn't as long as he was. That wasn't my fault, I told him. I didn't send him away to military school.

I asked him only one more time if he were having sex with Alex and Nicky. He took too long to answer, and his denial was pretty weak. Well, even if it were true, he was making it with somebody, because he had never sucked on my nipples the way he did now. Nor licked my perineum. But I kept my mouth shut. Sometimes a guy needed more than a hand, as I was proving every time he came home.

But for all of the hot sex, we were growing apart. I knew he still loved me, and I still loved him. I knew I always would. Until the day he brought his roommate, Ted, home for a visit. Not only didn't we sleep together, I knew exactly what he and Ted were doing in his bed, because I listened at the door. Therefore, I was glad to see my brother leave.

One guy my mom came to really like: Master Lao. I have to admit that he was pretty slick for a shyster. He was a monk of some Buddhist sect. He would even come to the house, if he were on his way from Boston to New York. I didn't know that monks drove cars, but he did. A Lexus. Silver. I got the impression that he freelanced, because his little temple didn't seem to have other monks—only cute boys with shaved heads, wearing short robes. Although I had never been in a Buddhist temple before, there just seemed to be something phony about it.

I have to admit that sometimes I would replace Sea with one of the boys at the temple for my nightly fantasy. We always kissed and masturbated each other before I would submit to the hairless boy. Well, not down there. Curiously, each boy always had the same arrangement of pubic hair. It was a carefully-fashioned heart, although why I made their bushes into hearts, I hadn't the vaguest idea. And every time I did, I would wonder why Master Lao would have those pretty boys at his temple. Even more than I wondered why he drove a Lexus. And boy was I going to get to find out.

I don't know if my mother got the idea, or if Master Lao planted the idea in her head. I suspect the latter. Since seeing him, exclusively, she didn't seem all that much weirder than she'd been, but that wasn't saying much, because she was already plenty weird, as I said. Yet that day she was pretty lucid. Almost her old self, in fact.

"Ty, I've been aware of your unhappiness at Sea being away." Hardly. What day is it, Mom? Tell me that. For starters.

"Well, he's the only brother I have left." I bit my lower lip, but my eyes still rimmed with tears. I wondered if there were some kind of Buddhist exorcism that could be done to magically remove the loss I still felt over Christopher. Then I felt hope. "Is he coming home?"

"No, dear. And your grades have been slipping. Your report card said that you're lethargic."

"Well, so much has happened over the last couple of years. It's still tough dealing with losing Chris and my dad. And not having Sea here." I was desperate to have Sea home, hoping that getting him away from Ted and all of the other boys he seemed to be smitten with, although he wouldn't admit it outright in his damned teasing letters, would rekindle his love for me. Because even the cutest boys in middle school didn't do for me what my brother still did in my fantasies. Besides, it was so much easier not to date at all, than to go out with guys. "Are you going to send me to a shrink?"

"No, Ty. I've talked with Master Lao. He said that you have an especially large aura about you. Radiant and white. The pureness of an angel." Did Buddhists believe in angels? "He thinks that you might be a reincarnation of Buddha." Oh, please. Get us both to a shrink. Please.

"And how would he know that? Except that you give him tons of money."

"What I contribute to his good work is none of your business, young man." She didn't have Seatons and Tylers in her family for no reason. And she did give him a lot of money, I just knew it. "And you need more discipline in your life, without your father and Sea here. Master Lao has agreed to take you on as an apprentice acolyte and try to determine if you're divine." I was only divine, or at least felt like it, when Sea fucked me. Pure, I was not.

I put up a spirited protest, but that only made it worse. I was not going to win, but I was not going down without a fight. And I went down all right. I also realized that loon was too kind a word to use for my mother.

Four

It was simple. Foolproof, really. Ask any fifteen year-old the definition of that word, and you'll know that he's the first part of it. My plan was to wait until we got to Boston to bolt. I'd thought about feigning a need to pee along I-95, but realized I had no idea where I would run. Once we made it to the temple, however, I would bolt. Even though Lao appeared to be a fairly young guy, I was certain that I could outrun him and lose myself in the big city. So I was playing it to the hilt, as a docile, shaved wannabe.

I should have tried "the pee gambit." Wouldn't you know that when we arrived, he drove the car into an underground garage, whose door slapped shut like the bars of a prison cell?

He turned off the engine but didn't make a move to exit the car. I sat as still as he did.

"Master Tyler, I truly want you to be happy here at the temple. I will do everything in my power to see to it. All I ask of you is cooperation. You, Master Tyler, are exquisitely beautiful. Your aura is splendid. It is the purest. You have been blessed with both beauty and spirituality. And with the happiest of all flesh. You have a penis and scrotum, Master Tyler. You are the embodiment of maleness. Quite simply, I believe that you were created to greatness. Perhaps to be worshipped." His right hand caressed my hair. I heard every word he said. It was imprinted on my brain. No thought of running now. He had me.

He took me to his private quarters, where he continued the seduction. Slowly he undressed me, telling me again and again how beautiful I was. First the tie, tugging on it gently, unraveling it. Then the shirt buttons, one by one. He kissed my nipples as he undid my belt. And unhooked my pants. And unzipped my fly. He stopped kissing my chest to remove the shirt. He kissed me again. "So beautiful," he sighed into my ear and licked it. I shivered.

I began to kick off my loafers, but he stopped me. He knelt and unshod me. He sniffed the shoes, and my socks, and smiled. The fresh fragrance of boy, he said. Without rising, he pulled down my pants and helped me out of them. He stroked the outsides of my legs and the downy dark hairs responded to the attention. Now the insides of my thighs. Calves. He closed his eyes and leaned into my crotch, kissing it. Having finished this act of reverence, he grasped the waist of the white briefs and pulled them down. I stepped out of them as he stared, transfixed by my cock. "Gorgeous." He looked up at me. "Just gorgeous—from your silken hair to your well-formed feet."

Then he cradled my ass cheeks and took me into his mouth. The warmth engulfing me felt great. It had been a long time since anyone had gone down on me. Sea didn't like sucking. He liked getting blown and fucking. Well, fuck him. I had an oriental mystic on his fucking knees, his nose buried in my black pubic hair, my boyness in his hungry oral cavity. Up and down I watched him go, watched his hand tease my sac into a ping-pong ball before returning it to knead my cheek. I was hard in him now, and he moved on me with orgasmic determination. He caressed my sides and back. I closed my eyes and pictured Chris, but that seemed sacrilegious, so I let my mind go blank and enjoyed my mounting excitement. I wondered if he would always suck me off. If the other boys there would, too. My breathing quickened as I began to throb from his slick lips. My toes bent to grab the carpet. I let out a sigh and spurted in his mouth. He swallowed greedily, as if I were a boy god, and my semen had magical powers.

He had me lie on the bed while he undressed. He surprised me by having a good body. It was obvious that he worked out. His cock was kind of little, but that was fine, because I knew where it was going.

When he crawled onto the bed, he kissed me again. I played with his prick to get his motor revved. I had him hard in no time. He took me the way Sea did, on my back. He really was a good-looking guy, I decided as he pounded away in me, all the while telling me that my body was divine. If sex was the price of being a deity, I would be one.

When I awoke the next morning I was lying on my stomach. I realized that I had been awakened by a tickling in my rear end. His face was buried in my crack, his hands holding my cheeks apart. I spread my legs wide to accommodate him. His tongue was probing up into me now. The delicious sensation made me wiggle my ass. He moaned into my rectum, making my cock respond fully. He tongue-fucked me as a finger petted the back of my sac. I sighed from the pleasure. The tongue inched up inside me, massaging my sphincter into purrs as it made its way to my rectum, where I would shortly beg him to put something else.

I sighed again as he entered me, the fullness spreading and filling me. I savored the snugness of his hardness against my walls. I thought briefly of how I had come to love having Sea plow me with his enthusiastic boy cock. The remembrance made me sad, so I banished it.

He was lying on me now. His weight wasn't oppressive. Although taller, his body was lean, so he felt good against my back. His hot breath was on my face as he praised my tight ass. Unlike my brother, Master Lao took me slowly, his strokes measured, experienced. I was lying with my eyes closed, head on my arms, focusing on the good feeling in my bowel. I was stiff from his fucking. I knew that the longer he lasted, the likelier I was to shoot. Sea had never done that, as fast as his fucking had been. But Master Lao....

I felt it as he humped me faster. My sap rising as the master would put it. Then I cried out. This seemed to push him over the edge, because he thrust two more times and froze, sending his reproductive fluid up my smooth muscle. Then he turned me over and licked my abdomen and sucked my cock to clean me. He told me that I was special, kissed me good morning and led me off to wash.

The other couple of times that I'd been at the temple, the boys had worn short white silk robes, sleeveless dresses really. But I found out in quick order that it wasn't their dress when there were no visitors. The master produced a white silk sock, which he called a lotus covering for modesty. He fitted it onto me and adjusted the sheath until it hugged me just right. He told me again how good-looking I was before we left his quarters to meet the other boys.

I had seen them on previous visits, of course, but now they would be my daily companions. Craig, Justin and Chad were really pretty and so sexy in their lotus coverings. Their shaved heads gave them an exotic look. I knew that I was going to like making it with them. Craig was a year older and was taller than I. Justin was nearly my age. Chad was twelve. All were from well-off, if troubled, families. I would come to find out that, although he was a charlatan, Master Lao really did care about us boys beyond sex. We were almost a family.

All three of the boys were white, and given my mixed heritage, only my eyes and honey-colored skin were any different from them. But I did look more like Master Lao, which made me wonder if they would see me as a threat to their lives there.

I liked my fellow acolytes right away, and they were ecstatic that I was joining them. They remembered me from my visits with my mother and told me later how chastely they had lusted after me. I wondered if "chaste lust" wasn't an oxymoron. I didn't wonder how chaste we would be together. They all had cute, adolescent bodies, which I found a real turn-on. Not that Master Lao's lean, muscular body wasn't. Maybe it was that his body was more like Sea's, who was lost to me, and that theirs were like Chris's, whom I found myself missing.

I spent a great day with my new friends. They took me through the routine of the temple. The place itself was really a multistory townhouse. There was a garden with a pond in back surrounded by a high masonry wall. There were daily chores, classes, meditation, and prayers before a golden image of the Buddha. None of us had any idea that the religion that we were participating in was a blend of beliefs, including boy worship on the master's part. We dressed for dinner in our robes, because a cook came in to make that meal. Otherwise, we had spent the day in what Craig referred to as our lotus socks, or lotuses. Master Lao returned home and joined us for dinner.

My arrival at the temple was a complication, I found out that evening. Usually, one boy spent the night with the master, and the other two had sex with each other. Now there would be an odd boy out. It was Chad's turn to serve the master. Actually it had been the night before, but I had interrupted the routine. They hadn't had any sex the night before, as a result. But both Craig and Justin wanted to make it with me, so we found the solution.

After Chad went off to serve his master with his body, the three of us piled into Craig's bed. We still had on our socks as we sat kissing and stroking each other. The silk felt so good against my sensitive skin, and I was aroused in no time, as were my new playmates. But three guys trying to kiss each other was awkward. So we talked about what they wanted to do with me, and I agreed readily. We took off our lotuses and got down to it. Justin sat back against the head of the bed, spreading his legs. On all fours, I began to do serious oral on his dick. Meanwhile, Craig finger-fucked me. I went down farther in front, raising my ass higher and reached under me to search out his equipment. He must have seen the hand, because he placed his scrotum in it and then put a second finger into me, while I played with the seat of his maleness. I massaged and tugged on his sac. Sea had taught me that little trick of making my partner feel good before a doggy fuck. One of several he magically learned at the academy, of course.

I felt Craig remove the fingers and replace them with his cock. The head and shaft slid into me in one motion, and he set up a steady pounding while holding me by the waist. I concentrated on pleasuring Justin. I used the free hand now to put my second finger to his rosebud and had him squirming from the attention. You see, I wanted to make a good impression on my new sexmates. And I was happy to be sucking one of them and being fucked by the other. I hoped that the symbolism of my willingness to submit to them like that wouldn't be lost on them. My finger and mouth on Justin weren't. I had him going crazy to the point of bathing my throat with his essence long before he was ready. He seemed amazed that he had come so quickly. When I straightened back up onto all fours after having drained him, he leaned forward and kissed me.

I wasn't surprised when Craig came mere minutes later, he had been so intent on getting off as soon as possible. When he slipped from me, I lifted up and he took hold of my cock and masturbated me while Justin licked the underside of my prick to help me along. I announced my orgasm so that Justin could catch me as I came. He did, surprising me with his deftness. He missed only the last of my volleys, which dribbled out. But he licked what was left.

I slept soundly that night, happy that I had pleasured my new comrades, and that they accepted me as one of them.

Five

We ate breakfast after prayers to the Buddha. Then we had morning classes, for which we also wore our robes, such as they were. A man from the Burberry School, which was in the same block of townhouses, taught us our lessons. A different man conducted the afternoon classes. The cook was from the same school. It was ostensibly a boys' school, but despite its high-sounding name, it was more like an orphanage. And much more.

It was between lunch and afternoon classes on that second day that I had my first encounter with Chad. He was a self-proclaimed twinkie, whose mother had sent him to Master Lao to change him.

"I'll go home the same as I was, but with a hell of lot more sex under my belt than if I had stayed there. The master will simply tell mummy that I'm truly a homosexual, and the Buddha approves. Of course, he'll keep all of the money she showered on him, and I'll know things most teenage gay boys don't know. It'll make me that much popular."

"But you're already a really pretty kid, Chad."

"Thanks for calling me that, Ty. I'm serious about being a twinkie. I like being fem, because it's the way I am. So do Craig and Justin."

"So do I." I held and kissed him to reinforce it.

"I'm glad. You're beautiful Ty. Let's fuck."

"Can you?"

"Since the day I discovered beer bottles." That, unsurprisingly, made me laugh. And he had figured out their alternative purpose years before I had.

I took him on his back and kissed him the whole time I moved in him. We didn't have the luxury of time, but I didn't want to slam him the way Craig had me. I also wanted to taste his cherry-red lips, which seemed to curl into a pout whenever he wasn't talking. His ass was really tight, but that was no surprise. That he accommodated my cock was. But then I figured that he was probably used to Craig, who was close to me in size. He masturbated as I fucked him, and we both came after a few minutes, we got so into our physical contact. Then we dressed again.

To do our chores and say evening prayers, we wore only our

lotuses. And at dinner, if the cook wasn't in that night and we microwaved something frozen. I think that Master Lao liked seeing our near nudity as much as being naked. But the pretext of covering our genitals was to be modest for the Buddha.

One day I did get to see some of the students from the Burberry School leaving in a van traveling down the alley behind our building. I mentioned seeing boys in caps and white shirts to Justin. He said that they wore uniforms, although he hadn't seen more than I had. We had no contact with them, he said. Craig walked up to us.

"Talking about the Burberry boys?"

"Yes. I saw them leave in a van."

"Well, from having heard parts of conversations I shouldn't have, I think those kids are prostitutes. They may be school kids, but they also turn tricks over there, from what I've been able to gather."

"Really?"

"Master Lao would never do that to us," Justin said.

"No. But imagine young school boys wrapping their knee socks around an older guy's neck."

I could, and liked the images my mind visualized. A pretty, slim, fair-skinned young boy, with freckles dotting his nose and cheeks, was wearing only wide-ribbed white socks, which covered his lower legs. The tops were turned down twice just under his kneecaps. His stockinged feet were in the air in anticipation of being fucked. The older, handsome man now penetrated him, sliding his big prick slowly into the little body, as the boy sighed in happiness. Then he locked his slender ankles behind the man's neck as he surrendered completely to the organ pushing deeply into his colon, stretching it and pushing it against his sensitive prostate. The stimulation made his youthful sex hard, and he urged the man to fuck him silly.

However, despite that fantasy, I didn't imagine the boys wearing all sorts of fetish outfits and making films, having no idea that they did.

In fact, I did spy on two of the boys once without meaning to. We were in the garden meditating on the stone benches scattered around it. My perch was under the feathery foliage of an old Japanese maple near the house. At the end of my meditation, I looked up through the branches to see them standing on the roomy third-floor balcony of a building a couple doors over from ours. They were bare and tanned all over. That was where they sunned themselves in warm weather, on the two chaises set out there, I found out shortly. The two were gorgeous kids, from what I could see at that distance. And definitely young. Without a doubt, I would have wanted their stockinged legs around my neck. As I watched, they lay down on the chaises to sun themselves.

While they were lying there turning darker, a third boy came out onto the balcony, and I finally got to see the uniform. The pretty chocolate-skinned boy of perhaps nine or ten looked adorable in it. His knee-socks actually were white and ribbed and matched his shirt. His cap, tie, short pants and strapped shoes were navy blue. I was able to see the straps and buckles clearly, because he pointed the toe of one of them into the iron slats, which comprised the floor of the balcony, as he talked to his housemates. I envisioned myself kneeling before him and unzipping him. Then taking out his little brown dick and sucking on it as he stood there in his schoolboy glory.

Sitting there with my lotus blossoming from seeing the beautiful young flesh, I wondered if I could get admitted to the Burberry School, because I would dearly love to make it with those youthful beauties with their smooth, browned skins.

When we weren't ruminating out there, we also played handball at the back of the garden, where there was a patio next to the rear wall. Besides getting exercise and having fun, we were visual treats dressed only in our lotuses and white athletic shoes. I especially liked seeing the other guys' sexes swaying when they were returning shots. It was the only time we wore footwear, unless we went for one of our walks along the banks of the Charles River nearby. That was also the only time that we wore our "civilian" clothes.

Although I liked the three boys about equally, Chad was my favorite sex partner and Craig my most satisfying conquest. Taking him from behind while kneeling and holding him to me was my favorite sexual moment there, because I envisioned that he was my older brother, while I was doing it. I hooked his arms behind mine. I proceeded to pinch his nipples and stroke his body, leaving his bobbing cock waving helplessly. I nuzzled and kissed his neck as I took him in short, slow strokes. I had him begging me to come in him by the time I was nearly through using his body. Chad just sat there, mesmerized, watching us teenagers locked in sweaty congress. Until I made Craig shoot. Then the boy exclaimed and lunged to take the spoils of the erupting cock. Neither boy could believe what I'd done to Craig.

I don't think that it was that particular act, but I became the first among equals with my friends. And, by all accounts, I was the best-looking of the four of us. Master Lao seemed completely pleased by my ascendancy. I guess that it helped him to make comments about my possible divinity. Those stuck with the other guys, and they seemed to be excited by the possibility that I could be a reincarnation of the Lotus Boy. Another meaningless term, I know now, but as I said, the master's religion was mixed nuts, with Buddhism being the majority peanuts.

And that was how I would come to need my brother's help. It all started so innocently, for it being so dishonest to begin with.

Six

Life went on pleasantly at the temple. From time to time we had visitors. Mostly women, to whom we showed our pretty faces and arms and legs during the spiel by Master Lao. And to their adorable sons, whom they brought along, as my mother had brought me. And who, one by one, seemed to end up as our brothers, eventually. Lao really was a slick operator. But, as I said, life at the temple was good. We lost Craig but gained John, Ashley and Tony.

Despite his name, Ashley was one tough nut. He was really cocky, and he upset the placidness of the temple by his snide comments and pretty-boy strutting. Before the end of his first week there was out, I had had it. I told him that we were all brothers and he had to conform and act like one. Well, that offended his feeling of superiority, and a wrestling match ensued. He thought it was about physical dominance. I wanted to win, but I knew I wouldn't, because all of the grappling with his gorgeous body did was arouse me.

Finally, he got me on my back and straddled me, triumphant. He smirked, which was his last mistake. I lay there defeated, until I lifted him and shoved my erection into him. The look on his face was priceless. I might have shot him, he looked so shocked. He tried to get off me, but I was the one on adrenaline and testosterone now, and I held him fast on me as I bucked into him.

"You're, you're...."

"Inside your body, Ash. It belongs to me now, cocky boy," I said thrusting again and again.

"Stop it, Tyler! Let me go! You're raping me!"

"Not until, ahhhh!" I came in him. He was still in shock, but all of the other guys saw me take him, so he became quite docile after that.

Of course my conquest of Ashley did nothing to dampen the speculation that I might be a god. And that seemed to be the catalyst for what happened soon afterward. I guess it sealed my fate, but fucking Ashley had been great.

We would have special sessions at Buddha's shrine each week, where we would bare ourselves to the statue and lie nude in front of it, offering our naked selves to the deity. By this time I was really into the religion. My depression had lifted, which, to me, was a miracle. I loved my master and my fellow acolytes. Even Ashley, who loved me, too, I'm happy to say. In another ending to this story, I could have imagined us as lovers, we became so intensely attracted to each other.

It was one such evening that it happened. It was my turn to lie in front of the Buddha and offer my life, my body to him.

"Master Lao, make Ty lie on his belly. He should offer his buns to our god, they're so pretty," Chad said. We laughed, but Master Lao enthusiastically agreed to it, considering that mine were pretty popular with my templemates. Not to mention Chad, who loved to have me sit on him and smother him with them, so that he could achieve ecstasy.

So I showed my hemispheres to the statue. Then, as I was offering them up to him, I got very sleepy. I started to slur my prayer and must have passed out.

When I awoke, I was groggy and still lying there.

"It is a sign!" Master Lao exclaimed, when everyone else had become conscious again, by the way, although we didn't know it. "The lotus." I turned my sleepy head to see it. Sure enough, there was the flower blossom sticking out of my ass. I was wide awake now. How the hell did that get there? The master looked at me with eyes showing wonder. He caressed the showy, fragrant blossom, whose stem was imbedded in me. "Pray, my children. Pray, at this wondrous sign, as I turn the lotus boy over." For what?

Well, shock could not begin to describe my reaction after the master carefully removed the flower and gently turned me onto my back. Everybody inhaled sharply. I looked down and saw why. My cock was a brilliant golden color. Even in the flames of the flickering candles, it was a glinting gold. I kept blinking, but it kept shining in the light. I had a golden cock. And balls. "It is a miracle!" Tell me. I was dumbstruck. So were the guys. Their mouths were open at the sight of my altered organs. One by one they began to murmur their disbelief at the wondrous sight. Master Lao lifted and kissed my golden equipment. Then he thanked the Buddha for the miracle.

I seemed to be forgotten in this marvel, but not my golden genitals. All of the boys kissed them, but I didn't feel much of anything down there. What should have had me rock hard, had no effect on me. Chad did kneel at my head and kissed the golden circle on my forehead, which we wore everyday. And Ash kissed me on the lips before the master forbade that sacrilege. But his kiss meant so much to me, because we were really becoming tight, as I said. We would again, until we were caught.

Seven

I became completely guarded by Master Lao. Ash and I had a couple of trysts, but he caught us the second time, at least after I had come in him and we were lying sated. And it wasn't easy for him to get to me. I lived in my own room now. I became isolated from my brothers, except for prayers, where I would sit in front of the Buddha in all my genital glory.

In fact, for days after the miracle, I didn't leave the room. I couldn't leave my bed, because the master would give me something to drink which would make me sleep. He had to help me to the room of worship, I was so unsteady. When he stopped giving me that stuff, Ash and I were able to make it together. God, Ash cared for me so much.

"Ty, you're being used," he said, smoothing my scalp.
"How?"
"How should I know? You're the one of us who's smart."
"That's not true."

"Well, you're the smartest, okay? And something doesn't make sense. I don't know what it is, dear. I just know I love you."

"I love you, Ash."

"And Chad misses you. So does Justin. But I love you."

"I love them a lot. And I do love you, Ash. But I don't know what this means."

"I wish I did."

"You and me both, believe me."

One of the things it meant was that I was not to have sex with any of my templemates. Further, not even Master Lao would partake of my body, at least at first. He seemed as baffled as the rest of us by the sudden, dramatic change in my genitals, although he averred that there was no doubt that I had been altered by Siddharta himself. It was really more like, "Okay, I've made him into the golden Lotus Boy, so now what do I do?" Only I didn't know that.

Not surprisingly I was entranced with my altered genitals. That is, once I was conscious enough again to enjoy them. I still didn't understand the potion stuff or the pills for a few days after that, but I sure as hell didn't understand how I suddenly had golden equipment. Except that maybe I was a god. But why? My childhood had been unexceptional, if happy, until Chris died. Well, having sex with my brothers might count as an exception, but that would more likely to be seen as kinky. Did my early sexual activity have something to do with this happening? For the time being, I decided that it didn't matter how I came to be the Lotus Boy. I was and had the way-cool golden cock and balls to prove it.

I admit that I spent hours posing in front of the mirror in my room, admiring my shiny sex organs. I would stroke myself to hardness and just look at my gleaming column of precious flesh standing up from my body. Man, what a turn-on. And my black pubic hair only seemed to make my sex look more golden. I would turn around and bend over to look at my honey-colored skin framing my gilded scrotum. I did lewd dances with my hips to make my stuff sway and reflect the light. What a rush it was to see them swathed in the precious metal.

That was the conclusion I came to at the end of my skeptical period. I tried to wash off the color; then scrub it off. I examined myself carefully for any hint that it was painted on me. It wasn't. It was real skin. Being newly religious, I decided to accept it as a miracle. The question was: what did that mean?

Nothing, for a while. Except for a resumption of sex with the master. He seemed to treat my body with a heightened sense of respect, a tenderness he'd never shown, and I'd never felt before. His touch, his kisses tantalized my receptive skin. He was respecting me, not using me as he had previously. And my body responded to his worship in complete physical surrender.

As with Ashley, Master Lao couldn't stay away from my enhanced genitals. As he licked and nibbled and sucked, he murmured as if he were praying. The first time he took me to bed after my transformation, he surprised me by asking me to fuck him. Then, once I was sheathed in him, he told me to tell him everything my golden cock was going to do with him. That was a trip. Outside of Sea growling Shit! or Fuck! when he was coming, I'd never experienced trash talk in bed. But I learned quickly as my glimmering hard-on reamed his ass. "Fucking you with my godlike prick, man. Reaming you good with my golden Roto Rooter. Making you beg for this shiny fucking beauty. Making you whimper for it all the way up your boy pussy. Desperate for it. Desperate to be fucked by a god. A fucking golden boy rod. A fucking golden god rod. With Lotus Boy come."

It worked. He begged and whimpered and even came without touching himself, I had gotten him so hot.

I saw my mates only at meals and prayers now. That way they couldn't play with the Lotus Boy. Although why, I couldn't figure. Neither Ashley nor the master had been struck dead from having sex with me. And the forlorn looks on the faces of Chad and Justin broke my heart. I tried not to look at them while we were eating and kept my eyes closed as I sat in front of the Buddha, exposed to them at prayers. But I missed having sex with them, especially Chad, as I said.

So one day I passed a note to Chad at breakfast, when the cook was not in the dining room. I preferred that, because he leered at me now that I had been altered. I had no doubt that he was dying to see what I looked like under my robe. Master Lao was also away that day, which was why I decided that it was time to play with my former roommates.

We met in my room. After handing over the note, I had had second thoughts. The reason was that I didn't know what kind of punishment, if any, Ash had received for having sex with me. I didn't want to get the guys into trouble. On the other hand, maybe their coming would mean that Ash hadn't been punished. Or that they missed me so much that it was worth it. Chad showed up first. We hugged and kissed. His slim, smooth body felt wonderfully silky pressed to mine. We nuzzled and caressed, getting the other excited.

"I've really missed you, Ty."

"Same here, Chad. Where's Justin?"

"He'll be along in a while. The master's gone all day, so we have a few hours until supper to feast on our Gilded Lotus Boy." He grasped my shaft to emphasize where the feast would be held.

He dropped to his knees, still holding me, and just stared at my glimmering boyhood.

"Man, this is awesome. I still can't believe it, Ty."

"Me, either. Trust me."

"God," he said, rubbing his nose and cheek against me. His soft skin, shining, glowing with youthful oils, aroused me further as I slid over it.

He took my head into his mouth, looked up and grinned. Then he sucked on me slowly, letting the metallic splendor of the mushroom expand in his cavity. When he had my prick pulsing, he came off me to admire at it again. He was entranced by its effulgent beauty. He licked down the underside of the shaft and set to work torturing my balls. He stopped and asked if they were golden, too. I shrugged. Why not? Cool. Then he mouthed and tongued them in turn until they retreated from his warm embrace. He licked back up the bobbing, glimmering column and then kissed all the way down again.

He opened wide and took my once-more relaxed sac into him. I moaned in pleasure. He echoed my sounds, causing the vibrations to radiate through my lower torso and making my erection twitch in sympathetic response. Then he made yummy sounds as he teased my balls with his tongue. It drove me crazy, but I continued to twitch. It was weird. Before my transformation, what Chad was doing would have made me shoot. Now I noticed that it took me a lot longer to come, for some reason. In a way, it prolonged my pleasure, loving what Chad was doing to me. But, on the other hand, sometimes when a boy wants to get his rocks off, he wants it right then.

And Chad wanted my cock in his mouth again, because he left my beleaguered scrotum to shrivel up in self defense and feathered his tantalizing tongue back up my shaft. "I want your lotus milk," he said. He swallowed me hungrily and inched down the shaft. The smooth friction of his wet lips made me sigh. He wrapped his hand around the base of my cock and pumped me as he sucked. I watched my goldenness disappear into his mouth and reappear in stark juxtaposition to his pink hand and head. Man, what a sight. It got me hotter and hotter. I pinched my nipples as I felt my lotus milk rise fast. "I'm gonna come." His lips gripped the shaft behind the glans and ran his tongue up and down my sensitive spot, which wasn't so responsive anymore. Still, he did drive me over the edge and nearly choked on all the lotus boy jism I spurted into his throat. When he finished milking me, he said, "That was sure worth waiting for," and grinned.

We lay on the bed, Chad still fascinated by my golden goods. He ran his hand over them. He confirmed that my skin felt real, although it didn't look like skin now. We talked about how all of us had been in a trance, when the change had occurred and how it truly was a miracle. A delicious one, he added, smiling.

After a while, Justin peeked his head around the door. "Hey, it's my turn," he said, when he saw Chad stroking my semitumescence.

"There's nothing left for you. Ty shot an All-American wad into me."

"Figures, you greedy little cum-eater."

He mounted the bed and sat on his calves between my parted legs. For a time he just beheld the shiny organs. Then he grasped my cock and pulled on it until it was hard. Then without a word, he got up and squatted down on it. He lowered himself steadily until he was sitting on my pubic bush. He put his arms behind him, planted his hands on the bed and began to fuck himself with me. Chad played with himself, while he watched Justin moving up and down on the gleaming tumescence.

"Man, it's so hard. Just like it was made of solid gold," Justin said, working up an intercourse sweat.

"I'm praying the Buddha will make us gilded, too," Chad said. He was jerking his hard little dick unhurriedly. "I'd even give up sex for a while to have one."

"Fat chance, cum-eater." I laughed at that. Justin was right. Chad couldn't get enough.

Justin took his own tool in hand and beat it fast. Chad speeded up, too. He leaned over and began to suck on my right nipple. I loved the attention and also being the fantasy for these cute guys. After he nursed at my swollen nub, he cocked his left leg and slid onto my body, lowering the leg onto Justin's foot. He began to go at my left nipple as he rubbed himself insistently against my smooth abdomen.

Justin's eyes were closed, perspiration making his face shiny, as he jerked himself on me. Chad was speeding up his movement on me as he suckled on my teat. I watched his young round buns flex as he masturbated himself in earnest on my soft skin. He came off my nipple and mewled as he froze in orgasm.

Justin followed soon after, sinking onto me completely and spewing hot cum onto those pretty-boy buns below him. He opened his eyes and grinned. "Phew," he said. As he scooped up his come with his finger and deposited it inside Chad, the boy lying on me kissed me tenderly. When Justin was done impregnating Chad, the latter got up and licked himself off me. Then he lay down and let Justin clean him. Then we just lay as they savored their orgasms. But not for long.

Although I'm sure it was much longer, it seemed that it wasn't five minutes after my two pals shot their rocks that Ashley poked his head around the door, grinning.

"Man, it smells to high sex in here."

"Golden boy sex," Justin said.

"For sure," Chad said.

"Well, count me in."

Ash walked to the bed and looked at my glistening cock, more effulgent than ever with Justin's mucous on it. He picked it up and held it lightly.

"I need to be fucked bad with this beauty."

"You want it, too, huh?"

"Yeah. I want you to drill me, Ty."

He decided that he wanted it standing up. I got off the bed to accommodate his wish. Thank goodness Justin hadn't made me come. He kissed me as his hand slid up and down the head and shaft, reigniting its passion. When he had me wanting again, he turned away from me, spread his legs and bent over. "Wait," he said, as my glans tip pressed against his lips.

He straightened and went to the closet door. He angled it so that he could watch himself being fucked. He returned and resumed his supplicant stance. I positioned myself behind him and nudged the head in. His sphincter swallowed it with a sigh. "All the way, man." I slid all the way into his beautiful boy body. He arched his back in response. I held his narrow hips and eased most of the way out, returning the golden sword to its hilt in him. He watched me take him with intense interest, as his tongue slid over his upper lip. He felt me fucking him good, too, because I could see the reflection of his pretty dick, and it was beginning to twitch.

Once more I was becoming mesmerized by seeing my shaft move in and out of Ash. However, when Chad came off the bed and knelt in front of him, I saw that he was waving up in the air now, thanks to my rutting in him. The cum-eater swallowed the bloated head, and I could feel those lips on me again, even though it was really Ash's bowel caressing me seductively. Evidently feeling left out, Justin stepped off the bed and knelt behind Chad. He buried his face in the boy's crack, no doubt intent on retrieving some of his own cream from its repository. I envied him Chad's sweet boy smell there, but not enough to want to trade places. I felt heavenly in Ash's tight ass.

So the four of us were joined together. These were the guys I loved most in the world. Certainly not Seaton, whom I rarely thought of. The other boys notwithstanding, I had a longer history of affection and sex with Chad and Justin. And as I said, I was falling in love with Ash. I stroked his sides as I continued to pummel him, my endurance as amazing as it was disconcerting.

"Oh, God, Ty. Well, just God, I guess. Your cock feels like a fucking broomstick in me."

Justin came out of Chad's ass to say, "I'd like to see one of those sticking out of your ass." Chad laughed on Ash's stick and choked.

I was frantic in Ash now, feeling so close but not so close. I held him fast by his hips once more and thrust up into him repeatedly. He was breathing heavily, and I knew that Chad was going to bring him off soon. Then finally I felt myself beginning to get off-center. That was when Justin mounted Chad and began to lick Ash's balls. Justin's boy butt was even rounder than his sexmate's, and I concentrated on it moving as he fucked the younger youth. We were all breathing, moaning and mewling as we hurtled to orgasm. I was getting really close, when I heard Justin announce his climax and saw his cheeks clench as he emptied himself in Chad. Ash cried out next, creaming the hungry come mouth. I felt his muscle clamp down on me as he shot. The further tightness sent me over the top. Then Chad made noises on the softening cock in his mouth, having brought himself off.

The three of them hugged me for a long time afterward, each telling me that he loved me. It was the neatest thing to be held by the three guys like that and told how much I meant to them. Then we four got into the tub in my bathroom and soaped away each other's smells from our bodies. The bedroom was still rank with sweat and jism, but Ash found a can of Lysol in the bathroom and sprayed a heavy mist all around. With any luck, Master Lao wouldn't catch on.

After supper I was exhausted and fell asleep, only to be reawakened by the master for prayers. And then to share his bed—just what I needed.

Eight

It got to the point where I thought that what had happened to me *was* a miracle, because Master Lao didn't seem to be taking advantage of my transformation for monetary purposes. True, we had a few more visitors than usual, but not the sideshow I thought it would be. And when those pilgrims came, I was demurely tucked under myself, so that all they could see was about an inch of my golden shaft. They were all impressed, if I do say so myself.

As a result of the increased visits, more boys came to live at the temple. A couple were really gorgeous, but I would never have sex with them. I envied Ash and the others partaking of their fresh, youthful bodies. I, however, belonged exclusively to Master Lao. My comrades weren't able to get to me with him around most of the time, and the tutor staying later on days when the master was away. In retrospect I think he had to know, or at least suspect, that we had had wild, wanton sex in his absence. If nothing else, my half-hearted performance in bed that night probably told him.

One day I was ushered into the master's office, which was strange, because he never took me there. There was a fat, bald man sitting there, when we arrived. He looked Asian, too, although I couldn't say from which country. The master took me to stand in front of him. He said nothing, but he stared intently at my genitals. "Hold your penis by the glans, Golden Lotus Boy," Master Lao said. I did as I was told, and the man scrutinized my shaft and scrotum. "Turn around and bend over, lotus boy." I did, spreading my legs, figuring that he wanted to see if my sac was completely plated.

"Amazing. Truly amazing," the fat man said, with a heavy accent.

"As I told your master, this is the Golden Lotus Boy."

"I shall report what I have seen." But not what you felt, I thought, spying his erection poking up in his pants as he continued to stare at my gleaming boy stuff and muttering now in a foreign language. Before I left the room, he knelt and bowed deeply, his head touching the floor. Wow. Then I was ushered out.

"Who was he, master?"

"I will tell you later, golden one."

Later was after supper, which we ate in his rooms, and after prayers. Then, Master Lao ravished my body with his lips and tongue. And that night I came before I could fuck him.

"So who was that guy," I asked as he held me afterward.

"He is the representative of a very rich and powerful man, who lives in a place called Montana."

"Helena's the capital. Big sky country."

"So you know of it?" Obviously. At least that much. Which wasn't much. Why Montana?

"He lives in San Francisco, but he has built a temple in Montana, because it reminds him of Tibet, where the Dalai Lama has been exiled from. And he is most anxious to have an incarnation of Buddha to dedicate his temple. I think that his representative will tell him that you are, indeed, the Golden Lotus Boy."

"Will I have to go out there?"

"Of course, golden one."

"But I'll come right back, right?"

"In due time, boy god."

"What's due time, master?"

"Whenever the Buddha says."

"I thought I was the Buddha."

"An incarnation." Somehow it sounded like I was evaporated milk or instant breakfast. Moo.

Nine

Don't ever fly from Boston to Helena, unless you love the guy a lot, or he has a big dick to scratch your bad itch. And certainly don't do it with Odd Job escorting you. Which is what I decided this "representative" looked like. He smelled worse. He was nice enough. Well, he was fawning. No, he was obsequious. Which was all right for a while, but that wore off quickly. His smell didn't. And he was hard to understand with his accent, even though he was speaking perfect English, as far as I could tell. Which wasn't very far at all. I wondered what the airline personnel thought of his carryings-on. I knew what our fellow passengers in first class thought. I was with them.

What was worse, I was dressed in a robe. Not the saffron robe of a monk, nor the short one we wore at the temple, thank God, whatever the real one is. Mine was white. It was actually two of them. The one underneath had slits up the sides to nearly my waist. The outer one probably made me look vaguely Buddhist, I suppose. It didn't help that I had the gold circle on my forehead, which I forgot to mention. I got that after my divinity was proclaimed. That was in lieu of a jewel. I couldn't imagine being with all of those passengers in First Class on the magnificent Boeing 747 with a diamond in my forehead, let alone at Logan airport. Small favors.

I really wanted to take off the outer robe and do a lewd dance for my fellow passengers, given that I had those slits up my sides, and I had pretty good, smooth boy legs. But it would have gone unappreciated, except by Odd Job, who seemed to be praying most of the way, when he wasn't drinking cocktails or watching the movie or pecking at the food. I loved the entree and all that went with it; he looked at my voraciousness doubtfully.

We stopped in Chicago. Our flight was going on to Denver. We didn't get off the plane during the layover. I told Odd Job that I needed to use the facilities, but he begged to accompany me. I refused, and he wasn't happy about it. My bladder was happy not to have him in the restroom with me. As I was shaking off and blowing a kiss to my beautiful golden glans, which I loved now, I heard a tentative knock on the restroom door.

"Your Holiness, the crew is waiting to empty the, uh, forward, uh, head."

I opened the door. "It's okay. I'm done. Empty away." Then I looked at the flight attendant. It made me draw in my breath. He was the most beautiful black man I had ever seen. I just stared at him, he was so stunning. I wanted to drag him into the head, ravish him, even renounce my godhood.

"This way, Your Holiness," he said, but he knew what my look meant by his wonderful smile. Unfortunately, Odd Job intercepted us and the black got a dirty look.

"I am perfectly fine, Yodo. Philip will escort me back to my seat." I wished that obsequiousness could kill. Or booze. God, Philip.

He was the head attendant, Holly, one of the other attendants said, in answer to my question. He ran things on the ground in the cabin, as the Captain and Co-Captain were out inspecting the plane. No, Philip was in coach on this flight, she said, in answer to my question. Oh, well. "Please tell him that his Holiness loves him. A lot." Odd Job didn't like that.

"I will, Your Holiness."

"We love all of our believers, don't we," I asked Odd Job. He didn't answer. He furrowed his brow and drank another cocktail. Have one more and pass out, I thought. Then I'll let Philip fuck me in whichever bathroom has already been hosed.

But it was not to be. Worse, while the other attendants bowed slightly when I left, Philip bowed deeply. I caressed his head but smelly Odd Job nudged me, accidentally, of course, before I could say anything to the flight attendant I was suddenly in love with.

In Denver, we boarded a private jet. I wondered why we hadn't flown it from Boston. I almost asked, but thought better of it. Then it was off to Helena, after every other jet took off beforoe us, it seemed. I thought that I would smell them for the rest of my days. Fortunately, Odd Job sat across from me on the other side of the Lear jet, so I didn't smell him now.

I fell asleep and dreamt of Philip. And Seaton. They were in swashbuckling boots and gauntlets and funny caps, but they were otherwise naked. They were dueling over me with sword blades coming out of their erect penises. Before the duel was decided, I woke up to the plane touching down.

Ten

Hello, Montana! Big Sky Country! It was *absolutely* beautiful, no exaggeration there, but that wasn't *all* it was—not by a long shot. The estate of our host was in the next county. I had never seen such sparsely-populated land, but there was something about the isolation that was comforting and threatening at the same time.

The estate was off a two-lane road, and it took forever to reach it, the place sat so far off it. But once I saw it, I was stunned by how big it was. Then I was even more surprised by how young and handsome the owner was. He told me his Thai name but asked me to call him Kip. Although formal, he was not fawning as Odd Job was. He was friendly and had a great smile. He took me on a tour of the house. He told me that his father had made a fortune during the period of time when Thailand was one of the so-called Asian Tigers. He had wisely invested most of his profits in the United States, so when the economic collapse came, he survived it. His heart didn't, however, and Kip inherited and became filthy rich, as he put it.

The temple was attached to the rear of the house by a glassed-in hallway. The place of worship itself was simple, although the Buddha was appropriately made of gold. It was there that Kip told me that I was beautiful, and that I could easily be mistaken for being of Thai ancestry, my Asian eyes were so soft. I thought that he was going to kiss me, but he didn't.

He showed me his suite, which was at the end of the glass breeze-way. He told me that I would be sharing his rooms, because they were convenient to the temple. Uh, huh. He did kiss me then. It was tender, as was his touch, and I liked that. But he didn't try to do anything more. Instead we went into an adjacent part of the house.

That wing consisted of bedrooms and a common room. It was there that I met two very pretty boys, who were also Thai. They didn't speak English, but Kip spoke to them in their native language. Both knelt and bowed immediately to me before my temporary master told them to rise. Not only was I struck by their beauty, but by their attire, too. They wore only a rounded gold triangular cup over their genitals, which was attached to waist chains and one running up their asscracks in back; a metallic G-string, in effect. I would see the lock at the juncture of the waist and ass chains later. They were harnessed like that until bedtime. Kip said it was for my protection, because he didn't want either of them fucking his household god. His what? I thought that I was supposed to be there just for the dedication. Then I realized that must have meant someone else, whom I hadn't met yet.

We ate dinner in a large dining room. The table looked as if it could seat twenty, easily. But it was just the two of us. We were served by two different teenagers. They were gorgeous boys, too. And they were naked, which made it even better. But that was curious, considering that the other two were neutered. I commented on that to Kip.

"They're eunuchs. They were castrated as boys and will always be boys. They're of no threat to you, because they never had sexual urges and now can't have them. They are our personal servants."

Kip called one of them to his side. He lifted the little penis, and I saw that there was no sac. However, there were interwoven gold threads up the seam of what was left there. They'd evidently been sutured with the precious thread after they'd been emptied of their boynesses. The boy smiled at me, as if he was truly proud of it. Man, I couldn't imagine not being able to have sex, but as Kip said, these two had no clue about what sexual desire was, so their ignorance was bliss, in this case. Still, it was kind of depressing, because they were so pretty. It would have been great making it with them. However, I doubted that Kip would allow me to fool around with them, or the other two either.

It wasn't until after we ate that we returned to the temple. It was dark now and there were candles lighted next to the Buddha. We were alone when Kip disrobed me. He knelt and gazed at my glimmering genitals for the longest time.

"This is no hoax?"

"If it is, it even has me fooled. The color doesn't come off. Trust me."

"You went to sleep and awoke golden?"

"On the ceremonial altar."

"A miracle."

"At least."

"Indeed."

He stood and explained that he was going to enshrine me. I neglected to mention earlier that the Buddha was anatomically correct. So enshrining meant lifting me up and impaling me on the statue's phallus. It wasn't getting fucked, but I liked the feeling of fullness of the hard organ in me. "Beautiful. Both of you together." Yep, me and the Buddha. I'll resist any crude comments about being fuck buddies, because I don't want to offend real Buddhists. But Kip, like Lao, had his own crazy brand of it.

He told me that the Golden Lotus Boy's semen was supposed to give immortality to those who ingested it. Lao had told me that it made the recipient more virile and be able to perform more often, as if Lao had a problem with that without my cum.

Kip knelt in front of me for a long time, praying. Then we got to the main event. He leaned over and kissed me down there. Then he took the cockhead into his mouth and nibbled on it, then sucked me in. I groaned in pleasure as his mouth and tongue moved all the way down my shaft. I swear I didn't have as much feeling anymore, but he was making my nerves happy enough. He moved slowly up and down, tasting and savoring me. When I was rock hard, he worshipped the seat of my life-giving fluid. He licked and sucked and had my cock bobbing from the pleasure rippling up from my scrotum. Then he licked back up my shaft. His fingers replaced his mouth on my sac, and he sucked me deliberately again. This guy was a World Class cocksucker, I decided. I also realized that I could get used to being done like that, especially with my ass filled with the golden dildo. And now that I was that way, it turned me on even more to watch myself get blown. I whispered to him that I was going to come, and he held me securely as I pulsed in his mouth. He moaned as if he were in ecstasy while I unloaded in him. He sucked every last drop out of me.

It made me wonder if there were a certain amount of come you had to swallow in order to become eternal. Like it's written in a book that you need to drink a gallon of boy goo in order to get the desired effect. Man, I hoped not. If I was coming an average of a teaspoon an orgasm, how many years would it take to make a gallon, even if I came twice a day? Which I was willing to do for the cause of immortality, you understand. And then I wondered if I were immortal myself now. After all, I was the Golden Lotus Boy producing the death-cheating stuff. And I could still beat off and swallow my own cum. Although maybe it was like a poisonous snake biting itself; a waste of perfectly good venom. And maybe I was just starting to think as wacko as these guys were. Still, there was no denying the fact that my boy parts were gold.

Afterward, Kip sat in the lotus position looking up at me for a long time.

"You are so beautiful, Lotus Boy." I realized that he hadn't used my name since I'd arrived.

"Thank you. You are, too."

"That is kind of you to say, but your beauty is the fairest I have ever seen." What can a god say to that? You bet your sweet ass, Kipper.

He answered my question about whether or not I was going to be sitting there helpless all night by finally lifting me off my sexual prison. He held me to him and told me how fortunate he was to have me. I resisted the impulse to ask him how much come he needed for his transformation, because I really didn't want to know that I might stuck in Montana till the timber wolves came home. I missed my friends back in Boston, and I also missed my mother. And if I weren't going to be able to play with the two adorable boys, I really didn't want to hang around there, cute Kip notwithstanding.

I did sleep with him, but he was a gentleman about it. After kissing me goodnight, he turned over onto his side of the king-size bed. That was fine. My cock and ass had been worked over, so I was ready for sleep.

Eleven

The next morning he woke me with his hands and lips. That was cool. He kissed down my body to my piss hard-on. I thought that he was going to fellate me again, but instead he inspected my organs. I wondered if he didn't trust me that they were real. But then I wondered if I would have if the positions had been reversed. He kept shaking his head.

"How old are you?"

"Um ... sixteen. I think."

He laughed. "You're not sure?"

"Oh, you see, I don't know how long I've been at the temple."

He told me the date.

"Still sixteen."

"You're pretty big for a sixteen-year-old."

I smiled. "Thanks."

One of the servants knocked and entered. I looked up. God, he was pretty, I thought. What a waste. He asked if we required anything; Kip said no. I guess. Well, the kid did leave, but not before staring at my cock and balls.

We got cleaned up and I found out that I would be spending my time around the place in the nude. I didn't mind. It wasn't much different than wearing the lotus sock at the other temple. Besides, as I said, I really got off on myself the way I was. I liked my flashy cock swaying in front of me. And I guess I had gotten big, now that I thought of it.

After we ate breakfast, we went to the temple for morning

prayers. This time Odd Job and the two acolytes were there. I could easily get off seeing them in their sexy G-strings. With the help of the phallus, which I was on again. The two boys knelt and bowed. Then they kissed my feet. Chris always said I had great-looking feet because of my high instep. But his and Seaton's were, too. That thought made me hope that my big brother had gotten fallen arches from marching, which wasn't a very lotus boy thought, I admit. But it still hurt that Sea had brought boys home and screwed them right under my nose like that. Then the thought hit me that if I was divine, maybe I could wreak some kind of vengeance on him. Fallen arches, hah! Or was that some other religion? Buddhism seemed so peaceful. Just what powers, if any, did a lotus boy have?

They were evidently allowed to kiss my penis and scrotum, too, because they did so with a reverence that surprised me. Then they put their foreheads to the floor. That reminded me that I had been seen at Logan, O'Hare and Denver, your typical backwater airports, with the golden dot on my own forehead. Which I had dutifully reapplied with temporary glue after showering.

The four of them prayed to us in Thai for a while. Kip had a mustache, which made him look debonair. I decided that I wanted him to fuck me and wondered if I could maneuver him to do it. Just how divine did he think I was? Well, he had touched me down there with his fingers that morning.

When they were prayed out, Kip came over to the boys, who were still kneeling in front of me. He produced a key and unlocked them. That was when I knew that they had them. He lifted the metal G-strings out of their crotches. They had small, cute dicks. They bowed to me once more and then turned to each other. They proceeded to kiss each other as if the world were going to end in seconds. Their bodies were pressed together, and their hands were all over each other's body. They had nice ass cheeks, I noticed, seeing them in profile. It dawned on me that I was seeing two guys make love for the first time in my life.

I responded to their rabid hunger for each other. The neck-kissing and licking, the grinding of hips together, the kneading of buttocks. I was saluting their passion in no time. But they were unaware of it, being so lost in each other. It was probably the neatest sight of my young life. These boys, who couldn't have been older than I was, were so into each other. I wanted them to break their love-drunk clench so that I could see how much bigger they'd gotten from all of their ardor. Finally they did. They might have been about three or four inches, but it was a beautiful sight. Except, I guess, if you're a size queen. Your loss, because their little rods looked so neat standing up in arousal.

One of them, whom I decided to call Abe, lay down, and Ben lay on top of him. They went at each other again, Ben rubbing himself against Abe while they did it. Abe wrapped his legs around his partner, as if they were in intercourse. Well, they were, just not connected. They kept on kissing and rubbing and writhing until I couldn't take it anymore.

"Fuck him, Ben!"

Kip looked at me. "Ben?"

"Sorry. Did I say something wrong?"

"No, Golden Lotus Boy. But who is Ben?"

"The boy on top."

"Ah." Then he barked a command in Thai. Or Swahili, although that was less likely.

Ben got off Abe, and the latter reared back and spread em. God, their bodies were so smooth. I know a lot of people like bears, but I preferred the silky, unadorned skin of these two. My brothers and I were like that, too, in spite of the English genes we had. Well, Chris had. I wondered if I could bring him back from the dead. Man, I would give up my divinity, and my golden jewels, for a lifetime with the neatest guy I ever knew: Christopher.

I came back to the action in time to see Ben's cockhead nudge Abe and disappear. He held himself like that. Great. There was something about seeing his shaft without the point that was so cool. Then he rammed it in. He leaned forward onto his hands, and Abe locked his ankles around Ben's neck. He fucked the supine boy steadily, but he did withdraw enough for me to see his glistening maleness. I pictured it golden. And Abe's, too, but that didn't do anything for me. Must have been narcissism. Well, a god's allowed. I think.

Abe took his flaccid, brownish cock in hand and jerked himself as he was being taken expertly. He squirmed under Ben's assault, loving the cock in his rectum. I closed my eyes and envisioned his sphincter turned to putty, embracing the hard boyness that was subduing him. Stroking it. Loving it. Come in me, cock. Caressing it with all of the firm gentleness that it was capable of. Come in me, cock. You own me. Come in me, and mark me as your own, cock.

Just then Abe cried out. His hand was a blur on his organ, and the blur made him shoot. Ben rutted now, frantic for one of those boy O's that can't come soon enough for nerves stressed from excitement. He froze and uttered curse words, I swear, his release was so emphatic. Abe was muttering at being come in. God, such gorgeous boys, such great sex.

I was still at full mast when they finished, sweaty and giggling. Then Ben slipped out of Abe and pulled him up to sitting. They both knelt and started to lick my scrotum. Oh, no, I was not going to last, as exhausted and wired as I was by their lovemaking. Then Kip approached me, bowed and went down on me. Blessed relief was just two lips away. Then I realized that he was naked. So was Odd Job, who looked like a Sumo wrestler on a diet, albeit not SlimFast nor Weight Watchers. I didn't see Odd Job's tiny cock before it was too late, and Kip moaned on me as it went into him.

I thought it was really cool that the boys were so enthusiastic about worshipping me after their own orgasms. It really did pay to be a god, I guess. And Kip was going down on me with fervor, if nothing else. Odd Job was already sweating, he was so enthusiastic. Ben kept tonguing my sac, while Abe took his master's cock into his mouth now. More moans from Kip, which was fine with me. Sympathetic vibrations might have brought down the walls of Jericho, but what was that compared to bringing a boy to orgasm?

Odd Job suddenly looked as if he had been shot, but then I realized that he was the one shooting. Kip was desperate for my essence, but I wasn't giving it up so easily, strangely. Abe was frantic on Kip and had a finger fucking his come-lubricated hole. Odd Job cried out in Hebrew and looked shot again. Was he coming a second time? Kip seemed to be mewling on me, he was so desperate to have me spurt in him. Or maybe it was Odd Job creaming him again. He'd have to sit on the toilet after the guy got done with him, it seemed.

His noises on me finally worked, but not before Abe shot another wad, and Ben wet my leg. Kip veritably screamed on me as he came, and I gave it up to him. One more teaspoon.

One more day in paradise. Oh, all right, Montana. Well, it could be—but don't tell San Franciscans that.

Twelve

As I had feared, I wasn't there at the temple in Lewis and Clark County, or whichever one it was, only to open the newest Buddhist shrine. It could have been worse, I suppose. I could have been doing it for McDonald's. Welcome to Paleface, Alabama or Knotty Hair, Mississippi.

Instead, I was among some of the most breathtaking scenery I'd ever seen. Along with two beautiful boys I desperately wanted to make it with but didn't have the key, and two boys I wanted to put in my mouth, just because they had given up their sexuality without their consent. Kip told me that he had bought them in Bangkok, when they were fixed. He assured me that they were eight when it had been done, and none the wiser.

Strangely, I remembered Seaton accidently butting his head into Christopher's groin, when we were horsing around in the back yard with a football once. Chris went to the turf immediately, in great pain. It was accidental, because there was no reason ever for us to hurt our brother. Okay, he wasn't a saint, but he was the neatest guy any guys could have as a brother. Chris went up and lay down on his bed, and I asked how he felt.

"As if there's no sex."

"None?"

"I don't feel a thing. I don't even know what sex is. And I sure as hell don't miss it."

That surprised me. Maybe it's always contingent on the feeling down there, although Chris told me once that it's the brain that tells your cock what to do. But maybe even if these two gorgeous boys, with the golden threads, had felt like boys once, perhaps they didn't miss the feeling. Why I cared, I don't know, but I did. But they seemed happy the way they were. I had been there too long already.

My coming in Kip's mouth wasn't limited to our temple sessions. We spent part of the day in bed watching Abe and Ben on video, making it in leather, nylons, dildos, diapers, nooses, whatever variations there were. And that was an education, believe me. But they were so beautiful, that I always gave up my cum to Kip. I decided that getting fucked by a dog was cool, if he really, really liked you. And he did Abe and Ben. It was a blond cocker spaniel, and he had a hell of a time with them. And then afterward.

I resisted asking the fatal question for as long as I could, although it didn't come out the way I thought it would.

"Do you need a gallon of me?"

"A gallon of what?"

"My come. Is that why you're keeping me here?"

"No. I have the only Golden Lotus Boy in modern recorded history in you. And I'm not going to let you go."

Figured. "So you do need a gallon of my semen."

"To do what?"

"To be immortal."

"Possessing you, I already am." Lucky me.

But life there wasn't so bad, except that I couldn't make it with Abe and Ben. So life was bad there, to a certain extent. At least I didn't have to make it with Odd Job. But the boys were extraordinary in their costumes and passion.

In their diapers they were adorable, and they played with each other like excited babies. They had their hands in each other's thick, cotton diaper and were obviously jerking off, but you had to use your imagination, because you couldn't see them actually running their smooth hands up and down each other's stiff little dicks. It was so cool to watch them having sex but not *seeing* them have sex. I mean, masturbating each other but having it hidden by the white diapers.

Another intriguing video was of the boys dressed up as girls in scanty lingerie.

"It is a custom among some young men in Bangkok, especially. They are called Lady Boys and do striptease shows or prostitute themselves. Or both."

"Really?"

"Yes, but the boys, who *ten ram*, that is, dance, at the popular bars, also prostitute themselves, mostly to western foreigners."

"Wow. But Abe and Ben look so cute in their girl things."

"Indeed. Sexual expression is a wonderful thing."

"Yeah, but so is a golden cock."

"You need not remind me. I think that a visit to the temple

is in order."

Which is why I said it, of course. When you have the best cocksucker in Montana hot for you, you exploit it. Well, it helped to have a gold-plated organ that he panted for. And I was getting very used to being filled by the Buddha's considerable endowment as I sat with him at the shrine. It was a sunny day, and the light slanting into the temple windows made me squint so much that I started to get hard even without Kip's hot mouth. "Ah, the fortune of youth, my Lotus Boy," he said, and then went down on me. I choked him and bathed his aching throat muscles with my cum.

Thirteen

Kip decided that he had to get back to San Francisco. That meant we had to go, of course. It also meant that Odd Job would accompany us, lucky me. And that Abe and Ben would be unfettered during our absence. And that they would fuck the eunuchs, in addition to each other. I'm glad I didn't know that, because, honestly, I was coming to love the two teenagers who served us, and I wonder if it was cruel for them to be taken, in retrospect. But I didn't know that when we left. However, I was also coming to love Abe and Ben, too. And they were stunningly beautiful—and they had scrotums, so maybe if I were a boy without one I would submit gladly to a superior male, who did.

We took the private jet to San Francisco. Actually to Oakland International, across the bay. A car met us. I was dressed in normal boy clothes, with my gold dot, but that was somewhat hidden by the baseball cap I was wearing. I was dressed in regular boy clothes; jeans, sweatshirt, athletic shoes.

"There won't be an earthquake, will there, Kip?"

"Highly unlikely." I remembered the one before the World Series game and the havoc it had wreaked. Parts of Candlestick Park had fallen. "In fact, after the earthquake of aught six, two biddies supposedly climbed up Knob Hill to look across the bay. One is said to have noted that Oakland was still standing. The other said, 'My dear, there are some things even the earth won't swallow'."

"So? A lot of people died in Oakland during the last one."

"I know. I should have known that you would be so

discerning."

And completely lost in another strange place. I have to admit that I was coming to love my new master, and the thought of staying with him was becoming appealing to me. He was handsome and rich, plus he could suck my brains out. The drawback was the isolation of the mansion in Montana. But I was quickly taken with San Francisco. It was a welcome break to be in the hustle and bustle of a city again. Kip told me that a lot of gay people lived there.

We drove through a particularly gay part of town. There were lots of male couples walking together. Christopher and I could have lived here and been able to be a couple, I thought. Except that there was no more Christopher. Or Seaton. If he hadn't turned out to be such a creep.

There was a cute blond leaning against a building. He had on a leather tank-top and shorts, high, thick-soled lace-up boots. There were elaborate tattoos on each bicep and thick silver rings in his ears. A heavy chain choker encircled his neck. Wide leather bands hugged his wrists. Man, he got my motor running. I wondered if he were waiting for another leatherboy.

At a corner waiting for the light to change, I saw a beautiful, slim Latino girl in a tight, short lavender dress, black stockings and high heels. "She's a boy," Kip said, when he saw me staring at her.

"Really?"

"Kid's in high school. He dresses up, puts on nail polish and makeup and comes to the city on weekends."

"Wow. He's really pretty."

"Indeed." Even Odd Job smiled and nodded. I shook my head, the boy had me so completely fooled.

Kip's apartment was large and reflected his wealth. It had a great view of the bay. It also came equipped with a houseboy named David and, involuntarily, I licked my lips when I saw him he was so yummy. Fortunately, Kip didn't see me do that. Nor David's furtive wink. Then I realized that I didn't need the complication of being around a servant who was worth ten Brandon Lees, at least.

I was going to ask Kip how he was going to worship me without a temple, but it turned out that there was a miniature one in the alcove of the bedroom. It had a Buddha sitting behind a low altar mounted with a golden dildo. He undressed me and let me impale myself on the huge, shiny phallus.

When I was comfortable, he went down on me. I closed my eyes and let my nerves speak to me in slowly growing whispers. Flesh on flesh. Hot, needy breath. Tickling, teasing tongue. Erect in his mouth. Glistening with his spit. Wiggling on the cock inside me, growing harder still from the stimulation. Building. One anguished nerve after another beginning to cry out in tormented happiness. The tongue on my vulnerable spot, insistent. Subduing me; making me spasm; making me give it up to him in spurt after spurt of pleasure jolting my body. Relaxing my curled toes. Opening my eyes. To see him still in possession of me. Sucking on me still. Taking every last drop of cum from me. The Golden Lotus Boy.

I slept for several hours afterward until I was awakened by a body moving against mine. A soft hand touched, then caressed my smooth body. I knew who it had to be. I sighed from the pleasure. David was tender yet intimate. I turned my head, and he kissed me. His lips were electric, his tongue tentative. I melted into him, determined that he could have me any way he wanted me. I was rock hard in his hand, when he stopped his oral assault.

"The Golden Lotus Boy is very beautiful, and I haven't even seen what makes him a god."

"You are, too, David. A god, I mean."

"I know. As one god to another, I want to worship you and then fuck you."

"I'm not supposed to be fucked, except by a golden phallus."

"Except that I don't believe that you're divine, so it's okay."

"Really?"

"Yes. Otherwise it would be a sacrilege. But since I don't, it's just fucking the most beautiful boy I've ever seen."

"Fuck me, David."

"First the worship."

He inhaled when he saw my cock. He was taken aback and taken, at the same time. "It is so big!" he gasped. He sucked on me, savoring the golden skin. He mouthed my balls, he licked up and down my shaft, covered my golden mushroom with his lips, until he had me throbbing. Then he lifted my legs and spread them. He entered me, letting my rectum feel the presence of his cockhead, before moving all the way in. He fucked me slowly, and I watched his ripped abdomen undulate as its extension pleasured me. Once he had set up a steady pace in my body, he took my cock in his hand. I had my feet on his chest, which was fine, because he was about fucking, not making love. So I didn't impede him, given that he had no desire to kiss me during our coupling. He also wasn't interested in masturbating me to climax, just wanting to keep the resplendent shaft and glans hard.

"How old are you?"

"Eighteen. I've been his boy toy since I was nine. Now he has you. Oh, he's had many others, but I thought I was special. I found out I wasn't. But this is my revenge. I'm defiling his god. His beautiful, golden god."

"Defile away, David."

"You are a miracle."

"I guess."

"It's real."

"And it responds to another boy's hand."

"Sorry. I'm being selfish."

"No, your cock's giving me a lot of pleasure."

"Good. I think you're a nice guy."

"Thanks. I really am. I didn't ask for solid gold equipment. I just woke up with it."

"Well, I believe your divinity. And I don't doubt that you're real. I just don't believe in *you*."

"That's cool. I've never believed in myself, so join the club."

"Believe it now, because you're fucking gorgeous, lotus boy."

"And you're fucking me."

"Hang on."

David still didn't do any more than hold me, but his rutting cock stimulated my prostate enough to make me shoot before his sweaty body unloaded a different liquid into me.

Afterward we lay on our sides with him holding me.

"So why don't you believe in me?"

"Because I'm a Christian. Although I admit that you are golden, no doubt about it."

"For sure."

"I probably shouldn't tell you this, but as much as he supposedly loves you, your master is at a private sex club tonight, fucking every pretty black and white boy he can."

"Really?"

"Well, he can't fuck you. And he gets tired of fucking the eunuchs in Montana. Poor, sweet guys."

"He fucks them?"

"And the sluts. The temple slaves."

"Abe and Ben."

"Who?"

"That's what I named them."

He chuckled. "You know, for someone so innocent, you have a sense of humor...what is your name?"

"Tyler. Ty, David."

"Ty, you have the most awesome boy things I've ever seen. And a tight ass to boot!"

Fourteen

That and a buck will get you a visit to a Buddhist temple, I guess. We went to a gay one the next day. I was in my robes, with the gold dot screaming 'Look at me!', as if the robes didn't. I really wished that I'd danced in my side-slit under robe for Philip. God, the thought of that stunning flight attendant remained with me to the point of making me stir, whenever my brain's photograph album brought him up. I think that I was using him to distract my mind from what David had told me that Kip had been doing the night before. I had asked him how his business meeting had gone. He'd simply smiled and said fine.

Unlike me, the monks we met wore saffron-colored robes. With no slits, I noted. Their loss. Well, maybe not, because I didn't find any of them attractive. I guessed we were going there so that he could get their imprimatur on my lotus boy status. But Kip said that they didn't believe in the lotus boy legend. His intention was to show them that they were wrong.

They led us into a small room, where Kip told me to disrobe. There were two monks present, but it didn't bother me. I was used to being naked all the time now. Needless to say that the monks were impressed, when they saw my stuff. They thought nothing of touching my cock and balls, maybe because they were gay. Naturally they made me hard, which seemed to impress them all the more. One monk left and returned with another one who looked pretty old.

"Well, I thought I had seen everything, but I stand

corrected." He stared at me for a while, during which time I went soft again, to the others' chagrin, I saw. "This isn't paint?"

"No, master, it does not rub off."

"When did this happen to you, my son?"

"I fell asleep on the altar at the temple in Boston. When I woke up I was golden, and a lotus flower was coming out of my, uh, rear."

"There were witnesses to the miracle," Kip said.

The monk nodded. "As you are well aware, we consider the Golden Lotus Boy a myth and outside mainstream Buddhism. But you, my son, have golden genitals. I shall have to consult those unofficial texts that mention the legend, considering the reality of you." He smiled. "They are beautiful, like the rest of you."

Kip had more business to do after the visit, so I was dropped at the apartment. David was waiting for me; when I entered.

"Well, are you divine?"

"They don't know. They have to look it up."

"Well, I'll take you as you are, because you are divine, if not sacred."

We went to his rooms, where we got naked and into each other's arms. Then on each other's mouth. Man, he could kiss. My hands roved down his smooth, muscular back to his ass cheeks. They were round like melons and hard. David was more muscular than I was but not much taller. Our cocks began to bloat from the foreplay, so David suggested that we retire to his bed. He had me lie down and he lay on top of me. Now our erections were pressed between us the way our lips were pressed together. I had no doubt that I would fall hopelessly in love with him, he was so sensual, in addition to being gorgeous. He came off my mouth in order to wreak havoc on the blood flow to my nipples now. He licked around the little brown areolas before attacking the short peaks in the middle. He sucked and nipped them, and it felt wonderful.

Then I noticed it. The bed was the canopy variety, and there was a mirror mounted to the top. It was strange but somewhat kinky to watch David making love to me as he moved down my body now. He tongued my navel and then skied down to my straight, black pubic hair. He slalomed around that and attacked my cock. Man, that was so cool to see. The best seat in the house, so to speak. I watched myself get hard again. When he was satisfied that I was ready and able, he said, "Okay, this time you fuck me with your solid gold stallion."

He lay down and reared back. He told me to hold his legs apart, which I did. I realized that this would give him an unobstructed view of me moving in and out of him. Like me, he was tight, and I had no trouble keeping my erection in him. Besides, I was looking at him when I wasn't watching myself doing him. He was so beautiful, and for some reason he reminded me vaguely of someone, but I didn't know who. I just knew that some day soon I would want to be with David forever, ever though I also knew that Montana would be in my future again sooner. "Oh, man, this is awesome," he said, staring up at the mirror.

"You're awesome."

"Face it, Ty, we both are."

"Yeah, and making it with you is great."

"Same here. We'll have to figure out how to get Kip out of the way, so we can fuck undisturbed."

I wished that he'd put it a little more romantically, but at least he admitted the mutual attraction. And my cock's attraction for his asshole was sending me steadily higher. Without stopping his peeping at his deflowering, he took his own rod into his hand and beat off in measured strokes. "God, this is so cool," he said, staring and pulling. I kept up a steady lunging into him, trying to withdraw about halfway each time for his entertainment. But once my prick was getting very serious, I buried myself in him and took him with short strokes. He didn't seem to mind. He just stroked himself faster, and took what glimpses of gold he could.

Then he cried out and his white jism erupted from his slit. More dribbled down his shaft. I felt him tighten around me and was able to give it up a few seconds, and strokes, later. When I plopped out of him, I let go of his ankles and bent over to lick up the come from his penis. Then I cleaned his chest. I lay down on my side next to him and took his soaked hand. Slowly I sucked on each of his fingers. He liked that.

Afterward, I stared at him again, certain that I knew someone who looked like him.

"Why are you staring at me?"

"You remind me of someone I know."

"Lucky you."

"Tell me about it." Then it hit me like a three hundred pound linebacker. "Oh, my God."

"What? What's wrong?"

"I just remembered who you look like."

"And?"

"And it's my older brother, Seaton."

"You're kidding."

"Let me tell you how much I'm not." And I did, to his amazement and amusement.

When Kip came home that evening, we had dinner and retired to the TV room to relax together. I sat on his lap, and he played lazily with me, while he nibbled and nuzzled me. After a time, David came to the doorway to announce that Kip had a phone call. He took it in the room. His back was to me, and he didn't say much, which I thought was strange. He usually did a lot of talking on business calls. When he got off the phone, he turned around and had a mean look in his eyes. What in the world was that for?

"That was the monk. He researched the Golden Lotus Boy, and the sects that believe in him all agree that he is always uncut."

Uh, oh. "Really?"

"You perpetrated a hoax on me!"

"I didn't perpetrate anything. What ever that means."

"It means you pulled a fast one, you little shit."

"How could I? These are real."

"But you aren't."

"I didn't do this to myself."

"Maybe not, but whoever did it to you was ignorant of the entire legend. You're a fraud, Ty."

"I'm a sixteen-year-old boy who has been altered, Kip. I'm not trying to rip you off. I love you."

"Well, I have been ripped off. Do you know how much I paid Lao for you?"

"No, and I don't want to." I really did, but I wasn't going to give him the satisfaction.

"I'm going to get back at him, but in the meantime I'm going to get rid of you. Out of my house. Out of my life. Now!"

"But I don't have any clothes or money or any place to go."

"Wear your robes and sandals. Go to the temple. Perhaps they'll take your sorry ass in."

"But..."

"Get the fuck out of here, asshole!"

I ran from the room, fearing the distinct possibility of physical violence. I dressed as quickly as I could. David came in as I was slipping into the sandals.

"I'm sorry, Ty. I guess the shit hit the fan."

"And I'm covered with it. What am I going to do?"

"He said to give you this." It was five hundred dollars. Well, it was a start. "And I'm going to call a friend of mine in the building. Another houseboy. His master's away on business. He's older and has connections. He may be able to fix you up more permanently." He drew me into his arms.

"I have to get out of here, David."

"You have time. He's gone out. Probably to his sex club to cool down. I love you, Ty."

"I love you, David." We kissed, not knowing that we wouldn't see each other again.

Fifteen

I was really feeling lost when I knocked on the door of apartment number 1241. I had tried to call Master Lao but got only the machine, then I called my mom and got no answer. I realized that I couldn't remember what military school Seaton was attending, or even if he was still there. I admit that I was desperate by that time, willing to call my two-timing, asshole brother. I tried a couple of airlines and found out that my five hundred dollars wouldn't get me back to the east coast. David said that he might be able to get some money, but where would I go? I didn't want to go back to Providence. I did want to go back to Boston, but it now seemed that Lao had somehow had me altered when we were all conked out. I mean, what other explanation was there? A lotus boy was always uncut, so it had to be Lao somehow. But how, I had no clue.

So I really didn't react to the handsome young man with the sparkling blue eyes and neatly-trimmed beard. His name was Ricardo, David had told me. He greeted me cordially, although I missed the leering curl of his mouth. As I said, I was feeling pretty abandoned.

"Come in, Tyler. David told me all about the fix you're in. I'll do what I can for you. My master is in the orient trying to see if he can salvage any business there. He'll be gone for at least another week. Have you eaten?"

"Yes. It's really nice of you to take me in like this."

"No trouble at all. Besides, it gets awfully lonely. I don't have a revolving bed the way David does. But then I don't have his looks, either."

"I wouldn't say that. You're cute."

"Aren't you a dear. Well, if you're not hungry, how about a nice, relaxing hot bath?"

"A shower would be fine."

"No, I insist. After all, I am a houseboy."

Somewhere in his twenties, I figured, although the beard could have made him look older. "Oh my god," he said, when I was naked.

"It's gotten me into my current mess, so I'm not real happy about having gilded organs."

"Tell me about it while I wash you."

I did. He was all ears. He was also non-sexual in bathing me. I felt the tension begin to lesson, the longer I soaked and he scrubbed. I thoroughly enjoyed the way he was gentle with my body. When he had dried me off, he said, "You're still way too tight. I think you need a massage."

"Really?"

"You'll love it."

I lay on his bed on my stomach. Ric, which is what he told me to call him, took off his clothes. His toned torso was a mass of short, dark hairs, which continued on down his legs. He was the hairiest guy I'd ever seen. He had a good body and an uncut cock. Figured. We were both in the wrong churches and wrong pews.

He applied oil to my skin and rubbed and kneaded my muscles, making me feel great. With the hot bath, I was ready to conk out. He kept talking to me, though, probably to keep me from doing so. He told me how beautiful my slender body was and how impressive my buttocks were, given the leanness of my body. It felt so cool to have my cheeks manipulated and my crack brushed without having my hole entered.

Then he made me turn over and repeated the routine. He started at my shoulders and worked down all the way to my toes. I was semi-tumescent by then but also relaxed. He worked back up my legs, giving my inner thighs some welcome teasing before taking my cock into his slippery hand. It responded like a good massagee. A finger from his other hand did go inside my rosebud now, as he told me that I was the most beautiful boy he had ever seen. I figured that David must have been stingy with his favors, because he was the most stunning guy I knew. And Seaton, the shit.

He finger fucked and masturbated me, making my subdued body want to float away. I would never have guessed that I could have come with such ferocity after how low I'd felt upon arrival. But I did. Ric called my coming a moonshot, and he lapped up what I'd expelled.

I slept with him that night. He didn't demand any sexual favor in return. He just held me as I drifted off to sleep.

However, the next morning I awoke to a full feeling in my colon. Surprise, Ric was in there. "Are you awake?"

"Yes."

"Is it okay?"

"Yes." I lifted my leg and his hard-on drilled me good. He was a panter and a whiner and a moaner and groaner as he pounded into me. For a few minutes, anyway, because he was a screamer in orgasm, which took him no time at all to achieve. Then he blew me with the same gusto. Maybe that was why David didn't like to make it with him.

He took me shopping, which I did not want to do. I wanted to save every penny I had and hoped that Kip would either forgive me or at least give me more money. But Ric was right; I needed clothes sooner or later. I wore some of his during our shopping spree.

"Couldn't we just stop at Target?"

"And where do you see one?"

"I'm not familiar with the city. This is my first time. You aren't scheduled for an earthquake, are you?"

"Honey, we don't schedule them. They're a come-as-you-are party. And we're going to one that isn't. The annual houseboy party."

"Will David be there?" He looked hurt.

"Doubtful. He always has something pressing that night. Against his prostate is my guess." David? I had thought that he had me fuck him only because of my enhanced cock.

We managed to squander nearly half of my money with little effort. And with not much to show for it. Okay, the nylon jeans were cool, as was the transparent mesh top. The boots were shit-kickers a Maine woodsman would have been proud of. Ayup. The other stuff was cool, too, but how was I going to get back east now?

"Why would you want to?"

"Because I live there?"

"My beautiful, beautiful Tyler. As we say here, a day in San Francisco rather than a lifetime elsewhere."

"It's nice here, but I'd like a lifetime."

"You'll meet thoroughly fascinating people at the party." Among houseboys? And David wouldn't even be there?

Okay, I looked adorable, as Ric put it. Fortunately the jeans weren't sheer, and Ric promised not to tell anyone that part of me looked like the golden calf. The best part, if you're into animals.

The party was being held in the penthouse of the building. We were greeted by the host, who was a handsome young black named Fletcher. Evidently, in the hierarchy of things, Fletcher ranked at the top floor, although I got the distinct impression that David was among the elite, whatever floor that apartment was on.

Granted, the houseboys were all pretty. They were mostly slim and a number were effeminate, which was fine. No, it was kind of endearing. They were my brothers, even if I wasn't one of them, per se. I thought of having taken down Ashley several notches by fucking him. Yet I came to love him and he me. I thought of the other people I had loved and decided that I didn't want to again. It never went anywhere. To love is to be disappointed, I decided. To have sex is to make your rocks happy. I wished that I hadn't learned the difference yet.

Ric showed me off all around the apartment. There were guys with their tongues practically hanging out. Some just stared at my chest, which I didn't think was all that developed and worth ogling. Others made snide comments after meeting me, which Ric said was jealousy and a sure sign that I was a star. I figured that he wanted me to be one, for his ego's sake.

The lighting in the penthouse was dim, but I was enchanted by the waiters catering the party. They were all nude, except for white bow ties, which stood out on their tanned and brown bodies. But what was really cool was that they had light sticks coming out of their penises. They shone on their own, these little thin sources of light swaying from the boys' bodies. They also illuminated their great, oiled bodies. Awesome. Light my way to boy paradise, I thought.

It was in the music room, where there was a parlor grand Steinway piano, that I saw my own paradise. I knew who it was, immediately. He was dressed in a leather shirt, jeans and boots. When he saw me, his smile spanned the continent. He ignored the person he was talking to, and headed straight for me.

"Your Holiness."

"Not anymore. But it's great to see you, Philip."

"You remember my name."

"Always."

"You two know each other," Ric asked, obviously annoyed.

"We've met."

"So why are you here," I asked.

"I finally got the San Fran route. I'm based here now. Thank goodness I'm out of Chicago."

"But how did you get here?"

"I know Fletcher. Old flame, when he was into flight attendants. Frankly, I'm into gods."

"I'm not one anymore."

"Oh? Should I be sorry?"

"Not as sorry as I am."

"Really?"

Ric had a fit, but Philip seduced me in front of every reveler there, and I wanted to be taken by the beautiful attendant. I also had too much to drink.

Sixteen

I awoke the next morning in his bed. It smelled of him, and my olfactory nerve was greedy for it. As new as it was, I knew whose it was. It was Philip's. I felt the arms tighten around me.

"Are you okay?"

"I think. A little bit of a headache."

"That's reasonable. You had several glasses of champagne."

"I was happy to see you."

"Well, at least you remember that."

"I remember most of it. I think."

"You do. You were the perfect young gentleman. I was the one who insisted that you were coming home with me, to Ricardo's chagrin."

"I do remember that. I guess I was just tired."

"Holding and smelling you was wonderful."

"I like the smell of you, too."

"Good. And, Ty? I've never ever wanted to do this with anyone before, but I want to taste your morning breath."

That was easy. Despite those mouthwash commercials, you forget about how lousy the other person's breath is a couple of seconds into kissing him. Maybe it's a mutual thing that cancels itself out, but Sea and I always kissed when we woke up. His boy taste and mine mingled into erections. So did Philip's and mine. I was hard in no time. I felt that Philip was, too. I swiveled my body on top of his and sat up. I raised up and guided his cock into me. It had been thoughtfully lubricated by Ric, who would probably never speak to me again, but I decided that I needed to apologize, anyway. But not right away.

Philip was hung, but he slid up my colon easily, because his was a modest endowment. Like Seaton's. I banished that thought in a hurry. A day in San Francisco, he said, having the stunning Philip in his body.

"So this was what made you a holiness, I gather. They're beautiful, Ty."

"Thanks. I don't know how they managed to do it to me, but it's real. Unfortunately, a real god is not circumcised."

"Pity. I think you could become mine."

"I feel the same way, Philip."

"Shall we start to see?"

I moved steadily on Philip, his long prick, which I would find out was almost black, ascended halfway up my descending colon. He touched my penis and scrotum with reverence, evidently in awe of the aural magnificence that my boyhood was. He kept me hard and longing. I decided that older guys knew more about sex than I and my other young sex partners. The bonus was that he was as sensual as David, and I deep-sixed my feelings for that houseboy by reminding myself that he resembled Seaton. Then all of a sudden I stopped moving on Philip.

"What's wrong, Ty?"

"Philip, I'm only...." He hesitated, looked away.

"Only what?" Sheepishly, he looked back at me.

"Sixteen."

"Well, I'm not surprised, as young as you look. But if you were twelve I'd fuck you, as long as you could take me."

"Really?"

I nodded. "Look, you're my dream come true, Ty. I want to be yours, too."

I did, and he did. My orgasm occurred with his cum already coating my walls. I wriggled on his insistent hard-on as he teased me into a climax that made me shoot him in the face, it was that emphatic. Man. I lay on his hard, silky brown body with him still in me. Not since Christopher. Not since ... no, I was not going to acknowledge the shit.

Philip's body fascinated me. It was muscular, and smooth, like mine. It was an absolutely wonderful Hershey's milk chocolate color, which he didn't take offense at, when I said it.

We spent the two most wonderful weeks of my life together. It turned out that Philip had taken vacation before starting on the new route. He bought me a bunch of clothes, despite my protestations. We ate out and saw movies. We drove north across the Golden Gate bridge. We rode cable cars and did a lot of other touristy stuff, both getting acquainted with our new home.

"Would you live here, Ty?"

"With you I would."

That wonderful smile again. "Great. Are you homesick?"

"Honestly? Yeah. But I'd rather be with you."

"We'll go back and visit your mom."

"And tell her what? That I'm shacked up in San Francisco with an adult? She'll be thrilled with that."

"I see your point."

"Besides, she doesn't answer her phone. Which, under the circumstances might be good, now that I think about it."

"Whatever you think is right."

"You are. That much I do know."

Life was as sweet as it had ever been. On his layovers, Philip got into the leather scene. Well, so did I, except that I didn't go to the bars with him. He went to make contacts. He wasn't into pain or anything, although I did really come to like being tied up and made to be submissive. As time went on, we became friends with a number of leather guys. The conjugal unit line was that I was eighteen. I don't think anyone believed that for a minute, but they had the good manners to go along with the lie. It was neat, too, to have friends who were older. Philip was twenty-seven, but he looked a lot younger, so we looked kind of like cool, hip teenagers together on the town. I especially liked dressing up with him. Naturally, he insisted that I had to have a leather wardrobe, so that he could show me off. It felt liberating to be able to go out in the city in my skins. Everything seemed freer here, I was noticing. We sometimes even held hands while we were walking.

And making love in leather became a real turn-on to me. We almost always wore our high engineer boots. I liked wearing chaps to be fucked. Seeing Philip in his really got my motor running, framing his dark cock and balls the way they did. I especially liked being tied or cuffed to the bedroom door. That made me helpless, and the way I would stand would make my round butt exposed and vulnerable to him. I loved being taken that way. Fucked silly while helpless.

Or just taking me on my back wearing the chaps. It was the reenactment of a video scene we'd watched. "This is the way a boy likes to be with his master," the voice says. "Together in chaps and boots. The master loving his boy with his mouth, showing him how much he cares for him. The boy's legs raised in submission to his master, exposing his ass while he's being sucked. The master pleasuring his boy before putting his big cock inside the now-excited youth, his body begging to be fucked, his surrender to the man complete in revealing shiny black leather." And Philip would take me that way—how I loved to be fucked with his long tool!

My genitals were not a big deal. Philip liked them, but he didn't fixate on them. "I'll take an almost-god, who's an adonis, any day," he would say. He did like to fit me with a plain black leather cock and ball harness, because it looked dynamite against my golden skin. Sometimes that and my collar were all I wore around our apartment.

He showered me with love, and I returned it as much as I could. That made what happened so devastating.

Seventeen

It was a cool, sunny day. The sky looked like a meadow massed with cornflower blooms. I thought of Philip up there in that gorgeous blue sky at about thirty-seven thousand feet and missed him terribly. I forget exactly where I had been, but I was walking back home when I saw Ricardo pulling up alongside me.

"Hey, Ty. Nice duds."

"Hey, Ric. Thanks. Philip's into leather, you know."

"You guys are really together?"

"Uh ... huh ... and never happier."

"Great. How about a ride home?"

"Thanks, but it's not that far."

"Look, I haven't seen you for at least a year, more like two. If you've got time, maybe we can go somewhere and catch up on things."

I shrugged. "Sure." I got in and he drove off.

"Care for a beer?"

"I usually don't drink." He popped one open anyway.

"Go ahead. Treat yourself. A little buzz never hurt."

"Well, all right." He handed me the brew.

"I still can't get over you meeting that flight attendant and falling in love."

"I had met him before on a flight to Denver. It was kind of mutually hormonal."

"And became love."

"Oh, did it ever."

"I'm glad for you, Ty."

Well, I'm sure I've been lied to more times than I know, but that one was a whopper. I don't remember falling asleep, but I woke up with a headache in a darkened room. What the hell? Was I at home? I found and switched on a bedside lamp. No, I sure wasn't home. I sure wasn't wearing anything, either. I shook my head to get rid of the headache, which of course did no good. I wonder if guys are genetically stupid. I suspect. I looked around the room. The furniture looked expensive. I was lying on a king size poster bed with a satin comforter.

(Philip had told me that his parents had one, and he would sneak into their room as a kid, when they weren't around, and rub himself on the slick material. That is, until he started to come. He told me he was scared shitless. First by what his dick had ejected, and second that he'd stained the comforter. He had turned it over, and his mother didn't see the stain for months.)

I got out of bed and walked to what I figured was a closet. It was, but there were no clothes in it. Another doorway showed me a bathroom. That left one more, which had to be the way out. And it was locked. Great. I was being held prisoner somewhere. I peaked out one of the windows, but all I could see was shrubbery. Past the bars. Shit. The second one was the same way. Now I was scared. I tried to think back on what had happened. I was sitting in Ric's car drinking a beer....

The door clicked and opened. A cute guy in his twenties and wearing a golden diaper entered. He was followed by a middle-aged Asian guy with a beard. He spoke.

"Ah, the Golden Lotus Boy has awakened."

Not again. Philip, where are you? "I'm not the Golden Lotus Boy. I'm circumcised."

"I can see. Delightfully so," he said, leering. You are also golden, as the legend says."

"But the legend says that the boy is uncut."

"Tut, tut. Most American boys are circumcised. It is the nineteen nineties after all." Whatever that had to do with it. "So it is perfectly reasonable that the incarnation of Buddha would be altered. Buddha, himself, if he were alive today, would be." Of course I was ignorant of the fact that it was a Jewish custom, which gentiles adopted for health reasons. The Buddha would no more have gotten circumcised than been baptized. "Those at that temple are narrow-minded and misinterpreted the texts. As is your former master."

"How do you know about them and him?"

"It is of no consequence."

"Who are you?"

"Your humble servant and communicant."

"My what? Never mind. I want out of here."

"You are not Tyler Langston, as you suppose. You are the Golden Lotus Boy, and I will not have you defiled and clothed by an unbeliever." I was using Philip's last name as mine now.

"Philip? He's my lover."

"No. The Golden Lotus Boy has many lovers, but he is not

one of them."

"Like Hell."

"There is no discussion. You are a god and will be worshipped like one."

Then he and the diaper left me to stew. I tried the door on the off chance that they'd forgotten to lock it. Silly me. That was genetic, too, probably. I threw myself back onto the bed and wondered what in the world I was going to do. After a while the diaper came back. He really looked sexy in it, I hated to admit. He had a tray of food with him.

"I'm John, Your Holiness. I will attend to your needs. You can ask me any questions you want while you eat."

"How can I get out of here?"

"You can't. The property is fenced and guarded. To protect you."

I snorted. I also saw that there was a salad, rolls and chocolate cake on the tray. I lifted the silver keeper with trepidation. "Veal parmesan?"

"We don't know your tastes in food, but we'll cater to them, of course."

"I thought you'd all be vegetarians."

"We aren't that kind of Buddhists."

"You aren't any, because they don't go around kidnapping people."

"Eat your food before it gets cold, Your Holiness. You don't understand that you're a god, and you must be protected and worshipped. I worship you. You are the beautiful god of the prophecies."

"Oh, come on, John. This isn't another of those crazy millennium things, is it? Besides, gods don't eat. Boys do."

"You are a boy god. We know that you're human. As was our God at one time. But like him, you're divine now." *You're divine, even if you aren't sacred.* Who had said that?

I ate everything, because I was starving. When I finished John knelt before me and kissed my feet. Then he mumbled something about being forbidden and took my cock into his mouth. He swallowed it hungrily, as if mine were the last male organ on earth. He moaned as I grew in his cavity. He almost seemed to be in some kind of ecstasy. Man, you met all types when you were a god. Just when I was throbbing and primed, he froze and cried out on my shaft. Damn, he had come simply from blowing me. I, of course, had not before he relinquished me from his warmth. He looked up at me sheepishly, guiltily, and said, "Thank you, Your Holiness." Yeah, and holiness says thanks for nothing, but I didn't.

Soon another boy came in wearing a diaper and bearing a pillow. He was really cute, too. And I admit that as upset as I was, I wouldn't have minded making it with either of them, although John's guilty demeanor seemed to indicate that I was off-limits to them. That made me bite my lip to keep from crying.

I didn't try to make a run for it through the open door, because John told me that I was well-guarded. Besides, I had no clue about the layout of the place. On the pillow was a necklace with what looked like a diamond. John took it and put it on my head so that the diamond sat on my forehead. I also realized that my head had been shaved again. I had worn a brush cut as Philip's lover, but it was billiard ball revisited now. And they'd measured my head while I was out cold. Geez, that was disconcerting.

The temple was right outside my door, I saw, as we walked into the large room. It was sparsely, but ornately, furnished. I was led to an altar, which I was made to mount and assume the lotus position. There were a few more handsome boys there in the blousy metallic diapers. However, the two who stood on either side of the altar were naked. They were young but they had wonderfully buffed bodies that were tanned and shining with good health, enhanced, it appeared, with a light coating of oil. Their heads sported striking golden blond hair. They were nude, so their fat, meaty cocks draped down enticingly in front. I licked my lips and wondered if the lotus boy could name his sex partners. Then I had a terrible thought. My eyes shot to their crotches, in turn. I let out my held breath. Their ball sacs were not only intact, they were cradled in fine gold mesh. I breathed a sigh of relief. I didn't need any more eunuchs on my behalf. Nor on my conscience. But I *did* need those two beautiful boys in my bed. I really did.

Funny how I'd forgotten about Philip all of a sudden. In my defense, I think I realized already that I had no hope of rescue. No one knew where I was. Except for Ricardo, I had no doubt. But Philip had no idea that I'd had the unfortunate encounter with the houseboy. So who would know where to look? The answer: no one. Simply no one.

The prayer service was boring but mercifully short. Odd Job's cousin, whose name was Zhao, approached me and bowed. Then he told me that he already felt the spiritual energy descending on him and his followers and that many others were sure to follow and convert at the sight of the lotus boy. Great. Another Sun Yung Moon in the making. And I was the accomplice. He asked me what my wishes for bed were, and I said, "These two gorgeous specimens." Without turning their heads, they both smiled, which I took to be approval. Zhao scowled. Figured.

"We will discuss this, holiness."

So we went back to my room.

"What's to discuss. I'm the lotus boy, and I want to have sex with my acolytes."

"Of course, of course. But you are going to be famous, holiness, and I will be the reason. So, I thought that you might show your thanks by giving me some of your favors, too."

It was a lost cause. I reconciled myself to having to put out for him, if I wanted to have the pleasure of those studly buffed boys in my bed. Besides, he held all the cards. I was his prisoner. He wasn't much to look at with his clothes off, either. However, I noticed immediately that he didn't know what Degree or Mennen or Ban were. I was going to have to ask John for a can of Lysol spray.

Naturally he wanted to kiss, and his mustache was scratchy. I hoped that he wouldn't want to rim me. And he didn't. After I kissed him passionately and he was fully erect, he lifted my legs and pushed his little penis into me. He rutted for the better part of two minutes before coming. So it wasn't as bad as I expected. I could handle a five-minute drill every now and then, certain that it would be more now than then.

After he left I sat on the toilet to get his junk out of me. While I was on there, I heard someone call me. "In here." The two beauties appeared at the door, grinning. "I need to take a shower, once I get this gunk out of me."

"We won't tell, but there's another way," the one said, pulling back the shower door. "Yep, it's got one."

"One what," I asked, standing.

"An enema attachment. Oh, sorry, holiness. I'm Matt, and this is Steve." I kissed them instead of shaking hands.

Matt turned on the water, and we piled into the tub. We let the warm spray warm our skin as we did some three-way kissing. Their lips were surprisingly full, and they felt oh-so-good on mine. We were all kind of waving happily at each other in no time. I said that I was ready for the enema and braced myself against the long wall of the tub. Matt inserted the stainless steel phallus into me gently. Steve hit the diverter, and a gush of hot water churned into me. I arched my back from the sudden filling pleasure

"Are you okay, Your Holiness?"

"Great. It feels fucking great." I looked down at my belly and smiled at the slight distension there. I was getting hard again, too. Just then Matt withdrew the nozzle. For a few seconds, nothing happened. Then I had world-class diarrhea. I kept shitting water in prolonged steams for about five minutes. "Man, that was good. Now you two." I did them in turn. It was so cool to see the pleasure they got from being filled with the water, and then to watch it flow like a waterfall from them. I cut loose with a couple of enema farts that echoed off the tile and made us laugh. The others did, too. After we were finished peeing the wrong way, we showered. Not surprisingly, we hadn't expelled only the water, given how much had been pumped deep into us.

In bed they lay on either side of me and kissed me. They worked down my body slowly, stopping at my armpits to subdue the straight, soft black hairs there. I shuddered to think that Zhao might have wanted me to do that. They thought it was from the pleasure they were giving me. I noticed that their eyebrows were brown and saw the dark roots. The golden color of the dye job was beautiful. It looked even better juxtaposed with the dark underlayment and eyebrows. Brown eyes, too. Over cheekbone cliffs. God, what gorgeous guys!

I played with their finely jeweled pouches, fascinated by the sexy enhancements. Then I stroked their cocks as long as I had access to them. After that I just enjoyed looking at their muscles rippling under their light brown skins. They had hugged me between them in the shower, and the feel of their muscles pressed against mine was wonderful.

They were both at my genitals now, licking my scrotum and then up my cock. They sucked my head together. That was the first time I'd had two guys suck on me. It felt cool, but it looked even hotter. Two blonds with thick, pouty lips worshipping me as if I really was their god! Well, come to think of it, I was. I was curious to know how they had come to live wherever we were living. Steve let Matt have my glans. He spread his lips sideways and moved up and down my shaft. "Guys, I'm going to come in a minute, if you keep that up."

They stopped immediately, if reluctantly. They got me up to kneeling. Matt sucked on my nipples while Steve made love to my rosebud. Then when I was going soft again, he resumed sucking me. I could feel Steve's tongue dart in and out of me. At least we were all very clean down there. Then I thought how much I was already looking forward to another enema with them. Yeah, I'd let Zhao fuck me for the chance to spend hours of playtime with these two stud puppies.

When I was solidly erect, Matt came off me. Now the problem. They both wanted me to fuck them. Well, they didn't care which one I came in, they just wanted my gold rod in them. We solved the logistical problem by Steve lying down and Matt on top of him. Steve raised his legs, spreading Matt's. So I had easy access to both of their holes. And it was so erotic to see their metal pouches pressed together. Not to mention their bubble butts begging me to use them. I entered Steve first and pumped away as Matt rubbed his body against his fellow acolyte's. They were kissing deeply, too, which was a further turn-on. I moved quickly into Matt and pumped away. I smiled, noticing what I had glimpsed in the shower. On his right buttock was a tattoo of a golden lotus blossom. They belonged to me. I wanted them to belong to me. I wanted sex with them at least once every day, they were such beautiful creatures.

I divided my time between the two of them, enjoying cleaving their hard asscheeks until I came in Steve. The two of them spasmed from Matt's frottage soon after me. Afterward, we lay and talked for a while to await our recovery. I fingered their chained sacs, still captivated by them.

"How come you guys wear these?"

"The master wanted us to. He thought they'd look sexy on us," Matt said.

"He was right."

"Yeah, we love them," Steve said.

"How do you take them off?"

"We don't. The guy who fitted us closed the final link with a pliers," Steve said.

"Besides, guys with pierced nipples don't take the rings off," Matt said. That was a point.

When we went at it again, we repeated the scene. This time I came in Matt long after they did, because they had the luxury of their luxurious natural lubricants still on their bodies from the first time.

"I'll be your slave and follow you anywhere, holiness," Steve said.

"Me, too. For sure."

"Thanks, guys. How old are you?"

"Fifteen," Matt said.

"We've been pumping iron since we were thirteen."

"And shaving our bodies for almost that long. Not that we have that much to shave. You know, a boy can't wait to shave his beard. A buff boy can't wait to shave his legs and armpits." We laughed. I knew that I was going to really, really like these guys.

We spent the night together. I was nestled between the two muscle studlets, and it gave me a strange sense of security, even if they were younger than I was. And I had no doubt that we would get to the point where we would be practically inseparable.

I found out that they had been recruited by Zhao in San Francisco at a Chinatown speakeasy, where they could drink beer. I wouldn't have been surprised if he owned it. Anyway, he made them an offer they couldn't refuse; plenty of sex and sun and weights. In return, all they had to do was to be naked and beautiful. And let him suck them off once in a while. They knew that I existed, from Zhao's talking, and they admitted that they had wanted to faint, when they actually saw me emerge from my room and saw that I was real.

They did have sex with one or two diapered boys, but they had been groomed to serve me, whenever I appeared. The others were temple slaves, who were the real acolytes, but who also templed more with Zhao than they did with the temple.

Eighteen

Zhao decided that he was going to push the Cult of the Golden Lotus Boy through direct mail and over the internet. I guess he got cold feet about having throngs of people come to his house. That was fine, because I really didn't need to sit exposed to hundreds of strangers, even as exhibitionistic as I was finding myself to be.

I was photographed in numerous poses, not all of them for cult solicitation. I had the distinct feeling that Zhao was going to sell photos of me unrelated to my godheadedness. And I wasn't sure if I was eighteen yet, so he was taking a chance.

One day he decided that I needed a diamond in the cleavage of my glans. I was incredulous.

"Isn't that gilding the gilded boy?"

"No, it is enhancing him with the most precious stone known to man. Also a larger one for your forehead."

"Oh, no you don't. You can implant one in my cock but not my forehead."

"I can implant one anywhere I want, because I own you boy/god."

He was right, of course. It was times like that when my spirits would ebb dramatically. It made my missing Philip that much more severe. Honestly, I always missed him, except when I was with Matt and Steve. Even once then. I was telling them of my exploits as the lotus boy. Naturally Philip became the central part of my life after Kip threw me out. I broke down while telling them how wonderful my life had been with that most beautiful, loving man. And I would never see him again.

Philip had taught me so much about myself. He'd shown me my submissive nature, which of course had always been there. In fact, he made me celebrate it, without degrading me. We were equals in our marriage. But more importantly, Philip had shown me what love between two people could be. The intensity. The beauty. The mundane made special, because it was shared by two people, who cared deeply for each other. I wore my boots and my collar proudly. Philip wore me proudly. I grew up in that relationship, secure in the knowledge that no one in the world loved me more and that no one in the world would safeguard me the way he did. My taking his name, unofficially because I was underage, was testament to that.

Tyler Cho Langston. Now I was somewhere else again. I had no name, except for my divine designation. And I had no rock, no Philip.

However, I did have Matt and Steve. As time passed, sex became more fluid among us. It didn't become mechanical, just more comfortable as we became attuned to each other's body. We even got to the point where they could each take each other and me up their asses at the same time. In order not to lose muscle tone, we took enemas, of course. It was fun to have water fights with our asses. We were silly, I admit, but I loved these two buffed muffins. They kept me from despair.

Zhao's demands on me were surprisingly few, but odious nonetheless. Still, I had the comfort of Steve and Matt with me every night now. I had also come to like John very much. He was unfailing in his devotion to me. He also never again tried to suck me.

"You know, you're really pretty, John. I appreciate how you serve me more than I can say."

"It's my pleasure, Your Holiness. I was born to serve. I'm glad you've forgiven me for my sacrilege during your first day here."

"There was nothing to forgive. You were just being a horny teenager."

"Always, I'm afraid."

"Why? There are so many beautiful boys here." He blushed but said nothing. "Come here, John."

He approached me, tentatively. I pulled his head down and kissed him. His hunger shocked me. I met his own passion and felt his pouch. That stopped mine. We looked at each other. I undid his golden diaper. "Please don't, holiness." I did, anyway. The sight was heartbreaking, in a much greater way than what people do to the tails of cocker spaniels.

"Oh, god. How did this happen, John?"

"I'm sorry you saw it. I displeased the master."

"And he cut off your cock?" He had only a stub above his fat scrotum. He had no glans, which outraged me. I put my mouth on it. The little thing twitched.

"Please, holiness."

"John, I want you to feel good."

"I can't."

"We'll see."

I tried my damndest to make love to the stump but failed. I apologized to him and then remembered that he had been able to come by sucking me off. I told him to do it. I would deal with Zhao later. It was heartbreaking to watch John suck on me, knowing that I was his only salvation. I had felt his scrotum as I was dutifully sucking on him. His balls were almost the size of walnuts. He came once more, to our mutual relief. The amount was amazing.

"You don't know what this means to me."

"I do, of course. Blow me whenever you want, John."

"You are a god."

But that was the problem. I wasn't. I was being used. After seeing how John had been mutilated, I went on the offensive with Matt and Steve. I needed to secure their support. They were flabbergasted that John had been altered like that. Then outraged.

"Zhao did it, for some reason."

"You never do that to a boy," Steve said.

"Unless you're a sadist with a divinity complex."

"And he is?"

"He did it to John."

"Wake up and smell the real god, Matt."

"I'm not a god, guys. By now you know that I'm just a boy with golden stuff. That Tyler Langston misses Philip Langston, you guys notwithstanding. That sex with you is making love, because we love each other. I'm not a god. But John is a boy to whom an unspeakable thing has been done."

"He has only a stump?" Matt asked.

"Why would you doubt Ty?"

"I don't know."

"He has a fucking stump, Matt!"

It got a little contentious from there. One of the guards looked in on us. Standing on the bed, I smiled sweetly and told them that I'd had a hot flash. I made my long gold cock sway for effect. Then we retired to the bathroom and closed the door, in case we started shouting.

"Remember, he's done this and they've let him," Steve said. John had told me that he wasn't the only one. I figured all of the diapered boys had been altered, but they hadn't been, because my playmates had had sex with a couple of them, who were normal.

"Why?" Matt voiced my question, too.

"I don't know. Power, I think. But if you castrate a boy, he ceases to have sexual urges. I learned that from Kip's boys. They didn't know what the urges were or why Kip's penis got hard and wanted to fuck them. But cutting off these guys' penises is so cruel, because they still want to come. Except that they don't have enough nerves in their little penis stumps to make it happen."

"You never do that to a boy," Steve said, with a bitter edge to his voice. We were silent. Revenge for John would come, but we needed to be rational about it. As I was thinking that, the possibility that I might have some hope of escaping that place rose just a little bit.

I took John to bed, not knowing whether or not I was doing the right thing. I began by kissing him and caressing his smooth, silky body. Once more he responded ferociously to my kisses. He squirmed under my touch. I was determined to find a trigger that would make him shoot, literally.

I sucked on his nipples and they responded. John sighed in appreciation. Licking his navel didn't help much, nor did my tongue on his abdomen. I kissed the tip of his penis to try to tell him that I found what was left of the organ beautiful, even if it wasn't, because he was. Instead of playing with the stump, I concentrated on his big scrotum. I had no idea if low-hangers had a correlation to cock size, but these were impressive, as were his balls, as I mentioned. I went about licking, kissing and lipping him. I teased the nuts and got a response from everything I was doing down there. First it was a cooing, but it soon escalated into moans. I touched the back of his pouch, and he yelled, "Oh god, oh god...." and shot me in the forehead. It dribbled down my face, and I licked it off my nose, rightfully pleased at having been creamed. Unfortunately, it also brought back memories of kneeling before Philip and having him come on my face. I loved that, it was so humbling.

We lay quietly, embracing and snuggling. Then he thanked me and kissed me. I told him that I wanted to try something else, when he was ready to go again. He asked what, and I told him he would see.

This time I simply fondled him with my fingers as I kissed and nuzzled him. Within a few minutes, he shot another wad as his body shook in delight.

"Man, I mean, God, I can't believe this."

"You still have your ball sac to get you off, John. Try what I did and see if you can do it to yourself." To make a short story shorter, he could. Oh, happy day!

Nineteen

Well, the 'Oh, happy day' was a little premature for me, but not by much. In fact, it was the night before I was supposed to be implanted with the diamonds. Matt and Steve and I had just finished screwing for the third time, so it was late. The lights were out, and we were cuddled and just getting down to serious drowsiness. Then the commotion.

We heard voices and running. Something crashing loudly. More voices. Then what sounded like fighting outside the bedroom door. There was slamming into the wall, grunts, then silence. Then the door was flung open, the overhead light snapped on. And there, dressed in black with a blackened face, stood Seaton Cho. Another, taller blackened face stood behind him.

"Ty!"

"Sea!" Then he made a move as if he were going to attack my playmates.

"No, don't, Sea! They're good guys!" I knelt and put my arms out to shield them.

"Are you sure?"

"Positive. They're my protectors."

"Your what?"

"Never mind." I stood and hugged him.

"Jesus, Tyler, your cock's gold."

"And my sac. That's how I got here. How in the world did you?"

"The hard way. Jesus, Ty, your stuff's gold."

"We've established that."

"Come on, let's go. Put on your clothes."

"I don't have any clothes. And neither do Matt or Steve."

"I don't care about them. I care about you."

"Well, I care a hell of a lot about them. They're coming with us."

"We're taking them," Sea's companion said.

"You're all naked."

"And you're still a master of the obvious."

"They're not coming."

"Yes they are! They ran away from home and are underage. I don't want the authorities to get a hold of them. Come on, guys. He suffered brain damage as a kid."

"Brain-damaged, they are definitely coming with us. And coming soon, I hope," the companion said.

There were guards sprawled here and there, and I wondered how two young guys managed to take out all those people. Then a third person appeared and joined us. Sea hastily introduced them as Alex and Nicky. Then we hurried off. As we did we heard shouting behind us. It was Zhao. He was running toward us. Seemingly out of nowhere, John appeared and tripped the fat man, sending him lurching onto the toppled knight's suit of armor, and the lance was now sticking up through his back. I watched his eyes get big and his arms reach for me in what appeared to be one last, desperate entreaty.

Then he appeared dead. John smiled, blew me a kiss and gave me the thumbs-up sign. I wanted to go back and hug him, but Sea grabbed my arm and yanked me along. I looked back once more. Man, his mutilated penis really did look sexy. I smiled.

They had a sexy black Jeep parked outside the estate. It was awfully cozy with four of us in the back, but cozy was good, because I was sandwiched between Steve and Matt. Well, next to Sea, who was holding me. But he didn't seem to mind the arrangements, either. Besides, it just felt so cool to be naked with Matt and Steve in the back of the Jeep. Well, and to be held by my older brother.

"How in the world did you find me?"

"Ty, my momma had a stroke. She's coming along, but she's in a nursing home for rehabilitation. Her left side's still a little weak. But eventually she'll be okay."

"That's why I couldn't get her on the phone."

"I turned off the machine. Her close friends knew what happened, so I just thought it was better to forget the phone calls. Anyway, I called Boston, because that's where my momma said you were at. At some religious school. So I called and all I got was dog breath from that charlatan Lao. That's when I called Alex and Nicky. We were together at Valley Forge, remember I told you?"

"Vaguely, but it's good to meet you guys."

"Likewise the adonis of the Cho family," Nicky said.

"You got that right," Alex said.

"Okay, he is. Satisfied? Where was I? Oh, we paid Lao a visit and extracted the information on your whereabouts, although he was not happy about our methods. Then we chased you across the whole damn country. And lost you again when we met Philip. Nice guy, by the way. I like him."

"Gorgeous nice guy you mean, Sea," Nicky said and winked at me.

"Yeah, yeah, he is."

"Are you jealous, Sea?" I asked.

"He is," Alex said.

"Why?"

"Because you're my kid brother, and you were my first love."

"Christopher was your first love."

"You both were." He kissed me.

"Thanks. You both were, too. And thanks for the comments about Philip, guys. I really love him."

"It's obviously mutual. He was distraught when we caught up with him," Alex said.

"That's an understatement," Nicky said. "Honey, for him the sun rises and sets on you."

"Well, a master's lost without his slave."

"Master? You're a leather slave? And with a black guy, at that?"

"What's that supposed to mean?"

"Nothing. I just never knew you were into black guys."

"Only one. Who's more accurately into me." The guys laughed. Sea didn't. Figured.

"Anyway, we hit the brick wall with Philip. He told us he'd left for Chicago that morning, and when he came home you were gone. He reported you missing as soon as he could. He knew something had happened, because you had a great relationship and you were even using his surname. Is that true?"

"Yes, Sea, I love him that much. Go on."

"So, we didn't know what to do, except that we were back to square one. So we went back to that Thai guy's houseboy and grilled him."

"He was so grillable. Yummy," Nicky said. Alex laughed. I could tell that Matt and Steve were really getting into the spirit of things from their laughter.

"Will you stop interrupting? Anyway, we found out about the party where you met Philip. David knew, because Ricardo told him."

"That's who drugged and kidnapped me."

"I know! One more interruption and I'm shutting up."

"Interruption!" Nicky. I liked him. Alex, too.

"Very funny. Anyway, we leaned on this Ricardo, having nothing better to do, and he finally cracked."

"He was not yummy. But we cracked him, too," Nicky said.

"In a nutshell, he confessed that he'd taken you to this guy in the Berkeley Hills, who believed in the Golden Lotus Boy, and he thought that was you, from what he understood David to say," Alex said.

"Uh, huh. Ric saw my genitals. I'm glad you cracked him."

"How did he see them?"

"It was before I met Philip."

"Slut. Why didn't you ever call me?"

"I couldn't remember that you went to Valley Forge."

"Hell, that's ancient history. I graduated from there this past June."

"Then how was I supposed to get in touch with you? And are you going to be a big military guy now?"

"Now that you're married, I guess so."

"Matt and I aren't, Sea," Steve said. That made us all laugh.

Twenty

Homecoming was indescribable, especially in light of the fact that there were two nude buffed boys with me. Philip overlooked that and offered the guest bedroom to Matt and Steve. I knew that I had a lot of explaining to do to Philip about my unfaithfulness, but I didn't care. I was home again, and I would gladly exchange any punishment, any debasement, for being there. None was forthcoming, he was so thrilled to have me back. It was mutual. And to have Seaton there, too.

Philip and I were touching and kissing on our bed after some pretty intense lovemaking. It was so good to be with him, so wonderful to melt into his hard body. Then we heard the first noises. We tried to ignore them, but they became insistent.

"We're going to be thrown out of this apartment."

"But what a way to go, it sounds like." He looked at me and smiled his fabulous smile.

"It's so good to have you home, dear." We went to explore the building disturbance taking place next door in the guest room.

The guys were already sweating from their seminal attractions and exertions. Specifically, Alex and Nicky with Matt and Steve. Sea was trying to be involved, but he looked lost. I looked at Philip, who smiled and nodded. I kissed him and headed for the bed. I knelt next to my brother, hugged and kissed him.

"Seaton, shit that you were, you've become an absolute fox, and I want you to fuck me." You should have seen the eyes of the little cadet from Valley Forge. As I pumped his penis, I said, "Of course my master will have to fuck you."

"Anything for one last chance at you, Ty."

When he was hard, I lay down and reared back. As in olden times, he took me easily, sliding all the way in. He waited for Philip to fill him, eyes closed, the hint of a smile on his lips as he was being possessed. Then they set up a steady coordinated rhythm. I loved having Sea in me again and making it with him together with Philip. After looking up at my beautiful, muscular brother for a while, I turned to look at the accompanying action next to the bed.

I guess that it was then that I realized that Alex and Nicky were identical twins. They were kissing with my temple playmates, heatedly. Matt was running his right leg up whoever's left leg it was. Seeing that I started to get hard. He and Steve were so sexy for such young guys.The sexy leg play continued as did the lengthening of my gilded cock.

Then the two boys almost simultaneously dropped to their knees and took the identical arousals into their mouths. Their bubble butts were touching, and I thought how cool it would be if a double-headed dildo were inside them, keeping them joined. I knew that Philip had one, although he had no use for it since we fell in love. Unless....

Alex and Nicky were making out like crazy now as the boys continued to worship them. Watching my friends enjoying themselves on the twins made me happy and sad. As I mentioned, they ran away from their homes to live a freer life at the temple. But it was sad that their home lives had forced them to do it. On the other hand, I was happy that they were able to celebrate their sexuality, and their glorious teenage bodies, so freely.

Now the twins were fucking them bent over. They were holding each other's head and kissing as Alex and Nicky were taking their measure with pretty impressive endowments. Both of which had been in my brother's body, I was certain. They were masturbating my buddies as they fucked them. This was okay with me, as I wanted Steve and Matt to have as much physical pleasure as humanly possible.

The twins were going at it fiercely now, holding onto hips and driving their cocks home. The boys were doing themselves, as a result. I swear that Alex and Nicky came at the same moment, both their faces screwed up in pleasure, simultaneously. The guys followed, spitting and dribbling their essences in relief.

I returned to being fucked and fucked by extension. My legs were around Sea's neck, and Philip was licking the soles of my feet. I know, a master usually doesn't do that, but he can do whatever he wants with me, sexually, so it was no surprise.

Just as his breathing got really ragged, Sea pulled out of me and jerked himself to orgasm. His come splashed onto my golden sex and flowed down it. He got on all fours and went down on me as Philip took him doggy style. It was really a rush to see and feel my brother blowing me. He had never sucked me off before. I'll bet he had Alex and Nicky many times. But at that moment it didn't matter. It was a kind of rite of passage for me to have him do that. Maybe confirming that I was an adult now, if barely. I warned him that I was going to come so that he could pull off, but he took everything I shot and swallowed it. Maybe military schools had been good for him.

Twenty-One

"So, how did you figure out it was a tattoo, Ty?" Sea wanted to know.

"When I saw these guys with their tattoos. Gold, like me. And that must have been why Lao had me drugged and on painkillers for so many days. I'll bet it would have hurt like a bitch. I suppose it also explains my decreased sensitivity. And all those hours we were all out."

"Man, I can't get over how really golden it is," Nicky said.

"We couldn't, either," Steve said, grinning, then looked at Philip and turned sheepish.

"What a racket," Sea said.

"You're just jealous because you don't have gold jewels and your brother does," Alex said.

"So are you guys going into the military, too," Matt asked.

"Oh, heavens no. Eight years of that shit is plenty," Nicky said.

"And my dad's given up trying to make Nicky butch. He's just praying that he doesn't end up as my wife."

After we paid the tab, we wandered out into the Castro. Philip and I were in our boots, T-shirts, vests and caps. Sea was in his combat boots, black jeans and T-shirt. The twins had on sleeveless gray T-shirts, black jeans and these really cool, tight, high boots they got when they took a gay paramilitary training course. The boys were the most conventionally dressed in T-shirts, denim shorts and sneakers. Well, we had to get them something to wear. They looked really hot in clothes.

"You know, we're going to have to get you guys a whole wardrobe for the trip," Alex said.

"What trip?" Matt asked.

"Well, that's where we live, and you guys are going to live with us, aren't you?" I swear that Matt's and Steve's faces lit up like flares. They hugged and kissed the guys excitedly. "And we're driving back in the Jeep. We bought it out here, and obviously we have to get it home. Which means stopping at lots of motels for...."

EPILOGUE

Steve and Matt are having a blast as the twins' buffed boy toys. They got one added benefit out of it that they hadn't expected. The twins' family was loaded. So now they're showered with love and fucked regularly and have no material worries. Better still, Alex and Nicky adore them, as they should.

Sea and I flew back to see our mother. Philip came with us. I really felt bad for her. It had been almost two years since she'd had the stroke, but she had fought back and was now amazingly close to her old self. She was thrilled to see me after all those years, and to have us both home. And she liked my hubby. Of course it didn't hurt that Sea had laid it on thick about Philip in advance.

By the way, Sea didn't go into the service; he lives with Mom and goes to see the four other guys down in Pennsylvania regularly for fun and games. He also visits Philip and me several times a year. I think it's great that we're close again. Philip says that he thinks it's also because Sea just can't get enough of the boy with the golden cock. My master should talk!

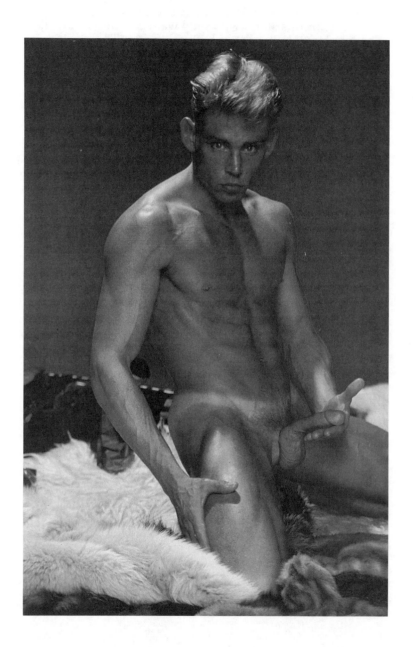

The following novella is based on the life of the legendary early porn star Casey Donovan (aka Calvin Culver). If we were to film this story, we would want one of our favorite bottom boys, hottie Kevin Kramer, to star. The inspiring picture on the preceding page is courtesy of Kevin Kramer, whose life history, as told to John Patrick, appeared in the book *Beautiful Boys*.

*For boys like Casey,
nothing is out of bounds....*

The Sex
Trade

The Lives & Loves of
Casey Cassidy

A Series of Related
Erotic Tales by
JOHN PATRICK

*STARbooks Press
Sarasota, Florida*

"I think the thing that makes guys kind of tap out on me is that when I walk in, they're expecting an attractive guy, but they're not expecting somebody who's intelligent and perceptive and honest. That's the last thing they're expecting.

"When I walk in the door, the whole thing changes—they get really attached, quick. But it's like, Look, can't I just come in here and do my job and leave? Do you have to probe into my past to be able to, you know, understand things?"

—Casey Cassidy, Seasoned Porn Star and Aspiring Stage Actor

Prologue

The apartment is dark, but there is enough moonlight coming through the windows so the lights don't need to be turned on. I like fucking in the dark. As a kid, I discovered that illusion is more exciting than reality, more compelling. I feel stronger when I am in darkness, sensing my surroundings rather than seeing them. One of the reasons I love sex so much is that senses more imaginative than sight—touch, smell, taste—are the most important.

At an early age it became second nature to me to use my sexual power: why was I given it if not to use it? But no matter how calculating I can be, some amount of pleasure is always there, some touch, some taste, some smell. People ask me how I can go to bed with certain men they might find repulsive. I always respond that I believe what my father always said, "You can find some good in everyone," one of many stupid homilies my father lived by. Granted, my father was a jerk and a total drunken loser, but he was right about that—but only when it came to sex. I also learned very early in life that the rest was all bullshit, there are plenty of people you can't find anything good about. The majority of people, in fact.

Besides, I love being wanted, being desired. I love the buzz of the unknown, of potential, of possibility. Being wanted so bad that the john can taste me before he's tasted me. I love the feeling of new hands on me, not knowing how they'll move, where they'll go. The smell of a new client, familiar but unique. The slick slide of sweaty flesh. And the sounds a john makes when he's about to come. The sounds that come from so deep down they seem to be coming from his very depths. I want him to talk to me. When I first meet a man, I don't care what he has to say. I just want to see his mouth move. I want to see how he punctuates his conversation with his hands. I want to see his hands moving. I want him to have to lean in close to share some confidence with me. Then, when we are comfortable with each other, which might take a moment or a couple of hours, I want to hear what matters to him, what he wants to tell to me before we fuck.

But tonight my late-night caller, Gardner, and I skip all the preliminaries. He is not even a paying client; he is my "mentor," my acting coach. He strides into the little apartment

I share with another "mentor," a businessman named Jackson, kisses me hello, and soon he's sitting on the worn leather couch; his shoes are comfortably off, and I, wearing only my skimpiest briefs, start to go down on him. When he is fully hard, I take him by the hand, pull him up from the couch. "C'mon, stud, I'm horny."

He smiles at my own erection, tenting my briefs. "You're always horny," he says.

In moments, his shirt is off, and he's sitting on the bed taking off his socks.

I strip off my briefs, dab a bit of K-Y on my hole and bend over, shoving my ass in his face. I am ready for him, but I don't rush him; I let him go at his own slow, agonizing pace.

His finger rubs ever so lightly around my butthole, lubing itself as it does, causing my ass lips to pucker and then open up. Slowly he inserts his finger into my hungry hole, which I know is by now pouting eagerly, although it is so dark Gardner can't see it, but he moans when two fingers pop in easily. "You've been fucked today?" he asks, full well knowing the answer.

"At noon. That guy from Japan."

"Can't get enough?"

"No...." I groan, because he shoves three in, then four.

He groans a low animal growl, and I know he is loving my talking about my earlier sex as much as I had. He finger-fucks me, slowly at first, then faster. I go on about how the Japanese visitor does it, doggie at first, then ends up missionary, so he can watch me come. Gardner loves it when I describe how my clients come inside my ass. He begins twisting his finger inside me and I can't hold back any longer; the heat is too much.

My skin is now copper-colored from my days in the sun at Fire Island so I present a stark contrast to the pasty white of Gardner's skin as I move onto the bed. The dark and the light. The top and the bottom. The young and the older. I love contrasts.

"Put it in!" I cry out. I get on all fours with my ass in the air, and he gets behind me. I can feel his heavy breath on my asshole as his tongue darts in for a moment or two. He squeezes my cheeks, rubs my crack. Finally his big cock is poised at the entrance. I push back, and he thrusts into me.

He goes in all the way to the base without effort; I have been well-prepared. I don't tell him that the Japanese client paid to do it twice today. After the first fuck, he took me to lunch, and then he took me back to his hotel room for another round. I earned an extra hundred. Hearing that might be too much for even Gardner. I only tell my men what I want them to know, what I think they need to know, whatever I know will turn them on.

Sometimes, after I have been fucked out, Gardner will just face-fuck me with his thick, smooth cock, his hands holding firmly to my head as he thrusts, deeper and deeper into my throat. But this is what I prefer, having him bang away for at least half an hour, and come deep inside me. This is my idea of heaven.

Now he climaxes, and I am groaning loudly as the power of his punishment of my aching asshole pushes me over the edge. I jerk myself to orgasm, my piddling load barely marking the sheet beneath me. It feels so good, to be consumed with pleasure and pain in equal measure—too good really.

"When's your lover due?" I ask after I return from washing myself off.

He's sitting up in bed, smoking a cigarette. He never showers after sex. He says he likes having the smell of me on him as long as possible.

"Tomorrow night, I think."

"I'm jealous of him, you know."

"Why?"

"How can I not be?"

"Don't," he says, cutting me off. "Don't get started...."

"I'm not starting...."

"I love Chad, you know, it's just that...." he hesitates.

"Just that what?"

"Well, he's ... well, he's cold."

"Cold?"

"Look, that's all I can say. Cold."

"But...."

"I love him very much. I wish I didn't."

"I hope he never finds out about us, then."

"Oh, he won't."

The apartment is hot and still. We sleep naked on top of the sheets and I fall asleep in the strong arms of someone else's lover.

I. The Beginning

"There's a swagger to the boys in L.A., caused in part by the bulge in their pants. There must be a sign in Kansas that reads 'Over 9 inches, head West' because out here big cocks are the rule rather than the exception."
—Edward Patrick, writing in Blueboy magazine

It all began on celluloid, where so many exotic yearnings begin, where the boys are put up before you, infinitely desirable. Yes, believe it or not, people in Hollywood still say, "You ought to be in pictures." Hollywood is a town on the make and, to many, it still is the dream capital of the world. Guys who come from all over and think that a handsome face and a big dick will open all the doors. Their bulging baskets are their passports to success, and for a new face in town, there is a brief moment when all those small town dreams do seem possible.

But my own dreams, while furthered in Hollywood to be sure, began in Manhattan. I had never even *thought* of going to Hollywood. Not far from where I was born, in Brooklyn, I was discovered—immortalized, if you want to stretch it a bit—on celluloid in "Fire Island Fantasies."

Granted, I had always dreamed of being in a movie, but being in a movie where I would suck and fuck was something that had never occurred to me.

That fateful weekend when I was approached at a friend's house on Fire Island. At first I said, "Thanks, but no thanks," but everybody kept telling me, "Go for it!" So, what the hell, I thought. The clincher was that my co-star for one sequence was to a black youth known to me only as Aaron. He was tall, handsome, hung—true carved-ebony perfection. I had never even been with a black man before, but when I saw Aaron, I knew I wanted to venture into new territory.

He smiled at me, and I thought we clicked, but his eyes were covered by dark glasses and I had no idea what was hidden beneath them. He had a high-pitched musical voice, reminiscent of Smokey Robinson. I could see him appearing on *Soul Train*. Instead he was working for an escort service in Manhattan and now would be fucking me in a porn film.

Pinky Blake was to be the director; his partner had a house on the Island and we would be making that home base for the filming. I had known Pinky casually; he was rather plump, with bland features, a ruddy complexion and, with his puff of blond hair, I thought he bore a striking resemblance to Liberace.

His partner, the man with the money, was Carmine, of Sicilian origin. Carmine's hair was patent-leather black and greased back, his eyes brooding, his nose too long, and his mouth too thin. He was handsome in a cold, mean way. Guys who had been with him said he was hung like nothing they had ever seen, and that he should be before the cameras, not behind them. He wasn't interested, but he was flattered when they told him that. Pinky had told me that Carmine's brother was somehow connected to the Mob in Detroit. Like a lot of guys I was later to meet in L.A., Carmine was, in effect, being paid to stay away from home.

When Carmine was present there was a weird tension on the set, as if everyone was afraid to bust loose, act crazy, or they might end up missing one night, or at least have their legs broken. It was Pinky's dream to make movies in Hollywood, not Fire Island. I got the idea he wanted to be bi-coastal, with his lover and money-man on the East Coast and him having fun on the West Coast.

The plot, if you could call it that, had me playing the boy-toy of a gentleman of inherited wealth. This was hardly a stretch for me, of course, because I had several wealthy gentlemen in Manhattan who were helping to put me through acting school. In the film, I spend most of my time cruising the bushes and beaches looking for new dick to suck in a teeming Fire Island bleached by the sun. Aaron meets me, filmy with sweat, and I take him back to my wealthy patron's house (he was conveniently in Manhattan making more money).

As porn was in those days, this is a silent movie, with music dubbed in later, so the gestures and facial expressions had to carry the day. Pinky shot it so that you could see I was responding to the elegant angles of the young black's face, the beauty of his body. Then, at the house, when Aaron removed his bathing suit, his long, thick, cut cock seemed to shimmer on his frame like golden chocolate. We hugged, and I brought my hand to the cock. I gasped at having it so close and finally in my hand. I kissed and licked his erect nipples, feeling his chest hairs on my cheek. He nibbled my earlobe and breathed hotly into my ear, making me crazy with desire. It was so exciting that I put away my fears of being filmed and got down to business.

I got down on my knees to sample his goods. I licked his cock-shaft and lightly tongued his piss-hole. I closed my lips upon the tip and slowly took the whole, throbbing cock into my mouth. He gasped as I worked on it. When I released it, he began slapping it against my cheek, coating my face with saliva and pre-cum. I was amazed by how big it was hard. He moaned as consumed every inch of it, then slowly brought it back out again and twirled my tongue around the head as Pinky moved in for a close-up.

I continued to worship Aaron's cock, starting at the base and working my way up, flicking the tip with my tongue. Then quickly I wrapped my mouth around it again, taking in as much as my throat would allow. My head bobbed up and down over it, and I could feel my saliva spilling from the corners of my lips and down the sides of the now fully hard cock. He moaned and gripped my head with firm hands. I hungrily sucked his cock, starting at the tip and then working down in fast, fluid motions to his swollen bull's balls. "Yeah," he whispered, "take it. Take it all." He started to fiercely; I felt his warm cock pressing on my tongue and sliding in and out of my throat. I sucked it slow and hard. I took my own hard, throbbing cock in hand and began jerking it.

"Oh yeah, baby, you know how to suck dick."

The words were music to my ears. He pumped his groin against my face. Pulling back on my hair, he pulled me off.

"You want this? You want this in your ass, don't ya? I see your ass down there humping. I'll give you something to hump."

I lay on the luxurious Oriental rug and he dropped between my legs. He thrust a finger into me. "I want this ass." He stuck another finger in and rotated them.

I softly moaned at the intrusion. I pushed my ass back toward the invading fingers. He stuck another finger into me.

This was going to be great. I spread my legs wide, begged for more. Pinky zoomed in to film the finger-fuck of my life in close up.

Removing the fingers from my ass, Aaron spread me wide apart and I pressed back, anxious to feel the hard cock fill me. Aaron reached down and placed his hands on my hips. He forced the head of the cock into me. My breath became heavy; I was panting. Pinky was going crazy.

The cock entered me. Aaron sighed, "That's right, you can take all of it."

He smiled seeing my contorted face agonizing with the strain of the thick member forcing its way inside my ass.

The tears burned my cheeks as they coursed down my face. Pinky didn't see that; he was concentrating on the entry.

"You've almost got it." He had almost all of it in me. Then, a final thrust. "There...." He was snugly inside. Pinky was delighted. "Oh, perfect," he said.

But being filled was not enough. I could feel my muscles begin to contract. I pushed back onto the cock as much as I could. I gasped as I felt him pull the cock nearly all the way out and then force it back in.

"Oh, great ... great," Pinky gushed as he zoomed in to get the re-entry in close-up.

Aaron began fucking me slowly at first and then harder and faster. He was a masterful top.

"Yes!" I shouted between breaths. As Pinky and his camera watched us fuck from straight on, all I could see was Aaron's sweating, straining shoulders, and all the effort he put into the fuck.

Aaron now pumped harder and faster. I closed my eyes and raised my ass higher in the air to greet each of his thrusts as they came down.

Suddenly he slowed. I opened my eyes and, looking up, I saw a wild man staring back at me. He was ready, too soon for me. I raised my ass even higher to accept the final thrusts. Aaron came quickly and painfully. He pulled the cock from me just in time, his load spewing all over my ass. Pinky zoomed in again, telling Aaron to shove it back into me, which he did, gleefully. Now the black began pulling and pushing my hips to-and-fro, rocking my body back and forth on the still-hard cock. The base of it pressed against my pubes as I rocked, bringing me closer to my own orgasm.

I jerked myself and my moans filled the room. I pushed and pulled against the cock stuffed inside my ass, my muscles contracting against it. I began to explode, and Pinky was right on top of me, shooting it all as I came across my belly.

Aaron withdrew the cock, and pulled me closer. He could feel me shuddering still, and it turned him on. Lying on his stomach, he pushed his face into my crotch and began to lick. I could only twitch in response, my orgasm having drained all of my energy. I meekly trembled while he licked me clean and Pinky recorded it all, every last lick.

It was a scene I will never forget, a scene that, if I'm low, always lifts my spirits—to say nothing of my cock. Thank goodness for the VCR.

II. Going Hollywood

To this day, I swear that scene with Aaron is my best. Come to think of it, I did only ten scenes in a total of eight hard-core movies in my entire two-year porn career. Today's so-called "stars" make thirty movies right away and then wonder why nobody calls them anymore. Hell, even after all these years, guys are still calling me! But I tell them, "How could I top what I've done?"

Following the extraordinary success of "Fire Island Fantasies," Pinky demanded that I do a sequel, "Hollywood Fantasies."

In those days, the Century theater in L.A. was featuring dancers on stage in addition to showing porn films. Pinky got the idea that a bodybuilder named Kane and I would be on the bill together and he could film us performing before a live audience. The audience in this case was invited by Pinky.

Kane first appeared in his cop uniform drag, while I was playing his pick-up outside the theater in the alley. Pinky filmed Kane frisking me and shoving me inside, thinking the place deserted, and I then lured him onto the stage.

There was a general murmur of agreement in the audience when I started to strip Kane out of his uniform. He probably didn't really have any idea what was about to happen, because he hesitated a moment and tried to leave the stage when I ripped his shirt off. But the crowd jeered and cheered him to have a go at it. He didn't have any choice.

There was a big hurrah when I finally undressed him to his shorts. Now he stood on stage, tall and proud, and worshiped by all—he was more than six feet tall, massively built, with a smooth body, large chest, muscular torso, washboard stomach, narrow waist, full buns, tree-trunk-like legs, dark curly hair, pouty lips, and blue eyes accentuated by his golden tan. I kneeled before him and worshiped him.

It was obvious that Kane knew he looked good, because he started to pose with a wide grin on his face, lapping up the applause. When I ripped his white boxer shorts off, there was even wilder applause. Kane had not been blessed with an enormous cock that would have been too much to expect, really, considering everything else but what he had was very respectable, and I sucked it to full hardness. The crowd began clapping and shouting, and I played to them, working vigorously on Kane with my mouth.

Finally, pushing me down onto my back, Kane straddled me. We kissed deeply, my fingers moving over his biceps, plucking at his hard nipples. When his eyes closed with pleasure, I lifted myself slightly, taking the cock in one hand and pressing the head against the entrance to my ass. Kane's hands came up to grasp my pecs as I fed the length of him inside me, slowly, inch by inch, until he was all the way in.

He gave a sigh as I began to move up and down. I had meant to tease him a little, to push him out, to prolong the fuck, but I was apparently irresistible to him. "Oh, god," Kane breathed as he surged against me, his climax imminent. He knew he had to allow Pinky to film his climax, so he pulled out just in time. Watching him, I felt powerfully alive, his face contorted before me at the moment of orgasm, his cock spewing cum all over my belly. The crowd went wild.

Kane left and I was told to take a shower while Pinky served some "refreshments" to his audience members.

After showering, I was drying off when Pinky came into the bathroom. I protested as Pinky yanked the towel from my hand. "What are you doing?"

"Starting," Pinky said. He pushed me down a dark hallway and back out onto the stage. Pinky had obviously been doing some kind of strong drugs because he had gotten that mean look in his eyes. I didn't want to argue with him. I had seen that ugly look in his eyes only once before and I never wanted to see it again (at least that time I hadn't the one who had had to survive his torment, I only got to watch). When we got to the stage, I saw there were five men sitting there on little chairs. So I was to be their very own live sex show—filmed by Pinky for posterity! Of course, I could have gotten out if I'd wanted to. All I needed to do was laugh at them, turn it into a joke, and I'd have been out of that stage door and on my way to a client call I had made for midnight. But I didn't laugh. I played along. I don't know why, but I did. But even if I was to perform for them, I wanted them to know I wasn't easy; and I wanted them desperate. Desperate men appreciate it so much more. And then I guess I wanted to show them that whatever they came up with, they wouldn't shock me. I had a dirtier mind than they (or Pinky) could ever imagine.

But I couldn't help being a little nervous as they sat in a row on the stage, because, as I danced around in front of them, Pinky served more "refreshments," washed down with Coke. For me, drugs and sex just don't mix, especially in a group scene. Still, as I danced around them to the accompaniment of the draggy music on the sound system, I could literally feel the excitement in the air.

Eventually, when I had removed my G-string and my cock was bobbing up and down in their faces, they were desperately turned on, high on drugs or not. They leered in silence as I pulled at my cock. I looked at each of them in turn, and their lowered eyes and open mouths made me excited. As I glanced at Pinky, he looked up and smiled slightly. He was impressed, and not just by my hardening cock. He admired my guts, too. He motioned me to start the action. I went to the first man in the row and stood in front of him. He was tall and lanky, and my cock was level with his face. He stared for a moment, his lip quivering slightly. He glanced from left to right, making sure all eyes were on him, then buried his face in my crotch. Soon he was licking and kissing my cock. Sitting forward on the edge of the chair, he pulled me closer and reached around behind me to rub my ass.

As he pulled back and revealed my cock at full hardness, slick with spit, someone whistled softly. Five pairs of eyes caressed me; I'd never held so much undivided attention in my life, and I loved it. Man #1 was still for a moment, just staring.

Then he remembered he had other options than staring and swirled his fingers all over me. Dipping his head, he took me deep. He was carried away by now, and he knew exactly what he wanted. He unzipped his jeans, reached into his underpants and brought out his long, thin cock. He stroked it while fondling and rolling and caressing my cock, giving Pinky a really good show.

I could hear the sounds of him jerking his cock, and he groaned and looked up. He was deep in concentration, focused on my cock and pumping hard with his hand. He was close to coming, his orgasm no doubt building quickly because of the total weirdness of this whole situation and the drugs he'd done. He grunted as the first drops of cum spattered on the floor before him, captured by Pinky's camera. It was then that I noticed Man #2, who had stripped completely, had been jacking off while this was going on and he cried, "Oh fuck," and shot his load all over his exposed belly. Panting slightly, he slumped back.

Well, that was it. The ice was broken. With the cum still dribbling onto the floor from Man #1, Pinky spoke up. "Go over there," he said, pointing to the last man in the row. His cock was out. It was huge. My eyes popped as I knelt down and he put his big hand behind my head and brought it into his lap. He tasted vaguely of cigar smoke, but I gave it all I had, licking and sucking and flickering my tongue as if I weres auditioning for Pinky, as if I hadn't already been cast for the part. I showed him how much I wanted him by taking as much of his cock into my mouth as I could. I even massaged the base of his balls as he was about to come and made him moan appreciatively. Pinky caught the orgasm with his camera as it flew onto my cheek.

I lifted my head at the feeling of someone behind me. I quickly stood and I could feel my asslips opening and swelling and I arched my back against his chest with pleasure. "Hmm," he whispered. It was Man #1 again, and he rubbed his cock in my crack. I loved that the others were watching me as Man #1 prepared my asshole with his spit. "Oh Jesus," I sighed as the head of his erection slid in.

Pinky whispered, "Do it," and Man #1 didn't hesitate.

"Oh, yes," I moaned, leaning forward, kissing Man #5. I needed something inside me.

Pinky came round from behind me and stood at my side to get a better view. I watched him as he watched Man #1 easing in and out of my ass. I felt myself starting to come. This was amazing: it usually took me at least ten minutes to bring myself off. The extra tension caused by all their attention was making everything faster, deeper and wilder than it had ever been before. The climax hovering just beneath my fingertips was like an electric current. It made me twitch uncontrollably. My inner thighs started to tremble and my hands went into overdrive, pumping my cock feverishly. "Oh God," I moaned, "I'm coming."

Everyone groaned appreciatively. Everyone except Man #5, who was getting my load in his face.

The fucking of my ass continued even though I had come. Man #1 did not come. He let Man #3 in. He pulled my shoulders down, manhandling me as he shoved his thick prick into me. It hurt, and brought tears to my eyes, but I loved it. He came quickly, pulling out, spurting his load across my ass as Pinky got his close-up. Man #4 was up next. He was nice. As he kissed and stroked my ass, he put his hands on my hips and forced me down on all fours. I was pulled up towards him and his cock was soon sliding inside me.

"Ooooohhhh," I groaned. He was big. While he fucked me, the rest lined up to get blowjobs. Five men at once. Five times the pleasure.

Man #4's cock was thrusting hard and deep as he took me doggy-style. His fingers were tight around my hips, keeping me still. Someone had crawled under me and cruel fingertips were pulling my nipples so hard I cried out; but no sound came out because my mouth was full of cock. Underneath me, lying sideways like a mechanic, doing some fine tuning, Man #1 was sucking and nibbling on my cock, setting off fireworks in the pit of my stomach. Suddenly, out of nowhere, Kane re-emerged, fucking me once more while they all stood over me, eventually coming onto my belly. It was at that point I realized I wasn't me any more. I wasn't a person, I was just a body—a receptacle for their lust.

Kane joined me in the shower, then asked me to go to the bar next door for a drink.

Without waiting for an invitation, Pinky joined us and pulled up a chair and sat down beside Kane. He was quite gallant to the bodybuilder and to me, even ordering several rounds of beer for us. And while he was sitting next to Kane, he joked a lot with him, telling him stories of his last trip to Fire Island, sometimes slapping Kane's bare back, or gripping parts of his huge thighs, or brushing Kane's crotch with his hands. Pinky plied Kane with so many drinks that the young stud finally passed out, slumped on his chair.

I left them there; I had surely had my fill of amusement that night. My head was light from so much excitement, and I was queasy from too much beer on an empty stomach. Walking back to the hotel where I was staying, I puked several times in the streets and one more time, very violently, in front of my hotel, retching slime and my guts out. I swore I would never drink again.

III. The Roar of Applause

Back in Manhattan, I was back on stage, in acting class, and with the sudden roar of applause, I had reaffirmed that appearing on stage was what I wanted to do for the rest of my days. To hell with film; I loved the applause. I was just performing a lesson, but it went very well and strenghtened my desire to be in the theater.

Fiftyish, balding Gardner, my acting coach, told me my scene was "very good," quite a compliment coming from him. He rarely had anything good to say about anyone's performance. But I think he knew I had given it everything I had that night. I had been gone for some time doing the film and traveling with clients. I needed to get back on stage.

On my way out of the building, Gardner stopped me. "There's a great little cafe on the next block. I was going to stop in for a bite to eat. Care to join me?"

I hesitated; I felt unsure. Gardner certainly knew my story; Alexander, one of my patrons, was a close friend of his, and I knew that Gardner had a boyfriend. I closed my eyes, then quickly gathered my wits, looked at the director and smiled. "Yes, that would be very nice."

"Good," Gardner said with a warm smile.

A bite to eat that night with Gardner turned into candlelit dinners, movies and long walks in the Village. Then one humid evening, we had taken a walk down Christopher Street and stopped for some light appetizers at a favorite sidewalk restaurant of Gardner's. It was there that he said, "My lover is away tonight," narrowing his greedy, pleading, dark eyes. "I'd like you to stay with me tonight."

"I'd like that," I said.

It was the first time he had extended an invitation to his place. When we got to his apartment, without so much as a word between us, we fell into each other's arms. I had been expecting this for so long, yet I was still shocked by it.

There wasn't a single part of my body that did not ache for his touch that night, and I had had a client in the afternoon.

I wrapped my arms, thighs and even the tips of my toes around him, wanting to feel every inch of his warmth against my own. I could smell the spicy aroma of his cologne as I kissed his neck and face.

"I've wanted to do this for weeks," Gardner said in a husky stammer. I teasingly thumbed his nipples, then took them one by one into my mouth. He responded in writhing delight as my soft lips caressed each pec. In between the exhilarating moments of arousal, there were deep kisses and intimate glances.

He forced me down on the bed and his tongue worked a slow, delirious magic in my ass. At the same time, with the forceful movement of my hips, I drove his tongue deeper into me. My body trembled in his arms when he said, "How beautiful you are, Casey."

I was grateful for every day that I was being coached by him, and now I could show it in the only real way I knew. He had helped me overcome my innate shyness. His complete and matter-of-fact acceptance of me at a time when I was untested was now to be rewarded.

"You light up a room, Casey."

"I'm just so glad to see you happy."

"You've got no idea how good it feels to finally hold you in my arms. I have always wanted to fuck you. You know I did."

Before I knew what was happening, he was doing it. Nobody had ever gotten it into me as quickly as Gardner did. He started with me on my hands and knees, but I wanted to see his face, to see his gratitude and watch the coldness in his eyes melt into pleasure. I wanted to hear him moan in ecstasy; I wanted to make him come. He slid his cock deep inside me.

I shuddered and sighed, and he sighed too, knowing that at last I would be his, even if it was for just a moment.

His long, intense thrusts made me squirm. He held on to me, showing me how much he wanted this; how much he'd thought of it, how nothing else mattered right now but this.

Finally he rolled me over and my body was open and vulnerable and waiting for him. He held on to my hips and plunged his cock back inside me.

His groan was full of anguish. I smiled at the sound and grimaced at the sensation of being filled by him. I raised my knees and spread my legs wide.

He watched me now as he fucked me. He was silent, the only sound his breathing as with every stab of his cock I felt the short bursts of breath on my face. Finally he thrust hard, wanting to come, wanting to leave his mark, to claim me as another of his victories.

In the afterglow of our sex, Gardner leaned back into a mass of pillows. He ran his fingers through my hair. I lay, soft and still, against his legs.

"Are you happy now?" I asked him.

"Now that you're here?"

"No, no. I mean, in your life ... generally."

"Oh, I'm pretty happy," he said.

I rolled over on my tummy and looked up at him. "I ... don't even know why I asked that. What does 'happy' mean, anyway?"

"I think it's like porno, you know it when you see it."

"You've been really generous to me, Gardner."

Gardner shrugged uncomfortably.

"Do you know why I don't have a lover?" I asked. I could literally feel his heart thudding.

"No." Gardner shook his head. "I can't imagine why you don't have a lover."

"Because I would miss nights like this, having a different man whenever I wanted...."

He laughed, a touch dramatically. "You're so funny. So free. I mean, Chad's really serious. A very serious young man. He works too much ... he has a family to support."

"Like in wife and kid?"

He nodded. "Two kids, in fact. He married for money."

"Where did you meet?"

"At the baths. He was in town on family business...."

"His wife's family?"

He nodded. Now I understood; I had met many men who had done what Chad had done, but this was a bit different in that Gardner kept insisting that Chad was his "lover." How could this be? How can you have a lover who is a thousand miles away? Yet maybe that was what Gardner wanted, what suited Gardner.

He took one of my hands and tangled his fingers in it. I stayed there, holding on. He kissed me full on the mouth for the first time. And I was kissing him back, and that shattered me and put me together again in one instant.

I left his lips and grazed my teeth along his tight belly and went for his cock. I sucked it to hardness again. Every once in a while I would look up from his crotch; his eyes remained closed. A moan stuck in my throat, dry and half silent. He opened his eyes at last. He looked at me as if I was a complete stranger. In that moment, I felt further from him than ever. He shut his eyes again and his head turned away and his hands were now grabbing the blanket as if he was close to orgasm. I didn't stop the rhythmic motion of my hand until he came.

The phone rang. "Don't answer it," I said.

"I have to," Gardner said, turning away. "It's Chad." He slid to the edge of the bed and slowly launched himself from it, pushing his weight up with his arms. "Wait for me. I'm going to take it in the living room."

I could hear him on the phone, talking to someone who may well have trusted him to be faithful, or maybe not. Chad thought Gardner loved him, probably, and maybe he did.

All I knew at that point was that, just once, I wanted to be the priority of someone who really wanted me, and not just a substitute.

When Gardner came back to bed, I pretended I was asleep. I guess I fooled him, because he left me alone and promptly fell asleep, his back to me.

In his hurry to get to an appointment with his therapist, Gardner had left a closet door open at an angle that allowed me to see a narrow slice of myself in the mirror: propped against the pillows, resting the mug of coffee Gardner had brought me against my belly, my unshaven, suntanned face nearly brown in the bedroom gloom. I threw a pillow at my reflection and cursed Gardner. I had many idle hours ahead of me today. No class to attend, no clients to tend to. I had a chance to brood over the fact that I had no boyfriend in my life, no "'Chad" in my life like Gardner had. I envied Gardner that. I looked at Chad's photograph on the dresser. Would I cheat on Chad, fuck one of my students, even if he was Casey Cassidy, while my "lover" was gone, at home with the wife and kiddies? The whole business made me sad, so sad that I finally called my service. Yes, I had a client if I wanted him. Yes, I wanted him. Anything to keep my mind off Gardner and Chad....

When I stepped from the apartment building, I found it was still velvety warm, though not as suffocatingly hot as it had been the day before. I love it when it's hot. Summer is made for me. I was born in summer when the sun was at its highest. My body is made to receive heat. Now the heat sucked the chill of Gardner's apartment from my skin. It raised the hair on my arms and soothed the knot between my shoulders.

I finally relaxed. I waited outside in the sun for the john to appear. I closed my eyes, and inhaled/exhaled.

Instinctively I lifted my hand to my crotch. My hand stroked downward, my cock responded. When Vince, the john, appeared, he could not help but notice. He smiled. "I'll take you upstairs," he said

He hadn't wanted to meet me in his room in the hotel. I sensed fear right away from him. Yet, by the time we arrived at his room, he was relaxed, rubbing my bulge. In the room, my jeans were soon down around my ankles, and Vince was blowing me. I held his head and thought about Gardner, then Chad. Chad just wouldn't leave my mind; I nearly came thinking about Chad and what I wanted to do to him.

I could tell that Vince was really getting into my fucking him. Getting fucked by a man was one thing, but fucking one is quite another. I enjoy it all. Now, on my knees behind Vince, I was really getting off on it. I picked up the pace, sweating and grunting from the effort, getting slick and hot again myself, imagining I was fucking Chad, Gardner's secret lover.

I lunged all the way into Vince's asshole. The rush almost tore him in two. Then I took my free hand and brought it to his tiny pecker, and just like that he came.

It was a massive orgasm. It seemed to take all of my strength to hold on to him and keep us from falling off the bed. The guy must not have come in weeks. As Vince came, he howled like a dog, the cum pouring out of him onto the bedspread. For moments, I heard nothing beyond my body's pounding into him. Then I faked an orgasm for him, groaning, acting as if I were filling him. It was the least I could do.

IV. A Weekend in London

Like limousine drivers, escorts tend to wait for the calls from prestige clients. And so, when my agent Jerry Grand called me with the news that film director Stanley Howard wanted to know if I was free to see him, I cancelled my other plans. Howard made lots of movies: comedies, dramas, even romances. He preferred never to repeat himself. That's why I was so surprised when he wanted to see me again. The first time had been a quickie at his hotel in New York, and I had no idea who he was at the time. Just another john needing some sexing in the middle of the afternoon.

Now, Jerry told me, Stanley did not haggle and my agent did not push him too hard. He wanted to see me, "Sooner the better," he said. The trouble was, Stanley was in London, renting a house while he finished a horror film.

Stanley sent a car to pick me up at Heathrow. I sat in back, feeling like quite the visiting celebrity. We drove along a country road, and, after many twists, turned left through ornate green metal gates. We forked left, past signs announcing "Private Property," and proceeded over some speed bumps to another gate, which was closed. The driver got out to press the necessary buttons. He had to do it again at still another gate, sixty yards farther on.

The house was a low, very wide Victorian place, with a pillared facade. The estate was heavily protected, but why, I wondered; had Stanley received death threats from hustlers who figured he was an easy mark?

Stanley himself opened the door. He was wearing blue overalls with black buttons. He was a rotund man with a beard that blurred rather than defined his features. His black eyes were enlarged by big spectacles. His hands were curiously delicate and white. I recalled how those hands had been all over me, massaging, caressing, tweaking, while he sucked my cock.

"Ah," he sighed, "you got here." He spoke as if he was not really comfortable with company, even when he had invited it, paid for it even. I felt that he might have suffered some trauma as a child that had made him lose confidence in himself as a lover.

He led me into a long room at the back of the house where large windows looked onto a walled lawn. No other houses were visible. He invited me to sit down.

I knew that Stanley had told Jerry that he had regretted that we had not fucked when he saw me those many months ago, and had thought of me often. He served a good red wine and we sat in upright chairs and talked. He asked about my theater work. He seemed to know all about me, so it was easy to tell him little stories about my stage experiences. This was, I knew, the warmup.

I didn't reveal any names, knowing of his obsession with secrecy. His secrets were safe with me, I was telling him. He looked at me through those large glasses as if I had, just by showing up, fulfilled one of his fantasies. He became more relaxed.

We talked and talked, and would have talked some more had I not looked at my watch and seen that it was nearly half past two.

He said, "Do you want something to eat?"

"Beats having a migraine."

"You suffer from migraine?"

"If I don't eat, and I have to ... perform."

"Let's go in here, see if there's anything we can eat. Is that what you're doing now? Performing?"

"I hope to perform, let's put it that way."

We walked from one long room into another. In the massive dining room there was a lunch already laid out. A tureen of soup, cold breasts of chicken, fruit salad in a big bowl.

Stanley said, "Feel like eating any of this?"

"Looks fine," I said.

"Then let's eat it."

It was as if there might be some other rooms, with fancier meals in them, and I had settled for the first deal I was offered.

At one point, he asked, "Do you like the wine?"

He was already opening another bottle. Again, I was aware of his delicate white hands.

Perhaps I was not alone in being nervous. As soon as I made a comment of a sexual nature, he backed away. We ate and talked, and then we just talked, finishing the second bottle of wine.

I knew he had gone from directing tear-jerkers with Lana Turner and the like to a job as Chief of Production at Warner Bros., only to wander off into self-imposed exile. There was a hint of scandal about his leaving. One rumor had it that he had propositioned one too many office boys. Anyhow, few in Hollywood ever mentioned his name after that. But in moving to London, he re-emerged as a director of horror movies, which were highly successful at the box office.

He told me he preferred making movies in Britain, where there are no real stars, just fine actors. "Directors don't operate in a vacuum," he said. "The movie business dictates that directors need stars. Stars also need directors, of course. They need to bully and intimidate them. When you are directing a star, you must be ready to answer questions like, What was my character's relationship with his father? Was he popular in junior high school? Does he have facial hair? Is he hung? And having explained all that, you must be prepared to have the star come back at you with his own answers to all those questions—ideas that usually cause weeks of rewriting the script."

I shared with him how, as a kid, I loved imagining things. How I would go outside and put on a cape and just imagine I was some great action hero. He told me that, in his judgment, acting was believing. "Acting is not acting. It isn't putting on a face and dancing around in a mask. It's believing that you are that character, playing him as if it were a normal day in the life of that character."

While he directed lowbrow movies, his personal tastes were unabashedly elitist, and he showed me to his library where he picked out a copy of Radclyffe Hall's *The Well of Loneliness* for me to take along for the plane trip back to the

U.S. "I read it once a year, to keep myself alive," he said. "It's really the story of my life. Except," he smiled, "Stephen is really a lesbian."

"Oh," I responded, promising to read it.

He told me he enjoyed going to bookstores in London, picking up rare editions, and buying bowlers at the royal hatter James Lock and Co.

After a while, we finally went to his bedroom. By that time, the high all the wine had given me had worn off a bit so I was feeling horny again.

"You know what I'm going to ask you to do, don't you?" he asked, dropping his pants.

"Of course." I was taking my sweet time undressing.

"Is that what they all want?"

"No. You didn't, remember?"

"I was terribly nervous that day. I just wanted to meet you. ... I came too quickly." He was naked except for his boxers.

"Better that than never coming at all...."

"You have some who don't come?"

"I have. Yeah." I stayed in my briefs. I stroked myself so that he could see I was getting hard.

His hand reached down to caress my ass, a finger finding its way into my hole, which was moist, warm, and mildly pungent after the long trip.

"Hummmm," he moaned, dreamily. He got some lube and began again. I parted my legs just slightly so that he could slip two fingers inside me. He pushed deep, and my body responded with an undulating rising and riding of my ass against his hand and penetrating fingers. He drew them in and out in a slow, steady rhythm. He pulled me back so I lay back against his chest. And, as one hand played in my ass, his other massaged my cock.

"Oh, God," he breathed, "I don't know what I like better, your cock or your ass."

I was fully hard now, responding to his lusty manipulation. "Oh God, put it in me," I whispered. I felt how hard he was behind me and I wanted the feel of his thick, swollen penis moving in me. I wanted to squeeze it, and massage it with my ass muscles. He turned me around to face him, and he pushed my legs farther apart, and spread the wet lips of my ass, he thrust himself into me.

"Oh, yeah," I said, and he responded, his strong hips thrusting against me. With his hand around me, he held my butt tightly and pumped rhythmically, with a steady, unrelenting pounding.

"Ah, oh, God!" I moaned, as my ass rose and fell under his hand, meeting every thrust with one of his.

He squeezed my cock firmly. I groaned again.

He could tell that I was about to come, the way my body was grinding against his, the way my ass muscles grabbed at his cock from within, the way I flung back my head, and the way my cock was throbbing in his grip. My moans became louder. He thrust against me harder, realizing, intuitively or because he had seen my movies, how I loved it vigorous and constant just before I peaked. I gasped, "Oh yeah...."

And he lurched against me. "Aaaauuuugh!"—his own gratifying need gratification surging through him. "Aaaaaaaauuuugh!" He held me tightly, pumping into me furiously. "Aaaauuughr!" he gasped

As the last, smaller thrusts pushed into me, I clung to his cock. He collapsed against me. We were both sweating. He was hitting bottom with his cock so far inside me that I could hardly bear it. I squeezed against him as he began to move in and out again methodically.

He asked, almost humbly, whether I was· willing to go through it one more time.

"Of course I am," I said.

He seemed relieved, even grateful. I was not grateful, but I was relieved.

I loved his unrelenting energy, consuming me totally.

"I come too fast," he whispered. "I will make this last," he promised.

Yes, I wanted it longer, I wanted more; I wanted it to last an hour if he could do it. He rolled me onto my stomach and began again. My hips ground against him, thrusting toward his body towering over me. He fucked me for ten minutes like this, then one jolt, then another, then another. I felt him as he ejaculated inside my ass. I relished the feeling of being really filled.

Over the next full day of my visit, I determined to show Stanley that I was better than others whom he might have recruited, and I finally had him begging for me to stop, to rest, to leave him alone for a bit.

The morning I was leaving, Stanley came out onto the forecourt as the car that was to transport me back to London approached the house through the last of the barriers.

"So listen," he said, "thanks for... well, for coming out. And for everything you did."

"No, thank you."

"Worked out pretty well, didn't it?" He put his arm around my shoulder. I was aware of the small white hand gleaming in the bright sunlight. The warmth in his embrace was more flattering than anything he'd ever said to me.

I said, "I wouldn't have missed it, Stanley."

I got into the car and was driven toward the first gate. I waved to him through the window as if—although I would never trade on it—we were now close friends.

• • •

When I returned from London, there was a message from Gardner. He wanted to meet me for lunch. I returned his call and explained that I had just been to London, was exhausted, but I would be happy to meet him. I wanted to lower expectations, but with Gardner that really wasn't necessary. We met at our favorite little sidewalk cafe. I think he started to ask whom I had seen in London (he wa always curious about my tricks), but then stopped himself. "So *what* did you see there?" he finally asked.

"Not much, I'm afraid. I was picked up at the airport and driven to the country, then back again."

"You should have stayed a few days, taken in the theater, the museums. It is quite wonderful there."

"I never thought of it, really. I suppose I should have. But I just had all of this arranged for me and...."

"I shall take you one day," he interjected. "That's what. *I* shall take you."

Toward the end of the meal, Gardner looked at me and said, "What do you charge for such a thing?"

"What?"

"A weekend in London, for instance."

I felt the heat in my belly. "I ... well, I get a hundred an hour, a thousand a day."

"My," he said, looking away.

I hoped from this that he would know he was getting something for free that was highly prized. Instead, he became anxious. I was soon to find out why.

Gardner told me Chad hadn't been in town for a couple of weeks and he was horny as hell. I was to come to his place. "I have a little diversion planned," he said, acting more like a director than Stanley.

I hadn't been in the apartment more than a few moments when the front doorbell rang and Gardner sent me to answer it. When I opened the door, I found a very cute boy standing there. He was a couple of years younger than I, wearing shorts and a tank top.

"Hi, I'm Joey," the boy said, smiling knowingly.

I was too puzzled to say anything; I asked the boy to come in, closed the door, and brought him to Gardner.

Gardner smiled at the boy, looking at him in that critical way he had. "Well, you're dressed for the weather."

"It's so hot today," Joey said.

"Have a drink if you like. You can find whatever you need at the bar over there."

"Sure, thanks."

Gardner smiled at me as the kid walked to the bar. "He's pretty, isn't he?" In a subdued voice, so the boy would not hear, he added, "He wants to enroll in the school."

I thought I understood it now. Gardner had indeed arranged a little "diversion" for us. As I thought about the possibilities, I could feel my pulse racing. I would have charged $1500 for such a "scene," but Gardner, impudent Gardner, was getting it for free. Then I told myself I didn't care one way or the other about that; the kid was too attractive, too tempting. Besides, he couldn't be doing this without liking it, and I imagined at the end of it, the boy would go home to some hovel in New Jersey where his mother would be screaming and his father would be drunk. At least thinking that made it more palatable. Yes, it must be like that.

As if reading my mind, Gardner said: "He's a sad case, really. Down on himself, no self-esteem at all. I thought meeting you would cheer him up."

I smiled, trying hard to remain cool. "Well, I'll see what I can do."

As Joey carried back his drink, he said, "This is a nice place," his eyes roaming around the large, expensively furnished room. He looked even younger now. I felt like telling him this luxurious apartment was being paid for by a handsome, spoiled rotten kid who happened to be married to a woman, and had kids. If Gardner had to rent his own place.... I guess my attitude was steaming off of me.

Now Joey's smile was quiet, a question in his eyes about whether or not I would accept him.

Yes, he passed, all right.. For me, anyway. I could easily fuck him, if that was what Gardner wanted. I thought I could spend three hours having fun with Joey and still want more at the end of it. As much as I would enjoy it, I would tell myself I was doing it for Gardner.

"Joey wanted to meet my most illustrious student," Gardner said.

"Who is that?" I asked, smiling broadly.

"The star of 'Fire Island Fantasies'."

"Is Joey even old enough to get into the theater?"

"Oh, yes. I took him last night. They didn't even question it."

"Of course not; he was with you."

"Of course," Gardner said smugly. "No one questions me!"

"Least of all me," I said, playing along.

Joey set his drink down and went to the bathroom.

Gardner looked at me and smiled. "I'd like to watch the two of you. Do you mind?"

"No, hardly." I quickly peeled off my clothes as I followed Joey into the bathroom. He was just finishing when I opened the door. Seeing me nude, he smiled. "Hmmmm. You know, Gardner said it would be like fantasy made flesh...."

"Gardner would say something like that. But you know what I look like. I'm the one who is curious."

I cupped his heavy balls with one hand while I slid the other hand down behind him into his asscrack. He gave a throaty squeak and his face flushed. He closed his eyes and moaned softly as my fingers worked in and out of his sopping ass.

"Oh, I like that!" he said.

Abruptly, I pulled my fingers out. "You have prepared yourself."

"Yes. I was hoping, of course."

With a whimper, he immediately sank to his knees on the bathroom tiles and buried his face in my crotch.

Holding my ass with his hands, Joey sucked my cock with abandon. Gardner was now sitting on the bed no more than six or seven feet away from us, his eyes intent as he watched me being sucked.

I wasn't thinking about Gardner now; I was thinking about the kid's tongue and lips, his tongue sliding everywhere with such an expert twisting motion. It was obvious he was not new at this game. He was good, very adept, expert in the way he moved his tongue and mouth.

When I looked at Gardner, he had removed all his clothes and was now sitting on the edge of the bed naked, jerking his cock. I was aggressively face-fucking Joey and was close to coming, so I stopped and, helping Joey up, I brought him to the bed for Gardner. Gardner proceeded to suck Joey, then he sucked each of our cocks while we kissed each other. Gardner even managed to get both of our cockheads in his mouth at once for a few moments.

Finally Gardner leaned back and moved his legs apart, his dark cock erect, his hands stroking it. "There's plenty of room on the bed," he said.

Joey blushed and hesitated, but finally he did what Gardner wanted. Gardner was holding an audition for his school, wasn't he? Joey wanted to pass, I could tell. Joey scrambled onto the bed and got between Gardner's thighs and began sucking his cock. When Gardner was erect, Joey turned around and, squatting on his haunches, he pushed Gardner's cock deep inside his ass. I climbed on the bed and Joey resumed sucking me while he fucked himself with Gardner's prick.

"Oh, God, that's good!" Gardner gasped as he orgasmed inside Joey.

After that, Joey lifted himself off Gardner and got on his back, opening up for me. Gardner lay there watching us as Joey hooked his legs over my shoulders and met each of my thrusts as I came deep in his ass. Gardner played with his cock but did not get erect again. The grand finale was Gardner and I taking turns sucking Joey to orgasm. After he came, as only a teenager could, we lapped it up off the boy's chest.

Gardner sent the boy home after that, walking him out of the living room to the front door. As they did that, I stretched out with my eyes closed.

Then Gardner returned to me, knelt down on the bed and kissed me. "Damn, that was exciting," he said. "You're the best there is. But you know that." He lit a cigarette.

"I know, but it's nice to hear it, especially from you." Then, as I always did, I fixed my gaze on one of the many framed portraits of Chad and wondered where he was at that very moment. I cursed the fact that I was always seeking him, looking for him in all those places where he was not, and where he might never be.

V. In Baghdad By the Bay

Pinky was the one who came up with the idea of a film based on the intimate lives of a group of dancers at a sleazy bar. Carmine, who I didn't know could write anything but his own name on checks, wrote the script after a "treatment" had been done by a scriptwriter in Hollywood. When they were done, they decided it would really work better as a legit play, and they could tour the country with it if they had a "name" in the lead. Of course, who would they turn to?

Surprisingly, Gardner was all for the idea of my having my own starring vehicle on stage. In fact, he coached everybody once we went into rehearsals in New York. Pinky was the director, but Gardner really ran the show. Gardner had the time of his life, especially because it gave him more opportunity to see me. After several weeks of rehearsals, Pinky decided we would "try out" the show—in San Francisco, where a friend of his owned a small theater near the Castro District.

We spent two weeks in San Francisco rehearsing the play and staging "previews." The play was generally well-received by the audiences, especially when, in the final scene, I have a nude love scene with my co-star and we simulate anal sex.

The play opened in the locker room of a sleazy bar where the strippers would get ready. I always got applause when I entered, stage left, and quickly moved over the dirty floor, layered with discarded condoms, dirty underwear and old jockstraps, and went to my locker. I threw my bag on a nearby chair, undid the lock and took a deep breath. I pulled my baggy old sweatshirt up over my head, unbuttoned my jeans and stepped out of my underwear.

With my back still to the audience, on went the tiny black g-string. I moved to the mirror, looked herself up and down in the mirror, critically appraising every inch of my golden body before releasing a slow, seductive smile. Casey Cassidy was a "star."

I walked to the door leading to the bar and waited. Steve, one of the bartenders, greeted me with a knowing wink before bringing me a double shot of whiskey, which I downed in a single gulp while I let the loud music flow over me, possessing me with its beat. Its pulse became my pulse, pounding through my veins and arteries, sending blood down to my cock, making me gyrate my hips to its rhythm, making me hard.

I turned to Steve, slowly taking him in with my best bedroom-eyed gaze, while a knowing grin came to my lips. He brought me another drink, which I gulped down, and then wrapped my arms around his thick shoulders, drawing him close He pushed his pelvis against me, letting me know he was ready whenever I was.

He asked, "Why don't we go in the back?"

"Maybe later," I responded, knowing damned well that later would never come, then turned and bounced onto the small stage.

Two other dancers, Joey and Jimmie, were already on stage, dancing around on their little platforms, wearing only their g-strings. The flashing, colored lights dancing were over skin that was already wet with sweat. Jimmie's black skin contrasted against the near-alabaster of Joey's untanned, skinny body.

I strode to the center of the stage, moving my hips and glancing over the audience with a sultry, unseeing gaze. I spun around and suddenly Jimmie was pressed up against me, his hands wandering over my body, taking liberties by running them over my ass, up my legs and into my crotch.

I felt Joey against my back so that I was sandwiched between the two men. I leaned back against Joey and hooked my fingers into Joey's tiny g-string. Jimmie reached around me and grabbed Joey's ass, while Joey's hands squeezed my already-hardened nipples.

The audience always yelled their appreciation at this scene, and Jimmie dropped to his knees so his breath was hot on my already-throbbing cock. I reluctantly cupped Jimmie's head and brought him back to his feet. Joey turned and went out into the crowd to tease them while we gradually broke away from each other, each to dance alone on the stage. Eventually, Joey announced that the men could approach us and slide tips into our g-strings as we moved among them. As each tip was deposited, we would allow brief dalliances—a hand on a leg, a touch of a crotch, an ass.

Jimmie moved out into the audience, and another dancer, Toby, joined me on stage. At this point I noticed a guy walking up to the make-believe bar to get a drink before going to his table at the back of the stage. Dialogue between Toby and me made it plain that he was a new face and that I wanted him.

He was slender and rather short, probably only about five-four, and was dressed in a neat double-breasted blazer, slacks, and a tie that was still fully tightened.

I could see that he was already turned on, and it was a monster. I wanted to look away from him, do my thing with the audience, but couldn't. His dark eyes met mine across the smoky room just before he sat down, adjusting himself along the way, I noticed.

When I left the stage to begin the greeting the audience, I stopped by the bar to allow Steve to quickly re-fortify me. I ignored the man with the big dick, working my way around the bar, moving to the music, swaying just inches away from their hardened dicks while they laid their hands on my thighs, getting a free feel. Finally, I found myself doing a dance at the table next to his. I glanced over at him while I rode the thigh of a man in the audience. And so began the love story of an erotic dancer and the uptight businessman who loves him.

Like my character in the play, I have never had a

relationship with a man I liked because he couldn't live with the fact that I was in the sex trade. I wasn't quite sure if it was jealousy or fear or what that caused them to take off, but all I knew was I never had a lover of my own.

While the play ended happily, with the dancer and the dark stranger fucking in a make-believe bedroom for the climax to the show, and presumably living happily ever after, my search for my own lover continued in every city we played. I recalled what Matthew told me about refusing to do a TV series: "What I like least about acting in that kind of thing is that when you're only in one place, you're missing the other part of life." It seemed by taking my show on the road, I wouldn't miss a thing.

During the run of the play in San Francisco, I couldn't help but notice the boy: he bought a ticket for every performance. He was always waiting at the stage door when the cast left the theater. It got so I would wait until everyone had left in hopes he would give up and leave me alone, but that didn't help. He'd wait. I tried leaving out the front door, but that was no good either; he knew where I parked my rental car and would meet me there. I'm an easy-going guy, and I appreciate my fans, so as much as he bothered me, I couldn't be rude. After a week, he gave up on asking for my autograph and just wanted to wish me a good-night. As annoying as it was, it became endearing. I began to wish he were cute. He was a teenager, nicely dressed, thin, but homely. I might have been attracted when I was younger, but after all the men I've had, he just didn't have any appeal.

On the last night of the engagement, everybody was going to a party, but I was drained. I had done two tricks that afternoon, and so I begged off, telling my fellow cast members I would go back to the little apartment where I was staying, away from the rest of the cast so that I could entertain clients, and take a little nap. I promised to join them at what had become our favorite hangout later.

Of course, the boy was waiting at my car. "I'll miss you," I told him, unlocking the door.

"I'll miss you," he responded.

I looked to the street. The cast was piling into a cab. I waved at them as they pulled away, then turned to face my young stalker. "What will you do now?" I asked.

"I don't know," he said, looking sad. There, in the streetlight, he suddenly appealed to me. I know it wasn't pity. Maybe it was because I was just so tired that I let my guard down.

"You want to come to my place?" I asked before I really had a chance to think about it. I climbed into the car.

"Yeah," he said, smiling for the first time, as he rushed to get into the car.

In the five minutes it took to get to the apartment that I had been allowed to use while I was in town by a long-time client who was away in Europe, the kid finally introduced himself to me: Buddy, which I thought was perfect under the circumstances.

As we drove along through deserted streets, he stayed close to the door, made no move towards me.

"Do you like Chicago?" he asked at one point, referring to the play's next engagement.

"Oh, I've never been there, except to change planes. It couldn't be as good as San Francisco. Anyway, it's only for a week."

"Then where do you go?"

"New York. That's the real deal. This is really just a warm-up."

"Try out, right?"

"Yeah." He was so cute now, the theater-buff.

"You should do well in New York," he said, relaxing a bit as we neared our destination. I parked the car and I put my arm around him for a moment and he leaned against me. "You gonna let me fuck you?" I asked.

He didn't say anything; he simply nodded. I took his hand. He was trembling. I drew him into my arms and kissed him—just a peck, really—before drawing away.

We stepped from the car and, even though I had warmed to him, I didn't want anybody to see me with him. I made him walk several feet behind me, like Chinese women are taught to do. I told him it was because I didn't want to see seen bringing anyone into the building, but really it was just him. Even inside the building I made him walk a flight behind me up the stairs.

I put on a record, took out two beers and a joint, turned down the lights, and sat next to him on the couch. I stared at his pale, soft skin, his close-cropped head, and my loins stirred.

The beers and the drug did their work and he was finally relaxing. The trembling stopped and he leaned against me. A wave of total peace washed over me and I shut my eyes. Whatever happened, happened.

His hand fell to my groaned, and he could feel my hardness, my desire. He leaned down and kissed the bulge, then chewed on it.

"Go ahead," I said. "Suck it. Suck it good."

He unzipped my jeans and freed my cock, now almost fully hard. He immediately began sucking my cock.

The record was done. I thought about getting up and turning it over, but I didn't. Then the silence became interesting. I was spaced-out from the marijuana, and I realized how tired I was of being even a little bit in charge. Of anything. I just let the kid do the work as bits of songs played in my head like a movie soundtrack. I realized how rarely I was with another person without some kind of music in the background. I wondered if Buddy was playing something in his head too. I cleared my throat to speak, but I stopped. The silence, except for Buddy's slurping, grew more and more awkward.

As he adored my cock, I wondered if he realized how many men I had entertained, let do what he was doing, for $200, during the run of the play. But there would be no fee for Buddy, who had spent far more than that in tickets. He deserved a fuck as well, and I intended to give it to him. But he was so good at sucking I had to pull him off or I would have come.

We went to the bedroom, where I finished undressing while he tore off his clothes. It was when he turned around that I was stunned by what I saw: Buddy was equipped with the thickest cock I had seen in months, a virtual beer can of a cock. It was not especially long, maybe two inches shorter than my often-photographed nine-incher, but incredibly thick. I dropped to the bed and pulled him towards me. The monster bobbed and weaved in my face. Pre-cum oozed from the tip. "Wow," I murmured as I drew it closer to my face and stroked it. I soon was struggling to wrap my mouth around this cock, and here it had been there, waiting for me, for two weeks! I decided to make up for lost time. I sucked on it a bit but what I really needed to do was feel it up my ass. After moistening it and my asshole with spit, I leaned back on the bed and brought Buddy with me. I remained in control, guiding it toward my asslips, holding it there, taking Buddy's ass in my hands and pushing him forward. It was as if I hadn't felt any cock there before in my life. Buddy shoved, and I had to struggle to get even the head of it in.

"Am I hurting you?" he asked.

"No, no, that's okay."

The head and an inch or two slid into me. I groaned.

"If I'm hurting you, I'll stop." He started to withdraw the cock.

My body sucked after it. "No, no. It feels good," I whispered.

"Okay."

He sounded pleased. I suppose he was; he had hounded me for two weeks and I had finally relented, and now he was fucking the infamous ass of Casey Cassidy, one-time porn star and now stage star. In any case, he spread me wide, and shoved it in to his pubic hairs. Now this really did hurt, in such a way that was hard to tell whether it was pleasurable or not. And yet I was pushing my legs as far apart as possible, wanting even more.

I moaned when he put his teeth around one nipple, then the other.

I was soon sweating and messy as he slammed into me. He was incredibly cool, almost clinical as he proceeded, which not only aroused me but made me like him better; he was no longer a homely little kid in my eyes. I thought of the dick that was invading me, of my first glimpse of it, and wished I had a camera so I could have a souvenir picture of me salivating to the first sight of it—and ever after I could torture myself over what he had done to me. And what I had done to myself by not taking him home the first night of the engagement.

Abruptly he pulled out, then I heard him stand up. I kept my eyes shut, wondering what the hell he was doing. I heard him walk away, then behind my lids I saw, or perhaps felt, the warmer glow that I pretended was sun, but that was really a distant light in the apartment. I heard the toilet flush.

He came back. His hands made me shiver as he rolled me over. He said nothing, just positioned me. Apparently he figured my being on my knees would make taking it easier. This manipulation of me both embarrassed me and turned me on.

"Ow," I moaned as he entered me again. But I didn't push him away. In fact, the lower part of my body gyrated towards him.

"Oh that hurts," I cried.

"Just relax." He ran his fingers over my ass, and I felt the goose bumps again. I realized I was tensing my muscles, and told myself to let go. As I exhaled he pushed it in farther.

"Ow!"

"I told you—just relax." He placed his hand on my erection as his cock slid all the way in.

"Ohhh," I moaned. I had relaxed enough to open myself to the pain again. Although intense, it was made bearable by the thought of my strange submission to this homely youth. Not just bearable, pleasurable, at the thought that my body was possessed, not by just anyone, but by this boy who had disgusted me for two weeks. Had it been someone I cared about, it might have been different, but since I did not know him and there was nothing I could do about it, I might as well relax and enjoy it. No doubt I would have been happy enough with him on a desert island, where he could make love to me all day and no one would ever know. I began to imagine us on some white-sand beach, him fucking me day in and day out ... and yet, with all the time in the world, who knows, perhaps I would not have wanted to let him do it, or he himself might not have wanted to do it.

Then, beyond the pain and mental pleasures, came a powerful sensation of peace. I was really doing nothing now, just kneeling on the bed while he jerked my cock and slammed his cock into me. I was tired and I wanted to go to sleep. The sweat on my body was drying up. I had had two orgasms earlier in the day and had come close to it when he was sucking me, but now I knew I didn't really want another one. I did, however, want him to come inside me. He kissed the back of my neck, which made me shiver even more. He pulled the monster out a little; then he slammed it in all the way again. His pace quickened and he finally came.

He didn't leave it in; instead, he lifted off me rather abruptly and the cock popped out. "Ow," I said. But what I really felt was sadness. Amazingly, I had gotten used to it in there. The peaceful sensation was still inside my body, but less so. I collapsed to the bed. When I turned my head I saw that he had picked up a sheet. He placed it over me, then went to the bathroom.

When he returned, he crawled on top of me, turned my head to the side, and kissed me. His lips were incredibly soft, and he rubbed my ass through the sheet. My loins stirred again.

"What can I do for you?" he whispered.

"Nothing."

"You sure? I can finish sucking it."

"No. I'm fine."

"Did I hurt you?"

"It hurt, but the more it hurt, the more I liked it."

"You really didn't mind?"

"No."

"Very few can take it. But I knew you could. I just knew."

I closed my eyes. When I opened them again, he was dressed, bending down to kiss me goodbye. Then he headed for the door. He opened the door, looked back at me. The words "I love you" played through my mind, although I knew they weren't true. "Bye," I said.

I shut my eyes. Neither awake nor asleep, I thought of boys I had never regarded as sexual objects. I pictured them doing unspeakable things to me ... and soon was fast asleep.

VI. Warm Bodies in Chicago

I lay on the bed writhing. The john, whose name was Darrell, washed over me, warmed me, kissing, pressing, licking. I felt his smooth back, his armpits, and his erection against my belly. I pulled him to me to kiss him. I sucked his lips, his cheeks, his neck, as he lifted up and pressed his erection against my asslips. I gasped. I kissed him, I bent into him. But his kiss was slow, to calm me. The slick head of his cock slowly caressed my ass, over and over, then down, then up. Back and forth. I was so horny for him I thought I would scream. I spread my legs wide, my back arched.

He whispered, rasping, breathing hard, "Oh God, Casey, I've waited so long for this." His cock slid in slowly. He pushed up, steering the head of it into me. He shoved in slightly, then out, then back in, each time his cock crept a little deeper. "I don't want to hurt you," he gasped.

"Oh, please, please ... oh my God!" I grabbed his shoulders, bringing up my knees, and exquisite tremors erupted somewhere at the base of my spine. I could no longer control myself and reached for his buttocks, pulling him down and pushing up. His penis rammed and rocked to the hilt, the walls of my ass undulated.

Darrell let loose; his deep thrusts awed me. I clamped him to me, crying. The shaft of his penis pulsed again and again. I could feel this penetration, the surging of his cock filling me. Our hearts pounded. I wept silent tears as he held me dearly, gasping, murmuring, "Oh, it's as good as I dreamed."

"Yeah? I'm glad," I moaned as Darrell's cock exploded inside me.

He withdrew and lifted up. His lips grazed in my pubic hair, kissed my erection, then gently, ever so gently, licked my asshole clean. I felt his tongue explore, search, as if to heal any damage his big dick had caused, kissing me over and over. Then he cradled me in his arms and looked at me adoringly. He pulled me up to kiss me. I tasted his cum ... and his tears.

"Let's spend a week in the desert," Darrell said next, absently playing with my cock. "I'll tell my wife I'm visiting my aunt in Palm Springs. She owns a gallery there, and my wife'll be happy to think I'm making contacts."

I know I did not look eager. "I don't know; it might be hard for me to get away."

I loved playing hard to get, but in Darrell's case it was not a game. I didn't need another married man in my life, not then. He had been to the theater four times, tipping me generously when I dropped to the edge of the stage in front of him and wagged my cock in his face.

Four times he saw the show, four times he tipped me $20, and four times he said he'd be back and we'd have a date. The last time, I offered to have him come to my hotel. I knew he was married, and I felt safe having him there. At my place, I fixed him a drink, which I knew he'd never finish, and led him into my bedroom. He mentioned that his wife was probably wondering where he was and we strained to make conversation. It didn't take long before our bodies took over and communicated for us....

Lawrence arrived at my hotel just after Darrell left. He wanted to take me out to dinner, but I ordered a hamburger for him from room service. I couldn't eat anything myself. Then I took a long, hot shower. When I smoothed the creamy lather over my cock, it stiffened. I didn't want to masturbate though. Lawrence was paying for it; let him have it.

Wrapped in my robe, I went to the bedroom to find Lawrence finishing his dinner. I was feeling slightly decadent, having just had Darrell, but the thought of it had kept me erect and I was beginning to get a stomachache, which is what happens to me if I got too excited without climaxing.

When we lay down on the bed, Lawrence finally removed his clothes and I saw his erection for the first time. It was incredibly beautiful, bobbing out in front of him like a sword. His foreskin had been pushed back because the knob had grown so large. It made him irresistible. I no longer wished to keep myself under control. I reached out and encircled his cock with one hand, pulling the foreskin down the shaft and exposing the full head of his cock, a shiny deep-red knob already glistening with pre-cum.

Lawrence shuddered, but moved closer to me. I took the tip of him into my mouth and felt its heat on my tongue. Lingering on the tender underside with my lips, I took his balls in my other hand and scraped them gently with my fingernails. Lawrence was moaning. His eyes were closed. He clearly loved what I was doing. He was even making humming sounds like one who's enjoying a good meal.

So I laid my head back into the pillow and slowly began to let myself relax. Now it was his turn to enjoy my cock. The more I relaxed and released my body's tensions, the better what he was doing to me felt. Soon all of my attention was centered down there, on my prick and his mouth. I became aware of an orgasm rising within my body.

He stopped, but only for a moment. He stopped to say, "You have the sweetest cock. I could suck you forever." Then he went back to it. His words turned me on almost as much as his actions and I was on my way. My hips lurched up and grabbed for that orgasm.

My legs were trembling and I had to struggle to keep them from closing down on Lawrence's head. Involuntary gasps escaped my throat.

Lawrence inserted one finger into my asshole and my inner muscles grabbed hold of it like a vise, as if trying to squeeze fluid from his fingertip. I bent my head into the pillow to wipe off some of the sweat. And all the while he kept talking to me: "You're so beautiful. You look magnificent, the way you move on stage is a sight to behold...."

When the shuddering finally ceased, Lawrence came up toward me and gently inserted his cock into my ass. He did it so slowly I could feel the folds of my inner skin scrape past the ridge of his cock. He felt big inside of me and when he was fully inside, he began a steady fuck.

Lawrence was a strong man. I could see his muscles flexing even in the half-light of the television. When he lifted my pelvis up in the air to meet his, the biceps of each arm exploded under his skin. His shoulders and chest were gleaming with sweat. But it wasn't only his chest I was looking at. His face turned me on too. If I had a mental image of what the perfect man for me would look like, Lawrence would have fit it perfectly. His eyes were large with thick lashes. The blue was paler than the sky, in sharp contrast with his dark, tanned skin. His hair was thick and curly and his mouth full and sensuous.

Each time I was sure we were through, Lawrence started

up again. He turned me over and pulled me up doggy fashion and fucked me from behind. I thought I would never like this position, but he made it feel good. He stuffed a pillow underneath my belly and tilted me in such a way that nothing hurt. I came this way too and when I finished, he moved me again, this time to the edge of the bed.

My legs fell over the side and Lawrence knelt on a pillow on the floor. He could fuck me this way without either of us having to exert much energy. He began to fuck with very rapid strokes. I was starting to wonder if he would ever come at all. His thrusts grew more demanding, his body heavier against me. And then he exploded in me with a strangled cry and I came myself without even touching my cock.

Then we were on the bed and I was on top of him. He seemed to be resting, so I took over. I was straddling him, my knees bent on either side of his torso, his hands up on my pecs. I began a vibrating, gyrating motion with my pelvis that forced my ass down to rub against the base of his shaft. It forced the cock to move from front to back inside of me. I can come very easily this way and when I did, I fell onto his body, spent.

The last position was the same as the first, with him on top of me. My cock hovered on the brink of orgasm constantly. I sobbed, fiercely. "You're beautiful!"

"And you," he laughed gently, "are nearsighted."

• • •

The party was large, noisy, with disco-loud music with a deep beat that appealed to hungry bodies on drugs who desperately wanted to mingle with others. Many of the guys wore suits but some just wore sport shirts and pants, or even T-shirts and jeans. Sitting with the people Jerry, my agent, had arranged for me to meet, I saw a tall, very young black across the room; he was smiling at me. He was very sexy, but I was there on business. Not only was I meeting people who could help me in my post-porn stage career, I was always looking for another john.

It had been a busy week what with Darrell, then Lawrence. Then, today, I had entertained a john at lunch, after which he blew me in his hotel room. Then another john, Bill, wanted to see me. Late in the afternoon, we met at a bar and taxied to the baths. Bill had a little coke, to "get in the mood," as he put it. I wet my finger. The wet digit slipped up my nose to grease the passageway. I was handed a small snowy peak of powder, offered up on a golden spoon. Snorting it was like a blast from the past. It was all still there: the rush, the burn, and the feeling of euphoria. Blessedly the coke was all for me: he said he couldn't come if he was coked up. One more toot for me before I left. Coke was one of those things you build up a tolerance for, but I had not done coke for a couple of years. I was wired for sound, here in this filthy bathhouse. We walked around. Bill was parading me, I thought, showing off his prize. But hardly anybody really noticed. There were men in the shadows, grunting and moaning, cocks exposed.

Bill wanted an audience and since he was paying generously for it, we went to the orgy room. On his knees, a mat under us, Bill jerked his cock. I had no trouble getting hard. This was, as far as I was concerned, just another performance, and one I was quite capable of giving. I didn't need to act. At least, not much. He had lubed his ass in the room so my cock slid right in.

As Bill responded to the pain, I gave him more. Another man stood over Bill and Bill took the man's cock in his mouth. The man fucked Bill's face the way I did his ass. All his holes were filled and ready to fire. Overwhelmed, the need to come rushed over him. He dropped his hand to his erection and started rubbing himself in time with the fucking and the sucking. He came, but the man went on fucking his face till I stopped the rapid-fire pummeling of his ass. As I pulled out, another guy came right up and shoved his hard dick into Bill's sloppy ass. Another man moved towards me and started playing with my filthy erection, then knelt before me. He licked my balls and had me close to coming, but it was no use. I rubbed the sucker's head and told him how good he was. I also told Bill how good he was, patted his ass and went back to the room.

Cash in hand, I left the baths. Outside, in the cold, I stood there, all fucked out, looking at the cars going by in a blur.

Now, at the party, I had a headache, coming down from my coke high, and I was trying to concentrate on what was being said, but I couldn't take my eyes off the young black.

He had luscious dark brown skin and long, straight hair. I had to admit he was stunning. He seemed a bird out of a jungle paradise, alien and irresistible. Our eyes met and he held my gaze. If I hadn't known better I would have thought he had me hypnotized. I admitted to myself that even though I was coked-up, I still wanted him. The thought of his body over me, fucking me, warmed me all over.

I raised my wet hand to cool my flushed skin. The feeling was electric as I watched the black move gracefully across the room towards me. Seeing me watching, it seemed as if he was showing off for the handful of people, both men and women, whose eyes turned to look at him. When he was halfway across, he stopped to speak with a woman seated on a low sofa. The woman was short, heavy, and blond. He did this, I imagined, to make me jealous, knowing that it would make me want him even more. Waiting on him now became almost unbearable. I saw him give the woman a small kiss on her rosy cheek.

Even though I returned to my drink and the conversation of the producer next to me, I felt the presence of the black standing behind me. It was as if I was somehow drawn to him, forcing my eyes up to stare at his reflection in the mirror across the room. When I looked at his face pictured in the cloudy glass, he was smiling slightly. His cold eyes looked back at me intently, daring me not to smile back. We stayed locked like this for a few moments and I gave in, my lips rising up in a pouty greeting. It was only then that he touched me.

"Hello," he said, his breath warm on my neck. His voice was mellow, seductive. I felt his hand on my shoulder as he pressed in closer. He smelled of cologne, a light musk scent that mingled sweetly with the sweat rising on his skin. "Have you been waiting long?"

"No," I lied, settling back against him so that my head was resting against his chest. He knew exactly how long I had been waiting, and wanted me to be angry that it took him so long to come and pay his respects to me, the world-famous gay porn and stage star.

I studied him again in the mirror. He was the most beautiful man I had ever seen—and he knew it. He also knew that he had power over me, knowing instinctively that I wanted him so much. He moved onto the tall chair next to me, sitting with one hand on my knee, his fingers pressing points of heat into my skin. He leaned in and boldly kissed me softly on the mouth, his tongue teasing me momentarily. "Shall we go?" he asked.

I nodded, extended my apologies to the prodcuer, who smiled knowingly, and I obediently followed the black.

As we made our way through the crowd, he kept turning to look at me, to make sure I was following. I smiled, because there was no way I would change my mind now.

In the cab headed to my hotel, he finally introduced himself as Leon. He said he was an out-of-work actor. I told him I couldn't believe he would ever be out of work, and he laughed. I told him I was appearing in a play in town.

Only then did he admit he knew exactly who I was. He took my hand in his. "I've wanted your body ever since I saw you in 'Fire Island Fantasies'."

I had heard this before, of course, from other black men who had been astonished that I had bottomed so eagerly for Aaron, the big black bodybuilder. Most of them had never seen a blond boy bottom for a black on screen or off.

"At least you know what I like," I would tell them, and then they would proceed to follow Aaron's lead and rip me apart.

Now I stroked the bulge in Leon's trousers and would have done more except we arrived at my hotel.

In my hotel room, I turned on one of the table lamps, and lovely golden light pooled across the double bed that occupied the center of the room. As soon as the door was locked, Leon pressed me against the wall and kissed me hard on the mouth. Taken by surprise, I gave in to him.

I resisted the urge to get down and kneel before him, to worship that magnificent body. There was no way to know what his reaction might be to that. I moved to the bed and sat on the edge of it. Leon looked at me, like a doctor looking over a patient. I tried to imagine he was a prospective slave buyer, examining the merchandise before trying it out himself. "You like?" I asked, watching for a reaction. No change; he just kept on examining me in the light as he removed my clothing. He glowed; I glowed. Time to initiate something. "I'm ready for you whenever you are." There, that was almost like something a slave would say. Leon ran his hand over my thighs and I shivered, back in a mental game of slave for sale. I turned over onto my stomach and waved my ass in the air.

Leon quickly stripped and then approached the bed.

"Well, here," he said. "If you suck me some I'll be hard enough to fuck you, okay?"

I pretended that was an order and went at the flaccid penis with gusto. The thick, uncut cock was slow to harden. Now it appeared that Leon might be having second thoughts about stuffing his big one where Aaron had been. I began to worry that maybe he wouldn't get hard. I imagined being punished for failing to do my duty, but I couldn't really imagine what the punishment would be, only that there would be some. I moaned around the cock in my mouth. Leon was getting hard. He didn't wait long before pulling away from my mouth and positioning himself at the end of the bed. I applied some lube, then began to rock back on all fours.

"You ready?" Leon said, spreading my asscheeks with one hand and guiding his cock with the other. I nodded, pretending that he really had no choice. My black master was just toying with me, asking like that as he was when he later asked, "This okay?" when he changed to a faster rhythm and, "You getting close?" a bit later on. I didn't answer either time—it would have broken the spell. The truth was, I was getting close, and I wasn't able to hold it. Not like a good slave would have. And Leon didn't seem to care much either, as he slicked himself in and out of me as fast as he could, straining toward his own orgasm.

"Are you okay? Am I hurting you?" Leon asked. "Do you want me to stop?"

I shook my head, smiling at the memory of the homely boy in San Francisco. *Heavens, no, Leon, you are not hurting me!* In response, I clenched his butt tight. This sent him over the edge into orgasm.

But he wasn't done. He went back to fucking me vigorously. Trembling, I tried to pretend he wasn't there. I closed my eyes this time. He was brutal, and the pain didn't lessen, not for a second.

"We're almost through," he said. I could almost feel the clenching of his teeth. "I'm sorry. I wanted to come twice with you."

"Hmmm," I mumbled, my eyes popping as his cock slowly slipped out of me.

"Can you stay the night?" I asked him.

"Of course."

I had to leave the next morning for Manhattan, but I did manage to get fucked by him in the shower before heading to the airport. We promised to meet again some day.

VII. Back in Manhattan: The Harder the Better

When I returned to Manhattan, beginning an open-ended engagement in "Cockteasers," Peter called me at the theater to tell me he had managed to convince his new boyfriend that three-ways could be fun.

The next afternoon, I was in bed with them. The initial penetration was a single, very brutal thrust. I don't know why, but Peter liked it this way, the harder the better. He groaned as I let myself fall forward, sliding into his by now well-lubricated ass. I felt his long, hairy legs being wrapped around me as he pulled me deeper into his ass, which tightened on me in urgent contractions. I cupped my hands around his butt and dug my fingers into those meaty mounds while he screamed "Fuck it," over and over, maniacally, his heels drumming on my bare butt.

In response, I rammed into him, fucking furiously, my cock churning in his hot, juicy depths. The exquisite feel of his tight, slick ass muscles wrapped around my cock was thrilling, and I pumped into him with wild enthusiasm.

In this wonderful moment, while I was fucking Peter, I turned to look at his new boyfriend, Eddie, whose clenched hand was pumping his cock to full hardness. I realized Eddie's cock was not a "grower," five inches at best.

I felt my control slipping away as Peter tightened his grip, his eager body straining up to meet my thrusts, his hips bucking against me. Eyes clenched tight, he tossed his head from side to side, and he gyrated in a frenzy of passion that sent me over the top. As my cum filled him, Peter opened his eyes and looked into the smiling face of Eddie. I looked down to see that Peter, always in total control, had taken his hands off his penis; he was holding off his orgasm until I was out of him and Eddie was in him. While I may have been the fuck of choice, the one he had paid for, Eddie had to be given his due.

I pulled out and stood over them while, grinning, Eddie got on the bed behind Peter and shoved forward. I figured that, by this time, his prick had to be aching for release. As he approached the sopping, well-fucked ass of Peter, Peter's slightly parted legs seemed to beckon him. Eddie fumbled there, shoving himself in and slipping out. Eddie lost some of his potency and might not have been able to get the cock in had Peter not reached down between his legs, taken him firmly in hand, and inserted the cock into his ass. Eddie lovingly rubbed and massaged those mounds and Peter stirred impatiently as the cock popped in.

Peter groaned and offered his boyfriend no respite, begging to receive his orgasm. But Eddie, having watched me spend fifteen minutes deep inside Peter, was in no hurry; he settled into a steady rhythm, fucking his lover with a cold determination, attacking Peter's heaving bottom with quick thrusts. I knew from my own experience with guys with small cocks how much this was hurting Peter. Peter had, the first time I visited him, agreed we would always rather have a big dicks than tiny ones, but that was before Peter met Eddie. Small dick or not, Peter fell hopelessly in love with Eddie, who was a beautiful, blue-eyed blond who reminded me very much of Chad.

I stepped in front of Peter and allowed him to suck me while Eddie slammed into him, but I knew nothing would lessen the pain. My cock in his mouth, Peter jacked himself. He had become stoically resigned to the savage pounding. After a few more minutes of this relentless punishment, I sensed that Eddie, at last, was close to orgasm.

I was impressed with Eddie, despite the small cock. He had a marvelous physique: small waist and hips, broad chest and shoulders. Except for the small tufts of hair beneath his arms and at the base of his cock, his torso was silky smooth. I reached over and began tweaking his nipples as he began his orgasm. We kissed as his cum shot into his lover. Eddie was one more thing: a great kisser.

Still unfulfilled, Peter rolled over onto his stomach, and

Eddie pulled the cheeks of his ass apart. I gazed wantonly at the small, pink pucker nestled in the mat of wispy hair that I knew so well. Eddie bent down and put three fingers into his lover's ass. Peter moaned softly as Eddie finger-fucked him and Peter began jacking his cock again.

"Casey," Peter cried, "please?"

Nodding, I moved over, slid behind him and shoved my cock back into Peter.

I had just started the fuck when I hissed sharply as Eddie poked a single finger up my butt.

The hot, slick walls of Peter's rectum suddenly tightened around my cock.

"I'm gonna come!" he panted.

"Oh, thank god," I mumbled, fearing Eddie would try to fuck me while I was fucking Peter.

Cum spurted from Peter's cock. As I continued pumping into Peter, Eddie aligned the head of his cock with the center of my asshole. I felt him push. The pressure was strange, but pleasing. He pushed again, harder this time, and his helmet-shaped knob burst into me.

I cried out in agony, "Oh fuck, it hurts!"The pain coursing through my legs and up my spine was causing me to lose my erection and my cock slipped from Peter's ass. I kissed Peter and kept kissing him; it helped take my mind off the pain Eddie's tiny prick was causing.

Eddie began moving his hips, causing the head of his cock to wiggle around inside me. "Oh yeah, that's it," he said, shoving his cock as far as he could into my ass. "It's not so bad now, is it?"

I refused to take my mouth away from Peter's to answer him. I had hoped this would not happen ever again, that I would never give another of Peter's much-too-young and too-cute-for-words lovers the pleasure of sticking his cock in me, but because it had, there was simply nothing I could do about it.

In my fashion, I probably loved Peter more than anyone else in the world, even more than Gardner. He was not a handsome man, but he made the most of what he had: tall, gym-toned, a nice mat of chest hair. And I did love to suck on his meaty cock.

As I kissed Peter passionately now, I was remembering

how, at one point when I was eighteen and out of work and needed a place to stay, Peter let me stay at his apartment. At that time, he had another young lover who was not responsive to sharing Peter with anyone. So we had to meet in dark movie theaters, at the baths and , once, he even gave me a blowjob in the park.

Now, dizzy with ecstasy, Eddie was getting close to orgasm. My ass began to respond to his insistent efforts. My whimpers and moans had done nothing to discourage him. I stopped kissing Peter and turned to look up at Eddie. His fingers tightened in my hair and a look of utter determination came over his face as he ravaged my rectum. The air whistled in and out of my lungs with each punishing stroke of his vengeful little dick. I shuddered and writhed beneath the sweating youth as he finally came inside me. He didn't linger; he slid off the bed and went to the bathroom. A strange silence settled upon us.

"Well, you're welcome to stay the night," Peter said after a couple of minutes. I blinked. "Oh, Eddie doesn't mind," he said. "In fact, I think he finds you quite as delicious as I do."

I smiled and looked up as Eddie returned from the toilet. He sat nervously on the edge of the bed next to me. He stroked his semi-hard cock, avoiding my face as I studied him. Oh, he was so adorable, I thought.

"Yes," I said, looking back at Peter. Peter smiled, looking like he did the first time I was with him, the first time I learned what lovemaking could be.

Eddie continued stroking his cock slowly. He looked at me nervously.

I liked Eddie too, and might even fall in love with him if I were to give him half a chance. Eddie stared at me, taking in every inch of my body but keeping his hands busy with his cock, which was hardening a bit. It was a cute cock, now that I really looked at it, and while it lacked in length and girth, Eddie made up for that with enthusiasm. I saw his roving eyes pause at my cock, which was becoming erect again as a result of my thoughts. Moving towards him, I kissed him, feeling the stiffness of his mouth as I ran my tongue across his lips. I pushed my tongue harder against him, and his lips opened to me slightly, allowing me inside. I kissed him for several minutes, then Peter's voice broke the magic. "Fuck him, Casey," he said. "Fuck him. I want to see you fuck him as hard as he fucked you."

I looked up into Eddie's eyes for his permission. Eddie shrugged. I watched, enthralled, as Eddie got down on his hands and knees. His ass shifted heavily as he obediently positioned himself before his lover. Peter placed his hand under the boy's chin, drawing his face up to look into his.

As they kissed, with great passion, I got behind Eddie and pushed forward, sinking a couple of inches of my prick into him. He wiggled, and I had to hold him steady. He was not really fighting it, and he quickly took his mind off the pain by bringing his lips to Peter's cock. "Oh, that's right," Peter murmured, "Suck it. Fuck, him, Casey. Fuck him good."

As I pushed another few inches into his lover, Eddie's back arched. At one point, when I rammed it all the way into him, he cried out, then went back to sucking Peter.

As I was nearing orgasm, Eddie raised up and held on to the frame of the antique iron bedstead. He inhaled sharply and his body rose as I lowered myself on top of him. His young flesh was soft and yielding, and I finished in him, fucking him forcefully. I stopped for a moment, pulled out, and slid my cock up and down his crack, getting it fully hard again. Eddie was writhing and crying out for me not to stop. But I had to, momentarily, catching my breath before resuming my assault on his ass. I knew Peter was watching, getting off on the sight of me on top of his lover, and I wanted to put on a good show for him. I leaned over to see his hand rising and falling along the length of Peter's cock. I drenched Eddie's ass with my jism. I felt Eddie's body stiffen. At this point, Peter took his lover's cock in his hand and jacked it along with his own. I listened to the soft moans that escaped from Eddie's throat. I was consumed by lust, grinding myself into him even though I had come.

Later, resting, I agreed to stay the night. I knew what that meant, that there would be more fucking in the morning, but now, instead of worrying about it, I was looking forward to it.

• • •

I had another three-way the following weekend. It began

on one of those glorious nights when they'd let all the stars out. I wanted to reach up and pluck a few; instead, I found myself catching the train to Connecticut to see a man who had met me briefly after the show one night. I admit I was intrigued by Randall Cunningham. His almost-handsome face was bony, almost but not quite too narrow, his lips thin. His eyes—which were an indefinite gray—the kind of eyes that change colors, I thought—had tiny flecks of gold in them. They were sad, intelligent, wry. I wanted to fuck him, please him, free him from whatever was paining him.

Randall's rented country house was a huge stone monstrosity with a spacious living room and a wide staircase leading to the solitary bedroom.

"I love it," I said.

"It's cheap," he said.

"Cheap's okay," I responded as he showed me to the upstairs sanctuary. He asked me if I wanted to take a shower first, and I did. When I was done, I moved across the room to sit on the edge of the bed. He stood at the window; he was naked, his buns glorious in a soft light. When he turned to face me again, I could see that he was fully erect; his lovely long prick bobbed and swayed in front of him as he stepped over to me.

He drew me into his strong arms and kissed me. He was gradually over on top of me, still keeping his lips glued to mine. Our lips finally parted, and I started licking his face and ears. Soon my tongue and lips were moving down his body. There wasn't much of his firm body that I didn't lick before I got to his cock. I massaged his crotch, reaching back occasionally to his asshole. He spread his legs, almost like he was asking for me to fuck him with my tongue. I did so, and he took vast intakes of air all the while I was doing it. Then I took the cock in my mouth. It was not an especially large cock, but it was a nice one. It was a good sucking cock, with its large head. More than anything in the world, I love sucking a beautiful cock, and his sighs signaled that my talents were being appreciated.

He suddenly pushed me away and knelt, straddling me.. He put his hands on my shoulders and started his hips moving. I opened my mouth and just let him do it. His rapid piston motions over my lips and deep dives down my throat sent me into orbit. I loved how he was using my mouth. My cock was ready to explode but I took my hands off it so I could play with his balls as he fucked my mouth. With every plunge down my throat, he moved a step closer to orgasm.

"Oh, God!" he suddenly howled and jerked his cock out of my mouth. He shot all over my face.

He grabbed my cock; it was as hard as wood and he pulled on it, not so gently, and it swelled so much he could not contain it in his hand. I sighed with pure pleasure as he stroked me. He positioned me, arms up and out to the side, legs spread wide. He bent his head and tapped my cock up and down on his ready mouth. He ran his tongue round and round the tip. I wanted to shove it into his mouth, but he wanted to admire it. "What a pretty one," he said.

I knew Randall was a best-selling author of mystery novels, but I had never read any of his books. Still, I pretended I had. He saw right through that, of course, kidding me that I needed to go to acting school. A good school, not Gardner's. I shot back that I couldn't afford any better, and he laughed. He said he was willing to bankroll me, but he already had his hands full with another actor who had attained some level of fame in motion pictures. When he showed me the young man's photograph I recognized him instantly. "You're Matthew Lane's lover?" I asked, incredulous.

He chuckled. "Well, yes. I guess I have become somewhat famous in some circles for being Matthew Lane's lover. Isn't that a sad commentary for a serious writer?"

I held the photo, elegantly framed in silver, and stared at it. God, I thought, all the times I had seen Matthew making passionate love to all those women on screen! Talk about a good actor...!

With the exception of Randall, it seemed Matthew Lane shunned possessions, preferring to live out of a couple of suitcases and hiring limos to take him from place to place. I was to learn that Randall and Matthew had an on-again, off-again relationship that spanned the continent. When in New York, Matthew holed up at Randall's apartment on Central Park. That was where he was at this very moment. When he was making a movie, Matthew stayed in a rented house in Beverly Hills. Often Randall joined him there and that was where he finished his novels. He said he started them in New York and finished them in California. "They always start dark and end light. Full of hope at the end. There's always hope."

I thought my weekend respite at Randall's expense might come to an end much sooner than I had anticipated. After lunch, I went down to the beach and took a long swim, and when I returned to the house, I found Matthew giving a blowjob to Randall in the living room.

My first thought was to race up to my room, pack my stuff, and beat it, leave them to it, but Randall told me to enter the room. Matthew looked up from his action enough to smile at me and say, "Nice to meet you," before he went back to work. Matthew was even more gorgeous in person than on screen. And here I was seeing him completely nude! His hairless backside was perfectly formed, and there was a nice tan line that only added to his beauty.

So, with nothing else to do, I found a comfortable chair and watched Matthew, silver screen adventure hero, suck his lover's cock.

Matthew was kneeling between Randall's spread thighs. And Randall was comfy on the couch enjoying the view as Matthew's head was bobbing up and down. Randall did not ignore me for long. "Come closer," he said, waving me over. I stood, stepped over to them, and parked my buttcheeks on the arm of the sofa.

The hunky young star of Hollywood action movies was sucking the big cock as if he weres licking the dripping ice cream off some super-deluxe sugar cone, lapping up the pre-cum and his own saliva.

Randall was loving it too, his head arched back, moaning "Ohhh" and "Yeah" like he was in some other world. Well, he'd never acted that way with me.

When Randall was close, Matthew ran his tongue up and down the length of Randall's cock, licking his balls and then working his way back up to his big purple head. When he got there he brushed his lips over the tip and then sucked his entire cock deep into his mouth again like he was trying to see just how much of it he could inhale. Let me tell you, it was a lot. I'd tried doing that a couple of times, but it always made me gag.

Matthew just kept sucking his lover deep down his throat,

farther and farther, until Randall didn't have any more to give him. And then he started moaning again, louder this time, as he moved his body in slow gyrations, as if he were trying to fuck Matthew's mouth like it was a pussy. Matthew actually let him do it for a few seconds, but then he pulled his mouth away from his cock, leaving it glistening wet in the dim light of later afternoon. I was amazed. Randall's cock had never been that big or hard with me. Never!

Randall looked disappointed that Matthew had stopped sucking him off, but Matthew either didn't notice, or didn't care. He just sat down on the sofa next to his lover, spread his legs and said, "Your turn now." He was talking to Randall, not to me.

As obedient as a schoolboy, Randall moved to the end of the bed and made himself comfortable between Matthew's legs, and began licking his ass. I couldn't believe it: he was licking his ass from top to bottom, bottom to top, sucking and fucking the sopping-wet hole with his tongue. He had never done any of those things for me. Never! Matthew began to buck and grind his sex against Randall's lips. He could barely control himself.

"Oh, that's it!"

It looked and sounded as if he were going to have one hell of an orgasm. And, although I couldn't take my eyes off the two of them, it was hurting me to watch. Matthew, I could tell, had attitude—that's what gives stars this thing that makes them attract attention when they walk into a room. They give off an energy, a supreme self-confidence, a presence. You either have it or you don't. I wondered then whether I had it. I thought I did, but wasn't sure. If it was possible, perhaps, by osmosis, I was acquiring it. All I know, I was mesmerized by Matthew, and, as he watched me watching him, I knew he found it pleasurable too.

"God, I've been thinking about what you could do with this," Randall said to me, stroking Matthew's cock after taking a break from his rimming.

I had to admit it was a lovely, cut cock; not as big as Randall's, but perfectly formed, with a slight bend to the left.

I swallowed hard. "Sorry," I said. "I feel light-headed. Too much sun this afternoon."

"You're refusing this?" Randall spat, waving it at me.

"Matthew came back early just to meet you."

Yes, for me to do this was unheard of. I was being paid to do whatever he wanted, but this whole scene had gotten the better of me. I got up from the sofa without answering him.

I started to leave the room, go upstairs, pack my stuff and split.

Randall yelled at me, "What is it? The money?"

No, it wasn't—not entirely. I was intimidated by Matthew, but I would never let them know that. Money, I decided, was as good an excuse as any. I turned to face them. "I was paid up front for you. That was the deal."

"Oh, shit, you know I'll make it good."

"I've been through this before," I said, turning away. "I don't like surprises."

I raced up the stairs. Randall had Matthew follow me. He followed me right into the bathroom adjoining my guest room.

I was having trouble peeing because I was nearly fully erect. Matthew saw this as he entered the bathroom and chuckled. "Well, at least you're not turned off."

"No, I'm not turned off," I said curtly.

He left me alone to finish peeing, if I could. But he was back in moments, and a fistful of dollars was tossed at me.

"That's five hundred. Is that enough?"

As the dollars fell to the floor at my feet I shook the pee drips off my cock. "This is seven inches. Is that enough?"

Matthew said nothing; he just dropped to his knees before me and began kissing my cock.

This was really more than I could stand; meeting someone I had fantasized about was one thing, but having him actually performing for me was beyond comprehension.

My body was exploding with pleasure. I felt giddy. My crotch was buzzing, asking to be touched. On their own, my hips began grinding against him, a rhythm I gave myself over to. He licked my balls next and I held his shoulders for balance. I was now looking down on the top of the head of the greatest cocksucker I had ever experienced. Suddenly, he looked up. "I want to fuck you."

I hesitated, mainly because I wanted the suck to go on a bit longer. He stared at me with desire in his eyes. I stared silently back, taking in the lines of his powerful pecs, his rock-hard biceps, and the thickness of his forearms. His handsome face was lit in shadows by rays of light pouring in from the bedroom. We stayed like this a moment, not speaking or touching, just breathing each other in.

Then he went back to sucking. Again and again I was at the brink of coming, and as he held my thrusting hips with his strong hands, I was literally swimming in desire. Squeezing my eyes shut, I let him guide and carry me to the edge beyond myself. We rocked together on the waves of my orgasm, he taking all of my cum down his gullet. Crying out, my voice mingled with his, and I clung to him with a tight grip, gasping and panting wildly until my breathing slowed. I was still gasping for air when he finally released my cock.

And then gently he turned me so he was behind me and soon we were both on our knees. Then he guided me forward onto my hands and knees. He was on his knees behind me, making soft noises between breaths. His hands on my hips pulled me back so that my ass felt the warm flesh of his thighs and stomach. As he rocked us softly, the lukewarm coolness of his hard dick bumped against the cheeks of my ass provocatively. I looked back over my shoulder for a moment at his handsome face as he reached for lube, which he generously smeared over his seven-inch, nicely cut cock. I was waiting to be filled, and when he touched me lightly with his finger, then pressed his thumb slowly inside me, I pushed back, taking it in, aching and taking.

"I want you in me," I said, my voice cracking, nearly failing me. Now he pulled me back against him, and with each thrust, my fleshy butt slapped pleasantly against his thighs and abdomen. Each thrust was agony, but I endured. Finally he achieved a pleasantly rhythmic pulsing, and he came. I collapsed as he held on, and an exquisite peace flowed through me.

"Well, you boys look like you have gotten better acquainted," Randall said, entering the bathroom.

"He's as good as you said he was," Matthew said, pulling his cock from my ass. "This is one hot piece of ass."

"Can I finish inside you, Casey?" Randall asked.

I nodded, and started lifting myself up. Matthew took me in his arms, kissed me and then led me into the bedroom.

Once I got on the bed, Randall started kissing my ass, and

twirling his tongue inside me. Then he decided I needed a good shaving. That was better than a good spanking so I kept my mouth shut. He started at the outer edges, the razor tugging gently against the hair and leaving a clean path behind. Every time he applied the lotion he rubbed it gently through my hair to be sure the skin beneath was lubricated.

As he shaved closer and closer to my crack, his touch sent shivers through me as his fingers tugged and pulled my asslips this way and that. Occasionally his fingers reached inside as he held the skin taut for the razor. My fantasies were becoming more and more explicit as he continued, his warm hands on my inner thighs to spread them farther apart as he put the finishing touches on my clean-shaven ass. By the time he finished and used a moist towel to clean up any remaining shaving lotion, I was hotter than a firecracker and nearly panting.

"There," he said, "just like a newborn baby." And then he slowly pulled my asslips apart. He fingered me, saying "Hmmm, let me admire your beautiful body for a while, okay?"

I moaned in response. The longer he held out the better. As he ran his hands all over my body, I quivered with excitement. He rolled me over and squeezed my nipples, gently licking and sucking them. His soft lips on my nipples lit a fire in my crotch, and I started wriggling around on the bed. He moved down my torso, beneath my navel, ending with his tongue lapping up the precum oozing from my cock. He flicked his tongue around my cock and, when it was hard again, he lifted me up so that he could stick his tongue in and out of my newly shaved ass, then inserted two fingers deep inside. He smiled at me and said, "I love licking your ass."

He continued probing my ass with his tongue until I begged him to stop, to fuck me.

Matthew joined us and positioned me on all fours. Now Randall was ready. His crotch was level with my ass. He pointed his throbbing cock at my spasming hole and drove forward. With one stroke, he impaled me right to hisballs. The gaping orifice was warm and slimy, stretched out nicely by Matthew's fat cock.

I was soon thrashing like mad, but Matthew held me tight. "Oh God, you're good," he told me as Randall began to thrust in and out, working up a burning friction in seconds.

My body jerked and squirmed all over the bed. Randall grabbed hold of my ass and rammed his cock home, pummeling my hole as rapidly as he could manage. The cum Matthew's had deposited there spilled out to drip down my crack and onto his balls. My hole felt as if it were on fire. Matthew had merely warmed me up; I shoved my ass back over Randall's cock just as wildly as he was thrusting into me. I lifted my face and managed to slide my mouth over Matthew's raunchy dick, which I could see was getting hard again.

Randall came after about ten minutes of this steady reaming, shooting a his cum into me while Matthew was thrusting upwards into my mouth, his own lust rekindled. It was enough to push me over the edge again. I shot another load, groaning into the bedcovers.

I napped alone In Randall's big bed. It was dark when they awakened me for dinner, and I had a hunch what dessert would be that night.

• • •

When I returned from Randall's country place, there was a message from Mom. My dad had been on one of his binges and was insisting I clear what remained of my stuff out of my room. He was planning on renting it out. "He doesn't really mean that, of course, but he does mean for you to take everything out. I'm so sorry, hon."

There was always a special thrill of anticipation when I made the trip to Brooklyn to see Mom again, no matter how brief the separation had been, but this time it was mixed with the slight dread of having to listen to her tell me my dad had decided I wasn't welcome there any more.

I walked across the room into Mom's waiting arms. She said, "Oh, honey, I don't mean to fuss at you. You know that, don't you? It's only that Dad always manages to hurt you ... I don't want you to be hurt!"

"I know. Please just let me pick up the few things that I have left and I'll be on my way ... no lectures, please."

"I haven't had time to pack for you, but your suitcase is on your bed and I'm making some sandwiches for you to eat on your way back."

Mom always gave me food to eat on the way back into Manhattan, as if I was making a long journey to another country.

"Egg salad, your favorite, on...." she said as she moved toward the kitchen, finishing the thought under her breath as she adjusted her apron.

"You don't need to bother...."

She gritted her teeth as she trimmed the bread. "I've got a good mind to go with you, son. But I've gotta stay. I gotta stay with it till the end."

The end for Mom would come when Pa finally breathed his last. Every time I went to Brooklyn to see Mom, he'd show up, as if he knew I was coming, and cause a scene. Finally he put his foot down: I was not to darken their door again.

Okay by me. I went into the bedroom and began pulling assorted items of clothing from drawers and closets and dropping them into my small, battered suitcase. Then, overcome with memories of my early teen years living in the house that had ceased to be a home, I relived that awful day when I was fifteen and heard Pa's hateful voice when he caught me sucking Frankie, the neighbor boy. "What are you doing, you filthy kid?" And later, "You dirty little pervert! You get out of this house, you filth. You don't live here anymore with decent people!"

"Are you okay, honey?" Mom's voice interrupted the painful memories. She crossed to the bed and bent to touch my shoulder.

Seeing the concern on her creased, but still-lovely face, I embraced her gently.

"I don't know why Pa is the way he is...."

"Don't worry about it, Ma. I'm fine, really. I turned out to be exactly what Pa thought I was. To his thinking, what I did to Frankie was a shameful thing and he was right to send me away." I sighed.

"Oh, I didn't mean to get you started, honey."

Finally I closed the bag and turned to Mom.

"I don't really want you to go," she said bleakly.

"I know. But he's bound to show up any moment and....."

"Remember I love you."

I think I invited her to come into Manhattan for lunch one

day, but maybe I didn't. My mind was so filled with painful memories that I almost forgot my sandwiches. "Don't worry about me, Mom. I'm leaving the tears behind me."

On the subway, I ate the little sandwiches and thought about Frankie, wondering whatever happened to him. He and his family had moved away shortly after I was discovered blowing him. In fact, that was why I did it then, because it was really my last chance. He had been such a tease. He was two years older than I and a beefy player on the football team. He had come over to sneak a peek at my dad's collection of *Hustler* magazines, which I had discovered one day down in his workshop in the basement. Frankie was looking at the pictures and rubbing his crotch.

Finally, he said he had to take it out, it was just too painful. Somehow I knew exactly what was going on; I guess I realized very early that the only way "a real man" could do it with a fag was if he was drunk or, as in this case, looking at pussy and "allowing" a fag to "help him out a little." I had practiced on a couple of other neighborhood pals, but this was the big league for me. Frankie's cock was at least eight inches long and thick, uncut. I nibbled the foreskin, a new sensation, then began the suck. Frankie went wild, and I held off his orgasm, sending him higher and higher into uncharted territory I was sure. Delicious waves of pleasure rolled over me as I discovered the power I had with my mouth and hands. It was as if I had been born for the sole purpose of sucking cock. Suddenly, the door banged open, flooding the darkened room with furious light. There was Dad, his black eyes searing me with hatred. Frankie pulled up his pants and made a hasty retreat, leaving me to suffer the worst beating of my young life.

Now as the subway car jostled me to and fro, I saw the swarthy youth reclining in the seat directly across the aisle from me had fallen asleep and was apparently dreaming of his girlfriend's pussy, because I could see an admirable bulge at his crotch. Or he was trying to entice me. I hoped that was it. I concentrated on his bulge and it worked. He opened his eyes, rubbed them. He looked out the window, then back at me.

He was an adorable youth: dark curly hair, olive skin. I guessed he was Greek. He wore a brightly colored T-shirt, a pair of worn jeans that were torn in strategic areas.

He noticed where my eyes had strayed and smiled. "Hi there," he said casually. "You going or coming?"

I blinked, then realized I had my old suitcase next to on the seat. "Oh, both."

He smiled at this, not knowing what to make of it. He looked me up and down, then asked, "You got a place?"

I nodded. "Just got settled in." I slapped the suitcase. "This is the last of it."

He moved across the aisle and sat next to me. "You need any help movin' in? I'm lookin' for work."

"No. Like I said, this is the last of it."

"I really need to earn some money...."

I knew what the story was but at this point I didn't care. After Mom and thoughts of sucking Frankie's cock, I was ready to lose myself in this boy's crotch. He introduced himself as Jason.

I shook his hand. "Okay. I guess I could use your help. My roommate is out of town...."

Once in the apartment, thoughts of unpacking fell away as I stroked the incredible bulge, and fumbled with his zipper. Reaching inside his jeans, I felt the sticky moisture of precum soaking his underwear.

When I withdrew it from the briefs, I saw his prick was long,, nearly as thick as mine, and uncut, his ample foreskin hanging low over his cockhead. At the tip of his dick, a small pearl of dew glistened.

"Suck my dick, man. Let me feel your mouth," he whispered urgently.

I followed the boy's instructions with pleasure, taking his skin into my mouth and savoring the sticky, sweet taste of his lube. Jason placed his hands behind my head and stuffed my mouth full of his young meat, my throat expanding easily to accept his length. I sucked him for a good ten minutes, jerking myself as I kneeled before him. He was leaning against the wall, holding my head. Finally he pulled me off and asked, "Can I fuck you?"

I nodded, stood and led him to my bedroom. Nude, he was a vision. I worked on his nipples, then his balls, before going back to his cock. I was hoping he'd come because after the weekend with Randall and Matthew, I simply didn't want to get fucked. But he saw the jar of lube on the nightstand and he stuck his finger into the jar and spread the gel into my ass. I decided I wanted to take him on my back so I could watch him over me.

Before I could urge the Greek boy to be gentle on my aching hole, he slipped the head of it into me effortlessly, his thick shaft slowly, and painlessly, spreading my anal walls apart.

I spread my legs a bit wider and placed my hands on the furry cheeks of Jason's ass, urging him deeper into my butt. His cock was making squishy sounds as it plunged in and out of my hole, and Jason's eyes were closed in rapture, his face a picture of ecstasy.

Jason read my mind. "Your ass was made for my dick, man," he said as he picked up the pace, thrusting into my stretched hole faster and faster.

I was rewarded as I watched his shaft plunging in and out. I jerked my cock only a couple of times, then he began to shoot along with me, filling me as my cum flew across my chest.

Breathless and exhausted, Jason sprawled on the bed next to me. I could smell the warm, musky scent of his dripping body. His beautiful face had the stubble of several days' growth of beard. When I licked the salty rivulets of sweat from his stomach and chest, my cock began to harden again. The smell, the taste of him was so intoxicating that I was almost ready to go another round. I sucked his nipples until they hardened between my lips, then nibbled the roughness of his neck and chin.

When we kissed, it was very tenderly. Our lips soon parted and he said, "I've gotta go, man."

"I appreciate your helping me out."

He smiled, looked about the room. "Seems you really didn't much help."

"Oh, just having you in bed was a great help. It'll help me make it through the night."

"That's what it's all about, man."

He was thrilled when I gave him one of the hundreds that Matthew had thrown in my face. I am a firm believer in spreading the wealth.

VIII. Invitation to a Gang Bang

The taxi pulled up to the hotel of my drunken client for the night. The cab driver, who barely spoke any English, was more than a little annoyed I wasn't getting out with the john. As the client tearfully slammed the door, I shifted my full attention to the cabby, who really had no interest in driving me across town. I pleaded and negotiated, promising him $10, $15, then $25 to get me to the place where Matthew said he would be staying. Shaking his head and muttering under his breath, he jerked the cab into Drive and headed down Fifth Avenue.

Traffic was heavy that night and the drive seemed terribly long. My head leaned and bounced against the slimy window of the cab as the city rushed by in a dreamy blur.

Intimidated and intrigued, terrified and transfixed by Matthew Lane, I agreed to come to a party one of his pals was hosting. I placed the agreed-on $25 in the driver's sweaty hand, knowing and not caring that I had no money left to get home. I climbed out of the cab on woozy, rubbery legs. I had matched my dinner-date john drink for drink, something I never do, and then simply could not go through with it, another thing I never do. A deal is a deal, in my strange world, but the thought of seeing Matthew again had affected my judgment.

He was standing inside the iron-gated door of the basement apartment in the Village, his beautiful face framed by the wrought iron. A sweet stab of excitement rushed through my body, slowing to spread itself gently over my cock.

"I'm glad you're here," he said with a glassy-eyed, squinty grin, fingers fumbling with the keys in the gate's lock. His tousled, blondish hair looked wet, and his breath stank of liquor.

He pulled me inside and re-locked the iron gate behind me. I stood in the foyer and bent to untie my shoes, feeling a rush of panic. I couldn't believe I was there with this movie star again.

"This is a nudie party, Casey. Will you take your clothes off for me? Your body is so beautiful."

I barely heard his words, hearing instead the rhythmic cadence of his sensual Southern drawl. I still hadn't said a word. A wave of heat washed over my face in embarrassment.

"Here?"

"Yeah, take them off here. Put your clothes on that chair there."

I looked about me. There were five chairs there, all but one with piles of clothes on them.

"I'll get you a drink."

I ordered a Coke. He smiled. "Okay, I'll be back in a moment." He touched my arm and winked, then turned and headed toward the kitchen.

I was alone in the marble-floored foyer, but I felt as if I were being watched. My trembling hands rested on the buckle of my black leather belt, making me think about what I was letting myself in for. This was no ordinary "party" and I began to think I had let Matthew and Randall pull a fast one on me, or at least try to, once again. I thought of running while I could. Beads of sweat began to form on my upper lip and forehead. I was drunk enough to just say "Fuck it," and I pulled off my turtleneck, then peeled off my slacks and socks and tossed them onto the chair designated for me. I fingered the elastic band of my crotch-soaked briefs and slowly slid them over my hips and down my thighs. I stepped out of them slowly, one leg, then the other, and brought them up to my mouth and nose. Eyes closed, I breathed deeply of my own powerful essence, my senses heightened beyond belief.

The beat of a Marvin Gaye album blaring through the apartment, resonated up from the hardwood floor through my body, and bounced out like a sonic sounding device, testing my endurance. I was sweating and flushed with furious desire as I made my way down a long corridor to the kitchen. Matthew handed me my Coke, his eyes riveted on my crotch. "Your cock is so beautiful," he said, approaching me. He slid his hand down my belly to my thighs, over my ass, and back around, finally, to my hungry cock. My pelvis arched to meet his touch, legs spread wide.

He slid his fingers inside me, first one, then another, letting his desire guide him, letting my ass muscles massage them in a rhythmic dance of its own, until I shuddered and cried out, my ass gripping and releasing his fingers. "You are *so* good," he said. "C'mon, let's join the others."

The first man I was introduced to was Brian, a tall, handsome man who looked me over with hazel eyes. "Hmmmm." He held a tight smile.

I grinned back at him, and turned my attention to Sal, at least two hundred and forty pounds of chiseled muscle, and his close buddy Gino, who was hanging all over him. Gino was shorter and slimmer, lithe and sleek. "So, you wanna play with us?"

Brian gave Gino and Sal an inebriated look.

"A foursome?"

"Nah, a gang bang," Matthew replied.

"Oh, I don't think so," I said, cool as I could manage, sipping my Coke at last.

Matthew came up behind me and his hand began massaging my ass. "You like big dicks, Casey. I know you do." I didn't pull away. Matthew's voice was a seductive murmur, "Shall we tie you up and use you for our pleasure? Would you like that, Casey? All of us using you?"

Resistance was futile, but I put on a good show for them; I was an actor, after all.

They led me to a black leather sling in what one of them called "the playroom," and strapped my legs and arms in and locked them down, then put the blindfold on me. Matthew tore the blindfold off. "He wants to watch. He gets off on watching."

I silently thanked him, one actor to another.

Matthew started by donning a latex glove and slathering it with lube. He caressed the crack of my ass, teasing me. I arched, and Matthew slid his hand up and down the crack. I was tight; I hadn't been fucked in several days. All my johns had wanted me to fuck them, or blow them. Matthew was surprised, and smiled as he teased my hole, inserting the tip of his finger and massaging the sphincter until it relaxed. Sal and Gino watched, playing with each other's cock. Brian played with Matthew's cock while Matthew worked on me. Matthew was as skilled at this as he was at everything else. He kept talking to me, making me answer. "You like that, you like something hard in your ass?"

I was gasping and pulling on my cock.

Matthew now said, "I want you to suck a nice big cock for

me. Take it all the way down your throat." He nodded to Gino, who unfastened the head of the sling, lowering my head so that my mouth hung open. Gino began fucking my face. Gino slid the uncircumcised crown of his dick between my lips and I sucked convulsively. Matthew stroked my ass with one hand and fingered my hole with the other. Gino worked his dick inch by inch into my mouth, getting harder and hotter all the time. Soon Gino's pubes were shoved against my face, the black hair tickling my nose, and the low-hanging balls draped over my nose. Sal stepped up to us, wanting me to know he was there, watching. A silent look passed between Gino and Sal, and Gino held his dick deeper and longer, choking me in the sling. Sal watched for him, deciding how much I could take. I struggled as I realized I had no control over what was happening to me, but with a mouth full of Gino's succulent cock, I couldn't say anything at all. During the rare moments when I was permitted to breathe, I was too busy gasping for air to get a word out. Then Gino slammed back into me, making his body arch, and cutting off all further conversation.

Meanwhile Matthew watched the ass squirming around his fingers and fiddled inside. This caused me to jerk and struggle harder as my dick got stiffer and stiffer. I wanted desperately to come; I guess the whole idea of being their slave had turned me on. This was a much heavier scene than I had ever expected.

Matthew apparently felt my tension because he started his low, seductive talk again: "We've been planning this, you know. We thought that since you wanted it so much, we'd give it to you in a way you'd never forget. You could never do this in one of your movies, I know."

Then his hand slapped against my ass. I jerked and twisted, but I was impaled on Matthew's stiff fingers and Gino's dick, and his own cock was standing up, throbbing. Matthew continued slapping my ass, reddening it, making the sling sway so that I was shoved into Gino's groin, then almost pulled free of the cock. We eventually got the rhythm going good: slap, impale, swing, gasp, over and over again. Meanwhile, Brian was jacking Matthew's dick. Tears streamed from my eyes and my ass was burning hot.

"Now that's a butt that looks like it needs to be fucked, and fucked good, doesn't it, Brian?"

Brian nodded, not letting go of Matthew's prick.

"Yeah, it sure does," Sal agreed, and Gino grinned.

"Want a piece of this?" he asked Sal.

"No, I'll wait until you're done."

I cried out as Matthew entered me, his cock being guided to the target by Brian's trembling hand, not that that cock needed any help. Matthew let out a groan, then bracing his hands on my waist, began to fuck me.

Gino reached out and grabbed his lover by the neck and kissed him, as they fucked my body.

Then Gino and Sal switched places and Sal shoved his thick, squat dick down my throat. His eyes locked on Matthew's, and the two of them shoved hard, fucking my body between them, feeling one another's thrusts as if in their own flesh. I had been reduced to being a medium of communication between them. I was suffocating now, and tears were streaming down my face, trying to kick loose of the two invading pricks, to get some air, but this only inflamed the two fuckers. Gino pushed Sal away from Matthew and slapped him for kissing the movie star. Sal pulled out and let me have a breather while Matthew continued ramming my ass.

Gino grabbed my nipples and twisted. That diverted my attention from the merciless fuck, and Gino played them skillfully. I began to whimper. Now Sal moved out of the way to let Brian fuck my face. Sal played with my nuts; my dick was hard and purple with frustration and pain while every muscle in my body strained. I could feel the balls against my butt as Matthew shot his jism deep into my body.

"Your turn," Sal said to Gino. "You know I like your sloppy seconds."

Matthew moved aside, breathing heavily, while Gino quickly took his place at my ass. He rubbed the head of his dick up and down the crack, added more lube, and stimulated himself to even greater hardness by teasing his foreskin against the wrinkled sphincter. I knew I was loose after the fucking Matthew had given me, and the head of Gino's massive prick slipped in easily. He let the head rest there a moment. Then he pulled it out and began teasing me. Finally, as Sal began to suck me, Gino treated himself a nice, leisurely fuck. At one point, he moaned, "He feels just like a pussy," then began to thrust more forcefully. Brian let up on my mouth so that I could lift up and see Gino when he finally came. It was glorious, almost in slow motion. Then Gino sagged and Sal grabbed him; Gino seemed on the verge of total collapse. His bodybuilder boyfriend helped him to a chair nearby and then came back to stick his thick meat into me. Covered in sweat, beads of it rolled down his body and onto my belly. Brian proceeded to lick my chest and then suck my cock while Sal had his fun.

I screamed, more in joy than pain. Matthew wanted a show, and I was going to give him one. I began to come, what with Brian's expert mouth action. I kicked in my bonds, but resistance was futile.

Suddenly Sal began to moan; I looked up to see that Brian had left my dick and gone round to stick his prick into Sal as Sal fucked me. Being the middle of a double fuck while Gino watched must have been one of his fantasies come true because he blurted that he'd never been so happy.

The two men were in sync, coming together, with Sal's hand dragging on my dick, as if he was trying desperately to revive it so that I too could fuck him.

I left them all in the living room, fearing what would happen if I stayed any longer. I dressed quickly and left without saying goodbye. I decided to walk; actually, I had no choice since I was broke after having spent my last $25 on the cab. But then I stuffed my hands in my pockets and felt something had been put there. I reached in and pulled out a wad of cash. I stopped under a street lamp and counted out $2,000: five hundred per man. When I got back to my apartment, I called the number Matthew had given me and left a message: "Matthew, I love you. Thanks."

I hung up the phone and turned to see Barry standing there. He had heard what I had said, and was curious. "Matthew? Matthew Lane again?"

"Yes. It was fabulous."

Now, I knew, it was time again, time for Barry to move in and claim some of his "past dues," as he called them. Barry was an old friend of Peter's, and took me in when Peter could no longer have me there. Barry, forty, balding, with a little tummy he always said he was going to work on, had many businesses and traveled incessantly, so, in the beginning, I was left alone in the apartment on Riverside Drive much of the time. Then I began acting school, the movies came out, the hustling started. Barry's businesses went through hard times, he traveled less, and he had to get through so many dark nights alone. For those nights of loneliness, I had to pay—but only occasionally.

"Did you like Matthew's fuck as much this time as last time?"

"Yes ... no," I moaned weakly, barely thinking, eyes closed, smiling, arching my pelvis to meet his hand as he stroked my ass.

"No, you didn't?"

"No, there were four of them, Barry. Four."

Barry was the only one I told about my tricks. He loved every minute of my confessions. Now he slipped his fingers inside and my ass muscles spasmed and grabbed. I gasped, missed a breath, my heart pounding.

"Do you like feeling my fingers?"

"Oh ... yeah!"

"But you love my cock more, I know. I'll have it hard for you if you'll talk to me. Tell me about it, Casey," he said.

Secretly, I loved Barry, in my fashion. I loved his physical passion and passion for life: he was exuberant, theatrical at times, but always genuine and not like the fakes and flakes I met most of the time.

Gently, he pushed me onto his bed, and we kissed a long time, slowly at first, then with more passion. He took his small prick, now as hard as it ever got, and slid it in. I winced, but just for effect. I drew my legs around the back of his thighs and pulled him in. Soon we were gliding together faster, more urgent, pressing, his raw power and my reckless confessions driving him insane with desire. The rhythm increased, my ass ached, swollen with the beating it had just taken.

"God, I love fucking you, Casey."

"I know you do. God, how I know."

Finally he came and collapsed on the bed, sweaty, satisfied, with a shit-eating grin lighting his flushed face. He pulled out and lay back on the bed. Nuzzling my face under his chin, I settled into the glorious warmth of being held by a man who loved me above all others. All I wanted in life was to love someone as much as Barry loved me, and have him love me in return.

IX. Mad, Mad Love in Miami Beach

I asked the cute Latin boy what his name was, and he blushed.

"What's *your* name?" he asked, and his eyes narrowed in the smoke of the bar.

I told him. He acted as if he didn't know me. But then he said, "What's your *real* name?"

The boy seemed to talk in italics. He must have heard I was performing up the street in "Cockteasers." I told him my real name. Then I added, "If you want to see my driver's license, I'll show it to you."

Just then Jesse and Paul came back from the john. "Where did you find this kid?" I asked them. They were two guys who lived in Miami Beach, working as flunkies for the theater where the play had been booked. We hit it off immediately and they were always looking for boys who wanted to meet Casey Cassidy. But, after two weeks, it was beginning to bore me.

"We met at the movies," the boy said, and Jesse said, "Yeah, the movies, right?" The three of them laughed, and the boy blushed again.

"I love the movies," I said. "What movie did you see?"

They laughed again. "Yours!"

"Mine?"

"Yeah, they started running it at the Triple X when they knew you were going to be in town in your play."

"Which one are they showing?"

"Oh, 'Fire Island Fantasies' of course."

"Of course."

Jesse laughed along with me, then said, "Miguel wanted to meet you, so here we are."

Paul added, "He didn't believe we knew you. So...."

"So here you are and here I am," I said, batting my eyelashes at Miguel.

Conversation ceased because it was time for the strip show, which was preceded, as usual, by a brief message over the loudspeaker by the man in the sound booth: "Put your hands together for Larry," and no one even bothered to clap.

From our ringside table, Miguel seemed to genuinely enjoy the show, especially when Larry whipped off his rip-away running shorts, and, having sniffed them, cast 'em over to the boy, who caught 'em, sniffed 'em and waved 'em in the air. Jesse and Paul roared and signalled the waiter to bring us yet another round of drinks.

Larry worked on his erection, pulling on it through the jockstrap, and finally letting it snake out into the air along his thigh. The boy stirred uncomfortably, although a bit pleased, when Larry came over to him and dared him to touch it. As the boy reached out, Larry bounced away, on to the big tippers seated at the bar.

I downed my drink and moved my chair closer to Miguel. "I have something special for you," I said to him, pinching his arm. He curled his lip and rolled his eyes, clear indication that the stiff drinks were having the effect on him that my two co-conspirators had planned. What they didn't count on was that I liked the boy more than even they imagined I would, but my idea was to save him from me, them, and himself.

"What *is* it?" Miguel asked, still emphasizing every other word it seemed.

"You have the won the door prize tonight."

"He didn't even get a ticket," Jesse protested. "We paid for him. We should win."

"No, no. I'm the fuckin' judge and I declare *him* the winner."

"What *do* I win?"

I smiled. "A night with Casey Cassidy, of course!"

"My, oh my. That's worth a grand at least!" Jesse hooted.

Just then, Larry returned, leaping into our midst, pulling the front of his jockstrap down and wagging his semi-hard cock in our faces. We all sat up straight and widened oureyes as if they were hallucinating.

Jesse, closest to it, drooled over the cock, and Paul said he would buy it for his long-time lover. Paul gave Larry a twenty dollar bill and got a knowing wink in return.

As Larry danced away, Miguel collapsed upon the table. I pulled him back and helped him up. "We're leaving," I said, and I dragged the kid outside, and pushed him into a conveniently waiting cab.

"Where *are* you takin' me?" he moaned.

"To where it is you live. As quickly as possible."

"What? I thought I won the door prize."

Now, in his advanced drunken state, I couldn't imagine taking advantage of this boy; I was only going to drop him off, let him get on with the rest of his life. But he still wouldn't believe me, and he wouldn't give me his address. He kept babbling about the "fuckin' door prize" and falling into my lap. I had the driver let us out at the all-night diner that was next to my motel. I bought him coffee and a strawberry shortcake smothered by whipped cream. I nibbled on a chocolate chip cookie and drank coffee while he virtually inhaled the cake. Miguel said very little, nothing really, except "Thank you" after he'd finished. I handed him what was left of my cookie and he inhaled that as well.

"You're really going to take me to your room?"

"Of course. You won the door prize, remember."

As we walked across the parking lot to my room, I took his hand and squeezed it. "You know, you better learn who you can trust or you'll never get anywhere in this world."

"I'm not as dumb as I look," he said, pressing into me.

In the room, I softened. I grew quiet under the touch of his long, tender fingers. My hand went out to his, and he drew my palm to the soft inside of his thigh. "Do you like me?" he whispered after a moment, urging my hand upward.

I grinned. I liked the sound of his voice. The eagerness was there, coiled tensely inside his throat. But with the eagerness was submission, total submission to my will.

"So you want me, do you?" I asked quietly.

He nodded. He put his hand on his chest and trailed a route across his tight stomach to the bulge in his running shorts. "Yes," he answered weakly, "I really do."

I said nothing, but my grin broadened. My fingers played on his bare legs, and I tugged off his shorts. Then I slowly filled my palm with his huge piece of uncut flesh. For several minutes, we lay silent and motionless, except for my stroking his cock to full erection. It was nearly as thick a cock as the boy's I had met in San Francisco. I dared not look at him for fear I would let him know just how much I wanted him. I bent over him and my lips brushed the hair at his crotch. My nostrils quivered as I breathed in the strong, pungent odor of his Latin maleness.

As I took his cock into my mouth, I remembered the men back at the bar, all the envious eyes around us as we left. *Oh, if they could see me now*, I thought. I was in heaven with this young cock. I couldn't remember when I had a better time sucking a cock. So many times, when you are getting paid to please, you go through the motions, become numb. But now my lust kicked into overdrive. I withdrew the prick after a while and took my hands off it. There it gleamed, towering next to my face, my saliva rolling down the heavily veined shaft. What a killing I could make with this one in Hollywood, I realized. I wanted to see if he could perform on cue.

"Touch yourself, boy," I groaned. "Spread your little asshole for me. Open it up for me."

Miguel presented his buttocks, spread his thighs. He moaned crude words entangled with those of affection: "I want you to fuck it, Casey Cassidy," Miguel begged, saying my stage name as I had never heard it, elongating the vowels of my name, making it sound downright exotic.

I climbed back on the bed for a feel. Miguel moaned some more under the touch of these unfamiliar hands.

I had fantasized watching Miguel finger-fuck himself as soon as I caught sight of him. Motionless and fascinated, I stayed there on the bed and watched Miguel eagerly suck his middle finger with delight, as though it had been dipped in Orange Blossom honey, then slip it into his ass, only to offer it to me like some exotic sweet. I pulled it into my mouth, licked it, savored it, and returned it to him glistening with my saliva.

Miguel was beginning to enjoy this game. His legs wide open, with slow motion gestures, he turned toward me to allow a better angle of observation.

He plunged his finger in. Then two fingers assaulted his ass. Then three. He raised his hips, to bring his ass close to my flushed face.

"God," Miguel moaned, "I'm so hot. Fuck me!"

I rushed to get between Miguel's thighs and rammed myself into the boy, who was supporting himself on his hands. I didn't want to lie down on him. I needed to see Miguel's adorable face contorted with pleasure as I slid into him. I was determined to live up to my exalted reputation; I plunged deep into Miguel's ass and began my patented jackhammer fucking.

"Yes, yes...." Miguel cried as inch after inch of my cock was shoved in and out of him.

Finally I told him, "I want to see you come. I'm sure you're absolutely beautiful when you are coming."

Miguel gasped with each of my thrusts, but it was not enough after a while.

"Tell me that you like it," I ordered.

Miguel's only answer was to grip me tighter with his legs.

"Tell me," I persisted. "I need to hear it. To hear that you like it."

"Oh, yes," Miguel groaned. "Yes, I do. I love it. You know I love it. I am being fucked by Casey Cassidy."

I kept on, jacking that huge cock while I fucked. He came, a gusher unlike any I had ever witnessed, in or out of porn. I came too, then, deep inside him, and we fell asleep in each other's arms.

In the morning, I picked up our clothes strewn on the floor. Miguel was still asleep. I took a hot shower and attempted to regain my spirits. I was smitten. Miguel was a natural sex performer. I knew what it meant to give a performance, and Miguel had given a performance like no other.

Awake now, Miguel said he was hungry. I invited him to join me for breakfast. After breakfast, Miguel wanted to return to the room for more sex. I delivered an awkward apology that, no, he could not return to the room, that I had things I had to do before returning to the theater that night. I wanted to go further, to explain that the reason I couldn't have him back to the room was because I had fallen for him, and that our relationship could not go anywhere, there was no possibility of love between us, and that was that.

That night, after my show, I went back to the bar, only to find Miguel there, as I hoped he would be, but I was shocked to see he and Larry were dancing together, bumping and grinding, teasing the customers.

My sharpened excitement was tinged with fury. I saw man after man pay their respects for Miguel's incredible gifts of seduction. I was determined to enjoy Miguel again tonight. And tonight I wanted prolong the foreplay, making Miguel want me even more. And, I was determined to have Miguel's cock up my ass as well. He saw me, smiled, as if he had expected me to come for him, and, of course, was leaving with me.

Back at my room, Miguel was lying down upon the bed, like the sleeping prince, waiting for me to wake him. I leaned over his smooth, muscular body. I brushed his skin lightly, caressing him, every sensual inch of him. When Miguel tried to touch me, I drew back. This form of punishment excited him. I took a firm hold of Miguel's wrists, signifying that he'd better behave. Then I turned Miguel over on his stomach.

Miguel panted, writhing on the bed, begging me to put it in. My caresses aroused him uncontrollably, as did the role he was supposed to play in our little game. I lifted up his ass, spread his legs, and his asshole seemed to be winking at me.

But I still did not stick it in. I loved the way Miguel was responding to the game, begging me, "Please, Casey Cassidy, fuck me!"

Miguel's expectation made me harder than ever. The sight of the boy on the unmade bed with his ass rotating, surrendering his manhood to me again, had driven me over the edge. I had never wanted to fuck anyone as much.

Again I woke up before Miguel. He had slept in my tightly clinched embrace; we had not even tried to disengage our bodies from one another. I looked at him, smiled. Like a child with a new toy, I held his miraculous cock in the palm of my hand as if laying my claim to it.

"Is it late?" Miguel asked.

"Twelve-fifteen."

"I'm hungry," he said.

"So am I. But let's eat something first."

The air outside our love nest was humid, the sun intense. Glutted with sleep and pleasure, I was no longer concerned with keeping this affair secret. I wanted to take Miguel with me wherever I went. I would brazenly expose my lust for this boy now for all to see. I savored the looks we got as we sat down for lunch at a funky fish place down the road. Feeling like nothing more than a tourist, I ordered the crabcakes. I was still high from our sex, yet I wanted him again so badly my cock throbbed. Still, I was tempered by the knowledge that my limited engagement was coming to a close, and I knew how hard it would be to say good-bye to him.

As we ate, I could feel myself swelling at the sight of him, so enjoying his food. He saw the look in my eyes, and reached under the table to squeeze my knee. With a mischievous grin, he lightly ran his hand up and down my thigh. Gradually he moved his hand up farther. My crabcakes were quickly forgotten. Under the cover of the tablecloth, he twisted his hand to push my legs apart, then moved it back and forth near my crotch in his charming, teasing manner. I could hardly believe I was sitting in a crowded restaurant with this Latino's hand near my cock, and I picked up my wine glass and sipped it in a foolish attempt to look natural.

The cute waiter came by and asked if everything was all right. Still with his impish grin, Miguel answered that it certainly was, and at the same time, rubbed his hand over my swollen prick. The waiter glanced up at my sharp intake of breath, but I smiled and nodded at him. I was relieved when he moved away to another table. Miguel chuckled, like a schoolboy playing a prank, and took a forkful of crab. Meanwhile, his other hand was busy teasing and stroking my throbbing cock.

Finally, I had to warn him that I would come in my pants and then not be able to leave until it dried. He only laughed and increased the motion.

I could feel the heat from my belly right down to my thighs. Miguel played me like an instrument, knowing just when to rub hard and when to pull back and gently caress. Any attempt at sipping my wine was forgotten. I felt as if the whole restaurant must know what was going on, but I was beyond caring. All that mattered was Miguel's hand touching me. I tightened up, so close, so close, and then the hot, sweet wave rose up out of my cock and moved up my spine in a rapid, blissful sweep. I bit my tongue to keep from crying out as I came. Miguel's hand rubbed every last wave out of my cock, and I could feel that my pants were soaked with my hot cum.

I struggled to pull myself together. Playing the schoolboy still, but with a shit-eating grin, Miguel was now finishing his crabcakes, the very picture of cool. Orgasms always relax me and I seemed to need all of my strength just to lift my hands and finish eating my lunch. When coffee came, Miguel, still hungry, ordered a slice of cheesecake, and was right back at it again, nibbling at it and running his tongue over the fork when he slid it out of his mouth. No boy I had ever met loved sex as much as Miguel did, or made me want him more.

I had begun to feel as if our only purpose on earth was to love and satisfy each other.

My pants spotted with cum, we returned arm in arm to the motel, and some other visitors glanced shyly away, embarrassed by the sudden glimpse of gay life opening up before their eyes.

In the room, Miguel's sexual vigor was undiminished. He grabbed my hips as I was undressing. "Your ass is quite somethin'...."

"Not as nice as yours."

I did not move. Goaded by my seeming passivity, Miguel slipped off his shorts, sliding them down his thighs. He grasped his hardening cock and swept my ass slit with the tip of his cock.

"If you don't tell me to stop," he hissed, "I'm going to fuck you in the ass."

I did not say a word. Relishing the delicious thought, I could only murmur my consent. He thrust the entire length of his cock into me, again and again, one long stroke after the other, while I rubbed my own cock. Like the surge of high tide, his rhythm increased. It was so painful, yet I was suffocating with pleasure, tilting my hips to meet each incredible assault, amplifying the impact of his cock in my ass.

I uttered a long, modulated shriek, wrenched from the pit of my gut. I emerged from my orgasm with the knowledge that the pain was increasing as Miguel rammed himself in.

"Do you want me to stop?"

"No, go on. It hurts, but I like it. Just go a bit slower.

Please."

When he judged himself sufficiently lodged within me, Miguel began a to-and-fro motion. I clenched my teeth, and howled, whitened knuckles gripping the sides of the bed.

Soon my pain subsided, and at that point he asked, "Yes, you love me fucking your ass, don't you?"

"Yes," I cried out, "I love it!"

"I'm going to come!" he bellowed.

He shoved himself in all the way, came, and I was left limp.

Miguel gathered me into his arms, and we kissed. We continued kissing for several moments.

"I love you," Miguel said to me, in Spanish, pulling away to catch his breath..

I told him I loved him, and, in a way, my own way, I did.

Miguel asked me where I was going next.

"To Hollywood," I told him. "I have a client call."

"Take me with you, make me a porno star."

I didn't laugh, although I should have.

X. Return to Hollywood: Fucking for the Cameras

They weren't fucking for the cameras, but they obviously didn't care that the cameras seemed to b e there. They were used to cameras, so no one else was there, really. I couldn't look at Paul's sweet face without thinking how good he looked sucking cock, John's in particular: those moist lips wrapped around the thick shaft, those puppy-dog eyes turned upward in supplication, and John's meaty hands on Paul's head, pushing and impaling. God, they were good. I felt honored just to be in their presence. I had completed my scene with Paul. I just lay back and jerked off, awestruck at Paul's capabilities. He had just been fucked for three hours straight, but still he was horny and he was getting ready for his lover. This event had turned out far better than I had ever expected. Pinky said he had to get back to making movies; he had suffered some losses from the long tour of the play, due, I was sure, to his high living in the cities where we played. I avoided him when I could; I was busy with clients and my searching. I noticed that he made no trip to Miami Beach at all. I knew something was wrong. When I called him, he said he was glad to hear from me. Always devious, he said that he would use Miguel in his new film provided I would do a scene as well. He had two new sensations, John and Paul, whom he had nicknamed "The Apostles." I agreed, provided he paid Miguel the same $1,000 he was paying me. Pinky agreed without hesitation. My, I thought, how the business had changed since I did my first film. Back then, each of us was paid $200 a scene.

My scene in the new film would be done before Miguel's. I left Miguel at the motel and went to Pinky's house high in the Hollywood Hills. Carmine, he said, visited, but not very often. John and Paul were lovers in real life; in fact, they could have been brothers: both muscular, blond, blue-eyed.

The fucking started eventually, of course, and John soon was crying out in ecstasy. He pounded with every last inch of his might, filling Paul as I had attempted to do an hour or two earlier. All at once Paul screamed, and swayed up, rigid—and then swooned back, his cum spewing out and dropping on the bed, captured forever on celluloid.

They lay there, spent. After a while, John rolled off the bed and went into the bathroom and turned on the shower.

As John was drying off with a leaf-green towel, he heard me laugh behind him and he turned slowly around.

I leaned against the doorway, naked, smiling at him.

"So, how was it?"

"Great," I responded.

He came over to me, took my cock in his hand. His intimate approach gave me pause. I was thrilled at being desired by him, wanting to be possessed, consumed by such an appetite. His desperate mouth found my cock and stretched and moaned and sucked and got it all the way down.

He seemed to forget his lover awaited him in the next room, to think only of feeding his hunger. In moments, we were writhing on the floor, and I was nourishing his desire, stronger than my own. He wanted to fuck me, and who was I to refuse? "C'mon. No cameras."

The next day, Miguel arrived for his scene. We had abstained from sex, so intent was I that Miguel be successful before the cameras. He insisted that I tag along.

Now I could see by the monitor that Freddy, the lean, long-haired cameraman, was concentrating on Miguel's beauty as the boy crouched between the two standing studs, Bo and Thomas, sucking on one big cock while jerking the other, equally large, with his hand. Freddy was obviously as taken as I was when I first saw Miguel. I looked up to watch the action and see what the cameraman was not getting: how the two studs were running their hands down Miguel's back, teasing him.

I could see how hard they were, and so could the second cameraman, Jeff, who had just arrived in the room, ready for work at last. "God," Jeff gushed, "they're all so fuckin' hard. Just look at 'em."

Even Miguel was hard, harder than I had ever seen him. Maybe it was okay, letting him do this, I decided. He'd nagged and nagged me. I was afraid he'd sign with some other studio and I wouldn't get the chance to repay Pinky for past favors and opportunities.

Both the studs, Bo and Thomas, had impossibly long and thick cocks, made for porn. Thomas was black and uncut; Bo, a swarthy farmboy, was cut. I swallowed hard watching as Miguel's mouth stretched to accommodate both cocks for the end of the sucking sequence. Jeff said he was ready and the scene could now move away from Miguel's hungry mouth and Freddy got a close-up of Miguel stroking his own cock.

Jeff directed Miguel to get on the couch and told Thomas to start licking away at Miguel's asshole. Bo moved to permit Miguel to continue sucking him. He saw that Thomas was so good that it was hard for Miguel to keep the cock in his mouth. "Oh, man," Miguel groaned, over and over, cries that were all too familiar to me. I could not believe how skilled Thomas was at rimming, but Miguel couldn't take much more of it. He had to have it, I knew. He stopped sucking Bo and looked up at Jeff. "Please, I want it in me—now."

Thomas grinned at this and he quickly placed himself over Miguel and entered him. He was slow, deliberate, and eventually he got the entire thing in Miguel. Miguel kept on sucking Bo, but I saw tears coming to his eyes as Thomas pressed farther and farther in. Jeff asked for a couple more penetration shots, then Thomas slid right in, all the way down to his pubic hairs, and began a more heated fucking. At that point, Miguel cried out, letting Bo's cock drop from his mouth. Thomas's balls were soon slapping furiously against Miguel's backside, the sweat running down his ebony body and dripping onto Miguel's back as Jeff pulled back for a wide angle shot.

Just then, Bo decided he wanted some of Miguel's ass. Thomas moved away, then shoved his hard-on into Miguel's mouth. Bo mounted Miguel and the entry must have been rough because Miguel let Thomas's cock drop from his mouth and reached behind him to spread his cheeks wider. Thomas took Miguel by the hair and jammed his cock back into Miguel's gaping mouth.

"You suck that prick," he demanded.

I decided I couldn't take much more of this spectacle. I could not protect Miguel any longer, and now I doubted I could even truly love him any longer. The money shots could not come any too soon for me, but Jeff got the idea that Bo and Thomas should go back and forth at the ass, leaving the boy free to scream and yell. Miguel gave it everything he had now, jacking himself wildly as Bo and Thomas took their turns, a few minutes each.

At last Jeff had Thomas and Bo stand over Miguel and come on his stomach, about where his cum had landed minutes before while he was being fucked by Bo—or was it Thomas? I closed my eyes again, not really wanting to watch their final kiss, but when I opened them again, Bo and Thomas were gone. There was no final kiss. This thing must have had a story line because in came a huge Italian stud, acting indignant at discovering Miguel in his bed. The grimace Miguel's face disappeared in short order and he was moaning, begging the Italian to fuck him.

When the long, thin, uncut cock began mechanically going in and out of his ass, Miguel's mouth was open wide and suddenly Thomas was back, shoving his prong into it. After a couple of minutes, Thomas had taken the Italian's place, digging even deeper into Miguel's ravaged asshole. Thomas put on an amazing show, coming once again, in what must have been the finale. The thought of all of these guys having Miguel had proven both frightening and, strangely, exciting.

Later, in the rental car, we kissed and I held Miguel. I had the terrible feeling that this had all gone too far, too far over the edge, and it was all my fault. He started sobbing, but I realized soon enough they were tears of joy. He started talking, wanting to tell the truth for once, to let it all out. "God, Casey, I loved it." He gestured wildly, as Latins do when excited. "I fucking loved every fucking minute of this fucking day!"

I smiled. "I'm glad."

"But you didn't come," he said, stroking me.

Now he showed his thanks by pulling out my cock and going down on me as I drove toward the hotel. He worked me expertly, trying to milk every ounce of cum out of my body. I pulled over to the side of the road and he let go of the cock to watch it erupting. My body jerked and shook with the power of my orgasm. Suddenly light-headed, I felt him cleaning me up with a towel.

Back at the hotel, we were silent as he fell asleep leaning against me, his head on my shoulder, and I began to wonder about what I could do for an encore.

Epilogue

When I return from California, I find there is a message, three days old, from Gardner. He wants to see me at his apartment tonight. Exhausted, I set the alarm, then sleep.

I am on time, as always for Gardner. I am buzzed into the building. I see the door to the apartment is hanging open as I make way down the corridor. The apartment is uncharacteristically dark. I close the door behind me and a voice I do not recognize tells me to come into the kitchen. I fear it might be another of Gardner's new students. I don't know if I am in the mood for that tonight but....

But, no, it is not a new student for me to indoctrinate. It is not Gardner. It is ... Chad!

"It's about time we met," he says, holding out his hand. He is even more gorgeous in person than in his pictures. I am speechless. He is so sexy; no wonder Gardner has put up with what he has for so long.

I shake his hand, sit on the stool opposite him at the counter. Finally, I am able to speak. "Where's Gardner?"

"I should have called you. I saw he had written your name

in his appointment book...."

I begin to sweat. "Has something happened to him?"

"Heart attack. A mild one. He'll be fine. He'll have to cut back on his schedule, and finally give up smoking, but...."

"Can I see him?"

I carry on for a few moments, asking questions, trying to feel my way through the most awkward moment of my life. Any other time, I would be full of confidence, but this is Chad, my dream lover, the one I have been longing for all these years. I wonder if he has any idea how much I have wanted him, desired him. And he is even more blond, more blue-eyed, more muscular than I had even imagined!

Finally, he says, "I've always wondered what it would be like."

"What *what* would be like?" I ask, knowing full well what he is talking about.

"To fuck Casey Cassidy."

It seems neither of us wants to be alone tonight, not after this.

Now he smiles. "Come on," he says, and our eyes meet and I melt on the spot. Our kiss is deep, kisses so deep and ardent; we are all mouth and hands.

Soon he is pushing me back against the kitchen wall in one movement. A twisting movement of his hips against me lets me know he is packing a hard cock under his jeans, pushing against my crotch. I moan and kind of slip down against him.

He chuckles, very pleased. "Oh. You like that?"

"Yes."

"I thought you would. It's not Gardner's but, frankly, it's better than Gardner's."

"Chad," I moan. I just slide right into the space, whimpering a little and enjoying the feeling of my knees going weak.

He abruptly steps back, unbuttons his jeans. I'm moaning as he pushes me to my knees and shoves his cock in my mouth.

Oh God, this is what I've thought about since I first saw his picture. My mouth full of Chad's dick, my throat being assaulted by it, my tongue all over it and being able to suck it as hard as I can, over and over. His fingers are in my hair, urging me to take his cock and I can hear his running commentary from above, hear him saying, "I've been waiting for this for so long," or "Oh yeah," or just groaning as I take another inch of his splendid, thick dick down my throat. This is what I've thought about while I masturbated alone in my bed, stroking myself with one hand and working a dildo in and out of my ass with the other.

Now it's for real. Chad is sliding it in and out, like I like, like I've fantasized, fucking my mouth with the same mixture of ruthlessness and tenderness Gardner does. Just when he gets a good rhythm and it starts to be easy, sucking him, he changes it, shocking me and making me moan around it.

His other hand, the one not holding my head on his cock, reaches down and squeezes my nipple. I feel the pain-pleasure jolt in my crotch, feel myself get harder than I am already, and I feel my throat open up. I'm inhaling his cock now, my lips all the way up the hilt. "Oh yeah," he murmurs urgently, "suck it, suck it, you cocksucker." I can feel my eyes rolling up in my head as the head of his dick slides down my throat. A gag reflex washes over me, making my nose run and tears roll down my cheeks. It passes and I'm even harder than I was before. I'm choking on Chad's cock and I'm going to come any second and his hand pinches my nipple, viciously, and I go over the top, coming hard, and I'm sucking him harder than I thought possible.

Pretty soon, I know, he's going to pull out of my mouth and fuck the hell out of me, but I'm not thinking about that now. Right now, heaven is coming while I suck Chad's cock.

When I am done, Chad pushes me away slightly. He caresses and toys with my spent cock. I am still aching with need when his hands travel back to play with my ass.

I stretch my arm just a little and stroke my fingers across his moist, swollen cock. It is a beautiful cock; no wonder Gardner put up with so much so he could have it, whenever, wherever. Chad moans and shifts his hips to give me better access.

"Please?" I beg him. I drag him back down on top of me. My teeth capture his lower lip, and he surrenders, at first reluctantly and then with enthusiasm. Foreplay disappears, replaced by fierce determination. We are in no mood for games.

His fingers spread my asslips and are sucked into the

depths. He pulls them out, slides them back in. In and out. Again and again until I moan, my back arching, and my muscles convulsed.

A moment to breathe, then he is between my legs, and all I know is that Chad is there. I am not dreaming it. Electricity sparks through me as he rims my asshole. His tongue traces, flickers in and around. Sucking and licking, over and over until I scream and grip his shoulders.

"Stick it in me," I beg, and he does, slamming it in all the way to the base.

"God, if you only knew how long I've waited to do this," he says.

"Me too."

"Really?"

"Yes. From the first time I was in this apartment and saw your picture...."

He kisses me as he plunges in and out. He comes—quietly, relaxed, satisfied. He pulls out of me and lies next to me, breathing hard. "God that was good. I knew it would be."

"I did too."

I draw him into my arms. He's sweating even more than I am.

"You know, I have you to thank for so much, Casey."

"Me?"

"Yes. Gardner and I ... well, for a long time it was boring, but once he met you, I don't know what happened, he just came alive again. He didn't want me to know, of course. But I knew something had happened so I snooped in his appointment book. I saw your name, over and over. I checked out your movie...."

"Oh shit...."

"No, it was great. I would go home and when I was doing it to my wife, I'd picture scenes from the movie...."

"No kidding?"

"That's the only way I can get through it now."

And now what? I don't push; I will let him make the moves. And, after all that time bottoming for Gardner, I see he is pumped up with his success at topping—and not topping just anybody: topping Gardner's "secret" fuck, Casey Cassidy, porn superstar.

Minutes later we are taking turns under a hot shower,

erasing the lingering musk of sex.

I am putting on my pants when he leans over, takes my hand. The bravado I saw immediately after sex has evaporated. Now he is the little puppy dog again; the little boy Gardner found at the baths one afternoon. "This'll be just between us, right? Gardner doesn't need to ever know."

"No. He'll never hear it from me."

He shook his head. "God, now I want to see you again, too."

"You can...." I want him again, right now, whenever.

"It's just so fuckin' complicated...."

I take him in my arms, hold him tightly against me.

"You know that I love Gardner," I say, matter-of-factly.

"Yes, I know. I love him too."

"If only...." He hesitates, fearful again of showing too much emotion. "You know, Casey, in the beginning," he goes on, on the verge of tears, "Gardner and I tried to tell each other that it would get easier, that we'd grow accustomed to it ... but...."

Now, as he breaks down, the tears flowing freely at last, I can tell he has been a victim too, as much as Gardner has, to the pain and pressure of saying hello and goodbye so often.

And now tears form in my eyes as well; I realize that I have been part of it, an integral part of it at that, all along—and have never known it.

The Classic Book
SEDUCED
Now Available on CD-Rom

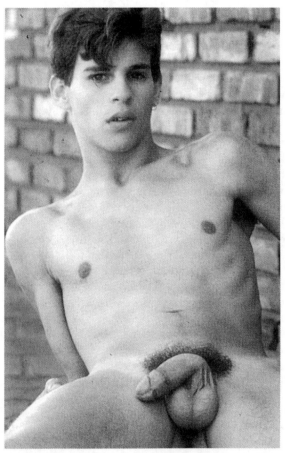

Technology has now made it possible for us to make available classic books of the past that are now out of print. In the book industry, these are known as e-books, meaning that you can obtain them via the internet by going to a website and selecting the book of your choice. The book is then made available to you on disk or CD-Rom. Write us for more information at STARbooks Press, P.O. Box 2737, Sarasota FL 34230-2737 for more information, or e-mail us at starrxxx@gte.net.

IN A FOREIGN PLACE

A Selected Story by John Patrick from the Classic Anthology " Seduced"

It was the defining moment, the split-second when the handsome young stranger returned my stare. And smiled. It was nothing much, just a half smile. But it said, interested?

Oh was I ever. He was a dark-haired youth, slim, muscular in a natural way. He was neatly dressed in jeans and a matching jacket, unbuttoned to the navel, exposing his deeply-tanned skin and well-defined pecs with dark brown nipples. He stood there, leaning against the wall of the pavilion, his fingers in the belt loops.

I soon became aware of him next to me. I didn't want it like this, not in a tearoom. Yet, I knew where his eyes were fixed and I stroked myself to semi-hardness.

I dared not look at him; I stared at my own cock, as if encouraging it and encouraging him at the same time. His touching of it was tentative, then more aggressive. He slid the tips of his fingers across the full extent of it. It swelled under his tender touch to my maximum length.

"Yeah," he groaned. "Over here."

He wanted this even more than I did. As he stepped over to the cubicle, I admired the perfection of the denim that stretched across his ass.

Once inside, I slammed the bolt shut. He sat on the toilet and looked up into my eyes. Fluttering his long dark lashes, his sad blue eyes were pleading with me.

I nodded.

He reached inside and pulled out my cock. He gasped, as if genuinely surprised at the size of it. He slipped his hand into my trousers and felt the warmth and weight of my balls. He looked up at me again, as if seeking my permission again. I turned my face to the ceiling and closed my eyes.

The boy extended his finger and stroked the quivering head, traced down the blue tracery of a vein. Now I moved closer, eager for it. He smiled and with delicate precision bowed his head and with the tip of his tongue licked the pre-cum from the head of it. Holding his lips firm, he put his mouth to my cock. Soon he was sliding the warm stiffness of it through his taut lips until he had the head completely in his mouth. Then, as he inched down the shaft, I put my hands on his shoulders. Soon he had it all inside of him, his nose buried inside my trousers. He was aware of my trembling and put his hands over mine. I began to ease my cock down his throat, as if fucking him. He gagged a bit as it slid past his tonsils. Apprehensively, he brought his hands to my balls and moaned. His head began to bob back and forth on my dick and his other hand began caressing my butt cheeks.

For several minutes we stayed that way, my watching the boy's head sliding back and forth, helpless under his spell. It was an ecstasy I seldom experienced. Somehow, he sensed I was ready and he stopped moving. He let the cock fall from his mouth and he took it in his hand. I pressed his head into my crotch as the cum came hurtling from my cock and splashed onto the floor. The boy moaned again.

Outside, a car door slammed. The boy scrambled to his feet, shoved his way past me, and raced from the room. I returned to the urinal and stood there, bringing my hands to the side of it, holding on.

I went back the next day but the boy was not there. I got back into my car and drove further up the road to the park that surrounded the boat ramps. On weekends it was a busy place but during the week I could read there in solitude.

A pickup truck pulled up towing a jet ski. The driver, a youthful sandy-haired blond, backed it to the water's edge. As he climbed from the cab, I saw there was a sweet disorder in his dress, a wantonness about him that appealed to me. He became a fine distraction from my proofreading. I had grown bored with the novel. He busied himself getting ready to ski. He tugged off his jacket, then his jeans, revealing a sleek black nylon suit that masterfully defined his genitals.

As he started the machine, he noticed me staring. He waved. It was a winning wave, accompanied by a smile. I waved; a tiny acknowledgment, considering what I really felt.

He proceeded to roar across the bay, around the fishing pier, and back again, the sound deafening. He was adept at it, staying his course.

I returned to my reading but only briefly. I put one book down and took up another, a book I can read in a certain way, just for the pleasure of it.

As if I was caressing his skin, here, there, everywhere, I slowly turned the pages.

It clouded over and the calm bay became a tempestuous sea. I folded my chair and began to make my way to my car.

As I put my things into the trunk, he was returning to the shore. The wave again. I acknowledged it with a nod, slammed the trunk and walked over to him.

The sea had soaked his trunks, giving new definition to the crotch. I detected the full outline of the head of his penis as well as the shaft, the ballsac. I imagined how tasty they would be soaked now in sea water.

"Storm coming," I said.

"Happens every day about this time." He slipped off the life jacket. "I was hoping it wouldn't, though, my only afternoon off."

"I guess we'll just have to find other amusements."

He looked deep into my eyes, then smiled. "Why not?"

At his apartment, I asked to use the shower.

"Sure thing," he said. "It'll give me some time to tidy up. I hadn't expected visitors."

When I came out of the bathroom, a twoel wrapped around my middle, he said, "I put some music on. I hope you like it."

"Yes, it's fine." Rock 'n' roll, but mellow, like my host.

"I can change the station...."

"Please, no. It's fine."

"I don't have a bed. My sofa is my bed. See, I lift it and presto. There it is."

"It's a very nice one."

"Yes, I got it on sale."

"No, no ... I meant this," I said, reaching over to stroke his obvious erection.

Lying there on the sofa which so magically became a bed, I looked up at him, so large over me as he leaned on one elbow to stare down into my face. I saw him but what did I know? I knew I had a sad life, being a married man, forced to seek comfort wherever and whenever I could, and that I had many problems, and certainly he had problems too, but in this moment, there were no problems, just possibilities. After years of furtive encounters, I knew the best sex is often between people who do not know much about each other. And, as I entered him, I no longer had a sad wife, I had only this boy, no other. Outside there was darkness; inside there was only light.

As I hovered over him, braced by my hands firmly planted on each side of his head, my relentless penis sank into him deeply and the wind blew the curtains and rustled the newspapers on the coffee table.

As the light began to fade in the sky, he came jerking himself off while I fucked and I, still hard and pumping, began to worry I would be late, have to make excuses. I had pleased him, that was all that mattered, really. I pulled out and retreated into the bathroom. The vision of him enjoying it would come to me while I was pleasuring my wife, and then I would come and it would be in his memory.

On the way back to my condo, where my wife was undoubtedly pissed because I was so late, I passed the pavilion on the beach. There he was, the boy from yesterday, leaning against the wall, his fingers in his belt loops.

I pulled into the parking lot, stopped in front of him. I leaned over, looked at him. "Got a date?" I asked.

"Now I do," he answered, smiling, sauntering over to the car.

As I pulled out of the parking lot, he began leafing through the manuscript I had left on the seat between us. "You write?" he asked.

"Yes."

His finger traced down the list of my books. "What was this one, 'Hard,' about?" he chuckled.

"Life. Life is hard. When I wrote that I was married. I was still with my first wife, not the last one, the first one."

"How many times have you been married?"

"Three. And too many lovers in between. I can't make up my mind."

"Are you married now?"

"Yes. In fact she's down here with me. We've rented a condo for a month."

"And life's still hard?"

"Yes."

"Yeah," he smiled, pressing my crotch. "Hard as your cock."

He shifted his body toward me and dropped his head to my chest. Again I felt his eyes fixed on my crotch.

I rented a cheap motel room on the North Trail. Inside, he ran his finger along the full measure of my cock, licked the pre-cum from the head. He looked at me, at the cock, then back at me again. His hand moved up and down on it.

When he was nude, he laid on the bed on his stomach, undulating his hips. I knew what he wanted. He didn't have to ask. He was slender, practically hairless. His buttocks were small, unblemished. I squeezed them.

"Relax, it'll be okay, " I said, re-assuring him as I parted his asscheeks, applied the lube.

My fingers probed the asshole, stretching the taut ring of muscle. After sliding on a condom, I thrust once and again, then again until the full length of my penis was in him. He moaned, lifting himself up so that he could fondle himself while I continued thrusting. The springs of the old bed squeaked monotonously and the head of the bed banged against the wall. I hurried it. At the moment of my climax, his buttocks flailed up and down so wildly and his moans of ecstasy so loud that I thought he had come.

But when I returned from the bathroom, he was lying on his back, his hands behind his head, and his perky erection pointed toward his navel.

"It's a fine cock," I said, lowering myself to the bed.

He lay motionless while I stroked it. Licked it. Sucked it.

He laid back, enjoying it. Soon he was grabbing my head, shoving it deep into his crotch. I struggled, managed to pull away just as cum began spurting from his cock. He came copiously. I loved his cock, and told him I wanted to suck it again.

"I'm hungry," he said, once back in the car.

"I'm not surprised, you're a growing boy."

"Do you think I'll grow bigger *everywhere*?"

"God, I hope not. Like I said, it's such a fine cock. And I want to see it again."

I needed this encounter solely for myself, but he has

enjoyed himself; now time pressed upon me. I worried that I was so late in returning. "I'd buy you something to eat but I'm late. Very late."

When I pulled into the beach parking lot, I left the engine running. "I must be going," I said.

He nodded, then reached out and touched my crotch. I put my hand over his and squeezed gently. As I caressed him one last time, I knew I had a strange love for him and no time to say it.

At first I thought my encounters with men happened to me once, in a foreign place and were not a part of time, not a part of my life. But I learned I could not leave it that way. The memories of these boys are not easy to lose. They are really not far away from me and, even if I never see them again, I will not forget them.

The Contributors
(Other Than the Editor, John Patrick)

"Rupert Bare"
Tony Anthony

The author says he is a "handsome young stud (in his wet dreams)," who has been a draughtsman, storeman, truck driver, prospector, ship's steward, miner, hospital technician, technical writer, and physical security designer. He has boxed as an amateur, hunted big game, played rugby, cricket, squash, tennis and men's lacrosse, ran a half-marathon, and raced on bicycles and motorcycles. He has traveled in Africa, Australia, New Zealand and Europe. He says he has won the fabled Pulitzer Porn Prize no less than twice (again in his dreams), and enjoys writing fiction, especially for STARbooks.

"Red-Hot, Iron-Hard"
Barry Alexander

The author is a frequent contributor to gay magazines and has had stories published in several anthologies.

"Hot Summernight Rendezvous"
Antler

The poet lives in Milwaukee when not traveling to perform his poems or wildernessing. His epic poem *Factory* was published by City Lights. His collection of poems *Last Words* was published by Ballantine. Winner of the Whitman Award from the Walt Whitman Society of Camden, New Jersey, and the Witter Bynner prize from the Academy and Institute of Arts & Letters in New York, his poetry has appeared in many periodicals (including *Utne Reader, Whole Earth Review* and *American Poetry Review*) and anthologies (including *Gay Roots, Erotic by Nature,* and *Gay and Lesbian Poetry of Our Time*).

"The Boy with the Golden Cock" and "Smooth"
Kevin Bantan

The author now lives in Pennsylvania, where he is working on several new stories for STARbooks.

"HEAT"
K.I. Bard

The author's first story for STARbooks appeared in *Juniors 2.* Future stories are in the works. He lives and thrives in Minnesota.

"At the Car Wash"
Donald Patrick Beavers

Based in Los Angeles, the popular author's last story for

STARbooks was in *Boys on the Prowl*.

"The Playground"
Blaise Bulot
This is the author's first story for STARbooks. He is a major contributor to gay journals and has published two novels, *Starr Lyte* and *Dark Waters*, from Croker Sack Books.

"The Voyeur"
Frank Brooks
The author is a regular contributor to gay magazines. In addition to writing, his interests include figure drawing from the live model and mountain hiking.

"Rocky Mountain Fever"
Jason Carpenter
Texas-based Jason's last work for STARbooks appeared in *Juniors 2*.

"On A Hot Saturday Night..."
Corbin Chezner
The author is an experienced writer of erotica who lives in Tulsa, Oklahoma. His credentials include a master of arts degree with mass communications. His first story for STARbooks appeared in *Sweet Temptations*.

"Hot and Wet and Ready"
William Cozad
A frequent contributor to gay magazines, William lives in San Francisco, where, it seems, he is continually coming up with new and exciting material. He is currently at work on a new novella to be published exclusively by STARbooks.

"In Certain Situations..."
Carl Miller Daniels
This new contributor of erotic poems lives in Virginia. Carl's first chapbook, *Museum Quality Orgasm*, is currently available from Future Tense Books, Portland, Oregon. His new chapbook, *Shy Boys at Home*, is available from Chiron Review.

"Jedediah, My Tadzio"
Peter Eros
The popular author's work also most recently appeared in *Play Hard, Score Big, Boys on the Prowl*, and *Sweet Temptations*.

"Hot Wheels"
J. Freeman
This is the author's first story for STARbooks.

"Giving A Boy A Hand"
Frank Gardner
The author lives in Maine where he is working on many more hot stories for STARbooks.

"Tally-Ho Teens" and "Learning the Hard Way"
Peter Gilbert
"Semi-retired" after a long career with the British Armed Forces, the author now lives in Germany but is contemplating a return to England. A frequent contributor to various periodicals, he also writes for television. He enjoys walking, photography and reading. His stories have swiftly become favorites of readers of STARbooks' anthologies.

"Tower Park Boys"
Ronald James
The author is a graduate student in Fine Arts at a university in St. Louis, Missouri. He is working on more stories in this vein for STARbooks. His first story appeared in *Fresh 'N' Frisky*.

"A.K.A. Dick Adams"
Mike Johnson
A close pal of Daniel Miller's, this is the talented Mr. Johnson's first story for STARbooks.

"Best Laid Plans"
James Hosier
The youthful author lives in a little town that is "definitely not sleepy." He says he is straight but admits that he lets guys do what they want: "I need the money and I happen to have a good body (thanks to the swimming club). Provided they're prepared to pay, I let them go ahead." Stay tuned.

"That Sizzling Summer" and "In Heat"
Thomas C. Humphrey
The author, who resides in Florida, is working on his first novel, *All the Difference*, and has contributed stories to First Hand publications. A memoir appeared in the original *Juniors*.

"At the Ole Swimmin' Hole," "White-Hot,"
"Sweet Revenge," and "Getting Off, Cooling Off"
David MacMillan
The author was born in London, England, and entered the U.S. after the Korean conflict. He earned his masters degree from Columbia University and returned to England as a political analyst and organizer as well as a stringer for a number of publications before returning to the US permanently in 1977. His writing efforts are devoted to crime

fiction, historical fiction, and dark fantasy. He is the well-trained pet of Karlotte, a 16-year-old calico dominatrix. She strokes him on average once a week—but only if he has followed his assignments faithfully and with at least some creativity. He has contributed to *The Mammoth Book of Historical Erotica*, and is editing books for Companion Press and Idol, London.

"Lockerroom Heat" and "Twice the Heat"
R. J. Masters
The author, who lives in Maine, is a frequent contributor to gay erotic magazines under various pseudonyms. His first novel, *Foreign Power*, an erotic tale of sexual awakening, a young man's introduction into the world of S/M, was published by Nocturnis Press.

"Provincetown Heat"
Matt McCarthy
A close pal of Daniel Miller's, this is the talented Mr. McCarthy's first story for STARbooks.

"Heatwave"
Daniel Miller
The author, who lives near Boston, is a frequent contributor to gay anthologies and skin magazines. Two of his stories appeared in *Juniors 2*.

"Hot Reunion"
Rudy Roberts
The author's previous stories for STARbooks have appeared in *In the Boy Zone*, *Pleasures of the Flesh*, and *Secret Passions*. He lives in Canada.

"Crazy from the Heat" and "Beyond Beautiful"
Lance Rush
The popular author is a frequent contributor to many of the leading gay publications.

"Horny As Hell"
Sonny Torvig
Based in London, this is the author's latest work for STARbooks. His stories have appeared in *Pleasures of the Flesh*, *Intimate Strangers*, and *Naughty By Nature*.

"Crowning Achievement"
Thomas Wagner
A close pal of Daniel Miller's, two of the talented Mr. Wagner's stories appeared in STARbooks' *Fresh 'N' Frisky*.

THE CLASSIC: BARELY LEGAL
NOW IN ITS SEVENTH PRINTING

COMING SOON! TABOO!

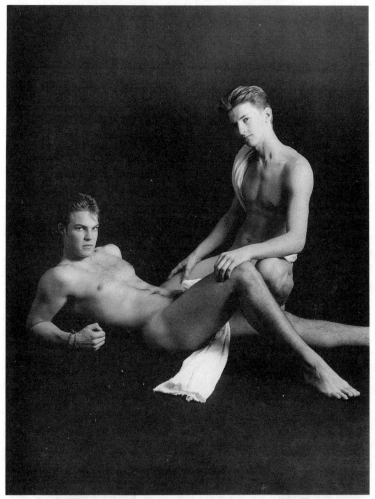

Principle photography for the forthcoming anthology *Taboo!* will be provided by David Butt. Mr. Butt's photographs may be purchased through Suntown, Post Office Box 151, Danbury, Oxfordshire, OX16 8QN, United Kingdom. Ask for a full catalogue.

E-mail at SUNTOWN1@aol.com. A collection of Mr. Butt's photos, *English Country Lad*, is available from STARbooks Press. *Young and Hairy*, David's latest book, is enjoying huge success currently and is also available from STARbooks Press.

ACKNOWLEDGEMENTS
AND SOURCES

The main cover model appears courtesy of Mike Arlen, whose magazines enjoy extraordinary sales throughout the world. "Mike Arlen's Guys " are available from Wetherby Studios, 23 Wetherby Mansions, Earls Court Square, London, SW5 9BH. A limited number of magazines are available from STARbooks Press and at specialty bookstores throughout the U.S., Canada, and the U.K.

Also featured on the cover are Pagan Prince and Danny
Sommers, stars of the classic video "Seamen First Class" from
Studio 2000. Current video offerings are on view on the
internet at: studio2000video.com. You may e-mail them at:
studio2000jt@earthlink.net. This video is also available from
RAD Video. The above photograph of Pagan Prince courtesy
Studio 2000.

You may contact Studio 2000 via fax: 1-800-435-2445.
Catalogue and mailing service is free.

ABOUT THE EDITOR

After a very hot time in bed, the editor relaxes with porn performer and escort Pagan Prince, who is featured on the cover.

John Patrick is a prolific, prize-winning author of fiction and non-fiction. One of his short stories, "The Well," was honored by PEN American Center as one of the best of 1987. His novels and anthologies, as well as his non-fiction works, including *Legends* and *The Best of the Superstars* series, continue to gain him new fans every day. One of his most famous short stories appears in the Badboy collection *Southern Comfort* and another appears in the collection *The Mammoth Book of Gay Short Stories*.

A divorced father of two, the author is a longtime member of the American Booksellers Association, the Publishing Triangle, the Florida Publishers' Association, American Civil Liberties Union, and the Adult Video Association. He resides in Florida.